COMPLETE SUBMISSION

COMPLETE SUBMISSION

THE COMPLETE SERIES

CD REISS

SUBMISSION

PART I
BEG

CHAPTER 1

At the height of singing the last note, when my lungs were still full and I was switching from pure physical power to emotional thrust, I was blindsided by last night's dream. Like most dreams, it hadn't had a story. I was on top of a grand piano on the rooftop bar of Hotel K. The fact that the real hotel didn't have a piano on the roof notwithstanding, I was on it and naked from the waist down, propped on my elbows. My knees were spread further apart than physically possible. Customers drank their thirty-dollar drinks and watched as I sang. The song didn't have words, but I knew them well, and as the strange man with his head between my legs licked me, I sang harder and harder until I woke up with an arched back and soaked sheets, hanging on to a middle C for dear life.

Same as the last note of our last song, and I held it like a stranger was pleasuring me on a nonexistent piano. I drew that last note out for everything it was worth, pulling from deep inside my diaphragm, feeling the song rattle the bones of my rib cage, sweat pouring down my face. It was my note. The dream told me so. Even after Harry stopped strumming and Gabby's keyboard softened to silence, I croaked out the last tearful strain as if gripping the edge of a precipice.

When I opened my eyes in the dark club, I knew I had them; every one of them stared at me as if I had just ripped out their souls, put them in envelopes, and sent them back to their mothers, COD. Even in the few silent seconds after I stopped, when most singers would worry that they'd lost the audience, I knew I hadn't; they just needed permission to applaud. When I smiled, permission was granted, and they clapped all right.

Our band, Spoken Not Stirred, had brought down the Thelonius Room. A year of writing and rehearsing the songs and a month getting bodies in the door had paid off right here, right now.

The crowd. That was what it was all about. That was why I busted my ass. That was why I had shut out everything in my life but putting a roof over my head and food in my mouth. I didn't want anything from them but that ovation.

I bowed and went off stage, followed by the band. Harry bolted to the bathroom to throw up, as always. I could still hear the applause and banging feet. The room held a hundred people, and the audience sounded like a thousand. I wanted to take the moment to bathe in something other than the disappointment and failure that accompanied a career in music, but I heard Gabrielle next to me, tapping her right thumb and middle finger. Her gaze was blank, settled in a corner, her eyes as big as teacups. I followed that gaze to exactly nothing. The corner was empty, but she stared as if a mirror into herself stood there, and she didn't like what she saw.

I glanced at Darren, our drummer. He stared back at me, then at his sister, who had tapped those fingers since puberty.

"Gabby," I said.

She didn't answer.

Darren poked her bicep. "Gabs? Shit together?"

"Fuck off, Darren," Gabby said flatly, not looking away from the empty corner.

Darren and I looked at each other. We were each other's first loves, back in L.A. Performing Arts High, and even after the soft, simple breakup, we had deepened our friendship to the point we didn't need to talk with words.

We said to each other, with our expressions, that Gabby was in trouble again.

"We rule!" Harry gave a fist pump as he exited the bathroom, still buttoning up his pants. "You were awesome." He punched me in the arm, oblivious to what was going on with Gabby. "My heart broke a little at 'Split Me.'"

"Thanks," I said without emotion. I did feel gratitude, but we had other concerns at the moment. "Where's Vinny?"

Our manager, Vinny Mardigian, appeared as if summoned, all glad-handing and smiles. Such a dick. I really couldn't stand him, but he'd seemed confident and competent when we met.

"You happy?" I said. "We sold all our tickets at full price. Now maybe next time we won't have to pay to play?"

"Hello, Monica Sexybitch." That was his pet name for me. The guy had the personality of a landfill and the drive of a shark in bloody waters. "Nice to see you too. I got Performer's Agency on the line. Their guy's right outside."

Great. I needed representation from the The Rinkydink Agency like I needed a hole in the head. But I was an artist, and I was supposed to take whatever the industry handed me with a smile and spread legs.

Vinny, of course, couldn't shut up worth a damn. He was high on Performer's Agency and the worldwide fame he thought they would get us. He didn't realize half a step forward was just as good as a full step back. "You got a crowd out there asking for an encore. Everybody here does their job, then everybody's happy."

I listened, and sure enough, they were still clapping, and Gabby was still staring into the corner.

CHAPTER 2

Darren took Gabby home after the encore, which she played like the crazy prodigy she was, then she blanked out again. Her depression was ameliorated by music and brought on by just about anything, even if she was taking her meds.

She'd attempted suicide two years before after a few weeks of corner-staring and complaining of not being able to feel anything about anything. I'd been the one to find her in the kitchen, bleeding into the sink. That had been terrific for everyone. She took my second bedroom, and Darren moved from a roommate-infested guest house in West Hollywood to a studio a block away. We played music together because music was what we did, and because it kept Gabby sane, Darren close, and me from screwing up. But it didn't even keep us in hot dogs. We all worked, and until I got my current gig at the rooftop bar at Hotel K, I had to give up Starbucks because I couldn't rub two nickels together to make heat.

Because Spoken Not Stirred had drawn more people than the cost of our guaranteed tickets, we'd made three hundred dollars that night. Fifteen percent went to Vinny Landfillian. Sixty-eight dollars paid for Harry's parking ticket because he figured if he was loading his bass and amp, he could park in a loading zone on the Sunset Strip before six o'clock. We split the rest four ways.

Hotel K was a spanking new modernist, thirty-story diamond in a one-story stucco shitpile of a neighborhood. The rooftop bar thing in L.A. had gotten out of hand. You couldn't swing a dead talent agent without hitting some new construction with a barside pool on the roof and thumping music day and night. The upside of the epidemic was that waitress service was the norm, and tall, skinny girls who could slip between name-dropping drunks while holding heavy trays over their heads without clocking anyone were an absolute necessity. The downside for someone tall and skinny like myself was my replaceability. You couldn't swing a tall, skinny girl in L.A. without hitting another one.

Darren and I had taken too long discussing who would watch Gabby. He convinced her to stay at his place for the night, though "convinced" might not be the word to use when talking about someone who didn't care about where she slept, or anything, one way or the other.

I ran from the elevator to the hotel locker room, the fifty bucks I'd made for holding a hundred people in my palm light in my pocket. I peeled off my jacket and stuffed it in my locker, then pulled my shirt off. I didn't have a second to spare before Yvonne, who I was relieving, started chewing me out for stranding her on the floor. I yanked a low-cut dress that showed more leg than modesty out of my bag and wrestled into it.

"You're late," Freddie, my manager, said. He stank of cigarettes, which I found disgusting.

"I'm sorry, I had a gig." I kicked off my shoes and pulled my pants off from under my dress. I had no time to worry about what Freddie thought of me.

"Bully for you." Freddie crossed his arms, scrunching his brown pinstripe suit. He had a mole on his cheek and wore a puckered expression even when he looked down my shirt, which was almost every time we talked.

I didn't wait to argue. I slipped back into my shoes, slapped my locker shut, and ran toward the floor.

"Yvonne!" I caught her in the back hall as she folded a wad of tips into her pocket.

"Monica, girl! Where were you?"

"I'm sorry. Thanks for covering my tables. Can I make it up to you?"

"I don't get home in time, you can pay the sitter an extra hour."

"No problem," I said, though it was a big problem.

"Jonathan Drazen is at your table." She put her hand to her heart. "He's hot, and he'll tip if he likes what he sees. So be nice." She handed me the tickets for my station.

Drazen was my boss's boss. He owned the hotel, but we'd never crossed paths. Apparently, he traveled a lot, and he spent little or no time on the roof when he was in town, so we hadn't met. This development was more annoying than anything. I'd just gotten the ovation of my life at a really cool club and was bathing in the warm validation. I didn't need to prove myself all over again, and based on what? If it wasn't my music, I didn't care.

The place was packed: wall-to-wall Eurotrash, Hollywood heavyweights, and assorted hangers-on. The pool was a big rectangle in the center of the expanse. Red chairs surrounded it, and a large cocktail area with tables and chairs sat off to the side. Little tents with couches inside outlined most of the roof, and when the curtains closed, you left them closed unless someone looked as though they'd taken off without paying.

I stood at the service bar, flipping through my tickets. Five tables, two with little star punch-outs in the upper right hand corners. Put there by Freddie, they meant someone important was at the table. Extra care was required.

My first tray was a star punch-out. I put on a smile and navigated through the crowd to deliver the tray to a table in the corner. Four men, and I knew Drazen right away. He had red hair cut just below the ears, disheveled in that absolutely precise way. He wore jeans and a grey shirt that showed off his broad shoulders and hard biceps. His full lips stretched across flawless, natural teeth when he saw his tray coming, and I was caught a little off guard by how much I couldn't stop looking at him.

"H-Hi," I stammered. "I'll be your server." I smiled. That always worked. Then I thought happy thoughts because that made my smile genuine, and I watched Drazen move his gaze from my smiling face, over my breasts, to my hips, stopping at my calves. I felt as if I were being applauded again.

He looked back at my face. I stared right back at him, and he pursed his lips. I'd caught him looking, and he seemed justifiably embarrassed.

"Hello," he said. "You're new." His voice resonated like a cello, even over the music.

I checked Yvonne's notes and picked up a short glass with ice and amber liquid from the tray. "You have the Jameson's?"

"Thank you." He nodded to me, keeping his eyes on my face and off my body. Even then, I felt as if I were being eaten alive, sucked to fluid, mouthful by mouthful. A liquid feeling came over me, and I stopped doing my job for half a second while I allowed myself to be completely saturated by that warm feeling. In that moment, of course, someone, a man judging from the weight of impact, pushed or got pushed, and my tray went flying.

For a second, the glasses hung in the air like a handful of glitter, and I thought I could catch them. I felt the sound of the impact too long after three gin and tonics splashed over each guest. I was shocked into silence as everyone at the table stood, hands out, dripping, clothes getting darker at crotches and chests. A collective gasp rose from everyone within splash distance.

Freddie appeared like a zombie smelling fresh brains. "You're fired." He turned to Drazen and said, "Sir, can I get you anything? We have shirts—"

Drazen shook a splash of liquid off his hand. "It's fine."

"I am so sorry," I said.

Freddie got between me and my former boss, as if I would beg him for my job back, which I'd never do, and said, "Get your things."

CHAPTER 3

Fuck it. Fuck that job and everything else. I'd get another one. I promised myself I was going to make it big, and when I did, I would come in here with my freaking entourage and Freddie was going to serve me whatever I wanted for no tip at all. Not even a cent. And Jonathan Drazen was going to sit by me and look at me just like he did before I spilled gin and tonic all over him, but like I'm an equal, not some little piece of candy working for tips.

I slammed my locker shut.

I had to find another job soon. I always paid my housing expenses first, but we owed the studio money, and I couldn't take another dime from Harry.

Freddie strode down the dim hallway, toes pointed out and walking like a duck on a mission.

"Fuck off, Freddie. I'm leaving, and by the way, you're an—"

"Mister Drazen wants to see you."

"Fuck him. He can't summon me. I don't work for him anymore."

Freddie smiled like a sly cat. "Sometimes he gives the short timers a severance if he feels bad. Nice chunka change. After that, you can get the hell out if you don't want to sleep with him. I'd like to see him not get laid for once."

He took a step closer. I didn't know why he'd get close enough to touch me, so I didn't back away, and when he slapped my ass, I was so stunned I didn't move. He ended the slap with a pinch.

"What did you...?"

But he was already waddling off, elbows bent, as if someone else's life needed to be miserable and he was just the guy to make it so. I stood there with my mouth open, seventy percent mad at him for being a complete molester and thirty percent mad at myself for being too shocked to punch him in the face.

CHAPTER 4

I had pride. I had so much pride that heeling at Jonathan Drazen's beck and call for a "chunka change" was the most humiliating thing I could think of doing. But there I was, in front of his ajar door on the thirtieth floor, knocking, not because I needed the money (which I did), and not because I wanted him to look at me like that again (which I also did), but because I couldn't have been the first waitress ass-slapped, or worse, by Freddie. If Drazen wasn't aware of Freddie's douchebaggery, he needed to be.

The office looked onto the Hollywood Hills, which must have been stunning in daylight. At night, the neighborhood was just a splash of twinkling lights on a black canvas. He stood behind his desk, back to the window, the room's soft lighting a flattering glaze on the perfect skin of his forearms. He wore a fresh pair of jeans and a white shirt. The dark wood and frosted glass accentuated the fact his office was meant to be a comforting space, and even though I knew the setting was manipulating me, I relaxed.

"Come on in," he said.

I stepped onto the carpet, its softness easing the pain caused by my high heels.

"I'm sorry I spilled on you. I'll pay for dry cleaning, if you want."

"I don't want. Sit down." His green eyes flickered in the lamplight. I had to admit he was stunning. His copper hair curled at the edges, and his smile could light a thousand cities. He couldn't have been older than his early thirties.

"I'll stand," I said. I was wearing a short skirt, and judging from the way he'd looked at me on the roof, if I sat down, I'd receive another stare that would make me want to jump him.

"I want to apologize for Freddie," he said. "He's a little more aggressive than he should be."

"We need to talk about that," I said.

He raised an eyebrow and came around to the front of the desk. He wore some cologne that stole the scent of sage leaves on a foggy day: dry, dusty, and clean. He leaned on his desk, putting his hands behind him, and I could see the whole length of his body: broad shoulders, tight waist, and straight hips. He looked at me again, then down to the floor. I felt as if he'd moved his hands off of me, and at once I was thrilled and ashamed. I wasn't going to be intimidated or scared. I wasn't going to let him look away from me. If he wanted to stare, he should stare. I placed my hands on my hips and let my body language challenge him to put his eyes where they wanted to go, not the floor.

Because, fuck him.

"Freddie's a douchebag." I could tell from his expression that was the wrong way to start. I needed to keep opinions and juicy expressions to myself and state facts. "He said you're going to try and sleep with me, for one." He smiled as if he really was going to try to sleep with me and got caught.

"Then," I continued, because I wanted to wipe that smile off his gorgeous face, "he grabbed my ass."

The smile melted as though it was an ice cube in a hot frying pan. He took his hungry eyes off mine, a relief on one hand and a disappointment on the other. "I was going to offer you severance."

"I don't want your money."

"Let me finish."

I nodded, a sting of prickly heat spreading across my cheeks.

"The severance was in case you didn't want to continue working here," he said. "Even though I can't stand the smell of the gin you got on me, I don't think you should lose your job over it. But now that you told me that, what should I do? If I give you severance, it looks like I'm paying you off. And if I unfire you, it looks like I'm letting you stay because I'm afraid of getting sued."

"I get it," I said. "If he said you'd try to sleep with me, then you've got your own shit to hide, and nothing would bring it out better than a lawsuit." I waited a second to see if I could glean anything from his eyes, but he had his business face on, so I put on my sarcasm face. "Quite a terrible position you're in."

His nod told me he understood me. His position was privileged. He got to make choices about my life based on his convenience. "What do you do, Monica?"

"I'm a waitress."

He smirked, looking at me full on, and I wanted to drop right there. "That's your circumstance. It's not who you are. Law school, maybe?"

"Like hell."

"Teacher, woodworker, volleyball player?" He ran the words together quickly, and I guessed he could come up with another hundred potential professions before he got it right.

"I'm a musician," I said.

"I'd like to see you play sometime."

"I'm not going to sleep with you."

"Indeed." He walked behind his desk. "I assume no one witnessed this alleged ass-grab?"

"Correct."

He opened a drawer and flipped through some files. "I hired Freddie, and he's my responsibility to manage. Your responsibility is to report it to someone besides me." He handed me a slip of paper. It was a standard U.S. Equal Employment Opportunity Commission flyer. "The numbers are on there. File a report. Send me a copy, please. It would protect both of us."

I stared at the paper. Drazen could get into a lot of trouble if enough reports were filed. I intended to tell the authorities what happened because I couldn't stand Freddie, but I felt a little sheepish about getting Drazen cited or investigated.

"You're not an asshole," I said.

He bowed his head, and though I couldn't see his face, I imagined he was smiling. He took a card from his pocket and came back around the desk. "My friend Sam owns the Stock downtown. I think it's a better fit for you. I'll tell him you might call."

When I took the card, I had an urge I couldn't resist. I reached my hand a little farther than I should have and brushed my finger against his. A shot of pleasure drove through me, and his finger flicked to extend the touch.

I had to get away from that guy as fast as possible.

CHAPTER 5

Los Angeles weather in late September was mid-July weather everywhere else—dog's-mouth hot, sweat-through-your-antiperspirant hot, car-exhaust hot. Gabby seemed better than the previous night, but Darren and I were on our toes.

Gabby said she was going for a walk and, trying to make sure she wasn't alone, I suggested she and I get ice cream at the artisanal place on Sunset.

We sat on the outside patio so the noise would mask our conversation. I poked at my strawberry basil ice cream while she considered her wasabi/honey longer than she might have a week ago.

"It's good money," she said, trying to talk me into a Thursday night lounge job. "And no pay to play. Just cash and go home."

"I hate those gigs. I hate being background."

"Two hundred dollars? Come on, Monica. You don't have to learn any songs; one rehearsal, maybe two, and we got it."

Gabby had spent her childhood getting her fingers slapped with a ruler every time she made a mistake on the piano. Her playing became so perfect she barely had to work at it. She was so compulsive her every waking moment was spent eating, playing, or thinking about playing, so the word "rehearse" couldn't apply to her because it implied an artist taking time out of their day to get something right, not a compulsive perfectionist basically breathing. She was a genius, and in all likelihood, her genius plus her perfectionist nature drove her depression.

"I only want to sing my own songs," I said.

"You can spin them. Just, come on. If I don't bring a voice on, I'll lose the gig, and I need it." That hitch in her voice meant she was swinging between desperation and emotional flatness, and it terrified me. "Mon, I can't wait for the next Spoken gig. I'm twenty-five, and I don't have a lot of time. *We* don't have a lot of time.

Every month goes by, and I'm nobody. God, I don't even have an agent. What will happen to me? I can't take it. I think I'll die if I end up like Frieda DuPree, trying her whole life and then she's in her sixties and still going to band auditions."

"You're not going to end up like Frieda DuPree."

"I have to keep working. Every night that goes by without someone seeing me play is a lost opportunity."

Performance school rote bullshit. Get out and play. Keep working. Play the odds. Teachers told poor kids they might be seen if they busted their violins on the streets if they had to. Dream-feeders. Fuck them. Some of those kids should have gone into accounting, and that line of shit kept them dreaming a few too many years.

I looked at Gabby and her big blue eyes, pleading for consideration. She was mid-anxiety attack. If it continued over the coming weeks, the anxiety attacks would become less frequent and the dead stares into corners more frequent if she didn't take her meds regularly. Then it would be trouble: another suicide attempt, or worse, a success. I loved Gabby. She was like a sister to me, but sometimes I wished for a less burdensome friend.

"Fine," I said. "One time, okay? You can find someone else in all of Los Angeles to do it next time."

Gabby nodded and tapped her thumb and middle finger together. "It's good," she said. "It'll be good, Monica. You'll knock them out. You will." The words had a rote quality, like she said them just to fill space.

"I guess I need it too," I said. "I got fired last night."

"What did you do?"

"Spilled drinks in my boss's lap."

"That Freddie guy?"

"Jonathan Drazen."

"Oh..." She put her hands to her mouth. "He also owns the R.O.Q. Club in Santa Monica. So don't try to work there, either."

"Did you know he's gorgeous?"

A voice came from behind me. "Talking about me again?" Darren had shown up, God bless him.

"Jonathan Drazen fired her last night," Gabby said.

"Who is that?" He sat down, placing his laptop on the table.

"He didn't do it. Freddie did. Drazen just offered me a severance and referred me to the Stock."

"And apparently he's gorgeous." He raised an eyebrow at me. I shrugged. Darren and I were over each other, but he'd rib me bloody at the slightest sign of weakness. "I haven't heard you talk like that about a guy in a year and a half. I thought maybe you were still in love with me." I must have blushed, or my eyes might have given away some hidden spark of feeling, because Darren snapped open his laptop. "Let's see what kinda wifi I can pick up."

"I don't talk like that about men because I prefer celibacy to bullshit."

Darren tapped away on his laptop. "Jonathan Drazen. Thirty-two. Old man." He looked at me over the screen.

"Do not underestimate how hot he is. I could barely talk."

"Earned his money the old-fashioned way."

"Rich daddy?"

"A long line of them. He makes more in interest than the entire GDP of Burma." Darren scrolled through some web page or another. He loved the internet like most people loved puppies and babies. "Real estate magnate. His dad lost a chunk of money. Our Jonathan the Third..." He drifted off as he scrolled. "BA from Penn. MBA from Stanford. He brought the business back. Bazillionaire. He's a real catch if you can tear him away from the four hundred other women he's getting photographed with."

"Lalala. Don't care."

"Why? It's not like you've had sex in...what?" Darren clicked around, pretending he didn't care about my answer, but I knew he did.

"Men are bad news," I said. "They're a distraction. They make demands."

"Not all men are Kevin."

Kevin was my last boyfriend, the one whose control issues had turned me off to men for eighteen months. "Lalala... not talking about Kevin either." I scraped the bottom of my ice cream cup.

Darren turned his laptop so I could see the screen. "This him?"

Jonathan Drazen stood between a woman and man I didn't recognize. I scrolled through the gossip page. His Irish good looks were undeniable next to anyone, even movie stars.

"He *has* been photographed with an awful lot of women," I said.

"Yeah, he's been a total fuck-around since his divorce, FYI. If you wanted him, he'd probably be game. All I'm saying." He crossed his legs and looked out onto Sunset.

Gabby had a faraway look as she watched the cars. "His wife was Jessica Carnes," Gabby recited as if she was reading a newspaper in her head, "the artist. Drazen married her at his father's place on Venice Beach. She's half-sister to Thomas Deacon, the sports agent at APR, who has a baby with Susan Kincaid, the hostess at the Key Club, whose brother plays basketball with Eugene Testarossa. Our dream agent at WDE."

"One day, Gabster, your obsession with Hollywood interrelationships will pay off." Darren clicked his laptop closed. "But not today."

CHAPTER 6

I think one could be at Hotel K, get blindfolded, taken to the Stock, and believe they'd been driven around and dropped in the same place they started: same pool, same chairs, same couches, same music, and same assholes clutching the same drinks and passing off the same tips. What was different was that there was no Freddie. The Stock had Debbie, a tall Asian lady who wore tight, crisp button-front shirts and black trousers. She knew every superstar from just their face, and they loved her as much as she loved them. She could tell a movie mogul from an actress and sat them where they'd have the most professional friction. She coordinated the waitresses' tables according to the patron's taste and coddled the girls until they worked like a machine.

She was the nicest person I'd ever worked for.

"Smile, girl," Debbie said. I'd been there a week and she knew exactly how many tables I could handle, how fast I was compared to the others, and my strong suit, which appeared to be my magnetic personality. "People look at you," she said. "They can't help it. Be smiling."

It was hard to smile. We'd had three good shows in a row, then Vinny disappeared into thin air. We'd banged on his office door in Thai Town, went to his house in East Hollywood, and called four hundred times. No Vinny. Every gig he had lined up for us fell through. My momentum was slowing and I didn't like it.

"What's your freaking problem?" said one dude as he threw a dollar bill and three dimes on my tray. "You need a blast of coke or something?" He'd looked like every other spikey-haired, fake-blonde, Hugo Boss–wearing douchenozzle who namedropped from zero to sixty in three beers. But Debbie had put his name on the ticket, probably as a favor to me. His name was Eugene Testarossa, the one guy at WDE I'd wanted to meet for months. In my depression over stupid Vinny, I hadn't recognized him.

I stalked toward the bathroom on my break and bumped into a hard chest that smelled of sage green and fog.

"Monica," Jonathan said. "Hey. Sam told me he hired you." His green eyes looked down at me and I wanted to break apart under the weight of them. As he looked at me, his face went from amused to concerned. "Are you okay?"

"Fine, just a bad day. Whatever." I stepped toward the bathroom, but he seemed disinclined to let me go so easily.

"I got your report. Thanks. It was very professional."

"You assumed a waitress couldn't put together a sentence?" His glance down told me I'd been a bitch. He didn't deserve my worst side. I tried to think fast; I didn't want a barrage of questions about my life right then. "The Dodgers lost and I'm from Echo Park and all, so I got a little down."

"The Dodgers won tonight." His pressed lips and bemused eyes told me he understood I was half joking.

I shuffled my feet, feeling like a kid caught lying about kissing behind the gym. "Yeah. Fucking Jesus Renaldo pulling it out in the ninth like that."

"He's got five good pitches in him per game."

"He tends to throw them in the bullpen."

"Or trying to pick a guy off." He shook his head. He looked normal just then, not like the guy behind the desk undressing me with his eyes.

"I'm sorry I was such a bitch just now."

"I'm used to it."

"No, you're not. Come on. People are nice to you all day."

He shrugged. "You lied about why you were upset. I get to lie about how people treat me."

"I'll keep that in mind."

"Yeah," he said, clearing his throat. "I have season tickets on the first base line."

I felt my eyes light up a little, and getting so excited over something someone else had embarrassed me.

"I could bring you sometime," he said.

"You haven't seen a Dodger game until you've seen it from the bleachers. Six dolla seats, yo."

He laughed, and I laughed too. Then Debbie showed up at the end of the hall.

"Monica!" she called out, tapping her wrist.

"Shit!" I cried out and ran back to my station, turning to give Jonathan a wave before rounding the corner.

I put on a smile and made myself as intensely personable as I could. I saw Jonathan at the head of the bar, talking to Sam and Debbie, laughing at some joke I couldn't hear. When I went to the station to pick up my tray, he looked at me and I felt his sight. He was gorgeous, no doubt. I could write songs about that face, those cheekbones, those eyes, that dry scent.

I wished he'd go away. I tried not to look at him, but he and Sam were still talking at one in the morning. Debbie stood at the end of the service bar, counting receipts, when I came by with a ticket, and I couldn't take it anymore.

"I'm sorry I was talking to Mister Drazen in the hall," I said. "I used to work for him."

"I know."

"How often does he come around here?"

"He and Sam have been close since they went to Stanford together, so… once a week? Should I arrange for him to be here more often?"

My cheeks got hot. To Debbie, who read people like neon street signs, the blushing was visible even in the dim lights. I glanced at him across the bar. He was looking at Debbie and me. He lifted his rocks glass, a bunch of melting ice in the bottom. Sam had gone to take care of some late-night hotel business, and Jonathan was alone.

"Perfect," Debbie said to me. "You will bring him his refill." She hailed the bartender, a buffed out model who worked his body more than his mind. "Robert, give Mister Drazen's drink to Monica."

"Debbie, really," I said.

"Why?" asked Robert, pouring a glass of single malt from a shelf so high I would have needed a cherry picker to reach it. "I'm not pretty enough?"

"You're plenty pretty," Debbie said. "Now do it." She put her hand on my forearm and spoke quietly. "You need more practice dealing with his social class. For you, as a person. Getting used to it will only benefit you. Now go."

Being mothered was nice, I guess. My mother had been more or less absent since I went to high school, which was about when she and Dad moved to Castaic. I never felt abandoned, but I could have used a hand with the day to day bullshit.

Drazen watched me come around the bar with his scotch. I wondered if he knew that made me uncomfortable or if he even gave it a thought. I wondered if the difference in our relative positions bothered him or turned him on. He was a bazillionaire and a customer. I was a waitress with two nickels making heat. This had to be a turn on.

"Thanks," he said when I placed the napkin and drink on the bar, a job Robert could have done in half the time.

"You're welcome."

We looked at each other for a second or ten. I had nothing to add to the conversation, but his magnetic pull made words irrelevant. I was stepping away to leave when he said, "I meant it, about seeing a game."

"I meant it about the bleachers."

"I like to get to know someone before they drag me out past centerfield." He clinked his ice against the sides of his glass. "The company has to be pretty engaging that far from the plate."

I wanted to mention the stunning color of his eyes. I wanted to touch his hand as it rested on the edges of the bar. Instead I said, "Your fellow fans keep you on your toes, especially if you wear red."

"Can I see you after work?"

The clattering noise in my chest must have been audible. It wasn't that I hadn't been asked out or the object of a proposition in the last year and a half; all of the men who wanted me were simply too easy to politely reject. If I had a brain in my head, I would reject Jonathan Drazen right out of hand. Politely.

"Maybe," I said. "Company's got to be pretty engaging at two thirty in the morning."

Sam showed up, and since I didn't want to be seen talking up my ex-boss, I walked away without confirming that he'd feel engaging at that ungodly hour.

CHAPTER 7

I spent the next hour and a half talking myself out of meeting with Jonathan after work, if he even showed. He was going to be a distraction, I could tell. I couldn't be in the same room with him without feeling like I needed to touch him.

I thought about Kevin. A fine specimen of a man, he'd had much the same effect on me as Jonathan Drazen, complete with fluttery stomach and tingling cheeks.

I'd been with Darren over six years when he admitted to kissing Dana Fasano. We were in the process of either breaking up or getting married. I went to a party downtown with a friend whose name eluded me right then, and there he was. Kevin was talking to some girl in the corner, and when he glanced over her head, his eyes found mine like he was looking for them. I froze in place. He had brown eyes and thick black lashes, and when we saw each other, the distance between us became a plucked cello string, vibrating, making a beautiful sound.

I didn't see him again for another half an hour, yet I had felt him circling me, tethered, even when we talked to different people. Finally, in the crowded kitchen, he was behind me, and I knew it because I could feel him before I even saw him reach over me to slide a beer from the sink.

"Hi," he said.

"Hi."

He held the beer bottle toward me, his hands slick on the glass, cold water pooling in the crevice between his skin and the bottle. "Is the opener over there?"

I took the bottle from him, overreaching, as I'd done with Drazen, so I could touch his cool, wet hand. Then I put the bottle cap on the metal edge of the counter and pulled down swiftly. The cap bent and popped off, clinking to the floor. I held up the bottle for him. "Here you go."

"Thanks." He considered the bottle, then me. "See that girl over there?" He pointed at a girl about my age with short, dark hair and striped leggings.

"Yeah."

"In twenty seconds, she's going to come over here and ask what I'm working on for my show. I don't want to tell her."

"So don't."

As if on cue, the girl saw Kevin and walked over. It was the first time I experienced him as a charmed person, and it would not be the last.

"It would be better if she didn't ask. My paintings are secret before a show. If I tell her, she'll own them. Her soul will own them. I can't explain it." The kitchen was crowded, slowing the striped leggings' progress and pushing us together, forcing us to whisper.

"I get it," I said. I would have gotten anything he said at that point. I would have claimed to understand quantum mechanics if he explained it to me. "They aren't born yet," I continued. "If she sees them while they're being made, she knows them as children. Their insides."

"My God, you get me."

I had no snappy reply. I wanted to get him. I wanted to get everything he said from now on. He touched my chin. "If I kiss you, she'll turn around and go away."

In retrospect, that was the lamest come-on imaginable from him. He'd done much better in the year following. But at the party, the word "kiss" breathed from his beautiful lips, was all I needed. I put my hand on his shoulder, and he slipped one around my waist. Our lips met, and I held back a groan of pleasure. I'd only ever been with Darren, and I loved him. I would always love him, but kissing that man, like that, with his taste of malt and chocolate, uncovered physical sensations I didn't know could come from a kiss. I felt every pore of his tongue, every turn of his lips. The world shut off and my identity became a glow of sexual desire.

I went home barely able to walk from wanting him and completed my breakup with Darren the next day. If desire was supposed to feel like that, I needed more of it. I felt awake, alive, not just sexy, but sexual. Thoughts of him infected me until I saw him again and we tumbled into bed, screwing like wild animals.

When I finally walked away from him, weeping, I realized I'd let my sexuality control and manipulate me through him. He took my music and crushed it under the weight of his own talent. He ignored what I created, dismissing it, degenerating it, so that within three months, I couldn't sing a word and any instrument I picked up became a bludgeon. I'd never felt so creatively dead and so sexually alive.

When I got the strength to walk away from him, I vowed never again.

CHAPTER 8

I snapped my locker closed, thinking about those Dodger seats on the first base line. A corporation gets a skybox. A real fan gets tickets at field level, luxuries be damned. I'd never seen a game from that angle.

Debbie came into the locker room, buzzing with talk and flirting and locker doors banging, and handed out our tip envelopes. "A good night for everyone," she said, then got close to me. "Someone is waiting for you at the front exit. If you want to avoid him, go through the parking lot, but be nice. He's a friend of the hotel."

"Can I ask you something?"

"Quickly, I have to count out."

"How many drinks did he have?" I asked as quietly as I could.

Debbie smiled as if I'd asked the exact right question. "Two. He nurses like a baby."

"I know you don't know me that well yet, but... would going out the front be a mistake?"

"Only if you take it too seriously."

"Thanks."

Debbie walked off to hand out the rest of the envelopes. What she said had been a relief, actually. It made the boundaries that much clearer. I could hang out, be close to him and feel the buzz of sex between us, but I had to be careful about climbing into bed with him. Fair warning.

CHAPTER 9

Jonathan stood in the lobby, talking to Sam, laughing like an old buddy. I wasn't going to approach him with my boss right there. Sam seemed like a fine guy for the fifteen minutes we'd talked. With his white hair and slim build, he looked like a newscaster and had an all-business attitude. I just pushed through the revolving doors, figuring fate had lent a hand in deciding whether or not I'd see Drazen outside a rooftop bar.

I was three steps into the hot night when I heard him call my name.

"You stalking me?" I asked, slowing my steps to the parking lot.

"Just wanted company to walk to my car."

We strolled down Flower Street, the long way to the underground parking lot. Any normal person would have gone through the hotel.

"How do you know Sam?" I asked.

"He introduced me to my ex-wife, which I'm trying not to hold against him."

"You're a good sport," I said. "Have you always been blue?"

He tilted his head a few degrees.

"Dodger fan," I said. "I would've taken you for more of an Angels guy."

"Ah. Because I have money?"

"Kind of."

"I like a little grit," he said, that smile lighting up the night.

"Is that why you met me after work?" I asked, turning toward the parking lot entrance.

"Kind of."

He let me go first into the underground passage, and I felt his eyes on me as I walked. It was not an uncomfortable feeling. When we got to the bottom of the ramp, we stopped. I parked in the employee level and his car was in the valet section. I held up my hand to wave good-bye.

"It was nice to talk to you," I said.

"You too."

We faced each other, walking backward in opposite directions.

"See you around," I said.

"Okay." He waved, tall and beautiful in the flat light and grey parking lot.

"Take care."

"What do I have to say?"

"You have to say please," I said.

"Please."

"Where do you think you're taking me?"

"Come on. Text a friend and tell them who you're with in case I'm a psycho killer."

CHAPTER 10

The early hour guaranteed a traffic-free trip to the west side. I'd gotten into his Mercedes convertible thinking most killers don't drive with the top down where everyone could see, so I just let the wind whip my hair into a bird's nest. Jonathan drove with one hand, and as I watched his fingers move and slide on the bottom of the wheel, the hair on the back of it, the strong wrist, I imagined it on me. I grabbed the leather seat, trying to keep my mind on something, anything else, but the leather itself seemed to rub the backs of my thighs the wrong way. "So, you pick up waitresses a lot?"

He smirked and glanced over to me. The wind was doing crazy shit to his hair as well, but it made him look sexy, and I was sure I looked like Medusa. "Only the very attractive ones."

"I guess I should take that as a compliment."

"You definitely should."

"I'm not sleeping with you."

"You mentioned that."

So maybe the rumors were true, and he was a total womanizer. Well, I'd already told him sex was off the table, so he could womanize all he wanted. Didn't matter to me at all. I was driven by curiosity. Who was this guy? What was it like to be him? Not that it mattered, I told myself, because again, I had no time for a heartbreak.

"What's your instrument, Monica? You said you were a musician."

"My voice, mostly," I said. "But I play everything. I play piano, guitar, viola. I learned to play the Theremin last year."

"What is that?"

"Oh, it's beautiful. You actually don't touch it to play it. There's an electrical signal between two antennae, and you move your hands between them to create a sound. It's just the most haunting thing you ever heard."

"You play it without touching it?"

"Yeah, you just move your hands inside it. Like a dance."

"This, I have to see."

When he tipped his head toward me, I thought, oh no. He wants me to play it for him. Never gonna happen. For some reason, the idea of this guy seeing me sing or play made me feel vulnerable, and I wasn't in for that at all. "You can watch people play it on YouTube."

"True. But I want to watch *you* do it."

I didn't know where we were going, so I didn't know how much of a drive we were in for. I wanted to get off the subject of me before I told him something that gave him a hold over me. I had to remember he was my new boss's friend, and I really liked working at the Stock.

"What do you do besides own hotels and pick up very attractive waitresses?"

"I own lots of things, and they all need attention."

He pulled the car to the side of the road. We were on the twistiest part of Mulholland, the part that looked like a desolate park instead of the most expensive real estate in Los Angeles County. A short guardrail stood between the car and a nearly sheer drop down to the valley and its twinkling Saturday night lights.

"Let's go take a look," he said, pulling the emergency brake.

I got out, thankful for the opportunity to uncross my legs, and slammed the door behind me. I walked toward the edge overlooking the city. My heels kept hitting little rocky ditches, but I played it off. They were comfortable, but they weren't hiking boots. I stood close to the guardrail, leaning against it with my knees. I felt him behind me, closing his door and jingling his keys. I'd been to places like that before. There were thousands of them all over the city, which was surrounded by hills and mountains. Way back when, before I'd even kissed Darren, I'd been up to a similar place to squirm around the back of Peter Dunbar's Nissan. And after the prom, I'd come up to drink too much and make love to Darren behind a tree.

"Do you live up here?" I asked.

"I live in Griffith Park." He stepped behind me. "Those bright lights are Universal City. To the right, that black part is the Hollywood reservoir." I could feel his breath on the back of my neck. "Toluca Lake is to the left." He put his hands on my neck, where every nerve ending in my body was now located, following his touch as he stroked me, like the little magnet shavings under plastic I'd played with as a kid. When the pen moved, the shavings moved, and I arched my neck to feel more of him. "The rest," he said, "is hell on Earth. Not recommended."

He kissed me at the base of my neck. His lips were full and soft. His tongue traced a line across my shoulder. I gasped. I had not a single word to say, even when I felt his erection against my back and his hands moved across my stomach, feeling me through my clothes. God, I hadn't been touched like that in so long.

When did I decide men were too much trouble? A year and a half since I shed Kevin like a too-warm coat? I couldn't even say. Drazen's lips were more than lips; they were the physical memory of myself before I shut out sex to pursue music.

I twisted, my lips searching for his, my mouth open for him as his was for me. We met there, tongues twisting together, his chest to my back, his hands moving up my shirt, teasing my nipples.

I moaned and turned to face him. He pushed me against the car. The hardness between his legs felt enormous on my thigh. He moved his hand down and pushed my legs open, gripping tight enough to press my jeans against my skin. He looked down at me, and the intensity of the lust in his eyes was nearly intimidating, but I was way past sense. Miles. The thought of saying, "No, stop, I need sleep so I'm fresh for rehearsals tomorrow," didn't even occur to me. He pushed his hips between my legs and kissed me again. I was hungry for him. A white hot ball of heat grew beneath my hips. We kept kissing and grinding, hands everywhere. I pinched his nipple through his shirt and he gasped, biting my neck. I hated my clothes. I hated every layer of fabric between myself and his cock. I wanted to feel skin sweating above mine, his dick rigid and hot, his hands at my breasts. I wanted those hard, dry thrusts to be real, slick, sliding inside me.

The siren blast split my ears. I almost choked on my own spit. Jonathan looked over at the police car and the tension in his neck was the last thing I saw before the light got too bright to see anything. I lowered my legs, and when he got off me, he held his hand out to help me off the hood.

"Good morning," came a male voice from behind the driver's side light. The passenger door opened, and a female cop got out.

"Good morning," Jonathan and I answered like two kids greeting their third grade teacher. He wove his fingers in mine. The female cop shone her flashlight in my face. I flinched.

"You okay, miss?"

"Yeah."

"Can you step away from the gentleman, please? Come toward me."

I did, hands out so she knew I wasn't reaching for anything. The cop pulled me out of earshot.

"Do you know this guy?" she asked, shining a little light into my pupils to see if I was on anything stronger than pheromones.

"Yes."

"Are you here of your own free will?"

"Yes."

"That was pretty hot." She snapped her little light down. "Next time, get a room, okay?"

CHAPTER 11

Things cooled on the way home. I kept my legs crossed and his hand stayed on the gear shifter. When I told Jonathan the lady cop said we should get a room, he laughed.

"If only she knew who she was talking about," he said. After a few seconds, he stopped at a light and turned to me. "So, what's up with you saying you're not sleeping with me, then pushing up against my dick on the hood of my car?"

I was a little annoyed with the question, because he brought me there and he started kissing my neck, but I also couldn't pretend I wasn't just as responsible for the raw heat of the scene.

"I just..." I had to pause and think. The light changed, and when he turned his head back to the road, I felt like I could talk. "I have things I'm doing. I can't be up all night fucking because my voice gets messed up. I can't think about a man, any man, nothing personal, when I should be writing songs. Carving out enough nights for song writing, between gigs and working, is hard enough without making time for a boyfriend. So, I mean, I had to give up something in life, and it's men."

He nodded and thought about it. He rubbed his chin, which had a little bit of stubble. My neck remembered it very fondly. "I get it."

"So, I'm sorry I led you on. That was careless."

His laugh was loud and inappropriate, considering what I'd just said, but he didn't seem embarrassed.

"What's so funny?" I asked.

"You're taking all my best lines."

"Didn't mean to steal your thunder."

"No problem. I enjoyed hearing it."

I leaned back and watched the scenery change from the twisted forestation of Mulholland to the expanse of the 101. How did I end up in this car, at four in the

29

morning, with a known womanizer? Yes, he was gorgeous and warm and knew all the right places and ways to touch me, but really? How stupid would I be? How many women had fallen for this crap, and I was going to be another one in line?

The wind made it hard to talk until he pulled off downtown. "What's with you and sleeping around?" I asked.

"What do you mean?"

"All the women. You have a reputation."

"Do I?" He smirked, not looking at me as he drove. "And that didn't chase you away?"

"I trust myself. I trust my instincts and my resolve. You just make me curious is all."

He shrugged. "What do you think your reputation is?"

"I don't have one."

"Of course you do. Everyone does. When people talk about Monica, what do they say, besides that she's beautiful?"

I let the compliment slide. Coming from someone who had almost made his way into my pants, it didn't mean much. "I guess they say I'm ambitious. I hope they say I'm talented. My friend Darren would say I'm cold."

"Did he try to get you into bed, too?"

"Shut up." He glanced at me and we smiled at each other. "I was with him for six and a half years, so it's not like he had to try for a long time."

"Was it a hard breakup?" He stopped at a light and turned his gaze to me, ready to offer me sympathy or words of wisdom.

"No. It was the easiest thing we ever did." I couldn't discern what he was thinking from the way he looked at me, but he got serious, draining his tone of all flirtation.

"Easy for *you*?"

"Both. It was dying for a long time."

He looked out his window, rubbing his lips with two fingertips.

"You want to say something you're not saying," I said. "I don't want to be your girlfriend, so being honest isn't going to come back and bite you on the ass."

The Stock, and my car, were a block away. He pulled up to the curb. He put the Mercedes in park but didn't turn the key.

"You really want to know?"

"Yeah."

"Why?"

"Because you make me curious."

He smirked. "My wife and I were married that long. It wasn't easy." He rubbed the steering wheel, and I realized he regretted answering even the first part of the question. It was too late for me to give up on him now, so I waited until he said, "She left and took everything with her."

"I don't understand. Are you broke?"

He put the car into drive and turned to me. "She didn't take a dime. She took everything that *mattered*."

I felt sorry and then I felt stupid for feeling any kind of sympathy. I wanted to hold his hand and tell him he'd get over it someday, but nothing could have been less appropriate.

"I'm kinda hungry," I said. "There's this food truck thing on First and Olive. In a parking lot? You can come if you want."

"It's four in the morning."

"Don't come. Your call."

"You're a tough customer. Anyone ever tell you that?"

I shrugged. I really was hungry, and nothing sounded better than a little Kogi kimchi right then.

Jonathan was right in mentioning the time. Four in the morning was pretty late, as evidenced by the fact that he found a place for the car half a block away. We walked into the lot, against the traffic of twenty- and thirty-something partiers as they filtered out, one third more sober than they had been when they got there, carrying food folded in wax paper or swishing around eco-friendly containers. The lot was smallish, being in the middle of downtown and not in front of a Costco. The only parked vehicles lined the chain link fence, brightly painted trucks spewing luscious smells from all over the globe. My Kogi truck was there, as well as a gourmet popcorn truck, artisanal grilled cheese, lobster poppers, ice cream, sushi, and Mongolian barbecue. The night's litter dotted the asphalt, hard white from the brash floodlights brought by the truck owners. The truck stops were informal and gathered by tweet and rumor. Each truck brought their own tables and chairs, garbage pail, and lights. The customers came between midnight and whenever.

I scanned the lot for someone I knew, hoping I'd find someone to say hello to on one hand and wishing Jonathan and I could stay alone on the other.

"My Kogi truck is over there," I said.

"I'm going to Korea next week. The last think I need is to fill up on Kogi. Have you had the Tipo's Tacos?"

"Tacos? Really?"

"Come on." He took my hand and pulled me over to the taco truck. "You're not a vegetarian or anything?"

"No."

"*Hola,*" he said to the guy in the window, who looked to be about my age or younger with a wide smile and little moustache. "*Que tal?*" he continued. That was about the extent of my Spanish, but not Jonathan's. He started rattling off stuff, asking questions, and if the laughter between him and the guy with the little moustache was any indication, *joking* fluidly. If I'd closed my eyes, I'd have thought he was a different person.

"You speak Spanish?" I asked.

"I live in Los Angeles," Jonathan replied as if his answer was the most obvious in the world.

"You don't speak it?" Little Moustache asked me.

"No."

He said something to Jonathan, and there was more conversation, which made me feel left out. They were obviously talking about me.

"He wants to know if you're as smart as you are beautiful," Jonathan said.

"What did you tell him?"

"Prospects are good, but I need time to get to know you better."

"Anywhere in that conversation, did you order me a *pastor?*"

"Just one?"

"Yes. Just one."

"They're small." He made a circle with his hands, smiling like an old grandma talking to her granddaughter about being too damn skinny.

I pinched his side, and there wasn't much to grab. It was hard and tight. "One," I said, trying to forget that I'd touched him.

We sat at a long table. A few trucks were breaking down for the night. There was a feeling of quiet and finality, the feeling he and I had outlasted the late nighters and deep partiers. I finished my taco in three bites and turned around, putting my back to the table and stretching my legs.

He took a swig of his water and touched my bicep with his thumb. "No tattoos?"

"No. Why?"

"I don't know. Mid-twenties. Musician. Lives in Echo Park. You need tattoos and piercings to get into that club."

I shook my head. "I went a few times, but couldn't commit to anything. My best friend Gabby has a few. I went with her once, and I couldn't decide what to get. And anyway, it would have been awkward."

"Why?" He was working on his last taco, so I guess I felt like I should do the talking until he finished.

"She was getting something important. On the inside of her wrist, she got the words *Never Again* on the scars she made when she cut herself. I couldn't diminish it by getting some stupid thing on me."

He ate his last bite and balled up his napkin. "What happened that made her try to commit suicide?"

"We have no idea. She doesn't even know. Just life." I wanted to tell him I'd found her, and been with her in the hospital, and that I took care of her, but I thought I'd gotten heavy enough. "I have a piercing, though," I said. "Wanna see?"

"I can see your ears from here."

I lifted my shirt to show him my navel ring with its little fake diamond. "Yes, it hurt."

"Ah," he said. "Lovely."

He touched it, then spread his fingers over my stomach. His pinkie grazed the top of my waistband, and I took in a deep gasp. He put a little pressure toward him on my waist, and I followed it, kissing him deeply. His stubble scratched my lips and his tongue tasted of the water he'd just drunk. I put my hands on his cheeks, weaving my fingers in his hair.

It was sweet, and doomed, and pointless, but it was late, and he was handsome and funny. I may not have been interested in having a boyfriend, but I wasn't made of stone.

When Little Moustache had to break down the table, we had to admit it was time to go. The sky had gone from navy to cyan, and the air warmed with the appearance of the first arc of the sun.

We got to his car before he had to feed the meter. We didn't say anything as he pulled into the parking lot at the Stock and went down two stories to my lonely Honda, sitting in the employee section. I opened the door with a clack that echoed in the empty underground lot.

"Thanks," he said. "I'll probably see you at the hotel sometime."

"We can pretend this never happened."

"Up to you." He touched my cheek with his fingertips, and I felt like an electrical cable to my nervous system went live. "I wouldn't mind finishing the job."

"Let's not promise each other anything."

"All right. No promises," he said.

"No lies," I replied.

"See you around."

We parted without a good-bye kiss.

CHAPTER 13

Gabby and I lived in the house I grew up in, which was on the second steepest hill in Los Angeles. When my parents moved, they let me live in the house for rent that equaled the property taxes plus utilities. I was sure I'd never need to move. I had two bedrooms and a little yard. The house had been a worthless piece of crap in a bad neighborhood when they bought it in the 1980s. Now it had a cardiologist to the west of it and a converted Montessori school that cost $1,800 a month to the east.

The night Jonathan Drazen took me up to Mulholland Drive, I returned to find Darren sleeping on my couch. We had agreed to not leave Gabby alone until we knew she was okay, and she'd gotten no better after a week on her meds. The first blue light of morning came through the drapes, so I could see well enough to step around the pizza box he'd left on the floor and get into the bathroom.

I looked at myself in the mirror. The convertible had wreaked havoc with my hair and my makeup was gone, probably all over Jonathan Drazen's face.

I still felt his touch: his lips on my neck, his hands feeling my breasts through my shirt. My fingers traced where his had been, and my pussy felt like an overripe fruit. I stuck my hand in my jeans, one knee on the toilet bowl, and came so fast and hard under the ugly fluorescent lights that my back arched and I moaned at my own touch. It was a waste of time. I wanted him as much after I came as I did before.

My God, I thought, how did I do this to myself? What have I become?

I needed to never see him again. I didn't need his lips or his firm hands. If I needed to take care of my body's needs, I could find a man easily enough. I didn't need one so pissed at his ex-wife he'd make me fall in love with him before apologizing for leading me on. He wanted to hurt women, and nothing froze my creative juices like heartache. No, I decided as I went back out to the kitchen, anyone but Jonathan.

Darren was already making coffee.

"Where were you?" he asked. "It's six thirty already."

"Driving all over the west side with I-won't-say."

"Mister Gorgeous?" He said it without jealousy or teasing.

"Yep."

"He's nice to you?"

"He wants to sleep with me, so it's hard to say if he's being nice or being manipulative," I said. "How's Gabby?"

"Same." He got out two cups and a near-dead carton of half-and-half. "She's volatile, then deadened. She started shaking because she wasn't playing last night. Missed opportunity and all that. Then she rocked back and forth for half an hour."

"Did you sit her at the piano?"

"Yeah, that worked. We need something to happen for her."

"She'll still be who she is," I said. "She could play the Staples Center, and she'd be this way."

"But she could afford to get care, the right meds, maybe therapy. Something." I nodded. He was right. They were stymied by poverty. "And Vinny? I haven't heard a damn thing from that guy. I tried calling him and his mailbox is full." He was losing his shit, standing there with a coffee cup in his hand.

"We have six more months on our contract with him and we're out," I said.

"She doesn't have six months, Mon."

"Okay, I get it." I held him by the biceps and looked him in the face.

"She's like she was the last time, when you found her. I don't want—"

"Darren! Stop!"

But it was too late. The stress of the evening had gotten to him. He blinked hard and tears dripped down his cheeks. I put my arms around him, and we held each other in the middle of the kitchen until the coffeemaker beeped. He wiped his eyes with his sleeve, still holding the empty cup. "I'm working the music store this morning. Will you stay with her until rehearsal?"

"Yeah."

"Can I shower here? My water heater's busted."

"Knock yourself out. Just hang the towel."

He strode out of the kitchen, and I was left there with our dripping sink and filthy floor. The roof leaked, and the foundation was cracked from the last earthquake swarm. It had been nice to sit in that Mercedes and drive around with someone who never spent a minute agonizing about money. It had been nice to not worry about anything but physical pleasure and what to do with it for a couple of hours. Real nice.

Darren's laptop was on the kitchen table, set to some Pro Tools thing he probably hadn't gotten a chance to touch in the middle of taking care of Gabby. I fixed my coffee and slid into the chair, opening the internet browser. We stole bandwidth from the Montessori school during off hours, so I checked my email. I remembered my conversation with Jonathan about his ex-wife, so I did a search for her: Jessica Carnes.

I got a different set of pictures than Darren had shown us the other day. Jessica was an abstract and conceptual artist. Searching under Google Images brought back a treasury of pictures of the artist and her art, which despite Kevin schooling me in the vocabulary of the visual arts, I didn't get at all.

Jessica had long blond hair and an Ivory Girl complexion. She might have worn a stitch of makeup and maybe used hot rollers. She wore nice flats, but flats nonetheless. Her skirts were long and her demeanor was modest. She was my exact opposite. I had long brown hair and black eyes. I wore makeup, tight jeans, short skirts, and the highest heels I could manage. And black. I wore a lot of black, a color I hadn't given a thought to until I saw Jessica in every cream, ecru, and pastel on the palette.

On page three, I came across a wedding photo. I clicked through.

The page had been built by her agent, and it showed a beachside extravaganza the likes of which I could only aspire to waitress. I scrolled down, looking for his face. I found him here and there with people I didn't know or side-by-side with his bride. A picture at the bottom stopped me. I sighed as if the air had been forced out of my lungs by an outside force. Jessica and Jonathan stood together, separated from the crowds. Her back was three-quarters to the camera, and he faced her. He was speaking, his eyes joyous, happy, his face an open book about love. He looked like a different man with his fingertips resting on Jessica's collarbone. I knew exactly how that touch felt, and I envied that collarbone enough to snap the laptop closed.

CHAPTER 14

I tapped my foot. Studio time was bought by the hour and not cheap, yet Gabby and I were the only ones there. She was at the piano, of course, running her fingers over the keys with her usual brilliance, but it was only therapy, not real practice. Darren's drums took twenty minutes to set up. The chitchat and apologies would take another fifteen minutes, and I still had to practice some dumb standards for the solo gig at Frontage that night.

I sat on a wooden bench facing the glass separating the studio from the control room. The room stank of cigarettes and human funk. The soundproofing on the walls and ceiling was foam, porous by necessity, and thus holding cells for germs and odor. Though I thought I'd rubbed away the ache Jonathan had caused, I woke up with it, and a good scrub and an arched back in the shower did nothing to dispel the feel of him. I needed to get to work. Letting this guy under my skin was counterproductive already.

I whispered, "I've got you, under my skin." Then I groaned the rest of the lyrics like I was in heat. No. But yes. It was a good song. It was missing how I really felt: frustrated and angry. So I belted out the last line of the chorus without Sinatra's little snappy croon, but a longing, accusatory howl.

"Hang on," Gabby said. She took a second to find the melody, and I sang the chorus the way I wanted it played.

"Wow, that's not how Sinatra did it," she said.

"Play it loungey, like we're seducing someone." I tapped her a slower rhythm, and she caught onto it. "Right, Gabs. That's it."

I stood up and took the rest of the song, owning it, singing as if the intrusion was unacceptable, as if insects crawled inside me, because I didn't want anyone under my skin. I wanted to be left alone to do my work.

Having the guys here to record it so I could hear it would have been nice, but I could tell I was onto something. The back room at Frontage was small, so I needed less rage and more discomfort. More sadness. More disappointment in myself for letting it happen, and begging the pain away. If I could nail that, I might actually enjoy singing a few standards at a restaurant. Or I might get fired for changing them. No way to know.

I did it again, from the top. The first time I sang the word, "skin," I felt Jonathan's hands on me and didn't resist the pleasure and warmth. I sang right through it, and when Gabby accompanied, she put her own sadness into it. I felt it. It was my song now.

My phone rang: Darren.

"Where the hell are you?"

"Harry just called me. His mother is sick in Arizona. He's out. For good."

I would have said something like, *so no bassist, no band,* but Gabby would have heard, and she wasn't ready for any kind of upset.

"And you're not here because?"

He sighed. "I got held up at work. I'll be there in twenty. Tomorrow night, I have a favor to ask."

"Yeah?"

"I have a date. Can you get her home after your gig and make sure she takes her meds?"

"Yeah."

"Thanks, Mon."

"Go get laid."

I clicked the phone off and used the rest of the time to work on our performance.

CHAPTER 15

Thursday afternoon shift at the Stock was slow by Saturday night standards. I earned less money, but the atmosphere was more relaxed. There was always a minute to chill with Debbie at the service bar. I liked her more and more all the time. I tried to keep it light and hold my energy up. Just because this gig tonight wasn't my own songwriting, I still wanted to do a good job. But after Darren's call and the sputtering dissolution of the band, I lost the mojo, and I just sounded like Sinatra on barbiturates. I had no idea how to get that heat back.

Debbie got off her phone as I slid table ten's ticket across the bar. Robert snapped it up and poured my rounds.

"I think he likes you," Debbie said, indicating Robert. He was hot in his black T-shirt and Celtic tattoos.

"Not my type."

"What is your type?"

I shrugged. "Nonexistent."

"Okay, well, finish with this table and go on your break. Could you go down to Sam's office and make a copy of next week's schedule?" She handed me a slip of paper with the calendar. The waitstaff hung around waiting for it every week as our station placement and hours determined not only how much money we'd make over the next seven days, but our social and family plans as well. And here she was giving it to me two hours early. She smiled and patted my arm before walking off to greet three men in suits.

I went to the bathroom and freshened up, then headed for Sam's office.

It wasn't a warm, fabulously decorated place like Jonathan's at K. It was totally utilitarian, with a linoleum floor and metal filing cabinets. The copy machine was in there, and I put the schedule on the glass without turning the lights on. The windows gave enough afternoon light.

The energy saver was on, meaning the copier was ice cold. I tapped start and waited. Lord knew how long it would take. I stretched my neck and hummed, then whispered, the lyrics to *Under My Skin*.

I gasped when I smelled his dry scent. When I turned, Jonathan stood in the doorway with his arms crossed. That was the first time I'd seen him in daylight, and the sunlight made him look more human, more substantial, more present, and more gorgeous, if that was even possible.

"Jonathan."

"Hi."

I realized the deal with the schedule copying just then. "Debbie sent me up here."

"You didn't know she was a yenta?"

"You're very persistent."

"I just kept telling myself I didn't want you, but we said no lies, and I think that includes lying to myself. How about you?"

I didn't know what to say. I had shut out thoughts of him for almost a week. I thought about baseball, chord progressions, and getting a new manager whenever he came into my mind. So having him in front of me was like opening a closet door and having all the stuff come tumbling out.

I took a step forward, and he did, too. We were in each other's arms in a second, mouths attached, tongues twisting. He reached back and closed the door.

Okay, I was going to get this over with now. Me and him. Right there. Just get it done so I could move on. He thrust me onto the desk and I opened my legs, wrapping them around his waist. He was pushing against me again, like on the hood of the Mercedes, a million years ago.

He put his hands up my shirt, across my stomach and to my breasts.

"Yes?" he gasped.

"Yes," I whispered. "Yes to everything."

"Yes," he whispered in my ear, then pushed my bra up and cupped my tits, finding my nipples and rubbing them with his thumbs. My hips levitated from the desk, and I made some noise deep in my throat. Damn, he was good. Lots of practice. He knew exactly what to do.

He looked down at my chest, nipples hardening from his touch and the cool air. "My God, Monica, you are magnificent."

I laughed, because being admired like that made me nervous, but he shut me up when he put his mouth on one nipple and his fingers on the other, pressing and twisting. My legs tightened around him, hitching my skirt up to my waist. With only my panties between me and his jeans, he felt harder and more forceful. He pushed against me, and I flowed with him, my hips to his rhythm as I gripped his hair. I'd almost come like that, eons ago, with some guy in freshman year I couldn't even remember now, and it felt like it might happen again.

As if reading my mind, he pulled away. His own breathing was heavy as he looked at me, not as if he was undressing me with his eyes, but as if he was making plans for the body in front of him. He moved his hands down my sides and pulled my skirt up, bunching it at the waist. My underwear bottoms, which I hadn't given a thought to when I'd dressed in the morning, were the only thing between me and the world.

"Listen," I started, "I don't know if Sam would think this is ok."

He put his fingertips to my mouth, and I shushed. Let him explain to Sam. Let me get fired. I parted my lips and took two of his fingers in my mouth, sucking them down to the back.

"Ah, Monica," was all he said as he pulled them out, slowly, and pushed them back in at the same pace. I cupped my tongue around them and sucked. Not too hard, just enough. I knew I was doing it right when his eyelids closed just a little, and he opened his mouth for something between a gasp and an *aah*. He rubbed them over my bottom lip, curling it back, then put them back in my mouth. I took them eagerly, tasting his skin, feeling his warm breath on my face.

He slid his fingers out and stepped back, taking his crotch away from mine. I suddenly felt exposed and started to close my legs, but he pressed them apart. I reached for his buckle, but he pulled away.

"I want to touch you," I said.

"Not yet."

"I'm going crazy."

"No, you're not. Not enough."

With that, he moved the crotch of my panties to the side and put the finger he'd just removed from my mouth onto my wet folds. We both gasped. Then he slid two fingers into me. Slowly.

"Oh, God," I whispered.

He slipped them out without a word and put his thumb on the thin strip of cotton covering my clit. Lightly. Barely touching it. Just enough so I knew it was there, and he leaned over to kiss me, flicking his tongue in time with his thumbnail as it gently scratched the fabric of my underwear.

I thrust my hips forward. His fingers went deep into me, but the thumb wouldn't press down any harder. It just grazed the cotton as he glided his two fingers in and out.

"What do you want?" he asked.

"I want you to fuck me."

"What's the magic word?"

"Now?"

His fingers worked my body while he bent down to whisper into my ear. "You have three minutes of break left."

"I don't care."

"I'm going to spend hours fucking you."

My hips pushed against his hand, but he kept control: a light touch of the thumb and a slow grind with the fingers. I was on fire. I thought I had known what that meant, but I didn't.

"After your shift."

"I have a gig right after. We have to do it now." He might have considered it for the next three thrusts, but he didn't give my clit more than a stroke through fabric. I couldn't decide if that was pleasure or torture.

"After your gig," he said. "I have a dinner meeting anyway. Meet me at the hotel tonight. Room 3423."

"I have to take care of my roommate."

"Figure it out."

He pulled his fingers out of me. I felt the loss of them and his tormenting thumb so deeply I moaned. Sitting there, splayed and nearly naked on Sam's desk, I felt foolish and exposed, not to mention ravenously aroused.

"Don't." I didn't have anything more to say, except don't stop there; don't leave me like this. My eyes must have pleaded with him for some release, because his face, with its parted lips and heavy lids, shone with a lustful satisfaction. He knew I wanted him to fuck me for hours, starting on that desk. "You are despicable," I said.

He pulled my skirt down, and when he leaned down to kiss me, I returned it with no little anger on my lips. "Too true. And tonight, you're mine."

"What if I don't show?"

"You'll show."

After opening the door as little as possible, as if to protect my destroyed modesty, he was gone.

I had another three hours to work, and I couldn't keep my mind on the task at hand: pouring drinks. A moron could do it. First example: Robert. A hunk by any measure, but dumb as a post.

He slid the tray over the service bar. Each had the requisite alcohol as listed on the order ticket, clockwise from twelve o'clock, where he'd put the ticket. My job was to fill each glass with mixers from the soda gun and juice bin.

Like I said, a moron could do it. But I stood there, with Debbie next to me checking stuff off the inventory list, and I put soda in a whiskey. I stared at the glass and watched it over flow and why? Because the pain between my legs was uncomfortable and exquisite, and I was counting down the hours before I could get home and release it.

"Whoa!" Robert shouted, waking me up. "You got soda all over the tray!"

"I'm sorry!"

"Monica," Debbie said, slipping her pen onto the top of the clipboard, "come sit with me."

She pulled me over to an empty table by the kitchen door. We tried to keep it clear until the bar got too packed. I pressed my legs together when I sat even though my skirt was long enough. I felt like she could see my arousal.

Debbie placed her clipboard in front of her and leaned forward. "What's happening? You took the wrong order to Frazier Upton; you stepped on Jennifer Roberg's foot. That's not how we do service here."

"Why did you do that, Debbie? Why did you set me up to meet Jonathan upstairs?"

"I saw you looking at him the other night. I thought it would be a nice surprise."

"If you could avoid doing that again, that would be great."

"Of course. I'm sorry, I thought I was doing you a favor."

"You were. It's just..." I looked at my hands in my lap. "He's... I don't know." I felt suddenly embarrassed talking about a man's hold over me with my manager. I should have been mad at her, but in the world I lived in, she had done me a kindness, and it wasn't like he'd raped me. I'd loved it. I hated it ending when it did. "I just don't need to be with anyone right now. Or ever. I had this boyfriend, Kevin, a year and a little ago. He wouldn't let me sing. It was awful, but what I'm trying to say is, I don't want to be that person again."

"Okay." Debbie sat up straight. She pushed her long, straight hair out of her face with a single, French-manicured finger and got down to business. "I am going to tell you things you need to hear, but don't want to. Are you okay with that?"

"Sure."

"Jonathan Drazen is not going to stay with you long enough to care what you do with your spare time. He is very attracted to you, that much I can see. But he is in love with one woman, and one woman only."

"His ex-wife."

Debbie nodded. "When Jessica left, he begged her to stay. She wouldn't. He broke down at a shareholder meeting. It was ugly. He was humiliated. He's *still* humiliated. He won't put himself in that position again, I promise you. So if you like him, I suggest you enjoy yourself with him. He will treat you very well, and then you'll go your separate ways. He can be a valuable friend."

I nodded. I got it. I felt comforted, in a way, that I could meet him later, have mattress-bending sex, then go home without worrying. I knew I wasn't getting involved, and if he had the same idea, I was safe.

Debbie gathered her things and started to stand, but I wasn't done.

"Why did she leave?" I asked.

"Another man," she said, "and everyone knew it."

"Ouch."

Debbie nodded. "Ouch is right. It should never happen to any of us."

CHAPTER 17

I hated gigs like Frontage. I had to sing songs someone else wrote to people who weren't there to see me. I had to sing through waiters taking orders and customers being seated. I couldn't sing too loud or I'd disturb everyone, and I couldn't improvise at all. Ever. I was background.

But it was money, if not a lot, and it was practice. It wasn't as if Vinny had shown up and booked anything fabulous. It wasn't as if he'd shown up at all in the past two weeks. I simply had nothing else going on.

We had a dressing room with a smudged mirror and filth on everything. Sometime in the eighties, a tube of lipstick had been jammed into the seam between the two pieces of plywood that made up the counter, and the red goo that was out of reach of a folded paper towel had turned brown and crusty. The carpet stank of beer vomit, and the bathroom had been casually wiped down a few days previous. I felt like a superstar.

Gabby was already out there, tinkling the piano. She had a jazzy way of rolling her fingers across the keys, creating a melody from nothing, building on it, and landing into something else without a hitch. Her bag was open on the counter, and I did what Darren and I always did. I took out her meds and made sure she had one less Marplan than she had last night. Ten milligrams, twice a day. Eleven pills in the bottle. Darren had texted me this morning with the number twelve. Good.

I called him. He was headed out for another date with this girl whose name he wouldn't reveal.

"Hey, Mon," he said.

"Eleven," I said.

"Thanks."

"What are you doing tonight?" I asked.

"Date."

"Are you going to tell me her name?" I sat on the torn pleather chair, letting my short skirt ride up since I was alone. My hair was up, and red lipstick coated my lips like lacquer. I looked like a 1950s pinup.

"Not yet," he said.

"Is it an early date or a late date?" I swallowed hard. I was about to ask a lot.

"Maybe both. Why?"

"I wanted to…" I drifted off, because I wanted to meet Jonathan and relieve the ache he created, but I didn't want to get into too much detail with Darren.

"Ask. I'm shaving and it's messing up the phone."

"I wanted to see Jonathan Drazen tonight. After the gig. Right after. I can be home to watch Gabby by eleven."

"Can't. My date's boss got us tickets to *Madame Bovary*."

Great. A date including a musical would go from dinner at seven p.m. to curtains at eleven thirty. He must like this girl.

"Sorry," he said. I heard the water running.

"No problem." I hung up.

Eight months before I ever worked at K, I found Gabby sitting at the kitchen sink, on the high stool I'd used to get cereal as a kid. Her head was on the counter and one wrist had flopped over, spilling blood onto the floor.

I'm so sorry I messed up the floor, Monica, she'd said the next day, in her hospital bed. That was what she was worried about: That I would be mad I had to clean up the floor. I'd just ripped up the whole thing and put in new press-on vinyl tiles. I couldn't find another way to think about something besides how dead and cold she looked when I pulled her off the stool, or the blood trapped in the drain catch, or the way I'd screamed at her the day before for eating graham crackers in the living room, or the way she'd wept when Darren and I broke up, eons ago. I cried over cracking linoleum flooring because the ambulance had arrived a full nine and a half minutes after I called, and I spent them slapping her because it made her groan and I didn't know what else to do to prove she was alive.

So though I wanted Jonathan to treat me like his own personal toy for a few hours, I had to get Gabby home and stay there until the next morning, when Darren would show up.

The lights kept me from seeing any of the diners. I smiled at a bunch of silhouettes because even though I couldn't see them, they could see me.

Gabrielle hit the first song, *Someone to Watch Over Me,* then went to *Stormy Weather.* I had my groove on then. I sang with the feeling she and I had practiced, but as I got to the middle of *Cheek to Cheek,* I caught a whiff of cologne I recognized: Jonathan's. Someone was wearing his cologne, and the weight between my legs came back from the memory of the afternoon. I sang about his cheek on mine, about the scent and feel of him. *Under My Skin* came out like a seduction. I sang the words, but all I could feel was sex, the need for it. I begged for it with the lyrics, the snappy little Sinatra tune gone, replaced by a moan for gratification.

When my voice fell off the last note, I was ready for that hotel room.

They applauded, quiet but earnest. You weren't supposed to clap at all at these types of gigs, and I said, "Thank you" with an embarrassed smile. I was convinced they could see my arousal like a dark patch soaking through my dress. I looked back at Gabby, and she gave me a thumbs up. I think I must have been a hundred shades of blush. I put the mike down and the spotlights went out. The diners started up their conversations again, and I headed back to the shitty dressing room.

Jonathan was in a booth, staring at me.

Of course that was where the cologne smell had come from. The source. It wasn't like he'd gotten it at Barney's. If it wasn't a handmade scent, I'd eat my shoe. But I hadn't even thought of that until I saw him in a booth at Frontage with a gorgeous redhead sipping a cosmopolitan. He tipped his glass to me.

He leaned toward the redhead and whispered something to her. Right into her ear. Like tipping his glass to me and breathing on her in any ten second interval was perfectly okay.

I was going to run and get as far from him as possible. I couldn't believe what I'd almost done. I wasn't kidding myself into thinking monogamy was on the table, but I'd think a day would pass before he'd put his hand up someone else's skirt, or that he'd take the trouble to not shove it right in my face.

But instead of running away like a sensible person, I walked up to the booth. "Hi, Jonathan."

"Monica," he said. "This is Teresa."

I nodded and smiled, and she held her glass up to me. "That was beautiful."

"Thanks."

"You were incredible," Jonathan said. "I've never heard anything like that." I stared at him. Something had changed in his face. I couldn't pin it down. Softer? Was he tired? Or did Teresa have a relaxing effect on him? His happiness made me feel evil and sharp.

"I've never heard of a man trying to sandwich another woman between fingering me and fucking me in the same day."

Teresa, who looked as though she was one hundred percent lady, almost spit out a mouthful of her cosmopolitan. Jonathan laughed too. I personally didn't find any of this funny. I stepped back, and Theresa stood as well. Maybe she was pissed. Maybe her laugh was the nervous kind or maybe I'd just shocked her. But she was as composed as possible as she turned to Jonathan and said, "I'm going to the ladies'."

He nodded, then scooted over once she was gone. "Would you like to sit?"

"No."

"For someone who doesn't want to get involved, you have a way of being involved."

"Even I have limits."

"She's a natural redhead." His look was full deadpan, and though what he said had a hundred filthy connotations, the one non-pornographic one became apparent with the straight-faced look.

"She's your sister," I said.

"Two years between us. She'd appreciate it if you assumed I was older."

"I'm so embarrassed," I said. "I have to apologize to her."

"Are you going to sit? Or am I just going to stare at your body without touching you?"

I slid in next to him, and he put his arm around me, his fingertips brushing my neck.

"What are you doing here?" I asked.

"I was having dinner with my sister. No, I was not stalking you, though I have to say again, I think you have a gift. I think I felt a half a tear, right here." He touched the inside corner of his eye.

"Are you making fun of me?"

"No. I promise you. You were... I don't have a word big enough." He looked at my face, and I noticed his eyelashes were copper, like his hair. I was overcome by his presence. "Now I know what you're protecting by not getting entangled."

"Thank you," I said. "I appreciate that. I really do."

He ran his finger over my collarbone with just enough pressure to make me breathe a little more deeply. "Am I seeing you tonight?"

I tried to stay cool, but I wanted him all over again. "I don't think I can. I'm not avoiding you. I have something else going on. Tomorrow?"

He shrugged. He must have thought I was playing games with him, which he'd probably be exquisitely sensitive about after the cheating wife. But I wasn't playing a game. Not at all.

"I have a flight out at five tomorrow. After two weeks, you might forget me."

"I should do to you what you did to me this afternoon," I said.

He let out a short snort of a laugh into his whiskey. "You don't have the self-control."

"What?"

"You heard me."

"You're wrong."

"Wanna bet?"

"Yeah. I wanna bet."

He pulled me close and spoke so softly I could barely hear him. "You get me to beg for it, and tomorrow I will take you to Tiffany on Rodeo Drive where you can pick out anything you want."

"Anything?"

"Anything."

"And what if I don't? Which I won't, but just for argument's sake."

"Then you cancel whatever it is you're doing, and I take you back to my house, where you will obey my every command until the sun comes up."

"I am not scrubbing your kitchen floor."

He smirked. "That's not what I had in mind."

I hadn't noticed the piano had stopped until I mentioned the kitchen floor.

"I'll be right back," I said, getting out of the booth before I had a chance to explain that I wasn't ditching him or manipulating him. I'd let Gabby go off by herself, and I didn't know if she'd seen me with him and taken a cab home.

I ran into Teresa in the hall on the way to the dressing room.

"I am so sorry," I said. "I was rude and unbecoming."

"My brother's an asshole, so I don't blame you." She said it with a smile, taking my hand and squeezing. "We both loved your voice."

"Thank you. I have to go. I'll try to see you on the way out."

I got into the dressing room just as Gabby shouldered her bag.

"I was looking for you," she said.

"I was talking to Jonathan. You ready to go? I want to see him on the way out."

"He's here? Oh my God, Mon, he can help us get an agent or something. Another manager. Anything."

"He's not in the business, Gabs, please come on."

She tugged my sleeve. "Wait. First of all, everyone's in the business, even if they're not. Okay? And what are you hiding from me? What?" She was a few inches shorter and looked up at me like she could pierce me with her eyes.

"Nothing."

"Monica."

"I want to go home." I took a step toward the door, but Gabby leaned against it. I dropped my bag, giving in. "Fine, he wants to make this bet, and it has to do with sex, and I'm not hanging out with him tonight, I'm hanging out with you."

"Cancel with me."

"No."

"Why not?"

"Because Darren would kill me."

"God damn the two of you!" she shouted.

"Gabs, please. Give me a break."

"No, you guys won't leave me alone to take a dump and you think I'm too stupid to notice? Now you have the chance to get the ear of a major fucking player—"

"He's not—"

"Shut up. Because you don't know anything. He teaches business at UCLA where Janet Terova heads up the Industry Relations board, and you know who that is, right?"

I sighed. I felt like I was taking a quiz.

"Arnie Sanderson's ex-wife?"

"Eugene Testarossa's boss. Right. Him."

"Gabby, if something happened because I went to have sex with some guy I barely even know…"

She put her hands on my arms and looked up at me with those big stinking blue eyes, the ones that had rolled to the back of her head and could only be brought back with a slap in the face, and said, "I promise I will not try to kill myself tonight."

"Your word is the last thing I should believe."

"I tried to kill myself because I felt hopeless. You do this, I have hope. Okay?"

"You're whoring me out."

"Am I taking a cab home or not?"

I had to admit, the temptation was painful, almost physically so. Here she was, not only giving me permission to leave her alone and promising not to hurt herself, but pushing me out the door.

The exquisite ache between my legs grew to a distracting level when I thought about being with Jonathan. The afternoon's frustration had turned into a longing that seemed bigger than my body.

Right then Darren's face showed up in my mind. He looked disappointed and angry.

I pushed past Gabby and went out to Jonathan and Teresa, who had moved to the bar. He put his hand on the back of my neck when I got close enough, and I whispered in his ear, "If I win, you cancel your flight and see me tomorrow night."

"And no Tiffany?" he asked, smirking.

"Yes, Tiffany. If you win, I'm at your command until sunrise. And after the sun comes up, I'll scrub your floors." He laughed. I didn't know exactly what he was laughing at, unless it was the presumption that he didn't already have a team of people to sterilize his house, but I smiled back at him because it was a stupid offer and I knew it.

Gabby situated herself at the end of the bar and ordered something. I hoped it was soda. Alcohol's a depressant, and she could assure me she had hope all she wanted. I didn't believe she had as much control as she asserted.

"You drive a hard bargain." He put his drink down. "And you're funny. I never know what's going to come out of your mouth next."

I had a million jokes about what was going in my mouth, but I kept them to myself as I pulled him into the back room.

The dressing room was locked. I was momentarily stumped, but I remembered there was another one for men. I took his hand and led him deeper into the back, passing the kitchen and backmost hallway, to the least populated part of the club.

"I'm really liking this scrubbing idea," he said as I pulled him into the second dressing room, which was as gross as the first, and slammed the door behind me. If he had more wisecracks, they got swallowed in a kiss. I ran my fingers through his hair, pressing his face to mine, then ran them down the length of his body. I pushed him onto the chair, which squeaked when he fell into it.

I kneeled in front of him, the industrial carpet digging into my knees, and opened his fly. I stroked the hardness under his boxers until I teased out his cock. It was rock hard and gorgeous.

"You ready?" I asked.

"You are really cute."

He held his arms out as if to say *come at me*.

I pulled up his shirt and kissed his stomach, which was hard and tight, down the line of hair, until I got to his base. I put him between my lips, kissed it, sucking the length on one side, then the other, running my tongue up and down the taut skin, tasting the sharpness of it. He took a deep breath. I flattened my tongue against the underside and ran it up to the end, then put the head in my mouth, sucking it on the way out. I tasted a salty drop of moisture on his tip.

I looked up at him as I slid it into my mouth again. His lips parted and he looked straight at me, moving my hair from my eyes. Perfect. I moved down, sliding the whole huge length of him into my open mouth.

"Oh," he whispered as I took him to the bottom. I moved my head up and down, taking all of him with every stroke, sucking on the way out, rubbing him with my tongue on the way in. I looked up at him again, going slow, letting him see every inch of his dick going in my mouth. I picked up the pace slightly, then gave three really fast strokes. He sighed and thrust his hips forward, jamming himself down my throat. I had him. All I had to do was slow down and tease him so close he'd beg me to finish him.

But he put his head back and looked at the ceiling, groaning deep in his throat. It was such a position of surrender, I couldn't do it. I couldn't stop. I was going to make him come way before he begged.

He was going to have me at his beck and call until sunrise.

I didn't like jewelry that much anyway.

CHAPTER 19

He'd smirked when he'd given me his address and tried to give me directions, but I knew where he lived, give or take. He was up in the park, where the lawyers and magnates play. I remembered Debbie's edict to just have fun, but the fact I'd failed in my mission to get him to take me to Tiffany rankled. Not that I really had anything to go with the carats I would have made him buy me, but failure wasn't something I took lightly, especially if it meant I'd been weak.

The valet pulled up with his dark green Jaguar. "Can I drive you to your car?" Jonathan asked.

"I'm in the lot," I said. "It's fine."

He put his face close to mine, until I could feel his breath in my ear. "If you don't want to go home with me, I won't hold you to it. We can wait, or we can call it off."

"A bet's a bet."

He brushed his nose on my cheek. "You sure? I can be demanding."

"So can I."

He stepped back and smiled. "Not tonight, you're not." He moved onto the curb. "I'll leave the gate open for you." He got into the car and drove off. I watched it head down La Brea, swaggering just like he did.

When I went inside, Gabby had already called a cab. I could smell a vodka tonic on her breath, but she seemed relatively sober.

"Are you sure you're going to be all right?" I said.

"Monica, you want to go, so just go. I'm tired of being babied."

And that was that. I put her in a cab and walked to my car.

My phone buzzed as I got into my little Honda. It was Vinny. Fucking Vinny.

"Where are you?" I asked.

"Vegas, baby." He was somewhere loud and unruly, yelling into the phone.

54

"We've been looking for you. The band broke up."

"I can't hear you. Listen, Sexybitch, you did a gig tonight at that shithole on Santa Monica?"

"Fron—"

"Eugene Testarossa's partner was there. Testarossa himself wants to see you. So you text me when you're up next, and I'll call him back and he'll show up. Bang! You're in."

"Vinny, I can't—"

"Text me, baby. Love you."

He cut the call.

What an asshole. He goes to Vegas for how long and now he wants his fifteen percent because I got my own gig? Oh no. That wasn't going to work. I texted him.

—You're fired—

I was at my car when the phone dinged.

—Fuck I am. You signed
a contract—

—The band signed a contract.
The band didn't play tonight.
I played solo—

There was a longer pause, and I sat in the driver's seat waiting to hear back, my night of subservience forgotten.

—Good luck getting WDE to
take your call—

I shut off my phone. I wanted to throw it, but I couldn't afford to replace it when I smashed it into a million pieces. He was right. No one at WDE was going to take a call or email from me. They'd contacted Vinny. I wouldn't get past the first round of assistants. Their job was to filter out artists. I could sing *Under My Skin* a hundred more times and never get another opportunity like this.

I think I looked out the window for fifteen minutes, resigning myself to the fact that I had a manager I hated and distrusted, and he was going to take a chunk of money from me from now until I accepted my Grammy.

I started the engine, but I had forgotten where I was going. Then that weight between my legs came back. Shit. I had an evening of wild sex planned with a rich womanizer who liked cute broke chicks. I was worrying about Vinny Landfillian. Fuck him. I hated Los Angeles.

All money and connections.

He can be a valuable friend.

All I needed was a lawyer to unravel that contract, and I was about to screw a guy who must have had a hundred sharky lawyers on speed dial. All I had to do was let him boss me around all night. The pleasure would be all mine.

I put the car in drive and headed east to Griffith Park.

It was wrong. My mother didn't raise me like that. She raised a nice girl who cared about her body more than her career. I didn't know who that girl was or what she wanted out of life though. I knew who I was. And the only thing I wanted more than Jonathan Drazen's body was an agent at WDE.

CHAPTER 20

The houses north of Los Feliz Boulevard aren't dream houses. A dream house in Los Angeles has four walls and a roof and maybe heat, but no one can afford it. The houses up in Griffith Park are scenery. They're owned by other people, the people who live on the other side. Not nouveau riche rock stars and actors. Old money. Generations' worth of trust funds. Three thousand square feet was a palace behind ten-foot hedges. I drove up the winding pass. Never having looked at the addresses before, I was at a loss to find them. It was as if you were supposed to just *know* where you were going because you belonged there.

I finally found the address under a gigantic fig tree with a brass plaque next to it, announcing the tree's status as a protected landmark. The gate opened for me, and I went up the drive and parked next to the Jag.

I sat in the car and looked at the house, convincing myself I still had a choice between going in or going home. The house was a craftsman, all warm lighting and dark woods. The porch was as big as my living room, leading to a wide, thick door. It was closed.

I took a deep breath.

Bottom line: He was hot, he was charming, and he didn't want anything out of me but the same thing I wanted. Unless he wanted me to clean his bathroom. I took hours to clean a bathroom, and I wasn't cleaning his.

I slid my phone out of my purse and called Darren.

"Hi," I said. "How was the show?"

"Fantastic. What's up?"

"I thought you should know…" I swallowed hard. "I sent Gabby home in a cab."

"You what?"

"She's tired of being followed around."

57

"And where are you?" He was pissed. He sounded like he was in the middle of a street, with people everywhere.

"Griffith Park. I can explain more later."

"No, explain now why you let a suicidal woman go home alone when her meds obviously aren't working and she's showing the same behaviors she did just before you found her bleeding into your kitchen sink."

"She's fine."

"This is completely irresponsible."

He hung up, which was a huge favor. I didn't want to tell him *why* I'd ditched Gabby.

I got out and walked up to the porch. Stained glass windows bordered the door. The light on the other side was soft and inviting. *This would be all right. Just fine.*

I knocked so softly, he couldn't have heard me unless he'd been waiting. I needed to see if he'd found something else to occupy him or if he was looking forward to seeing me. That could set the timbre for what I could request in the way of a warm call to WDE on my behalf.

The door opened immediately.

He wore the same button down shirt and jeans he'd worn at Frontage. His feet were bare, and in his right hand, he held a glass containing whiskey on ice.

I stood with my bag in front of me, which didn't stop him from looking at me as if he wanted to eat me alive. He leaned on the door jamb and swirled his drink. "I thought you weren't coming. I was starting to think I was losing my touch."

"This is a nice house."

He paused, and I waited. Despite the distractions of the past half hour, I was back to wanting to put my tongue all over his body. "All bets are on?" he asked.

"I'm yours to command."

He took my bag and put it on a side table. "Turn around."

I put my back to him. My car sat in the drive, next to his, the gate to the street wide open. He clicked the button on a little handheld box, and the gate slid closed.

The ice in his glass clinked, and I felt the touch of his hand at the base of my neck, then a tug as he unzipped my dress. "Jonathan..."

"No one can see."

The zipper went down past my lower back, and he slowly pulled it open. The sleeves slipped off a little when his hand, cold from the drink, touched between my shoulder blades. He ran his hand up to my neck, then over my right shoulder, pushing the dress off. Then he ran his hand to the left shoulder, until the dress slipped off and pooled around my ankles. I felt a breeze over my body. He slipped his finger under the bra strap. "Take this off."

I did, dropping it to the porch floor. He stroked under my waistband. He wanted that off too. I knew it, and I complied. I was fully naked except for my shoes, with my back to him.

"Face me."

I did. I'd never felt so naked in my life as he took his time looking me over.

"Hands behind your back."

I think if anyone else had gotten to command number four, I would have started laughing, but he wasn't anyone else.

"You doing okay?" he asked, stepping up to me. He put the glass to my lips and tipped it. Warmth filled my chest. It was good whiskey. The single malt I'd suspected.

"It's warm tonight," I said.

He put his face up to mine and whispered, "Infield fly rule. What is it?"

He kissed my neck as I answered. "When there's a force play at third, any fly hit inside the baselines, whether it's caught or not, means the batter's automatically out."

"Why?" He bit the corner of my neck and shoulder, and I gasped.

"To prevent an intentional error that would manufacture a double play."

"You are very real." He enunciated each word.

He drank the last of the whiskey and took an ice cube in his teeth. He put his face to mine and pressed the ice cube to my lips. I sucked on it, then took it from him, holding it in my mouth.

He took half a step back. I must have been a sight: naked but for my heels, hands behind my back, with an ice cube in my mouth. "And you are stunning," he said, lifting his glass. He put the cold base of it to my nipple, and I groaned as it hardened. He touched the other one, chilling it to a rock.

He bent down and warmed my breast with his mouth, sucking on the hard tip, pulling on it with lip-blunted teeth. I gasped, but couldn't open my mouth farther or I'd lose the ice. I guess that wouldn't have been the worst tragedy, but I knew the game was to keep the ice in my teeth. His attention to my breast made me groan, awakening the warmth in my crotch. The ice in my mouth melted, dripping down my chin and neck, tingling a wet path to my stomach. He licked the droplets that found their way to my breasts, warming cooled skin with his tongue. When I thought I couldn't take another minute of his attention without falling down from the pleasure of it, he stood straight and put his mouth over mine, sucking the ice back.

He crunched it and said, "Come on in."

I stepped past the threshold, and he closed the door behind me. The living room was impeccable in dark woods and Persian carpets. The bookcases were full. The whole place was the exact opposite of the cold modernity of his hotels.

Jonathan stood in front of me, watching my eyes take in the details of his house. The paintings. The stained glass. The clean corners and fluffed pillows. He kissed me again and, having forgotten the edict about the position of my hands, I put my arms around him. His hands warmed my back, his touch solid and strong. He kissed my cheek and neck. "Go upstairs. There's a room with the light on and an open door. Sit on the end of the bed. I'm going to lock up down here."

"Okay," I said because I needed to hear the sound of my own voice at the end of so many commands. I backed up, and he watched me as I turned and went up the stairs.

The room he wanted was right in front of me. There were other doors, all closed. I heard him banging around downstairs with locks and lights. I could peek in one room, just to see, then say I was looking for the bathroom, but the idea lasted the time it took for me to step into the room with the single, glowing lamp.

I sat at the edge of the bed. It must have been a guest bedroom. There were no pictures, no personal effects, just a hardwood bed and matching craftsman style dressers.

He seemed to take forever, and just as I was about to get up and see if he was all right, I heard him coming, one slow step at a time, up the stairs.

He was still dressed and had a bottle of water. He held it out to me.

"I'm good. Thanks."

"You look uncomfortable."

"You took a long time."

He kneeled in front of me and touched my knee. "I'm sorry, Monica. Can you forgive me?"

Before I could answer, he kissed inside my knee. "I think so," I said. "If you keep doing that."

He looked up at me, all green eyes and messy red hair. He moved his lips up my thigh, spreading my legs. A tingle went up the inside of my thighs as he ran his hands up them, the edge of his watch made a light scratch on sensitive skin. He picked my leg up, and I fell back as he lightly kissed the outside of my mound.

"Ah, Jonathan," I whispered, stroking his hair. He spread my legs farther, kissing between them. He slipped his finger into my wetness, and I gasped and remember the afternoon and Sam's desk. This time was different. When I looked down at him, his eyes were closed with intensity as he flicked his tongue over my clit. I think I said his name again. He flicked again. He was so light with it. Like he didn't want me to come.

As if he read my mind, he stood up, undressing so quickly I had only a second to admire his body, with its light hair and perfect angles. He flipped a condom out of his pocket and got it on without missing a beat, then lodged himself on top of me, his dick like a rock and everywhere it should be except inside me. We kissed. He tasted perfectly of whiskey and desire. I wanted him. I wanted every inch of him. He was right outside, pressing in, the head of his cock a tingle at my opening. I twisted my hips to move him in, but he backed off, picking his head up to look at me.

"Please," I said.

"Not yet."

He slid his dick up my folds without entering me, rubbing the length of him on my clit, sending waves of pleasure through me. I was so wet, he slid back and forth. I spread my legs as far as I could and moved with him. I could come like this, but I didn't want to. I wanted him inside me. This would feel like masturbation compared to his cock being where it belonged.

"Please," I said again.

"Not yet."

"Jesus, Jonathan. What do you want?" My sex ached for him. It didn't feel empty. It felt full to bursting, a throbbing, pounding hunger filling my skin.

"I want you to want it," he said.

"I do. My God, I do."

In response, he pushed harder, increasing the pressure without entering me. "No, you don't. Not enough."

I knew what he wanted, and I was willing to give it to him. "Please. I'm begging you. I'm begging. I'll do anything you want. I'll be anything you want. Just don't—"

He drove his dick into me with a ferocity that shocked me and turned the last word into a cry. He stopped for a second, as if he'd been shaken by the violence of his initial thrust.

"Don't stop," I gasped. "Don't make me beg again."

He buried his face in my neck and fucked me, pushing inside, pressing his body against my clit, his cock rubbing with each stroke, until I couldn't take it anymore, and then he stopped.

"What?" I groaned.

"You want to come?"

"Yes. Fuck. Yes."

"Beg for it."

"Fuck you." I pushed his chest. I was on fire, so close to orgasm, nearly unable to think complete thoughts. He pushed himself in me once, then stopped. It was a burst of sensation between my legs, then nothing. I looked up at him. He was enjoying himself, and he could keep going as long as he needed to.

"Please. Fuck you."

"Close." He stroked again, a taste of what I could have. He went slowly, too slowly, moving enough to keep me hot, but not enough to get me off. I put a hand between my legs and he grabbed both my wrists, holding them against the mattress with all his weight, rocking his hips back and forth just a little.

I had never felt anything like that. It wasn't an orgasm, because I had not an ounce of release, only the firing nerve endings and blasting heat between my legs. I was sweating everywhere. Tendrils of hair clung to my face, but his hands held mine down,.

"I want to come," I groaned.

"I want you to come."

"Let me. Please." I said it so softly I didn't even think he'd hear me. "Please. Please. *Please*..." With every *please,* I got more desperate and more quiet. On the last plea, he pulled out of me and pushed back in, all the way, and then again, until everything went hot red. I said his name over and over, going limp everywhere, and still the orgasm went on and on. His mouth was at my ear, and I could hear his groan as I finally stopped coming. His arms wrapped around me, tightening as he came, a guttural *ahh* rattling his throat with each slowing thrust.

"Holy fuck," he whispered into my neck.

"Thank you," I said. "Thank you."

He propped himself up on his elbows and kissed my face from my chin, to my right cheek, to my forehead, and back down my left cheek, and to my chin again. His eyes flicked to his watch.

"Sun rises at 5:38 a.m. You're mine for four more hours."

"I don't think I can take four more hours of that."

"Don't sell yourself short." He rolled off me, and we just stared at the ceiling, letting our breathing get back to normal.

I had never experienced anything like that, not with Kevin and certainly not with Darren. I didn't know I could sit on the brink for that long or just how many brinks there were. I didn't know I could give someone else control over what I felt.

It felt as though, after that orgasm, I should have to sleep for hours, or I wouldn't want sex for at least a month, but neither was the case. I was energized, and I wanted it again.

"Where are you flying off to tomorrow?" I asked.

"Korea. I'm putting a hotel up in Seoul."

"Can I ask you a question?"

"Uh oh."

"Your house. You have all the original everything in here, and the hotels are, like, white and chrome."

"This house was built for a family a hundred years ago. It was a home. People want to feel like they're *away* from home when they go to a hotel."

"Right. That makes sense."

"I thought you were going to bail on me."

"I got held up talking to my manager. Ex-manager. Jerk-off." I tucked my head on his shoulder and ran my fingertips up and down his chest. I couldn't keep my hands off him.

"This the guy who disappeared?"

I propped myself up on my elbows and kissed his shoulder and down his chest. I could still smell some of the dusty cologne past the sheen of sweat built up from our sex. "This guy from WDE was at Frontage and called him. He wants his boss to see me. But I fired Vinny, and now he won't give me the contact."

"Why'd you fire him?"

"Because he's an asshole. I'll find a way to get Testarossa to take my call myself." I worked my way down his stomach, over his hip bones, with my lips and tongue. I was aroused all over again. He put his hands on my shoulders.

"WDE? That's Arnie Sanderson, right?"

Arnie Sanderson owned WDE and was the single most inaccessible person in the world. Even his own clients had to make appointments to get a call, and regular schlub WDE clients, who were some of the top paid people in entertainment, never met the guy.

"Arnie Sanderson. Yeah," I said. Jonathan's dick was hard again already.

"I'll call him for you."

"I'm not about to suck your dick so you'll make a call for me."

"And I'm not making the call so you'll suck my dick. So, now that we've cleared that up, can you get on with it?"

I looked up at him. He smiled from ear to ear and put one hand under his head. I licked his dick's length with the flattest part of my tongue. When I got to the top, I slid the entire length of it down my throat.

He breathed a deep *ahh* and said, "Where did you learn to do that?"

"Los Angeles High School of Performing Arts," I said. "They taught me how to open my throat to sing. Then Kevin Wainwright taught me how to put his dick down it."

He laughed. "I'd like to thank LA Unified and Kevin Whatever for this moment."

I couldn't help but grin, which kept me from engaging in the task at hand. "I like you, Jonathan."

"Feeling's mutual, Monica."

CHAPTER 21

We collapsed from exhaustion around five thirty a.m. Two hours later, I woke up with a sore sex and a dry throat. Jonathan's arm was draped over me. His breath came in heavy, slow rhythms. I looked at him sleeping, closely inspecting him for the first time. His copper-colored lashes fluttered under soft brows. Faded freckles dotted his nose. He was truly beautiful, and seeing him with those eyes, I realized I could easily fall for this man. I was walking on a precipice even letting myself stare at him for this long.

I slipped out from under his arm and went to find my clothes.

My dress and underwear were draped over a chair by the door and smelled like last night's whiskey and fresh porch air. I slipped into them and went into the kitchen for water.

I looked onto the backyard, with its dark green furniture and bean-shaped pool, sipping my water. I ran over the night in my mind, which was hard, because after a certain point, it just became a blur of skin, sweat, and orgasms. I must have said his name a hundred times, starting with me begging him to fuck me and ending with an orgasm he'd delayed eternally. When he finally let me come, it must have lasted fifteen minutes.

The first time he had thrust into me with such force, it was almost like he wanted to shut me up. Like he was saying, "here, take it, but please stop."

Please. I'm begging you. I'm begging. I'll do anything you want. I'll be anything you want. Just don't—

I was going to stay *don't stop*, but in a different circumstance, when the love of your life was walking out the door, you might say *don't leave*.

The buzz of a phone brought me back to my senses. I was making stuff up. The phone buzzed again. I didn't know if it was mine, but I located the source on the kitchen counter, plugged into the wall. Jonathan's phone, and it was facing up.

The caller: *Jess*.

Ex-wife.

Fuck.

I threw the rest of the water down my throat and put the glass in the sink. I had to go. I didn't want to get in the middle of whatever that was.

"Good morning," he said, sleep all over his face, T-shirt stretched over his perfect body.

"I took the glass from the rack and got water from the little thing in the fridge door. Didn't even open it." He shrugged, and I relaxed. He didn't seem to feel invaded.

"Can I make you coffee?" he asked. "I can scramble eggs if you want."

"No, I'm okay."

As I rinsed the glass, he came up behind me and kissed my neck, fingering my zipper. "How about another go?"

"The sun is up," I teased. I wanted another go. On the counter. On the floor. His lips caressed my earlobe, and I leaned my head back.

He slipped the dress's zipper down. "You need to beg again. You're good at it." He kissed my back. I wanted to. I wanted to cry for it, one more time, before he became a memory. He pushed my dress off my shoulders with a perfect touch that rode between firm and light, a touch on a collarbone, maybe, like the one caught on camera from his wedding day.

"Your phone rang," I said. Stupid. Another go would have been nice, but it was too late now.

"It's always ringing." He reached inside the dress and caressed my breasts, nipples hardening at his touch.

The phone buzzed. His lips left me, and I knew he was looking at it. His hands fell, and a palpable chill filled the room. I cleared my throat.

"I think I need to take this," he said, zipping me back up.

"Sure," I whispered. "My shoes are upstairs."

I walked to the door, and when I looked back, he was popping the cable from the phone. His hands might have been shaking. I couldn't tell.

I scooped up my shoes from the bedroom floor and went back to the kitchen. He was on the patio, elbows on his knees, looking at the flagstones with the phone pressed to his ear. His hands gestured, but I couldn't hear him. It wasn't my business.

"Good-bye, Jonathan," I said before I slipped out the front door.

PART II
TEASE

Jonathan was master of my nudity, my positions, and my orgasms, and though the first screw of the evening should have satisfied any normal woman for the night, minutes after it was done, I wanted him again.

His dick was beautiful: proportional, with a head just the right size and a straight and hard shaft. I'd only seen two other dicks in person, and though I'd seen those two a lot, I wouldn't pretend I had enough experience to judge if he was as huge as he seemed. But as we talked and he stroked my hair, his penis got hard again, and I couldn't resist putting it in my mouth. Minutes later, he twisted my hips around, and we became a gorgeous ball of sweat and heat, sixty-nining with me on top. I took the whole length of him while he put his tongue into my pussy. He grabbed my ass hard, digging his fingers into my skin, and drew his tongue out, then stuck it in again.

"Jonathan," I'd groaned, kissing the head of his prick, "I'm going to come if you keep doing that."

"No, you're not," he said, giving my clit a peck before turning me around. He guided my body around until I was on top and facing him. He grabbed my ass again, fingers in my crack where it was sensitive, and pushed me down. His penis went flush with my lips, and he pulled me toward him, then away, rubbing my lips against the length of his dick.

I put my face to his, breathing on his cheek, and said, "I want you."

"You want what?"

"I want you to fuck me."

He reached into the nightstand drawer and got a condom while I rubbed myself on him. I rolled it on, my hands shaking. When I started guiding him in, he said, "I want to see."

I moved my hips up so I squatted over him. He looked between my legs and watched as I slid his dick into me. I put my knees back on the bed and moved up and down. He put his hand between my legs to shift my hips. My ass stuck out, and the triangle between my legs pressed against his cock, making my clit rub right against it as I moved.

I shuddered from the heat and friction. I didn't think I could keep any kind of rhythm, but I did, because I had to. He moved his hand to my breast, but I knew what to do. The way I held my hips was everything, and I'd never forget it. The direct clitoral contact, him inside me, surrounded by his smell and his voice and his touch made me blind to everything outside my pussy.

As if he sensed how hot I was, he rolled over and got on top. "You're close."

I couldn't answer. If I agreed, he'd probably have gone to do the laundry. "Harder," I said in a breath.

He pulled my legs up and apart and pounded me. I cried out, clawing at his back. He pummeled himself into me until I was about to come. I tried to tell him, but I didn't have any words.

Then he slowed down.

"Oh, God no," I moaned.

"Take it easy," he breathed in my ear, rocking so gently, so slowly.

"You're killing me." I hovered at the edge of climax. Tension and pleasure tugged at each other inside me.

"I don't know how much longer I'm going to last," he said. But he lasted, at that pace, until the buildup almost pushed pleasure over the edge. I thought, for a second, *I'm going to come without telling him, because he won't let me.*

"Please," I gasped, my resolve gone, "I need to come."

"No, you don't."

"May I? Please?" As much as I wanted to come, I wanted to ask even more. I wanted to beg for it. I wanted him to make me lose myself in him.

He pushed against me, and I groaned. He didn't answer.

I was supposed to know what to do. "Jonathan, please. Please let me come. I can't..." He put his nose to mine and looked into my eyes. I felt surrounded by him and safe in his attention. "I'm going to lose it...please. Please do it so I come."

"Do what?"

"Fuck me hard. Please. I'll do whatever you want. I'll suck anywhere you want. I'll be yours. It's all I have, but please fuck me so I come."

"Come then." He pushed into me, slowly but forcefully, and I felt my world tip over as he grunted and heaved with his own fulfillment. My hands went over my head and clutched the headboard. My back arched, and I must have screamed, because I felt his hand on the side of my face, his thumb hooking into my open mouth. He kept moving, churning his hips and gasping, and every push sent a new wave of sensation through my lips, my pussy, my clit, everything.

Warmth had shot up the curve of my spine. The feelings went on and on with changing breaths and sensations. My voice wasn't my own, but the expression of a built-up explosive detonating inside me. When he bit me hard, at the base of my neck, another point of gratification had been found. The pain was a counterpoint to everything else, bringing me back to consciousness and reigniting my orgasm. I cried out again, pushing myself into his dick, feeling nothing but wetness and hardness and shocks of pleasure between us. I'd entered a timeless zone, and when I realized he was softening inside me, I slowed down, even as my orgasm took on a life of its own.

"Monica?" asked Debbie's voice, not Jonathan's.

"Huh?" I was at work. Early afternoon, Thursday. I had five full tables and a tray of sucked-dry glasses in my hand.

Debbie, my boss, looked at me with concern and a little irritation. "Are you all right?"

"Yeah, I was just thinking."

"About what? You just stopped dead in the middle of the floor."

"Nothing. I'm sorry."

"You have Ute Yanix on seven. Please, if you need a sick day, let me know. Otherwise—" She twisted her hand at the wrist to let me know it was time to get moving. I ran to Ute Yanix's table with a smile and an apology. I took the actress's order with a temporarily clear head that got muddied by thoughts of Jonathan's belly hair just three minutes later.

Two weeks ago before I'd met Jonathan, I felt like a normal person. I worked. I sang. I bitched about my manager. I took care of Gabby and drank a little too much. I pleasured myself maybe once a week if I thought of it. I went from place to place, daydreaming about winning a Grammy or ruining my ex-boyfriend's life forever. I didn't realize how much time I'd spent plotting Kevin's demise, but when I stopped, I filled the spaces with Jonathan.

After Jonathan, my brain seemed hard-wired for sex. I walked around in a state of constant arousal. The past year and a half had caught up with me like a train crashing into a wall. After the initial impact, the rest of the train kept moving, pushing into that front car until eighteen months of desire got squashed into two weeks.

The afternoon following my first night at his house, he sent me a text message from some lounge at LAX. He thanked me for a great night and made promises I didn't believe he meant at all, and then... nothing. I didn't expect anything. He wasn't my boyfriend. He wasn't even my lover. He was some guy I used to work for who happened to get me into bed after I'd spent a year and a half intentionally celibate. He opened a jack-in-the-box of sexuality by turning a handle I didn't even know I had.

He'd done a whole list of little things before that, naturally. He'd been confident and charming and vulnerable all at once. He had a way of touching me that felt like static electricity without the shock, and he made me come like no man ever had before. Scratch that. I'd never even made *myself* come like that.

The hot heaviness between my legs was why I ran home from work most days, shut the bathroom door behind me and masturbated like a thirteen year-old. I had trouble functioning outside of work, too. I'd sent my band manager, Vinny, a termination notice littered with typos, fielded a call from Eugene Testarossa's assistant mid-masturbation session and stopped eating. My friend Darren had started cooking for me and watching me like a hawk.

The only thing I could do better than ever was sing.

Fuck, I was on fire. Rehearsals with Gabby, my pianist and best friend, were almost as good as the sex eating my mind. She and I could do no wrong. I could make changes on the fly, and she went with it. Two weeks ago, I'd been ashamed to sing old-time standards at a dinner club, but the performances of the past two weeks had drawn the attention of the agents at WDE. That night, they were coming to see us. Our version of *Under My Skin* would send Sinatra running and *Stormy Weather* would make it rain in L.A. In my life, I'd never felt better about my work.

I just needed to keep my mind on the paying job.

"You playing again tonight?" Robert asked as he poured alcohol into iced glasses.

"Yeah," I said. "Late set."

"I'm glad I saw you last week. You were hot."

"Thanks." The compliment was about the extent of Robert's vocabulary, and I accepted it with a smile.

"You been okay?" he asked. "You just stopped moving for a second earlier. I wondered if you were going to fall over or something."

"I'm fine. Just a little distracted."

"Probably the music. Got your mind in the game." He winked and clicked his tongue on his teeth. He was a nice guy but a bit of a douchebag.

I took care of Ute Yanix and the rest of my tables, making a concerted effort to smile and keep my mind on my job.

Toward the middle of my shift, I saw Debbie talking to a tall woman by the door. The big woman wore grey, pleated pants and a matching grey jacket with darker velvet lapels.

"Who's that with Debbie?" I asked Robert as I handed him a ticket.

"Dunno, but I wouldn't wanna meet her in a dark alley."

The woman built like a six-foot-four hourglass. Her left ear was encircled by small silver hoops from lobe to helix.

"I'm sure it's a her," I whispered. "She doesn't look like a customer."

"She probably has a script under her shirt," he murmured, keeping quieter than the white noise of the instrumental trip-hop.

"Rolf Wente's at table six. Maybe she wants to drop it in his lap."

"He'll read page one if she sucks his dick."

"He can read?"

We giggled, trying to keep quiet for the lunchtime crowd. I swooped up my tray and delivered my drinks, took an order, and checked on the rest of my tables. I forgot about the lady in the grey suit until I went back to the service bar and saw her standing with Debbie, looking at me as though I was the reason she was there. Robert arched an eyebrow at me, and I told him to shut the hell up with my pursed lips and narrowed eyes.

"Hi," I said when I reached Debbie and The Rectangle.

"Monica," Debbie said, "this is Lily."

"You can call me Lil." She had a genuine smile and feminine voice.

"Hi, Lil." I slid my tray onto the bar and pressed a damp terry towel to my soda-sticky palms before offering my hand. She shook it, but only for a second, as if the familiarity made her uncomfortable.

Lil handed me a small beige envelope that seemed only wide enough for a check. My name was scribbled on the front in blue ballpoint.

"It's not a subpoena, is it?" I joked.

"Nah."

I looked from her, to Debbie, and back. Lil gave me a short nod and said, "Thank you," before walking out.

"What was that about?" I asked Debbie.

"Yeah," said Robert, appearing like a bad penny, elbow on the bar, peering at my envelope. I smacked him with it.

"Take your break," Debbie said to me. "Maddy has you covered."

I took my little envelope to the back room, which had a few long tables, a vending machine, microwaves, and our lockers. I was alone. I opened the envelope.

Dear Monica,

Can you meet me at the Loft Club after work? I'd like to talk to you, at length, until morning if possible.

Lil will meet you out front after your shift.

If you can't make it, let her know.

—Jonathan

The print was tightly written with the same blue ballpoint. As though he'd dashed it off without thinking, or as if he had been in a rush. For the billionth time that afternoon, I counted the days since we'd last seen each other. He'd said he was going to Korea for two weeks, and it had been just about that. I put the paper to my nose and got his dry smell full in the face. A controlled scent, it was truly original.

I had no idea how I would get through the second half of my shift. I had a gig that night, and it was an important one. According to the assistant's assistant I had spoken to at WDE, half of their talent agents would be at Frontage to see me and Gabby, though she and I were still a nameless pairing. I had four hours between my lunch shift and my gig. I could squeeze Jonathan in. Making plans with him before the gig was foolish and reckless, but I wanted to see Jonathan Drazen almost as much as I wanted to play.

CHAPTER 23

Lil waited out front, leaning on a grey Bentley in a loading zone. When she saw me, she opened the back door.

"Hi. Uh…" I felt weird getting into the car without knowing where I was going or who was driving.

Lil spoke as if reading my mind. "I'm Mister Drazen's driver. I'll take you there and back. If you're going to be out late, you can give me your car key, and I'll take care of your car for you."

"How?"

"Take it back to your house."

"How would you get back to your car?"

Lil smiled as if I was a seven-year-old asking why water floated down, not up. "I'm not the only staff. Don't worry. Please. I do this for a living."

I smiled at her, broadcasting pure discomfort, and slid into the back seat.

I'd never been in a car like that before. Darren and I had taken a limo to prom, but it smelled of beer and vomit and the carpet was damp from a recent shampoo. I'd ridden in Bennet Mattewich's Ferarri down the 405 at two a.m. He thought the ride bought him a blow job, but it almost bought him a slashed tire. We'd stayed friends, but he never took me out in his dad's car again.

The Bentley was huge. The leather seats faced each other and it had brushed chrome buttons I didn't understand without a crumb or speck of grime anywhere around them. The paneling was wood—real wood, dark and warm—and though the ride took about ten minutes, I felt as if I'd been transported from one world to another via spacecraft.

The car stopped on a dead end street in the most industrial part of downtown, somewhere between the arts district and the river. Next to the car was an old warehouse with a top floor made exclusively of windows. The side of the building facing the parking lot was painted in matte black with modernist lettering listing each tenant. No mention of a Loft Club or anything like it.

I'd seen enough movies to know I should wait, and Lil was at my door in two seconds flat, as if I was incapable of opening it myself.

"Go on in to the desk, and the concierge will take care of you." She handed me a cardboard rectangle the size of a business card with a few numbers printed on the front. The word LOFT was printed on the top, in grey.

"Thanks," I said. I walked up the steps and inside. When I showed the card to the Asian gentleman behind the lobby's glass counter, I was still convinced I was either in the wrong building or the whole thing was a cruel joke.

He checked the card against something written in a leather book in a way that wasn't rude but was somehow officious. I shifted a little in my waitress getup: a black wrap shirt and short skirt, from Target and the thrift store on Sunset respectively. I felt as though my clothes exposed me as an outsider or worse: a liar and sneak. But he looked up with a smile and said, "Down this hall behind me. Pass the first elevator bank and make a left. I'll buzz you through the doors. There's another elevator at the end of the hall. Take it to the top."

"Thank you."

My heels clicked on the concrete floors. I shrugged my bag close. I passed the first set of elevators and made the left. A pair of frosted glass doors stood in my way, and I noticed a camera hovering above them. A second later, a resonant beep preceded a click, and the doors whooshed open.

Beyond those doors, the hallway changed. The lighting was softer and came from modernist chrome sconces. The walls were a softer white, and when I got close, I saw the texture was silkier, somehow more nuanced. The oak and brass elevator didn't look like a refrigerator, as most do, and it hummed in D minor and dinged in the same key before it whooshed open.

I stepped onto the floral carpet and hit the button that said *Loft* in block letters. The door closed, and the elevator took off without a sound. I closed my eyes, focusing on the force under my feet. The elevator's movement somehow added to the pressure between my legs that maybe had more to do with the fact I was seeing Jonathan than the perfect speed of the vessel I stood in.

The doors opened onto a room made of glass overlooking the city. I could see the library, the Marriot, the whole skyline, and the miasma of smog hovering over it all. The marble floors had a gravitas all their own and were buffed to a shine that didn't look cheap. The woodwork seemed to have gotten seven extra turns of the dowel.

The lobby was lightly populated with people speaking quietly. A clink of laughter. A klatch of young men in perfect suits. Leather couches. A chandelier as big as my garage. I couldn't take it all in fast enough.

"May I help you?" The woman clasped her hands in front of her and bent a little at the waist. Her hair was twisted in an unremarkable bun and was an equally unremarkable color. She smiled in a way that was attractive but not stunningly so.

Even though she wore a blue Chanel suit, her job seemed to be to appear as unthreatening as possible, and she was very good at it.

"Hi," I said. I smiled because I didn't know what else to do.

She noted the card I'd crumpled in my hand. "May I?"

"Oh." I was so nervous I was being an ass. I was entitled to be there. I was invited. I had no reason to feel unworthy just because I didn't know where I was. I handed her the card and stood up straighter, no thanks to my thrift store skirt and two-year-old shoes.

She thanked me and looked at the card. "Right this way. My name is Dorothy."

"I'm Monica. Nice to meet you."

She gave me a courteous smile and took me down halls and byways. When I noticed how many outer walls had windows, I remembered how the building had looked from the street. Places all over the city looked mysterious and inaccessible from the outside, and that warehouse was one of them.

Finally, Dorothy stopped in front of a door. "If you need anything, I'll be your concierge. My number is on the card."

She gave me a white card the size of a playing card, then opened the door.

"Thank you." I didn't know if I was supposed to tip her or say anything in particular, so I just slipped in. Dorothy clicked the thick wooden door shut behind me. Two walls were made of windows. A third wall made of shelves included wine, glasses, a bucket of ice, and a wet bar. The fourth wall had a huge oil painting that looked like a Monet or a damn good copy. The Persian carpet looked real. Antique couches flanked a six-foot long coffee table cut from a single tree.

I had no idea what I was supposed to do.

I spotted a bottle of Perrier and two glasses on a small table on the opposite side of the room, against a window, and walked over to it. The leather chairs next to the table were worn in the right places and their arms were bolted with brass studs. An envelope with the word "Monica" printed on the front balanced between the two glasses. I slid the note out. Printed on the club letterhead, which was embossed with silver, was,

Five minutes late — Jonathan.

I looked at my watch, then poured myself a glass of water and waited in the chair, humming and looking at the skyline. I was looking forward to seeing him and feeling his touch, the curves of his body, the heat of his mouth on mine.

When the door opened, it startled me. I stood up, still holding the short glass of bubbling water.

Jonathan tucked his phone away with one hand and carried a briefcase in the other. I'd only seen him at night, naked or in casual clothes and late day scruff. I'd never seen him clean-shaven and wearing a three-button herringbone tweed jacket with a windowpane white shirt and a tie the color of coal. A black silk square stuck out of his left chest pocket. Matte black cufflinks. All that was really nice. It brought out the shape of his body: straight, tall, with shoulders that didn't need padding and a waist that didn't pull his front buttons.

"Hi," I said.

"You came." He seemed genuinely surprised and placed his briefcase on the short table by the couches.

"Lil didn't tell you?"

He stepped toward me. "She doesn't answer the phone if she's driving, which is most of the time." He stood a foot from me, and I felt his gaze on my face. "And in a way, I didn't want to know."

I leaned into him, breathing a little heavier, just to take him in. "I have a gig later."

"How much later?" He seemed to lean forward, too, though I couldn't tell if it was a physical lean or the spear of his attention.

"Later."

"Would you like to sit down?"

No, I didn't. I wanted to put my body all over his. Instead, I sat when he did.

He poured himself a glass of Perrier and leaned back. "How have you been?"

"You had a driver pick me up to ask me that? You could have sent me a text and gotten the same answer."

"What's the answer?"

"I've been fine. Thank you."

"Just fine?"

He wanted more. He wanted a way into a conversation about what he and I did really well. At least, that was what I was reading. "Fine," I said, "and a little aroused most of the time."

He smiled a true and genuine smile. "I think I missed you."

"You think?"

He leaned forward, putting his elbows on his knees. "I'm not going to pretend I missed you the way I'd miss someone I know very well. But, okay, here's an example. I'm in the office of the Korean Minister of Tourism. This is the guy who can approve the hotel or send me packing if I say the wrong word. My Korean is fluent, but not nuanced, so I have to pay attention."

I leaned forward as well. "You speak Korean?"

"I live in Los Angeles. Do you want me to finish my story?"

I wanted him to bend me over and fuck me, but instead I said, "Yes. Finish."

"He's rattling off numbers, and somewhere in there is a mistake that will cost me a fortune if I only pay attention to the total, but I have to translate the numbers and find the flaw. Like he'll say the permit is one, the fees are two, something else is three, and it all equals ten, meaning the mistake is four. He considers that his bribe, which I'm not paying. But the numbers are bigger, and he's talking fast so no one else in the room will get it. I can't keep my mind on what he's saying or who I'm paying because all I can think about ..." He paused as if he'd reached the important part. "All I can picture in my mind is spreading your legs."

I cleared my throat to keep from smiling, but my face still split in a wide grin. For a second, I wondered if he hadn't been trying to be funny, but when I saw his pleased expression, I knew I hadn't insulted him.

"I wasn't even thinking about sex," he said. "I mean, I was, but just that moment when I put my hands on your knees and pulled them apart, and you leaned back and let me do it. I kept replaying it. That moment when you *let me*. Couldn't add and subtract worth a dime. I'm sure I overpaid the man."

My legs tingled, wanting the pressure of his hands between them. I pressed my knees together, waiting for him to do what he'd fantasized. "Well," I said, "I've started sucking on ice cubes all day."

"Ah. The porch."

"I just smile until it melts. Debbie thinks I've lost my mind."

He plucked a cube from his glass. "Maybe you have." He reached out and put the ice to my mouth, brushing my bottom lip. I opened my mouth and circled around the edge. I flicked my tongue out, but he wouldn't give it to me. A drop of cold water trailed down my chin, and he took the cube away, popping it into his mouth and crunching. "I want you," he said.

My spine felt like a piano someone had just done scales down.

"I want to have you in ways that surprise me."

"I'll take that as a compliment."

"But I think we need clarity first." Nothing followed but him looking into his glass.

I leaned back and sipped my water. "Go on."

He tapped his fingertips together and looked out the window, stalling. I wasn't about to interrupt.

"I've imagined a hundred ways to say this. They all sounded like I was trying to hurt you," he started.

"Unless your dick fell off in Seoul, it can't be anything that bad."

He laughed and rubbed his eyes. "I'll say it straight. I love my wife. My ex-wife. Nothing will ever change that."

"Okay."

"I can't love anyone else."

I got it. We could like each other forever, but he wouldn't cross that line into love even if I did. I considered myself fair-warned. I had to let him know I was good with that, but I wasn't his doormat either.

"I don't want your heart," I said. "I want your attention for a few hours at a time. I understand I'm one of many women you carouse around with."

He raised an eyebrow. "How much carousing do you think I do?"

"A lot."

"Based on what?"

"Rumor. And pictures on the internet." My face burned red hot.

"The rumors are based partly on fact, I admit," he said. "But carousing's only carousing if I take them out. The pictures on the internet, I had my clothes on?"

"Parties and stuff." I couldn't look at him. I felt silly accusing him of being a whore with so little evidence.

"I have seven sisters. Most of them have been there for me since the divorce."

How many women had been in the pictures? Not a hundred. But I assumed they were like roaches. If you see one on the counter, there are fifty more behind the cabinets. "How many times will this sister thing bite me in the ass?" I asked.

He smiled. "They're a slippery bunch. All older. And protective."

"You're lucky. I'm an only. I attach to friends."

He put his glass down and slipped his icy fingers between my knees, but he didn't part them. A chill went up my thighs, to my belly, where the heat I'd been tamping for weeks raged. I could have closed my mouth right then, said nothing, opened my legs, and let him do whatever he wanted.

"I have something else to say," I whispered.

"Tell me."

"I'm a musician. It's what I do. You can't interfere. Even for the best sex of my life, you can't get in the way of one rehearsal."

"That's the last thing I'd do," he said.

"That also means if I start feeling as though my heart's getting shredded, even if you're being a pure gentleman, it won't matter. We're done. Even if you haven't done anything wrong. I don't have time for it."

He ran his palms along my thighs, then back to my knees, his thumbs grazing the insides. I kept them closed. I wanted him to open me. I wanted the pressure of his fingers on my flesh, and I wanted to resist, just a little.

"I have another thing I've been thinking about," he said.

"Go."

He put his hands up my skirt and slid his fingers under my panties as if they weren't even there. The intrusion was delicious, and my cheap knit skirt rode up until the triangle of my underwear was exposed. When he looked down, I felt like I was being touched again.

"I own your orgasms." He pulled me forward to the edge of the seat before I could respond. His move was forceful, demanding, and left no room for questions.

"I don't know what that means," I gasped as he slipped my panties off. He put his finger under my right knee and placed it over the arm of the chair. I let him. I wanted him to. The less I resisted, the more aroused I became, especially when he did the same with the left leg. I was spread-eagled on the chair. My skirt rode up, leaving nothing between him and me.

"It means," he said, running his hands up the insides of my thighs, "you come when I say. Not before. If I send you home without, you just deal with it until I see you again." He looked at me as though he wasn't sure how I'd react. His green eyes darkened in the afternoon light.

"My fingers reach, you know," I said.

"Honor system," Jonathan said, running a thumb on each wet lip, leaving a vibrating hum behind them, like a plucked string.

I groaned. Had it only been two weeks? With my butt sliding forward, my legs over the chair's arms, and my pink wetness under his fingers, I felt as though I'd been pent up much longer.

"Ok." I would have agreed to anything.

"Ok, what?" He knelt in front of me and kissed the inside of my knee before running his tongue up my thigh. I touched his shoulder, and he grabbed my wrists, placing my hands on my knees. "Say it."

"You own my orgasms."

"And?" He bit down, deep where my thigh creased into sex. The pain was sharp and perfect. I lost words for a second. "When do you come?" he asked. His hands gripped my thighs, spreading my legs farther apart. It didn't hurt. It felt like surrender. It felt like giving myself over to his control. It felt safe.

"I come when you say," I whispered.

"I've thought about nothing but this," Jonathan said and put his tongue on my clit. He warmed it with his breath, not moving his tongue. I gasped and gripped the back of his head. He pulled his tongue away, and when I tried to push him back, he held my wrists in one hand. He sucked my clit, keeping my wrists in his tight grip. I was helpless under his tongue, the gentle counterpart to his rough hand. The tip of his tongue traced a line from my clit to my opening, teasing it, then sucking lightly. Warmth coursed through me. I threw my head back, breathing hard.

"Part of this," he said, moving his tongue back to my thigh, "is you have to tell me when you're close."

"Okay."

"You're very agreeable today." His green eyes looked at me over my crotch. I'd agree to anything that face asked.

"Next time, ask when I'm wearing pants."

He crawled up and kissed me, and I tasted my juices on his tongue. My legs were still spread, and he was still fully dressed. He let go of my hands to brush his fingers over my breasts. I reached for his belt with one hand and felt the hardness through his pants with the other.

"Let me," I said.

"Later."

"Now."

"I own my orgasms, too," he said.

"God, you are a greedy bastard."

He kissed me again, then stood back, staring at me. I started to move one leg down, but he held my ankle.

"Don't move yet," he said. Then he stepped back.

I saw his erection under his perfectly fit trousers, and he seemed disinclined to hide it. All he did was stand there, smiling, and look at me with my pussy out. I knew he wouldn't fuck me, and I knew he wouldn't let me come. Despite how unfulfilled that made me, because my body wanted him without a thought to any kind of agreement or rule, I knew he would draw our encounter out until I peaked with desire. I wanted him, and I'd wait as long as he told me to.

"It was a long flight," he said. "I could use a drink."

"And after that?"

"You said you had a gig." He kneeled again.

I hoped for a second he would put his tongue back between my legs and finish the job, but he gently took my knees off the arms of the chair instead.

"Oh, man," I said. "This orgasm thing is going to break me into a million little pieces."

"What if it's worth it?"

"I'm counting on it."

Jonathan scooped my panties off the floor and held them open while I put my toes through, then he slid them back into place when I stood. He was still kneeling, with his hands up my thighs, when he said, "Pick up your skirt." I did. He put his hands on my ass and kissed between my legs, through the fabric of my underwear. Nerve endings I didn't know I had fired like rounds of ammunition.

A million little pieces, for sure.

CHAPTER 24

"What do you drink, Monica?" Jonathan asked, as if realizing for the first time he had no idea. My mother would not have approved of our intimacy so soon, but Mom had never been at the raw wood bar in the lobby of Loft Club, either. She'd never seen the view of Los Angeles facing west, from downtown to the water, never been with a man besides Dad, never served drinks to seventy-five people a night or sung a note outside church. I stopped taking life lessons from my mother right about when I left my first love and started sleeping with Kevin.

"Same as you, actually," I said. "Single malt if they have it."

"I presume you'd like some ice to suck on?"

"You presume correctly."

The bartender, an old guy who looked as though he could mix a bull shot or Harvey Wallbanger without checking the book, scooped ice into two glasses and poured two fingers of MacAllan into each.

The room was huge and not too crowded. Mostly, the members wore creative class outfits, movie executives, talent agents, entertainment lawyers, ad agency people, and they all sat in square-cushioned armchairs around low tables. The waitstaff flitted between them, making as little fuss and being as unassuming and invisible as possible. I checked to see if everyone was out of earshot.

"How long have you been a member here?" I asked.

"My father got me a membership to the Gate Club when I turned eighteen. I moved over here a few years later."

Iggy Winkin, the sound guy at the studio, had a girlfriend who worked at Club KatManDo. It was probably the same kind of thing, and he said memberships ran about 35 grand a year. Obscene, for sure, but who was I to say? I was trying to get around to a different point entirely, and bringing up money would sidetrack the conversation indefinitely.

"They must know you in here," I said.

"Pretty much. The old guys. Like Kenny over there." He indicated the bartender. "He used to work at the Gate. Knew my dad. Told me stories I didn't want to hear."

"Like what?"

"You're full of questions."

"I'm trying to keep my mind off this feeling between my legs."

He leaned close. "Describe it."

I sipped my drink. I didn't have a single word or even phrase to describe the raw hunger of the physical sensation. I whispered, "Kind of like someone hooked me up to a bicycle pump and put too much air in. I feel overfull. It's your fault. Now, tell me. Kenny and your dad. Make something up, I don't care."

"Does it have to be true?"

"Honestly? No."

"My dad's a drunk. A passive, pathetic drunk, and Kenny poured him a few thousand gallons of vodka over three decades. His stool was at the end of the bar, right there." He pointed at a space occupied by a thirty-something year-old guy in a cream suit and blue tie.

"I don't believe it."

"That hardly matters. I want to hear more about what's going on between your legs."

"It's eating my brain. Your body just looks like a bunch of surfaces I want to rub against. I can't think in this state. IQ points are dropping off me. I can only speak in short sentences. Back to Kenny. How many times has he seen you here with a woman who wants to rub herself up against you?"

"Does it matter?"

"No, because it doesn't. And yes, because I want to know if I should steal a matchbook now or next time."

He laughed softly, covering his mouth. "I want to kiss you, but there's a guy here from acquisitions at Carnival Records and I don't want to embarrass you."

"Who?" I brushed my hair behind my ears and tried so hard not to look around that I must have looked everywhere at once.

"Eddie, hey," Jonathan said to a man behind me. He was Jonathan's age, bulky and handsome with receding black hair he brushed forward in a way that suggested he did it for style, not to cover a balding head.

"Jon, what's happening? Did you watch the game? We got killed."

"I can't watch anymore," Jonathan answered.

"Falling down on the job, as usual," Eddie said before he looked at me. "I'm Ed. We played for Penn together."

"Played what?" I was embarrassed I didn't know, but not too embarrassed to ask.

Eddie looked at Jonathan, then back at me. "You're not one of the sisters?"

Jonathan smiled, so I knew Eddie wasn't implying anything terrible. "This is Monica. No relation," Jonathan said.

"Ah," Eddie said, holding out his hand to shake mine. "Sorry then. Nice to meet you. Jonathan pitched. I played the bench."

"Nice to meet you, Ed."

"Monica's a singer," Jonathan said, "but she finds time to follow the Dodgers."

"My sympathies to both of you," Eddie said.

"I'm from Echo Park," I said. "I don't know this guy's excuse."

Jonathan took mock offense, looking at his watch. "Don't you have a gig?"

I sipped the last of my scotch. The ice cubes were huge, so I couldn't hold one in my mouth for Jonathan's benefit the way I wanted to. "I do. The late dinner crowd at Frontage awaits. Ed, it was nice to meet you."

"Oh, that's *you*," he said.

"Maybe. I guess that depends on what you heard."

"I heard someone's taking the house down over there."

"I doubt it was me."

Jonathan put down his drink. "It's her. She's not as modest with a microphone in front of her." He addressed me, "Come on, let me get you down to the car."

We said our goodbyes, and when Jonathan walked me out, he put his hand on my back. My skin shivered where he touched.

"Thanks for that," I said in the hallway outside the elevator. "That guy, he's important in my world. You put my face in a good context."

"My pleasure, and just so you know, I wouldn't have said anything if you didn't sing the way you do."

The elevator was empty. I kissed him on the way down, not as a lead into sex, but because he'd moved me by talking about me the way he did. His arms went around my waist and cradled my back, his mouth returning my affections, matching the tone and substance of what I was trying to say. That he wanted my body was enough for me, but supporting my work was a new and different thing, and it required a different kind of kiss. I wished there were more floors, because the doors opened before I'd appreciated him enough.

Lil got out when she saw us approach. I had enough time to make it back to my car and get to Frontage early enough to get made up.

"After your gig," Jonathan said, "text me?"

"I usually go out after with my friends."

He looked me up and down as if he was eating me raw, just like he'd done and tried to hide the first time we'd met. Only now he didn't have to conceal it. "If you don't mind unfinished business, it's okay with me," he said.

I got into the Bentley, and he walked back into the club.

CHAPTER 25

The dressing room at Frontage hadn't improved a single bit since my first night there two weeks earlier, but my attitude toward it had. We'd begun on a Thursday night, and they'd asked us back for Sundays and Tuesdays as well, until we dried up or found something better to do. Bitch and moan though I might, they paid in cash and didn't suck us dry for incidentals. After that first show, we brought people in, so they started feeding us dinner and slipping a few drinks our way after the set. I enjoyed being treated like something besides a piece of drink-slinging eye-candy or a desperate whore singing for nickels.

Gabby was already there, smearing beige under her eyes. Tonight was our night. WDE had booked a table. Rhee, the hostess, confirmed it was true, and at my request, she put them by the speaker on the left, which had the warmest sound.

"Did you check your seat for gum?" Gabby asked.

"No gum," I replied, clicking through the bottles and tubes in my makeup bag.

"Vocal chords attached?"

"I hope you get carpal tunnel."

"Bitch," she said.

"Snob," I replied. We smiled at each other through the mirror.

I'd met Gabby during my first day in L.A. Performing. I was tall but gangly and awkward. Glasses and braces, the whole thing. All the other kids seemed to know each other. They'd all come from a music charter on the west side, slipping into ninth grade at the exalted magnet as planned. I'd filled out my application and bussed myself to the audition behind my parents' backs. I informed them of where I was going to high school when the acceptance letter came.

So in that first week, while I was getting my bearings, Gabby and her crowd had themselves completely together. Totally unprepared for the competition, I was subjected to laughter that may or may not have been directed at the fact that I was

85

off half a key, fell victim to broken guitar strings, and found a blue gum wad on my drum skin. During last period on my first Thursday, when I sat down on a stool and it broke under me to the music of everyone's laughter, I ran out crying.

The last person I'd expected ran out after me: Gabrielle. She laughed the loudest, stared the hardest, flipped her blonde hair with the most vigor. Before she fell apart at twenty-two, she was the most together girl I'd ever met.

"What do you want?" I'd shouted when she followed me into the bathroom. "Why are you all so mean to me?"

"What are you talking about?"

"You laughed when I fell."

"It was funny. I mean, you've been here a week, and if there's a broken chair or a guitar with a busted string, you pick it. The guys have a pool about when you're going to break your glasses in P.E."

I'd wanted to fight harder with her. I'd wanted to blame her for a week's worth of misery, but the fact was, I had chosen that guitar because it was blue, and I didn't check the strings. The gum did look pretty old, but I'd blamed them anyway, and I'd sat in that chair because it was far away from everyone.

"Everyone says you're a snob," said Gabby.

"I am not a snob. I'm a bitch."

I'd chewed the inside of my cheek for a second, because awkward girls weren't supposed to risk saying things like that to cool girls. After a second, she laughed, and I did too.

"Come sit with us at lunch," she'd said. "I think my brother has a crush on you, so… gross. Okay?"

She'd folded me into the in crowd from that lunch on, like a complementary voice in a symphony, just adding me as if I was naturally in the same rhythm and key, and my entrance simply hadn't been arranged for the first few measures.

"You calm?" I asked Gabby in the dressing room as she poked at something nonexistent on her face. She had to be. Since my night with Jonathan when he'd promised to call Arnie Sanderson, she'd been blissed out. The call had been totally unnecessary, but any light at the end of her tunnel was a positive.

"No, I am not calm." She giggled. "Look!" She held her hands out. They were shaking. Generally, one wouldn't want that in a pianist, but in Gabby's case, as soon as she sat down, her fingers and body would quiet, and she'd be completely on top of it. "I got everyone from school in. I called in every favor. And the whole gang from Thelonius? All here. Darren, too."

"He bring his new girl?"

"I have no idea. Do you feel strong on *Cheek to Cheek?*" We'd worked on a rendition that sounded as though Gershwin had been talking about more than a little facial contact. All the songs were shaking out that way, and it brought them in.

"We're good on *Cheek to Cheek.*"

"It's happening, Mon. Really happening."

"This is a long process." I took out my makeup bag and smeared back on what

Jonathan had kissed off. "We're not signing any contracts in the morning. We don't even have a disc or anything."

"You said not to worry about that."

"I didn't worry about it until Jonathan introduced me to Eddie Walker as if I didn't know who he was, and if he'd asked me for a disc, I wouldn't have had one."

I watched her in the mirror and saw her eyes go blank. She was doing a calculation in her head, and she took a second to come up with the answer.

"Penn," she said.

"Yes, they went to University of Pennsylvania together, but do you know what sport they played?"

When Gabby didn't know something, she didn't pretend she did, so her answer came quickly. "No."

"Baseball."

She pushed her mascara stick into the tube slowly, staring at it. I could almost see her filing the information and cross-referencing it with every other piece of Hollywood intelligence in her head.

"Thanks for doing this," she said. "I know you didn't want to do a restaurant gig, but I feel really good about it, and I couldn't do it without you."

"Well, I was wrong. I should have said yes right off. I mean, the thing about performing is you have to perform, otherwise you're all talk, right?" I said.

"That's exactly what I'm saying. If we get WDE behind us, we can maybe start doing *your* songs."

I shrugged. My songs were rage-filled punk diatribes and wouldn't translate into the loungey thing I was doing with Gabby. If we landed an agent as a piano-driven lounge act, I had no idea what I would do with him. I couldn't go from eXene to Sade on a dime. As a keyboardist, Gabby could play anything at any time, but I would be in a world of shit at the first hint of success working at Frontage. I had zero songs ready.

"I didn't tell you something about meeting Eddie today," I said, trying to sound flip.

"He cute?"

"Yes. And he'd heard about us."

"He was trying to get into your pants."

"No, he didn't know it was me singing here when he mentioned it. I mean, he did, but he could have just said something polite like, *oh, how nice*. But he didn't. He was all, *Oh, that's* you?"

"What did he say, exactly?"

"He'd heard someone was bringing down the house at Frontage."

"Some*one*?"

I got defensive. She'd gotten me through high school. I'd never abandon her. "He didn't phrase it like it was just one person. Could have been a swing ensemble from the way he said it."

Gabby tossed her sticks and tubes back in her little bag. "I'd better get out there," she said. "I have to warm them up."

We hugged like sisters, and I went back to making my face presentable.

When I told Jonathan he was lucky to have sisters, I'd meant it. I hated being an only child. I hated when my mother looked at me as if I'd somehow disappointed her by being her first and last, as if it was my fault they found cancer during the C-section. I hated being the only kid in the house. I hated being responsible for every success and failure of my parents' children. The attention was great, except when I wanted to die from it.

If anything happens to the only child, there's no backup. If she's a drug addict, all the kids are drug addicts. If she dies in a car accident, suddenly the family is dissolved.

In one way, I never felt right around people, and in another, I craved their company. I needed them too much. So I had tons of acquaintances, maybe four hundred people in a loose music-scene around Echo Park and Silver Lake. I could fill a club when I needed to, but outside the guys who wanted to screw me, I inspired no closeness in anyone besides Darren and Gabby, who were orphans and needed me as much as I needed them.

CHAPTER 26

I poked my head out into the restaurant. Darren was at the bar with a huddled group. I recognized them: Theo, Mark, Ursula, Mollie, and Raven. Darren was Mister Popularity. He could bust out an inside joke with anyone he met on the east side. He had an ear for language and a way of listening that gave him a vocal "in" with whoever was in earshot.

I didn't see a girl I didn't recognize, so he either came without her or I knew her. I deliberately didn't look at the table by the warm speaker. I didn't want to see if they'd shown or if it was a table full of assistants getting drunk on the company dime. I didn't want to see an empty table with a big "reserved" card on it. I didn't want to see anything at all; I only needed to feel.

I'd been drawing off the energy from my night with Jonathan for two weeks, and after that afternoon at the Loft Club, I felt renewed and concerned. I couldn't let myself depend on him getting me all hot and bothered so I could sing to the throb between my legs. I had no idea how much longer he'd drag me around by the panties, but it surely wouldn't be long enough to make a career.

Rhee stood by the door at the opposite side of the room, hair up, a big smile her default setting. A black woman in her forties, she didn't look a day over thirty. She winked when she saw me and tilted her head to the table by the warm speaker, which I couldn't see from where I stood.

It was go time, as my dad would say.

The management always put fifteen minutes at the beginning of the schedule for the talent to walk around doing a meet and greet. My disdain for that type of gig had evaporated when I realized what shrewd businesspeople ran the operation. My job wasn't to fade into the background as I'd originally thought, but to make the diners feel as though they'd walked into a place where they were known, and

89

special, and wanted. The goal was repeat business, and though new customers were encouraged, the management found people who came back regularly were better tippers, better customers, and better friends than a constant stream of trend followers.

Gabby was already improvising something on the piano in the center of the dining room. Her eyes were closed. She wouldn't even know it was time to start until I put my hand on her shoulder in twelve minutes. Darren was in the middle of an earnest discussion with Theo and Mark, and I broke in to greet them.

"You guys," I said to Darren, Theo, and Mark as a group, "please look like I'm cheering you up when I sing, okay? You're talking like you're at a funeral."

Theo, who had Maori tattoos crawling up his neck despite being a skinny Scottish dude, pointed an unlit cigarette at me. "You tell him to get his sorry ass over to Boing Boing Studios. He's a man without a band. It's a crime."

Darren rolled his eyes, and I put my hand on his arm, speaking for him. "He told you he wants to mature as an artist before selling his ass to the man, right? He told you he wants to develop his process before he starts playing for other people's glory?"

"Oy," Theo said. "My ears hurt with this."

Mark cut in. With his narrow-lapel jacket and horn-rimmed black glasses, he couldn't have been more Theo's opposite. "You need to get in your ten thousand hours, buddy. That's the rule. You can't master an art in under ten thousand hours. Documented. You can't develop a process in a vacuum. Bank on that."

Darren looked at me with his big blue eyes. Poor guy. He and Gabby had enough to live on from their inheritance, but they couldn't do much more than live. The cash flow they enjoyed seemed to keep them from doing the things they needed to do in order to grow.

"Darren, try it," I said. "Be a studio musician for fifteen minutes. You're making a big deal over nothing."

Over Darren's shoulder, I saw a face I recognized, and though I took a second to put a name to her face, she knew me right away and waved, smiling.

"Thank you," Theo said. "Nicely done, lassie."

But my mind was on the woman in the green dress. "I have to go," I said, making my way to her.

Before I got half a step away, Darren grabbed my arm and whispered in my ear, "Behind you, at a deuce up front. Kevin."

"Fuck."

"Bad idea," he said.

"Can you get rid of him?"

"Nope." He smiled at me, our faces close enough to kiss. I'd left Darren for Kevin almost two years before, and though he forgave me, he'd never forgotten.

"Fuck. What do I do?"

"You go and act like this is your room."

Right. This was my room. Kevin was the interloper. I stood up straighter and continued toward the woman in the green dress: Jonathan's sister.

"Theresa," I said, "hi. I'm so glad you came."

She kissed each of my cheeks. "I had to, of course, since I was the one who told Gene about you."

"Oh, it was you," I said. "Thanks again, then. I had no idea you worked at WDE."

"I run the accounting department. Not glamorous, but it keeps me busy. This is my sister, Deirdre."

Deirdre stood close to six feet tall, and she wore jeans and an Army surplus jacket. Her auburn curls stuck out everywhere, and her eyes were as big and green as the emerald isle itself. They were also glazed over, with lids hanging at half mast. She was drunk, and dinner hadn't even been served yet.

"Hi," I said. "Nice to meet you."

She looked at me, then made a point of looking away. I was being ignored, and somehow it was deeply personal. I turned back to Theresa with a big fat smile. "I hope you enjoy the entertainment tonight."

Deirdre made a huffing noise, and Theresa and I looked at each other for a second. She seemed as embarrassed as I was as she said, "I'm sure I will. Come by the table after."

I thanked her and left. I looked at Rhee. She spoke with a customer, nodding and serious, her dark skin a flawless velvet despite her knitted brows. If she wasn't on me, I had a minute. Scanning the room, I saw Kevin sitting with his buddy Jack. Kevin waved me over with one hand and pushed Jack's shoulder with the other. Jack gave me a quick wave and vacated the seat. Apparently, I was supposed to sit there. I glanced to Rhee again. She held up five fingers. Five minutes left. Perfect. I slid into Jack's empty chair. Kevin didn't get up or pull the chair out for me. He never did.

"Nice to see you," I said.

"You changed your number." He gave me the sorry eyes. They used to put me in a state of panic that I'd done something to hurt him. His huge brown eyes, big as saucers, hung under eyebrows that arched down at the ends. He had the textbook cartoon sad face. His hair had that greasy hipster look, a perfect complement to the ever-short beard that broadcast he was above such trivial concerns as looking nice in company. I used to think that made him smarter, more intellectual, more spiritual, but really, he'd just hit a lucky triple in the looks department and made it to home plate on a force play.

"I'm sorry," I said. "You know where I live." I smiled because I wanted Rhee to see me engaging a new person, not looking like an alley cat about to defend a fishbone.

"That's stalking," he explained. "The fact that you didn't want to talk to me was enough of a message."

"Yeah, well. We're grown-ups, and that was a year and a half ago. So, I have four and a half minutes. It is nice to see you." I plastered my friendliest smile across my face as I delivered the last line, and he bought it. He took a sip of his beer and relaxed.

"I heard about you singing here. Everyone's talking about it. 'This girl at Frontage will make you cry.' As soon as I heard it, I thought it was you. My canary." I think I blushed a little. No. I *know* I blushed a little. With all his degradation of my music toward the end, I'd forgotten his pet name for me. The memory of the time he did honor my talents went straight to my heart.

"And once I thought about you..." He stopped himself and reached into his pocket. "I thought, man, I'd like for her to see what I'm doing too. Thought we could hook up again. Artistically. You know? As creators in this mad city."

He handed me a brochure. The Los Angeles Modern Museum had a Solar Eclipse show every time there was a full eclipse somewhere in the world. It was a group show of the moment's hottest visual and conceptual artists, and an invitation to show could open doors to new artists, reinvigorate the careers of established artists, and solidify stars in the historical lexicon.

Kevin's name sat in the middle of the list.

"Congratulations," I said. "Tomorrow night, huh? Have you hung it already?"

"Did it today. It looks amazing. This is my best work yet. I have one last invite, and well..." He made his deep artist face, where he looked away and made a pained expression before he blanked it off his face. "You contributed to my work. You were my muse. I want you to be there."

Either he had a new expression or he really meant it, because his face was nothing if not completely sincere.

"I'll try to come. I'm happy for you."

He smiled, and I remembered why I'd loved him. Not for the serious crap, but the smiles that lit up his face and my heart at the same time.

I caught sight of Rhee out of the corner of my eye and stood up.

"I'll put you on the list," he said as I walked away.

I walked to the piano and touched Gabby's shoulder. She opened her eyes.

I gave the flyer one last look before slipping it onto my music stand. Jonathan's ex-wife, Jessica Carnes, was at the top of the list. I folded it over.

Gabby started *Stormy Weather.* The room quieted, though I could still hear the occasional fork or clinking glass. I had to close my eyes against the spotlight. I sang it the way we'd rehearsed, of course, with the sexual longing intact, but something was missing.

Jonathan's ministrations that afternoon had done their work on my body, but my mind was on Kevin, and everything he said to me and didn't, every expectation I couldn't meet, every time I'd failed him with my own ambitions. My disappointment at the inadequacy of his love came in a flood.

I had nothing to do but use it because I started *Someone to Watch Over Me.* I growled it from my diaphragm. I used the breakup I'd caused, cutting me off from friends I depended on because I was the aggressor. I wasn't allowed hurt. I wasn't allowed to grieve. Without Gabby and Darren, I had had no one to love me during that time. No guarantees. No sisters to protect me from bad decisions or whatever predatory lover followed. No Deirdre to defend me. No one would shelter me or worry about me. When I found that emotional place, I roared the last notes of the song, getting rid of all the accumulated junk feeding the angry girl in my heart.

Then I felt clean. I went through the rest of the songs the way we'd planned, with the dynamics and inflections coming from the right place. We culminated with *Moon River*, our gentle send-off from the emotional roller-coaster of the set.

I breathed. And they applauded. I was getting used to that. I didn't get filled-up like a balloon anymore, probably because they weren't my songs. What they applauded over their dinners was my craft, not my songwriting, and that artistic distance made all the difference.

I nodded, glancing behind me. Kevin's table was empty. Typical. I thanked everyone, and just like every time before, I slipped into the dressing room. Gabby came in right behind me.

"What happened to you?" she demanded.

"What?"

"I thought you were falling apart at *Stormy Weather*."

Ah. I remembered. Gabby the perfectionist. "I pulled it out, I think."

"Every. Song. Counts."

"Thanks. No pressure, right?"

"This was not the night to find your footing, Mon." She pointed at me, accusing me of ruining the set.

"Hey, you know what? Lay off. And you might consider pulling your weight at the meet and greet. The Gabby I knew in high school didn't hide behind a piano."

I didn't wait for a reaction. I just walked out. I'd been underhanded and cruel. The Gabby I knew in high school wasn't coming back, not after the depression and suicide attempt. That Gabby hadn't shown up for years, and bringing her up was unfair. I was fighting with some core, self-fulfilling loneliness that made me push people away.

The room was crowded, with the bar area customers bleeding into the dining area. The servers had trouble navigating the people and tables and mislaid chairs. I made it to the table by the warm speakers and found it full of men in fitted suits with colorful ties and women in button-down shirts and spiked heels. Agent-wear. Theresa had her back to me, and Deirdre, with her dismissive glare, was nowhere to be found. The eleven of them were having so many heated conversations in groups of two and three that I was going to pass the table and pretend I hadn't been on my way over.

"Monica Faulkner!" I heard my name and almost had a heart attack. Eugene Testarossa, who I'd been a creep to a couple of weeks before at the rooftop bar of the Stock, called out to me.

"Hi," I said, waiting for him to recognize me. From his expression, he either didn't remember me or didn't care.

"Nice set."

"Thanks."

"I'm Eugene. I'm a recording talent agent at WDE. You've heard of us?"

"Yes, of course." I was spinning smiles into gold, trying to keep from hugging a guy who, without his job and connections, wouldn't have gotten more than a courteous rejection.

"I'd like to sit and talk with you about something. Not a big deal. We're headed out to Snag. Can you come?"

A dream invitation. But no. I wasn't talking business over drinks. And if it wasn't business, I didn't want to be trapped at a douchebag bar on the west side.

"I have plans, I'm sorry."

He handed me a bright red card I knew had the WDE logo on it. "Call me then, and we'll set something up."

"Thanks. We hoped you'd come tonight."

"We? You've got representation already?"

"No, me and Gabby." I indicated her at the bar, next to Darren.

"Oh, the piano player? I thought she came with the club. Huh. Well. You don't gotta bring her if you don't want." My face must have been dragging on the floor, because he stood up straighter and held his hands out. "But no problem. Yeah, sure. Both of you. A set. We can talk."

"Great."

"Okay, you call tomorrow," he pointed at me, then put a phone to his ear. I smiled, but I knew more douchebag representation was in my future.

I started walking backward out into the aisle. "Will do," I said, nearly crashing into Iris, the waitress who'd been there long enough to be considered furniture. With one last wave, I went to the bar as fast as I could which, after the kind words and handshakes with everyone between Eugene Testarossa and Gabby, took about seven minutes.

"What happened?" Gabby was all over me. "What did he say?"

I showed her the card. She hugged me as if I'd just told her it was a healthy baby.

"Nice work." Darren held up his beer.

"Don't all huddle around the card, guys. Act cool, okay? It's not a big deal," I said.

"Ah, lassie," Theo said, "there's nothing coolish about you." He took my chin in his thumb and forefinger and shook my face. I playfully slapped his hand away.

"Let's go out," Darren said. "We can take every word you two said and give it major surgery."

Oh no. That wouldn't be good at all. I'd have to tell Gabby she was an optional part of the set or make something up I'd get busted for later. If she found out I'd had to rescue her before she'd even met Testarossa, she would spiral into Shitsville, and I didn't want Darren and me following her around again. Our recent freedom had been delicious.

"I made other plans," I said, glancing from face to face, landing on Gabby's last.

"Uh oh," Darren said. "Kevin's back."

"It's not Kevin," I said.

Gabby's eyes narrowed. "Cancel them."

"I don't want to. Tomorrow, you and I can call WDE. Testarossa's assistant will pick up. We'll make the appointment during lunchtime so he takes us out. Until then, you guys go out and have a good time. Come on. Give me a hug."

She did. Thank God, because I didn't know how much more convincing language I had in me.

CHAPTER 27

I texted Jonathan as soon as I got outside.

—Are you up?—

—I'm on Asia time. Wide awake.—

—Me too—

—So, why aren't you here?—

—Coming—

—!—

—j/k—

I'd been debating seeing Jonathan when a late night with the crew was the standard procedure. Testarossa had handed me the perfect incentive, but I'd almost wished he hadn't. I'd rather tell them I was ditching them to get laid than that Gabby's dream agent wanted to rep her as an optional attachment, or not at all.

I wouldn't abandon her.

I couldn't. I didn't know how.

She wasn't just my first lover's sister. They'd both become my family. We'd been through *stuff* together.

CHAPTER 28

I remembered where Jonathan lived, up by the historic fig trees. I had no idea how many cars he owned, but the little Fiat in the drive didn't look like his style at all. At ten p.m., he shouldn't have had any guests, but he stood on the porch with his arms crossed, talking to a blonde a few years older than me. She wore a printed, ankle-length dress and a loose jacket. He saw me pull in and waved. The blonde kept talking. I didn't know if I should get out or hide until she left.

That was ridiculous. I had a right to be there. I gathered my things and got out of the car. As if on cue, the woman turned and stepped off the porch, tapping something into her phone. As we passed each other, she glanced at me, but she got the phone to her ear in time to avoid greeting me.

"That was awkward," I said as I stepped onto the porch.

"Not really," Jonathan replied. "Or, I mean to say, not yet." He wore a sweatshirt and jeans, but not old, grey things. He wore designer clothes that were new at the edges and fit as they should, bringing out the beauty of his body without showing an inch of skin.

He looked behind me at the Fiat as it pulled out.

"Your assistant?" I asked.

"One of them." When the Fiat got into the street, he clicked a button on his remote box, and the gate slid shut. He leaned on the door jamb. "How did your gig go?"

"Fantastic. We're about to land a very good agent." I suddenly felt exposed, standing out on the porch again in a sleeveless, button-down shirt dress and heels.

"Oh, really." He put the remote on a table by the door.

"Really."

My dress had a fabric belt on sideseam loops. He pulled the bow loose and yanked the belt off. "Can you unbutton that thing and tell me the rest?"

"Is there some superstition about me entering your house with my clothes on?"

"I prefer you without them. And I like fresh air. Come on, I want to hear about your career." He wrapped the belt around his hand, which was muscular and square with a little hair on top.

I slipped my top button through the hole. "You want me to undress or tell you about the agent?"

"Yes to both. Tell me how it went."

I slipped the next button through, exposing the space between my breasts. "I almost screwed up the entire thing. I wasn't in the right frame of mind for the first song."

"My fault?"

"No. Actually..." I didn't want to bring up his sisters or my ex-boyfriend. Not with me getting down to my belly, and him watching the buttons' progress. "The agent wanted to go out tonight and talk about things." I finished the last button and stood in front of him.

"You could have gone." He stepped out of the doorway, reaching for the split in the dress. When he touched my throat, I lifted my chin. "We didn't have definite plans."

"He wants to ditch Gabby. I can see it. I'm not ready to tell her, and if we went out with him, she'd know."

He ran his hand down my body, only touching what the open dress revealed. "You think you can protect her from getting ditched?" He slipped his hand into the front of my panties. He stopped before he hit my growing wetness, but the electricity of his touch under my clothes made me gasp.

"Probably not for long." I stepped toward him. He pulled the dress off me. I unhooked my bra and let it drop to the floor.

Again, I stood almost naked before him. He unwrapped my belt from his hand, put it around my neck, and used it to pull me toward him. Our tongues and lips met. He let go of the belt, leaving it draped over my shoulders, and moved his hands under my panties, onto my bare ass. He grabbed it, pulling me to him, grinding me against his erection. I slipped my hands down his shirt, and he pinned them behind my back.

"I have a call with Seoul in seven minutes," he whispered in my ear.

"You couldn't make *yourself* come in seven minutes."

"That a challenge?"

"You tell me."

We kissed again, and he let my wrists go to hitch my legs up around his waist. He pushed me against the doorjamb, moving our hips together in a rhythm.

"Actually," he said, "I don't think I can get you upstairs in seven minutes."

"Don't sell yourself short."

He smiled, his face close to mine, where I could see every crease in his skin, every freckle, every thorn of stubble. His scent was everywhere around me. I wanted to fall into him. As if hearing my thoughts, he pulled away from the doorway, carrying me with my legs still around his waist. He shut the door behind us as he carried me to the stairs, kissing me. I wound my fingers in his hair. He bumped into a chair, then a bannister. We fell onto the soft wool carpet of the stairs, him on top of my nearly naked body, our hands everywhere, our hips joined in a fabric-sheathed tease.

His phone rang.

"Oh, no," I said.

"There wasn't going to be a good time."

"Don't answer it."

He looked right at me as he slipped the phone out of his pocket, smiling as if he knew he was tormenting me and felt nothing but sweet delight. He answered the thing, right there on the stairs, after putting his finger to his lips.

He said something I'd never be able to repeat, his Korean was so fast. His face hovered so close to mine I tasted his breath as he had a conversation I couldn't understand. The corners of the stairs bit my back, and the pressure of his hips on mine hurt, sending shocks of pleasure up my spine.

He put the phone to his chest and lifted himself off me. "I'm on hold. Get upstairs."

We ran up the stairs and into the room we'd been in two weeks before, laughing like teenagers. He landed on top of me on the bed, still fully clothed against my naked skin. He kissed me with his phone to his ear, putting his free hand on my breast, groaning into my mouth when I ran my hands under his shirt.

"Hey, Tom," he said into the phone. He put his finger to my lips and got off me, leaving me spread out like a bear-skin rug. I sat up.

"Yes," he said, his eyes on me. "I heard. Janice told me half an hour ago." I considered getting up and making myself a sandwich or something. I closed my legs. Who knew how long he would be? From his tone, it sounded urgent, but that could mean an hour or five minutes. If I left, I could still catch the guys for a drink, and I could glaze over the thing with Testarossa if Gabby was tipsy enough.

Jonathan put his hand on my shoulder and pushed me back down. He grinned and spoke into the phone. "They're insane. The Seoul Hilton is two miles away. If the North Koreans want a target, they already have one." He put his knee between my legs and parted them. I gasped, and he put his finger to his lips. Part of me thought he was being rude, disrespectful, and deserving of a desertion, but part of me found the third person in the room exciting, yet safe.

I reached for his belt, and he let me feel his erection through his clothes, but no more. "I am not taking five stories off it," he said. "I'm taking exactly zero stories off it. This whole Pyongyang alarm is a scam. Tandy Burton from the Hilton paid them off to give me a hard time." He tucked the phone between his shoulder and ear and used both hands to spread my legs wider, bending them at the knees. He nodded at something Tom said. Tom couldn't see us, but he was there. Jonathan lay beside me and slipped his fingers under the crotch of my underpants, sliding his finger along the length of my wetness. I bit my lip so the man in Korea wouldn't hear me.

"No, don't do that." He ran his thumb along my clit. "You'll have to back it up, and I can't." I gasped. I'd entered the room on fire, and his touch was charged with electricity, just hard enough on my bump before he put two fingers inside me. I was wet and ready, and after the past weeks of longing, and an afternoon with my legs spread over the arms of a chair, I was already close to coming. He would give me my orgasm. He had to. We had all night. Except for Tom, who could be a real wrench in my works.

"What you need to do," he said, eyes on me, fingers inside me, thumb rubbing my clit under the fabric, skin to wet skin, "is get a council of Koreans. Natives. Have them work up numbers, odds, and projections. See what they come up with on a North Korean attack."

His thumb circled me. I wanted to moan but couldn't, or I'd be heard. I just spread my legs wider, hitching my hips forward and into his fingers. Tom babbled. It sounded like gobbledygook. Jonathan said, "yes, yes," periodically as he spoke to Tom, but he looked at my face as he fingered me. With his phone tucked at his shoulder, he grabbed my nipple with his other hand and turned it absently as if he was fiddling with a pen on his desk, except the "pen" was connected to my sexual center.

My back arched. My breathing got short. I mouthed to him, *Let me come.*

He tilted his head as if he didn't understand me.

I mouthed again, *Please let me come.*

He took his hand off my nipple and put it behind his ear, mouthing, *I can't hear you.*

"No," he said into the phone, "we're paying them. Tom, listen. The hotel is not a target, okay? Seoul is a major city. Everything's a target." He rolled his eyes as if Tom was just some annoying employee, and he and I were watching TV on the couch. Oh, funny guy.

His fingers left my hole and ran up to my clit and back. Once, then twice. I mouthed, *Please let me come please let me come....*

He made the *I can't hear you sign,* and I got the game, but I was about to explode into his hand hours after I'd given him control of my orgasms. I couldn't show so much weakness so early.

I rolled off the bed, letting his hand slip out of me, and ran out of the room.

I stood in the hall, back against the wall, and tried not to make a sound, but I started laughing. I couldn't help it. I crouched, balled my fists up in front of my mouth, and just laughed.

I saw Jonathan in the doorway, phone to his ear, fist in the same position in front of his mouth as he tried not to crack up in the middle of a business call.

"Okay." He cleared his throat. "Tom, I have to go." The last word came out in the squeak. Tom, however, wouldn't shut up. "I get it," Jonathan said.

I got myself together, but I knew I could burst into audible laughter any second. I went back into the bedroom and hooked my hand in his waistband before I kneeled in front of him.

"Okay, that's fine," he said. "Just let me know if you hear anything else." I unbuckled his belt and got his dick out of his pants. He leaned back against the wall. "Yes, and keep your ear to the ground on the other thing."

I gave him a taste of his own medicine, licking the underside of his dick with the flat of my tongue from base to tip, then throating him.

"It's an expression, Tom. It means listen hard." He put his fingers in my hair and pulled my head into him. "Yes, okay. Really, it's late here. Let me know tomorrow." He hung up and threw the phone on the chair. "You," he said, looking down at me, "are very naughty."

I couldn't respond. I had a dick in my mouth. When I pulled back, leaving it slick with my spit, he bent down and caught me under the arms. I laughed as he threw me on the bed, and I tried to get away until he crawled over me.

"No, you don't." He grabbed my arms. We laughed together as I tried to wiggle away, but he flipped me over onto my stomach and pinned my wrists behind my back.

"You shoulda let me come while the coming was good," I said.

"Oh, you're going to come." He slapped my ass, and the sting made me catch my breath.

"You didn't just ..." I said, knowing he did and wanting him to do it again.

He did. One hand held my wrists behind my back and the other thwacked my ass as if I was a wicked, naughty child. I made some noise, like a breathy cry, that might have sounded something like "yes."

I felt him bend down and whisper, "Have you ever been tied up, Monica?"

"No."

"Why not?"

"Never came up."

I waited for him to ask, maybe a formal request for permission, but he just bent backward while holding my wrists. I felt the pressure on the bed change, and I knew he wasn't asking for permission or anything else.

He let go of my wrists and laid his body over mine, slipping his forearms under my face. I saw him holding the belt of my dress. It had fallen on the floor at some point, and he was making sure I saw it.

He kissed the back of my neck as he said, "I understand words like *no* and *stop*. Outside of those, your body is my playground."

"Yes, sir."

"You're like a prodigy at this."

Before I could answer, he pulled me up to my knees. I felt him behind me, still clothed, as he stroked me from my neck to my crotch and back up again. He ran his hands from my shoulders down my arms and placed my hands on the wooden headboard. The railings and runner across the top were roughhewn. He looped the belt around my wrists, binding them together, then around the railing. It was a good knot, firm and tight.

I wasn't frightened. Nervous. I was nervous in the best way possible as he got off the bed and stood there in his jeans and sweatshirt, staring at me. Me, on my knees with my wrists tied to his headboard, hair in my face, ass out; him with his arms folded, checking out his work.

"Well?" I said.

He smirked a dangerous smirk. I felt the tingle of liquid dripping down my leg.

He pulled his shirt off, and when his face was covered and I only saw his body, another shiver went through me. His tight torso, with its patches of light hair, was a feast for the eyes, and when he got his shirt over his head, messing up his hair, he smiled as if he knew I was admiring him.

He took his time getting the rest of his clothes off. The condom went on, and he put his knee on the bed, tilting the mattress, and put his arms around my waist. One hand landed on my breast and the other between my legs. He found where I was wettest and rubbed gently, then harder. I rotated my hips, my tethered hands a fulcrum I rocked against, his dick waiting against my ass.

"Jonathan." My voice was husky. Breaths without a voice. I didn't know what I was trying to say. Just his name, as if that would tell him what I wanted. As if that would connect us to my pleasure. As if him binding my hands wasn't enough for me to feel possessed, owned, protected.

He stopped rubbing my clit, pulled my ass up, and put the head of his cock at my pussy. I felt as if it would be sucked inside me by the sheer force of my desire. But no, he let it hover there, just touching the skin. I pushed back, but my tied hands held me. He kept himself just out of my body's reach.

"Go," I said with a squeak of desperation.

I thought I'd have to beg him to fuck me, but I didn't. He slid in easy and sweet, pulling my ass up. The slow slide was good, the wet inches rubbing inside me and pushing against my hole. He moved so my wrists felts trapped and burned, the feeling of being held still almost stronger than the feeling of his stomach hitting my ass. He was doing everything right. He was fucking the hell out of me. But something was missing. He was holding back.

"Jonathan," I said.

"Monica."

"Hurt me."

"What?"

"Do it so it hurts. Break me apart. Make it hurt so I scream. I want everything. All of it."

He paused and slid his hands down my back. "Say it again."

"Hurt me, Jonathan. Hurt me. Please."

After a long exhale that sounded like a decision being made, he started moving faster, but that wasn't the half of it. He gripped my ass, a hand in each cheek, and spread me apart until I thought he'd rip me. When he pummeled me then, he was in my pussy so deep I felt the head of his cock hitting the end of me. But he didn't ease up. His fingers dug into my skin. My ass became dough in his hands. My wrists kept me steady against him. I wanted to scream, but I couldn't, or he'd stop. I didn't want him to stop because the pain was exquisite, focusing me on his pleasure as it peaked my own.

He took a hand off one cheek and grabbed my hair. I moaned so loud it came out as a bark. He pulled my ass up again, his fingers digging into my skin, as he fucked the shit out of me. I was damp all over from sweat and juice.

"Say my name," he gasped.

"Jonathan."

"Again."

"Jonathan, Jonathan, oh God, Jonathan."

He came as if he'd hurled himself off a cliff, with a long grunt and a longer groan. He pumped at me from behind, still groaning, going on forever. Nothing had ever given me more satisfaction than hearing him come so hard.

He stopped and fell on top of me, his chest to my back, his dick falling away from me. We breathed together for a minute, our bodies still in tune.

"Are you okay?" he asked, brushing the hair away from my face.

"Never better."

"Give me a minute. You'll be even better."

He kissed my neck, then between my shoulder blades, down my back, then to my ass cheeks, which hurt. I groaned and arched my back.

"Stay still," he said. I dropped down. "Very still."

"Okay."

The skin of my slit was sore and bruised from his fingers. The sting felt wonderful as he licked the insides of my thighs, then my soaking pussy, which throbbed with the hurt and pleasure of him. His tongue went up and down my folds, landing on my clit, teasing the tip with tiny, imperceptible motions. Then he drew his lips around it and kissed, ending in a light sucking.

"Oh, Jonathan..."

"Don't move."

"Please let me come when I'm ready. Please don't make me wait more."

"Only if you stay still. Move, and I take you out for coffee."

"Yes."

He spread me apart, which hurt until he slipped his tongue inside me, then drew it out, along the slit, which was so sore, and over my clit, slowly. Then back, into my hole and down until he sucked on my clit one last time. I went rigid, crying out with everything I had. My back wanted to arch, but I couldn't let it. My hips wanted to thrust, but my mind overrode the impulse. I became a vessel for my pussy and my clenching ass and the pressure on my wrists. My body's stillness drew out my orgasm, because I couldn't surrender to it until the final moment when I lost all sense to his touch and tongue, screaming his name at the top of my lungs. He sucked gently on my clit until I was a shuddering mess, way past the point of agony.

CHAPTER 29

Kevin had been the fuck of my life. That didn't mean much as he'd been one of two. Darren had been serviceable, but we were young and inexperienced and *in love,* so we had no idea how boring it was.

Kevin had seemed like a white hot ball of fire. He was all hands and lips. He masturbated in front of me, and I tried not to giggle because I thought hot people would be very serious. He told me I was pent up and repressed in a way that made me want to get unrepressed, but I didn't know how. I tried to get wilder by wearing lingerie and groaning louder. I sucked his dick more. I danced for him. All that seemed wonderful at the time, like really being grown up and sexual. But he didn't know how to take my repression, wring it out, and throw it out the window. He didn't know how to fuck it out of me or quietly tell me to get undressed in the night air while he watched in such a way that wouldn't make me laugh. I couldn't have given Kevin my orgasms, because he didn't want them. I could never have asked him to hurt me, because he would have.

I watched the sun come up through Jonathan's window, felt his breath on my neck, and thought *don't fall in love don't fall in love don't fall in love.* I didn't look at him while he slept. I didn't stroke the top of his hand where it rested on my belly. I didn't think about him. Nothing. Not his scent or the sound of his voice. Not his sharp wit or his easy smile. My job there was to enjoy him, and sense sooner rather than later when it was time to move on. That was the only way I would get out intact.

I heard steps in the hall, and some loose, non-English muttering between a man and woman, which alarmed me. But then I heard a broom on the hardwood. The staff. They probably lived in a house out back and were like furniture to him.

My bag was on the floor. The second and last time we'd fucked, I went downstairs for it because he ran out of condoms. I'd rooted in the pockets and found a little latex sack a month from its expiration date.

I had to grab that, and my clothes, which were probably still on the porch. That would be tricky. It was broad daylight, and I couldn't leave the room naked with the cleaning staff around. Or maybe I could. Who knew how people with money lived?

I closed my eyes and tried to sleep again, but Jonathan's phone buzzed. When I looked at him, his eyes were open.

"You gonna get that?" I asked.

"No."

"Your cleaning staff's been knocking around."

The phone stopped buzzing. Jonathan stretched as if two hours of sleep had left him refreshed. "I have to go get your clothes. You don't want to flash Maria, or she'll start sprinkling holy water all over the place. Makes a mess."

He kissed me and swung his legs over the side of the bed. I sat up, aching everywhere. I was so sore I could barely sit straight. Jonathan looked down at something and didn't move.

"What?" I said.

"I don't want you to think I'm prying or that I was looking in your things."

"Okay, I won't think that."

He picked my bag up off the floor. It was open, and Kevin's flyer for the Solar Eclipse show stuck out. I showed him the name list. I knew the only name he would see was Jessica's, so I pointed out Kevin's.

"Kevin Wainwright," he said. "The guy with the dick."

"He came to Frontage last night."

"And invited you to a show for tonight? Late notice, don't you think?"

I shrugged. "It's Kevin. He thinks courtesy is for non-creatives."

"Like me."

"You're plenty creative." I slapped his arm with the brochure. "With your body."

"You going?" he asked.

"I don't know. You?"

He sighed and ran his fingers through his hair. "I have to. It's unbecoming if I don't. The divorce looks anything but amicable, and people are watching."

"What kind of people?"

"She got custody of most of our friends. I do business with some of them. Others have just been in the same circles too long."

"Which sister you taking?"

"Deirdre, I think. Are you going to pretend you don't know me?" His phone buzzed again.

I slid off the bed. "We'll see if I even go."

I went into the bathroom, a huge white room with a separate shower and tub. Every corner was clean, as if little gremlins lived under the sink and scrubbed the place while he flattened women on the bed.

I had no idea if I was going to L.A. Mod. It was a black tie thing, and I didn't have anything to wear. And there was the Kevin issue. Jonathan would be there with Deirdre, who had given me dagger eyes just the night before. If I were being honest with myself, I would admit I was just making excuses. I didn't want to be in Jonathan and Kevin's line of sight at the same time. I couldn't stand any unmanageable drama just as my career was rousing itself.

I heard Jonathan through the door, mumbling. Not a business call. Then it went quiet. I peeked into the bedroom. He was gone, but my dress was laid out on the chair. I put it on and fished my underwear and shoes out from under the bed.

I went downstairs. Though I'd been to Jonathan's before, I hadn't paid attention to what he had on the walls.

One couldn't go through music school without an immersion in all the arts, and Kevin had continued my education with his passion for all things visual. So once I was fully clothed and paying attention, I recognized a Kandinsky in Jonathan's living room. I saw the Holbein over the mantle and the Mondrian studies in geometry in the corner. I didn't linger though, because I heard him in the kitchen. I didn't want him to think I was prying.

I followed his voice to the kitchen, realizing he wasn't speaking English, Spanish, or Korean. A middle-aged, dark-skinned woman with Asian features and wearing a cleaning smock smiled at me.

"Do you drink coffee?" Jonathan asked when I walked in.

"Not really." I leaned on the counter. "I like it with milk, and dairy's not good for my voice. So, let me guess. The lady you're talking to is Filipina?"

"Good call."

"I do live in Los Angeles." I smirked. "You speak, what is it called?"

"It's called Tagalog, and yes—"

"You live in Los Angeles."

He smiled. "Ally Mira washed your dress."

"That was very kind."

"She is. So, seriously, are you going to this thing tonight?"

"Kevin dragged me to a thousand art shows when we were together, and I'm just not into another one."

"That was Teresa on the phone," he said. "She says you met Deirdre last night?"

"Briefly. Very tall. Big curly red hair."

"She got alcohol poisoning."

"That's terrible."

"That's Deirdre. Theresa was watching her, and she didn't know Deirdre had a flask. So Theresa's counting drinks and Deirdre's off to the bathroom twelve times. Do the math on that." He came toward me. "They have her on a B vitamin IV drip, and she's already cursing the nurses." He put his thumb on my cheek, and I raised my face to kiss him. "You sure you're not going?" he said. "I can give you a lift."

"That would be like us going together."

"Would that make you uncomfortable?"

"No." I put my hands on his chest to caress him through his T-shirt. "I think it might make *you* uncomfortable."

He wrapped his arms around my waist. "Tell me more about me."

"You take your sisters out, and you meet your women in private. You said you and your wife, sorry, ex-wife, still hang around the same circles. You don't want her to see you with an actual woman. And don't make a crack about your sisters being women."

He looked up for a second, and I got a full view of the muscles and veins in his neck. I was right, or at least close.

"I can go alone," he said, looking at me. "I'm a big boy. But I don't want to. So if you're going, this non-creative wants to go with you, courtesy be damned."

The offer was compelling. I hadn't planned on going because I didn't want to stand in a corner and watch Kevin work the room. I didn't want to make small talk with his friends, and I didn't want to get the death-eye from whatever little hipster groupie was chasing him. Jonathan would be a nice buffer.

"Fine," I said. "I'll let your handsome ass drag me to a black tie thing at L.A. Mod. But you'll owe me."

"What exactly will I owe you?"

"You pick." I stepped away. The call Gabby and I had to make had started worrying the back of my mind. "Whatever it's worth to you. If it makes me scream and yell your name, even better." I kissed him quickly. "I have to go."

I walked toward the doorway, but I didn't get past it before I heard him say, "What are you wearing?"

I stopped and turned. "Why?"

"Because you're a beautiful woman, and what you wear is important."

"If I'm going to embarrass you, I can just stay home."

He stepped forward and grabbed me around the waist. "Jessica makes art because she has so much money she's bored and because she has the sharpest eye I've ever known. If she's going to see me with you, she's not going to see you wearing Target."

I looked him in the eyes. "Really, Jonathan? You never seemed like the catty type."

"*I* also want to see you in something better. I'm sorry. Come on. Go to Barney's and talk to Lorraine. She'll fix you up and bill me."

"Now I'm the one who's really uncomfortable."

"Please? Just go. And if you spend less than three thousand dollars, I'm spanking you and sending you back to Wilshire Boulevard."

"I'll come in *just* under three large then. And not because I have any intention of returning to that side of Wilshire."

CHAPTER 30

I stood under the shower head with my hands on the wall, letting the water scald my back. My head drooped, and my hair fell in front of me. I couldn't move without aching, and when I opened my eyes, I saw the insides of my thighs through the steam.

At first I'd thought they were dirty. When I touched them and felt a sharp pain, I knew they weren't dirty. They were bruised.

I got out of the shower and looked in the mirror. My ass, the area just below it, and between my legs were black and blue. It hurt to move. My pussy was so sore, it had hurt to clean myself. I heard a soft tap at the door, and Gabby asked, "Mon? Is that you?"

"Yeah. You need to pee?"

"Yeah." She started to open the door. Gabby and I saw each other naked and stood in the same room to pee all the time, but I couldn't let her see me that way. I looked as if a shark had tried to bite me in half. I grabbed the door handle and pulled it closed. "Are you okay?" she asked.

"I'm fine, I just...." I had no excuse. "Give me a minute."

I wiggled into a tee and jeans I pulled from the hamper, cringing from torn muscle and broken blood vessels. I snapped the door open. Judging from her clean clothes and brushed hair, she'd been up a while.

"Where did you go last night?" she asked.

"I saw Jonathan." I brushed my wet hair while she peed.

"Oh, really. Well? How was it?"

"He knows how to fuck, that's for sure."

"Better than Kevin?"

"It's the difference between a man and a boy." I slid my toothbrush out of the cup and got to the point. "I figure we should call WDE at about ten-thirty. Those guys don't get in until ten, and I want to give him a chance to get his jacket off and bang his secretary, but I want to catch him before he goes into a meeting."

"I'm nervous. Are you nervous?"

"Yeah. Actually, I am." I lathered up my toothbrush, and Gabby leaned toward the mirror, picking some nonexistent crud from the corner of her eye. "But you know how it is," I continued. "You get all nervous for a call, and you make it and they're not available. Then they call you back when you're going eighty on the 101."

"Since when can you go eighty on the 101? Give me a break." She held up a tube of aloe moisturizer I got from the farmer's market. "Can I try this?"

"Go ahead," I said, brushing my teeth. After I spit, I said, "I want to be clear we come as a set. You and me. Okay?"

"Why?" She seemed unfazed by my suggestion.

"Suppose he can't get a keyboardist for some band, and then you're off touring, and what am I supposed to do?" I pulled my hair into strands so I could braid it.

"We should give ourselves a name." Gabby pushed me onto the toilet. I winced, but she wasn't looking. God, sitting was going to be torture today, and maybe tomorrow.

Gabby had braid mojo. Our first year of Colburn, we made ninety percent of our friends because she could braid like a magician. She picked up the strands I'd started. I turned my head so she wouldn't see me grimace at the pain in my behind.

"I really liked Spoken Not Stirred," I said. "But Vinny reps them."

"That wasn't the last cool name we have in us," Gabby said.

"I guess it depends on what he wants out of us. Am I recording my own stuff? But how could he want that? He doesn't even know if I can write a freaking song." I gestured with my hands and saw the bruising around my wrists. Fuck. I slipped them between my legs, wishing I'd worn long sleeves.

"You can, Mon. Your songs are amazing."

I let her ministrations tickle my scalp. "What I'm saying is, if it's my stuff, then that's one name, but we'd need a whole band. If it's just you and me, that's a totally different sound. Which is fine, but even then, are we writing new material? Or are we doing Irving Berlin?"

"He might not even know what he wants." She concentrated on the strands, looping one around the other, tugging and pulling, straightening and separating the lengths with a black comb.

"He knows," I said. "Those sharks don't start swimming around unless they've smelled blood. Some label is looking for a specific something he thinks we can do. Otherwise he wouldn't have come out. Trust me."

She pulled my hair off my neck. "Whoa, Monica."

"What?"

"Hickey City back here."

I stood and looked in the mirror. Gabby held up a handheld mirror so I could see the trail of bruises at the back of my neck.

"Fuck," I said. "Can you braid it to cover it?" I sat on the toilet again and

Gabby undid her work. My ass, my wrists, and now my back. If it hadn't felt so good, it would have been assault.

"Sure, but what's the diff?" Gabby asked. "It's a phone call."

"I'm going to the Eclipse opening at L.A. Mod tonight."

"Fancy. Did Jonathan invite you?" Gabby moved my hair around in a way that soothed me, and I wanted to purr like a kitten.

"No, Kevin did. But Jonathan is taking me."

"Kevin?"

"This is such a long story."

"Are you wearing your little black mini with the bow on the shoulder?"

God, no. Even in my mind, that thing looked cheap and worn. Jonathan had been right, despite my hurt feelings. I had a closet full of black and nothing nice to wear to a black tie function.

"How about this? It's almost nine. You go take your meds. Come back in here and braid while I tell you everything about last night without the dirty parts. Then, at ten-thirty, we make a call on the speakerphone in the kitchen."

"Deal."

CHAPTER 31

Barney's New York was on the best part of Wilshire, close to Rodeo Drive and near all the big agencies. WDE was half a block away, in its own slick black phallus of a building.

Jonathan had given my name to an apparently very difficult-to-get personal shopper. She called me, and we made an appointment.

A valet drove my shitty Honda behind a Bugatti and a Jaguar and treated me like a princess when, as Lorraine instructed, I asked for the elevator that went to the fifth floor. I was handed off to a guy in a burgundy jacket who led me right down the hall, then right again, and pressed the button for me as if I was too good to lift my arm.

The elevator doors opened into a room rich in wildflowers and tapestries. The white leather couches were empty, but the antique desk was manned by a woman about my age with smooth skin and a ready smile.

"Good afternoon, Miss Faulkner," she said.

"Monica's fine."

"My name's Shonda. Lorraine will be right with you. Would you like some coffee? Or we have herbal tea?"

"If you have a green or a white tea, hot and plain? I'd love that."

"Great." Shonda seemed genuinely pleased to get me tea. She didn't have the same face I wore when I wanted to seem genuinely pleased to get someone their drinks, but I really wasn't. Or maybe that was exactly what I looked like.

I didn't sit but stood at the window, staring at the WDE building. Our call with Eugene Testarossa had been as quick as a hot fuck. Our meeting was in four days at twelve-thirty. High lunch. Location TBA. That meant we were important to him. He wanted to be seen with us. One day, I'd walk into that big black building from the parking lot and take the elevator up as if I belonged there. I'd be a moneymaker, a golden ticket, their canary.

"Ms. Faulkner?"

I turned to see Lorraine, a sixty-ish woman a few inches shorter than me with pixie cut white hair and not a stitch more makeup than was appropriate.

"Hi," I said.

"So nice to meet you." She held her hand out, and I shook it.

"I'm sorry," I said. "I want to be honest. I don't know exactly how to do this. I mean, usually, I'd just go shopping, so, if you could kinda guide me through?"

"Of course," she said, folding her hands in front of her. "You're looking for something for the Eclipse show?"

"Yes."

"Follow me." She smiled slyly and winked at me. "This will be fun. I promise."

We walked into a room with mirrors and a white carpet. My tea waited for me on a little marble table. Lorraine closed the door behind us.

"I set up some possibilities for you," said Lorraine, pointing to a rack of garments on hangers. Four mannequins wore other dresses. All of the clothes were black eveningwear. "You probably won't need any alterations. I pulled from size six per Mister Drazen's recommendation."

"He knew my size?"

"He said you were perfect, and it's my job to know every customer's ideal. Trust me, it's different for everyone. Size two to twenty two."

I didn't want to know how many women he'd sent up to Lorraine for her to know that. It wasn't a productive line of thought, and I had a bunch of clothes to look through. I usually loved shopping, but that was nerve-wracking. I felt like a Dodger's fan at Wrigley Field.

"If you sit," Lorraine said, indicating a chair, "I'll show you what I have."

I sat slowly when her back was turned. I didn't want her to see the pain in my face. She pulled things from the rack, one at a time, and laid them out. I rejected most as too dowdy or too slutty, which made her laugh. I didn't know exactly what I wanted, which didn't help. As she got to the last frock on the rack, and I knew from the length it wouldn't work, I imagined myself walking into the L.A. Mod. Who would I see? How did I want to present myself? I'd be with Jonathan, but who would see me besides him?

She didn't seem impatient or put out at all when I rejected the last thing and said, "I think I decided something."

"Oh, good."

"I want to look like an artist."

She looked at me for a second, hands folded in front of her again, and winked when she said, "I know just the thing."

She left and came back in a second flat. The dress was black, naturally, and soft to the touch, yet stiff enough to hold a shape. The skirt hit at the knee, with a raw edge and strips of fabric dropping from below the hem, like a deconstructed fringe. The bodice was plain, but the shoulder straps crisscrossed each other along the back and front, making an asymmetrical web of lines across the shoulders.

"It's gorgeous."

"Try it on."

I went into the dressing room. The dress felt like magic on my skin. The difference between a Target dress and a designer dress brought to me by a personal shopper wasn't the way it made me look, though I looked like the best version of myself. It was the way I felt inside it. I felt like a queen.

Until I got out of the dressing room, turned around, and saw the bruises on the back of my neck.

"Crap." My face went hot red.

Lorraine waved the concern away. "We have something for that down at the makeup counter. I'll get it for you. Don't you worry. I've seen much worse. And I've seen wealthy brats who wanted something that showed those marks off." She shook her head. I smiled at her. She made me feel comfortable, which I guessed was her job, but it was a gift. If she wasn't there, I'd be very, very ashamed.

"I love this dress," I said.

"You look lovely," she said. "Do you have shoes?"

I hadn't even thought of that. "I guess not."

"And something nice to wear underneath?"

"Oh, I don't need anything like that."

Lorraine looked at me in the mirror. "It's not about what you need, dear. And it's not for *you.*"

"I guess I should spend a little something on him then?"

"Exactly."

CHAPTER 32

After shopping the fifth floor at Barney's, my room looked messy and dim. My mirror made my body squiggle. The walls were cracked, and the floor was scratched down to the raw wood. Even through that, the dress was perfect on me. The bracelets I'd bought to cover my bruised wrists clinked and clanked when I spun hard enough to make the skirt wave. I'd tried to protest that the red soles of the shoes didn't go with the black dress, but Lorraine insisted they were fine, and since she'd rejected so many things on my behalf before that, I felt pretty sure she wouldn't bullshit me.

The bill came, and though I wasn't responsible for paying it, I had to sign off on what I was taking out of the store. Lorraine had slid it across Shonda's little desk with a smile. I checked the items and then the price. It came to two thousand, nine hundred, ninety-nine dollars.

"I know I spent more than this," I'd said. "I saw the price on the shoes."

"Well, you caught me," she'd said. "You're not supposed to see the price tags. So if you don't tell anyone you saw it…" She paused and smiled to let me know it really wasn't that big a deal. "I'll tell you. Mister Drazen asked that the bill say this number no matter what. He said you'd get the joke."

"I get it all right." I'd signed, trying not to smile too wide. But as I looked at myself in my bedroom mirror, I smiled again.

Gabby had done my hair to cover the bite marks, tsking the whole time and making me giggle. I'd told her what I could about the night before, leaving out the parts that made my thighs black and blue. She did a church lady voice that made me laugh so hard I thought I would break a rib. We were in the bathroom playing with my makeup bag when the doorbell rang.

"God," I said, "this is ridiculous. I feel like I'm going to prom."

"You didn't go to prom." Gabby ran some hand cream over her fingers. "You and Darren stayed in the limo making out."

"And you and Bennet Provist? In Elysian Park?" I popped tubes and pencils into my little makeup bag.

"Yeah. Excellent prom."

"Mon!" Darren shouted from the living room. "You have a gentleman caller!" Oh God, was Darren going to embarrass me? I ran out to do damage control.

Jonathan was by the doorway, looking too big for the space, wearing a tuxedo cut for him and no one else. He and Darren were smiling.

"Yes, sir," said Jonathan, "the dance is chaperoned."

"I want her home by eleven."

I stepped into the living room before the joke got old, and Jonathan saw me in my new black dress. He liked it. He pressed his lips together to suppress a smile that would have mortified me in front of Darren and Gabby.

"You clean up nice," I said.

"Obviously you were intending to clean up in that old thing as well."

I snapped my bag shut. "Good thing the Salvation Army was open late."

He held out his hand, and we laced our fingers together.

"You met Darren, I guess?"

"Yes. He mentioned his shotgun."

"This is Gabby."

"Nice to meet you," Jonathan said.

"Hi."

"Okay, great," I said. "Let's go." I pulled him out the door. I saw Lil standing outside the Bentley, which looked damn near vertical parked on my hill.

Darren stood in the door and wagged his finger. "Remember what we talked about. Not a minute later, young man."

Jonathan walked backward a step and waved to Darren. "Eleven tomorrow morning, yes, sir."

"Hi, Lil," I said. "How did you enjoy my hill?"

"Quite a ride," she said. "I want to try it in the Jag."

"Be careful."

"I was born careful, miss." She opened the door for us. I slid in, and Jonathan got in right after and sat facing me. Behind him, the partition between us and Lil was shut. We sat quietly for ten seconds. My eyes must have eaten him alive as much as his undressed me. By the time the car started rolling, we were on each other, lips searching, tongues twisting, hands testing how far they could get before we risked wrinkles and stains.

He put his hands up my skirt, and when he felt the garter, he whispered *oh* into my ear. But I cringed because he'd gone up high enough to touch the bruises. He pulled back and said, "Let me see."

I pulled the skirt to the top of the stockings.

"Monica, are you shy all of a sudden?"

"Don't freak out."

"I guarantee you I'll freak out." His tone told me he didn't mean "freak out" in the same way I did.

I pulled the skirt up to reveal the black silk garters, and though the fronts of my legs were fine, he could definitely see the damaged insides.

"I did this?"

"We did it. I shouldn't have worn garters, but they were so pretty."

"Turn around."

I turned to face the back window, my knees on the seat cushion, my hands on the back of the seat, steadying me. He touched me when he pulled my skirt up, his fingers barely grazing my skin. He didn't hurt me, but the anticipation of pain made me flinch anyway. He kissed where I hurt, lips soft and yielding. "I'm sorry," he said as he kissed the backs of my thighs.

"Don't be. It was worth it." He pulled my dress down and gently guided me back to sitting. I took his hands. "I just got a little bruised, but I was never scared."

"I feel terrible." His elbows rested on his knees, a posture I remembered from the morning I saw him talking to his ex-wife on the back patio. His eyes searched mine, looking for any hidden anger.

"Okay, stop it. Really. I've never had sex like that in my life. The bruises will heal. My brain chemistry is what's totally fucked."

"That's a high compliment. I should say thank you first."

"You're welcome."

He held his hands over my thighs. "I'm afraid to touch them."

"Do it."

"I'm going to San Francisco for a few days. By the time I get back, these should be healed enough I won't have to worry about hurting you."

"I remember asking for it."

"God," he whispered, "so do I."

He put his hands on my neck and kissed me all the way to the museum.

CHAPTER 33

We walked hand in hand to the L.A. Mod from the parking lot, taking an extra turn around the block. His dry palm against mine, the tracks of his thumb drawing circles on the base of my wrist, and the sound of his voice seemed to have a direct line to the heat in my crotch, which pulsed to its own beat after the make out session in the car.

The museum had been built on one of the busiest streets in the city, set back to leave room for a granite courtyard flanked by steps on either side that led to a patio a flight up. The gathering began in the courtyard. Jonathan introduced me to thirty people, none of whom stuck in my mind. Gabby would have had a field day drawing connections between everyone, but all I saw were the expensive dresses and cufflinks. I saw why Jonathan had insisted I go to Barney's. I would have stuck out like a sore thumb in my cotton shirtdress.

"When you sent me to Barney's, you were saving *me* from embarrassment," I whispered after another introduction. I held Jonathan's hand, leaning into him as if he was a string bass.

"I just wanted you to fit in."

I squeezed his hand and looked over the crowd, my eyes scanning the staircases.

"Why are you nervous?" he asked. "I'll introduce you to anyone you want."

"I'm not nervous."

"Yes, you are."

"Kevin." I looked right at Jonathan when I said it. I was a little ashamed to have my eyes peeled for my ex-boyfriend while I was with my current lover, but I had no illusions about my future with either man. "I'm looking out for Kevin. I'm sorry. I don't mean to be rude. I just suddenly want to avoid him."

"Monica, when you're with me, you don't need to be nervous about seeing Kevin or anyone else." He led me up the stone stairs.

"I'm not nervous."

"You better keep the truth on those lips."

I shook my head and looked away. I saw her at the top of the stairs: Jessica Carnes. She didn't photograph well. She looked gorgeous on film, but in person, she was exquisite. She wore a long white dress over her straight, slim figure and low heels on small feet. She saw us, or rather Jonathan, and excused herself from the couple she was speaking to.

Jonathan squeezed my hand. I looked in his direction and spoke close to him, keeping my lips as still as possible. "And this is who makes *you* nervous."

"I hate this," he said.

"We can lean on each other. Then you can take me home and bruise the rest of me."

"The things that come out of your mouth."

"They please you?"

"Yes." He looked at me and took one long blink before facing his ex-wife. "Jess, how are you? Congratulations!" His smile was so wide I thought his face would snap. It wasn't a happy smile. They kissed each other's cheeks, his hand on her bare shoulder.

"Thanks," she said. "I'm glad you could come." She made a quarter-turn so she faced me completely, her sky-blue eyes twinkling with icy delight. "We haven't met." She held her hand out.

Jonathan spoke before I could get out a word. "This is Monica."

I shook her hand, and to my surprise, it was warm. "It's nice to meet you," she said. "Very, *very* nice to see you here."

"Thank you," I said. As I tried to pull back my hand, Jessica put her left hand over our clasped hands for a second, then let go.

"Where's Erik?" Jonathan asked.

Her expression didn't change. Not a hair nor muscle moved. "He didn't come."

"Ah, too bad. Well, we're about to sign in. We'll see you in there?"

"Sure."

Another half turn and she was speaking to someone else. Jonathan put his arm around my shoulders and guided me away.

"Who's Erik?" I asked.

"The man she left me for."

I shook my head. "You people are too fucking mature for me."

He chuckled as if he had so much to say, but he didn't know how.

The galleries were designed to change. The vast space was chopped up by permanent-looking temporary partitions that still left enough room for huge sculptures. The lighting was flat, warm, and consistent, flattering the people in it. The space was so big, I stopped looking for Kevin and looked at the work.

Lynn Francis was still doing huge, photorealistic canvases of branded stuffed animals. Star Klein put out a bucket of meat encased in Plexiglas. Borofsky was still counting from one to a billion in ball point pen. Elaine Slomoff knitted pullovers with the names of the war dead. Jessica Carnes exhibited three sculptures thirty feet high that could only be accommodated by removing pieces of the modular ceiling and making the sky visible above them. The bottoms were shaped like Popsicle sticks and the tops, which reached into the night sky, were living trees. She'd cut them to look like a bomb pop, a fudgesicle, and one of the double flavor jobbies that had two sticks you broke in half and shared with your sister if you had one.

"Any insight?" I asked Jonathan, standing next to him under the leafy fudgesicle.

"She glorifies nature against popular culture. It's what she does. She's cut the trunks, so these are designed to die, like everything."

I turned to face him, feeling ornery and out of my depth. "I think its bullshit on a stick."

"The ability to talk about modern art is the sign of an educated mind." His voice was smug, yet inviting. He wanted a comeback.

I faced him but stood to the side and laced my fingers in his, speaking quietly into his ear. "Jeff Koons's grandiosity, plus Damien Hirst's embellishment of the mundane, divided by Coosje van Bruggen's extremity of the unremarkable ... equals bullshit. The presence of the stick is unimpeachable."

We regarded each other for a second. "Suitably erudite," he said. "And you pronounced van Bruggen's name right. What other tricks do you have up your sleeve?" He stroked the inside of my forearm, leaving trails of tingling nerve endings in their wake. I wanted to kiss him, but I was a stranger there, and I had no idea who I'd upset.

"I can throw a guy out at second from home plate," I said. "Arm like a rifle, as long as the pitcher gets out of the way."

Our noses sat next to each other, and my lips felt the heat of his. I smelled his sagey cologne and fennel toothpaste.

"Monica?" I knew that voice. It had uttered my name in the dark of night, with moonlight coming through the window, and had screamed it in the bright light of day with heat coming off the asphalt. My name had been on those lips between laughs and tears and rage and humility.

I turned my face away from Jonathan's. "Kevin."

"I'm sorry, I, uh ... didn't mean to interrupt, but I didn't know if I'd catch you again tonight." He was in a brown suit for a black tie event, with a lavender tie and a blue striped shirt. It should have been a mess, but he looked gorgeous, like he was *in* the world of the reception but not *of* it. The scarf in his pocket was folded into a peeking triangle, and his pants fit him as though they'd been custom made. He'd apparently been shopping for the event as well, and unless he had a rich girlfriend, the business of being Kevin Wainwright had been brisk.

"Hi, Kevin. This is Jonathan."

Kevin held out his hand. "Drazen?"

"That's me."

Of course Kevin knew Jonathan, at least by name and face. He made it his business to know anyone who could afford original art.

Kevin turned back to me. "Did you see my piece yet?"

"No, where is it?" Of course he was worried about himself. Of course he thought nothing of interrupting an intimate moment to ask me if I'd seen *his* piece yet.

"No rush," he said. "It's around that corner. I just wanted to see you first. I want to say..." He glanced at Jonathan, then back at me. "I hope you like it. Excuse me." He fell back into the crowd.

"That was awkward," I said.

"Looks like we'd better go see if it's bullshit on a stick." Jonathan held his arm out, and we turned around the next corner.

"Kevin Wainwright puts his bullshit in a box."

Kevin was known for installations. Two dimensions could not contain him or his big stinking ideas. His first set up was in a ten by ten storefront he rented in the worst part of downtown. When his parents moved to a one-bedroom apartment in the center of Seattle, he got shipped a basement full of every toy, game, and fetish object from his childhood. But to him, it wasn't crap. To him, it was media. He spent a month in that storefront hanging, pinning, pasting, and strapping things to the walls; setting up tables for *mise-en-scenes* with army men and action figures; deconstructed board games and decks of cards, mixing up the pieces to make new things. I hadn't known him then. I shared his bed after he was already an agented comet streaking across the art-world's night sky. I had heard of his downtown storefront, which had been titled *Arcade Idaho* and had spawned a hundred imitators but not one other success story.

Kevin was a shrewd businessman as well. Installations left nothing for the artist to sell. His art wasn't a painting a rich person could put in their living room or a sculpture for their yard. He sold the preparatory sketches and worked closely with a little hipster bookbinding outfit on Santa Monica Boulevard to create limited edition booklets containing silver halide prints of the installation, along with his wordy, over-modified prose describing what it all meant.

I knew his exhibit would be crap. I knew it would be manufactured meaning, and exasperating, and it would remind me of all his drama. But when I turned the corner and saw the doorway to the installation, I got a little nervous. Metal signs hung outside. CAUTION. HARDHAT AREA. NO TRESPASSING. The signs were typical Kevin overstatement, but the sign at the top concerned me.

FAULKNER COAL MINE

"Isn't that your last name?" Jonathan asked.

"Yeah."

"You sure you want to go in?"

"No."

But I pressed forward anyway.

From just outside, I heard a canary singing, a lone bird at top volume. The doorway was little more than five feet high. I bent a little to get in, and Jonathan bent a lot.

The room was dark, with spotlights to point where he wanted you to look. At first, I hadn't adjusted to what I was seeing. He'd scribbled a lot of words, floor to ceiling, on two facing walls and the other two facing walls had eight and a half by eleven copy paper pinned to them. Piles of objects were on the floor with papers on music stands, which I couldn't read because people stood in front of them.

Then, like a gunshot, the canary turned into the honking of a disconnected number. Everyone flinched, and some people got angry at the intrusive noise. Except me. I knew what the noise was about. I knew what the canary was about, and I knew, for damn sure, what that installation was about.

The phone noise drove out the people standing in front of one pile of about nine small objects. A black chalk line had been drawn around them. A music stand stood in front. The stand had a piece of paper clipped to it, and engraved on the paper:

1 (ONE) 13.5 oz bottle Purell shampoo. 50% empty. Current value - $2.39

1 (one) 13.5 oz bottle Purell conditioner, dry hair formula. Unopened. Current value - $4.79

5 (five) Tampax brand tampons, regular. Current value - $1.34

1 (one) Recyclable toothbrush, soft bristles. Used. Current value - $0
1 (one) 16oz bottle Kiehl's Crème de Corps moisturizer. 75% empty. Current value -
$12.50

I remembered a conversation over that tube. He'd questioned me about that and everything else, because he assumed I was too incompetent to manage my skin.

"How much do you spend on this stuff?" Kevin had asked, putting a blob of Kiehl's into his palm.

"This bottle will last me a year if you don't take that much."

Then he'd rubbed it on my thighs, and we did it on the bathroom floor. The bottle was 75% empty because that wasn't the last time.

I felt Jonathan behind me. "What is it?" he asked, just as the canary came back on.

"This is the stuff I left at his place."

Someone moved to my right, and I saw a pile of clothes. The pockets of my jeans and the T-shirt I slept in were folded neatly under a pair of simple cotton underpants. I didn't read the little menu. I knew what those jeans were worth. Any normal person who wasn't terrified of getting sucked back into their ex-boyfriend's life would have gone back for them.

To my left, a pile of hair accessories: a brush and a scrunchy. And a disk of birth control pills. Open. Half-used.

"Are you sure you're taking these right?" he'd said one month when I was a day late.
"It's easy enough."
"Not if you're knocked up."

The lights changed and illuminated the walls, making the little piles of my things disappear in the darkness. The scribbles became legible, and more than my things on display, more than the exact value of what I'd left behind, those words, written as one long, run-on sentence, brought months of sidelined emotion to the back of my throat.

I didn't say she was more important why do you have to make everything about you she needs me she tried to kill herself, Kevin, what the fuck do you think is going on in your life that's more important right now how can you tell me I can't practice how can you try to silence me again I've put everything on hold for you I can't do this I can't take care of everyone I can't be there for everyone I need to go I need to go I need to go I need to go.

"Bullshit in a box?" Jonathan asked from a safe distance, as if he knew coming closer would be inappropriate.

"These are the last things I said to him."

I walked to the other side of the room. More scrawled words on the wall.

I'm not telling you not to work I'm telling you to stay with me when I'm with those guys they make me feel inadequate and stupid and you're the only one I trust you're the only one I know who doesn't make me feel small without you I'm not a man you don't understand I need you I need you I need you I need you I need you.

I walked out as fast as the low-hanging entrance would let me.

CHAPTER 35

Having been inside the relationship described in the Faulkner Coal Mine, I knew how brave Kevin was to create and display it. We had been impeccable together. We looked good. We never fought in public. No one heard a word from him or me that anything between us was less than perfect. He dragged his confidence around like a skin he seemed to own. That installation fearlessly let his friends and admirers know that not only was our relationship imperfect, but he himself lacked confidence and swagger.

But that was Kevin. Mister one hundred percent. When he'd loved me, it was with all of his heart and soul. I never worried about his commitment or his fidelity. I never found a leak in his passion. I was his everything, and as suffocating as that was, I never wondered where I stood. That in itself was liberating.

But now all our friends would know our last straw. Tuesdays had been his poker night. All the guys would sit in Jack's loft smoking cigars and talking about didactics in postmodernism, or definitions of folk art from the twentieth century's cultural diaspora. The girlfriends would sit in the kitchen talking about sex and drinking wine. It was like the fifties.

Gabby and I had finally put together a band because playing music made her feel better. That burned his ass. Because ever since Gabby had tried to kill herself, I got less available. Harry got us free studio time on Tuesday nights, for rehearsals. Perfect. He could go play poker so I could rehearse. But he threw a fit. He needed my support. He needed me *there*. Why was I abandoning him for Gabby? And you know what? I felt *bad*. My first reaction was that he was *right*. Because that was the whole relationship. His needs, and they were plenty.

In the sculpture garden, behind a little pagoda, was a spot the lights didn't reach. I knew about it because I'd given Kevin a blowjob back there the night he helped his mentor hang his retrospective.

I was headed there when Jonathan grabbed my arm on the patio. "Monica?"

I took his hand and pulled him along with me until I caught a glimpse of Jessica. She smiled at us. I was trying not to burst out crying, so I nodded and let Jonathan do all the smiling.

He let go of my hand.

I glanced back. He and Jessica were talking. He half-faced her, one foot still pointing in my direction, like he wasn't committed to either one of us. I had no time for that. I didn't need him anyway. I ran down the stairs.

I was halfway to the courtyard when I heard his shoes tapping behind me. "Monica, wait up."

I slowed, and he took my hand again without another word.

When we got to the ground floor, I turned into the sculpture garden. It was empty, mostly, so I slowed down. I wasn't breathing well. That was how I cried: breathing badly. Then fat tears would come. I was a ladylike bawler, more or less, which was why I let Jonathan put his arm around me and slow me down. If I was a messy blubberer, I would have run away and gotten the bus home. He sat me on a quiet bench, slowly, as if remembering the damage he'd done to me.

"Are you all right?" he asked.

I put my finger to his lips, then I put my arms around him and rested my head on his shoulder. "I'm so sorry about all this."

"It's okay."

"Tonight was supposed to be your drama."

"I prefer it to be yours, to be honest."

I picked my head up. "That was why he invited me so late. He wasn't sure if he wanted me to come. And that was why it was a single space on the list and not me plus one."

"But you tricked him." He took a hankie out of his pocket and handed it to me. It was thick, possibly silk, and monogrammed.

"God, I feel like such a bitch leaving the way I did. What kind of person just leaves all their stuff and—" I took a hard breath, and the fat tears came every time I blinked. I dabbed my eyes with the hankie.

"Someone who's scared," Jonathan said. "Come on, he made that thing from his perspective. You didn't expect it to be fair, did you?"

I shrugged and dabbed, trying to get control of myself and not lose too much makeup. I sniffed hard.

"I just walked out on him," I said. "I had no closure. I know the way I did it was the only way, because I could be strong once and leave, but he had a way of making me forgive him. We would have been the couple that was always half broken up, and I knew I couldn't be strong another hundred times."

I dabbed the insides of my eyes with the hankie, but I didn't want to get mascara on it, so the wet blobs stayed on the outside of my eyes. Jonathan stroked the back of my neck and waited patiently.

"I don't know what this will make you think of me," I said.

"That any man who's with you better pay attention, or they'll find you gone."

A short exhale of a laugh shot out of me. I shook my head. If I wanted more from Jonathan than a casual fuck, my chances of getting there had just shrunk to nil. Who would want to be with such a psychopath?

"See, I was keeping you on a need to know basis," I said. "And now you know too much about me. I'm going to have to kill you. Sorry."

I looked up from the hankie. He was gazing at my mouth as if it was the most interesting body part he'd ever seen. He touched my lower lip with his thumb and brought it down to my chin.

"I know you're trying to be guarded, but you're too real for that." He brushed my lips with his fingertips, and I kissed them. "I think that piece up there wasn't bullshit. I think it's the most unkind thing I've ever seen. And to sell off the pieces to a stranger is a dirty trick."

I looked back down at my lap, where my hands sat. My wrists were covered in bangly bracelets to hide the bruises. I felt beat up.

"Thanks for listening," I said. "This can't be attractive."

"If you have never seen beauty in a moment of suffering, you have never seen beauty at all."

"Who said that?"

"Some German poet. Now, blow your nose. The sniffling's making me crazy."

I held up the hankie. "I can't. It's too nice." I sniffed again.

"Are you serious?" He snapped the hankie from me and draped it over his palm. He put it over my nose. It had his dry, foggy smell. "Blow," he said.

I looked at him over the silk fabric, and he looked back at me, tilting his head as if waiting impatiently for me to blow my nose into his hankie-covered palm. The corners of his mouth curled ever so slightly. He was trying not to laugh.

"Come on now," he said, squeezing my nose.

I couldn't hold it in. I burst out laughing.

He laughed too, even as he said, "Blow already."

"I can't when I'm laughing."

"Stop laughing then." He was a poor salesman for not laughing, of course, as he was mid-crackup.

I took the hankie back and turned away from him. I blew my nose right into that really nice, embroidered accessory, folded it, and blew again before turning back to him. He leaned back on the bench, his arm around the top of it. Streetlamps reflected blue on his cheeks and the tips of his hair. His finger brushed my bare shoulder.

"Do you want this back?" I said, trying not to laugh all over again.

"Keep it."

I waited in the back seat as Jonathan spoke to Lil outside. I wanted to see him naked again. I wanted his cock and his lips. I wanted his hands on my hurting parts. But I couldn't stop thinking about Kevin. After I'd left him, I thought he'd forgotten about me. I sometimes thought he might have been hurt, but I took only gleeful satisfaction in that thought. He had always been the strong and confident one, and I was the doormat.

Jonathan slid in across from me, and Lil slammed the door after him.

"You going to tell me to spread my legs?" I asked.

"I'll get to it."

He didn't. He just looked at me. My knees were pressed together. My nipples were hardened from the fierce air conditioning, and my hands lay folded on my lap. Once he was done with my body, he looked at my face.

The car moved, and the view of the parking lot turned into L.A. at night.

"I want to do things to you," Jonathan said, "but you're not in any physical condition for that right now."

"I'm not made of sugar." I tried to keep the disappointment out of my voice and feared I'd failed.

"Indeed." He touched my collarbone and drew his finger down, under my dress, pulling it down below my breast. The knit of the straps strained and held as he extracted my nipple. "Shift forward again." I pushed my hips to the edge of the seat, flinching with pain. He pulled the other side of my dress down and, getting off his seat, kissed the nipple he took out. I groaned and held his head to me. He sucked it hard, then bit on it, and I gasped.

"I want to tie you to the bed in a hundred positions and fuck you everywhere, but I want those bruises to heal first. I want a clean ass to bruise again."

"I shouldn't ask this."

"Then don't." He brushed his finger against my nipple.

"I need to know if you're like this with everyone. All the women."

He looked in my eyes for a second, silent, then cast his gaze downward. I didn't know what I wanted him to say, but the curiosity burned me from the inside out.

His fingertips touched my lips, and I opened my mouth for him. "Make these wet," he said. "You're going to need it." He slid two fingers in.

I put my tongue against them, and I felt them rub my tongue and slide down my throat. He pulled them out, then shoved them in again. I sucked hard, trying to get my saliva going.

"Come on, Monica, you can do better." He slid his fingers in and out of my mouth, hovering just at my lips then pushing them back in. I was sore. Pounding with heat.

I wanted him, despite the pain, or because of it.

His fingers were in my mouth up to his hand. My lips curved around them, and I was sucking. He used his fingers to pull my head up until I faced the ceiling, and his fingers fucked my mouth from above.

"Pull your skirt up. Gently." I heard the smirk in his voice as he pulled his fingers out then back. I shifted my skirt around my waist.

"Ah, this is gorgeous." With his free hand, he stroked under the garter at the tops of my legs where the pain wasn't so bad. "Now spread these beautiful legs."

A war raged in my pussy between the pain of soreness and bruising, and the intense fire of need. When I opened my legs, I groaned into his fingers, because I got warmer when exposed to him.

"More, Monica. Don't be shy." I moved them out a little more, but my muscles burned. With his free hand, he yanked my legs apart. I gasped with pain and pleasure. He pulled his soaking fingers out of my mouth, and with his left thumb pressed under my chin, he kept me facing the ceiling.

"You don't want a relationship," he said. "But you keep asking about other women." He put his fingers under the crotch of my underwear and stroked my clit. "Why is that?"

"I can't say." I didn't know how I made words instead of just sounds. The pressure between my legs was so distracting.

"Yes, you do."

"Ah, that's so good, Jonathan."

He put his two fingers in my pussy. They burned all the way in, and I thrust my hips forward. His thumb rubbed my clit, and I went with his rhythm. His left thumb stayed under my chin almost painfully, keeping me from moving freely.

"Yesterday," he said, "you mentioned something about rumors, and you asked how many women I brought to the club, and now, another question. Do you want to fuck or not?"

God, had I been so childish? "I want to fuck."

"So what's your intention? Why do you keep asking?"

"Curiosity."

He took his fingers out and moved my panties back in place. I thought *ok, now he's going to tease me all night, and let's face it, I'm going to love it.* But he did something that surprised me. I couldn't see it because he held my chin up, but it felt as if he flicked my clit the way he might flick a crumb off the table, with his thumb and middle finger. His thumbnail hit my engorged clit like a pebble tossed on a water balloon. I felt it as exquisite pain followed by sharp pleasure. I made a vowel sound in my throat, still looking at the ceiling.

"Tell me, Monica. Why so interested?" He flicked me again.

"Oh, Jonathan...." I moaned. Flick. I started to squirm.

"Tell me what's on your mind."

It was gorgeous torture. I had no idea when the flicks were coming, and they were sharp, excruciating, and beautiful. I'd never, ever be able to come even if he did it twenty thousand times.

"If I tell you," I said, "you tell me everything."

He flicked me twice in quick succession. I cried out. "No deals," he said.

"Don't make me scream," I said. "Lil will hear."

"Then talk," he said, flicking me again.

"Fuck you."

"Talk, baby," he said softly, as if cajoling me.

I breathed heavily, feeling the light pressure of his hand on my throat. I could have stopped him. My wrists weren't bound. I could have pulled his arm away. Honestly, I wanted to tell him. "I want you."

"And?" He rubbed over the now wet fabric of my underwear. It soothed the heat but not the arousal.

"I want you all to myself. I want to know what they didn't do so I can do it. So I can keep you longer."

"Ah." He took his thumb away from under my chin. My legs were still spread, and his knees prevented me from closing them. I looked at him, feeling ashamed. I was sure he'd drop me like a foul ball, right there in the back of his Bentley in a designer dress and new garter. "Three times is my limit. We're one fuck to our expiration date," he said.

"I hope it's a monster because I'm going to miss it."

He smiled at me, then pushed himself back. He closed my legs, and I pulled my skirt down, smoothing it against my thighs, pensive.

"I'll tell you what," he said. "I can't promise you anything long-term. I can't get past my marriage. But I like you more than I care to, and I'm not interested in anyone else right now." He pressed my hands in his and looked at them, then back at me. "Let's do it. As long as you understand where I can't go. Jess talked me through a lot of shit. She rescued me in ways you can't even fathom."

Asking him to explain would have been aggressively intimate enough to break whatever we had. Whatever indefinable thing that was, short-term monogamous relationship, friendly fuckery, exclusive fling, it was not what he had had with Jessica. Our connection didn't have the bandwidth to sustain the pain buried far enough in our past to cause the grind of our present. His past belonged to her, even though she'd cut the line, taking it with her, tugging at him, leaving no one else for him to give it to.

"I get it," I said, "and I'm okay with that."

"Not for long. That's what I'm afraid of."

I stared at him for a second, then down at our hands. "I didn't get into this car wanting anything more from you."

"Yes, you did. You just don't tell yourself the truth all the time." He put a finger on my chin. "You're a goddess, Monica. Never be afraid to ask for what you want."

Our faces were a breath away. I kissed him gently, minutes passing while the city zipped by outside the windows. I heard my phone bloop, and I ignored it. His dinged, and he ignored it. Our devices were like a chorus of bells in the wrong church. I felt the car drop from the nose to the back, as if it were falling off a cliff.

I looked out the window as we stopped. "You drove me *home*?"

"You're black and blue in just about all the places I want to fuck, and if you come back with me, I'm fucking them."

"The things that come out of your mouth," I said.

"Do they please you?"

"No, actually."

"Come on, Monica. I'll be gone for a few days. When I get back, we can pick up where we left off."

"You're leaving me like this for *days*? I feel like I'm carrying a baseball between my legs."

"No touching either. That orgasm's mine, and I'm trusting you to hold it for me."

I put my face to his, kissing his cheek, his nose, his lips. "It weighs ten pounds. Just release me."

"I'm going to release you when I get back," he said into my ear. "Repeatedly." He reached back and knocked on the window between us and the driver.

"You have a serious cruelty streak."

He smiled at me as though he knew good goddamn well what his streak was made of. Lil opened the door, and we stepped out. He kissed me by my porch steps, and my phone blooped again. From my porch, I watched the Bentley dip down the hill as if it was a feather thrown from a tall building. Inside the house, I heard the piano getting the attention I wished I was getting.

CHAPTER 37

JONATHAN

I WATCHED Monica close the door behind her and felt the car dive off that cliff of a hill. Her house would be a deathtrap in an earthquake, and the hill was probably already falling into the backyard. I considered rectifying it. She was no good to me under forty tons of clay and detritus. She was only any good writhing under my hips like a pinned kitten. God, she was one big nerve ending, that girl, and those big brown eyes got just a little wider when she was close. And those bruises. And how she begged for them.

I knew she was special the night I met her, I just didn't know how special.

I'd gone up to K with Eddie and two other guys from Penn. I was meeting Wendy afterward in one of the hotel rooms. I had one foot in LA from a disaster of a trip to New York, and the other in Seoul for a trip that could not, under any circumstances be anything but a roaring success, or I was going to have to answer questions. I hated answering questions.

So I'd just done the easy thing and took them to K. There had been plenty of nonsense before the tall girl with big, black eyes and long brown hair twisted into braids brought our drinks. The guys were bullshitting about ball and women, when we all stopped to watch waitress come toward us. The night was over. I couldn't take my eyes off her. Everything was in the right place, naturally. My staff has to look as stunning as the guests. But this girl wasn't just beautiful, because they all are, she was something else entirely. I was trying to figure out what it was, and she just looked right back at me, as if daring me to make an even bigger ass of myself.

Then she spilled gin on me, and Freddie fired her. The guys tried to reason with

Freddie, but the waitress was gone and I had to let him do his job however he saw fit. I was an hour to Wendy with her legs up in the air and I suddenly found the idea depressing. She was gorgeous and shrill and shallow. She blew too much coke and giggled at all the wrong times. She exhausted me. The thought of another night in one of my hotel rooms drained the life out of my limbs.

Freddie told me the waitress's name, and that she was a sexual harassment case waiting to happen. But I couldn't let the ebony-eyed girl walk away. I had to look at her again. Five minutes. I'd give her a severance. Whatever.

I heard her outside my office and I seized up a little. I wanted to look at her, but had to be discreet. She slipped in, and I wanted to fuck her immediately. She was so long, so curved, so smooth. Her skirt cupped her ass, and her heels brought her to a couple of inches shorter than me. As my eyes dragged over her breasts, and over the length of her neck, I realized she'd seen me looking again. She put her hands on her hips. Definitely a harassment case waiting to happen, especially considering she was telling me about Freddie's fucking stupidity. I looked into her eyes. Fire, and pride. Not an ounce of fear. What was going on with that gaze was ten times more interesting than the curves of her body.

"I was going to offer you severance," I'd said.

"I don't want your money," she'd shot back.

"Let me finish."

She obeyed not just with her mouth, but her heart. Her face got red and she cast her eyes down. Her fingers twitched, but didn't move otherwise. Holy fuck. I almost lost my breath. This gorgeous, proud creature was submissive.

I couldn't let her walk into Los Angeles and disappear.

And it had only gotten worse since. Of course, I couldn't fall in love with her, even if I tried, but I could pass a lot of time with her. A lot.

I wanted to know every twitch, every growl, every moment of desperate need, and eat her alive. If she needed me to be exclusive, I could do it. I'd just put Sharon on ice and stop looking around. How long could Monica last? A month? Two? How long could she make me laugh before she started asking for more? How many things could leave her lips that would make me want to put my face on hers? She couldn't stay so attractive for long. She'd burn herself out soon enough, but for the time being, I could not have created a more flawless woman.

I felt bad about bruising her, but I hadn't done half the damage her ex-boyfriend's piece had done. What a dick. And as soon as I saw that guy, what he'd done, and the way he looked at her, I wanted her for myself. I knew she was going to ask for exclusivity, I could see it in her face, and once I saw that piece, I was ready to give it to her. The thought of her getting hurt bothered me. It wasn't her personally as much as it was wrong to make their private business so public. It wasn't that hearing her cry made my fist clench, or that I felt as though I saw some shameful part of her she'd wanted to keep hidden. It was an overall, amoral wrongness. Could have been anyone, and I would have been just as mad.

Well, maybe not as mad.

Damn. I should have taken her home. I had a weird compulsion to reach out to her.

> *—Thank you for tonight. I'll*
> *call you during the week to*
> *check on that baseball—*

—You're welcome—

A flat, emotionless response. Odd. I regretted letting her out of arm's reach.

> *—Speaking of...They're playing*
> *the Mets the day after I get back—*

—Ok good night—

I sat back. Not even a joke or wisecrack. I shouldn't have cared, but I did. My phone dinged again, but it wasn't Monica loosening up. It was Jess.

Interesting that Erik wasn't there. He usually followed her around like a little beta puppy. Exactly what she needed. Half a man. I took a calming breath and called her.

"Jess."

"Jon. Where are you?"

She didn't sound good, and if I judged the whooshing background right, she was already home.

"Coming up LFB." Our shortcut for Los Feliz Boulevard, from when I was whole and had someone to make up little acronyms with.

"Are you alone?"

"Lil is driving. What's wrong, baby?" I could have guessed it was Erik, but she'd never admit it.

"Can I see you?"

I looked at my watch. My plane was scheduled out of Santa Monica at six. I could make it if I left Venice by four. If history was any indication though, I'd be out of there in an hour. I wished I could tell her no, but we had too much history, too much intimacy to just turn my back. So I let Lil take me home, then I got into the Mercedes and went to Venice.

Again.

~

JESSICA LIVED ON THE BEACH, as her publicly sunny demeanor demanded. I parked and walked up the long stairway to the back, where the pool overlooked the ocean. The furniture was gone, as was the barbecue. She stood alone at the half empty bar with her glass of white wine, still wearing her flowing white dress. It outlined the shape of her body in the breeze, making me think immediately of pulling her legs open, but gently. That brought my hot little goddess back to mind, because with her, gentle was optional. I should have nailed her in the car, bruises or no. I wasn't any less aroused than her, and now I was in a dangerous position. I wanted to fuck. I had a weight at the base of my cock that needed to drop, somewhere, somehow.

"Jess," I said when I could see her puffy eyes. "Wasn't there a party or something? After the opening?"

"I couldn't take it any more. Smile, talk about popsicle sticks and culture's effects on childhood memories. Smile. Answer process questions about keeping dead trees alive. Smile again. How are you?"

I snapped a glass off the rack, and Jessica poured me some wine. "I'm fine, really. You called me over here to ask me how I am? It looks like I should be asking you the question."

She barely paused before getting to the point. "Erik."

"I thought you were engaged."

"So did I. Do you want to sit?" She indicated the indoor patio behind sliding glass doors.

The thought of going inside and lounging on a couch with her, which I'd done a hundred times, somehow seemed too risky, so I slid onto a barstool. "Where's everything? Those hideous fucking lamps are gone."

She took a deep breath and swished her wine around. "Three days ago, he took them. They were his."

"Figured." I didn't know what she wanted. Was I supposed to sympathize? She had dozens of girlfriends, each with two shoulders to cry on. What the hell was I doing there?

"He found out you were coming to the opening. And he just went off. 'Why's this guy still hanging around? Why can't you cut him loose?' Blah blah." She downed her wine. "He doesn't understand. Or didn't understand. As you can see, he decided to stop trying, which I guess is for the best."

"I'm sorry to hear it, but I'm not taking the blame for it."

"Jon. You don't have to get defensive."

"Jess. What do you want, if not to blame me?"

She was a bundle of nerves, which no other person would notice because she never wasted a movement. She didn't have a set of sweet little tics like Monica. Jessica was still water, her tension revealed in her gaze, which sat in the middle distance.

"I should be frank," she said.

"You be anyone you want."

"Not funny."

I waited until she was ready, because she'd get to it if I stopped cracking wise, and I had the feeling I would want to hear it.

She took a deep breath. "I think Erik had something. I think he was seeing something I was pretending wasn't there."

She was squirming. Oh, this was good. Delicious even. I didn't say a word. I didn't want to assume she was going where I thought she was because I didn't want the rug pulled from under me again. It wouldn't be the first time she'd implied she wanted me back and then turned the conversation back on itself.

"You've always been there for me." She looked up, right at me.

"We were married," I said. "I told you, I take that seriously."

She took half a step toward me. I'd been through that before with her, and I wouldn't lean into her half a centimeter I didn't have to. I hoped with the same fervor, but I was gun shy. Even when she put her fingers on top of my hand, which she hadn't done in a while, I was torn. After the divorce, she'd still touch me, but she'd back off like a hosed down cat as soon as I went for her. I was impatient with the games and horny as hell from being around Monica. I felt like a caged animal.

So when she touched my face, I froze, convinced I would spin her by the hair and bend her over. That wouldn't do at all. Not if I was going to have her again.

"You're being shy, Jon. That's not like you."

"You going to push me away?"

"No. Not this time."

Fine. I put my hands on the sides of her face so she couldn't turn and pushed her against the bar. I choked off her squeak with a kiss. She kissed me back. She really did.

My stomach tightened. To have my life back. To be back to normal again. With my wife at my side, a sealed unit, unbreakable. I touched my old self when I put my hand on her breast. The old me, at my fingertips.

I wanted light to see her, to believe it. Oh, anything could go wrong between us if I actually got my dick in her. I remembered my promise to Monica, but I could explain the next day. I'd be sorry to see that sweet thing go, but she shouldn't tolerate infidelity, and I cared too much about both of them to sneak around. Jessica had to be my choice. I'd taken a vow, begged for it to be honored, and waited so long that turning away the possibility of a reunion seemed ludicrous.

"Are you sure, Jess?" She'd better be sure.

"Yes, baby. Make love to me like you used to. In the beginning."

Yes, I wanted to. And I might have. If she hadn't asked for the old me back, I might have been as sweet and gentle as our first night. But in my ear, as if she sat right next to me, I heard Monica moan, "Hurt me, Jonathan. Tear me in two." I got even harder, if that was possible, and I was at the point where I could expect to walk out of there with a pair of ten pound weights between my legs. I was too old for that shit.

I faced Jessica. She was beautiful. Exactly the girl I remembered. Her lips were parted, her breathing shallow as she pushed her hips into me. So close. I was so close to having her again.

"I'm sorry, Jess."

"For what?"

"This." I pulled myself away from her.

"What? Why?"

I stroked looked in her face, half cast in the moonlight. "Because. It's been too much. I just... I can't."

She touched my face, and I saw her hurt. She had a deep fear of loneliness. Leaving her alone would undoubtedly be the hardest thing I ever did. "I don't understand," she said. "Is this spite? Or revenge?"

I owed her honesty, at least, after everything we'd been through, after all I'd promised her, after all the times we'd hurt each other. "It's too late. I'm sorry. I'm not the same man."

"Is it that girl?"

"Which girl?" I knew exactly who she meant. I was suddenly sorry I'd brought Monica to the show. Had I known Erik had walked out, I would have kept her home and writhed around with her all night, just to shield her from my ex-wife's eyes. The thought of that bruised ass, and her attitude about it, even the guilt I'd felt at giving it to her, made my dick twitch to the point of pain. "It's a dalliance, Jess. Don't try to read more into it."

Jessica didn't answer. She just stared at me as if she was reading a book. She must have seen right through me.

"Just go, then," she said quietly.

I wanted to say more, to apologize again or offer some comfort, but in a quarter of a second, I thought better of it. The door. I just had to make it to the door. I took long strides, looping my fingers in my keyring as I stepped into the night air. My Mercedes was five steps away. It had been her favorite. That's why I'd brought it. Maybe it was time to get rid of it.

"Jon," she called out. I took another step, getting my hand on the car, not looking back. I didn't want to change my mind. I didn't want another argument. I thought maybe I could get back to Echo Park in time to not make a rude ass of myself in front of Monica.

I couldn't pretend I hadn't heard Jessica. I looked back, just to say good-bye. I didn't see her immediately, but once my eyes scanned the flagstone walk, I saw her, balled up on the ground.

The visit was getting more dramatic than I'd anticipated. Did she feel this way when I'd gotten on my knees and begged her to stay? I'd been such a mess of tears I couldn't remember her expression. God, I'd never do that again.

She cradled her arm. I went to her, and from the way she looked at me, I knew I wasn't getting to my little goddess of Echo Park that night.

Dr. Fuhr was in Aruba, but a few phone calls and he'd managed to get us skipped ahead in the emergency room if we could get to Cedars in twenty minutes. It was late enough that the 10 was clear, and we zipped along with the top up, an ice pack on Jessica's arm and a sulk on her face.

"She's pretty," Jessica said.

"Who?" I asked as if I didn't know.

"The girl from tonight. Are they all that pretty?"

"Mostly," I lied.

She looked out the window. "Do they all let you fuck them the way you like it?"

The foul language brought my breath in. That wasn't her way of speaking, and her tone prodded. I took the bait because it was late, my balls ached, and Dr. Fuhr hadn't been available.

"How do I like it, Jess? Maybe you can just repeat back to me what you told all your friends?"

"I needed to tell someone!"

"Everyone. You told everyone that I wanted to beat you. Beat you?"

"You changed, Jon. I was scared."

We'd been through it so many times, the tracks of the argument were smooth and well worn, but that felt different. It felt like the last time.

"I changed because you changed me. And I'll always be grateful. You made me right with myself."

"And right with yourself means you want to tie women up and hurt them."

"I don't want to hurt anyone. You're so fucking vanilla, Jess. It's like a religion. You can't see outside it."

I turned into the ER at Cedars, not facing her until I parked. Tears dampened her face. I hadn't heard her crying in the white noise of the freeway.

I put my hand on hers, but she shook it off.

"I wish we could go back to the way we were," she said.

"I don't."

~

ERIK CAME AN HOUR LATER, as she was in the x-ray room. We shook hands like gentlemen.

"Nothing happened," I told him. "She's all yours."

The blonde lock drooping over his forehead swayed. He owned a surfboard company, but his face was permanently tanned from twenty years on the waves. "She never was."

"Well, honestly, this is the last time I'm coming running. I'm done. And I'm sorry I had my foot in your yard for so long."

We shook hands again, and I put my hand on his arm because I was really, terribly sorry I'd caused him grief over a woman who was completely wrong for me.

~

IT WASN'T until I got on the 10 that I started to feel as if a weight had been lifted from my shoulders. I pulled off on Mulholland to feel the Merc take the curves like a lumbering behemoth for the last time. I hated that goddamn car. I would get rid of it immediately. A smile spread across my face, and I laughed so hard I had to pull over. Laughter overtook me, turning to tears and back to a deep, silent laughter in my chest again. From relief. From a break in tension. From sheer joy. I was free. Fucking free.

The car was too small to contain me. I got out and sat on the railing, looking over the city, quiet, tearful bursts overtaking me. I looked at my phone, wanting to say something, connect with someone, but I couldn't conceive the words.

When I recognized where I was, I sobered up. I'd kissed Monica for the first time there. I felt a stabbing twinge in my twisted balls. Oh God, I could have her. I could own her. She could be mine, without hesitation or reservation. Mine. The relief turned into excitement.

I looked at the time. I'd have to wait.

Thinking of Monica, I got calm and focused on my phone.

To: Matt.reynolds@harrywinston.com
   CC: KristenK@drazeninc.com
   Fr: Jon@drazeninc.com

SUBJECT: open a new account

MATT –

LONG TIME.

I need a favor. I need a diamond navel bar. Not a ring. The other kind. Platinum with a 1.25 to 1.375 carat stone. As perfect as you have on hand. Can you deliver it to the east side before noon tomorrow?

Address to come. Let me know.

J DRAZEN.

To: KristenK@drazeninc.com
   Fr: Jon@drazeninc.com

SUBJECT: Kevin Wainwright/Faulkner Coal Mine

KK –

IVAN SINCHOT IS on the board at the L.A. Mod. I need him on the phone first thing. I want to buy Kevin Wainwright's piece from Eclipse. All documentation. All copyrights. All assets, period. Do it through the Ibiza trust, immediately. Drop everything.

-JD

MY FINGER HOVERED over Monica's number. I wanted to talk to her.

No. I didn't want to hear her talk. I wanted to hear her scream my name. Hours. I wanted her for hours, and time was one thing I didn't have. I had real business in San Francisco that couldn't wait, and I had to break it off with Sharon if I was going to be honest. I texted my pilot, Jacques, telling him I was on my way.

I looked out over the city, feeling as though I owned it.

Beautiful goddess, when I get back, you are mine.

CHAPTER 38

Gabby was up. No one else could play like that. She didn't stop when I came in, but she nodded to me.

"It's eleven at night," I shouted over the music.

"So?"

"Can you play something a little less bombastic so the neighbors don't call the cops again?"

She stopped playing entirely. "Why are you home? Did you guys have a fight or something?"

"No. Where's Darren?" I dropped my bag and kicked off my shoes, draping myself across the couch. Even lying still on the couch made me think about sex, adding to the throbbing between my legs. Damn Jonathan.

"Fucker's on another date." She tinkled a fun little tune on the keys. I'd never seen her like that before, with so few words and a tone of such pent up anger. I wished I could have my old high school friend back. She was fun. The person I'd spent the last two years watching had a new personality every few weeks.

"So? We set you free. You should be happy."

"I am. I'm meeting Theo for a midnight show at Sphere."

"Scottish Theo of the tattoos? He's all right." As excited and approving as I tried to sound about her new fling, she seemed disinclined to take the bait. She'd always been that way, which I'd liked about her, but over the past two years, the trait had become less charming and more alarming.

"So," she said, "Darren has a mystery lady. You have mister bazillionaire."

"I don't have anyone. It's completely casual."

She ignored me and my half truth. I was falling for Jonathan, and she knew it better than anyone. She turned to the piano again and played something sweet and sexual that made me want to run to the bathroom and finger myself to orgasm just so I could sleep.

My phone blooped, and I finally looked at it. The number wasn't in my contacts, but I recognized it anyway.

—*see me*—

Scrolling revealed five more of the same.

—*see me*—

—*see me*—

—*see me*—

—*see me*—

—*see me*—

"How did Kevin get my number?" I asked.

"Darren. I told him not to."

"God. Fuck him. Is that a man thing? We're all too butch to admit something would be a problem?"

I held the phone out for Gabby so she could see the six texts. "You should see him," she said. "He met us after our show. I think he's over you."

"And these texts prove it." I held up the phone for her to see, then I texted him back.

—leave me alone—

"I'm going to bed," I said. "Did you take your meds?"

"Yep."

I stood behind her for a second. I didn't believe her, and I didn't know if I should say something or not.

I trudged to the bathroom and took out her bottle of Marplan. She'd just gotten a refill that past Monday. There were a lot of pills, and a month ago, I would have counted them. I would have checked Darren's text with the last number he counted and counted the number of hours since to see if she'd taken two per day. Then I would have texted Darren the results, and all would be well with the world.

But I knew I wouldn't count all those pills. Darren hadn't texted me a pill count in a day and a half, and I was tired, and horny, and my phone blooped again.

I put the top on the bottle and put it away. I brushed my teeth and went to bed, taking my phone under the covers.

—let me explain, pls. I
needed to make that piece.
I'm not trying to get you
back I know you're happy
with someone else—

Happy. Sure. Kevin had only known the Monica who was never casual about sex. He'd only known the fully-committed me. I was suddenly miserable with

Jonathan. Two fucks and a few illicit fingerings, and what would it ever be? A few more fucks and some more denied orgasms. In the end, we'd move on. He didn't have space in his heart for me. He'd made that clear. I'd never felt so empty in my life.

—good night Kevin—

Another text came in.

—Thank you for tonight.
I'll call you during the week
to check on that baseball—

—You're welcome.—

—Speaking of...They're
playing the Mets the day
after I get back—

I had snappy comebacks ready, but they turned to ice. Every bit of attention he gave me made me sad because it was fleeting and meaningless. I didn't have the will or the energy to play his game.
—Ok good night—
Bloop.
—see me—
I shut the phone and closed my eyes. The baseball between my legs shrunk into an olive, and I fell asleep.

CHAPTER 39

Impossible as it seemed, I was more sore the next morning. Gabby was already up when I trudged into the kitchen. She stared into the corner with a mug of coffee in her hands. If someone had put a gun to my head and asked, I'd have said her coffee was cold.

"Gabby?"

"Should we practice a new set for our meeting?"

"At WDE? No. It's a meeting, not an audition. Are you feeling okay?"

"Yeah." She looked at me as if I'd woken her from a nap. "We have rehearsal in an hour. Let me shower first."

We'd moved the rehearsal venue from the studio, which cost money but was necessary with a band of four people, to the living room, which was free and was fine for two people. We were as diligent about our appointments as we would have been if we were meeting at a studio.

I boiled water for tea as I heard the shower go on. The slap of metal on metal from the gate outside was barely audible over the noise. It was way too early for the mail. I got to the front door just in time to see a green Jaguar going up the hill and a bulky figure in the front. Lil, for sure. I got out onto the porch quickly enough to see the backseat was empty. When I turned to go back inside, I saw a little navy box with a silver ribbon. I scooped it up and ran into my room, clicking the door shut behind me.

I sat on my bed and undid the ribbon, revealing the silver HW on the top of the box. A little envelope had been attached to the bottom, and when the ribbon slipped away, the envelope dropped into my lap. I opened it.

Dear Monica—

Please take this as a token of my appreciation.
—Jonathan

I SLID THE BOX OPEN, then the box inside that. It held a three quarter inch long bar, silver or platinum, with a circular diamond set in the bottom.

A navel ring. A real one to replace the fake ring I'd gotten from the piercing place on Melrose. I held it up to the morning light, and I was again distracted by how shabby and cheap everything in my room looked, the mess of laundry in the corner, the old frames on my pictures, the smudges on my mirror.

I peeled my shirt off and replaced my crappy navel ring with that gorgeous thing. As I looked at myself in the mirror, loving it, I wondered what it was for. I read the note again. Appreciation for what? Me, generally? Or something else? The card was too small to write more, but I wasn't sure what to make of those nine words.

The shower went off. I held my concerns. I had to shower, dress, drink my tea, and show up in the living room ready to go. I couldn't be burdened by my worries about what Jonathan meant to me and what I did—or didn't—mean to him.

CHAPTER 40

JONATHAN

HAVING lots of money beat the alternatives, for sure. But having a plane didn't mean more privacy. It meant less, because everyone on board was there to serve me. I ended up in the bathroom taking care of the dead weight at the bottom of my balls, as if I'd taken a 727 like everyone else. On my mind was Monica, our first night, when we were so sore and tired I didn't think we'd have another go. She came out of the bathroom, naked, her dark hair a mess, mascara and lipstick worn to nothing. I sat on the edge of the bed waiting for her. She kneeled in front of me, looking up with those big, black eyes. Without a word, she kissed my dick, licking up the shaft, bringing the blood with her until it got hard again.

"Jesus, really?" I'd said.

"It's been eighteen months since I had sex. It might be another eighteen months before I do it again. I'm stocking up."

I'd laughed. I did that a lot with her. I pulled her up, sitting her on my lap, her back to me and my fingers between her legs and on her breast. Since she was stocking up and I thought I'd never see her again, I fucked her hard, bouncing her on top of me while our hands met between our legs. We connected, feeling each other sliding together. When her back arched, she lost her balance, and we wound up on the floor, laughing, her on her stomach and me coming at her from behind. She turned her head, and I saw the pleasure in her face, her eyes rolling up. She was a gasping, moaning mess, crying and begging for release without being asked.

In the tiny closet of a bathroom on my six-seater plane, my imagination replayed her brown eyes looking up at me while she took my cock in her mouth, then her lips saying *please please, don't stop* from underneath me... My use for the bathroom concluded soon after.

I texted Monica a few times, just a couple of pokes to let her know I wasn't running off and to let myself know I was really doing it.

～

SHARON HAD BEEN EXQUISITE. Attractive, willing, discreet and far away, she'd do what I told her without question, talk to me about anything, and never open her mouth about who she screwed four or five days a month. Exactly what I needed, when I needed it, and I had been the same for her, but in the end, she needed to make a lifestyle out of her sexuality, and I was just a tourist.

I'd texted her when I landed, but I was two hours early thanks to Jacques answering calls during his morning jog and my desire to clean up business before returning to Los Angeles. She didn't expect me until after my meeting, so I figured she wouldn't be in ready position, and we could talk.

She lived on a high floor of one of my buildings by the Embarcadero. When we'd started screwing, she was a wreck from a string of abusive, boundary-free masters who beat or fucked her confidence away, and I was broken from Jessica's complete rejection of my needs. We were two complete disasters trying to teach each other the meaning of safe, sane, consensual kink. Putting her in one of my apartments seemed like the kindest thing to do, considering she was teaching me as much as I was disciplining her.

The lobby was spare, in dark woods and chrome, with an Italian stone tile floor. I nodded to the doorman and went upstairs.

My phone dinged. It was Sharon.

—*I'm ready for you, Sir.*—

Shit.

Sharon had three ready positions. That confused her initially. I liked a little surprise. I wanted her to choose, and she was used to being told what to do from how she brushed her teeth, to what she wore, to which route she took to the grocery store. Having a choice of ready position was unheard of in her sexual life, which was why Debbie had set us up in the first place.

But I didn't want her in a ready position. I wanted her clothed and ready to talk.

I opened the door. The place was impeccably clean, every inch made of glass and steel. I could never live in such a space. The apartment was too cold and impersonal, but it was easy to rent or sell, and it was just fine for fucking.

The living room was a big open area with a leather sectional and a shag rectangle under a teak coffee table. Sharon had both hands on the low table, palms spread, arms straight. Her ass was in the air, perched on top of a pair of beautiful legs planted in heels high enough to make a lesser woman fall over. Her blond hair hung over her face, and I knew she was watching me in the mirrors and chrome all over the apartment. Besides the stilettos, she was naked. Naked or underwear was her call, unless I stated otherwise. She was a lovely creature, with curves in the right places and smooth skin she carefully maintained.

Normally, depending on my mood and demeanor after travelling, I'd taunt and touch her until she begged, or I'd slap her ass and fuck her without a word.

I held my hand over her ass, because touching it was the first thing I'd usually do, then I stopped myself. I couldn't tease her because I wouldn't finish what that touch would start. Or worse, I would finish it and make the whole thing a hell of a lot worse.

"You can get up, Sharon."

"I'm sorry, Sir?"

"Get dressed."

"Have I displeased you?"

Fuck. Her voice squeaked with nerves. Bad start. I should have told her to be dressed when I texted her. Total miss on my part.

"No, baby. You're fine. We have to talk, and it's hard to do that with your beautiful ass in my face."

I held out my hand and helped her up. Her face was a blank slate of fear. She had no reason to look scared with me. When we met, any implication of my displeasure was greeted by her acceptance of punishment I had no intention of meting out. It wasn't my thing, but history was hard to shake. She held onto my hand, then pulled it toward her mouth. I twisted away and cupped her cheek. Her grey-blue eyes were full of questions, and her lips were pressed tight, not a position I was used to seeing them in.

"Where do you want to go for breakfast?"

"Wherever you like, Sir."

"Can we not play right now?"

Her posture changed from erect to relaxed. "So," she said, "who is she? Or did the wife come to her senses?"

I smiled. She couldn't have dropped character like that two years ago. "Are you going to get dressed or is the whole town getting a look at you?"

Jessica hadn't up and left a perfectly happy marriage. This took a year or more for me to sort out. As I'd become more comfortable with my past, and the man I was, I changed. I became sexually dominant and emotionally controlling. I wanted her to submit to me in bed, which she wouldn't have any of. I wanted her body to be available to me more often, which annoyed her. I wanted her to dress for me, even if I wasn't there. I wanted her to do things during the day, when we were apart. Simple things. Touch herself. Roll her sleeves up. Open her legs. Say my name. It made me feel as though we were connected, but she didn't want to play the game, at all. I became frustrated and unsatisfied. We both dug in, and by the time I was willing to cave on both points to keep her, it was too late.

It had been my fault. I had no idea what I was doing. I didn't know what to ask or what I wanted, I only knew I had new ideas, new excitement, new desires. My requests sounded like demands, when they should have been demands that sounded like requests. I became, in two words, a controlling asshole.

To Sharon, however, I was a sweetheart, and through her and Debbie's stories, I learned just how kinky the kinky world was. I learned how her past men had done things and adjusted what I did to suit me and show her a life that wasn't based on fear, where her needs weren't just important but pleasurable for both of us. It was a shame I couldn't work up an emotion outside general tenderness in the two and some years I'd known her.

Sharon chose a place we'd gone to a hundred times before, with coffee handpicked by college graduates, roasted in the sun only during working hours, trucked in on fuel-efficient vehicles, and made onsite with organic water.

She had her hair tied back with a black velvet twist I'd used to bind her any number of times. No doubt she wore it on purpose. She was used to getting by on her looks and had little to recommend her in the way of conversational skills, but she wasn't stupid. She leaned on her elbows over her skinny latte.

"So?"

"So." I sipped my black coffee. "I wanted to tell you what you've meant to me. You helped me define things I thought had no definition. You've had a big part in making me whole again. I want to thank you for that."

"You never answered my question. The wife or someone else?"

Our relationship was built on honesty and trust but not on fidelity. She'd been on the lookout for a more permanent, full-time Dom, and I'd been searching for what I wanted out of a woman at all. "Both," I said.

"The wife's going to share? I thought she was vanilla?"

"No. Jessica's not going to share, but she did almost get me in the sack. I resisted."

"No *way*! And you turned her down? Why?"

Sharon was rapt. My life's dramas always interested her, yet she'd never betrayed a confidence. "Because I just didn't want her. Honestly. Just didn't. And also, there's someone I promised myself to, at least for the time being."

"Tell me."

"I probably shouldn't."

"What does she look like?"

I shrugged. "Nothing special."

"Oh, please."

I slipped my hand into hers and squeezed it. "You going to be okay without me?"

"You only show up once a month, and you're too gentle anyway."

"Without the tasks and the discipline and knowing I'm there. Are you going to be okay?"

"I think so."

"No assholes."

She took my hand in both of hers and looked me in the eye. "No assholes."

"The apartment. Do you want it?"

"I have some modeling things coming up. I'll pay you for it." I cocked my head at her. She knew what that place cost. "Installment plan."

"Fine."

"Is she short? Tall? How old?"

There is nothing like a woman's curiosity about other women. She'd never imply or even admit to herself she felt an ounce of competition between herself and Monica, yet she had to know so she could compare herself and decide if she was okay with it.

"I meet a lot of beautiful girls," I said. "She's... I don't know. The first time I talked to her, in my office, she was a waitress at my hotel. I looked at her, trying to figure out why she looked so tangible, so *present*. Every curve looked exactly right. Even her skin is this perfect color... Not even color. The texture of it. I wanted to touch it like I'd never wanted to touch anything before. She saw me looking, and she stood with her hands on her hips, daring me to get an eyeful. No fear. She filled that fucking room." I sipped my coffee. "She took my breath away. I was too stunned to even ask her out."

"So?" Sharon might have been watching the last fifteen minutes of a Lifetime movie, her attention was so focused.

"So I got her a job at the Stock, where Debbie works. I figured she could check her out, tell me if I was crazy."

"So smart, you. What did she say?"

"You know Debbie. She won't rest until everyone's happily coupled off but her."

I sensed rue in Sharon's smile. I rested my hand on her forearm. "You'll find someone, baby."

She shrugged. "Maybe. I don't think it matters. Can you stay for one last fuck?"

I checked my watch as if it was a possibility. "Got a meeting with Tim LaShaun from District 34. Then a tenant's advocacy group that wants my head on a stick. More bullshit tomorrow and the next."

She nodded. I always had at least that much bullshit when I came to San Francisco, but things was different, and she knew it. There wouldn't be one last fuck. I'd done it. I'd come out unscathed and true to my word. I was less confident about Sharon. She had a way of putting a nice face on everything until she decided the pain was too much to bear.

We parted outside. I gave her a hug and a kiss on the cheek. I felt that relief again, but unlike the previous night, when I'd walked out on Jessica, it felt less like getting hit in the head by a two-by-four.

My phone rang as I put Sharon in a cab.

"Hi, Debbie," I answered as I handed the valet my ticket. "Speak of the devil. I was just with Sharon."

As usual, she wasted no time getting to the point. "Jessica met Monica last night?"

"Correct."

"She came here and insisted on sitting at her station."

Ugly. It was just like Jessica to highlight any class difference she could tease out. Having Monica serve her would be a way to humiliate her with a smile.

Debbie continued, "I don't expect you to do anything about it. Except your wife—"

"Ex-wife."

"She said something to Monica. I don't know what, but now the girl looks like she's been slapped."

My fingers got ice cold. Jessica could have said a hundred things, secrets she could have revealed or implied. A million half-truths. Without a man to lean on, she was a cornered animal. I'd forgotten how dangerous she was when I was busy choosing another woman over her.

"Did you ask Monica?" I asked.

"She won't repeat it."

Apparently, my beautiful goddess was also a woman of honor. "I'll call her."

"She's working the floor, so her phone is off. Fix it, please. I don't like it. The power trip. It's sneaky."

"I will, Debbie. I will."

I hung up. My car came, and I parked it around the corner to give myself a minute to think. What did Jessica know? Everything. What was she willing to share? Or imply? Or use? I had no idea. I knew for sure I wasn't ready to share everything about my past with Monica, not a word or deed I didn't have to, because I'd lose her. Any woman would run for the hills.

I texted Monica before I drove away.

—*Can you call me?*—

WHEN I GOT out of my first meeting, she still hadn't called. She'd gotten the text, so her silence was intentional.

If I were her, what would I do?

Whatever Jessica had said, I'd be finding out if it was true. So I had to make the investigation impossible to complete. That meant moving Rachel, touching base with each sister, Deirdre especially, and stressing their silence. And Thomas. And the hospital. And dad, who would laugh in my face. And... Fuck. There were too many fires to put out. Too many pieces to move across the chessboard.

I put my phone in my pocket.

It occurred to me that I'd longed for Jessica because she knew all the ugliness of my past. I didn't have to reveal a thing to her. I didn't have to bear the uncertainty and loneliness of wondering what someone thought of me. But if she loved me through it, couldn't someone else? Couldn't someone else keep a secret or ten? Maybe, but I was getting ahead of myself. I was letting my excitement get ahead of my sense. I had to finish up here and get back to LA without panicking.

I made my way to my meeting with the tenant's rights group. That bunch would use that information to take me down, even if I gave them what they wanted. I had to deal with Jessica at some point, no matter what, unless I was willing to live without intimacy the way I wanted it. Or I would risk losing Monica before we even started.

If my unease came through during rehearsal, Gabby didn't say anything, but I could tell it was an off day. I'd texted Jonathan a thank you for the gift, hoping my uneasiness didn't come through. He didn't respond, and I was sure he was on a plane. I didn't want to hear from him right away anyway. I was too busy worrying. Nothing had changed. He'd given me everything I'd asked of him and more.

—Thank you for the gift. It's
really too much—

Especially for a meaningless fling. Way too much.

"How was your night last night?" asked Debbie. "I heard you went to L.A. Mod?"

Debbie, Robert, and I stood at the service bar. It was the slowest part of my shift, toward the end. All of my candles had been lit for the next shift. All of my chairs had been put into place, paper napkins twisted, and trays wiped. The sun got about its business of setting orange over the Los Angeles skyline, a sight I took for granted during the early shift.

"It was good. My ex-boyfriend did a whole piece on me, basically eviscerating me as a heartless bitch in front of everyone. Not sure what I'm going to do about that."

"Is that legal?" Robert asked.

"Only if I'm a heartless bitch. But I figure if it's not bad for my career, I should just close my eyes and pretend it didn't happen." Robert drifted off to make drinks.

"And how was the company?" Debbie smirked, a little wink flicking the bottom of her low-hanging bangs.

"Fine."

"He took you out in public. That's good. For both of you."

I shook my head and rearranged the lemon and lime trays. "I don't know."

Debbie didn't even hear the last word I said. She was up like a shot and already approaching a woman who'd just walked in by herself. She was tallish and blonde, and her skin glowed with health.

It was Jessica Carnes.

Debbie did her thing, smiling and double kissing, spinning conversation out of nothing. I was frozen in place. I didn't want to serve her drinks. Nothing in the world could make me serve that woman drinks for tips. Nothing except needing my job.

Debbie indicated the bar to her. I loved Debbie with a bursting heart right then, because Robert served the bar. I was the only waitress for the next twenty minutes. If Jessica sat at a table, I'd have to serve her.

Another woman came in behind Jessica, and more kisses were doled out. She had wavy brown hair and a face shiny with plastic surgery. A buffer? Or a team?

"I'm going to be sick," I said to Robert.

"Bathroom's that way."

Debbie led them to a table and handed them the drink menus. When she walked back toward the service bar, her face betrayed nothing.

"I tried," she said when she was in earshot. "You'll have to do it."

"I can't. I met her last night."

"That's probably why she's here." Debbie took my hand and squeezed it, her grip cool and firm. She looked me in the eye, unflinching. "Be a woman of grace."

I swallowed hard, glancing at Jessica. She and her plastic surgery buddy spoke closely. The couch they sat on left their arms exposed, and I saw Jessica had a slim nylon cast on her right wrist.

"Fine." I put my notepad in my pocket and strode over there as if I owned the place.

Jessica and Plastic watched me approach, two beige ovals with eyes seemingly in sync as they looked me up and down, much like Jonathan had when he first met me. I put a little lift in my step and smiled with closed lips.

"Hi," I said, "I'm Monica. Can I get you anything?"

They just stared until Plastic broke the silence. "You are just as cute as a button, aren't you?"

I smiled, showing my teeth, wishing for the pressure of Debbie's hand on mine. "Thank you."

"We met," Jessica said, "last night."

"Yes," I said, "that's right. I wasn't a hundred percent sure, so I didn't want to say anything. It's nice to see you again."

"Of course. Same here."

The awkward moment was broken by a phone ringing. Plastic reached for hers. "I have to take this." She smiled to me. "Grab me a mojito, would you, dear? Easy on the sugar." She pressed the phone to her ear and headed to the hallway.

"Can I get you something?" I asked Jessica.

"Yes, I'll have the same." She shifted in her seat. I was about to escape when she said, "You really had me scared last night."

"Why is that?"

"I thought you were an eighth sister."

Her gaze held me, and I felt just walking away would be rude. Debbie had told me to be a woman of grace, and I didn't know a better way to do that than to show I was interested in her. "What happened to your arm? You didn't have that last night."

"Hairline fracture. I spent half the night in the ER. I'm actually wiped out."

"Oh, wow. How did that happen?"

Jessica pursed her lips and looked away, then back to me. The movement was so smooth and quick, I almost missed it. "You know how it is," she said. "Jonathan can be a little rough."

My mouth went dry. I couldn't even swallow. I think I shook a little because I felt my knees knock once. I had to get away. I had to be somewhere else.

"Sure," I choked out. "Of course. I'll get those drinks."

I made it to the service bar. Debbie's eyes widened. "What happened? You're white as a sheet."

"I have fifteen minutes left in my shift."

"What did she say?"

"I'm not repeating it. I have to go home."

Debbie took both my shaking hands in hers, slipping the notepad away. "You finish your shift. And you smile. Another table just came in. Take care of them, but do not linger. Do you understand?"

Her face broached no arguments. My nod was so slight and forced, I was surprised she even saw it.

"Robert," she barked, "make two mojitos, *no* sugar." She looked back at me. "Let them ask for the sugar. Make them wait. Take care of your other tables. Smile. Maddy's here to relieve you, but you have to finish your shift. Grace, Monica."

Robert put two drinks on my tray.

"Yes," I whispered.

"Go."

When I went to their table to drop the drinks, Jessica and Plastic were deep in conversation. I made a nice face for them, and though Plastic opened her mouth to say something to me, I turned away before she'd engaged her vocal cords, giving me the opportunity to service my other table.

Twelve and a half minutes later, I came back to the service bar with a drink order and handed it to Robert. Maddy was made up, bright-eyed, and ready to go. I briefed her on the tables.

"Are you okay?" she asked.

"Fantastic. Where's Debbie?"

She shrugged. I didn't care. I went into the back without looking behind me to see if Jessica saw me leave.

I got to the break room and turned my phone on. I had to turn it off when I was on the floor, but now I would give that motherfucker a piece of my mind. He couldn't even keep it in his pants for me for how long? How many *hours*? They must have arranged to meet while I was busy running down the stairs. He'd promised fidelity and dumped me home with a lame excuse about not wanting to hurt me. What a joke. He went and got himself laid.

By his ex-wife.

Who he loved and would always love.

Because she talked him through a tough time.

'Til death do us part.

I had no idea what I would say to Jonathan, but something had to be said. If he wanted her, then fine, but why play with my clit while demanding I ask him for whatever I wanted? Why push me to tell him I wanted to be his only one, for however long, if he would turn the car around and fuck his ex-wife so hard he fractured her wrist?

I stared at my screen. He'd sent me two messages a few hours before.

—I'm glad you like it—

—I still owe you a spanking from Barney's—

And another one just three minutes previous.

—Can you call me?—

Darren:

—Have you seen Gabs?—

I replied:

—Try Theo—

There were another two messages, sent rapid fire an hour before. They were from an emotional fuckup, but one who had been open, sincere, and vulnerable with me. Someone who never, in the two years he had me, ever cheated on me. He'd never even looked at another woman. Never gave me a reason to doubt his devotion.

—last time I'm asking—

I'd forgotten what a persistent pain in the ass Kevin was. I replied because it wouldn't be his last text, no matter what he said. I'd opened the door a crack, and he was intent on barging in.

—*What*—

I waited for his answer. I didn't feel a hum between my legs at the thought of him, nor did he make me grin with anticipation. I didn't want him as a boyfriend, lover, or fuck—not that he would find the latter two acceptable. I wanted to just talk to him, to see the devotion and fidelity I'd slaughtered so heartlessly. I didn't want him back. I wanted to surgically remove the viable parts, label them, and put them in a case so I would recognize them if I saw them again.

—*see me*—

I answered it.

—*Where?*—

PART III
SUBMIT

CHAPTER 42

I was on my hands and knees at Jonathan's front door, my palms inside the house, my knees still on the porch. The smell of sage and dry morning fog surrounded me. The air was cold enough to harden my nipples even though the sun baked my bare back. I wanted to touch my breasts, but I wouldn't because I'd been told not to move my hands from the floor. I obeyed, though I didn't know why. My pussy was wet. I felt the weight of my arousal hanging between my legs like the clapper on a bell, heavy and swinging.

I wanted Jonathan, but he'd gone somewhere, leaving me here like *this*. I wanted to press my legs together to squeeze my aching clit, but I'd been told to keep my knees spread.

A voice called my name. Darren. Then Gabby. God, no. They couldn't be here until Jonathan finished.

Then, I felt his dick pressed up against me and hands on my hips. I didn't have a second to gasp before he was inside me, pounding mercilessly. Hands gripped my ass, pressing hard enough to bruise, and the pain was a counterpoint to the pleasure, making it sweeter, wetter, hotter. I moved with him, slamming onto his cock. He pulled my hips up and pressed down the arch of my back, stroking my clit with his shaft. I was this close to exploding in a burst of moans and cries when I saw a mirror in the house that hadn't been there before, and Jonathan wasn't fucking me, but Gabby. She was moaning, and the bedsprings were squeaking.

I woke up, sweating. In the room next to mine, the bedsprings squeaked, and Gabby let the neighborhood know Theo was fucking the life out of her. God bless them.

I was not in a clear emotional state. Two days before, Jonathan had left me with a promise of fidelity and a swollen nodule between my legs that I pledged not to touch. A day later, his ex-wife had shown up at my job, apparently to tell me he fucked her so hard the night before that he fractured a bone.

Yet, despite the fact that he may well have been a stinking liar, I kept my promise to save my orgasm for him. And I would, until I dumped him, at which time I was going to run into the nearest bathroom and relieve myself.

Theo finished with a Scottish-accented grunt. Thank God. I wasn't sure if they were making me uncomfortable or horny. Seeing them in the kitchen for morning tea was going to be awkward.

I went into my bathroom to shower and dress. Afterward, I walked out the back door so I wouldn't have to say good morning to anyone.

I felt constantly on the verge of an assault on something or someone. I got angry at the chair leg I stubbed my toe against. Traffic went from the cost of living in Los Angeles to a singular attack by a spiteful God. Mostly, I was angry at myself. I knew I wasn't capable of having a serious relationship because I got too involved and lost myself in the other person's needs. Nor was I capable of a casual encounter because I couldn't bear the thought of anyone I was screwing being with another woman in the same space of time. My only alternative was celibacy, a fine and viable option, but I'd broken a perfectly good sexless streak to be with Jonathan. So I was stuck. Our relationship was too serious to forget and move on and too casual to get upset over him fucking his ex-wife. I was a fool. A damned fool.

I got in the car and realized I hadn't put on any makeup. I looked in the rearview. Did I need any? I was only going to see my ex, Kevin. If I went in without makeup, it would be a sign that I wasn't trying to impress him, that I didn't want him back. I just wanted to talk, and I didn't need lipstick for my mouth and ears to operate. I didn't need mascara to see if I'd been crazy to leave him.

Kevin used to have a place Downtown, but when the market for crap industrial spaces exploded, his rent tripled, so he'd split for the strip of land between Dodger Stadium and the L.A. River called Frogtown. I'd helped him move there four months before I left. The building had changed drastically in the interim. The broken brick façade had gone from a soot-encrusted dark red to a multicolored mural, corner to corner, of a huge young girl peeking into the front door as if it were the entrance to her doll house. The side of the building had been painted to look like the wall was see-through, with depicted trees and buildings that matched the real landscape of the L.A. River, like a Road Runner cartoon where the bird painted a single-point perspective road on a brick wall.

Those were not Kevin's work. The girl looking at the door was definitely Jack's style. The *trompe l'oeil* thing on the side looked like Geraldine Stark, one of his contemporaries. She was a quite prolific whore in the art scene, and I found myself wondering if Kevin had fucked her at some point.

I rang the bell. I waited. I rang again. Waited. Just like him to beg to see me then get so involved in something else he couldn't answer the door. God, men were such fuckups. Every damn one of them.

The door finally opened, and I stood straighter so he wouldn't see me arched with annoyance.

"Monica," he said. "You came."

"I said I would."

He grinned his most gorgeous grin, straight-ish teeth a crescent of white in the pink dust of a set of lips that God himself must have used as a template for the perfections of the human face. I remembered kissing them. I remembered them running over the insides of my thigh, brushing against my pussy, bookends for his flicking tongue.

"Come in," he said, stepping to the side.

"Thank you." I grasped the strap on my shoulder bag for something to hang on to as I caught his scent of malt and chocolate. Jonathan left me with a throbbing ache of desire unquenched because he thought it made me think of him, but he couldn't have had any idea how dangerous that was. A different person would have been fucking anything that moved.

The hall was narrow, and I had to brush by him to enter. He closed the door behind me with a metallic *thunk*. I passed doorways on either side of the hall. At the end, the hall opened into a warehouse space with a forty-foot ceiling and a cement floor he'd had poured himself. Waist-high tables stood all over the room in what looked like a random pattern but wasn't. They were set up in an emulation of Kevin's process. Each table was inaccessible without passing a necessary step before it, so the visual story of whatever he was working on could be told from the start every time. The pattern would never make sense to an outsider, but in his mind, it brought his installations together.

"Can I get you something? Tea?" He seemed tiny in the huge space. His white T-shirt looked insignificant and plain. "I put in a kitchen."

"Wow," I said. "Can I see?"

He led me to the far end of the huge space, weaving past the tables down a path he'd left for that purpose. The kitchen had glass block windows to the outside and a wall covered in magazine pictures of food stuck on with silk straight pins. The cabinetry was white, the surfaces embellished here and there with perfectly placed stickers or an odd tile in an incongruous color that a person with anything less than exquisite taste would have screwed up.

"Green okay?" he asked, reaching for a box of tea on a high shelf. His T-shirt rode up, exposing the path of dark hair on his belly, and I shuddered with the memory of touching it.

"That's fine."

He nudged the box, and it fell, bouncing off his fingertips. He caught it and smiled like a shortstop fielding a chopper to left. He put a two-pint saucepot under the faucet, and by the time he got it on the stove, I noticed his eyes hadn't met mine since we'd walked into the kitchen.

"So," I said, pulling up a fifties-style chrome and pleather chair, "what the hell did you think you were doing with that coalmine bullshit?"

His back was to me, and I could clearly see the muscles there tense. His shoulder blades drew close, and he looked toward the ceiling as if pulling strength from the heavens.

He turned his head only slightly to answer. "I entertained every idea of what you'd think for the year I worked on that fucking thing."

"Did you ever consider sending me a letter and asking me what I thought?"

He turned and crossed his arms. His biceps were hard and lean from building, hammering, and climbing. Kevin's work was motionless in the gallery but very physical in its creation. "Yes, but honestly, Monica, once I decided to make the piece, what you thought was irrelevant. It wasn't about you."

Of course it wasn't. My stuff, my words, and our intimacy were his to use as he pleased. It was as if I'd never left. I didn't know what I thought I'd see by going to him, but he was the same old Kevin.

As if he could read my mind, his shoulders slackened and his hands dropped to his sides. "That's not what I meant," he said.

"Yeah."

"What *do* you think?"

"I'm really pissed I left those jeans behind."

He smiled again, a barely audible chuckle issuing from his perfect mouth. He dropped his eyes to the floor, black lashes shining blue in the fluorescent light. I wished I didn't have to look at him. He was screwing with my head.

"There were other things," he said. "I really struggled with what to put in."

"Did you miss a maxi pad?"

"Oh, Monica. Always ready with a joke when you feel uncomfortable."

"At least I don't flirt."

He looked me in the eye for the first time, and the gaze lasted long enough to make me shift in my seat. I looked away.

"I deserved that," he said. "Can I show you what I wanted you to come for?"

I stood up and turned the heat off the tea water. "Yes."

We wove back through the tables in the big room. Most were empty, as he'd just shown something, but as I went by, I noticed nudes in charcoal and ballpoint pen: men and women, some alone, some twined together in scribbled couplings. They were illustrations of what was on his mind, and what was on his mind was much the same as what was on mine.

The wall facing the front of the building had a row of doors, and unless something had changed, the rooms were meant to house draft installations. He opened one and flicked on the light.

The room was windowless and similar in size to the one in the Eclipse show, and it was a disaster. A quilted comforter hung on one wall, a table with more pornographic scribbles on the other wall. Stacks of boxes littered the floor.

"What am I looking at?" I asked.

"Early draft. But I really struggled with one object because I thought I should return it, but then, I got mad at you again, and I almost burned it. I had the barbecue going in the back, but I couldn't."

"What is it?"

He reached between two boxes and pulled out a hard plastic case with a handle. I noticed a pink and red Dirty Girls sticker by the buckle.

"My viola!" I held out my hands. He handed it to me then shifted some sketches so I could put it on the table. "I thought I left this up with my parents in Castaic the last time we went."

"Yeah. It was in the trunk. I... uh..." He put his fingers through his hair. "I didn't want you to play for me. It kept me from thinking straight about you."

Things between us hadn't been perfect before I left. I had no idea it was as clear to him as it had been to me. I opened the case. My viola was in there, exactly as I'd left it, with the bow tucked in the lid and a pocket with rosin, extra strings, and a pick I liked to use when I was feeling experimental. "Those last few months," I said, "I was very lonely. I could have used this."

He sat on a box. "I think hiding it was a mistake."

I should have been angry. I should have smacked the case across his face and run out with my instrument. But I couldn't. It all seemed so long ago. I touched the wood, running my finger over the curves. The gut core strings were dried out and would probably snap before I finished a song, and the fingerboard still had little grease spots from my hours of playing.

"That was really dickish of you, Kevin." I pulled the viola from the case. "You're an unscrupulous ass."

"Is that why you left me?"

I felt a sinkhole open in my diaphragm. I didn't want to discuss it. I had just wanted to break up with him, so I did. How did I get manipulated into going to his studio just to discuss an eighteen-month-old hurt?

Because I'd done it wrong. I'd done what was right for me, telling myself I'd just do without all the discussing and crying. I was just going to avoid all the emotional illness, but there were two of us, and Kevin hadn't been part of the decision.

I popped the bow from the clasps. The case was cheap, student-grade. The viola, however, was professional quality, purchased at a West Hollywood pawn shop for my fifteenth birthday by my father, who approved of me.

I tucked the viola under my chin and ran my fingers over the strings. They were loose. I tightened a couple of pegs, but the sound would only be barely acceptable. Barely. "I left you because I needed you," I said.

"That makes no sense."

I drew the bow over the strings and adjusted the tension, waiting for one to break in a snapping curlicue, but it didn't happen. I got the tension close and played something he'd know, dragging that first note across the bow as if summoning it from our collective past.

"You weren't capable of being needed." I played the next note.

"Don't." His whisper came out husky, as if the command had caught in his throat.

I didn't listen to him, but played the song my mind would never have recalled but my body knew.

Kevin didn't sleep well. Unlike workaholics and TV addicts, he wanted desperately to sleep a full night, and unlike most insomniacs, he fell soundly to sleep at a decent hour. But about four times a week, he awoke in the early hours of the morning with a pounding, anxious pain in his chest. I woke up when he shifted. I held him, stroked his hair, hummed, but nothing put him back to sleep except me playing the viola. We had a tune we shared, a lullaby I wrote for him with my fingers and arm. I never wrote it down because it became as real as the bond between us, and it ceased to exist when that bond broke.

So I played it for him in that first-draft installation that looked more like a storage room than a homage to a breakup. And he watched me with his butt leaning on the table, and his ankles and arms crossed. I let the last note drift off. The song had no end; I'd always just played it until his breathing became level and regular.

"Sounds like shit," I said.

"I don't know what you were doing, playing that."

"Maybe you can tell me what you were doing putting my shit in a museum without telling me."

"I was scared."

I laid the instrument in its case. "Of?"

"The piece was happening, and I wasn't fighting about it."

"I want my jeans back." This was ridiculous. I didn't give a rat's ass about my fucking jeans. I just wanted to provide him with the exact thing he didn't want. I wanted to fight him.

"The whole thing is sold. Even the books and catalogs are sold out. You'd be after me and some collector on a Spanish island. Our lawyers would have lawyers."

"This is not fair," I whispered, stroking the brittle strings of my lost viola.

"I know. None of it was."

I knew he didn't just mean his piece. He meant everything from the minute we met to the moment I finished playing our lullaby. I felt emotionally dehydrated and raw at the edges.

"I should go." I snapped my case shut. "Thanks for not putting this in the piece."

I turned to walk out, and like a cat, he jumped in front of me, putting his hands on my cheeks. "You're happy? With this new guy?"

"Jonathan. You know his name."

"Are you happy?"

"It's casual."

"You? Tweety Bird? I don't believe it."

I'd forgotten that. He called me his canary when he was feeling warm and affectionate. How convenient for me to overlook that when he felt confronted in the slightest, or distant, or overwhelmed, he called me Tweety Bird. I never knew if he even realized the name he used for me said more about him than it did about me.

"Take your hands off my face," I said. His fingers fell off my cheeks as if they melted away. "I don't mean to be callous, Kevin. I don't want to fall into life unintentionally any more. Jonathan has a purpose." His eyebrows went up half a tick. That had to be answered. "Get your mind out of the gutter."

Out of the gutter meant one thing to the rest of the world and the opposite to us. It meant, *Stop thinking it's about money*.

"You know, I didn't ask you to come here to talk about us. If you could give me another ten minutes, we can sit in the kitchen, and I'll make you some tea. Properly. I want to pitch something to you."

I looked at my watch. I had the night shift. "You have half an hour."

He leaned down a little to look me in the face with his big chocolate-coin eyes. "Thank you."

He walked quickly back to the kitchen. He made tea with efficiency and grace, speaking with a catch of thrill in his voice I hadn't heard in a long time. I couldn't have gotten a word in edgewise if I'd wanted.

"We all make art about these big concepts. We feel like we need to put it all under a cultural umbrella if we want to get into the lexicon, but I haven't cried in front of a piece of art since I was in college. It's because the whole scene is up in its head. Banksy's scribbling culture, Barbara Kruger's still yelling about consumer culture, John Currin's talking about sex and culture, and Frank Hermaine is ... I don't even know what that guy is talking about. No one's doing anything about the stuff that matters, stuff that gets us up in the morning and rocks us to sleep at night. When I realized this, I started being thankful you walked out. I mean ... not really, but it made me realize that nothing I was doing made a damn bit of difference or touched anyone, and I thought if I could take that pain I felt and put it in a room, so when someone walked into that room who was going through the same thing, they'd recognize it. They'd say, *yes, I'm connected to this. I'm feeling it.* Can you imagine it? The bond? The potential? The power?"

In the middle of his pitch, he'd sat down and, like a coiled spring, perched on the edge of the seat, his legs splayed, heels rocking his seat back onto the corners of the legs. His elbows were angled to the tabletop, hands gesturing.

How young I'd been to fall so deeply in love with his enthusiasm. "So this is what you were trying to do with the Eclipse piece?"

"I was trying to exorcise you with that, trying to figure it out so I could get rid of you. But it made me think about what something truly personal could mean as a visual narrative, and then I thought, maybe it's not a visual narrative. Maybe it's a multi-media narrative, with one party speaking to the visual and another to the aural." As if reacting to my expression, he leaned forward even farther. "Before you think anything, both narratives need to fight each other. There needs to be an aesthetic tension until it all goes black and silent. It's an experience of fullness before death. *Pow*."

I sipped my tea. He needed to wait for me to think. I wasn't fucking him anymore. I didn't have to jump like a brainless fangirl on every idea he pitched me. Except it was a good idea. Everything about it could be beautiful, a truly moving experience, a three-dimensional cinema of tone.

"You're not talking about a linear narrative," I said.

"Of course not."

"Yeah."

"Yeah, what?"

"You should do it. But without my toiletries."

"Fuck your toiletries. I want *you*."

I took a long breath through my nose and closed my eyes. I needed to avoid lashing out. He couldn't have meant it sexually. Couldn't.

"Let me rephrase that," he said.

"Please."

"It's a collaboration. You do the aural, obviously."

I pursed my lips and stared into my tea. "Kevin, I can't."

"Why not?"

"For one, it would be awkward."

"Only if we let it be."

He leaned on the wall, his posture relaxed now that the pitch phase of the process was ended and the artistic seduction phase was about to begin.

"And two," I said, "I haven't been able to write a word or make two notes together make sense. I'm stuck."

"Getting stuck is part of the process."

"It's a no."

"So you'll think about it?"

"Your thirty minutes are up, Kevin." I stood. "It was nice to see you."

"Let me walk you out." He smiled like a man who hadn't been rejected but had just gotten exactly what he wanted.

CHAPTER 43

Fifteen minutes after Jessica Carnes implied Jonathan's roughness in bed had broken her wrist, Jonathan had texted me.

—*What did she tell you?*—

I didn't answer, and I didn't hear from him again. Debbie, my bar manager and a friend of Jonathan's, had seen but not heard the exchange and had alerted him while he was in San Francisco. She'd admitted it with no guilt.

"If you saw your face," she said, "you would have called him too."

"Sometimes I think you're more invested in this relationship than either of us," I'd replied, arranging drinks on a tray.

"I like you both. Jessica, not as much. Now go serve those before the ice melts."

But I was glad I didn't hear from Jonathan again. I didn't want to have some drawn-out phone conversation about what Jessica had told me and why it upset me, whether or not he fucked her. I didn't want excuses. I didn't want conflicting stories. I just wanted to do what I was supposed to be doing: making music, being at peace with it, watching Gabby, doing my paying job without a sad look on my face or clumsy spills.

So when I got another call from Jonathan, I sent it to voicemail. I was driving. And I didn't want to talk to him. I knew he was back, because for all my posturing, I was counting the days until his return. He texted, and I ignored it. But when I got to a red light, I had to read it. I was only human.

—*If you're ending it with me*
just tell me, ok?—

Fuck. He had to go there. He had to undercut my delicious spite. I pulled the car over and drafted and redrafted a text. If I saw him before our studio time for WDE tomorrow, I could cut it short. No twelve-hour fuck sessions. Perfect. I needed to avoid hurting myself on his body.

—Tomorrow afternoon to talk?—

My screen told me he was typing, and I imagined his thumb sliding over the glass, the way it had slid over my body, and I shuddered a little as the car idled in a red zone.

—Public space?—

I started typing, then stopped myself. A public space meant I couldn't show that I was upset, and if I were honest with myself for a change, I *was* upset. The problem with a private space was that being alone in a room with him meant the conversation could only end one way.

—Private—

—Would the Loft Club be ok?
Not exactly neutral—

—It's fine. 1pm. Gotta go—

I tossed the phone onto the passenger seat and put the car in drive. I'd scheduled Jonathan three hours before a recording session in Burbank. The session had been set up by Eugene Testarossa at WDE because Gabby and I didn't have a track between us.

The lunch meeting with Testarossa had gone smoothly and lasted exactly one hour. We were stroked, complimented, and offered gigs and contracts that could never be delivered. I'd become convinced some time during college that the most valuable skill one needed in Los Angeles was the ability to tell the bullshit from the real shit. Only one piece of reality entered the conversation.

"Carnival has a new label," Eugene said as he finished his salad. He'd taken us to Mantini's and spent the whole meal looking at the door. "Singer, songwriters. Not folk, but a kind of trip-hop poetry. Lyrically heavy lounge."

"I don't have a lot of songs ready," I'd jumped in. I didn't want to say I didn't have *any* songs, but I couldn't lie completely without getting busted.

Eugene waved his hand. "We have a songwriter. We need your pipes." As an afterthought, he turned to Gabby. "And your compositional skills."

So we'd agreed to cut two songs written by a WDE client at DownDawg Studios in Burbank. Gabby and I were hip-pocketed, meaning they could take a portion of any money we made without committing to represent us over the long term. Gabby giggled the whole way home, but I felt as though I'd just had a fist removed from my ass.

The songs had been messengered the next day. For all Eugene's pretentions about lyrically driven vocals, they were lame garbage. I was going to have to work twice as hard to make them sound like anything. The last thing I should have done was make a date with Jonathan just before the recording session, but I'd been compelled. It was good timing. I'd have an excuse to leave.

When my phone blooped, I didn't look at it. If Jonathan and I were on, then we were on. If he had a change, he was going to have to wait for me to accept it. I wasn't playing games with him. I really needed to get to Darren's if I was going to talk to him and still get to Frontage on time.

I parked in my driveway and walked down the hill and right on Echo Park Ave. Darren lived in a two-story apartment building with a courtyard in the middle of a giant U. It was exactly like thousands of other buildings in Los Angeles: poorly thought-out, carelessly built, and hopelessly ugly. But the tall hedges and trees in the front gave it the appearance of a quiet hideaway, and its proximity to his damaged sister, who he had to watch if he was going to sleep at night, made it the perfect place for him.

The front gate was chocked open as always by the kids running in and out. I was thinking about how to ask him what I wanted to ask him and what answer I wanted as I trudged up the steps. I passed his window. The TV was on, so he was home. The front door was open, the screen was shut, and inside, Darren leaned on the kitchen doorframe and laughed. It was a relaxed laugh, done with his arms crossed, as an answer to something, and I felt as though I was eavesdropping. I raised my hand to knock, but a man with short sandy hair got up from the couch, and Darren laughed harder as he was engulfed in arms and kisses—wet and passionate—and four robust male arms tangled around each other.

I couldn't keep silent. "A*ha!*"

They pulled off each other and looked at me.

"Musical theater!" I shouted. "You're the mystery woman taking him out to shows!"

"Which one is this?" Sandy Hair asked.

They looked at each other, and Darren said, "You coming in or what?"

I went through the door and held out my hand. "I'm Monica. It's nice to meet you."

"Adam. Same here."

We shook. His grip was tight and dry. He was hot, with a little blondish stubble and grey eyes I knew would change color depending on what he wore. I tried to stay calm, but inside, I was giggling with delight. I was happy not only to uncover Darren's secret, but that he was only hiding happiness.

Adam picked up his jacket. "I gotta go." He approached Darren and went in for a kiss. Darren kept his arms crossed and turned his face to catch it on the cheek. Adam took him by the cheeks and turned his face, kissing him wetly on the lips. Darren was non-responsive.

"Oh, come on," Adam said. "Look at her. She's smiling."

"Kiss him! Kiss him!" I said.

He did, and it was such a lovely sight to see my friend happy that I had to clench my hands to keep from clapping.

Adam finally pushed him away. "God, slut. You're making me late." He winked at me on the way out.

I knew I was smiling again. It was the uncontrollable type of grin that hurt my face.

"You're embarrassing yourself," he said.

"I don't care. Are you going to tell me everything?"

He threw himself on the couch and turned off the TV. "We met in the Music House. He comes in all the time. I thought he was asking for me because of my expertise."

"But it was your hot body."

He threw a pillow at me. "Would you stop?"

I buried my face in the pillow. "I'm so happy. I worried about you all the time because you rarely went out with anyone."

"I was confused, as they say. And Lord knows I couldn't burden Gabby."

I flung the pillow back at him. "Why didn't you tell *me*?"

"We have a past. I didn't want you to feel like I was... I don't know, like I didn't love you the right way."

"You didn't, you fucktard. Now you do, but then you didn't. And why don't you tell Gabby now?"

He sighed. "Adam's last name is Marsillo. Which means nothing to you. But the CEO of Foundation Records? That's her maiden name."

"That's his mother."

"Gabby would know that," he said, "and freak out. She'd start making marriage plans. He's nice, but I'm not ready for her to start hovering."

I looked away, fondling the crease in my jeans. Gabby would handle her brother's homosexuality just fine, but he was right. Any connection to the music industry could send her spinning in either direction.

I jumped up and dropped into his lap, hugging him for all I was worth. I kissed his cheek.

He laughed and pushed me away. "Sorry, baby, you're not my type."

"I'm heartbroken."

"Did you come here to snoop or did you have something to say?"

"I saw Kevin."

"Uh oh?"

"Nothing like that. He wants to collaborate on a project. I'm totally stuck, and I thought if the three of us worked on it, I'd get unstuck, and we could be together again." I looked at my watch and bounced to my feet. "But now I have no time to even discuss it. Are you coming tonight?"

"Adam and I have tickets." He smiled. "Musical theater."

"You're a cliché."

He shrugged. "Don't tell Gabby yet. I don't like this thing with Theo."

"Why not?" I was annoyed that he'd deny her happiness just when he'd found his own.

"He deals scrips. He's the last person she should be messing with."

"How did I not know that?"

"Your head hasn't been in the game since you spent the night up in Griffith Park. Speaking of, did you see the pictures of you and Mister Gorgeous at the Eclipse show? They were all over the internet."

"God, no."

"Do you want me to pull them up? You look amazing."

"Absolutely not. I don't want to hear what anyone has to say about my life. Living it is hard enough." I went to the door but thought better of bolting out. I hugged Darren again and kissed his cheek. "I'm happy for you."

He pushed me toward the door. I felt closer to him than I'd felt since we were in high school. "Get out of here," he said. "Knock 'em dead or whatever."

CHAPTER 44

At first, I wore the outfit least likely to land Jonathan's dick inside me. My jeans were tight enough to cut the curve of my ass and accent the space between my skinny thighs, but so difficult to get off in a heat of passion that I'd have plenty of time to think about what I was doing and deny him access. I wore a bra with three hooks in back and a woven shirt that couldn't be pulled over the head without unbuttoning it. I looked hot and physically inaccessible.

I realized that made me very easy to lie to, because I'd walk into the room, he'd make plans to remove my clothes, assess the difficulties, and say whatever he had to in order to soothe my mind. I didn't want that. I wanted the truth about what had happened between him and Jessica the night he dropped me at my house. I wanted it in all its ugliness and gritty detail. I wanted all the pain and all the hurt. I owned it for trusting him and for asking more of him than he could give, even though I'd been warned. If he hurt me enough, I wouldn't make those mistakes again.

Despite the bruises that still stained the backs of my thighs, Jonathan wasn't the kind of guy to revel in hurting me, at least not emotionally. I was going to have to pull it out of him, and my suit of armor wasn't going to cut it. I had to weaken him. I had to make him tell me everything, even against his better judgment. I had to make him beg.

It was a garter, then, and a dress with a flared bottom. I got aroused just putting on that outfit. I'd go to the studio in Burbank directly after, so I stuck a pair of spare undies in my bag and called myself done.

CHAPTER 45

As I stepped out of the elevator into the club's lobby, a throbbing ache developed between my legs, and with each step down the hall, I got wetter just from being aware of the garter under the skirt. The upcoming conversation was going to be very difficult if I didn't get a handle on my sex drive.

I towered over Terry, the hostess, in four-inch heels. They made me about six feet tall, but I'd wanted to be looking Jonathan in the face. I needed to catch lies and half-truths before they dropped.

The room was a different one, smaller, with two sets of cocktail tables and a leather loveseat and coffee table in the center of the room. He stood by the wall of windows, and when he looked at me, my heart stopped for half a beat. It was the work clothes: the charcoal suit, maroon tie, and the cufflinks. The glass of Perrier in his fingertips.

But when I got close, something had changed. His scent wasn't the dry one I remembered, but something like sawdust, leather, and wet earth. The aroma was less beautiful, but sexier, and I felt the effects of it in the weight and wetness between my legs.

"Hi," he said.

"Hello."

The door closed behind me. I wanted to hold him, to forget everything. If I could only pretend Jessica hadn't come into the bar, I would have wrapped myself around him. I stepped close to him, until we were eye to eye.

"Can I get you a glass of water?" he asked.

"No, thanks."

"Flat water? I can get it without bubbles."

"No, thanks."

"I can order up some cookies."

"I don't want anything."

"Can you just tell me what she told you?"

"You're all aquiver, Jonathan. What do you think she told me?" My tone was sharper than I'd intended.

He swirled the ice around in his glass. "Something that upset you." He was going to dance around indefinitely. He was guarded and undoubtedly ready to be dishonest about something.

I had come prepared to make it very difficult for him. "Yes. She said something that upset me. A lot." I hooked my finger in his waistband.

"Did she say you looked fat? She can be very catty."

"Funny guy." I pulled his belt from the loop, yanking the tongue from the metal hook. "I'm going to ask you a question, and I want it answered in detail." His belt fell open with a metallic clank. I took the glass from his hand and placed it on the table. His fingertips went for my face, but I pulled them away. "Hands at your sides."

"You're joking."

"Do I look like I'm joking?" I unzipped his pants. "I'm going to be on my knees. No touching."

"Was there a question? You said there was a question."

I dropped to my knees and rubbed his organ through his underwear, hardening it. I put my lips to it and breathed a hot breath, then rubbed my teeth through the cloth covering his growing stiffness. He groaned.

I pulled out his cock, the gorgeous thing, and licked the tip. "Are you ready for my question?"

"No."

I put the head in my mouth to get it wet, sucking on the way out. "You stop talking, I stop sucking. Okay?" I looked up at him.

He reached for my hair, but I pushed his hand back.

"Okay," he said, and I could hear the smile on his lips.

I gave the head another suck, then said, "Tell me where you went after you dropped me at my house and what happened there."

"I don't need a blowjob this bad, Monica."

"I want your guard down, and I want your dick." I slid my mouth all the way down then, lips dragging along the length of him, tongue following, my throat open. I let it feel the whole of me for a second before drawing it slowly out.

"God damn." He reached for the back of my head, and I pulled his hand away again. "I'm tying your hands behind your back next time," he said.

"You went which way on Vestal Street?"

"I'm just going to cut to it," he said. "Jessica's. I went to see Jessica."

"An hour after we agreed to be exclusive?"

I didn't want to look at him when he answered, so I took his dick in my mouth and worked it while he spoke.

"She texted me. She wanted to talk. I was always there for her because she was there for me. I didn't see any harm in it. I didn't think anything would happen." He must have felt a hitch in my throat, because he added, "Wait. I don't want to phrase it like that."

"Phrase it any way you have to," I said, stroking his dick with my hand. My saliva made it slick enough to work, and his sharp intake of breath told me he could slip up anytime. A drop of pre-come oozed from his red tip, and I caught it with my tongue. I licked down to the base, his skin paper thin against my tongue, and what I was looking for, the scent of another woman, was nowhere on him.

"Monica, I like you. I don't want to—" He gasped as a tooth grazed his shaft.

"Speak. I can take it."

"I didn't fuck her. I don't know what she said, but I'm not telling you anything else while you're sucking me off." He grabbed my wrists and placed them on my head like I was being arrested. "Now, finish the job."

I looked up at his smiling lips. I didn't know what he'd done. Undoubtedly, there was more to the story, but was I going to swallow a load of his come to find out?

I opened my mouth. He held my wrists in his right hand, gripping them tightly. With his left, he guided his cock into my mouth, and unlike a second ago when I had controlled the situation, the taste and tautness of his skin sent a bolt of pleasure through me. I couldn't resist it. My pussy bulged when he tightened his lock on my wrists. Jesus, the motherfucker sucked away my resolve and turned it into orgasms.

He put his left hand to the back of my head and gently thrust himself down my throat, letting out a groan on the third thrust.

"You okay down there?" he asked.

I made a noise that indicated I was.

"Take it. All the way."

The act of obeying his command engorged my clit. It throbbed, demanding I notice the tone of his voice, his new smell, his hand tugging the hair at the back of my head.

"Flatten your tongue along the bottom. Ah, like that."

He pushed into my throat, my tongue stroking the underside of his throbbing, hot cock. He squeezed my wrists and thrust hard and fast, holding my head still. I opened my mouth wide to keep from biting him as he went down my throat to the base. The hairs of his stomach tickled my nose. All the concentration it took to keep my mouth open and take his cock only brought my own orgasm closer.

"I'm coming," he whispered. It was a statement, not a question, and I was meant to prepare to swallow.

He grunted and came, sharp and sticky down my throat. I breathed through my nose, taking him without gagging and letting his juice run out as he finished. When he came to a stop, I kissed the end of his cock. He released my arms.

When I put them down, I caught a shooting ache in my biceps. "I better not find out you're lying," I said. "That was the best blowjob I ever gave anyone."

He put himself back in his pants and zipped up. "You have a funny way of showing a guy you're pissed off." He reached for my hand to help me up, and I took it. He steadied me as I wobbled on my high heels.

"Welcome home," I said. "Now, I've been upset for days."

"I'm sorry about that. If you had called me, I could have told you sooner."

"But you did *something* with her."

He touched my chin with two fingers, then slid them over my jaw and down my neck, down my chest, stopping at my nipple, which was rock hard under my dress. He brushed his thumb against it and leaned his body into mine, kissing my lips softly while he stroked my breast.

"Why do you want to know?" he asked.

"I hate secrets."

"I have secrets I may never tell you."

"I only want this one today. I know she's yours. I know she has your heart, but you promised me your body, so I have the right to it."

He kissed my neck, finding the sensitive spots. "She has nothing of mine."

My hands went under his jacket, finding his waist. I stroked the shape of him while he moved off my breast and down to my ass.

He gasped in my neck when he felt what I was wearing under my skirt. "Monica."

"I was ready to do whatever I needed to so you'd tell me."

He stepped back. "Pick up your skirt."

"We didn't get to enjoy this the other night." I pulled up my skirt so he could see the garter, minus the panties. "So you're telling me, right?"

"No."

I put down my skirt.

He stepped closer and brushed his finger against my collarbone. "No games. I don't want to tell you because it's better that way. But I'll tell you this: I spent the past three days thinking about you, how much I wanted you, and realizing I was free to have you." He kissed me, a slow, soft grind of his lips and tongue, and I yielded to him. "Tell me you're mine," he whispered. "Say it."

I wanted to. I almost did. I almost promised him whatever he wanted, but the anxiety of the last few days nagged at my chest and throat. "Tell me what happened with Jessica."

"I'm afraid I'll chase you away, and I don't want to do that."

"I can take it."

"Fine then. Turn around."

I let go of my skirt and faced away from him. He put his palms on my ass, then moved closer and drew them up my back until his newly erect penis was pressed against me. He unzipped the simple black dress and pressed his hands to my shoulders in such a way as to turn me around to face him.

"Take it off," he said.

I let the dress slip over my shoulders and onto the floor. I stood in the black garter, black heels, matching lace bra, and a wet pussy. I stepped out of the dress and pushed it to the side. He watched me, and I could almost see his brain working. He stepped back to me and kicked my legs open with his foot, then stroked my forearms, down to my hands. He laced his fingers into mine. His eyes were not unkind, but hard and focused.

"I'd fuck you senseless," he said, "but I never got more condoms."

"You'll make it up to me."

"What did she say to you?" he asked.

"I asked her how she broke her wrist, and she said, 'Jonathan can be rough sometimes.'"

He made a little snort that might have been mistaken for a short laugh if the rest of his face hadn't been so hardened. "First of all, that's a typical Jessica contextual lie." He moved my hands behind me. "Lean back." He held my arms steady so I wouldn't fall, until my back was arched enough for my hands to lean on the back of the love seat. His body curved with mine, his breath on my shoulder as he drew his hands up my arms. "It's true as a statement, but false in context. Second of all, she doesn't know from rough. You, my darling, got me rougher than she's ever seen."

He stepped back from me, an artist working on a piece. I stood, legs apart, back arched, arms behind me leaning on the back of the sofa. I felt exposed, vulnerable, and turned on. He'd called Jessica a liar, and one with her own brand of lying. I noted the change in attitude. He put his hand on the small of my back and pushed up, arching it further, exposing me to him, and forcing me to look at the ceiling.

"She lives in Venice, on the water," he said as he lifted my bra, exposing my tits so he could stroke the rock-hard nipples. "And she was waiting. As soon as I drove up, she was in the doorway. She hadn't acted happy to see me in two years or more. And yes, I thought about you, but I figured only a few hours had passed. If I needed to get out, you'd understand. Or not. I wasn't on ethically shaky ground."

A drizzle of wetness dripped down my leg.

"She hugged me and pulled me into the house. I kept asking her what was wrong, and I mean, I shouldn't have been surprised, but there was so much shit missing."

"Her boyfriend left and took his stuff," I said.

"I was happy. I was excited. I felt like I'd won some kind of war." He reached down to part my thighs more than I thought physically possible. His finger grazed the drip. "A war of patience. She poured us some wine, and as soon as she started talking about how great she felt that he was gone, I knew something was wrong." He brushed his wet finger against my lower lips, and I tasted myself. "This is turning you on."

"What you're doing. Not what you're saying."

"She put her hands on me. I can't tell you how long I waited for her to touch me again." He put his hand between my breasts and moved it down my belly, touching the diamond in my navel and circling it before he drifted down to my crotch. He brushed against my crotch only long enough to feel the dampness then moved to my thighs again.

I moaned and pushed against him.

He pressed his hand flat against my pussy, letting me do the work of grinding against him. "And I kissed her. I admit it. I couldn't have stopped myself. She said, 'Make love to me, Jonathan, like you used to.' So I threw her on the couch."

I scrunched my face because I didn't want to show I was upset. I wanted to enjoy him and his touch and not hear what happened that had kept him from making love to his ex-wife. Had she pushed him away at the last minute? Or had the boyfriend walked in? I didn't care anymore. "I don't want to hear it," I said, staring at the exposed beam on the ceiling.

"Too late." He picked up his glass of Perrier and placed it on my chest. "Don't let this fall."

I couldn't look at him or the glass would tip. An icy cold patch formed at the center of my sternum.

He kneeled between my legs. "She smelled like I'd always remembered. Like cut grass." He kissed the inside of my thigh, licking away the juices from my pussy as he made his way upward. "And I thought, ah, I remember this smell. And I was kissing her, but..." He stopped and kissed my clit once. "I realized I didn't want her. And the cut-grass smell?" His tongue went from my pussy to my clit and back.

I moaned again, louder. He pulled me open. The air itself was a physical pressure on me, and I wanted him, just this once, even if it would be the last time.

"The cut grass smell wasn't love. It was gratitude. I felt like I was kissing one of my sisters." He gave my clit a suck, a fast, light thing that got a cry from me. "Then I thought of you, and I knew I had to get out of there. That was the end of that."

With that, he put his tongue on my clit, breathing hot breaths, wiggling his tongue until I thought for sure I was going to tip the glass. I felt gratitude, too, and it smelled nothing like cut grass.

"Kissing is cheating," I said. "Even if you had to do it to get over her."

"Yeah. But I figured if I got my lips on your cunt before I told you, you'd forgive me. I think we walked in here with the same strategy." He slid his fingers into me. "If that glass drops, I stop, and you go home with a baseball."

"I don't forgive you." Cold condensation dripped off my chest and down my sides.

"I know." He pushed his fingers in as deep as they'd go and used his other hand to expose the hard nodule of my clit. "You have a beautiful cunt, Monica."

I had not a second to think about how that word was foul and disgusting from anyone else's lips before he put his tongue to my clit and all thinking disappeared. Three strokes with the tip and a suck. Four strokes and a longer suck. Pushing fingers in and out, stretching me, while he licked me again, then he jammed his fingers all the way in and gently used his teeth on my clit.

"Oh, *God!*" I shouted. The pain was sharp but immediately followed by a pleasure I'd never experienced, as if the nerves were exposed raw by the bite and made more alive by the gentleness that followed.

"That a good 'oh, God' or a bad 'oh, God'?"

"Great, good, fucking *God.*"

He did it again, pressing his teeth a little harder and adding a suck to the grind of his teeth. The pain and pleasure coexisted, moving from opposite poles to the center of me. I writhed enough to shake water from the glass and onto my belly but not tip it.

He sucked my clit through his teeth, and I filled his mouth with stars.

"I'm coming. Fuck. Jonathan...."

He moaned into me, and I knew that meant I was allowed to come. And he didn't stop or pause long enough for me to stop the freight train of my orgasm. I tried to keep my body still, but toward the end, as the sucking felt as though his mouth was pulling every last bit of pleasure from me, I lost control of my body, and the glass tumbled, rolling along the floor. My back arched even more. The top of my head wound up on the loveseat cushions, and Jonathan stood to keep his head between my legs. He kept sucking even after I tried to push his head away, his pussy-wet fingers holding my thighs.

He moved his mouth away when I was a hot, shuddering mess. I breathed heavily, getting my bearings again. He put his hands around my waist and lifted me to standing. I still couldn't speak. He lowered my bra gently, then picked up my dress from the floor. I fell on him, and he laughed, holding me up.

"You all right?"

"I don't think all my parts are attached."

"You look just as perfect as you did ten minutes ago."

I breathed into him for a second, taking in the new, musty scent. "I don't think I have the coordination to get my clothes on." I got my bearings, feeling sexually satisfied in a way I knew wouldn't last. I could be ready for another go in minutes.

Jonathan found the neck opening of my dress and lifted it over my head.

I wiggled my arms through the sleeves. "What did she do for you that you're so grateful about?"

"I'm about to be cryptic," he said.

"Great."

"I went through some stuff when I was younger, and I was treated like it all happened *to me*. I was this victim. She showed me that I was responsible. She gave me my manhood back. That too heartwarming for you?"

I caught the sarcasm in the last sentence but also the defensiveness. I turned my back and moved my hair out of the way so he could zip me up.

"How did she break her wrist?" I asked.

He slowly zipped up the dress. "I said I was sorry and that I couldn't do this with her anymore, this whole dance we've been doing. She ran out after me and tripped on the walk. Fell on her wrist. I couldn't get my doctor on the phone, so I took her to the ER and waited with her. The only four words she said to me? 'Is it that girl?'"

"She was talking about me?"

"I assumed so."

"What did you say?"

"I lied."

I turned around. "You said I wasn't a girl?"

He smiled. "I said you were nothing to me. I think I used the word dalliance."

"Am I a dalliance?"

"Not for me. Not anymore." Looking pensive, he smoothed my dress. "But you see what she did when she thought you were. Made a special trip up to the Stock just to hurt you. If she knew I think about you all the time … well, she's possessive. Even after she left me, she made it a point to find out who I was with and what I was doing with them. I thought it meant she still loved me, but actually, it means she's crazy." He kissed my hands, then my cheek. His face smelled like my pussy. "Do you have a few more minutes?"

"Some. I'm going to record something in a few hours. I set it up so we couldn't be together too long."

"Clever girl."

"Well, now I just want to eat you alive."

He turned me back around and kissed me. The taste of our tongues was a mix of sex and sweat. I fell into him, a groan rising in the back of my throat. I wanted him again, and again.

He moved his mouth to my nose, my chin, and spoke into my cheek. "I need to wash up. Can you meet me downstairs in the bar?"

CHAPTER 46

I carried a toothbrush in my bag because I knew, at the very least, his dick would be in my mouth, and I didn't want to hit the high notes at DownDawg Studio with blowjob breath. I washed my face, readjusted my dress, and slipped on my panties. They made my pussy feel gagged, but if any part of me needed to shut up for a minute, it was the sopping cup of sensation between my legs.

He was waiting at a small table near the window, a bottle of Perrier and two glasses ready. He saw me come in, and I noted the appreciation in his gaze.

"How long do I have?" He scooped a couple of beige pistachios from a porcelain bowl. A metal bowl sat next to it, a couple of empty shells nesting inside.

"About ninety minutes. No time for another round." I sat. Our chairs faced the windows and were so close our knees touched.

"That's fine. I just want to talk to you."

"You smell different," I said.

He smiled. "The last cologne ... Jessica got it for me for Christmas seven years ago. I had something new made up north. Do you like it?"

"It's the other side of you."

He removed the meat from a nut and placed it to my lips. I glanced around. The bar was empty except for Larry, who was wiping glasses to an optic shine. I took the nut into my mouth like an offering.

"Which side is that?" He looked at me with those tourmaline eyes, his copper hair glinting at the edges from the afternoon sun.

I didn't know if I was allowed to fall for him, since he'd shed Jessica like an old skin. I didn't know if I was allowed to believe she was gone, or if that much had changed between us. "The side that makes me beg."

"You like that side of me?" He cracked another pistachio, tossing the shell into the metal bowl with a *plink*.

"You can't tell?"

"I want to make sure you're not tolerating it for other reasons." He placed the nut to my lips again.

I took it, letting the wet part of my lips graze his thumb. "If I were, I'd just lie about it."

"True."

"What do your instincts say? Am I a liar?"

"You're as real as anyone I ever met."

He turned his attention to the pistachios, popping another one open and dropping the shell with a *plink*. He ate that one, then another. *Plink, plink.* "I had business in San Francisco, but also, there's a woman up there."

The cold metal feeling that went up my spine must have made a sound loud enough for him to hear.

He glanced up at me and spoke in the voice he used when he was telling me to put my hands behind my back. "Wait. Let me finish."

That calmed me enough to remove the ice from my veins. "Go on," I said.

He fed me another nutmeat, *plinking* the shell with his other hand. "Her name is Sharon. We've been fucking on and off for a couple of years. We're very honest with each other, and she likes some of the same things in bed that you and I have done, but she's more experienced with it. When I got there, I saw her, and I told her about Jessica and you. I ended it with her, of course. Judging from your face you needed to hear that?"

"Sorry. I don't mean to be possessive."

He smiled. "You're fine." *Plink.* He put his face close to mine and brought his hand under my chin, a thumb on one cheek, and pressed lightly, opening my mouth.

My eyes went half-mast and a burst of pleasure blossomed between my legs.

With the other hand, he fed me the nut. "I want you, Monica. I want you on a regular basis. Constantly, actually. I don't think about much else." He let go of my cheeks and brushed his thumb against my bottom lip before taking his hand away and letting me chew. "I'm on the brink of being completely infatuated with you. I need to know if you feel the same."

I swallowed. Did I want him? Jesus fucking Christ, I'd never wanted anything so badly. I took a sip of water. "While you were away, and the last words I heard were Jessica's, I felt emotionally heightened. Sometimes, I just shook with rage. It doesn't matter that you didn't do anything, or didn't do much, or that you had to kiss her to get over her. The fact was, I had a hard time functioning. That's why I don't want a relationship. And the trouble is, you can't promise me I won't feel like that again."

"No, I can't." *Plink, plink.*

"But how am I supposed to walk away?"

"You can't. You're mine. The minute I told you to spread your legs and you did it, you were mine. When I told you to beg for it and you did, you were mine.

When you put your hands behind your back without being told, I owned you. You never had to say a word. You're a natural submissive."

Plink. When he turned away from the bowl to look at me, he had a nutmeat in his fingers, ready for my lips. His face, which had been so close to mine, slid half a step away. "Why the look?" he asked.

"What did you say?"

He smirked and got his face close again. "You are a natural submissive, Monica. You enjoy being obedient. You cede control with both hands. It's exactly right."

I was shaking. I wanted him, and five minutes ago, he was mine. He'd given up on his wife and wanted me, and the ache of holding back my feelings for him was quelled, if only for a moment. Until he called me a submissive.

I took my own fucking nut and cracked the meat out. "What were you thinking about us? You gonna put me on a leash?"

"You just turned into stone."

I chewed, not commenting. I wanted an answer. He stalled, pouring himself half a glass of Perrier, and I was immediately reminded of the glass I'd spilled on the floor.

"Women I take to bed, mostly they defy me, or act cute, or overdo obedience but don't mean it. Many pretend to like getting tied to the bedpost. One was so pliable it was disconcerting."

"And this Sharon person?"

"She's a submissive. That's what she does. So she nailed it, but it's not that kind of relationship. I could talk to her about what I liked, and we could try things together, but it's not like you. I want you. I can't get enough of you. You're strong. I want to see how you look with your wrists tied to your knees. I want to spank you red in the ass. Because you can take it." He paused, looking at me. "And I think I scared you. It's not what you think. I don't want anything from you that you already haven't offered."

"With both hands, apparently."

"It's beautiful, Monica. Don't make it ugly." He tilted his head, as if trying to see through me.

I tossed my pistachio shell into the bowl with a *plink,* feeling surly and confused. "Was Jessica submissive?"

"No. I think it's what drove her away."

I couldn't help but think Jessica's refusal to be dominated meant she was respected more than I would ever be. I'd always be the child, the one who could be bossed around, dismissed, belittled, and abused.

"Monica, what's on your mind?"

"No," I said.

"No, what?"

"No. Just no." I grabbed my bag. "But thanks for asking."

I took big steps in my high heels, nodding to Larry, who I'd probably never see again, and went out to the hall, where the elevator waited. There was an image in my mind, a thought, and I was keeping it at bay. Something about the nuts and the things he said was bringing a memory back to me.

He caught my elbow as I pressed the elevator button. "Monica."

"Don't touch me."

"What is it?"

The doors slid open. I didn't think he'd follow me in, but he did.

"Leave me alone."

"No. Fuck no!"

The doors closed him in, and we headed down.

He took me by the biceps. "What is it? Is it the word? We'll pick a different one."

"It's not what I want. Please. Just forget everything. I'm sorry. I can't."

"Why?"

I didn't want to think about why. I didn't want to answer. I looked up at him, thinking maybe I'd find some words to string together that would be reasonable or acceptable without letting through the image I held at bay. His face, his posture, everything told me I'd hurt him.

"I'm sorry," I said as the doors opened. I ran out, into the hall, through the lobby, and into the parking lot. Lil sat with the other drivers and got up when she saw me, but I ran past. I got into my car and put it in drive before the engine was even engaged.

The downtown streets jogged the car. I couldn't drive correctly. My mind was a soup of images I wouldn't acknowledge. I pulled over in front of a set of bay doors on an empty dead end street and put the car in park.

My hands were shaking. I had to calm down. I had to cut a song in an hour. In Burbank. Who knew what the traffic would be?

Breathe. Breathe.

As I relaxed, I felt a cord of arousal under my skirt. I closed my eyes, thinking about the silly junk I was going to have to sing, the clichés and simple chords. I had to add *me* to it. I had to breathe life into something dead. That was all I should be thinking about.

I heard a *plink* on the roof of the car. Then another. It had started to rain. *Plink, plink.* Through my relaxation, the memory came. The one I'd tried to shut out.

A club. Kevin and I went places and did things at night, in the odd hours, in the corners of the city, seeking out subcultures and twisted paths. Because we were artists, nothing was beneath our understanding or experience.

The club was dark. I'd been there before. There was nothing at all special about it. We sat at the end of the bar, by the wall. I'd been drinking something, and Kevin had my hand in his. His fingertips were cold from the ice in his glass, and I enjoyed the way he drew circles inside my wrist with them. I felt delicious and loved.

I heard a creak of old hinges above me. I looked up. The wall above seemed to have a hidden door, and a shelf and false wall swung out. A blindfolded woman about my age was tied to the shelf, on her hands and knees, hands and head facing the room. She wore a configuration of leather ties that bound her wrists to her knees. A silver ring with the circumference of a castanet kept her mouth open and her head raised. The leather harness holding it in place was strapped around her head and connected to a hook on the wall.

The bartender slapped a metal bowl under the shelf holding the girl and got on with his business, as if girls were tied to the wall all the time. Kevin barely glanced up, and though I tried to keep my mind on the conversation we were having with Jack and his girlfriend, my eyes kept going to the girl. She wore pink cotton panties that didn't go with the black leather garter pressing her tits to her ribs, but when I noticed a carefully placed mirror, I knew why. Her panties were soaked through at the crotch, and the pink showed off her arousal in a way leather wouldn't. I turned back to some conversation about process art in the 1980s.

I heard a *plink, plink* and followed the sound to the metal bowl. I craned my neck. It contained a few drops of clear, whitish fluid. I looked up. The girl, her mouth forced open by the ring, was drooling spit and semen down her chin and into the bowl. *Plink, plink.*

I caught sight of her eyes in the crease under the blindfold. She looked away when we made eye contact. I realized then that she could see through it. The blindfold wasn't there to protect her identity, nor was it to protect her from seeing us look at her, but to protect us from seeing how turned on she was.

I wasn't her.

That was submissive. I wasn't that. No, no, no.

Kevin and I had gone home, and neither of us ever brought up the drooling girl. We never judged. We were too sophisticated and cosmopolitan for that. We were too fucking cool to even let on that we'd noticed. I hated us. The people we were had been hateful snobs who never asked questions about anything real. Like why a woman would want to drool her master's load into a metal bowl and show her wet cunt to everyone.

So there I was, shaking in my Honda, because Jonathan had seen that girl in me. On his command, I'd opened my mouth as big as a castanet so he could fuck my throat.

Stop it.

I had to stop. I had to sing. But every time I heard the *plink* of rain on my hood, it was a pistachio shell, and I was drooling Jonathan's load into a metal bowl.

CHAPTER 47

On the way to the 101, I realized I still had that stinking diamond in my navel. It felt like a harness. I'd drop it at Hotel K after my session. My phone danced on the passenger seat. It could be Jonathan, but it wasn't as though he was the only thing I had going on. I was really glad I looked at it—WDE.

"Hey, Monica," Trudie said.

"Yeah, I'm on my way up there."

"We had a change. The set's at DownDawg in Culver City, not Burbank."

"Oh. Did you call Gabby?"

"Yeah, I talked to her. Here, let me give you the address."

I pulled over and wrote it down. I was glad I didn't need to call Gabby because it would probably take me an hour to get there without yacking with my pianist for twenty minutes, dissecting all the possible reasons for the venue change.

I did take a second to scroll through my recents. Nothing from Jonathan. Both my relief and disappointment were palpable. Then the phone dinged and buzzed in my hand.

—*I'm calling you now. Answer.*—

Oh, wasn't that just a juicy command? Answer the phone. Spread your legs. What was the difference?

When my cell rang, I rejected the call and sent a text.

—*I have to go to Culver
City. I can't talk*—

—*Let's talk about it again. I'll use
different words*—

—Not that way. I mean I won't
offend you—

He was no one to me, really. If I never saw him again, my life would be no different than it had been a month ago. No, that wasn't true. My life would be the same in all the surface ways. I'd live in the same house and have the same friends. But somehow I'd changed. He'd woken me from a dreamless sleep, and I couldn't roll over and close my eyes, because in my wakefulness, I'd started dreaming.

I read his text again. I could think about what he said, but I couldn't answer him. I couldn't be who he thought I was, but if I couldn't be that, then who would I be? I couldn't go backward, and somehow, in such a short time, he'd become the conductor of my forward motion.

I am not submissive.

I am not submissive.

I am not submissive.

I chanted the mantra all the way to Culver City, deaf to the buzzing phone and any thought for where I was headed or what I was to do there.

I didn't get my head back until I parked the car.

My name is Monica, and I am not *submissive. I stand six feet tall in heels. I am descended from one of the greatest writers of the twentieth century. I can sing like an angel and growl like a lion. I am not owned. I am music.*

CHAPTER 48

DownDawg Studios wasn't some little grunge house with egg-carton Styrofoam on the walls. It didn't smell of tobacco and fast food, and it most certainly wasn't a place we could have afforded on our own. There were three in Los Angeles. Burbank, which spent a lot of time servicing Disney, Santa Monica—home base for rich kids and middle-class rappers of the west side—and Culver City, where Sony did their ADR and apparently where WDE had their scratch cuts done.

The building was on Washington, in downtown Culver City. The renovated industrial box had the original casement windows in the front half, where they matched the three-ton metal-frame door. The back half was bricked in, a windowless green box with orange trim, the perfect modernist nonsensical combo.

A valet parked my car. A receptionist with more earrings than a Tiffany window pillow guided me to the back. I was seven minutes late. My excuse was the venue change. Right.

I opened the door and entered the engineering room with its bank of dials and window looking into the sound room. A man about my age with sandy hair and a linen shirt with the tails hanging below his sweater spoke to a guy with dark skin and a stiff-brimmed Lakers cap.

Linen Shirt held out his hand. "I'm Holden, your producer. This is Deshaun."

Deshaun offered a hand. "Sound engineer. My lady heard you play Thelonius a few weeks back. Said good things."

"Oh, thanks." I blushed a little. "Seems like ages ago."

"You got the song?" Holden asked. "What do you think?"

I thought it was a piece of shit, but honesty would get me nowhere. "We have a couple of takes on it. Gabby's on her way."

Holden got off the stool and threw himself on the couch. "Tell me how you're doing it."

I clutched my song sheet. I could do this. I could talk about the music. I knew what I had to do, and I was good at it, but the conversation with Jonathan had infected my mind, and I kept talking to Holden and Deshaun about dynamics and harmonies while thinking they somehow knew I was submissive. They were going to walk all over me and tell me how to sing the notes, how to breathe, how to open my mouth wide enough to take a cock. I knew they weren't laughing at me and my pretensions of vocal control, but I also knew they were.

Holden glanced at the clock. "It's getting late."

"Let me text Gabby," I said, slipping my phone out of my pocket. "She's probably in the parking lot."

—Where the fuck are you?—

—With Jerry, waiting for you—

I started getting a really bad feeling in my guts. I turned to Holden. "You know a guy named Jerry?"

"He does some production at the Burbank studio."

"Does he know Eugene Testarossa?"

"Yeah. Works with him all the time."

I typed fast.

*—There's been a mixup, I'm in
Culver City—*

There wasn't a text for a minute or more. "She's up in Burbank. She'll never make it here on time." I glanced toward the sound studio. A keyboard was already set up in there.

As if reading my mind, Holden said, "If you play, we're a go."

I did play. I generally didn't have to bother because of Gabby, but I played piano just fine. My phone blooped.

*—It's not a mixup it's a fucking
set-up Jerry never got an engineer
and he's been talking about the
fucking weather do you have
an engineer there?—*

I glanced at Deshaun, who was tapping away at his phone. I didn't know what to do. If I played, she'd never forgive me, and if I didn't, I was a back-bending little sheep who walked out with nothing. A nobody. A disappointment.

"We have time for a few takes," I said, turning off my phone and stepping into the sound room.

CHAPTER 49

The sun was dipping below the skyline when I got back in the car and turned on my phone. There was no use pretending I didn't see Gabby's messages, and there was no use listening to them. I just called her.

"Mooooooniiiiiicaaaaaa....." She was drunk. The white noise whipped like wind cut with the sound of music and laughter.

"Gabby, where are you?"

"I'm with Lord Theodore at the Santa Monica Pier. We're on the Ferris wheel."

"Are you okay?"

"You do the scratch cut?"

I rubbed the bottom of the steering wheel and stared at the building as if it could exonerate me, but the big green cube did nothing besides look squat and hip. "Yeah."

"We were set up, you know. I was. He don't want me, so they made it so you did the cut without me. You know that, right?"

She seemed okay with it, but she was wasted and on a Ferris wheel, so I couldn't take her forgiveness for granted. "Don't assume it was malicious, Gab."

"Oh fuck, when did you become such a ...whassa word? When you believe the best in people? Like you never lived in L.A. your whole life."

"Is Theo drunk too?"

I heard the phone muffle and Gabby say, "Hey, baby, you drunk?" Then her voice got clear again. "He says he's a little bit o' this and a little bit o' that."

"Great. Do you want me to come and get you?"

"Go fuck yourself, Monica."

The line went dead.

My car was the only one in the driveway, but the house lights were on. I got out and went inside.

"How did it go?" Darren was in my kitchen, wiping the counter. He had a key. He might as well have moved in. Fucker. I hated him and everything. He looked up at me when I didn't answer. "What happened?"

I had no words. I slipped my arms around his waist and held him tightly. He smelled nice.

He leaned his cheek against my head and stroked my back. "Is it the rich guy?"

"Yes and no."

"Where's Gabby?"

I let my hands drop and banged my forehead against his chest. "WDE set us up. It could have been a mistake, but it wasn't. I can feel it. We ended up in different studios, and she's with Theo right now, self-medicating."

"At least she's not alone. Theo's a fuckup, but he won't let her kill herself." He put his hands on my shoulders and pushed me away, looking into my face. "Did you do the scratch cut?"

"Yes."

"Oh thank God, Mon."

"I feel like I ditched her."

He shook his head. "They'd never reschedule, but if the cut's good, they'll send it out, and then you have a leg to stand on."

I dropped my bag on the floor and plopped onto a kitchen chair. "Well, we won't have to worry about that. It was the single worst performance of my life."

"Come on."

"Really."

"Because of my sister?"

I leaned on the table, lacing my fingers in my hair. "No."

"Do you want some tea?"

"Yes, please." I stood. "I'll make it. You don't even live here."

He pushed me back into the chair. "I can boil water." He pulled the teabags down. "I'm sure it wasn't that bad, Mon. Think about it. Are you just fighting the fraud men?"

The fraud men were the creatures that lived inside every artist's brain, rearing their ugly heads any time something good happened and telling them that they were useless, talentless hacks who had only gotten lucky. "No, I really blew it. Couldn't hold a note. I was ... distracted."

"By?" He plopped the teapot on the stove and turned to me, leaning on the counter with his arms crossed.

Could I tell him? And if I didn't, who *would* I tell? I took a deep breath and got ready for the red heat to rise in my face. "Jonathan's a little kinky."

Darren raised an eyebrow. "Oh, dear."

"Please don't embarrass me."

He yanked a chair out from the table, sat, and put his elbows on the table. "Kinky billionaire meets hot waitress. It's a cliché of a cliché. I love it. Does he make you spank him?"

The prickly heat finally hit my cheeks. "It's the other way around."

"*No.*"

I nodded while scratching a nonexistent piece of crud from the tabletop. "I mean, we haven't gotten that far yet, but basically, that's the nature of us in bed. He tells me to do stuff, and I do it. And he's rough. Really rough. He wants a more, I guess, *intense* version of what's been happening, and I'm freaked out."

"Does he have a dungeon?"

I buried my face in my hands and gave a muffled "No" from behind my palms. I opened them. "I don't think so."

He paused, rubbing his chin, then leaned even farther across the table. "And he wants you to be his *official* fuck toy?"

"Oh God, Darren!"

"I haven't heard you say that in years."

I got up so fast the chair dropped behind me. "I'm really upset, Darren, and all you want to do is make jokes." I turned off the burner and set about making tea. "He thinks I'm a natural submissive, which is code for, like, doormat and beneath him, and yeah, it's code for Jonathan's little fucking fuck toy. And I know what you're going to say. You're going to say I'm no man's whore. And you're right. I'm not. I'm not some submissive little kitten or his god damn punching bag. What the fuck is he thinking? And you *know* what I'm thinking."

"I have no idea what you're thinking."

I held up the teapot. "Do you want some?"

"Sure."

"Sugar?"

"Monica?"

"What?"

"You were saying something about what you were thinking."

I poured the tea. Darren didn't take sugar and neither did I, but I'd needed a second to avoid saying something stupid. "I can't say it."

"You're no man's whore."

I stared at the tea as it steeped. "I know."

"But you're falling for him."

The strength went out of my spine. I hated Darren for bringing it up and for seeing through me, yet I was grateful he'd said what I couldn't. "He's witty," I said. "And confident and affectionate. And he looks at me like I'm the only woman in the world. And you can make fun but ... the sex is ..." I searched for the right word and came up with nothing adequate. "I'm a fuck toy whore, aren't I?"

Darren got up for his tea, since I was falling down on the job. "I'll tell you the truth. I don't like hearing someone is treating you like that. It upsets me. I'd actually like to punch him in the face a little." He poured the hot water. "You've been alone too long. You're vulnerable. You're doing things you wouldn't normally do."

"Yeah."

"If you want to date again, you should have tried dating, you know?"

"I want to rib you for not dating forever, then turning up gay. But I can't. It's right for you. This ... I don't think this is right for me." I pulled the bag out of my cup and pressed it until it was a sack of damp leaves. "Too bad."

"Gabby was triangulating him against every other person in Los Angeles, and she said she came up with something she wanted to show you. It didn't sound good."

"Great. Secrets. Love those."

"Come on," Darren rubbed my shoulders. "Let's go watch a stupid movie and talk about Kevin's thing. I'm bored, and I've decided I'd love to make that guy crazy."

We never did speak about Kevin's thing. We never even watched a movie. We lay on the couch and watched a string of shows about rock stars with debilitating drug addictions who redeemed themselves in their fifties. I fell asleep on Darren's chest, where I felt as safe and comfortable as when I was with Jonathan.

I dreamed of some nether desert where the sky spoke in narrators, laugh tracks, and commercials, and I kneeled in the sand and put my hands in my pants to relieve the ache that had become water to me.

I woke up to the sound of Darren on the phone. Morning Stretch was muted. Darren's voice squeaked, but I thought nothing of it. The fullness of my bladder pushed against some sexual part of my insides, making me feel engorged and ready. I wanted to fuck.

I went to my room, crawled into bed, and pulled the legal pad I used for middle-of-the-night ideas from the nightstand. I wrote:

What if he collars me? Slaps me? Spanks me? Bites me? Fucks me in the ass? Whips me?

Hurts me? Displays me? Gags me? Blindfolds me? Shares me? Humiliates me? Ties me down? Makes me bleed? Fucks me up?

I couldn't write any more. My imagination kept coming up with new things to do, and they got more and more horrible as I dug deeper.

I went to the bathroom and sat on the bowl, in the dark, trying not to wake up too much. I'd defined something about Jonathan during my conversation with Darren, and though I was comforted at having come to a conclusion, I was saddened at the decision.

There was a tap on the door.

"Mon?" Darren whispered.

"Use the other bathroom."

"They found Gabrielle." He sounded so calm I thought he meant something innocuous. "I have to identify the body."

I stood up, my pants around my knees. "What?"

He asked softly, "Can you come with me?"

CHAPTER 51

In my life, I'd experienced grief like I experienced love. Deeply and with very few people.

My father had been taken from me when I was nineteen. I didn't see much of him, even when he wasn't deployed. My mother owned him, up in buttfuck Castaic, two hours north of the den of sin and temptation I called home. The news came through her, icily framed as a happier existence with a benevolent God. I didn't want to talk to her about how it happened. I ended up on the phone with his supervisor at Tomrock, who told me he'd taken mortar fire while escorting a Saudi prince to the central mosque in Kabul. I had told Dad he should have stayed in the military, that privatizing himself would leave him unprotected, but he was tired of listening to politically motivated orders dressed up as patriotism. If he was walking into death, he wanted it called that, and he wanted to be paid to take those risks. No fanfare. No dressing up in the flag. Dad was real. He wanted life so real it hurt. He'd been shot twice, stabbed once, and had his bell rung more than a few times in neighborhood brawls. He still held the door open for my mother after twenty years of marriage and loved her like a queen, even though she didn't deserve it.

When he was killed, I thought I'd go insane. I felt unmoored, unsafe, orphaned. I found myself pulling the car over and checking directions to places I'd been to a hundred times. I called Darren twice as often, just to hear the voice of someone who loved me. I didn't want to go outside if I could avoid it. The only thing that saved me, besides Darren and Gabby, was music. Dad had taught me piano. He approved of my pursuits. So when I played, especially when I played in front of people, I felt safe again. As the years passed, I found other ways to feel secure and loved, and grief slipped away so slowly I didn't notice when it became a dull ache of memory brought on by some corner of the house or Dad's mandarin tree in the backyard.

Grief had been hiding, ready for the next time. So when Darren and I listened to the lady cop tell us that Gabby had been found, drowned, two miles north of the Santa Monica Pier, I listened, but I was too busy trying to keep the bucket of grief from tipping. Darren needed me, and if I fell into a cacophony of emotion, I wasn't going to be there for him.

We stood by a Plexiglas window, watching a sheet-covered gurney get wheeled into the adjacent room. I felt that bucket of sorrow tip and empty, dropping its contents from my throat to my heart. It sloshed around when I moved, and I thought I would be emptying it with a teaspoon.

I didn't know what Darren was feeling, initially. He identified his sister, who looked bloated and blue, then turned to leave. He collapsed into my arms, weeping. I did my best to hold him up, but the lady cop with the inky curly hair had to help me get him to her desk.

Lady Cop brought us water and a box of tissues. "Was she on any medication?"

"Marplan," Darren whispered.

"Did she mix it with alcohol?"

He grabbed my hand. "We should have gotten her. We shouldn't have trusted Theo. Fuck. Of all people."

I wasn't buying it. "She was drinking, sure, but I thought she drowned," I said to Lady Cop.

"Technically, yes. But what happens is people overdo, and because their judgment is compromised, they go for a swim. Their breath is shallower, and their coordination is poor, so they succumb." She paused in a way that felt practiced and professional. "I'm sorry."

We signed some papers. They wanted to know where to send the body. I gave the name of the funeral home my dad went to because I had no room in my brain for anything else, and Darren was too emotionally brutalized to make any kind of decision. I didn't know how we were going to walk out of there, but we did, slowly, because the farther away we got from the police station, the farther behind we left Gabby. We stopped dead in the parking lot, holding hands, immovable.

"I don't think I can go home," he said.

"You can stay with me."

"No."

"What about Adam?"

Darren just stared into the distance, his face a blank. I didn't know what to do next. He had no family except Gabby. I was *it*, and I had no idea how to help him. His gaze fixed on something, and I followed it. Theo closed the door on his Impala and came toward us, his gait a little crooked. I squeezed Darren's hand tighter.

"Let's just go," I said. "Don't try and deal with anything today." I pulled him toward the Honda. "Please."

He looked down at me, big blue eyes lined with webs of red.

"We have so much to do," I said. "I need you. Please."

He blinked as if some of what I said got through.

Theo was getting closer, waving and trotting as if he thought he might miss us. I pulled Darren away and tried to shoot Theo a warning look. I wasn't a praying person, but I prayed there would be no fights. No accusatory words. No defenses. No excuses. I shoved Darren into the passenger side just as Theo reached us.

"Lassie..." he said.

"Back up, Theo." I strode to my side of the car.

"I have feelings about it too. I stopped her from jumping off the Ferris wheel."

"I'll let you know when we have the funeral if you have the balls to come," I said as I opened the door.

"You're the one who betrayed her. You did that scratch track without her."

I slammed the door before Darren could hear another word.

"I'm going to kill him," Darren said.

"Not today."

I knew that I had a limited time to figure it all out. I felt the thoughts I didn't want to have push against the defensive wall that kept me functioning. I needed that wall. It was the percussion section, keeping the beat, organizing the symphony of reactions and decisions that needed to happen. Without it, the whole piece was going to shit.

I pulled out of the parking lot. Theo got small in my rearview. "We need to make arrangements," I said. "Are you up for it, or am I driving you home?"

"I don't know what to do."

"Do you have money?"

He shook his head. "There was a life insurance policy. For both of us. In case. I checked it when she tried the last time."

"Okay. Let's take care of it. Then, I don't know." I took his hand at the red light. "Let's just keep our shit together until the sun goes down."

"Then what?"

"We fall apart."

We made it home before sunset. The funeral home had dealt with worse, and we did what the bereaved often did. We dumped everything in their laps and let them tell us what we had to do. Darren signed the forms to allow them to retrieve the body. We let them arrange a cremation. There would be no big funeral, no open casket, just a thing at my house. I didn't know what you called such a thing, but the funeral director seemed to know and nodded, letting it slide.

Then we ran back to my house and made phone calls, sprawled on the couch together. I'd called three people I knew weren't around, leaving messages and moving on, when I heard Darren weeping Adam's name into his phone. I felt glad enough to leave him alone. He needed someone besides me. He'd lost his sister, his only family. He deserved to have someone else to love him.

But my gladness was shouted down by something darker, more insidious, more selfish. A deep, evil stab of loneliness that I would have done best to ignore. I should have stayed in the living room to have Darren's warm body next to me, but he needed to be alone. He wouldn't want to go to Gabby's room, and I didn't feel right forcing him onto the porch. So I slipped into my room, crawled under the covers, and hugged my pillow, wondering who was going to braid my hair tomorrow.

CHAPTER 52

I texted Debbie, asking for a few days off and explaining that my best friend had died. She called, but I rejected it. I got dinged and blooped and buzzed a hundred times over by everyone we had ever known. I answered some, thanking people for their condolences, but I just wanted to be left alone, so I shut off the phone and cocooned myself under the covers.

I got out of bed the next night. The house was empty. I showered, ate a few crackers, and went back to bed.

I turned my phone back on, got under the covers, and scrolled through all the kind words and long messages. I resented them. I was grateful for them. I wanted to be around people and eviscerate the longing, lonely hole in my body. I'd earned the isolation and wanted nothing to do with another living soul. Fuck everybody. I needed them. I hated them.

I tried to remember things about my friend, nice stories to cheer me under the dark, damp covers, but my brain wouldn't jog anything loose. I could only remember our most hackneyed scenes. Graduation day. The last time I had seen her, the last time I spoke to her. Everything else was scorched earth, as if it had never happened, or like some mature, godly part of me was protecting the weak, repellent part of me from more hurt by refusing to release painful data.

Someone knocked on the door at some point, maybe just some delivery person, but it woke me up. I scrolled through my messages. *So sorry/That's terrible/Can I bring you something to eat?* Et cetera, et cetera. Everyone was so sweet, but I didn't know how to accept their kindness. The phone vibrated in my hand, and though I'd been ignoring it for however many hours, I looked at this message.

—Debbie told me—

I didn't know how to respond to Jonathan. We weren't in a place in our relationship where I could ask him for anything or expect him to intuit what I needed. His text made me feel lonelier than any other. I answered, feeling as if I were shouting down an empty alley.

*—Tell her I'm going to work day
after tomorrow—*

—What are you doing now?—

—I'm under my covers—

—Alone?—

—yes—

—A crime—

I smiled, and the feeling of levity cracked the brittle shell of sorrow, if only for a second, and tears streamed down my face.

—Don't make me laugh, fuckhead—

*—May I join you under those
lucky covers?—*

When I read the message, I didn't feel his request in my loins but on my skin. I wanted him to touch me. Kiss me. Breathe on me. Talk to me. Hold me for hours. The desire wasn't just between my legs, but in my rib cage, my marrow, my fingertips. Could I give up the consuming protection of loneliness and indulge in a few hours with Jonathan? Was I worthy of a little comfort? Probably not. And I hadn't forgotten the submissive thing. No. He was going to drag me into a pit of defilement and humiliation. Seeing him would only draw him closer to me than he should be, ever.

—I need you—

I hit send. I shouldn't have. I should have made a much cooler, more distant statement. At the very least, I should have been witty in admitting I was a filthy, repugnant mess of need. But I didn't. Three words and I'd debased myself.

I felt hopeful for the first time in days. I got out of bed and crawled into the shower, setting it for hotter than it needed to be. I had no idea how long I'd been in bed, but it was seven in the morning according to my clock. I hadn't seen or heard from Darren, and I assumed he was with Adam. I should have called him, but the idea of reaching out, even to the only person in the world who would understand my sense of failure, made me flinch as if my face would get slapped.

My skin was raw and pink from heat and friction when I stepped out of the shower. I dried my hair and pulled out my brush. A twisted black hair tie was wrapped around the handle. Gabby had put it there when she worked on my hair for the Eclipse show. I put my palm on my wet hair and stroked downward, curling my fingers to gather a strand, just enough to string a bow. The sensation was nothing like when Gabby did it with her care and artistry. And all that was gone. All that talent went into the nothing and nowhere. All the music she would have made would never exist.

I hurled myself under the covers, naked and half wet, grabbing my phone on the way.

—don't come nevermind—

I heard a phone ding from the living room and, soon after, a voice so close it shocked me.

"Too late," Jonathan said. "Your front door was open."

—go away—

A blast of cold air hit me as the covers were moved, and in the next breath, I caught his new scent. He pulled the covers over us just as his phone dinged. He pressed his front to my back, spooning me, his clothes taking on the dampness I hadn't gotten around to toweling off.

"I'm sorry, Monica." He put his face in my wet hair and draped his arm around me. "Ah. What's this text I have here? It says *go away*."

I sniffled.

He slid his arm under my neck and held the phone in front of our faces with both hands. His breath tickled my ear. "Let me text back. Hang on."

—I'd rather be here for you—

I waited for it to appear on my phone. He nuzzled into the hair pooling at the back of my neck as I typed back.

—And then what?—

His fingers flew across the glass.

*—And let's talk about the rest
later. Today, you are the goddess
my universe revolves around.—*

In the seconds it took my phone to bloop, I had a million thoughts, not the least of which was that he was crazy. Out of his mind. Didn't he see who he was curled against? For fuck's sake, I'd killed my best friend, first with carelessness and then with ambition.

201

I started texting back:

—*you have the wrong...*

But then I felt his lips on my shoulder and his warm breath on my skin, and my sorrow dropped out of me. I couldn't finish. My chest hitched and heaved, and the tears came so hard I couldn't breathe. His arms held me tight from behind, and his voice twisted itself into little nothings of comfort. I went into a timeless blackness where I let everything spill out, because he'd catch it. I knew in every cough and sob, every hitched breath and chest spasm, that he'd hold me together. Whatever fell apart, he'd put right. I couldn't curse him for not being everything I needed or failing to commit to me completely. I didn't have space to reject his idea that I was submissive or the will to deny him control over me. He was there, and he was exactly what I needed.

When the crying slowed, I turned to face him. In the dark, I found his lips by following his breath and kissed him. He opened his mouth, stroking my tongue with his in a gentle dance. I wove my legs into his.

"Thank you," I whispered, breathing it without a voice.

He started to answer, but I kissed away whatever came next. I pushed my hips into him. He was hard, and I was ready. I kissed him again, so I wouldn't hear any objections when I pulled his shirt from his waistband. I wanted him naked against me. I wanted to feel good, if only for a minute, and to forget everything for as long as it took us to bind together and fall apart. I hadn't earned it, but I wanted it.

A little light went on under the covers, and a bloop preceded a ding, but we ignored it. He rolled on top of me, mouth attached to mine, and stroked the length of my body. I gasped. The touch was so comforting, so distracting, a bow suddenly dragged across silent strings.

"Hello? Mon?" The voice sounded far away.

Jonathan and I separated.

"What was that?" Jonathan asked.

I twisted around. My phone was lit up under me. I must have rolled on top of it and answered the call by accident. Too late to reject the call.

"Hello? Darren?" I whispered. For some reason, I couldn't engage my vocal cords.

"I'm downtown."

Jonathan pulled the covers off us, and the light seemed as blinding as the air was cold. I already missed his warmth on my body.

"I need you to post bail, or I'm going to miss the wake." He sounded dead, emotionless. "I found Theo. I hurt him. There are bail places all around here. So can you come?"

"Yes, I'll come."

"Thank you."

I glanced at Jonathan as Darren started giving me the details. He was still fully clothed in a blue polo shirt and jeans, sitting up against the wall. I was naked and crouched beside him. He stroked my shoulder.

"What happened?" he asked when I clicked off.

"Darren beat up Gabby's boyfriend. I have to bail him out."

"Why are you whispering?"

I shrugged. I had no idea. All I knew was, I could whisper fine, but I couldn't speak out loud.

"You're not speaking at the wake, I guess?"

I shook my head.

"Where's it going to be?"

"Here."

He looked at his watch. "In seven hours? Are you prepared? How many people?"

"It's tomorrow."

"Debbie said it was Saturday. Today."

Oh God. Darren had said he'd miss the wake, and I thought he meant he'd miss it tomorrow. How long had I been under the covers? Had I slept more than I thought? I stood up, panicked. It was Saturday. I had to put out food. Clean the house. Make myself emotionally presentable. And I had to bail Darren out of jail? With what money? And what time?

I must have been a sight, naked in the middle of my room, hands out, not knowing what to do first. Jonathan got up and grabbed my wrists. I had no words.

"Calm down."

I nodded.

"I'm going to take care of it."

"No," I whispered. "It's my job."

He held my hands, pressing them together between his palms. He spoke in the voice that broached no questions, but he didn't tell me to spread my legs or come. "I have to work for a few hours today. I'll send a crew here to clean up, and I'll get food in. How many people?"

"Jonathan. Please. I don't want it to be like this, like I'm using you."

"You're not using me. You're mine. You are my own personal goddess. It's my job to make sure you're happy. And if I can't make you happy, I won't feel right if you're not taken care of as best as I can. So please, tell me how many people so I can feel right."

"A hundred?" I whispered.

How was I going to fit a hundred people in my thousand-square-foot house? Jesus, what were Darren and I thinking? Jonathan squeezed my hands and brought my attention back to his face. He seemed unfazed by the size of the guest list.

"I have this," he said. "I can take care of it between doing ten other things. Lil will take you downtown. I don't want you driving. Do you have enough to get him out?"

My mouth opened, but not even a whisper came. Did I have enough to bail Darren out of jail? I had no idea. How much did something like that cost? And how was I going to actually take money from Jonathan? I'd get my mother to mortgage the house if necessary. I'd supplicate myself before her, promise to stay on the narrow path, and eat four tons of shit on a hot tar shingle to get Darren out in time for his sister's funeral, but I wasn't taking money from Jonathan.

I nodded. "I have it."

He kissed me tenderly, stroking my cheek with his thumb. "I'll be in touch. Pick up the phone, okay?"

I nodded because I didn't want to whisper again.

Jonathan left gingerly, as if turning his back on me long enough to get to work making arrangements to prepare my house for a wake was going to give me enough time to fall apart again. He walked backward to the Jag, watching me, the red in his hair catching the morning sun. I waved and even managed to smile a little. I was determined to get through this, even if it meant pretending my shit was together long enough to restore his faith in me. When he drove down the hill, I felt as if he pulled part of me with him.

Lil showed up in Jonathan's Bentley spaceship thirty minutes later.

"Ms. Faulkner," she said. "How are you holding up?"

"Fine."

"Something wrong with your voice?"

I shrugged. I didn't know what was wrong with me, whether it was my voice or my mind or something else entirely, some trick of the universe. I was getting frustrated. The condition I'd initially attributed to too many tears and hurt was starting to feel like something more intractable.

"I wanted to say," Lil said, "and I hope I'm not being inappropriate, but my wife's brother took his own life. So my sympathies. It can be hardest on the family."

I screwed my face up, trying not to cry again, because she'd called Gabby family. She was exactly that. My sister. And having that recognized was like a bucket of cold water. "Thanks, Lil," I whispered.

"Where are we going today?"

"Going to bail my brother out of jail."

Five thousand dollars.

Apparently, Darren had gone after Theo with a broken bottle, which according to the State of California was a deadly weapon.

So, five large. Cash.

I swallowed hard.

The big lady with the skinny glasses behind the bulletproof glass seemed sympathetic. She'd tolerated my whispering and slid a notepad under the glass once she realized I could hear fine but couldn't speak.

"There's three bondsmen across the street. You pay five hundred, and they forward us the rest. But you don't get it back. Kaylee. That's the one I like. Best with first-timers and ain't no glass in between you so she'll hear that little voice you got. All right, young lady?"

I nodded, ripping the page from the notebook. I took the papers and forms she gave me that detailed Darren's infractions and went outside.

Lil stood by the car, which was perched in a loading zone, pretty as you please. She handed me a paper cup of tea. I didn't know how she knew I liked tea. I didn't know if Jonathan had detailed all my foibles and preferences to her or if she just paid incredible attention, but I took it and thanked her.

"I have to go to the bondsman." I pointed across the street at a yellow and black sign marked Kaylee's Bailbonds.

Lil opened the car door.

"It's just across the street." I had to lean in close to Lil so she'd hear me over the din of rush hour traffic.

"I told Mister Drazen I'd take care of you. So just get in. I have to drive around to the parking lot anyway."

I got in, feeling silly and childish. I could have run across the street in half the time, quarter-time if I jaywalked. But Lil was doing her job with sincerity and kindness, and I didn't have the heart to disrupt her. I sipped my tea in the backseat, hoping the hot liquid would reconnect my voice to my lungs, but when I tried to make a sound, there was only breath.

I felt that there was a choice at the deepest parts of my being not to speak, some fear that my voice would break the world or call up beasts that would rend me and everything I loved to tatters. But I couldn't locate that dark place and explain that it was doing more harm than good, that I needed the fear to go away, that everything in my life would be torn to shreds by simple inaction if I couldn't function as an artist and member of society.

I breathed. Panic was going to get me nowhere. I had to get through the day and bail Darren out in time for the wake. Sleep. Eat. Go to work tomorrow. Breathe. I would figure it out if I could keep the anxiety at bay.

Lil pulled in behind the bondsman place and let me out as if I were a celebrity arriving at a red carpet event. "Mister Drazen said if you needed anything, I should let you know he'll take care of it."

"Thanks."

"You should let him help you." She gave me a meaningful look that said she knew I had reservations about taking help from Jonathan.

I nodded to her and walked through the back door.

The space had no aesthetic pretentions whatsoever. The grey industrial carpet was worn in the high-traffic areas. The fluorescent lights buzzed behind the dropped ceiling, yellowing the piles of papers lying on every surface, every metal shelving unit, veneer desk, and unoccupied black chairs. The occupied chairs, three of them, held people of varying ages and ethnicities, all talking on phones or tapping into aged beige computers. Out the front windows, downtown Los Angeles hummed by.

A middle-aged woman in big dark glasses shuffled past in slippers and a multicolored shift. Her coffee cup was one third full of sludge.

"Hi," I whispered. "I'm looking for Kaylee?"

"Cat got your tongue?"

"Laryngitis." It was the only answer I could come up with that would make any sense. Telling her a part of me thought using my voice would shatter the world might have seemed a little crazy.

"You putting up a bond?"

"Yes. I don't know how."

"You got cash?"

"Some."

"Go on and sit by the desk at the front."

I did, slipping into the cushioned office chair placed in front of it. The bronze plaque that was really made of plastic had the name KAYLEE RECONAIRE cut into it. I had about two hundred dollars on me, which was more than usual because I'd never emptied my bag from my last shift at the Stock.

The lady with the sludge coffee placed herself on her chair with a sigh. "Do you have the forms?" She held out her hand.

I handed over the stack. She had exactly enough clear space on her desk to look at them, spreading them into three neat piles. The pink stub, the stapled and clipped form, all had a place.

"Any relation?" she asked.

"No."

"Boyfriend?"

"No."

"So?" She leaned her elbows on the desk. "We have to assess if he's a flight risk. It's our money you're talking about, so there will be personal questions. Like, does this gentleman care if you're responsible for him? This is not just assault." She indicated the papers. "It's battery with a deadly weapon, honey." She raised an eyebrow as if I were some girlfriend battered into bailing out her own personal douchebag.

I leaned in so she could hear me. "We broke up a long time ago. He's like a brother to me. He's not some ex I can't stop fucking because I'm insecure."

Kaylee looked at me for a second before laughing. "You nuts, girl. You got a job?"

"I'm a waitress at the Stock downtown." I swung my thumb behind me since it was about five blocks north.

"How much cash you got?"

"I have two hundred on me."

"You're short three."

"I can go to the ATM," I said.

"You can only get two hundred from the machine." She blinked. I blinked. Then she said, "I ain't letting you off the hundred. I'm running a business here."

"You take collateral?"

She gave a knowing, snorty kind of laugh. "Whatever collateral you got, I gotta hold in my hand, and it's gotta be worth ten times what I need. I don't see any jewelry on you I'd take."

I stood and picked up my shirt, showing her the Harry Winston navel ring. I was stepping in a pile of shit, and I knew it. Using my current boyfriend's gift to bail my past boyfriend out of jail was the stuff Jerry Springer shows were made of.

Kaylee leaned forward, dropping her glasses low on her nose. "That real?"

"Yes."

She held out her hand, her face a mask of disbelief. I took out the diamond and handed it to her. She snapped open the top drawer of her desk, pulled out a jeweler's glass, and used it to inspect the diamond, which to me, looked like the hugest, most sparkly thing ever dug from the earth. I sat back down as she made little humming noises, turning the rock around under the glass.

She slid it back to me. "I can get in big trouble, young lady. I don't think you understand I'm running a business here. I don't take stolen merchandise."

I gasped. How could she? Was she insane? I was absolutely stunned wordless by the implication.

A lone, male voice cut through my distress. "Whose Bentley's in my spot?" A man with a crutch and a leg of his jeans rolled up over a missing calf wobbled in.

I raised my hand, whispering, "Sorry."

He sat at a desk. "Well, have that driver move it."

I looked back down at Kaylee. She was already slipping my diamond navel bar into a baggie. "You come back with the rest soon, you hear? Or for the love of three hundred dollars, your new man's gonna be pissed."

CHAPTER 55

I hadn't realized how big the Bentley was until Darren sat on the other side of the backseat as if he wanted nothing to do with me. It had taken me hours to get him out. Money had to be wired, forms shot over the internet, phone calls made, signatures garnered, and he had to be driven from a holding area two blocks away.

When they'd brought him, he looked tired but made a funny face when he saw me waiting, as if to let me know he was okay. When they took the cuffs off and released him into my custody, he hugged me so hard I thought he'd break something.

"Thank you, thank you," he said into my neck.

"You're welcome. Now we have to go, or we're going to be missed."

He nodded, and I wondered if he'd gotten himself in trouble to avoid the funeral.

"Why are you whispering?"

"Laryngitis."

"What? You weren't sick—"

I pulled him into the hallway, wanting to be away from the bulletproof glass and linoleum flooring. Then I stopped and moved my wrist like Debbie so often did to let him know it was time to get moving on the story.

"I went to Adam's," he said. "He stayed with me all night, but he had to go to work, and I just walked around Silver Lake. I sat at a table at Bourgeois for half the day. Fabio knew what happened, so he just kept bringing me new cups."

The elevator doors opened, and a carload of people got out. I pulled Darren to the side.

"He should have called me," I whispered.

"He did."

Right. I'd rejected calls and ignored texts while I lay in my undercover cave.

We got into the elevator with twenty other people.

Darren spoke softly into my ear. "I realized while I was in there that I left you alone. I'm sorry about that."

I shrugged and waved his concern away. I was unhappy about it, but I didn't have the heart to hold it against him. And it had brought Jonathan to me.

Darren continued, "Theo came in for coffee, like he always does. I knew he went there all the time. I didn't realize I was waiting for him. But anyway, some girl at the table next to me had one of those pomello sodas. I smacked the bottle against the floor and went for his throat."

"Holy shit, Darren!" I managed to whisper loudly and with emphasis. I glanced around at the people in the elevator. No one was staring, but they must have been listening.

"He's fine. I got his cheek. I aim like the fag I am."

I pinched his side, and he cried, "Ow!" We laughed. The rest of the elevator population seemed relieved to get away from us when the doors slid open on the parking lot level. Lil was parked in an Authorized Vehicle Only spot, reading the L.A. *Times*.

When Darren saw the Bentley, he stopped in his tracks. "Where'd you get the money to bail me out? Five grand? That's a lot of cash."

"I put up a bond."

"Did one penny of that come from *him?*"

"Stop."

"I'm not having any part of you being a whore."

I didn't know what came over me, maybe the stress of the past few days, maybe the insult, or maybe the fact that I couldn't speak properly to defend myself. But a ball of kinetic energy ran from my heart and down my right arm, and in order to release it, the only thing I could do was slap Darren across the face.

The *clap* of it echoed through the parking lot. Lil looked up from her paper. Darren crouched from the impact. The feeling of regret dropped into my belly even as my hand wanted to slap him again and again.

I folded it into a fist and stuck out my index finger. "Get in the car. If you are one minute late for your sister, Theo's face will look handsome in comparison." My throat was getting sore from all the harsh whispering, but I was sure I could lecture him for another half-hour if I had to.

He looked enraged with the red marks across his cheek, and his mouth was set in stone, the muscles of his face making tense lines in his jaw. I was a little afraid. Just a little, because I could fight, and I could take a hit. I would do both if I had to.

"The car is ready," Lil said, suddenly standing beside us with her calm, professional demeanor. She held out her hand toward the open back door of the Bentley. "Please."

I thought for a moment he'd opt for the bus, but I knew he had no money on him, because it had come back to me in an envelope of personal effects, along with a pocket knife he wasn't allowed to carry and a few credit cards. He also knew that public transportation would take hours on a Saturday. Despite his self-sabotage, he didn't want to miss Gabby's wake.

I nodded at Lil and walked toward the car, not looking behind me to see if he followed. My shoes clonked on the concrete, made louder from the enclosed space. I climbed into the back seat of the car and slid over, looking out the window so I wouldn't see if he was coming or not. If he saw me watching him, he would be more likely to turn around and take the bus out of pride.

I heard him get in, and the door snapped closed. That was when I discovered how wide that car really was.

Lil dropped him in front of his house. He didn't wait for her to open the door for him. There was a pause. I didn't look at him, but I held out the yellow receipt from Kaylee as I whispered, "Three hundred. Cash."

I felt the paper get snapped from my hand and heard the door close with that satisfying, low-pitched *thup* you get with expensive cars. I only dared to look when he was walking up his steps, head down, yellow receipt crumpled in his hand. I wanted to run up and hug him. He couldn't be held responsible for acting like an ass after what had happened with Gabby, but I wouldn't apologize. Yes, he'd insulted me, but he'd also insulted Jonathan, and somehow, that rankled me even more.

CHAPTER 56

The house was transformed. The front yard was trimmed like a poodle, hedges cut back, fallen oranges picked up and put into bowls at the porch railing, weeds and dead things gone.

"I'll let you know if I have to go anywhere for Mister Drazen," Lil said as she blocked the driveway behind a catering truck with chocks under the wheels.

I nodded, my throat too wrecked for one unnecessary word.

"Monica!" Carlos, our neighbor from two doors down, ran toward me holding a manila envelope. He was a cop and very protective of everyone on the block. "Hi, I heard what happened. I'm real sorry about it."

"Thanks."

"She had me look stuff up for her sometimes. About people. Celebrities and agents."

"Really?"

"Yeah," he smiled sweetly. "She took me out to dinner or something in exchange."

I wondered what "or something" meant and decided I was fine not knowing.

He handed me the envelope. "This was the last thing."

I took it and patted him on the arm. "Will I see you later?"

"Yeah. I'll come by."

We parted, and I headed for the house. I walked up the steps to the porch, which had been swept. Potted plants had appeared, giving the sense that the porch was a well thought-out, finished space. Yvonne, who I hadn't seen since the night I stopped working at Hotel K, almost knocked me over as she strode out to the catering truck.

"Whoa! Monica!" She smiled and kissed my cheek. "You working this gig? Double time. Boo-ya."

Shit. I was going to have to explain, and I didn't have the time, inclination, or vocal capability.

"I live here," I said in breaths.

Yvonne opened her mouth, then snapped it shut, cocking her head. "Girl, they said it was Drazen's girlfriend." Her eyes were wide and her face accusatory in a good-humored way. "I saw a picture on TMZ from that art show. I thought that was you."

"Hello!" Debbie called from inside the house. "Let's keep it moving."

"Later. I'll explain."

"I want *details,*" Yvonne said before kicking up the pace to the truck.

The living room had been transformed as well, with chafing dishes on long tables, new lamps, and clean corners.

Debbie took my hands. "How are you doing?"

"You work at the Stock. Jonathan owns K."

"You do sound terrible. No more talking. I volunteered when I heard. No one from K could do it but Freddie, and he's on probation. Can't get within arm's reach of a waitress, or he'll be cleaning toilets, or so I hear. You know how the rumor mill works. You. Now. We had the bathroom cleaned, so don't leave a mess. Go."

She pushed me across my own living room. I knew three of the people working the wake. All were dressed in catering formals, and all looked at me an extra second before getting back to it. I was mortified. They all thought they were doing an emergency party for the hotel owner's girlfriend, and it was *me.*

I went into my room and closed the door behind me. My closet was full of black. I chose a pair of pants and a sweater. I didn't want anything fancy or special, no bows, sparkly buttons, or short skirts. It didn't matter that Gabby liked it when I went sparkly; I didn't feel sparkly. I felt shitty, and I was going to respect her by wearing something so down and boring I'd be invisible.

I stripped down for a shower, catching a glimpse of myself in the mirror. I was naked, sure, but without that diamond in my navel, I had a worried pang. I couldn't let Jonathan see me without it. I'd have to explain or lie, and I wasn't ready to do either.

I took my shower, dressed, and made up in nudes and neutrals in twenty-four minutes, then texted Jonathan.

—Thanks for everything—

The answer shot back in seconds.

—My pleasure. In a meeting. See you there—

There? He was coming? I didn't know why I hadn't expected that. He'd come to me in minutes when I needed him; he wouldn't sit out my best friend's wake. I kicked off the sensible shoes I'd chosen and slipped into the red-soled pumps from the Eclipse show.

Carlos's envelope lay on my bed. I cracked it open and slid out a single sheet of paper. The heading was for Westonwood Acres, an exclusive retreat that was actually a mental institution. The paper was an admission form, and I froze when I saw the name of the admitted.

Jonathan S Drazen III

His age was right next to the date, so I didn't have to calculate that he had been sixteen. Everything else was blacked out with thick lines.

That was what Gabby had to tell me. I shoved the paper back in the envelope and stuffed it in my drawer with shaking hands.

CHAPTER 57

Darren shuffled up the hill on time. He glanced at me as he passed into the house. I didn't know what he thought of the house's transformation, but I didn't care, and I was ready to defend Jonathan again.

People came, east-side hipsters, west-side musicians, and a few teachers from Colburn who would express sympathy for the vaporized talent. They were all going to want to talk to me. I knew about seventy percent of them by name at least, but the thought of talking to all of them and explaining my "laryngitis" was going to make it ten times the drag it had to be.

I put on my customer-service face. I cleared my throat, which hurt, and smiled at the first person who entered the gate. I nodded, said "laryngitis" while brushing my fingers across my throat, and moved on. After the first few people, it got easier. I just didn't think about anything at all except making the person I was speaking to comfortable. The outward focus helped.

As with the past days of constant calls and texts, I was surprised at how nice people were. They wanted to help, mostly. I left Darren to the inside of the house, and I stayed on the porch, shaking hands and kissing cheeks, smiling as if I were taking drink orders. I stopped seeing faces. I loved them all, *en masse*, without discernment. I was struck by an unexpected, sudden feeling of well-being. By the time Kevin rested his hand on my shoulder, I was at the maximum dose of endorphins.

I threw my arms around him and whispered, "Thanks for coming."

"I'm so sorry, Monica. I know what she meant to you." His hands rubbed my back, and I thought nothing of it.

I spoke softly in his ear. "The thing. The piece. I'm in. Just give me time."

He squeezed me harder. I remembered how he did that in the past, tensing his biceps until I thought my ribs would crack.

He let go, but we still stood close, and he spoke softly so no one else would hear. "I pitched it to the Modern of British Columbia in Vancouver. For Christmas. They had an unexpected opening. Can we make it?" He pulled back and looked into my eyes, keeping his hand on my neck, a touch too familiar, too intimate, but I didn't pull away.

"Let's talk about it," I whispered.

"Once you can talk," Kevin said, smiling.

His scent alerted me to his presence. The new one. Sawdust and leather with light harmonies of an ass-bruising all-night fuck. I turned and found Jonathan behind me in a black suit built for him, a grey shirt, and a black tie. The dark colors brought out his sleek ginger hair and jade eyes.

He held out his hand to Kevin. "Good to see you again," he said, voice tense and overly polite. His eyes were hard stones, and he smiled in a way that could be mistaken for baring his teeth. I'd never seen that look on his face before, and I didn't like it. Not one little bit.

I remembered the piece of paper in the manila envelope. Could I be seeing a symptom of whatever it was that had sent him to a mental hospital? Fuck, I knew I couldn't ask him about it, and now I'd always wonder.

"Of course," Kevin replied. Then he looked at me and did something that he had no right to do. He touched my arm and said, "I'll call you about the piece," before walking into the house.

Jesus fucking Christ, was I really being subjected to a male pissing match at Gabby's wake? Really? I missed the luxury of celibacy for a moment, then looked at Jonathan, whose face had softened. "What the hell was that?" I asked.

"Forget it. How has it been so far?"

"I have my game face on." I pulled away and showed him my stage smile.

"Gorgeous. Debbie said there's no casket?"

I shook my head and did everything to make my look tell him I thought the very idea was absurd.

"As a good lapsed Catholic," he said, "I feel the need for an open casket somewhere."

"Not me, and I'm lapsed, too."

He put his arm around me. "My mother is going to love you."

I swallowed hard through a ravaged throat. I had no idea how his parents fit in with me being his submissive whore fucktoy, or if that meant I was to be kept as far away from his family as possible. It was too much to absorb under the circumstances.

I looked away from him. My eyes found Darren and Adam, who were speaking softly in a corner. Darren looked up, and our eyes met. He came over, and I hoped Jonathan wasn't about to have another pissing match.

As if he thought Darren was no threat at all, while Kevin somehow was, Jonathan excused himself to the interior of the house.

"I'm not sorry," Darren said.

I shrugged. Neither was I.

"Adam's going to pick up your thing. Whatever it was."

"Okay." I wanted to ask how long it would take because I didn't want Jonathan to see me without it and end up giving Darren the same ice-cold stare he'd just given Kevin.

I looked at Darren's face. I'd slapped it just two hours ago, and it seemed healed. Gabby'd had bruises on her left cheek when I went to visit her in the hospital, and my hand hadn't fared much better for the nine and a half minutes I'd hit her, because I thought it kept her alive. Maybe it had. I'd never found out because she was in her hospital bed with apologies, and I'd done everything I could to distract her. Everything. There was nothing more I could have done.

I asked, "Did Gabby ever tell you what she had to say about Jonathan?"

"No, but it wasn't good. Why?"

I was suddenly exhausted. My eyes hurt. My shoulders felt as though they were carrying a huge weight, and my beautiful shoes pushed me too far forward.

"Monica?" Darren said, putting his hand on my arm.

I felt Jonathan's presence and stood up straight, shaking it off and putting on my stage smile. Jonathan put his arm around me and guided me to the backyard. I don't know if a look was exchanged with Darren or not, and I didn't care.

Dad had designed the small backyard with private spaces and fruit trees. He'd placed flagstones to make paths and let them get overgrown where they needed to be, bordering hard lines with low jade plants and rocks. I led Jonathan to the back, against the cinderblock wall that kept the hill from sliding over our house. I hadn't looked at the bench in months. It was dirty with leaves and dust. Jonathan wiped it off, and we sat.

"How are you holding up?" he asked, stroking my hair.

I put my arms around his shoulders and kissed the place where his cheek and neck met. "What was that with Kevin?" I needed to know who I was dealing with, and every new piece of information I got pointed to the fact that I had no idea.

"I'm not good at hiding when I'm pissed. I don't like what he did to you." His lips touched my neck and his hand pressed me to his mouth.

"Possessive and jealous are real turn-offs, Jonathan. If you can't trust me—"

"I'm not possessive. I'm protective."

I sighed deeply, forgetting everything as his tongue found the most sensitive place on my throat. "Jonathan ..."

"No talking."

The arm behind the bench brought me closer to him, and the hand at my cheek slid down my chest, landing over my breast, which reacted by getting tight, stiffening the nipple through my sweater. He dragged his fingernail over the hard lump, first lightly, then harder. He slid his face across mine until our noses touched, and I could see the blue specks in his eyes.

He squeezed my nipple hard through my sweater and bra. My mouth opened, but no sound came out. I reached between his legs, where I could feel his erection through his pants.

"No, Monica. This is for you. Put your hands to your sides."

I shook my head.

"I get off on this," he said. "You obeying me is what turns me on. Don't deny me."

I did as I was told, as always: submissive whore fucktoy to someone who neglected to tell me where he'd spent his sixteenth year. I decided to think about it later.

He put his thumb to my lips. "Make this wet."

I took his thumb, and he moved it against my tongue as I sucked, pulling the juices from my mouth to give him what he asked for. Anything he asked for. The tidal wave between my legs demanded it as much as he did.

Our noses still touched as he slid his hand up my sweater, pushing the bra up so he could cup my breast. I panicked a little as he went past my navel, where the diamond should have been, but he went right by it, taking the nipple between his first finger and his moist thumb. I let out a *hah* when he squeezed and twisted.

"Keep your eyes open," he said. "Look at me."

I did as I was told.

He filled my vision when he pulled the nipple. "This is who we are." As if seeing my objection through my arousal, he continued, "You and I. You know that."

He dragged his thumbnail over the stretched nipple, and I opened my mouth, but no words came.

"Your legs are crossed. Spread them."

I did, cursing that I'd worn pants. I wanted his touch on me. I wanted him to feel how wet I was for him. A pang of guilt shot through me for being so turned on at Gabby's wake, but it was drowned out by the roar between my legs when he twisted my nipple again.

"Open the pants."

I unbuttoned and unzipped, keeping the sweater down over my bellybutton.

"Put your hand between your legs," he whispered.

"I can't." Somehow, feeling his touch on me would be all right. Touching myself would seem too self-indulgent.

"Yes, you can. And you will. For me."

I slipped my hand into my panties then stopped.

"Please," he said, not like a plea but a mandate.

My middle finger found my wetness first, gathering over my engorged clit like dew. Jonathan sighed when my expression changed. I put my hand down to my opening, dragging the tingle and heat with it, and circled, gathering the juices between the two fingers, like a metal ball around a roulette wheel.

Jonathan kissed my cheek and stroked my breast, keeping the nipple stiff as I pulled my hand back up to my clit, which was as hard as a marble and soaking wet. I was so close already. My body remembered I'd been lying under the covers with Jonathan, even if my mind had moved on to other things.

"May I come?" I whispered. Things may have changed between us, but one thing did not remain undefined. He owned my orgasms, and I wanted him to have them.

"You are such a good girl."

"May I?"

He waited before answering, kissing my nose, my cheek, caressing my breast. I kept stroking while he surrounded me. My orgasm pushed against me, a pressure inside, asking to get out, begging, needing. I kept telling it, *not yet, not yet* until, all at once, he grabbed my nipple hard enough to hurt and said, "Come."

The tension released like broken strings, everywhere. My body straightened under my own touch, pulsing and clenching from pussy to ass. I opened my mouth, and though I screamed inside, only air came out.

"Don't stop," he said.

I kept my hand moving, and the orgasm continued. My knees bent, and my body crouched and again, like a shot, I went rigid, breathing *ah, ah, ah*. It hurt, and just as I thought I couldn't take it anymore, he said, "Stop."

I fell into his arms like a shuddering mound of jelly.

He laughed. "I think you needed that."

I just leaned my head on his chest, gasping for air.

"You didn't use your voice," he said, stroking my hair. "I thought for sure that would do it."

I shrugged.

"We need to get back inside," he said, "before all your ex-boyfriends come out here, and I have to kill them." He drew his hand over my belly and stopped. He picked up my sweater so he could see my naked navel. "Did you lose it?"

I put purest innocence on my face with a hint of lack of surprise. "Inside." I indicated the direction of the house, but downtown was in the same general direction, and unless it was in transport or being stolen, there was a good chance it was indoors.

He nodded and pulled my sweater down, then watched as I buttoned up. He seemed pensive, and I wondered if he'd become sensitive to contextual lies.

CHAPTER 58

When we got inside, much of the wake had broken up. The wait staff cleaned and put away, making beelines for the catering truck. Only a few people remained. Darren, in particular, looked lost, milling around the leftovers. Adam wasn't anywhere to be seen. Jonathan and Debbie spoke quietly at the door.

A man of about fifty, with round plastic glasses and long straight hair, approached me. "Are you Monica Faulkner?"

When I nodded, he held out his hand. "Jerry Evanston. I saw Gabby that afternoon."

I tilted my head. No memory had been jogged.

"Eugene at WDE asked me to go to DownDawg in Burbank to keep an artist company. It was crazy, but he got me my next gig, and I kind of owed him. I didn't question it. I wanted to say I'm sorry. I didn't know this would happen. Eugene's an asshole, but I knew him in college, and he's always got a favor lined up when I need it."

I nodded and pointed to let him know I knew he was the one who had kept Gabby company while I fucked up the scratch cut by myself. She'd been right. It had been a setup.

"I'd understand if you're pissed."

"It's okay," I whispered. "You didn't know."

"Your partner played for me, and she was brilliant. Eugene said you were really good."

I shrugged. It seemed the simplest way to communicate paragraphs worth of feeling. I was good. I was worthless. I was mute. I was music.

"Your voice okay?"

"Laryngitis."

"I have a proposition for you, because I feel guilty about what happened."

I nodded. The room suddenly seemed stifling with too many people around, and Yvonne giving me the old eyebrow as if I were her source for interesting news.

"Tell me," I said.

"I got this job. It's through Eugene, but that's not going to matter. Carnival Records. I'm working with the EVP to develop new talent."

"Herman Neville?" I asked, feeling like Gabby with her magic hat of names.

Jonathan came up behind me, and I took his hand. I wanted to lean on him more than anything. He and Jerry nodded to each other.

Jerry continued, "Yes. And I have this studio time I booked for Thursday. In Burbank. The talent cancelled this morning, and I thought, if you wanted to do something low production value, all you, we could put something decent together, and I could bring it to him. No promises. But I'd feel better."

"Could it be my song?"

"Well, it would have to be. If you have the voice to sing it, of course."

"Yes." My agreement came out in a breath, and I wondered what the hell I was doing. I had no song. Shit, I had no *voice*. What the fuck was I thinking?

"Great, here's my card."

"Thank you." I stared at it. It just had his name and number. Could have been anyone. And as he left, I thought, he was probably the last person to hear Gabby play.

Jonathan came up behind me as Jerry left, stroking my back, his touch electric even through my sweater. I glanced at Yvonne, who seemed to find our intimacy fascinating in a very "you go, girl" sort of way.

"Are you going to be all right?" he asked softly.

"Tired."

"Do you want to stay with me for a few days?"

My knees almost lost the ability to hold me up. I wanted nothing more than to crawl into the bed of his spare room, where we'd done all our fucking, and let him stroke and spoon me for days. His voice as I drifted off to sleep, the soft touch of his lips on me, and the feeling of being cared for, safe, partnered, were exactly what I wanted with all my heart. I looked into those jade eyes, which expressed none of the smug dominance of the club, only concern, and said, "I can't."

"Why not?"

"You're not a prince, Jonathan. You're a king. But I'm not ready." I touched his face and looked right at him, as if that could transmit the depth of my feelings for him, or my doubts about their prudence.

"I'm trying hard not to be a controlling asshole."

"You're doing a good job."

He left me with a tender kiss that Yvonne saw, and then Darren was gone, too. The staff and all their accoutrements disappeared with Debbie telling me I didn't have to come in tomorrow if I didn't want to. Then it was me in my clean house, alone. The door to Gabby's room was closed. I opened it.

My best friend's knowledge of Hollywood's web of relationships came from hours and hours of hard work. Her dresser was piled with manila envelopes, each with a name. Colored bars in felt tip pen decorated the bottom of each envelope, cross referenced by name, education, job, and personal and family relationships. Stacks of *Variety*, the Calendar section of the *LA Times*, the *New York Times,* and the *Hollywood Reporter* rose in towers around the perimeter of the room. I'd asked her repeatedly to make use of the recycle bin, but she always thought there might be one connection she missed, so she couldn't throw away a shred of paper. In the end, she'd just relegated the mess to her room and closed the door.

 —You ok?—

Jonathan's text came in just as I was considering locking Gabby's door for good.

—Feet hurt. Fine otherwise. I'm
going to bed—

—Good night, goddess—

—We still need to talk—

—When you can talk, we will.
Now get to bed. No touching.
I'll know...—

I was sure he would, somehow. The same way I was sure he knew about the diamond sitting in a baggie downtown.

CHAPTER 59

I wanted to stay in bed for days after Gabby's wake, but I couldn't skip work. I hustled in for the lunch shift dry-eyed and made up. I put on my stage smile for Debbie, who pursed her red lips and seemed generally unimpressed.

"Can you talk?"

I shook my head.

"So what do you think you're going to do?"

My face must have been a complete blank because I had no answer. Debbie sighed and called Robert over from the other side of the bar where he was flirting with two women who looked like cover models. She took my pad from my hands and said to him, "Monica's at the service bar tonight."

"Why? It's lunch."

"Question me again."

Robert was immediately cowed. The tone in Debbie's voice triggered something in me as well. A recognition. A wakefulness. When she glanced over at me and indicated I should go around to the other side of the bar, I knew what it was because I'd heard it from Jonathan's lips. Debbie was a dominant.

The fact that I recognized that told me more about myself than I wanted to know. I'd spent the morning and afternoon in busy sequester, puttering around the house, picking up Gabby's things, and putting them in boxes. The copies of *Variety* on top of the piano. The shoes by the door. The metronome she left by the TV. Music sheets. I'd separated them into *Keep* and *Toss* and then kept everything for Darren anyway. All that time, I heard not her voice in my head, but her music. I sat at the piano and played one of her compositions, the one she played when she was feeling threatened and powerless, the bombastic thing she'd been at just the other night, and I stopped mid-way. I didn't sound as good as she had. Some keys were off, but she never wrote down her own stuff. She only did notations on pieces she heard and was trying to figure out. I'd snapped up a few sheets of the notepaper abandoned in the *Toss* bin and played again, writing down the notes as I went. And then, as if the notes could not be contained as simple sounds, words flowed through them. I had to run for the legal pad by my bed.

What if he collars me? Slaps me? Spanks me? Bites me? Fucks me in the ass? Whips me? Hurts me? Displays me? Gags me? Blindfolds me? Shares me? Humiliates me? Ties me down? Makes me bleed? Fucks me up?

That fucking list. I could have added another hundred things.

Chocks my mouth open. Pulls my hair. Fucks my face. Calls me whore. Tells me to lick the floor. Destroys me. Makes me hate myself. Turns me into an animal.

And that was it, wasn't it? I was afraid of turning into something subhuman, not just to him or to the people around me, but to myself.

I'd remembered the tone in Jonathan's voice when he demanded something of me. The calmness, the surety, the note itself. A chord. I played it, toying with the sounds until I came up with something in D, and I checked the notations I'd made of Gabby's piece. I could do it. I could keep her alive. I could figure out how to continue with him, if at all.

Hearing that tone in Debbie's voice threw me for a second, and I stood silent. She raised her eyebrow and made a motion with her hand, indicating that it was time for me to go under the service bar and do my new job. As I passed her, she said, "You need to get to the doctor."

I smiled, not because I agreed, but because I knew it wasn't something a doctor could fix. I didn't know if I'd be able to sing in time to record with Jerry on Thursday, but at least I had the beginnings of a song.

I poured for the girls, dancing around Robert to get to the bottles, refilling the ice when necessary, and replenishing the beer. I was definitely stepping on his territory and his tip total for the shift, so I tried to be nice to him.

I was having a fun time just smiling and nodding as forms of communication, until I saw Darren at the bar, looking sullen.

"Hey," he said. "You're back there?"

I indicated the service part of the bar just as Tanya came up with a ticket. I filled glasses with ice, then the liquor, and stuck her ticket at six o'clock. It was still slow, so I leaned over the bar, wiping the space in front of Darren.

"Can you get me a beer?" he asked.

I shook my head. Robert was already giving me the devil eye. I pointed at the beers. Robert slipped it out of the case, poured it, and opened the ticket.

"I got your thing," Darren said. "Pretty big fucking rock."

I held out my hand.

"I left it on the piano."

I nodded and glanced at Debbie, who was on the phone and watching me.

"I'm not sorry," he said. "I shouldn't have called you a whore, but that doesn't change anything."

I had so much to say, starting with the fact that I had no use for his non-apology and ending with the fact that I didn't need his judgmental attitude. But I'd also evened it all out by slapping him good and hard, so it wasn't resentment I held as much as impatience. He needed to get over it so we could work on the Vancouver piece, whatever that would be.

Angie, another waitress, came by with a ticket, and I poured her drinks. Then Tanya. Then the new girl, whose name I'd forgotten. They were all working harder because I wasn't on the floor, and Robert was making less, so I tried hard to pull my weight. By the time I turned around, Darren was gone, and two hundred-dollar bills sat under his empty bottle. Robert went for them, but I snatched them first.

"What the fuck, Monica?"

Not being able to talk was getting on my last nerve. I showed him the money and grabbed him by the back of the neck, whispering as clearly as I could, "Paying back a loan." I looked him in the eye with all the intensity I had. I wasn't taking an argument for an answer. I pushed him away.

Then I saw Jonathan at the end of the bar. It was the same seat he'd occupied the night I'd kissed him overlooking the Valley on Mulholland and again at the food truck lot. He leaned on both elbows, talking on the phone and watching me. I hadn't seen him at the Stock since the day he'd left me hungry and begging for him on Sam's desk. I assumed he was intentionally and respectfully avoiding my shifts. I approached him. He opened his hand, and I took it just as he finished his call.

"Hello, goddess."

I mouthed, *Hello, king.*

"Still not talking?"

I shook my head, just staring at him. I was used to him, the curve of his jaw and the color of his hair. He was a familiar thing I was getting to know deeply, line by gorgeous line. I wanted to crawl over the bar and drop into his arms.

"When do you record with that guy?"

Thursday, I mouthed. He watched my lips move with an unnerving intensity.

"And what were you intending to do about this problem?"

I shrugged. I was anxious about the non-talking. I didn't think about much else, but I didn't have a cure. I knew it wasn't physical; fear kept my vocal cords from connecting.

"Do you have plans after work?"

I shook my head again. Yesterday, I would have been able to answer, but this thing had been getting worse. His concerned look told me he noticed. I caught sight of Sam approaching and slipped my fingers from Jonathan's and went back to the service bar.

Jonathan didn't make an appearance at the bar again, which was just as well. The dinner crowd was larger than usual, and we were busy enough for me to get a few grateful looks from Robert. My shift seemed to end in no time at all, but it was dark, and the heat lamps had just been turned on when relief arrived.

Debbie handed Robert and me our envelopes. "Nice night," she said. "Thank you both for working together. You—" She pointed at me. "—get that throat looked at. You did fine, but we don't need you at the service bar. We need you on the floor, acting witty and charming."

I nodded, mouthing *okay* while keeping my eyes downcast. She'd been very kind not to send me home as soon as she realized I couldn't talk, and I was grateful.

At my locker, I got out my clothes and stuffed my envelope in my pocket. I felt it then, a hard piece that was too rigid to be cash. I tore open the envelope. There was far less than I was used to, as seemed just under the circumstances, and a key card for one of the rooms in the Stock hotel.

My phone blooped right then.

—*room 522 be naked*—

A ripple of electricity coursed between my legs. Despite the fact that he and I had so much to discuss, despite the fact that I couldn't speak and should go see a doctor, despite everything, I wanted him immediately. I grabbed my bag and shuffled to the elevator, texting on the way.

—*Honestly, why bother if I
can't scream your name?*—

—*You'll scream*—

—*I think I'll just go home and
wash my socks*—

I was getting out on the fifth floor when I realized the one thing that should get me home right away. I cursed myself. I should have put him off with an honest rescheduling, if for even an hour. But now my jokey, sarcastic texts meant I was on my way up, and my diamond navel ring was on my piano. Fuck.

I stood outside the elevator, staring at my phone. I had to just do it.

—*Actually, can I…*

I never finished the text. Everything I considered typing sounded like a complete fabrication. I'd already told him I didn't have any plans. He'd already seen I wasn't sick or otherwise indisposed. I was just going to have to put on my big girl panties and deal.

CHAPTER 60

I didn't know what to do with myself. I was supposed to be getting undressed and waiting for him naked, but I couldn't stand before him in all my nude, diamond-less glory. He'd see the missing jewel at some point, of course, but I'd rather it not be in the first three seconds, with him clothed and me squirming and naked.

So I paced the room, looked out the window at the disputable glories of Downtown, and waited with an anticipation that lacked sex in its tension. When the door clicked open, I wanted to run out, but Jonathan blocked the way.

He looked me up and down, in my black jeans and T-shirt, then tilted his head as if trying to figure me out. "Something's not adding up here," he said, dropping his keycard on the dresser. He didn't seem angry, just stern. Even when I smiled and shrugged, with a finger in my cheek like a pure innocent, he didn't crack. He stepped so close to me I felt his breath on my cheek. "Naked, Monica."

I shuddered. I wanted to obey. My hands twitched for my buttons and snaps, but I held them down and looked into his eyes. There was a smile there, buried under the rigidity. I couldn't tell if it was humor or enjoyment, but there was pleasure. If I could get him to take my clothes off so fast or messily he didn't notice, I'd consider this a success.

"Is this the submissive thing?" he asked. "You're proving you're not?"

I kept my mouth closed. I couldn't speak, so I had the perfect excuse not to answer. I just kept my face close to his, feeling the heat come off him in waves.

He brushed his hand across the top edge of my jeans. "Are you taking that belt off, or am I?"

I gave my twitching hands something to do, yanking my leather belt though the loop and snapping it off. I was about to drop it on the floor when he caught it.

"Thank you," he said.

He slipped his fingers in my waistband, and I gasped as he unbuttoned my jeans, then pulled down the zipper. He folded back the corners of the fly.

"My intention was to get you to use your voice one way or the other. You chose the other." He took a handful of hair at the back of my neck and threw me on the bed, face down.

I landed with a bounce. He was on me before I had a chance to inhale, straddling me, his knees pressing my thighs together as he grabbed my arms at the elbows.

"Anything that sounds like 'no' or 'stop' is effective. But you have to say it." He pulled my elbows together behind my back.

The restriction brought a tingle between my legs, a sensation that started deep in my gut and ran to the very tip of my crotch. When he wrapped the belt around my arms just above the elbows, I gasped from the sudden rush of arousal that nearly blinded me. He pulled it tight. I couldn't move.

"You have to use your voice. Do you understand?"

I nodded, looking back at him, half my face on the bedspread, the other half covered with a mass of hair. He gripped my jeans at the waistband and yanked them down over my ass, taking my panties with them. I thought he was going to pull them all the way off, but he only got them down to mid-thigh before he stopped to raise my ass up and back until my knees were under me.

He moved the hair from my eyes, looking deeply into them as he brushed his fingers over my vagina. "You're wet, Monica." He circled the outside of it, pushing the lips aside.

I felt how wet I was in the way he touched me, moving smoothly. Watching my face, he drew his hand away, and in the half second I missed it, I thought he'd take off his pants or kiss my pussy, but instead, his hand landed on my ass with a hard *slap*. A *hah* left my lungs. Then he did it again, higher up. Hard.

The sting was intense, and the rush of arousal was undeniable, like the tide coming in. My arms tensed against their binds, but I wasn't going anywhere. I was under him completely, confined, aroused, controlled. I had no will of my own, just the enslavement of his palm on my ass as he stroked it once across, down to my folds, then brought it back up to slap me again.

"You okay, baby?" he asked.

I nodded, admitting to myself that I felt more than okay. I felt safe. He kept at it. Stroke, slap, caress, slap. I lost myself in the sting and heat on my ass, submitted completely to what was happening, what I allowed to happen. The seconds between his palm slapping me and the stinging whacks themselves were hot with anticipation, and he timed them so they came when I didn't expect, thrusting me forward. My breathing got harsh and guttural as he moved down my thighs, one side, then the other. I knew he was going to hit the center. I knew the next slap was going to cut right into my pussy, and as if he knew I knew, he held it back an extra second, then whacked the backs of my thighs and my soaking clit.

I grunted.

"Monica, was that you?" He was breathless himself.

I couldn't make the noise again until he slapped my cunt twice, hard and fast, and the sting, then the rush of pleasure pulled one long vowel sound from my throat.

"There it is. That beautiful voice."

I felt the pressure on the mattress as he took off his pants. I couldn't see what he was doing, but those seconds of anticipation were rewarded when I felt his cock against the raw skin of my ass. He pushed it down along the slick wetness of my crack, and it slipped in as if meant to be there.

"Jonathan," was the only word I had as I felt him glide so slowly into me. He felt better than he ever had, smoother, silken almost, and I groaned, using the vocal cords that never could or would have damaged my life.

He dug his fingers into my waist and pushed himself deep, hard. A grunt left his lips. He took me, owned me, used me, and I was going to come right there with my back to him.

"No," I said. "Not like this."

He stopped and laid himself along the length of my back. "How do you want it?"

"Be sweet," I whispered.

"I need to hear your voice."

"Make love to me," I said, more embarrassed to ask for that than to beg for a hard fuck. But after the spanking, I needed his arms around me, his face in my neck, his breath in my ear.

He undid the belt that held my arms in one motion and turned me around. When I was on my back and my ankles were in the air, he pulled my jeans off the rest of the way. His dick never left me. Once I saw his face, I knew something had just happened between us. The rigidity in his eyes was gone, replaced by a mask of longing, and the openness to reveal it. He kissed me as I wrapped my legs around him. We moved together, and the urgency between my legs turned into a fire. He put his hands on my cheeks.

"Look at me."

I took him in, all of him. We slid against each other, his cock rubbing my sensitive, reddened lips while he pressed my clit against his belly.

"Oh." I had not another syllable.

"Look at me when you come." He rocked back and forth, drawing his dick out just enough so my sore pussy felt the pain and pleasure of him thrusting back in.

I took his hair in my hands, bringing his face to mine, as I spread my legs as far as they'd go. My pussy became a bag of marbles dropped on the floor, as it opened and the feeling spread all over me, across the floor, and into the corners. Ice-cold and white-hot at the same time, to my toes in undulating waves, I pressed myself against him and screamed as the marbles reversed themselves and landed everywhere his dick touched me. Nowhere else. I couldn't feel another thing, hear another thing, not even my own cries as I came, my cunt clenching him over and over.

I was looking right at him, but I couldn't see a thing past my own pleasure or hear him over my own screams.

When I finally opened my eyes, his face had drooped, and his eyes closed, and he said, "Ah, no," as he jerked into me like a reflex.

I felt close to him, tuned together, breathing in sync. He would tell me what happened when he was sixteen. He'd tell me about Westonwood Acres, and I promised myself I wouldn't care. We were bound.

"I'm sorry, Monica." He pulled out of me, and from the way it felt and the slew of liquid that followed, I knew we had a problem.

"You weren't wearing a condom?"

"I was going to put one on, but when you asked me to flip you, I thought I had another minute. But you came and then—"

"Jesus *Christ*."

"We'll handle it, whatever happens."

"This is not about you keeping me and a baby in a nice lifestyle, Jonathan." I felt shrieky. That moment between us had been so short before it was broken, and I already felt withdrawal pangs. "How many women have you been with?"

He straightened his arms, separating himself further. "I'm always careful."

"How is that supposed to help me sleep at night?"

"Monica..."

I pushed him off me and rushed into the bathroom, closing the door behind me. Alone. Finally. I could think about what the fuck I was doing. Crazy. It was all crazy. I turned on the shower and leaned against the door, sliding down to the floor.

I was involved with a womanizing slut who got over his wife fifteen minutes ago, who just spanked me because he thought I was ball-gag submissive, and who had spent time in a mental institution. Was I fucking *nuts*? Kevin was more stable.

I stripped off my T-shirt and bra and stepped into the shower. I'd worried about that diamond. I didn't even give a shit anymore. That thing was going back in the box and getting sent back to his doorstep. I couldn't return it personally. I couldn't let my knees get weak for that controlling, irresponsible, manipulative motherfucker.

A vision of him came to me, at the club the second time, when I was so worried about Jessica. I saw him straight and tall in his suit and tie, ginger hair finger-brushed back, and that slip of a smile when he spotted me, because the smile I felt in my heart when I saw him was ten times the size of the one on my face.

I turned up the heat on the water, cleaning between my legs as if that was going to do a damn thing. But I had to get him out. The scent of him, the taste, every cell of his had to be gone. Of course, the problem was that I wasn't involved with him. I wasn't dating him. I wasn't casually fucking him.

I was falling in love with him.

And when I realized that, I felt the warmth of peace because I knew what I was contending with, and my choice was clear. Stay with him, love him, and deal with the consequences, or end it with the commitment to make sure it stayed ended.

When I got out of the shower, I hadn't made a decision.

Jonathan was gone.

CHAPTER 61

I sat in the Echo Park Family Clinic, checking my phone. I tapped at the letters, considering a message to him, but with nothing to say about what I wanted from him, how could I show him the disrespect of a message? And with no word from him, maybe he was going to make my decision for me.

Darren texted:

—Are we cleaning Gabby's room?—

Lately, he and I only discussed practical matters. I thought that would be okay for a while. Eventually, we'd have to discuss what had happened.

—Can we do later in the week?—

—k—

—BTW I got my voice back—

—good—

*—I want to use one of Gs comps. I'll
credit her as author so the
estate gets the royalties—*

There was a long pause after that, then:

*—You're a good and honest person
with an incredible right hook—*

"Monica Faulkner," called the Hispanic woman behind the desk. She wore pink scrubs and slippers. I stepped forward as she took a triplicate paper from a sleeve. "Okay, you had a dose of postinor for emergency contraception and a depo-provera shot. Sign here. Did the doctor give you a date to return for another shot?"

"Yeah."

"Anything else?"

"I don't know if this guy is worth it."

"They never are, *mija*. Not one of them."

CHAPTER 62

We wove words under popsicle trees,
The ceiling open to the sky,
And you want to own me
With your fatal grace and charmed words.
All I own is a handful of stars
Tethered to a bag of marbles that turns

WILL YOU CALL ME WHORE?
Destroy me,
Make me lick the floor,
Twist me in knots,
Turn me into an animal?
Will I be a vessel for you?

SLICE OPEN our lying box
Through a low doorway for our
Shoulds and oughts.
Choose the things I don't need,
No careless moments, no mystery.
And you need nothing.
My backward bend doesn't feed.

WILL I ever own you?

Tie you?
Can I ever collar you?
Hurt you,
Hold you, and own you?
Will you ever be a vessel for me?

"THAT," said Jerry from behind the glass, "is exactly what I'm talking about. That is a *song*."

"Thanks," I said into the mic as I took off my headphones. I'd laid down the piano track first to get the tempo down, then I'd sung over it as I listened. "I'd like to do that second chorus again."

"It's that or you lay in the theremin. We're short on time."

My little electromagnetic box sat in the corner. The second chorus was going to have to stay the way it was. I needed to lay in a track with an instrument played without touching it, or the whole song wouldn't work. The lyrics were the culmination of all my fears, but there had to be a portion of the music that was comforting and sweet. Anything less would have been unfair.

Jerry didn't know that I hadn't actually composed an accompaniment for the theremin. I told myself I hadn't had time, but the fact was, I didn't know what I wanted out of the thing. The sounds it made were the opposite of Gabby's percussive composition, and the two things together made no sense at all.

As I stood in front of it, listening to my voice and the piano together in my headphones, I reached for the instrument. My hand crossed the electromagnetic field and made a note. I moved the other hand between the metal poles, stroking the music, not touching a thing, the vibrations caused by the lack of physicality. The hand dance became a sensual thing, as if I touched an imaginary man who had come too close to me when I felt vulnerable, who had touched me when I hurt, and who had made the mistake of caring about me when I asked him to. For those sins and the mistake of letting his skin touch mine in a dangerous way, I'd shut him out.

"Can I start over?" I asked Jerry, who was flipping dials in the control room.

"Yep."

Then I played the thing with all my anger and sorrow, flicking my fingers into the air to create notes of apology in measures of longing.

CHAPTER 63

I got back from the studio feeling as though I'd just played to a stadium crowd. Jerry was going to remix the whole thing and review it with me in the next few days. Until then, I was high. I had to shower and change before meeting Kevin and Darren about the Vancouver piece.

A Fiat was parked in front of my house. I recognized it as the one that had been parked in Jonathan's driveway the second night we were together. On my porch stood his assistant in all her blond sullenness.

"Hi," I said. "I don't think we've met?"

"Kristin." She didn't shake my hand or smile, just handed me an envelope. "I'm supposed to wait until you read it."

I tore it open. Inside was a sheet from Trend Laboratories. In the top right corner, Jonathan had scribbled, *Sleep well.*

Under the header were the words TEST RESULTS. Smaller words lined up beneath that. Many were no more than jumbles of consonants, each with two checkboxes. Positive and negative. Negative boxed were checked all down the line. I did a purposeful check for HIV, and when I saw the Negative box checked, I breathed a sigh of relief.

"Do you want to come in?" I asked.

"I'm late."

"Can I give you something to pass back to him?"

"Sure." Though the word itself implied that giving Jonathan a note would be her pleasure, and though her tone was completely professional, her posture and stony face told another story. She was probably a Harvard MBA passing notes between her boss and his mistress.

I unlocked the house. "This won't take a second."

I had a box of receipts, and I dug through it until I came to the one from the

Echo Park Family Clinic. I circled the prescription for my morning-after pill and wrote, *You too,* in the upper right-hand corner. I stuffed it into the envelope, went back outside, and handed it back to her. I knew what I wanted to do.

He hadn't texted or called since he'd spanked me pink in the hotel room. I knew he was giving me space, taking the pressure off. He'd broken a cardinal rule by entering me without a condom, but I wasn't such a child as to think I had no responsibility to protect both of us. I could have checked. I could have been more diligent. When his dick felt so good in me, I should have known. It wasn't as if I'd never felt an unwrapped penis before.

I held my phone, feeling the heft of it in my palm. I could call him. I could reach out to him, and we could discuss him tying me up and hitting me with riding crops. Or chocking my mouth open so he could fuck it. Or sharing me with his buddies. How far did it go? How deep was the kink? I had no idea. I'd shut him down pretty quickly.

I put away the phone, deciding to give it an hour. I wanted him to have that receipt in his hands before I called.

CHAPTER 64

"Why should the space be limited?" Darren asked. "Space is visual, and it's your problem. Time is aural, and that's between Monica and me."

"This is a representation of human limitation," Kevin said, his posture twisted like a spring, leaning forward, fully engaged as always. "We have no authority over space and time in reality, and any control we wrest is, by its nature, false."

"So Monica and I will dictate the space, and you'll dictate the tempo. We work from there."

I leaned back, arms crossed, legs stretched, and ankles twisted. I had nothing to add. They were in an epic intellectual pissing match. None of what they said mattered, and it ran counter to the original vision, which was to remove the intellectual from the emotional. But they'd started the minute we entered Hoi Poloi Hog, also known as HPH.

The furnishings were found objects rescued from street corners and thrift stores. That included the lighting, the sockets of which had been fitted with bulbs that seemed specifically designed to cast as little light as possible. The sunless, dark blue sky of the October evening didn't help the lighting situation at all, burnishing the faces of my two companions a deep bronze.

It was lost on no one that I sat with two of the three men I'd shared my body with, but it wasn't discussed. Art was discussed.

"Either of you guys need more coffee?" I asked. They were both on their second espressos.

"I'll get it," Darren said. "You guys got the last two." He got up and went to the bar.

Kevin didn't say anything for a second, and neither did I. He'd get to it if I didn't try to fill the empty space.

"You need a partner for this?" he asked. "Because I didn't ask for a team."

"You would have had three of us if Gabby hadn't gone swimming while overdosing."

"Was that a cheap shot?"

It was my turn to lean forward. "I don't work well alone. You know that. I do my best work with other people."

"You have to get over that."

"You're not feeling threatened, are you?"

He leaned back in his seat and gnawed on a lemon rind. "You do *not* like being challenged, Tweety Bird."

My phone blooped, and I glanced at it. Jonathan.

*—Jesus Christ, the Echo Park
family clinic? Are you serious?—*

—Problem?—

—Let me count the ways—

I was considering what to reply when it blooped again.

*—Can we stop this and talk
before I have an accident?—*

I had a wisecrack at the ready regarding the meaning of the word "accident" and possible incontinence problems that could be serviced at the Echo Park Family Clinic for a nominal fee. I kept it to myself. "I'll be right back," I said to Kevin, not responding to his questioning look as I took the phone outside.

The street was active with dog walkers, phone talkers, deep kissers, and loud laughers. The traffic was loud, and I had to pinch one ear shut when he picked up.

"Hi," I said.

"You walked out of there with more diseases than you walked in with."

"You're being a snob."

"Snobbery is a defense against low social position. *Ego sum forsit.*"

"I can't believe you just said that. Even without the Latin part."

"Which I botched, really. Because I feel like I've botched everything with you."

I let the silence hang for a second, checking in with my memory of him, the way he moved, the way he spoke, his scent, his breath. Then, I thought of Carlos's blacked-out page from the institution, the ex-wife he may still love, the woman in San Francisco, and of course, the submissive thing.

I took a deep breath before I broke the silence. "We're both not saying the same thing."

If there was a way to hear a smile on the other end of a phone line, it would have deafened me. "I'll be home at ten or so, unless you want me to come there."

It hadn't occurred to me to do anything at my house, and the idea was appealing, except for Gabby's empty room and Carlos's envelope, which made a huge mental racket for an inanimate object.

"Ten is fine."

He breathed. Was it a sigh? "I look forward to it."

I went back in to watch the other two great fucks of my life talk about the dialectics of emotion.

CHAPTER 65

I got out of there at nine forty-five with a head full of multi-syllabic words and no solutions. The boys were still talking about what it all meant in the grand scheme of things and seemed to be enjoying each other's company more and more as the espressos went down. As I got into the Honda, I decided that if they ended up sleeping together, I'd promptly become a lesbian, then banished the thought.

Jonathan's gate was open like a mouth ready to swallow me whole. I parked in his driveway and shut the car, sitting there for a second and watching the bougainvillea vine swing in the autumn wind. The yellow pad I'd been working on stuck out of my bag. I'd dashed off some notes during my talk with Kevin and Darren, but the page with my fears about Jonathan remained.

What if he collars me? Slaps me? Spanks me? Bites me? Fucks me in the ass? Whips me? Hurts me? Displays me? Gags me? Blindfolds me? Shares me? Humiliates me? Ties me down? Makes me bleed? Fucks me up? Chocks my mouth open. Pulls my hair. Fucks my face. Calls me whore. Tells me to lick the floor. Destroys me. Makes me hate myself. Turns me into an animal.

I dug around my bag and found a pencil. I leaned the pad against the steering wheel and crossed out some things. It was probably wildly incomplete, but a starting point.

What if he ~~collars me? Slaps me?~~ Spanks me? Bites me? Fucks me in the ass? ~~Whips me?~~ Hurts me? ~~Displays me? Gags me?~~ Blindfolds me? ~~Shares me? Humiliates me?~~ Ties me down? ~~Makes me bleed? Fucks me up? Chocks my mouth open.~~ Pulls my hair. Fucks my face. ~~Calls me whore. Tells me to lick the floor. Destroys me. Makes me hate myself. Turns me into an animal.~~

My remaining list didn't leave him with much room to maneuver, but I didn't see any of the crossed-out stuff as negotiable. The front door opened, casting a brighter light on my paper. Jonathan stepped out and went to the edge of the porch. Clutching my little pad, I got out of the car.

He leaned over the railing. "I thought you'd passed out in there." His hand gripped the railing, and in the light, each vein, each bone, each hair came to life as I imagined it on my body.

"I'm fine." I went up the porch steps as I'd done twice before, more guarded than the first time and more turned on than the second. He stood to the side of the door, waiting for me to pass. I didn't.

"You're not coming in?" he asked.

"I want to say something first."

He leaned in the entryway. "Okay."

I had words. I had plenty of words, but they all ran together and made no sense. I handed him the pad. He glanced at me, then down at it. I'd never felt so naked in front of him, even fully clothed in pants and long sleeves. He was looking at my limits. I couldn't imagine anything more intimate. I felt tingly heat all over my chest and cheeks when he glanced back up at me.

"You forgot to cross off anal sex."

"I tried it once. Didn't like it. If you're better at it, I'll have another crack." I paused. "No pun intended."

He pulled his lips between his teeth. I blinked hard twice, but that was as far as we got before we started laughing. The joke was terrible, but the release of tension turned what should have been a groaner into a belly laugh. He tried to look at the list again but started laughing, which made me unable to stop, and we were both wiping tears before he reached for me. I took his hand.

"Your list is good," he said.

"Really? It seemed like I didn't leave much."

"Monica, this should be fun. If we're not having fun, we're doing it wrong." He looked at our clasped hands and softened. "The other day, I said everything in the worst way possible. I like playing, and I know how to do it safely, but I haven't made a lifestyle out of it. I wasn't out looking for a submissive, and I haven't set hooks in the ceilings."

"So no dungeon?"

"The Historical Society wouldn't allow it," he joked.

"Oh please, you could buy and sell the Historical Society."

I tilted my head up, and he took the signal, kissing me. He wrapped his arms around my shoulders and pulled me close. "Jessica was the last woman I cared about that I discussed this with, and it didn't go well. None of it did. I was scared you'd run away."

"And I did."

"Sure as fuck you did. I was pretty upset."

"You didn't seem upset."

"I have a rich inner life, but that's where it stays."

"Really? Nobody gets in?" I slipped my arms around his waist.

"Can you live with that?" He puts his hands on my cheeks and kissed me. His stubble scraped my face, a rough counterpoint to the softness of his lips and the slickness of his tongue.

"No. Not for long."

"I'd like to see how long." He kissed me in earnest, pressing his body to mine. He felt good. Delicious. Warm and supple with his hands on my back and his open mouth on mine.

I could have kissed him for hours, but I didn't have the luxury. I kept my body close to his while moving my mouth away. "I need a test night. Like a trial run. To see if I'm scared."

"Boo." He dragged his lips down my neck and pushed his hands up my shirt.

"I mean it."

"Okay. You just smell perfect. And also…" He pulled far enough away to look into my eyes. "I'm blocked. I have everything I want from you, and I can't think of anything to do. I have too many options."

I pushed him away, smiling. "You're supposed to stand in the doorway and tell me to get undressed."

He laughed and stood framed in the warm light of the open door. He looked me up and down. I'd come from the meeting in tight jeans, boots, and a woven long-sleeved shirt with a daunting number of buttons.

"That outfit's bulletproof," he said.

"Sorry." I started unbuttoning the shirt.

"No," he said, his smile an infectious disease spreading all over his face. "Stop. Let's start over. Come up the steps."

He slipped into the house and closed the door behind him. Okay. He wanted to start over in the right frame of mind. I went down the porch steps and back up slowly. I knocked on the door and stepped back, clearing my throat. It seemed like two full minutes before the door opened, and he was there again, wearing the same shirt and linen pants, in his sock feet, smile in dormancy, but there at the corners of his mouth.

"Monica."

"Jonathan."

"It's good to see you."

"And you."

"Turn around."

My breathing immediately got heavier, pooling between my legs as I turned my back to him.

"Unbutton your pants." His voice had gotten half an octave deeper and more staccato at the hard consonants. The change in it made laughter impossible.

I yanked my belt loose, unbuttoned my jeans, and pulled down the zipper, then put my hands back at my sides.

"Good girl."

I felt him get closer behind me. He stuck his thumbs in my waistband and tugged down my jeans. In three heaves, they were mid-thigh, with my panties still protecting my ass.

"Now," he said, putting his hand on my back, "when I say bend over, you do it from the waist."

"Okay."

"Do it."

I bent over until my nose was inches from my knees. He put his hand on my ass and a finger in my panties, slipping under them to feel me. I gasped.

"You're wet."

"Yes."

"What were you thinking about while you were waiting out here?"

"Nothing."

"This is only fun if we're honest." He pulled my underwear down and circled my opening with his finger. "So say it."

Through my knees, I could see his legs behind me and the open door of the house. I closed my eyes. "I was imagining you'd come through the door. You put your hand at the back of my neck and grabbed my hair. You kissed me. Then you pulled me down until I was kneeling. You had your dick out. I don't know how, but it's a fantasy, and you did it really fast. And you put your cock to my lips, and I took you in my mouth. You sighed really loud."

"Then what?"

"I started over. Did it a little differently. Maybe more kissing. Or I went to one knee instead of both."

"So it was that moment."

"Yes."

He put two fingers in me. I groaned.

"Another time. Maybe. When you trust me completely." He leaned over, brushing his free hand against my neck and shoulder, and pulled me up to standing, telling me what he wanted with a slight pressure. He pulled out his fingers and reached around me with his other hand, cupping my chin. "Open."

I opened my mouth, and he put in the two fingers he'd just removed from me.

"This is what I taste when I eat you."

I sucked his fingers, savoring the sex on them, the taste of arousal filling my mouth, my tongue licking his hard fingers. His erection pressed against my ass. His other hand pressed against my belly, pulling me against him. He took his fingers out of my mouth and put them back on my cheek, leaving dampness in their wake.

"You turned on?" he asked.

"Yes."

"If I do anything that changes that, you let me know."

I nodded.

"I didn't hear that."

"Yes."

"Yes, what?"

At once, I rebelled against the suggestion that I call him by an honorary, but at the same time, I wanted desperately to complete the act of surrender. "Yes, sir."

"You just gave me a little palpitation."

"I am at your service."

He brushed my hair from my ear and spoke softly. "Your knees, darling. Turn around and make use of them."

I stumbled a little as I tried to get on my knees in my half pulled-down pants. He took my elbow and helped me. Kneeling eye-level to his crotch, I watched him undo his pants and pull out his dick. I wanted it. I wanted to suck it dry. He took me by the back of the head and put his cock to my lips. I waited a second before opening my mouth and giving him complete power over me.

"Like you did it at the club," he said. "Open all the way for me."

He pushed his hips forward, and I took him, all of him, down my throat. I groaned for him, vibrating, concentrating on keeping open, accepting, concentrating on his pleasure, which peaked my own. It wasn't long before his thrusts became less gentle, more erratic.

"God, Monica. Get ready..." He groaned loudly, and the sticky bite of his semen filled my mouth and throat. He slowed, still coming.

I couldn't close my lips, so my mouth dripped his fluid. He thrust twice more then fell out of me. I looked up at him as he stroked my hair.

"Thank you."

"You're welcome, sir."

He whipped out one of those expensive hankies and wiped my mouth. It felt smooth and warm. "You change when you call me sir," he said as he helped me up.

"It turns me on."

"It's only for when we're together like this."

I nodded. He pulled me to him by the waist and kissed me hard and deep. I didn't know if I was supposed to put my arms around him, so I kept them at my sides until he lifted them over his shoulders, and I embraced him fully.

"You're both the best and worst submissive I've ever met."

"And you're the only dominant I've ever met."

"I want to be your last. I want to ruin you for other men."

"Better get cracking then, Drazen."

"Sir."

"Drazen, sir."

He smirked. "Leave your clothes on the porch. Then, upstairs with you. There's one door open."

He watched as I pulled my boots off, wiggled out of my jeans, then unbuttoned my shirt. I didn't do it in a lascivious way, using only the most functional movements to complete the task. When I was naked head to toe, he moved to the side so I could get past him. He took my hand, and I went upstairs in front of him.

My heart beat so hard I could barely breathe. I was doing it. The thing on the porch was an appetizer. Upstairs, I'd be his completely. I could do it. I had to. My soaking pussy demanded it. My hard nipples insisted on it. My come-covered throat required it.

I felt his eyes on my ass as I got to the top of the stairs. All the hall doors were closed except one, and it wasn't the one I'd been to twice before.

"Go on," he said.

I went through the open door. The difference between the two bedrooms I'd been in was more than the size, with the new one being bigger by fifty percent.

The room was finished, lived in, and full of personal objects and photographs. The rug was worn where a man might lay his feet in the morning and night. The night table on one side held books, a half-empty glass of water, and a box of tissues.

"This is your room."

"Yes, darling." He ran his fingertips down my arms. "Get on the bed. On your back, please."

The bed was higher than the other. I crawled up and rolled over. The down comforter was cool on my back, soft on the feather bed.

Jonathan put his hands between my knees and spread them apart, then pulled them up, bending them until my heels touched my ass. I groaned from his touch and the act of obeying it.

"Stay there," he said. He got undressed, tossing his things on a leather chair while I lay on the bed, pussy and asshole up in the air. I watched his biceps tighten and release as he got his shirt off. His cock bounced out of his pants again. Naked, he slid on top of me and kissed my breasts and the diamond in my navel. I put my hands on his head, trying to push him down, but he wasn't being moved.

"So, the receipt from the clinic?" he started.

"Yes?"

"When does that birth control thing kick in?" he asked, coming face to face.

"Because of when I had my period last... uuuuuhm.... I have to figure it because the doctor said it was real important." I pretended to count on my fingers and tapped my cheek like I was thinking, screwing my eyes around.

"Monica, please." He played at annoyed, but he was smiling.

"Immediately."

He buried his face in my neck. "And I'm clean. What do you think?"

"You're the boss."

"This has to be more of a consensus."

I touched his face. He'd already ruined me for other men. "Yes," I said. "I want to feel you."

"You've overwhelmed me twice in one night."

"Don't freeze up on me on my first night of submission."

He straightened his arms, holding his body over me. "What happened to freaked-out Monica?"

"She turned into aroused Monica."

He shifted to my side and sat up. "Roll over then, aroused Monica."

I rolled over onto my stomach, holding myself up on my elbows. He placed his palm on my back, dragging it down my shoulder blades and the curve of my spine, landing on my ass, which he squeezed before standing up behind me.

"Okay, I'm going to show you something." He picked my ass up off the mattress. "Bend your knees under you."

I did it. I had one side of my face against the down comforter, watching him as he touched me and shifted my body the way he thought necessary.

"Now, pick up your butt. All the way up."

I did as I was told, straightening my knees to right angles.

"Higher." He gave my ass a slap that made me groan, then drew his hand along my back again, as if feeling for the right curve. "Put your hands under you, between your knees."

I wiggled to get them under me. "Touch your ankles."

"Like this?"

"Exactly like that."

He touched me all over, and I did feel like his work of art, his living opus with my ass in the air, so far up and bent out that my cunt must have been saluting the room.

"Physically," he said, "are you comfortable?"

"No, not really."

"And emotionally?"

"Not scared, but I feel exposed."

He kissed my ass, using his tongue along my cheeks. My pussy twitched in anticipation. But he stood up. I heard fabric shifting behind me and his movements, but I didn't look. When he came into my field of vision, he was wearing sweatpants.

"Stay there," he said. "Don't move."

"Where are you going?"

"You don't get to ask questions. You get to wait."

And he left me there, butt up, bedroom door open behind me. I wasn't scared, but I should have been. My ass tingled. Was he getting something to spank me with? Some rough tether? Cuffs? Hooks? Yes, I thought I should be terrified, but all I could think about was how much I wanted him to come back and fuck the living shit out of me.

I heard clicks and steps from downstairs, then nothing.

Your ass is out to a psychopath.

You don't know that. He could have been in the institution for anything.

At sixteen? Drugs. Suicide. Depression.

Violence?

I heard him on the creaky wood stairs, then his feet padding down the hall, then I smelled his sawdust scent.

"Very good." His voice was close behind me. "When I tell you to go upstairs and be ready, this is what I mean, okay?"

"Yes, sir."

"How was it? Waiting?"

"Not my favorite. But also kind of good because I just stewed, wondering what you were going to do to me."

He stroked my ass, letting his fingertips brush the crack, inside the cleft, touching where I was wettest. "It turns me on knowing you're up here doing what I tell you." He put both palms on my cheeks. I felt something in his right hand.

He put his mouth on me, and I groaned when he kissed between my legs. He flicked his tongue over my clit. I bucked a little. I knew I wasn't close, but I felt as though I could come from a warm breeze.

He moved me onto my back. He had a length of brown leather twine in his right hand. It might have made a fringed bag or a shoelace, but long. He looked at me clinically again, as if I were a problem to solve, then he went back to my eyes. "You ready?"

"The anticipation is killing me."

"Me too." He took my left wrist and placed it against my left knee, then looped a length of leather around them, making a figure eight, binding them together. "Too tight?"

"No."

He knotted it off, then picked up my back while he ran the rest of the spool under me. He pulled, playing with the length until my tied knee and wrist were splayed. "I want to say," he said as he placed my right wrist and right knee together, "if you say stop, it's good enough for me, but we might want to set a safeword." He spread my legs to get the right length under my back and tied my right side together, letting the rest of the loop drop off the edge of the bed.

"Tangerine," I said.

"Tangerine?"

"I doubt you can keep doing whatever it is you're doing if I say tangerine."

"Fine, wiseass." He leaned over me and kissed my lips so sweetly I wanted to put my arms and legs around him, but I couldn't.

He got off the bed and looked at me. I couldn't close or lower my legs, nor could I move my arms. A trickle of wetness dripped down my crack, and the discomfort of it was exquisite. He bent over and kissed between my breasts, dragging his tongue across, to my nipple, sucking it gently. "I'm listening," he whispered. "I'm listening to your breathing, your heartbeat. I'm listening to your skin on the sheets. If you need something, just say it. I'm all ears."

"I'll let you know."

"In words." He sucked the other nipple, which was hard and tight. He pressed his lips around it and pulled.

"I'll say, 'Get the fuck off me and untie me, you animal,' but not when you do that. That's good."

"And this?" He kissed down, circling my diamond crusted navel and down to my left thigh. He ran his tongue over my folds to the other thigh.

"That needs a safeword."

He licked my clit with the pointy part of his tongue. "What should it be?" he asked before licking again, then giving it a light suck.

"Oh, God."

"'Oh, God' it is." He got on top of me, his dick just touching my exposed pussy.

He kissed me. I moved my hips against him, and he shifted away, keeping the head at the entrance to my vagina, waiting. He watched me gasp as he pushed a little. He must have felt the way I closed in around him, as if I'd suck him into me.

"Please," I said. "Please fuck me. Sir, please."

He slid his cock inside me so slowly it felt ten feet long. Inch by inch, skin to skin, soft against slick, until he hit the end, and he pressed against me, rocking while my clit exploded. Then he pulled out just as slowly, and the feeling was devastatingly sharp in the pleasure of its loss. The heightened torment continued as he slid in again, and I couldn't grab him or move. All the other stuff was dress rehearsal for the control he took as he tortured me with the measured, unhurried thrusts and slow rocks of him against my clit.

"Jonathan, Jonathan, Jonathan...." I forgot to call him sir or anything else but his name.

He sped up, dropping onto me, a splayed thing, open, bound, servile, utterly compliant mass of nerve endings and clutching, wet flesh. His movements turned to pounding, slamming fucking that brought me close enough to cry out.

He slowed, straightening his arms above me and changing the rotation so I felt his cock, but not enough to stimulate me to orgasm.

"No," I said in a voice so desperate I was shocked to hear it.

"Easy, Monica."

"Jesus."

"You're mine. Your orgasms are mine. Your pleasure is mine to give."

I wanted to rail at him. I wanted to demand it. But not only would that not get me what I wanted, it wasn't how I wanted it to go down. I wanted to be fully compliant. "Yes, sir." Saying it calmed me.

"Breathe slowly."

I did as I was told.

He moved against me, gradually, as before. "Look at me."

I did, seeing the sweat on his brow and the pleasure in his face. That pleasure brought me the greatest satisfaction. I had done that. I gave him what he was giving me.

As if sensing my thoughts, he leaned down and kissed me. "Will you come for me?" he asked, his voice low and growling.

"Yes, it's yours."

"Mine," he whispered.

He fucked me in earnest, then. He fucked me like he meant it, roughly, hitting the right places as if it was what he did to get himself off. My breasts bounced with the motion. My cunt was a pulsing strip of flesh under him, a swath of need. Then, like a rush from a firehose, I came, ass and pussy clenching over and over as I screamed and released it all. He kept going, hovering over me, thrusting, and the release continued to the point where pleasure met pain, and I came again, pushing my hips into him as he opened his mouth and grunted hard, then moaned. He slowed, rotating again, then dropped on me with a heaving chest and hot breaths on my neck.

He reached behind with his left hand and untied my right wrist and knee. They separated with a cramp. Sitting up, he untied the other side. I rubbed my wrists.

"So?" he asked.

"So, a needle pulling thread. You've ruined me."

He brushed the hair off my face, and I did what I'd been wanting to do. I put my arms and legs around him.

CHAPTER 66

I awoke slowly to a few sensations: the light of the sun cutting past my eyelids, my sore pussy, and Jonathan's fingertips stroking my hand as it rested on his chest. When I opened my eyes, he was looking at me.

"Good morning."

I grumbled and shifted closer to him.

"Are you working today?" he asked.

"Lunch shift." I spread my hand out on his chest, pushing it forward, brushing the hairs between my fingers. "Then I have to go to Frontage and see if we can work something out. I don't want to gig there without Gabby, but I don't want to be stupid."

He pulled me on top of him. "There's nothing stupid about you."

I kissed him, and that kiss got deeper and more urgent. My sore pussy twitched when I felt him harden. He ran his hands all over me, then over my arms which he guided to the headboard, until I was stretched over him.

"Oh, Jonathan. I'm so sore."

"Is that a no?"

"Just be gentle."

He guided himself into me, and it hurt, but with the most delicious pain. I used the headboard to leverage myself, and Jonathan guided my hips and then rotated his finger on my clit until I gave him a sweet orgasm that felt more like a long breeze than a tornado.

With his face beneath me, falling apart under his own pleasure, I knew something for sure, and I whispered it to myself as he came. *I love you, I love you, I love you.*

251

CHAPTER 67

My clothes had been washed again and were waiting for me when I got out of the shower. Living on a hill in a crap neighborhood my whole life, I'd never had industrial-strength water pressure, and it seemed a good water heater was pretty important if you wanted a nice, skin-scalding shower. I got into my clothes, and feeling so refreshed, I almost skipped down the stairs, where I saw Ally Mira sweeping the corners.

"Hi," I said.

"Good morning." Her English was accented.

"Did you wash my clothes?"

"Mister Drazen left them for me. I get up early and do it."

"Thank you. It's very kind of you."

"You're welcome. I have tea for you in the sitting room."

"The what?"

She leaned her broom against the wall and motioned for me to follow her. We went downstairs, into the living room and through an arch I hadn't noticed before, past a short foyer, and into an enclosed porch on the side of the house overlooking a flower garden. A silver tea tray sat on the low table. I could hear Jonathan talking on the phone in another room I couldn't identify. Ally Mira indicated the couch.

I sat down. "Thanks." I picked up the teapot to let her know I'd do the pouring.

She nodded, smiled, and slipped out. I realized Jonathan's voice was coming through the wood sliding doors on the side of the room. The sound of the morning birds was deafening, and though it was a lovely white noise to distract me from Jonathan's phone call, his voice cut through. He did not seem happy. I tried to tell myself I wasn't eavesdropping, but when I heard her name, I stopped pretending I wasn't listening and made an effort to shut out the sound of the bird's chirping.

"Jess," he said, "this is you being afraid of being alone." Pause. "No, you don't. That's right. I'm telling you how you feel."

There was a longer pause, during which I sipped my tea and hoped the conversation ended soon, but Jonathan's voice got stronger.

"Don't you dare." Pause. "Jessica, let me be clear. If you do anything like that, I will destroy you. I. Will. Destroy. You."

That voice. It was the sawdust and leather voice, the voice that got me to unquestioningly spread my legs or bend at the waist. I'd never heard him use it outside of a sexual context. His voice got too low to hear after that, then the doors slid open.

He walked in looking as if a blanket of sadness had been thrown over him and tied at the neck. "You're up," he said.

"There's tea left if you want some."

He stepped forward until he was standing over me. "How much of that did you hear?"

"I know who it was but not what it was about."

He paused, then kneeled in front of me between the couch and the table. I put my hand to his cheek and leaned forward. His eyes shone a troubled green, and his mouth set itself in a line.

"Jonathan, what's wrong?"

"I won't let anyone come between us. I want you to know that."

"She won't if you don't let her."

"If she says anything to you, you need to come to me with it right away. Do you understand?"

"What happened, Jonathan?"

"Just say you'll call me."

"I don't understand." I held his face in my hands, stroking his cheeks with my thumbs.

"Wherever I am in the world, before you think you know anything, you make sure you call me. Say you will." He wasn't using his domineering voice, but the voice of a man who needed, desperately, to be soothed.

"I will."

He rubbed his palms along the tops of my thighs and up around my waist. He laid his head on my lap and said nothing as I stroked his hair and hummed a melody that reminded me of the cadences of his voice.

We sat like that, me on the couch, humming, and him on his knees before me, long after my tea became cold and the morning birds silenced themselves for the day.

DOMINATION

CHAPTER 1

MONICA

"Get on your knees."

Even through the phone, I could tell Jonathan was using his dominant voice. I got nervous that I would dampen the expensive panties so badly the protective paper at the crotch would curl and peel off. "Yes, sir."

Facing the dressing room mirror, I got to my knees. The black garter and stocking I was trying on looked as though it had been taped on me. The black satin belt slung low on my hips held the straps that dropped down my thighs with silver rings.

"How does it look?" he asked.

"I think you'll like it."

"How does it make you feel?"

"You really want to know?" I asked.

"I'm sitting in the back of my car, thinking about you. It's wall-to-wall traffic. So, yes, I want to know how it makes you feel."

I heard women outside the dressing room door. Their soft conversations and laughter were muffled by the clothing draped around the room, lingerie with bows and clasps and metal rings set into lush satins and elastics. Every piece I'd tried on aroused me, and when he called, the addition of his voice to the mix brought me near tears.

"How do I feel?" I asked. The carpet dug into my knees, and I was goose bumped from the air conditioner, but that wasn't what he meant. The black satin bra cups were made of two panels that could be moved for access. It felt so comfortable, I didn't even know I had it on. The curves of the underwear accentuated the length of my pelvis. "I feel like fucking."

I heard him take a breath. I did enjoy shocking him. "Tuck the phone under your left ear."

"Done."

"Done?"

"Done, sir."

"Put your left hand on the mirror," he said. "Lean on it."

"Yes, sir." My hand spread on the mirror like a starfish. It would leave a mark.

"Put your right hand between your legs."

"Jonathan..."

"Do it."

My cunt clenched with anticipation. I stroked lightly through the string of cloth, sucking air between my teeth from the tingle of the touch.

"Get under the fabric," he said, as if he could see I hadn't put my fingers on my skin.

"Yes, sir." The word *sir* seemed to vibrate not just outward, to him, but inward, down a thick nerve connecting my vocal cords to my core. When I slipped my fingers under the panties, I shuddered.

"You wet?"

"So fucking wet," I whispered.

"Your legs spread?"

"Yes."

"Look at yourself in the mirror."

I did, and I was greeted by a face slack with arousal, flushed with sex. "Yes, sir." I watched myself submit to him, in that outfit, as if I needed to be more turned on. Outside the door, I heard a throat clear.

"How do you look?" he asked.

"I look like I can't stay in here much longer without someone coming."

"You got that right," he mumbled. Papers shuffled on his side. He was working while telling me to finger myself. A true multitasker. "Stroke your clit and all the way down to that beautiful hole." I groaned, my cheek caressing the phone. "Keep going. Work your clit. Go around it twice, then over the top."

I did, and the heavenliness came as much from my own touch as the knowledge I obeyed him. "Oh, Jonathan."

"Put two fingers in."

My pussy clenched around my fingers, kissing them, sucking them in. The heel of my hand found my clit as I pushed my fingers in and out.

He whispered, "Tomorrow night, when I see you, I'm going to put my fingers in you and lick you until you beg me to stop. Then I'm going to squeeze your clit with my lips until you come again."

"I want you."

"You will have me."

"May I come?" There was a distinct possibility he'd say no, and I was so far gone, holding off my orgasm would hurt. "Please let me come." His silence tormented me. "Please, sir." I smiled a little. I never thought I'd actually want to call a lover *sir*. But it felt good, and right, and fun.

I heard his smile as he said, "You may."

I pressed my whole hand along my wet cleft, feeling everything from the tingle around my pussy to the powerful ache at my clit, back and forth, slowly. My breathing got hard and short. I had to keep it down. If I could hear myself, someone else could as well. I closed my eyes and buckled. My hand left the mirror as my back arched, encompassing me in heat from my knees to my waist. I bit my lip to keep from crying out. My hips pumped as pleasure washed over me in impossibly long waves. The phone dropped to the carpet.

CHAPTER 2

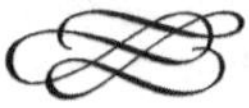

JONATHAN

I HEARD the phone hit the floor, and her groans fill the room. I looked out the window onto the parking lot otherwise known as the 710 freeway and imagined her touching herself. I imagined her expression, her smell as she writhed on the floor enough to drop the phone, all while wearing some elastic and satin configuration. A shiver went down my spine. I felt connected to her when I commanded and she obeyed. It was as close to touching her as I could get.

"Jonathan?" she whispered.

"How are you feeling?"

"I want to curl up next to you and go to sleep."

"Have I told you how amazing you are? You please the hell out of me."

She didn't answer right away. My little goddess of Echo Park must have been smiling. "Wait until you see the underpants I just made a mess of. They're gonna please you plenty."

"Buy everything."

The next pause wasn't as pleasant. "I want to talk about this."

"We can talk tomorrow. I'll pick you up at five."

"Are we going to lie in bed and watch the Dodgers lose game six?"

"You're not supposed to ask a man where he's taking you." She grumbled. My goddess was a big baseball fan. She probably thought I hadn't noticed or had forgotten.

After she'd left the previous morning, when I drifted off to sleep with her humming and stroking my hair, I leaned back in my office chair, looking out the window and thinking of her. Hours later, I called her and asked her on a date.

"A real date?" she'd asked. "Like dinner or a movie or something?"

"I know a nice place. We'll have some wine. Good food. You know, like people do." I'd looked out over the Hollywood Hills. I had to see her again. I had an ache for her that phone calls and texts wouldn't satisfy. It started the minute she left and had grown to uncontrollable levels in the hours since.

"Well, that's fine and all," she'd said, "but just so you know, I don't fuck on the first date."

I'd been laughing when my assistant came in. I indicated she should sit and took the schedule she offered me. "I need you to get something to wear," I said into the phone.

"Oh, not again."

"Again and again. I'm in a meeting." I looked over my schedule for the next day. "Can I text you?"

"You're avoiding my refusal."

"I won't be late. So be ready. *Dressed* and ready."

"Thanks for the clarification."

"You're welcome."

I'd tossed the phone aside, glanced at my schedule, and glanced at Kristin. "I have a meeting with my ex-wife at six thirty?"

"You said to take any meeting she wanted."

"I did. Cancel the meeting and cancel the standing order. She goes on the schedule like everyone else." Kristin shook her foot and nodded, her body a barrel of emotional tells. She was so transparent, I had no idea how she'd gotten through Vassar without those bitches eating her alive. "Yes?"

"Are you making your lunch with Eddie tomorrow, or do you want to meet Gerald Deritts from Council 12? He called and had an opening on the mixed-use ordinance."

"Cancel Eddie."

"Sheila's stuck on the 405. She's added this to the agenda." She'd handed me a folder.

"Ah, Jessica's trust," I'd murmured as I flipped through it. When we got engaged, I set up a trust for her that provided for everything she needed. Though she had taste and social standing, she couldn't manage a dollar. When we divorced, I'd intended to revoke her benefits, but never had. I'd been such a pussy. I'd told myself she hadn't taken a dime from me because I needed to believe it. The withdrawals didn't hurt me, but she'd continued to take money from the trust, and I owned the building her studio was in and didn't charge her rent. There were other incidentals I'd probably forgotten. "Tell Sheila I want to review all my financial entanglements with my ex-wife. Book that for next week."

Kristen had pursed her lips. I could have asked her what was on her mind, but it wasn't worth a conversation. Her crush was cute when I'd hired her, but it was getting less so. I'd said no, I didn't want to sleep with her. Further conversation about that, or why I wouldn't bend over backward to see Jessica anymore, would be unproductive.

After dismissing Kristin, I'd tried to get back to work, but my thoughts were consumed with Monica. In anticipation of our date the next day, I opened an account at Bordelle for her. When I texted her the info, she'd shot back...

—An account? For all the girls?—

—Just opened it. Go. For me.—

The next day, she called me from the dressing room to thank me, and I couldn't help it. I had to have her, and I did. She got on her knees when I told her to. She slipped easily into play and out again, becoming her witty, intelligent self seamlessly. She wasn't intimidated by me. She teased and challenged me. She kissed like she meant it, and from the very first night, she enjoyed fucking without reservation or shame.

Monica was, in a word, perfect.

CHAPTER 3

MONICA

I was bag laden as I walked to the café. Jonathan had called Bordelle and told
them to wrap up everything I'd put in the dressing room. So I went to Nordstrom's
and got my own goddamn dress. I hoped he liked it because it set me back two
weeks' tips, a lot of money for something that would end up draped over the chair
on his porch. But I needed to feel right with myself. I accepted him as a dominant
in bed, and that worked out very well for us. In the outside world, I was my
own woman.

Except for the eight hundred dollars in lingerie.

I rushed to the entrance of Terra Café. Yvonne sat at a patio table with her
fourteen-month-old, scooping ice cream out of a cup.

"Girl," she said as we hugged, "where the hell have you been shopping? And
what's with the shoes?"

I tipped my foot to make the red sole visible. I wore the shoes I'd gotten at
Barney's more often than I should, but letting them sit at the bottom of my closet
seemed a crime. Yvonne looked at me sidelong while she scooped ice cream. Her
afro was teased to four times the size of her head, her eyes lined with gold, and her
lips painted the exact chocolate color of her skin. She was simply gorgeous.

"You like them?" I asked.

"I know what they cost, so I know where you got them. So whether or not I
like them depends."

I sat down and ordered a green tea and a chocolaty cake thing. Aaron, in his
striped shirt and overalls, sat with his mouth open. Vanilla ice cream dripped out
of the corners of his mouth like he was a dairy vampire.

"I'm sorry about your friend," she said. "Were you close?"

"She was like a sister to me." I felt a little hitch in my throat, a sob pushing up from my gut. I swallowed it. I didn't cry in public. In private, the past few days had been a rush of tears and beaten-back sorrow. "Anyway. It's fine. I'm dealing with it. Still haven't cleared out her room. But anyway... how's school? It's your last year, right?"

"Tryna get my thesis accepted. Thinking about doing gender instead of race. Something with women's bodies and politics."

"Sexual intersections." My tea came.

"Oh, that's good." She scraped the bottom of the cup. "Now, I didn't ask you to lunch to talk about UCLA."

"The weather, then?"

"My boss? Your former boss? The hot motherfucker? Six two? Medium build? Reddish brown up top... and down below?"

"Not in front of the baby."

"I hear he's a freak." I spit my tea. "Well," she continued, "word gets around. So..." She slithered in her chair. "What. The. Fuck?"

"Yvonne, really. Totally inappropriate." I looked at her over my cup, wishing for a quick and painless death. I'd known she wanted to ask me about Jonathan, but I didn't know she was aware of his proclivities.

"He's really private about who he's..." She stopped herself. "... who he's spending time with. But we all saw your picture from the L.A. Mod show in the paper. And it was no secret at your friend's wake."

"I don't know what you'd call us at this point," I answered. Aaron made a long *aaaaaahhh* sound of pure delight. He kicked under the table and the silverware bounced. "He's cute, this baby. You made him?"

"Me and that creep. Can't deny he's a good-looking creep."

"Is he still stalking you?"

"Cops had to come last week. He put a camera at my bedroom window to watch me sleeping. Isn't that sweet? Oh, and he got my bank account information 'to put Aaron's child support right in there' to save me the trouble of going to the bank. I said, man, I hope narcissistic personality disorder isn't genetic."

"I'm sorry to hear that."

"I called you so you could help me with a little escapism, and so far you're a big fail."

I knew she'd ask, and I had prepared boundaries, but she immediately broke them down by revealing the freak rumor. The thing was, I wanted to tell her. I had no one to talk to. Darren didn't want to hear it. Gabby was dead. Debbie and Jonathan were friends. I knew some of my girlfriends better than Yvonne, but none of them had asked about the handsome man at my side at Gabby's wake. They'd raised eyebrows and introduced themselves. I got phone calls, roundabout questions, and invites to parties and gatherings. I refused everyone but Yvonne, probably because she was very up front about demanding information.

"We're having sex," I said. "Tomorrow night, we have a date, which we haven't done yet."

She put a board book in front of Aaron and leaned toward me, folding her long, skinny arms. "You're *having sex*? Who are you, grandma? Come on. I hear he's into whips and chains."

I pressed my lips between my teeth. I would have to deal with the rumors at some point. "I've never seen him hold or use a whip or a chain. Nor have I observed either one of those things in his house or his bedroom. However..." I let my voice trail off and sipped my tea, leading Yvonne along. "I won't deny there may be some truth to those rumors."

"Girl," she said with no little excitement.

I shrugged, wanting to play it off, but Yvonne had come to dish. She wasn't leaving with generalizations and vague admissions. "How is it?" she asked.

"It's incredible."

"Tell me." Her whisper was hoarse with anticipation.

"I can't," I whispered back. "It's not cinematic. It's not exciting unless you're in it. He speaks to me. He tells me what I want before I know it and before I can deny myself. I'm free with him, but not in the way you think." I turned my teacup around in the saucer.

I stopped. I could have said more. I could have told her he dominated me, and I submitted by letting go of everything I expected of myself. I ceded all control, all emotion, all physical boundaries, and in doing so, I found sexual honesty. I felt closer to him than I felt to anyone else because he saw parts of me I didn't. The quivering, weak, fearful parts that I denied existed, he brought out and caressed. Thinking about his demands made me want him again. I crossed my legs, convinced Yvonne wouldn't understand.

Her expression told me I was right. Her face was still, disentangled from the drama surrounding my adventures with a rich man. She wasn't exactly concerned as much as apprehensive. "So where's it going? Serious? Steady thing? Just sex?"

"I don't know."

"How do you feel about it?"

She was definitely not getting an honest answer to that. "Taking it slow. I like being around him. I'm trying to not get too attached, but I don't know if staying detached is working."

Aaron fussed, and Yvonne pulled him out of his chair. He rested his head on her shoulder. "You buy yourself the shoes and underpants?" she asked.

"Of course not. The shoes alone..." I pursed my lips. I didn't like where she was going, and I didn't have the heart to slap her the way I'd slapped Darren.

"I'm gonna ask you something because I like you. You can get your panties in a twist if you want, but you shouldn't."

"I may not answer."

"He abusing you?"

"No!" I cried. "God, Yvonne, what part of what I said makes you think *abuse*?"

My reaction was offense, not for myself, but for Jonathan. She didn't know him. She didn't know us together.

But I couldn't hold her to my level of loyalty. The twisting web of rage in my chest surprised me, though. Was the rage caused by her implication that Jonathan was an abuser? Or because I'd just found out he had a reputation?

Yvonne, who couldn't see my neurons pulsing like machine gun fire, continued, "Kink is often a disguise for abuse and exploitation. I know it's not that way yet. But if you get uncomfortable, will you call me?"

"No." Not only was I not calling her, I wasn't calling anyone. What Jonathan and I did, and how we did it, was private. Having even one person know was making me very uncomfortable.

"Sure, you will. Look, I know how a nice guy can turn into an asshole on the turn of a dime, so all I'm saying is..." Her expression changed, as if what she wanted to say fell dead on her lips. She smiled instead. "I'm totally jealous. If he's *not* abusing you, I might have faith in men again. That's all."

I exhaled a long, lung-emptying breath, as if I'd been holding it. I'd been unfair and insensitive. Yvonne's history included a brother who fondled her and a boyfriend who locked her and their son in the house when he went to work. Of course she was attuned to possible abuse when I came along with bags of expensive clothing and a man who tied me up and spanked me for our pleasure. I pushed my cake toward her. "Eat, please. I have to stay skinny if I want to look good in this shit."

CHAPTER 4

JONATHAN

Long Beach was the absolute last place I wanted to be. The sky was the color of a handful of quarters. Without the sun to warm the air, the wind off the ocean hit cold and hard.

I had to be quick. I had a meeting with the deputy mayor in Century City in two hours, and then I had a date. A real date, where I'd wear a suit and behave myself.

At the Port of Long Beach, the *Faulkner Coalmine* was set to be cataloged, packed up, and sent to a warehouse in Europe, never to be seen again. I'd bought it the night of the Eclipse show. Eclipse shows only ran a week, so the minute the show closed down, my dealer, Hank, had a team in to collect it. Wainwright was surprised, but the check cleared nicely. He showed up at the closing to chat up my dealer, trying to sell more work. Fucking hustler. Obvious how he got her into bed.

Lil pulled up to the warehouse. Hank strode out to meet me. He was six feet tall, early sixties, bald, and wearing a four-thousand-dollar suit. He could tell shit from chocolate, negotiate a deal, take up space at an auction, and determine true worth from hype. More importantly, he understood my taste, which was why he'd been so surprised I wanted that piece.

"Jaydee." He held out his hand. He had on a few big rings and a clunky watch, and his voice was thick with New York. He looked more like a truck driver than an art dealer, and that's why I liked him. He snuck up on people with his knowledge and erudition, and by the time artists and agents realized they weren't dealing with a rube, I had what I wanted.

"Hank." We walked through the warehouse. My companies used the space as a logistics hold for construction materials and imported food. The offices for the people routing it all over the world were inside the warehouse, too.

Hank waved his arm dismissively. "What the fuck did you buy this piece of shit for? You want something to spend your money on, I got a girl with a studio in Compton. Tears in your eyes. Tears."

"You called *me*. And not to question my taste, I presume."

"I question your taste every day."

"Really? Never would have guessed."

Hank stopped outside a conference room door. "It's good work, no question. But I don't know how much of it you saw before you went overpaying while I wasn't looking."

"Almost none."

"Fan-freaking-tastic. Can we not do that any more?"

"I have my reasons."

"Fine," Hank said, obviously annoyed. "Everything's here. All the documentation, the sketches, inspiration, all the history and work that went into the installation. That's what you bought, sight unseen."

"Can we go in now?"

Hank remained in front of the door. "Look, artists are crazy. I never met one who wasn't a little scrambled. Maybe they all got bit by a shithouse rat when they were babies. This? That I got behind this door? I'm thinking of calling the LAPD just so they can have a record of it. But I need your okay first."

"You've really intrigued the hell out of me, Hank."

He opened the door. The room was outfitted with a long table and black office chairs for impromptu meetings with the logistics staff, importers, and customs officials. Every surface was covered with sketches and tiny, three-dimensional mockups. Some cutouts, some collages, some mounted, all numbered to match the catalog.

"I left the good shit on the table, under that black matte," Hank said.

I moved the black cardboard. It was about the size of a placemat, but it hid something bigger than its actual size.

The top sketch was a black quill pen spaghetti scrawl, and only by looking at it carefully could I discern a woman with her throat cut and a blood-spitting dick coming out. The woman had dark hair. I knew who it was.

Next in the stack: her face split open and a target inside.

A gun between her legs. A dozen knives pinning her to the wall. Hands choking her. Squeezing her breasts blue. Pulling her vagina out. It got worse. The things he fantasized about doing to her body were sickening.

"Is this actual blood?" I asked.

"Your guess is as good as mine. The catalog says 'mixed media.'"

"Thank you for showing me this."

Hank slipped the black cardboard over the drawings so the violence didn't take up the whole room. "Should I shove it up his ass?"

"No. I want you to photograph it first. Then I'll tell you when to burn it."

"Do you know what this cost you?"

"Yes, I do."

He regarded me for a second. "You know the girl."

I held my hand out. "Thanks again, buddy. Make arrangements with your Compton girl if you think it's a fit."

"Will do."

On the way back up the 710, I couldn't think straight, much less work. I'd never wanted to hurt anyone as badly as I wanted to hurt Kevin Wainwright just for putting those images in my head. But he'd done nothing wrong. The purpose of his work was to exorcise his demons. He couldn't be held legally or morally accountable for its content. If he was angry at Monica for walking out on him, he had every right to draw her slashed open if that gave him closure.

So I couldn't call the LAPD, and I couldn't tell Monica. I'd have to admit I bought the thing behind her back, and she wouldn't think well of it. Worse, I could scare her for no reason. I didn't want to scare her. I wanted her to be the same, proud little goddess I knew. I was just going to have to watch her more closely in case they were more than just drawings.

CHAPTER 5

MONICA

I WORE one of my new garters, a purple so dark it could be black. Over that was the black lace dress I'd bought at Nordstrom's. The skirt fell just above my knees and the satin lining stopped just above the hem. The neckline was modest, and the sleeves covered my upper arms. It was skin tight but comfortable and classy. He could take me anywhere. I was only a slut underneath the dress.

I braided my hair. I tried to make it special, but I simply didn't have Gabby's skill, and my arms ached by the third try. I did my best, though, same as every day since she died. I wore my hair as a remembrance to her, as if I could call her back and whisper in her ear *I loved you.*

I didn't have a roommate to answer the knock at the door. Times like that made me feel gut-twisting loneliness. I ran out, winding a band around the bottom of the braid. Even though I knew it was Jonathan, I had to look out the window to check first. He leaned on the corner of the porch, looking at the opening of the crawlspace. His brown leather jacket hung over a suit and tie, and his expression was dead serious.

"See something you like?" I asked when I opened the door.

"Your foundation's slipping."

"Have you noticed the hill? And gravity? How they conspire?"

He glanced back at me without moving his body. Fuck, he was gorgeous. "I can get someone to fix it. I'm a real estate developer, you know. I've got guys."

I strode over to him and put my hands on his back. He looked at the foundation critically, as though he was doing calculations in his head. He looked at me again, and I put my fingers in his hair. We stood like that for a second as I drank him in.

"You're beautiful," I said.

"I was just about to say that." He turned and leaned on the railing with his legs spread. I stepped into the opening. He slid his fingers up my thighs, past my hemline, leaving my skin tingling in their wake. When he got to the lace tops of my stockings, he put his hands beneath my ass and stroked me gently.

I leaned down until my nose touched his, gasping when he fondled between my legs lightly. "Jonathan," I whispered, "what are you doing?"

"I just want to know what barriers I'm dealing with here."

"You always stick your hand up a girl's skirt on the first date?"

He caressed the insides of my thighs, keeping his touch soft. "I haven't bothered with an actual date for about nine years." He angled his face so his lips met mine. I put my hands on his neck and kissed him. The tip of his tongue found mine, and we weaved our mouths together until I was a ball of heat and desire.

"I hate to break this up," he said, "but we're on a clock here."

I groaned. I had no idea how I would make it through dinner.

"And you have to get a change of clothes," he said. "Jeans and a jacket."

"Why?"

"Can you let a guy surprise you?" He slapped my ass and pointed to the front door. "Go."

Still smiling from the delicious sting on my butt, I gathered up clothes, stuffed them into a bag, and ran back out to the porch. He'd parked the Jag in my driveway, right behind my little black Honda. He opened the passenger door for me and closed it when I got in. As he drove up the 101, I put my hand on his, stroking the top of it.

"You working tomorrow?" he asked. "Because I have the day off."

"Work, then Frontage."

"Without your partner?" he asked, then waved his hand. "Sorry. Obviously."

"Yeah. I wanted her on the piece with me and the boys, too. But, shit, I miss her."

"What boys and what piece?"

"I'm collaborating with Darren and Kevin."

The car swerved too far right, and he almost had an accident. A horn blared and a middle finger was raised. Jonathan waved in apology. "You were saying?" he asked.

"Don't have an accident." He pulled off at Los Feliz Boulevard. "Where are we going?" I asked.

"Small place in the hills." He turned up into Griffith Park.

"You're not just taking me to your house, are you?"

"No, not *just* my house. I have things planned, and they include my place. Initially." He glanced over at me. "I didn't suggest a date so I could take you back to my room and pin you to the bed."

"Are we going to watch the game from your bed?"

"Nope."

"Damn. Brad Chance is pitching."

"Why bother watching? He's going to overuse his screwball and wear out his elbow by the third inning."

"It's fun watching guys swing at them. Especially Den Adler. He practically falls over," I snickered.

"So," he said definitively, stopping at a light, "you've avoided this 'piece' thing for exactly three minutes, and I've been very good about it."

I put my hands on my knees. "Kevin asked me to collaborate on a thing with him for the B.C. Modern. We're on a tight deadline. I brought Darren and Gabby in." The light changed to green, and I was relieved of the weight of his stare.

"Why?" he asked.

"Because they're family, and I like working with them."

"Not as a buffer between you and Kevin?"

"No." I wasn't sure if I lied to him or myself.

He pulled the car to a wide space on the side of the road and put it in park. He faced me. "Why did you agree to work with him after what he did at the Eclipse show?"

Layers of emotion masked his face. The top was a cold calm, an understanding bordering on parental. Under that, something wilder, but laser focused and powerful, pushed to the surface. I took a nervous breath. He was pissed, and I'd never seen that before. Goose bumps rose over my arms, and I rubbed my thumbs against my forefingers. I wondered if he could hear the clatter of my heart.

"Having music at the B.C. Modern could make my career. Everyone will hear it. Everyone will review it. It was like being handed a gift, and if I'd refused, I would have regretted it the rest of my life."

"Your ambition outweighs your sense."

I tried to match his anger with my own, but I felt puny and unjustified. "We were pretty clear that my work is my work. That hasn't changed." I kept my eyes level with his even though I felt the weight of his stare. He didn't like Kevin. I knew that, but I wouldn't abdicate my right to live my life as I pleased.

"Everything's changed, Monica."

"Not that."

With those few words, I felt two wills pressing against each other, hard, straight, still. Nothing moved. No friction was created between them. His hands clenched the wheel, and mine were wound into fists. I couldn't bear it. I touched the top of his hand.

He grabbed the back of the neck and pulled my face to his, drowning me in a kiss so hard and hot, I almost forgot what I'd seen in his expression. What had he seen in mine? That my heart could be broken? That I was falling in love with him, and if I tried to stop, the inertia would crack me in two? I pulled my face off his.

I said, "I know you don't like Kevin."

"Understatement of the year."

"He's harmless. And I'm trustworthy."

"The latter, I believe. But men know other men." He stroked my cheek. "Can you not be alone with him? Can you promise me that?"

It was a lot to ask. Darren was involved, but who knew what situations would arise? I covered his hand with mine. He needed me to make an honest effort. I could do that. "Yes."

"Thank you." He kissed me and got back onto Los Feliz Boulevard. We made the rest of the trip in hand-holding silence. Whatever anger had manifested in his face got pushed away. He pulled into his driveway, and the gate shut behind us with a clang. He walked around the car and opened my door. I had never seen his house in daylight, never seen the art deco woodwork on the windows or the detailing of the roof shingles. He took my hand and led me up to the porch. The front door was open, and he went in, expecting I'd follow. But I stopped at the threshold.

"What?" he asked. "Cat got your feet?"

"I've never entered your house with my clothes on before."

"Ah. Well, first time for everything." He tugged on my hand until I crossed into his house. The living room was as it had always been but bathed in light from the setting sun. If the room could look warmer, more inviting, I didn't know how. He looked back at me and the sunlight dashed off the tips of his eyelashes as he pulled me through rooms and out to the backyard.

The pool was a huge, bean-shaped expanse in the center of the yard. Close to the house, a flower garden, sectioned by paths of flagstones, spanned from the main house to the pool house. Smaller, cozy areas with benches lined the right hedge, and on the left, wall-sized sliding glass doors opened into the sitting room where I'd had tea.

Aling Mira approached us in a modest black suit, carrying a tray of white wine.

"Hi," I said when I took a glass. She nodded and walked toward a little table set for two. A middle-aged man lit the last candle on one of the flagstone paths and then the two on the table. I told Jonathan, "You have a nice yard."

"Come walk with me." He held out his arm, and I took it. We headed toward the pool on the candle-lined path. "Aling Mira cooked a Filipino specialty for you called kare-kare. It's made from—"

"Oxtail stew?"

"You've had it?"

"I live in Los Angeles."

He smiled and squeezed my hand. "She saw you slept in my room. So she's very impressed with you."

"How long has she worked for you?"

"A long, long time. She's seen it all. She wants me to be happy as much as my own mother. Well, maybe an aunt or something."

We strolled around the pool while the staff set up dinner. The sun was setting fast, and the candles lining all the pathways became more visible as the sky darkened.

"You lived here with your wife?"

"Yes. Why?"

"The bed?" I cringed. "Was that...?"

He laughed. "New bed, don't worry. You're the only woman I've had in it, actually."

"I feel like a groundbreaker."

"You've broken some ground on a few things."

"Such as?" I swung to face him.

"This date?"

"And?"

"And showing you off at the L.A. Mod."

"And?"

"And taking care of you. And wanting to see you again and again. And dressing you for my eyes."

"You're making me feel very, very good." I kissed him gently and breathed in that leather and sawdust smell that was his choice, not his ex-wife's. "I have to talk about you dressing me."

He put his arms around my waist and pulled me close. "Yes?"

"It makes me uncomfortable when you buy me expensive stuff."

He kissed my jaw and neck, as if to belie my discomfort and turn it into heat. "But the diamond was all right?"

I pursed my lips. "No, it wasn't, but before I could think about it, stuff happened. So you got that one in under the wire. Don't let it happen again."

He put his lips to my ear and said, "I have a piano. A Steinway. Would you play it for me after dinner?"

I kissed him and whispered, "I'd love to."

"And you'd sing for me?"

"Yes." I dragged my lips across his cheek, listening to him breathing and feeling his hands at my waist. The idea of making music for him was so intimate, so arousing, I didn't think I'd be able to make it through dinner.

"When we met, you said you wouldn't," he said.

"Things changed."

"So, you'd take this talent, gifted to you from birth, and use it as an expression of how you feel about me?"

I pulled away. "Aren't you clever."

"Money is a blunt tool for expression. It's vulgar compared to art, I agree, but it's all I have. I want you to accept it. It would make me happy."

I didn't know how to argue without making the gifts he was born with somehow coarse and ugly, while mine were worthwhile enough to give. He really had me cornered. "You just did a number on me," I said.

He bowed. "Captain of the debate team at Loyola."

"Ah, a good Jesuit education," I said, walking away. "I suppose now I get to wear all my new underwear without guilt."

He grabbed my hand and pulled me back. "You said you were Catholic, so you have guilt somewhere."

"Only until eighth grade. I performed 'Invictus' for my graduation recital and earned my escape from parochial school. I entered Los Angeles Unified guilt-free."

He took me in his arms and kissed me. "Classic. We did that in sixth. Eighth grade was Kipling. 'If.'"

"Oh, that's a long one."

"I had to recite it with *feeling*."

I smiled. "Yes, me too. I still remember 'Invictus'. Let me see, '*Out of the night that covers me, Black as the pit from pole to pole—*'"

He completed the stanza. "'*I thank whatever gods may be, for my unconquerable soul.*'" He grabbed the base of my braid and pulled my hair as he drew his mouth to mine. He was so sweet. His kisses were hard and passionate, a controlled lack of restraint in every flick of his tongue, every grasp of his fingers. I pushed into him, feeling his erection against me. He pulled away at the sound of a throat clearing.

Aling Mira stood behind me. "I'm sorry to interrupt. You said I should let you know when dinner is ready."

"Thank you," Jonathan said. He rattled something off in Tagalog. Aling Mira nodded to each of us and went back to the middle-aged man who stood in a secluded area.

"What did you say?" I asked.

"I thanked her and gave her the rest of the night off." He put his hand on my back. "I'm perfectly capable of spooning you stew. And I'd like to."

We strode slowly to a table set with silver and porcelain. On the side table was a full setting with stew in a silver serving bowl. Aling Mira and the man went to a back gate.

"Who's the guy?"

"Her husband, Danilo. They live in the back house."

The metal gate clacked behind them, and we were alone in the yard. Jonathan pulled a chair out for me. I stood in front of it, between him and the table. I was ready to sit, but I wanted another kiss. I tilted my face to him, until I felt his breath on my face, and parted my lips.

He reached for me, and I thought he would put his arms around my waist. Instead, he met my lips with his and leaned into me. In one wave of his arm, he yanked the tablecloth, knocking the dishes off the table. They clattered everywhere, smashing and spinning. His weight continued forward, throwing more plates out from under me, until he pinned me to the table.

I opened my legs, wrapping them around him as we kissed. My dress rode up to my waist. I pushed into him. His cock was so hard, like a tight fist against me. He groaned into my mouth, then pushed his fist of a dick into me again. He fingered under the garter belt, twisting his fingers in it.

"I want you to wear these all the time. Under jeans. To bed when I'm not there. I'll buy you more. You be who you want when we're not together, but under your clothes, this is the reminder that you're mine. Understand?"

"Yes."

He unbuckled his pants. A shiver went up my spine as I watched him take his dick out. My panties were no more than a damp string at my crotch, and he pushed them out of the way, handling me roughly. His fingertips probed for my soaked opening. He jammed two fingers in me. I cried out in pleasure and spread my legs farther, kicking a bowl and sending it crashing to the ground.

"You're ready," he growled, sliding his fingers out and jamming them in all the way. He ran his finger across the front wall of my hole until I felt a shudder I'd never felt. He pushed, stroking, curving his finger over a hard nodule of nerves inside me while pressing the heel of his hand on my clit. I went weak with a radiation of pleasure.

"Do you want it?" he asked.

"Yes, Jonathan. Please, fuck me." He removed his fingers and lodged his dick in me. "Oh, God," I said, barely coherent.

He moved above me, his every stroke hitting the mark, bringing breaths of gratification. He put his fingers in my mouth, and I sucked on them, tasting myself. His dick spread me, pushing against my clit, the edge of my opening, and sending shockwaves through me as his thrusts found their rhythm. He removed his fingers and pulled my leg over his shoulder. He went so deep, I cried out. I pushed forward, wanting him inside me, a part of me. I was so close, and as though he could sense it, he slowed down.

"Take it easy, little goddess."

"Oh, I can't. I'm going to come."

"No, wait."

"I can't." I was desperate, on the edge of a cliff, a rope tied to my ankle and a boulder. The boulder was tipping over the edge of the cliff, and I would follow it to the bottom of the crevice.

"'Invictus.' Second stanza, Monica." He leaned over, still moving his hips. "Do it. '*In the fell clutch of circumstance…*' Slowly and with feeling, or you start over." His voice was a beacon of control and sense in the chaos of his every stroke, every inch a burning fuse to an explosion.

"You're joking," I gasped. "I can't recite 'Invictus' now."

He leaned down and sucked my nipple, leaving a trail of saliva when he looked up and said, "Do it."

Oh, God, how could he expect me to recall eighth grade while getting fucked on a dinner table? I had to stare through the pressure to give in to my orgasm, hold it back to remember. "'*In the fell clutch of circumstance, I have not winced nor cried aloud. Under the bludgeonings of chance.*' Oh fuck, Jonathan…"

He pinned my hands over my head and started on the next line. "'*My head is bloody…*' And no rushing, baby." His thrusts got faster, deeper, more willed.

I picked up, "'*But unbowed. Beyond this place of wrath and tears, looms the horror of the shade, and yet the menace of the years…*'"

"Ah, Monica. Go. Make it." His face was reddened with effort. He wanted to come too, and that, coupled with his searing thrusts, sent the boulder over the edge.

"'*Finds and shall find me unafraid,*'" I cried to the heavens. He moved to the rhythm of the poem as I continued, watching that boulder get smaller in the distance. "*It matters not how straight the gate, how charged with punishments the scroll.*"

He said the last stanza with me. "*I am the master of my fate. I am the captain of my soul.*"

"Yes, Monica."

"Yes!"

I was dragged off the cliff first. I cried out his name as I fell into a chasm of blackness and tingling lights. I clenched my thighs around him. My arms wanted to flail, but he had them tight as my pussy ignited, clutching for him, pulsing for him to be deeper. The orgasm came from deep inside, undulating up my spine and down the backs of my thighs. I lost myself in it.

I heard him grunt, miles away, then moan into a snarl of satisfaction. I gasped as he tightened above me, the base of his cock pulsing as he came. His eyes squeezed shut and his arms bent as he let go of my wrists and fell on top of me.

We twitched together, spent, still breathing in the rhythm of a poem.

CHAPTER 6

JONATHAN

I'LL COP to having plenty of sex, much of it of the "wild" variety. I'll admit I have memories that would beat most men's imaginations. I'll tell you I've had beautiful women do exactly as I tell them and we've gotten off on the control. But that? That was a new classification of fucking.

"Jonathan?" she whispered from under me. Her uttering my name brought me to my senses. I pulled my face out of her neck and kissed her collarbone.

"Monica."

"Are you all right?"

"No," I said.

"Really?"

I put my nose to hers. "Joking." My shifted weight made my cock drop out of her.

"Ah," she moaned as if she'd miss it. "I should use the bathroom."

"I'll set up dinner in the kitchen."

She smiled, and my world went on fire. "Let's eat it this time."

I got off her and she sat up. Her hair was falling out of her braid and the hem of her dress was bunched around her waist. One shoe had fallen off. I found it and slipped it back onto her foot, then helped her off the table.

"Thank you," she said.

"My pleasure." I kissed her because I had no choice. When she walked toward the house, I touched her neck as if I needed to tether her to me for another second. I brought the stuff on the sideboard into the kitchen and set the table. I had a handful of silverware and stopped myself.

Fork on the left, spoon above.

Or if it was a soup spoon, did it go on the right?

If she noticed I'd done it wrong, she'd tease me. I'd like that enough to throw her across the table again, which was not what I wanted to do. We didn't have all night, and I wanted to actually share a meal with her. I put the spoons on the right and set the tureen between the bowls.

I liked her. She was great. Outstanding. Gorgeous and smart. All those words seemed cheap, though. My rejection of them alarmed me, because they weren't good enough. I was losing control, and I needed to figure out why.

The lack of a condom was definitely something, but only part of the story. The fact that we were far enough along to feel each other's skin spoke volumes. Her looks were something also. She was beautiful, but not my type. I usually went for blondes, so maybe not. Her singing that night at Frontage ticked it up a few notches for me, but I had fucked other artists since Jessica. Monica was honest, real, and honorable. Those were commodities I didn't see every day, and those were words worthy of her, but those qualities didn't seduce the mind or calm the heart the way she did.

I forgot where the napkins went. Fuck. Where was Aling Mira when I needed her?

The issue with Monica was obvious, but I wouldn't allow myself to utter certain words, even in my mind. Certain commitments and feelings were simply inaccessible and needed to stay that way. I'd rejected my ex-wife, but the passions she'd thrown away were dead. I regretted that, grieved their loss, because if anyone deserved true, deep feelings, Monica did.

An honorable man would have given her up before she fell in love, choosing a small hurt over a bigger one later. But I wasn't that honorable. I wanted her more than I'd wanted anything in a long time, and I would have her until she couldn't bear it any longer.

I felt like an animal.

I heard her clopping down the hall in those cheap, sexy shoes. When she came into the kitchen, I sighed. Her hair was down, except for a thin braid at the side of her head. She was well put together, yet she looked like someone had just fucked the shit out of her. I held out my hand and she took it.

"I'm starving," she said.

I pulled out the chair for her. She glanced at the setting and said nothing. Instead, she tilted her head to see what was inside the tureen. What made me think she even cared where soup spoons went? She made me unsure about the simplest things.

She sat. "That looks good."

I ladled her stew, and then mine. She put her napkin on her lap and waited for me to sit before she took a scoop and blew on it.

"I'm sorry. I think it's pretty cold," I said.

"Ooh, good, she used banana blossoms." She pointed her spoon at a smaller dish. "Is that pinakbet?"

"Yes." I speared a piece of okra and held it to her lips. She parted them, allowed the fork in her mouth, and slid it out, her teeth barely scraping the silver tines.

"That's nice," she said, chewing.

"Have you been to the Philippines?" I asked.

She smirked. "I've been to Mexico."

"No farther?" I placed another forkful of pinkabet before her.

"No." She took the food I offered.

I poured wine for us. "I'm surprised. You seem more... worldly than that."

She shrugged. I noticed a little redness around her ears. "I'm not sheltered. There're plenty of ways to get into trouble in a thirty-mile radius."

"Do tell." She shrugged and took a spoonful of stew. "Come on," I said. "We'll make a trade. I'll tell you something that will make you run away if you tell me how to get into trouble in Los Angeles." The way she glanced at me made me think she had something more than a harmless exchange of stories on her mind. She obviously didn't realize the depth and breadth of the stories I could tell without touching the things I didn't want her to know.

"Deal," she said.

"Ladies first."

She took a sip of wine and straightened her shoulders, as if daring me to think less of her. Then she swallowed a little too hard, and I knew that down deep, she was afraid I might. I tried to remain impassive, but I was jumping out of my skin.

"One time..." she said, then paused.

"Go on."

"I shot up heroin."

I tried not to choke on my wine. "How was it?"

"Incredible."

"Really? And just the once? I don't get a whole story? Just six words and an adjective?"

"I'm gauging your reaction."

"I went to private schools. My friends financed dealers and producers to ensure their own product flow. So," I poured more wine, "how does a beautiful Catholic girl end up with a needle in her arm?"

"I've been tested since, you know. I'm clean."

I didn't say another word. I held out another bit of pinkabet, which she took. I was going to feed her until she told me about this tiny crevice of her life.

"Ok, well." She swallowed. "It was, like, the core of a laugh. You know that wavy good feeling you have inside before the laugh comes out? But the laugh is a release from that feeling, and when you're done laughing, it goes away. So without the laugh, and the release, it got huge. It kind of started in my heart and worked outward like a supernova and stayed there. Imagine that feeling, that happy feeling before you laugh, being big and *staying*. I was lying down, but I was flying, and at the same time. Well, at first it was just the good pre-laugh feeling, but then the tension came and I wanted it released, because it was painful. Emotionally painful. Like, if the tension got too much, and it broke, so much sorrow would come out."

She paused and took a sip of wine, not looking at me. "When I came down, I puked and I felt like crap. I mean, who wouldn't, right? But I knew the first time is the only really great time, and I didn't want to end up some sick addict. Not even to be Janis Joplin."

"But why do it in the first place?"

"Kevin… I know you're his biggest fan. He and I used to do things just to experience them. Just to see, you know, if there was something to it, or if we could translate it into our work. So we did some stupid things."

"But he never tied you to a bedpost?"

"No."

"He's a sad man."

She laughed. "We ran with our eyes closed. We walked through downtown barefoot. We slept on Skid Row a whole weekend."

I think I let the silence go a little too long. I was thinking about her huddled in filth under an overpass, broken glass underneath her, and strange, unstable people within arms' reach.

"What?" she asked, sipping her wine.

"Did he *sleep*? When you were on Skid Row?"

"I guess."

I took her hand. "I couldn't sleep knowing you weren't a hundred percent safe. I couldn't walk you into danger or watch someone put a needle full of drugs in your arm. I couldn't rest."

"Well, good, because the piss smell kept me up and I was hungry. Speaking of, I'm going to eat more oxtail stew, and you're going to tell me something that makes me want to walk out. Except I won't."

She took a spoonful of stew and glanced at me, so sure her feelings could survive any revelation. I had so many wonderfully juicy stories that wouldn't even half nudge her out the door. So many others would require a discussion that would ruin the evening.

I asked, "Are sexual escapades on the table?"

"Sure." She looked into her bowl. Maybe that was a bad idea. I didn't want her to get bent out of shape. If she told me a story like the one I intended to tell her, I'd get bent out of shape.

"Are you sure you're sure?"

"As long as your wife isn't in there."

"Why? Besides the fact that she's not the escapade type?"

"I'm not going to pretend your ex-wife's my favorite person ever. But to me, what goes on sexually in a marriage, you don't talk about. So—" she put her hands over her ears "—la la la, don't want to hear it."

In the five minutes I had to decide what to tell her, I'd prepared a story of bedding three women at once. It was absolutely true, terribly unsexy, and funny all at once. But she'd thrown me by respecting a woman who'd lied to her and caused her hurt, by honoring a vow she'd had no part of. Monica deserved better than a canned story I'd told a hundred times at the club.

I took her wrists and pulled her hands from her ears. She smiled at me.

"I agree," I said. "You're safe from my marriage bed. But not the rest." I took my hands away and picked up my wine glass, taking a deep breath. "There's a difference between a dominant and a pig."

"Really?"

"My father," I said, leaning forward, "is a pig." She looked as though she was ready to choke on her oxtail stew. "You all right?" I asked.

"I'm fine. I sense an example coming?"

"I hit puberty early," I said. "By thirteen, I was done. Close to my fourteenth birthday, my father wanted to know why I hadn't gotten laid yet."

She chewed, then gazed up me with those big, chocolate disks. "Okay?"

"He set me up on a date with a girl. Woman. Rachel. She was a couple of years older than me. That was my first time. And guess what? Turns out, she was his mistress."

She swallowed hard. "How old was she?"

"The math you just did in your head was correct."

"Wow. He whored out his underage mistress?"

"To his underage son. Like I said. Pig. And you should see the look on your face." Her heartbeat was practically audible. She pushed food around and I worked to control my nerves.

She sighed heavily. "Honestly, I didn't expect you to even have a story like that."

"You think rich people don't have sick shit in their houses?"

She raised her eyebrows and swirled her spoon in her stew. "Something like that."

I laughed. Partly because I was nervous about voicing a fragment of the story, and partly because I was relieved she hadn't run away. Not yet, at least.

She put her spoon down and sipped her wine. "Did you see her again?"

"I did but on different terms. It was messy for a while." I cleared my throat. "She died."

"Oh, I'm so sorry. How?"

"Car accident. I was about sixteen when it happened."

I should have shut up way before mentioning the accident. If she looked into it, I was deeply fucked. So I stopped talking. Just stopped.

She waited, slid off her chair, stepped over to me, and put her hands on my face. "You know you have to tell me the whole thing, right?"

"There is no more." I put my hand up her skirt until I felt the lacy top of her stocking. "You're going to have to take the dress off for where we're going next."

"Upstairs?"

I put my fingers under the lace and up the garter straps. "Nope."

"Where?"

"Have you finished dinner?"

"Yes."

I pulled her down, kissing her hard. She tasted of lovingly made Filipino food and cold white wine. I wanted her all over again, but we had someplace to be.

CHAPTER 7

MONICA

I slipped into my jeans, keeping my fancy underwear on. I felt filthy, sexy, sensual with garters under denim. When I reached the front foyer, I found the door open and a loud rumbling in the driveway.

Jonathan straddled a matte black rocket of a motorcycle with red touches at the rims. The back seat was suspended by nothing but air and the promise of velocity.

"Well," I said as I clopped down the porch stairs in my heels, "is this new or is it some old thing you found in the back of the garage?"

"I got rid of the Mercedes and saw this." He handed me a helmet in the same matte black as the bike. "You've ridden before?"

"Yeah." I slipped on the helmet. I'd dirtbiked with Kevin in the Sequoias until mud covered me from knee to toe and I walked like a cowboy coming home from a week on a feisty mare. Once, in freshman year, Ivan Ikanovitch took me out to Ventura on his new BMW. Needless to say, I had to take a cab home.

"Let's go then, little goddess. This trip usually takes forty minutes, and we have thirty five."

I slid onto the back seat and put my arms around his waist. "You shoulda let me recite 'Invictus' as fast as I wanted. We'd be on time."

The gate slid open as if by his thought waves alone, and we took off, my legs clenching the seat and my arms clutching his waist. When we stopped at a light, I heard his voice in my head.

"You're cutting off my circulation."

The clarity of his voice was shocking, and he turned to me, tapping the helmet.

"There are microphones in here?" He nodded. "Fancy."

The light changed, and we took off. We didn't talk much as we zipped onto the five, turning onto the 110 freeway. I tried not to squeal when he went really fast since he could hear me. Instead, I leaned on him, enjoying the softness of his leather jacket and the way it creaked against mine. Even though it was early November, the air was warm as it whipped under my clothes.

Another piece of the puzzle fell into place. He was fourteen when his father loaned him his mistress. His first sexual experience was coated in familial ties and discomfort. He went to the institution when he was sixteen, right about when she was killed. He'd given me a portion of the story. His time in the institution had something to do with his father's promiscuity and penchant for young girls, as well as his absurd expectations of his son's virility.

I was still missing some puzzle pieces. Something was very seriously off, but his explanation was a start, and I felt a sort of relief knowing that eventually, when he was ready, he'd fill in the blanks.

We traveled eighty miles an hour past the industrial tinkertoy skyline and outlet malls with their blindingly bright, sky-high screens, blasting high above neighborhoods still burned out from the riots, and back to a middle-class residential zone.

I slipped my hand under his jacket, then under his shirt. I felt his taut stomach and the little hairs on it, the warmth of his skin making me feel safe and cared for.

"Are you making a pass at me?" he asked in my head.

"Not at this speed."

"Okay, because I'm having you in a couple of hours."

"I know." I leaned my head on his back. "You're a big ho."

"Only for you these days."

I hoped my sigh wasn't audible through the microphone. I knew I was choosing to believe him, and that choice was conscious, and thus, fallible. I knew he could walk out on me at any minute, for any reason. If he really was over his wife, he could look for a more permanent mate with whom he had more in common, like money, and social standing, and similar friends and interests.

But I chose, maybe unwisely, to believe he wanted me for more than a short time because it made me happy to think it.

I was screwed.

He turned off the freeway at Carson, and after a few more quick pivots, he slowed in front of a grassy, floodlit field where a blimp was parked.

"We made it," he said, pulling up to the chain-link fence around the field's perimeter. A man in a white shirt and vinyl jacket approached us with a clipboard. Jonathan took off his helmet. His hair was a complete wreck, a school of wild-armed starfish backlit by floodlights. He fingerbrushed it and faced the man with the clipboard.

"Mister Drazen?"

"Yeah."

"You just made it. Park the bike in the lot to the left. Have fun."

"How are they doing?" asked Jonathan. I took off my helmet. I could only imagine what my hair looked like. A bunch of broken strings in the same backlighting, no doubt. And the little braid I'd left coming from my part probably looked like a dreadlock.

"Down two in the second. Having trouble getting men on base," the man with the clipboard said.

Jonathan shook his head and started the bike again. We cruised to the center of the lot and parked by a sheet metal trailer held up by a cinderblock foundation. He put the kickstand down and leaned the bike over until it was stable.

"What was that?" I asked, dismounting first. "The game? They're losing already?"

He got off and set the bike straight. "Apparently."

"Are we going on the blimp?"

"If you're good."

"And we're going to Dodger Stadium? Maybe? I don't want to assume, but the second blimp always comes about the fifth inning." I was trying to keep my shit together, but I'd lived my whole life in the Stadium's backyard and had never found a way to even get into a playoff game. When I knew the right people, the team had been in the basement. During good years, I'd been hanging with people who didn't "do" sports because organized team activities were uncreative, uncivilized, and boorish.

"Yes," Jonathan said. "We're going to see the game from the sky if you move that tight little ass. They won't wait."

I jumped on him. I couldn't help it. I'm only made of flesh and blood, and that blood is Dodger blue. I kissed his face and wrapped my legs around him. He caught me, hitched me up by the backs of the knees, and started for the blimp. The white noise was deafening, and before he let me down, I said in his ear, "Thank you."

He took my hand, smiling as if he was pleased to see me so happy, and we ran across the grass to the huge machine. It was bigger than I'd imagined. Massive. Overwhelming. A tire company's name was written across it in letters two or three times my height. I couldn't hear any of the men who greeted us, but I put on my customer service smile. In this case, it couldn't have been more genuine.

We were hustled into a gondola with six seats facing front. The two at the windshield were pilot and copilot. Jonathan and I were guided in behind that, and behind us were two men who appeared to be businessmen. We were surrounded by windows, but Jonathan made sure I got the seat closest to a view. I jumped in. I wanted to talk to him, but it was simply too loud. The copilot gave us headphones with mikes on them.

I heard Jonathan say, "Can you hear me?"

"Yes," I replied. "Can you hear me?"

"Loud and clear."

"Baby," I said, smiling until I felt my face might snap in two, "I'm a sure thing tonight."

Everyone in the cabin cracked up. Of course they could all hear me. Jonathan put his arm around me and pulled me to him, kissing my forehead while he laughed. I buried my head in his chest.

"Don't worry, miss," said the pilot, his voice loud and clear. "We get that a lot." After a pause, he continued. "I'm Larry. This here is my copilot, Rango. We'll be heading for East Los Angeles in a few seconds, set to arrive at Dodger Stadium in about forty minutes. Hold on, takeoff can be a little jarring for first timers. Buckle in."

The noise got even louder. I found my buckles and strap. Jonathan helped me click in, then he took my hand. Seconds later, I felt as if I was being launched from a rocket. Larry turned a wooden steering wheel set between his seat and Rango's.

"I'll have the game on," Rango chimed in. "We're in the bottom of the fourth against the New York Yankees. Cashen is pitching for the Yanks as we speak."

I closed my eyes and heard Jonathan's voice. "Open your eyes. These flights are hard to get, even for me."

I opened them and looked at him in the darkened cabin. He touched my cheek and smiled, and I felt protected and secure. Even if it was an illusion, knowing he was there made me feel less like I was shooting out a cannon and more like I was on a fun trip I wouldn't have dreamed up for myself.

The city spread beneath us in a blanket of lights made of a plaid of streets, freeways, and floodlit parks. I couldn't tear my eyes away. We were low enough to see cars and people but high enough to turn them into dots of velocity and intention. Everyone was headed somewhere, and we were above, passing in the wind.

The game wasn't going well for my team. I listened without discussion as another inning went by with three men stranded on base, a pitcher who threw balls that were fouled off until I knew he must be exhausted, and a beaner that may have left star hitter Jose Inuego with a concussion.

I felt Jonathan leaning over me to see the window. He rested his chin on my shoulder, then his lips landed on my neck. Leaning there, we looked out the window together. The gondola chilled as the minutes went by, and though we had jackets, I put my hand on his and found his fingers icy. I moved one of his hands between my knees to warm it and folded the other in mine. We stayed like that, looking out the window, his chest to my back, his chin on my neck, and his hands warmed by my body, until I saw Elysian Park. I probably could have picked my house out from there.

"Look!" I sounded like a kid. "I can see it!"

It seemed to take as long to get over the stadium from the moment I saw it as it took for us to get to Los Angeles from Carson. Another blimp passed us, heading away from the game. Larry and Rango waved at the pilots. I was filled with contentment and a feeling of rightness, of being a part of something bigger than myself. I'd only felt that during orchestra practice in college, and only when everything was going right. The percussionist was spot on, the conductor spoke in a manual language as easy to understand as the written word, and we all followed as if lifted by the same tide.

As the feeling slipped away, I wanted nothing more than to recapture it. I pulled my headphones off and faced Jonathan. His eyes were visible from the lights on the pilot's dashboard. He pulled his microphone out of the way. I kissed him, and I didn't care who saw. I molded my lips to his and fed him my tongue. He took his hand from between my knees and put it to my cheek, warmed from my body, gentle to the touch. I extended that feeling of rightness for another minute until the gondola seemed to blaze with light.

I opened my eyes. We were right over the stadium. I took one last look at Jonathan and mouthed the words, *Sure thing.*

He mouthed back, *I know,* and I smiled.

I'd never seen a game like that before, and I found it disconcerting initially. I was used to television, where I could see every twitch and nod of the pitcher, and live games from the bleachers, where I could tell the direction of the ball from the sound it made coming off the bat. From the blimp, the players looked like white flowers on a perfect lawn.

I put my headphones back on and leaned into the window. The announcer was going on about pitch counts and men on base, and I heard the guys in the gondola doing much the same. The Yanks were up. Men on first and third. One out. Harvey Rodriguez was on deck.

Larry cut the engine, and the noise reduced. "We're gonna hover until a commercial, then fire it up again."

Jonathan put his lips to my ear. "Rodriguez is a lefty. They're going for a double play. Watch the infield." The shortstop and third baseman took two steps toward first. "They step toward right field because a lefty pulls that way, and forward to get the ball on the jump so they can pop it to second on the force play. And they're playing it a little forward because there's a guy on third who can go for the steal on a wild pitch or a sac fly."

"But what if the fly is shallow? They'll miss it, and it'll be a mess. The outfield just came in a little, too. I mean, Rodriguez barely has to work to sac a guy in."

"You take your chances. They're down by two, so if a guy strolls home on a sac fly, it's a bummer, but there's not much difference in the middle of the game between being down two and down three. There's more to gain with the double play."

Rodriguez walked. Bases were loaded. Some moments in a ball game were more important than others. They weren't the grand slams or the fat, bobbling errors at shortstop. They were the bases-loaded, one-man-out moments where either someone scored or someone was stopped dead. They were unpredictable, uncontrollable, and oftentimes silent as death. Like the one extra foul ball that would have been a third strike. Or the pitcher catching the line drive that would have sent a man or two home. Or a walk to load the bases.

"I can't watch." I covered my eyes. I couldn't see anything from up there anyway. I just saw dots move around and heard the broadcast. But Jonathan reached from behind me and took my wrists, pulling them down.

"Come on. Play with me. Don't bail."

"Yes, sir," I said, joking on his use of the word *play*. The infield moved way in, practically to where the dirt met the grass, and Jonathan's arms tightened. His hands, now warm, draped over my crossed forearms. "I know they're playing in to catch the guy at home plate if they have to," I said.

"Yes." He kissed my neck once, twice, three times, each one softer than the one before. Each lingered longer than the last. I tingled all over, and it took all my self-control to keep from bending my head back and leaning into him. I would have looked exactly like what I was: a woman in heat.

We were interrupted by the crack of a bat through the headphones we'd taken off. The white flowers scuttled across the lawn. The shortstop fielded the ball, got it to second, and then Val Renault, an unimposing fielder known for his hitting, got the ball out of his hand and to first quickly and accurately enough to complete the double play.

Inning over.

An hour and a half later, the game ended with the Dodgers winning by a run and forcing a seventh game. The six passengers on the gondola erupted at the last out. We high-fived and cheered and headed back to Carson.

CHAPTER 8

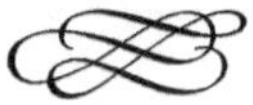

MONICA

I was a little wobbly getting off the gondola, but Jonathan put his arm around me and pulled me close as we went back to the bike. We thanked the employees we passed as they got the blimp back into place with ropes and pulleys. If their attitudes were any indication, managing a tire company's blimp was the most gratifying job in the world.

We approached the bike holding hands. "Thank you," I said. "That was probably in my top five dates ever."

"Top *five?*"

"Top four, maybe."

He faced me. "What?"

I shrugged. "It was a compliment."

He pressed his lips between his teeth. Before I could decide if he was suppressing rage or laughter, he ducked and thrust forward, throwing me over his shoulder. I squealed and kicked, bouncing as he ran. He pushed me against the side of the metal shed with a clang, pressing my shoulders to the wall.

"Name your top three. I'll beat them."

"With what?" I asked.

"I'll take you to the fucking moon and have you back in time for bed."

"Oh, Jonathan. The moon? Really?" I rolled my eyes.

He just smiled, all teeth and joy. "You're getting such a spanking tonight."

"Kiss me first," I said. "Maybe you'll get in the top three."

He took my hands and yanked them over my head, then kissed me. Or to be more accurate, he attacked me with his body. He pinned my hands hard and pushed his cock against me, grinding his lips against mine. His tongue filled me without finesse, as if he was fucking my mouth. I pushed myself against him in a rhythm until I groaned. I had to have him. He pushed back against me as if trying to get me, through our clothes, to beg for him.

"Hello," came a voice. Jonathan let my arms go and looked around. It was one of the guys who had wrestled the blimp to the ground. "We're closing up here."

"Thanks," Jonathan said without a hint of embarrassment or shame. He popped my helmet off the bike and handed it to me. A smile spread across his face like an uncontrollable oil spill. I took the helmet with the same grin.

The ride home passed with few words. I just rested against him with my hand under his shirt, feeling his warmth. I didn't stroke or caress him at eighty miles an hour, though the temptation was distracting.

He pulled the bike into my driveway. It was midnight, or close to it, and I was sore all over. "You coming in?" I asked, looping his finger in mine. He yanked me to him.

"We playing? Or am I just throwing you down and fucking you?"

Both options held appeal. Something hot and sweaty before an utter collapse into oblivion would be nice, and I'd be fresh and bright in the morning for work. But when he said "playing," I felt wetness condense between my legs, and a shiver went up my spine. I let my finger drop from his and put my arms to my sides. I wanted to be under his control, under his dominance, under *him*. I wanted to forget myself in him and to forget the shame of wanting it so badly.

"I'd like to play again," I said, then added, "Sir."

"Up to the porch with you then, and wait for me." When I turned around to go, he slapped my ass hard. I gasped and strode up the steps.

Jonathan dismounted and, instead of coming right up the porch, stood on the sidewalk. He looked up at the house, then crossed the street and did the same. He jogged back and came past my chain-link fence. "You're wide open to the street."

"Sir?"

"It means you have to keep your clothes on until we get inside."

My street, partly because of the hill and partly because of the neighborhood, was dead at night. If two people passed between midnight and eight in the morning, it would be a newsworthy event. I had the feeling it didn't matter. He stared at me, calculating. I knew that look. He was constructing the game. He faced the street and me, feet planted on my porch, and said, "Step over here, my little goddess."

I did it, heart pounding with anticipation. My back faced the street.

"Unbutton your jeans."

I popped them.

"Unzip, please."

I did, showing my garter belt and the tops of my new, already-christened lingerie. He stroked my stomach, his finger grazing the top of the lace.

"Touch yourself."

He watched my hand go down my pants. Between the sweet, secret caresses in the blimp, and the bike ride home, I was ready for him. I shuddered when my fingers found my swollen, soaked pussy. I buckled with pleasure, and he held my chin.

"Stand up." He put upward pressure on my chin, forcing my spine straight and my view upward. "How wet are you?"

"Very wet, sir."

"What would you like me to do about it?"

"I want you to fuck me, please."

"Hold up your hand."

I slid my hand out of my pants and held it up. The moisture on my fingers glistened. He kissed the tips of my fingers, then put them in his mouth. I gasped as he slid his tongue over them, sucking everything off. His lips might as well have been on my pussy, and I almost buckled again.

"You're delicious," he said.

"Thank you."

"Now, do you remember your ready position?"

"Yes, sir." I wondered how many more times I could call him *sir* without spontaneously coming.

"And your safeword?"

"Tangerine, sir."

"Go inside, get undressed, and wait for me in ready position. Be in any room you want. I'll find you." A smirk played at his mouth. "You have sixty seconds, and you'd better be ready."

I unlocked my door and entered the house. Where to go? I wanted to participate in the game. Surprise him. Make him earn it. So the bedroom was the first place I dismissed. The bathroom was in no condition. That was out. The living room had a nice soft couch, and I could be ready on the coffee table. That would be kind of cool, but the living room was right at the front door, and where was the fun if he practically tripped on me as he walked in?

I undressed as I walked through the house, dropping my shirt in the hamper and kicking my shoes into a corner. No. I retrieved the shoes.

I turned on hall lights and all the warm, indirect lamps. He preferred that kind of lighting, if his house and office were any indication. I'd yanked my pants off and slipped my shoes back on by the time I heard the screen door creak.

I crouched on the kitchen floor, behind the counter, knees and cheek on the linoleum, my hands between my legs until they touched my ankles. I had a wonderful view of under the counter. Not sexy. I turned my face to the kitchen table. Better.

I heard Jonathan close the front door, then his feet on the living room floor, down the hall, to the bedroom, where I wasn't. His smell permeated the air almost immediately, and I drank it in, waiting, my cunt high, a beacon of arousal.

His footsteps got closer. "The kitchen. Little goddess, you are beautiful." His boots came in my field of vision. "The kitchen," he repeated pensively. The refrigerator door opened and its light soaked the room. "What do you eat?"

"I eat at work. They feed us. And I order food out."

He grumbled. From his angle, I couldn't see him, but I felt the sting of his displeasure nonetheless. He closed the fridge, and the room was again lit by the two hallways on each side. He whistled, and though at first I didn't recognize the tune, it came to me at the chorus. "Under My Skin," the song I'd sung the night he surprised me at Frontage.

I heard some clacking and banging, a drawer opening, and the crumple of plastic bags. My heart seized. Plastic bags? Maybe something had been in them that he was managing? Or maybe he was moving something out of the way? Or filling one?

I simply couldn't see without getting out of position, and though I was overtaken by panic, I wasn't ready to give up on the game yet. But the panic wasn't fun. "Jonathan?"

A pause, then, "Monica?"

"You're not going to put a bag over my head, are you?"

Another pause. He came into my field of vision, looking into my face from six feet above. "Never."

I immediately relaxed. "Thank you, sir."

I realized, from the change in my throat's vibrations, that as much as Jonathan had a dominant voice, I had a submissive one. I used softly articulated hard consonants and breathy, aspirated vowels. I felt silly, suddenly, in such a position on the kitchen floor, ass up in stiletto heels, hands to my ankles, while my fully dressed kinda-boyfriend dicked around with the stuff in my kitchen. I knew the break in mood was my fault, but I couldn't have tolerated another second of being afraid.

His boots came in my field of vision again. They were brown, to match his jacket, and ridiculously sexy with his jeans. "Let's talk about ready position." He kneeled at my side and stroked my back and ass, letting his fingertips graze the crack. "This..." He slapped my ass and I gasped in surprise. "This is not ready position." He spanked me again. My cheek erupted in heat and tingles, which he exacerbated by stroking where he'd hit. "Up." He spanked the lower part, where meat met thigh. I straightened my legs. "More." I thought he would slap me, but he stroked instead, eliciting a groan that turned into a cry when he spanked me hard.

I jerked my hips up, not because I wanted him to stop spanking me, but because I wanted to do it right. My twat was fully in the air over an arched back. My breath heaved. I saw him at the edge of my vision, kneeling beside me in his long-sleeve shirt and suit slacks, his hand on my ass and pulling away for another slap that felt like a leather belt. The air left my lungs, leaving pleasure in the wake of the pain.

"The point of this," he said, "is that you are completely ready for me. I should be able to see your cunt is wet. Got it?"

"Yes, sir."

He ran a finger down my back, to my crack, and to my cleft, circling my clit before going back up again. "If you're crouched, I can't see it."

I couldn't form words.

"I'm sorry, Monica, I didn't hear you." He slapped the backs of my thighs, right at my pussy. It stung, and then pleasure blossomed like a thousand flowers.

"Yes."

He spanked me there again. "Sorry?"

I cried out.

"Shh. Behave."

"Yes," I gasped.

"Yes what?"

I knew that game. If I wanted him to continue, and I did, I knew how to do it. "Just yes."

He slapped me again, landing enough of his hand on my cunt to make me bite back another cry. "Monica, is there something you want?"

"Do it again, please." I don't know how I made words out of gasps, but I did.

He did. And then again, harder, and the sharper the pain, the more exquisite the pleasure. My ass must have been red by the third slap, but my pussy wanted more. He stroked me in between, to accentuate the tingle of pain, then held back his slaps until I thought I'd die with anticipation. When they landed, everything between my legs bloomed to pleasure. I thought I'd be overwhelmed with it, consumed, but he stopped, moved behind me, and took a cheek in each palm. He kissed my ass all over, softly, creating little stings of sore pain with his lips. He spread my cheeks apart while his thumbs stroked the sopping crack between.

"How do you feel, little goddess?"

"Beautiful."

"Good." He grabbed a handful of my hair and gently pulled me to a kneeling position. He came around to face me and got on his knees, a ball of plastic bags in his fist. "Your wrists."

I put them out. The plastic bags had been stretched and knotted together at the handles. When he touched me to tie my hands together, I felt arousal and relief. His touch was sure and gentle, his voice humming an old Sinatra tune that would always make me think of him.

When my wrists were bound, he eased me back, pulled my arms over my head, and looped my plastic binds to a drawer handle. He leaned over me, working the knot. So close, I breathed him in through his shirt. That smell mixed with the scent of getting tied up and fucked became the smell of complete release, of an orchestra connected by the simple movements of a skilled conductor. When he was done, he drew his hands down my arms, to my rib cage, thumbs stroking my nipples, and stretched me out across the floor until my arms were straight.

"Perfect," he said, more to himself than me. He pulled up my knees and spread them until they were to either side of my breasts. He leaned back and looked at his work. I saw his erection straining his pants, and I wanted to reach out and touch it. I was tied, and being stretched out added to the sensation of being exposed.

Jonathan pulled his shirt off, and I wanted to touch him even more. I wanted to run my fingers through his chest hair, to his belly, and follow the line of hair to his cock. When he pulled his pants off, it popped out, that wonderful thing. I hoped he'd stick it in my mouth. I wanted to eat it, take it down my throat with my hands tied to a drawer handle. I wanted to watch him come from below him, to see him throw his head back in surrender.

He picked up something off the counter before kneeling between my legs.

"Goddess, this has been done so many times before, it's almost boring." He held up a can of whipped cream. "You and I are too good for it. But it's two weeks from its expiration date, and we need to talk about the contents of your refrigerator."

"Yes, sir."

"Open up."

I opened my mouth, and he squirted some in. He kissed me before I could swallow. The cream mixed between our tongues and dripped down my chin. Still kissing me, he put the cold can on my nipple, sending shivers of pleasure down my body. He pulled away and kneeled between my legs. He squirted each nipple, topping me like a cake, the can making a *kkkkkkt* sound. He licked it off, then sucked each nipple, biting at the end. I gasped and threw my legs up higher. Pulling himself up, he regarded the can.

"This tip is interesting, actually," he said.

"Only you would find it interesting."

He placed the tip of the dispenser at my sternum, the pointed tooth digging into my skin. "Excuse me?"

"Only you, sir." I tried not to smile and wink. We didn't need to break the mood twice in one session.

The can had a pointed, plastic tip that made the whipped cream come out in a striated tube. When placed against the sensitive skin of the chest and abdomen, and slowly dragged while dispensing product, it created more than a sweet, decorative texture. It scratched, opening up the nerve endings so that when the cold whipped cream hit it, the sensation radiated out. Cold. Soft. More so than just cream on skin. Something multiplied by an order of magnitude. When he followed it with his mouth, the result was delicious for us both. He turned the coldness warm, and with the textured top of his tongue, he made the softness rough.

Jonathan dragged the can below my jeweled navel to the tip of my cleft, his tongue right behind. The anticipation made me gasp, which turned into a little squeal. "Shh, now. Be good," he said softly.

He drew the can, its sharp edge, and his warm, rough tongue inside my thigh. I was a throbbing, swollen hot mess by the time he put the can down and placed the tip of his tongue between my legs. He moved slowly up and down my slit, a tease that left me gasping, thrusting, pulling against the plastic bags binding me.

Bringing his tongue back up my abdomen, he landed on my mouth in a kiss. I opened my mouth for him, tasting the mix of cream and sex on his tongue.

"What do you want?" he asked.

"I want you."

"You have me."

"I want your dick in me," I said.

"When?"

"Please, sir," I breathed, "any time after right now is good."

He smiled and kneeled above me, spreading my legs. He dragged his finger up and down my pussy. My hips hitched, and I flung my knees farther apart, begging for him without a word. With one hand on my kitchen cabinet and another guiding his cock, he slid inside me, pushing in and rocking before pulling out. He closed his eyes and moaned. Seeing him feel pleasure brought my mind and body to the same focus. He thrust inside again, harder that time, and a sound left my lungs even as I tried to remain quiet.

"How do you want it, Monica?"

Could I ask? And how? Wasn't what I wanted exactly what scared me most?

"I want to please you," I whispered, telling the truth but avoiding the real answer. My pussy was almost in charge and doing the talking. As long as I had that last sliver of control, I didn't have to admit anything.

"You please me," he said, moving in and out of me in a slow, forceful rhythm. "How can I please you? Say it. Say what you want."

I was close, on the edge. Stoking a white-hot fire where his dick and my body met, I couldn't decide what to say. He sped up just a little, and the words came out of me unfiltered before I had a chance to be afraid. "Take me," I groaned. "Use me."

It took him one slow thrust to start pounding me, deep and hard. Fast. As though his only goal was to finish. He put a hand on my breast and squeezed it. The backs of my thighs, sore from spanking, ached with each thrust as his skin hit mine. Being under him, trapped, objectified, I lost all fear. With Jonathan, I felt safe. I felt a loss of control so complete, a surrender so honest that it became a luxurious indulgence.

"Jonathan, I'm..." I had no words. He was fucking the air right out of me.

"Go." He could barely get words out himself. "Yes."

"Oh..."

If he'd told me to be quiet, I wouldn't have heard the command over my own cry. The wordless sound, not even defined by a vowel, shot up from the base of my spine and out my mouth. I clenched around him, twisting. He held me straight, still beating me with his cock, as I came in a series of explosions that felt like the pounding of a drum hit hard, repeatedly, until it was hot with friction and resistance.

His name left my lips over and over. *Jonathan, Jonathan, Jonathan.*

He slowed down and fell back into a rhythm. He hadn't come yet, and I wanted him to. I wanted to own his orgasm the way he'd owned mine.

"Sir," I said. He put his face close to mine. "Use me for your pleasure. Please. Have me." God, what had I become? Such a whore that when he smiled at the thought of whatever he intended, I felt a surge of delight at pleasing him.

He kissed me, then reached up to the counter and retrieved a steak knife. I was still out of breath when he cut me from the drawer handle. My hands, however, were still tied together. He looked at me with a devilish grin when he stood up.

"On your knees, little goddess." I couldn't with my hands tied, at least not fast enough. He pulled me up by the bicep. My pussy throbbed, and when I got to a kneeling position, I felt warm fluid drip down my leg. Standing before me, his pussy-slick cock in front of my eyes, was my master. He was the ache between my legs, the desire in my belly, the tingle on my skin, the very embodiment of my gratification.

I felt his hand on the back of my head, grabbing a handful of hair and pushing my face forward. I opened my mouth, and he shifted, guiding his wet dick in me. I tasted the sharpness of my sex on him. Slowly, the length of him went down my throat, and he groaned, tilting his head back in that same position of surrender he had the first time my lips touched his cock. I breathed and took him again, slowly, my tongue coursing him. He jerked out a little, then shoved himself back in, all the way, until my nose touched his stomach. His full, hard shaft filled my mouth. I groaned, vibrating his head.

"Look at me."

I cast my eyes upward. His face was slack with arousal. I leaned back, still looking at him, letting his cock slip from my mouth.

"I own you," he said. He grabbed the back of my head harder, pulling the hair painfully, and pushed back in. His eyes closed a little, and a long breath escaped his lips. "Ah. That's right. I. Own. You."

We watched each other as his thrusts got shorter and faster. I had to breathe through my nose and concentrate on not losing him, not looking away, opening up for him totally as he fucked my mouth.

"Monica," he whispered. His eyes dropped lower and he whispered again, "Monica, Monica, I'm coming, baby. Take it. Ah."

I took him deeper, letting him come right down my throat, the base of his cock pulsing on my lower lip.

"Fuck," he whispered like a prayer, bending in supplication and release. His eyes closed, and after a final hitch in his breath, he pulled out, the last of his erection slick with spit and sex.

"How you doing, sir?" I was smirking. He'd tied my hands and forced the rhythm, but his orgasm was mine. He reached for the steak knife again, and I held my hands up. Slashing my binding, he bent down to take me in his arms. He lifted me, and I wrapped my legs around him, resting my head on his shoulder. He carried me out of the kitchen as if I was a child.

CHAPTER 9

JONATHAN

I DON'T KNOW how a man can feel ripped apart and whole at the same time.

Under her covers, on my side, and facing her wasn't close enough. I twisted my legs in hers, touched her face while she talked, and held her hand on the mattress.

When I'd carried her out of the kitchen, she'd been sticky all down her front. Her braid was a big knot. Her ass cheeks were pink and sore. Her throat was coated in my orgasm.

I took her straight to the bathroom so we could shower. We soaped, and kissed, and laughed, but she was wiped out. Her eyes drooped, and her hands worked over her body lazily. When we'd finished, I put a towel around her and brushed her hair. She insisted on a braid, so I put a loose one down her back, just to get it over with, and carried her to bed.

"I'm sorry about breaking the mood with the plastic bags," she whispered.

I stroked her cheek. "It's fine. I don't want to asphyxiate you, Monica. That's way past my threshold."

"I was scared."

"I know. And I don't want you to be scared, either."

"I should have put that on the list."

"We'll make a new list." I touched her forehead and drew my fingers down, forcing her eyes closed.

"You're my king, Jonathan." She'd opened her eyes, but they looked heavy. I kissed them over and over, eyelids, cheek, nose, lips, eyelids again, forcing them closed over and over. When her eyes stayed closed, I knew she was asleep, and I could rest.

300

But I didn't. I replayed the night in my head while looking out her window. Dogs barked. A police siren faded into range, then out. She hummed a little in her sleep, then stopped. She'd thought I was going to choke her. She'd thought I was going to put a plastic bag over her head until her body seized up. For thrills.

Obviously, she didn't trust me yet. It would take time and patience. I hadn't given either to a woman since Jessica because I gave her too much. My relationship with Monica could only go one place. Me, exposed to her, raw at the edges, breaking down at a shareholder meeting. Crying like—

I couldn't let myself finish that thought.

In the dead of night, when everyone else slept, was when it happened. I'd never been much of a sleeper, maxing out at four hours a night by the time I'd finished adolescence. Having business in Asia helped. I could make calls and send emails. Taking a lot of women to bed helped with the voices a little, but the dead-of-night hours were still spent alone. Then it took over.

It was my father's voice. The voice told me that the things I had done wrong were irreversible. My mistakes were yokes I could either break under or become strong enough to pull, but they could not be shaken. Marrying Jessica, which I had convinced myself was the only *right* thing I'd done, sat front and center. I'd screwed it up by trying to get her to fit into my sexual fantasies. If I'd stayed silent, just done things her way, I could have been happy. In the dead of night, the regret of putting my desires above love split me, gutted me, dragged me into despair. Come morning, the voice slumbered. The torment played on an infinite loop until I dreaded the sun's dip below the skyline.

The voice was quiet that night, just a hum of warning. I could be that man again very easily. It was no harder than tripping on a bump in the sidewalk or cutting myself shaving, a slip in concentration long enough to lose control. I could fall off the tightrope to either side if I blinked at the wrong time.

I forced my eyes closed and listened to Monica's breaths. Eventually, I fell asleep.

CHAPTER 10

MONICA

I WOKE up at 5:16 a.m., sore everywhere. My feet hurt from the stilettos. My knees from kneeling on the kitchen floor. My pussy from getting fucked hard, twice. My ass from the spanking. My tits from the biting and pulling. I wanted Jonathan again. I had about an inch of my body, somewhere, that wasn't throbbing and sore. He needed to find it and fuck it.

I heard his voice from far away, and I realized he wasn't next to me. He was on the side patio, facing the driveway and talking on the phone. After using the bathroom and getting into a robe and slippers, I joined him outside.

He sat at the little table I'd found on the corner of Echo Park Ave and Montana. His elbow was on the glass as he wrote something in a notebook and tapped something else into his phone.

"Good morning," I said.

He reached for me, pulling me into his lap. "Good morning." I flinched when my butt touched the hard surface of his knee. "Sorry," he said when he saw me lower myself slowly. "I mean, I'm not."

"Me neither." I leaned into the pain and sat on his leg.

"I have to go to Washington in a few days. I could be gone a week. A congressman from Arkansas doesn't want me building hotels overseas. I have an appointment to kiss his ass."

He wasn't just telling me he had to split. He was apologizing. I kissed him long and hard, running my fingers through his hair. "I knew you traveled a lot even before I met you."

"Will you keep yourself busy without me?" he asked.

"In all the most boring ways."

He slipped his hand between my legs and stroked inside my thigh. "What will you do?"

"I'll call you at night," I whispered.

"What else?" His fingertips touched my cunt just a little, like a threat of more.

"I'll text you every time I think of you. So, all the time." I opened my legs for him.

"Uh huh."

"I'll go to work."

"Yes." He breathed on my neck, his finger so close to finding me sore, wet, and ready.

"I have to work on the B.C. Mod piece. We're really behind."

His hand stopped dead. "When I'm away?"

I cringed a little inside. Shit. "You're away a lot. Should I stop working?"

"Maybe I should take you with me everywhere."

I stood and threw myself into the other chair. "You think I'm going to run off and fuck someone else as soon as your back is turned? What kind of person do you think I am?"

He put his elbow on the arm of his chair and rubbed his eyes. I had an inner, boiling-hot rage cooled only by remembering what his wife did. He needed reassurance, not defensiveness. Even if he didn't and couldn't love me, thinking he didn't have feelings or carry baggage was immature.

He said, "I trust you. I don't trust *him*."

I leaned forward and softened my voice. "It could be huge for me. Kevin is very important—"

"I don't want to hear that name."

"How are we supposed to talk about it? I mean, you trust me, but you don't trust him. Do you think he'll rape me?" I crossed my legs.

He took a long pause, looking at me. I would have bet two weeks' tips he was deciding whether or not to say something, or reveal a piece of information, but he looked away and tapped his notebook. "Do you think his Eclipse piece said anything about how he'll treat you?"

"He's Kevin Wainwright. He starts with the obvious emotions, then gets cold, then flushes what he can't use down the toilet. So that piece? I never saw the documentation, but my guess is someone just bought a pile of drawings of a dark-haired woman getting the shit beat out of her."

"How is he starting this piece with you? What's the early documentation look like?"

His eyes didn't waver from mine, so he must have seen my reaction. My ears got hot and my arms tensed, because Kevin's studio had been filled with raunchy sex drawings. Was that what he intended to work on with me? Were we talking about love or sex or the intersection of both? Had I been naïve and foolish?

"You can't get in the way of my work, Jonathan."

"He wants to hurt you, Monica."

"He doesn't know how."

"You're wrong. Very, very wrong."

I crossed my arms to match my legs. "Is there something you want to tell me?"

He swallowed, watching me. I watched him back. The tension made my heart pound, my palms sweat. My neck broke out in goose bumps, but I would not waver.

"I do have something to tell you," he said.

"Okay."

"When I say I own you, it's just a manner of speaking. It doesn't mean you don't have your own life, or you're a possession I can throw away when I'm bored. It means I am directly responsible for your well-being. If I sense a threat to your health or happiness, I will step in to protect you, even if you don't want me to."

Those words, so cold and practical, without a flowery phrase or hyperbole, made my lower lip quiver and a swelling, wet pressure collect in my eyes. Fuck.

"You can't keep me from working," I said, breathing hard, trying to forget the tears threatening to drop. "You have my word. I'm yours. You are the only man I want. I know what happened to you before—"

"Monica, you're not hearing me—"

"I am hearing you. You think Kevin wants to hurt me, and I'm telling you he can only hurt me if I give him my body, which I won't do."

He leaned forward as though he wanted to touch me, but wouldn't. "You said yourself he gets raw, then he gets cold, and then he does the piece. Maybe you're the piece."

I watched my hands fidget. "I can't stop my career for maybes." My eyes went back to him. "When I say you're a king, you are. You rule the world. You have everything. You can do whatever you want. I'm nobody. I have nothing to call my own. I could die tomorrow, and I'd be forgotten in a year. Like Gabby. If I don't record her music, it'll disappear, and if I let you stop me from doing whatever I have to do to make work, I'll disappear too."

I was crying full bore, with little sniffles and big, wet tears. He reached for his pocket, and I knew he would get out one of his expensive hankies. I hated that it was the second time I'd cried in front of him. I didn't make crying a habit. I hated it. I found no release in it, just sore eyes and shame. I grabbed his hand before it could leave his pocket. "Don't let my stupid crying get in the way of what you want to say."

"I wanted to say 'blow.'"

"No need." I cleared my throat, tilted my head, and pinched the corners of my eyes. Then I smiled a customer service smile. "See? All done."

He took my wrists and pulled me to him, gathered me up in his lap, and put my arms around his neck. "You think I'd forget you so easily?" he said, his face so close I could see the flecks of blue in his green eyes.

"L.A. is full of pretty girls. You'd find another one." He started to say something, some petty, pithy reassurance that would make me feel even more insignificant. I put my fingers on his lips before he could get a word out and whispered, "Shh. Behave."

He smiled under my hand, then kissed it. "We're all forgotten. Every one of us. Even artists and rich men. Eventually."

"My voice could survive."

"But with what meaning? This moment, here? On this little patio? This makes us who we are, and in a week, it's going to be a few pieces of memory. In a year... it's gone, and everything's changed."

"Are you a nihilist, Jonathan?" I stroked the hair on his cheeks as I teased him with my tone.

"I believe in plenty. You, for one. Your loyalty to your friend. The way you took care of her and still take care of her." He kissed my lips and kept his face so close to mine I felt his breath. "Will you let me take care of you?"

"To an extent."

"I want to get someone in to put food in your fridge."

"No."

"Your deadbolt is broken. That day when I said the door was unlocked, it wasn't. I opened the doorknob lock with a credit card. The deadbolt wasn't even set right."

"I'll fix it."

"I'll get someone in." His fingers found their way between my legs again, stroking inside my thighs.

"Jonathan, I put the first one in. I can do it again."

"Oh, is that why it works so well?" I pursed my lips. He pulled my hand off his cheek and held it. "I'm not questioning your competence, but I don't think you're defining yourself by your ability to set in a deadbolt. Or are you going to become L.A.'s first singing locksmith?"

I rested my head on his shoulder. "Fine. You have someone lock me up tight."

"On all the doors." His fingertips found a place between my legs where moisture gathered in response to his touch and his breath.

I sighed. "If it'll make you happy."

"It would keep unhappiness at bay." He dragged his finger up my pussy and across my clit. My breath hitched from the soreness and pleasure. "Open your legs for me."

"Another go?" I murmured.

"Yes."

We shifted so my back was to him. He released himself with the clink of a belt buckle and the purr of a zipper. I put my hands on the table as he reached around and pulled my legs farther apart.

"All the way," he said. "I want you to feel me." He stretched me apart to the point of pain, then pulled off my robe. Again, I found myself nude against his clothed body, exposed, vulnerable to him. His dick rolled past my ass and found the source of my wetness. I put my weight on it and groaned with how deep he went, how the soreness stung, and how the skin of my sex felt abused and loved.

Our hands met between our legs, feeling where we were coupled, taking turns touching my clit, stroking his shaft when it was exposed and feeling it enter me. I rubbed his balls under his clothes. Our hands went wild, fingers kneading, palms rubbing. He ran his damp hand up my belly and held my breast, twisting the nipple between two fingers. I was crazy with him, a circle of hunger and desire. He pulled me toward him until the back of my head was on his shoulder, and he whispered in my ear, "You are mine, goddess."

I groaned. Close, wrapped in a web of hands and wetness and throbbing shaft moving inside me.

"Mine," he said, pressing my hand to where were coupled, his sliding dick against my wet flesh. "This is us together. I own it. This body is my plaything. Your ache is mine. Your orgasm is mine. Your hunger is mine. Your dirty thoughts are mine."

"I'm going to come."

"Say it."

I was so close, but I wanted to say it before I exploded. I turned so my lips were close to his ear. "I'm yours. My pleasure is yours. My wet pussy is yours. You own me, Jonathan. You are the master of my fuck."

"Jesus, you are something else."

He thrust his hips forward. I sat up and matched him thrust for thrust. He moved my hand between my legs, my palm rubbing his dick and my clit at the same time. It was beautiful, soaking, earthy, celestial, electric. I slammed myself on him, driving him deep as I groaned, grinding my orgasm against the base of his cock, bending my body forward, winding like a spring, and unwinding with a shout.

A few gentle rocks, and I felt his hands tighten on my hips, grabbing flesh and digging in. He'd done it. He'd found the place I wasn't sore and bruised it, moving me up and down against him with decreasing gentleness.

He groaned, and with a final thrust forward, he yanked my hips down, coming inside me while whispering, "Monica, Monica, Monica."

CHAPTER 11

JONATHAN

I HAD A SINKING UNEASINESS. It wasn't necessarily about leaving her for D.C. It was about how often I left and stayed gone. I trusted her intentions, but I didn't trust her ability to make wise decisions. She'd basically admitted Kevin had vengeful thoughts about her, and dismissed them as part of his artistic process.

I wondered if she'd been bitten by a shithouse rat. If she expected Darren to protect her, she was sorely out of her league. He was a mother hen. He'd tuck her into bed and feed her soup if she got sick, but if that guy started doing the revolting shit I saw in those drawings, Darren was as good as useless.

I didn't feel much more useful.

Mostly because as soon as I hit the 101 and got too far away from her to turn back, I started planning the next time I'd see her. Nothing between visits occupied my mind. I already wanted to taste her again, feel her legs wrapped around my waist, and hear her sighs. I wanted to take action. Do something. Make some gesture that would bring her closer. Some sort of act that would bind her to me, even when I was away.

I felt greedy thinking about how much I missed her. I wanted more. More time. More sex. More laughing. I wondered if each of my sisters would like her. How each would react. Five out of seven would love her, and that thought warmed me. The warmth, instead of providing comfort, grew to a painful burn. I'd let my mind wander. I'd let something happen since last night when I kissed her eyelids. She was mine to protect and care for, a responsibility I relished.

CHAPTER 12

MONICA

J ONATHAN HAD LEFT only hours ago, and I'd gone right back to bed. A rumble in
the driveway woke me at eight a.m. It sounded like a farting tuba being played in a
closet. I peeked out the window. A Ford pickup as long as a bus pulled into my
driveway, blocking my car.

I threw on last night's clothes and ran out to the porch. He was obviously in
the wrong driveway. He was right at my door when I opened it. Six four. A solid
wall of muscle with a face to match and blonde hair that looked as if it had already
done a full day's work.

"Dr. Thorensen is next door," I said.

"I'm here for the Faulkner residence?"

I looked at his polo. The logo on the breast said The Foundation Guys, and the
name DAVE was embroidered above it. Jonathan said he had guys.

"I wasn't expecting you so soon," I said.

"Yeah, well, it's been slow lately. Anyway, coming to check it out. Get kinda like
a bead on the situation?"

"Yeah, well, I gotta get to work. Do you need me?"

"Nope, just your crawlspace. You got a dog or something? Gonna
bite me?"

"No, but I'll bite you if I'm late to work. I have to get the Honda out."

He laughed and ran to the truck, and I shut myself behind closed doors to get
ready. When I got out of the shower, I heard scuffling from Gabby's room.
Tiptoeing to the doorway, I found Darren stacking and restacking piles of
Hollywood Reporters.

"Mon," he said, indicating the towel wrapped around me, "I'm still a man, okay?"

"You could knock."

"I could if I wanted to sit on your porch for half an hour."

"Seriously. I have a boyfriend, and you could walk in on God-knows-what."

"Ah, right. Stay kinky, Monica. Stay kinky," he said, smiling. I whipped off the towel wrapped around my head and snapped it at him. "New trick?"

I whipped it again, and he grabbed it. I couldn't get it back because I needed to keep the other towel on myself with my free hand.

"Can you get dressed, please?" Darren threw the towel back.

I ran into my room and heard him through the wall as I wiggled into jeans and a shirt. When I got back to Gabby's room, he was sorting through manila envelopes absently, as if deciding what to do with the whole stack rather than whether or not to keep any individual file.

"What's happening with the work crews?" he asked.

"My foundation's slipping, or actually, *has slipped*."

"No shit. How you paying to fix that?"

When I didn't answer, he waved his hand, looking as if he was holding back a torrent of recriminations.

"Can we be done fighting?" I said.

"What fighting? Who's fighting? The thing in the parking lot?"

"Yes."

"I thought that was foreplay." Though his words were a joke, his voice took a serious timbre.

I felt a shudder that turned to heat on my cheeks. I didn't want him to know. I didn't want anyone to know. He must have imagined me tied up and gagged, like the girl suspended over the bar with wet underpants and come dripping out of her mouth. Would he avoid making eye contact with me? Would I always think he thought less of me?

I changed the subject, indicating the piles of papers and envelopes. "We should just throw it all out or keep it all. Going through it is just going to make you sad."

"She spent so much time on this stuff. It feels wrong to just trash it."

"It doesn't feel wrong," I said. "It feels too easy. And like a fast train to regret."

"Cheap. Like everything would feel cheap."

"It's not the same as throwing *her* away." I sorted through stacks, not really thinking. Some envelopes were thicker than others. Some had trees and webs of relationships penciled on them. Some were so thin they couldn't have been more than an idea. "I miss her. I think about her all the time. I should have called her when the location changed. I shouldn't have made that scratch cut without her. I'm sorry, Darren. I'm so sorry. I feel like I took your sister from you." I couldn't look at him, just the never-ending pile of envelopes left behind as her legacy.

"It wasn't your fault, Monica. It was a stupid accident."

"No, it wasn't. Stop defending me. She committed suicide because she was getting cut out. You know it, and I know it."

"No, you *don't*," he said with a pointed finger and raised voice. "You have two possible scenarios, and you believe the one that makes you responsible? Sorry, no. You want to get beat up during sex, that's fine, but this emotional masochism is bullshit."

"She committed suicide whether I take responsibility or not," I yelled back.

"No. She. Didn't." Darren ground his teeth. If I took responsibility, he'd have to as well. For not babysitting, for not watching more closely, for not counting her meds. It could go on and on in ever-expanding circles of self-blame.

"Fine," I said. "It was a freak accident. I'm still sorry."

"Me too."

Agreeing on everything and nothing, we looked through the envelopes as if we were doing more than touching what she'd touched so we could commune with our memories.

"I can take it all back to my place," he said. "Clear out this room. You need a new roommate."

I hadn't given that a moment's thought. I'd paid bills like a robot. Since they always came out of my checking account anyway, it didn't feel like anything had changed. But that account wouldn't make it another month without help.

I realized I didn't want the room cleaned. I didn't want anyone else living there. No one else was family. I didn't want a stitch removed until I was good and ready, which I wasn't yet. "How much are you paying for that place around the corner?"

"Not too much. Why? You want to move in?"

"Live here. With me."

"Here? In this room?"

"You can have my room. Or the living room. I can clean out the garage." It seemed like the most sensible thing in the world. We would stay together, which I wanted so much a knife of anxiety went through my chest.

He sorted through files as if he didn't want to look at me. "What would your new boyfriend say?"

"I don't care."

"Ask first."

"I don't have to ask permission to live my life, Darren."

"It's not permission. It's courtesy. Seriously." He glanced at me. "You and I were intimate, in case you forgot. Guys have a problem with stuff like that. Trust me. I'd like to move in, but not at the expense of whatever you have with him. Not that I understand it."

"Fine." I held my hand out, realizing too late my wrists were black and blue from straining against plastic bags tied to my kitchen cabinets.

"Jesus, Monica," he whispered.

Before I could even think about it, I hid them behind my back. Stupid. I was the cause of my own shame. "It's not a big deal."

He held out his hands. "Can I see?"

"No."

"Please? I won't give you a hard time." When I didn't move, he said, "Promise."

I put my hands in his. He turned my hands over, assessing the damage. I couldn't look at him. I knew what was on his face and what was in his head. It wouldn't be too far off from the truth. Me, naked on the floor. Knees up. Hands tied, straining. Add whatever darkness lay in Darren's imagination, and I'm getting choked, slapped, fisted... whatever act he decided was too sick to perform, too deranged to even think about, had a shape and a voice and they looked and sounded like me.

"Do we have a problem?" I asked.

He let go of my hands. "It's not a problem for me if it's not for you."

"You sure?"

"Sure? No. But close enough."

I put my arms around his shoulders and held on for dear life. He rocked me back and forth and gave me a big, hard kiss on the cheek. I heard another knock on the door and pulled away to go answer. I checked out the window and saw a rock-solid woman in her fifties carrying a beat-up leather case.

"Hi," I said when I opened the door. "You must be the locksmith."

"Sure am. Benita's the name."

I let her in. "Okay, well, this deadbolt isn't set in right, so if you could fix that."

She fiddled with the lock. "Uh, I was told to replace all the locks with Kleigs."

My face hardened. I couldn't afford Kleigs, naturally, but I'd agreed. "I have three doors. Back, front, and side."

"Done. Checking the windows, too."

Was there any use arguing? She was just doing her job.

"Fine. I'm going to work. You don't need me here, do you?"

"Nope, just your key. I'll leave it and the new ones in a box in the front. Code's 987. All you need to know." She handed me her card, and I saw her eyes widen when she saw my wrists.

I thanked her and ran back to my room. I caught sight of my wrists as I put rings on. That wouldn't work. I looked as though I'd been in a hostage situation. I put bracelets on to cover the bruises. I needed a more solid pair that didn't slide around so much. Whenever I lifted a tray, the bracelets would slip and reveal my weekend's activities.

Which was exactly what happened. I'd been at work thirty minutes when Debbie noticed. She flicked the bracelets, then looked at me when I got back to the service bar.

"How are you doing?" she asked. I knew exactly what she meant.

"Very well, thank you." I was pretty sure I blushed as I put empty glasses in the bus tray. She smiled at me then disappeared downstairs.

I serviced some tables, threw snide comments back and forth with Robert, and wore a ridiculous smile that was probably the exact opposite of the customer service smile I usually used. Debbie caught me on a bathroom run and handed me a black velvet bag with a drawstring.

"Put these on." She took off as if she had more important things to do than explain.

When I got to the bathroom, I opened the bag. Inside were two bracelets that were more like metal cuffs in hammered silver. Two inches wide, with red stones set into them, they looked heavy but weren't. When I put them on, they stayed put as I moved my arm.

"Well, there's a hint I can take," I said to Debbie when I saw her.

"I can't have customers thinking we tie you up in the basement."

"Thank you."

"Are you happy?" She indicated the bracelets, but I knew she meant the bruises underneath them. "This is good for you?"

Debbie knew Jonathan, and her voice often told me she was some sort of dominant. I knew she knew, if not the details, the broad strokes. "Inappropriate" was too mild a word to describe talking to her about my relationship with Jonathan.

"When I'm in the middle of it, it's very comfortable. But if I think of it any other time, I start to feel like I should be ashamed. As a woman. I'm sorry I'm..." I'd gone too far.

"Don't be sorry. You are what you are. You don't have to apologize for it to me or anyone. Especially yourself. And not feminism either. It'll get along fine with you doing what you want in private. Now, get to the floor."

"Okay." I ran back out to do my job.

When I got home that afternoon, the street was crowded with parked cars, and the foundation guy was still in my drive. I was stuck. I found a spot down the block and walked up the hill, wishing I'd worn sneakers. I crossed the street to my house next to a green minivan. I lived on a small block and knew most of the cars, but sometimes the odd car parked nearby when the lot at the coffee shop got too crowded. The minivan shouldn't have raised an eyebrow or a hackle. I looked at it anyway. Just a glance. I saw a glass circle enclosed in a larger black one tucked behind the driver-side window, near the side mirror. Must be a trick of the evening light. Why would a camera lens be pointed at my front door?

I peered into the car. A cord went to the eye of the camera, which looked like a webcam, and a red light blinked at the bottom of the cable.

That was not okay.

What was he trying to do? Make sure I didn't fuck the foundation guy? Check to see if Kevin came around? I stormed across the street, getting madder with each step. A camera was not protecting my health and happiness. It was creepy, stalker bullshit. I got my new keys out of the lockbox, then I remembered who paid for them.

Fucking great. He would have gotten the keys from Benita. I'd have to call her so she could take things out so I could have another locksmith, who I hired, put in new tumblers. Pain in the ass.

I took the whipped cream out of my fridge.

Asshole.

I couldn't even think straight. I was full on white hot rage from my core to my fingertips as I stomped back across the street and sprayed whipped cream all over the minivan's driver's side window.

Let's see what he saw through that. Motherfucker.

As I crossed back to my house, I texted him.

> *—WTF did you think you were doing with the stalker bullshit—*

Dave, the foundation guy, stopped me at the sidewalk, wielding a clipboard. "Miss Faulkner? I have an estimate." I took the clipboard. The number was insane. "Your house is falling down the hill. We need to jack it up and shift it. The whole thing. Then it's gotta be bolted. It's a big job."

I scanned the work list, then the line at the bottom for a signature. "I'm not the homeowner. It's my mother's house."

"Oh."

"I assume you can't continue without the homeowner's signature?"

He looked disappointed. The guy needed work, and I didn't want to screw him out of it. I read the estimate again. I couldn't afford the work, but since I found out Dr. Thorensen's house would meet my house on the day of "the big one," not getting it fixed was irresponsible.

"I'll bring this to my mom to sign and let you know."

He brightened. I didn't know if I was lying or not. Maybe my mother would shell out the money to protect her property. I could mail her the permits to sign. Or fax them. Or carrier pigeon. Anything to avoid Castaic.

But as God was my witness, I would not let some guy who couldn't trust me, and who put cameras on me, pay to fix my foundation or change my locks. Oh, fuck no.

My phone rang. Jonathan. I waved to Dave, and he walked to his truck. I answered the phone in a white heat. "I can't do this," I said.

"What happened? What are you talking about?" He was in a crowded place full of voices shouting. In my mind, I saw him pressing his finger to his other ear.

"I do not need to be watched. I don't need you if you can't trust me." He didn't answer. "Say something."

"I just want to make sure you're all right."

"I'm. All. Right." My voice was tight and firm, pure intention in every syllable.

"I didn't think it was that big a deal."

"Fuck? What? You don't think it's that big... Are you from another planet?" I paced my living room as Dave pulled his truck out of my driveway.

"Monica, calm down."

"Calm... What? No! I will not calm down. This is serious. This is a problem. And you know what? I don't have time for it. I don't have time to describe to you proper boundaries outside the bedroom."

"You're out of line."

"Don't you use that voice with me now. *You're* out of line."

"Monica."
"Jonathan."
"I'm coming over there."
"Don't bother."
I hung up.

CHAPTER 13

MONICA

I WANTED TO RUN. I wanted to somehow foil his stupid fucking plan to come over
and soothe the common sense right out of me. But I had to shower and change to
play at Frontage. Rhee and I had agreed to continue on a trial run, and I wanted to
be my best, not all screwed up. When I got out of the shower, my phone was
ringing. I picked it up without looking, thinking it was Jonathan.

"My doors are locked."

"Okay?"

Fuck, not Jonathan. The caller ID identified the caller as Jerry, the producer I'd
done a scratch cut with two weeks earlier.

"Hi, sorry. Thought you were someone else. How's it going?"

"Good, I'm having drinks with Eddie Milpas tonight. He's one of our
acquisitions guys. You playing that dinner club?"

"Frontage, yeah."

"You playing the song we cut?"

"I don't usually play my own stuff. I can ask."

"Do it. He's looking for something, and I think you have it."

My heart raced. "Thanks. I'll see you tonight."

"Great. Keep the doors locked."

I hung up. It had been twenty minutes since Jonathan called. I stuffed my crap
in a bag and ran out with my hair still wet.

CHAPTER 14

JONATHAN

"Lil." I knocked on the window. "Forget Sheila. Take me to Echo Park."

"Yes, sir."

Turning around was no small feat. She had to crawl off the exit of the 134, crawl back on, and sit in rush hour traffic. Dinner with my favorite sister and attendant children was officially cancelled.

When I got to Monica's house, she and her car were gone. I stood on the porch calculating my next move. She'd said something about a gig at Frontage, and I was tempted to go over there. I saw Dave pulling up the hill in his dually.

"Hey, Jon. The lady of the house home? I had a few more permits to pull."

"Nope. What happened today?"

He leaned out his window and offered me a fry from a McDonald's bag, which I refused. "What do you mean?"

"Did you say something about watching her?"

"No, man, I was watching, not telling."

"When I said to keep an eye on her, it was a casual keeping an eye. Because she knows, and she's pissed."

"Sorry. I didn't say anything. She did tag up that car with whipped cream. Don't know what that was about." He craned his neck to see the other side of the street. "Right there."

I followed his gaze to a green minivan. I got a sinking feeling as I walked toward it. The whipped cream wasn't just whipped cream. It was the kind from a can, and Monica was sending me a message.

I used my hankie to wipe the whipped cream away and saw a camera behind the glass.

Ah. She thought I did that. The thought had crossed my mind, but I did have boundaries.

And then the other question: who did it? Who wanted her watched?

I said good-bye to Dave and crawled back into the Bentley. "Lil, take me home." I needed my car, and Lil had been driving all day. Monica would be trapped behind that piano. I could still make it.

CHAPTER 15

MONICA

"One song," I said to Rhee. "The rest can be the same as we've always done."

She chewed the inside of her lip, glancing around the room. It was already getting crowded. "What's it sound like?"

"Like a woman on the piano," I said. "Here are the lyrics."

Asking permission to sing my own songs wasn't something I would have accepted a month ago, but so much had happened, and I depended on the job at Frontage to keep Gabby's memory alive.

The lyrics made me nervous, but I had to do it, just once. If I didn't take opportunities when they presented themselves, they'd dry up.

"Little hardcore, sugar," Rhee said. "Collar? Licking the floor?"

"It's metaphorical."

"I figured that."

Of course she did. What woman would have to lay that out for a man literally?

"It's important to me," I said. "Someone's coming to hear it. A producer and a record exec. And the composition, Gabby wrote it. I laid the lyrics over after..."

"Okay, okay." She handed back the sheet. "You're fine. Have fun. You deserve it."

"Thanks, Rhee." I dashed back to the dressing room. I'd played for Rhee earlier in the week to prove I could manage lyrics and music at the same time. I was only halfway into "Under My Skin" when she stopped me and told me I was fine to go back on my old schedule. I was happy for the distraction, but the feeling that Eugene Testarossa had been right, and Gabby had been redundant, nagged at the back of my mind. Some little guilt-inducing voice insisted that by playing her part, I was driving her deeper into the grave.

The dressing room was like a second home anymore, but it was lonely and my anger at Jonathan wasn't good company. I put on my makeup and hummed my new song. When it was time to go into the dining room, I looked at myself in the mirror and said, "I hope you get carpal tunnel and a frog jumps down your throat."

It wasn't the same, but it was the best I had.

CHAPTER 16

JONATHAN

NOTHING MOVED. The Jag was caught between a bus and a silver SUV. I should
have brought the bike. I could have gone between the lanes and been there already.
Even though I knew she wasn't going anywhere, I wanted to see Monica right away.
Had to. First, she was angry with me, and that fact bored a hole right through me.
The more I thought about it, the more I wanted to rush to her. Second, the
surveillance equipment across the street just turned the dial up on my concern.
That equipment wasn't a joke. Someone was watching her. I didn't know why, or
who, but I could buy those answers with money and time. One, I had plenty of.
The other, I'd have to manufacture.

"Margie," I said when my oldest sister picked up her phone. She was fifteen
years my senior and had been more of an aunt to me. Her law firm had a huge
criminal litigation division and billed thousands of hours keeping celebrities from
going to jail.

"Jonny, you never call anymore."

"Because I don't have any problems."

"But tonight? You have a problem?"

"Are you sitting?" Western Avenue opened up just as I had to turn down Santa
Monica Boulevard. Too bad all the money in the world wouldn't buy me a flying
fucking car.

"Sure, I'm sitting."

"There's a woman."

"You just gave me a migraine. That poor girl. What did you do to her?"

I'd squirmed when she litigated my divorce and I had to tell her it was about

320

sex; what kind of sex and how I'd been rebuffed. She needed details and received them only after I'd drunk half a bottle of scotch.

"It's not that," I said. "She and I, we're good. It's something else."

"Where does one find a woman who likes—"

"Enough." I knew all the wisecracks already. "I'm not in the mood, Margie. I found a camera outside her place. Temporary surveillance inside a car. I need her house swept for more. I think you might know someone who could do it."

"Do you have access?"

"No, and irony of ironies, I just had new locks put in."

"You're not doing that controlling thing again, are you, Jonny?"

"Just round people up and I'll get you access. Okay?"

"*She* might like it when you're bossy—"

I hung up. My sisters knowing I had a kinky streak wasn't easy. Another thing I could thank Jessica for.

I got Hank on the phone at the next red light.

"Jaydee."

"Did you burn those drawings?"

"Not yet."

"Can you pack them up and have them to my Wilshire office tomorrow morning?" I asked.

"You want them packed to archiving standards?"

"No. Put them in an envelope. No more. I'll let you know how to proceed." I hung up.

I was sure it was Kevin. He'd been at the funeral and could have planted cameras then. Video of Monica entering and exiting the house would be perfect for an installation, especially with her music over it. Another homage to a breakup. He knew her well enough to know that once he presented her with the footage in the completed work, she'd buckle and let it happen for the sake of art and her career. Or he'd neglect to mention it until the show was installed. She'd be even less likely to gripe since her name would be on the thing already. A humiliating stab in the back. If there were cameras inside the house, I would have to kill him.

I felt as if every cell in my body needed to be near Monica. To protect her from whoever watched her and to soothe her anger at me. I just had to brave the traffic and the ridiculous synchronization of the lights on Santa Monica Boulevard.

CHAPTER 17

MONICA

WITH GABBY GONE and the promotional machine at a standstill, the room's body count went back to normal. It was the same-sized crowd as the first night we'd played: just tables and a few people waiting at the bar. Any buzz we'd had about our shows died with Gabby. Basically, I was starting from scratch, which was fine. I didn't think I could take much more than that without her to lean on.

The table by the warm speaker had a RESERVED sign. Jerry and Eddie were meant to sit there, if they came at all. I said hello to some lovely couples by the front and asked if they had any requests, which I'd play if I knew. A group of frat boys had heard about me and come for dinner. They were half drunk already, and their appetizers hadn't even arrived, so I didn't linger. I made a last visual sweep around the room and cast my eyes to Rhee. She was leading two women to a table in the corner. I recognized both of them. One was Jonathan's sister Deirdre. One was his ex-wife.

My skin burst into tingles and my throat closed. I couldn't feel my fingertips. Then I remembered I was playing that song. Jonathan's song. I hadn't shown it to him or told him about it yet. Jessica would hear it. And she would know.

She would *know*.

I wasn't ashamed of what I was doing with Jonathan, but letting her hear my fears as if I'd whispered them in her ear was sickeningly intimate. A cold trickle of regret ran down my back. I should never have made the thing, never written it down, never set it to Gabby's music. Though I wasn't hiding it from Jonathan, at the very least, I should have shown it to him before playing it publicly. I hadn't even thought of that.

I sat down at the piano and touched the keys. No, I'd skip it. Play something else. Jerry wasn't there, so no one would be the wiser. Rhee didn't really care. I started playing. Yes, I'd hide behind Irving Berlin, then Cole Porter. I'd stay safe. I'd still paint them the colors of Jonathan. I'd still feed them his lust, his touch, his voice. But Jessica would never hear it because I was protected by dead men's lyrics.

I was coming off "Someone to Watch Over Me," the middle of my set, when I saw Jerry with two men at the bar. He tipped his glass to me. They weren't sitting at the table. Stopping by, maybe? Well, shit. I'd have to play it.

With the lights in my face, blinding me to half the room, Jessica didn't loom as large. After warming up with the standards I knew so well and hiding behind that shiny, black baby grand, I didn't feel as vulnerable. I could play that song.

I could do it. I could belt it out. Fuck her. Fuck her to Sunday. Fuck her with the lights on. Fuck her fuck her fuck her. It was my room. My song. My audience. My rules.

Rule number one? Fuck her.

I hit the keys, owning them, and I launched into Jonathan's song as though he was naked and I was jumping him.

WE WOVE words under Popsicle trees,
    The ceiling open to the sky,
    And you want to own me
    With your fatal grace and charmed words.
    All I own is a handful of stars
    Tethered to a bag of marbles that turns

OH, her ears would burn off at the mention of Popsicle trees and a ceiling open to the stars but guess what?

Fuck her.

My questions and fears were pregnant with heated longing, a desire for encouraging answers, begging for appeasement. My list of acceptable and unacceptable behaviors became a list of exciting possibilities.

WILL YOU CALL ME WHORE?
    Destroy me,
    Make me lick the floor,
    Twist me in knots,
    Turn me into an animal?
    Will I be a vessel for you?

SLICE OPEN our lying box

Through a low doorway for our
Shoulds and oughts.
Choose the things I don't need,
No careless moments, no mystery.
And you need nothing.
My backward bend doesn't feed.

AND JUST TO CALL TO her, just because she'd hurt me, and just because I could, I changed the last chorus on the fly, turning questions into statements.

I WILL OWN YOU.
Tie you.
I will collar you
Hurt you,
Hold you, and take you.
You will be a vessel for me.

FOR ALL MY INNER FEROCITY, the song had to complement the rest of the set, so I didn't scream or wail. I didn't hit the top of my range, but the ragged emotion was there as I hit the last note at low, dinnertime volume. A whisper even. I moved right into "Stormy Weather." The lights blacked out for half a second. Jerry and his buddies were leaving, blocking the spots. I felt a core of relief. I didn't think I could deal with managing them and Jessica.

I finished my set, thanked my audience, looked humbled for the applause, and strode back to the dressing room with my chin up. I didn't start shaking until I got the door closed and locked. My breath became ragged and my eyes filled. Jesus, fuck, what was she doing there? With Deirdre? Who was going for gold in the family Olympics, for fuck's sake? God damn it. Which lie was incoming? Which bomb would she drop? I would stay in the dressing room. I'd tell Rhee I was too upset about Gabby to do the good-byes, and I'd stay in there until the bar closed.

That actually seemed like a viable plan, but when I scrolled through my contacts so I could text Rhee an apology, I slid past Debbie's number. Her words came back to me as if whispered in my ear.

Be a woman of grace.

Yeah.

Maybe it was time to grow up. Maybe if I knew I wasn't doing anything wrong and if I stood by my right to be with any man I liked, I didn't have a reason to hide in a filthy dressing room.

I texted Rhee.

—I'm a little upset about Gabby—

She got right back with a bloop.

—Can I do anything?—

*—If you could bring back two
Jameson's? One shot and one on
the rocks for my nerves?
And I'll be out right after—*

—Sure sugar—

I straightened my dress, wiped mascara from under my eyes, and reapplied my lipstick. A waitress came. I cracked the door to thank her for the drinks and remove them from her tray.

Once the door closed, I knocked back the shot. The other one was my prop. I looked in the mirror and tried out my customer service smile. Awesome. I was just smashing. And fuck her.

I went out to do my job. I entered the room and said a few hellos, smiling and graciously accepting compliments. Deirdre was at the bar. Jessica was alone at the table, half paying attention to her phone and half pretending she didn't see me.

I went to the bar and squeezed next to Deirdre. "Hi, I think we've met," I said.

She was more polite than before and nodded, a noncommittal smile playing at her lips. "Yeah. Nice singing." She tucked a strand of tight curls behind her ear. They bounced right out.

"Thanks. I, uh, I don't want to launch into this and be rude, but I couldn't help but notice you came with someone?"

"Yeah. She's family. She wanted to see you. I knew where you were, so..." She ended with a shrug.

"She's borderline malevolent."

"She's my brother's wife."

"Not anymore."

"You have a lot to learn." She tried to put the hair behind her ear again, but it sprang in front of her eyes.

I took a deep breath. She was one of seven, and I was alienating her. "I'm sorry. I just don't understand."

She considered me deeply. There was something about her, some sadness, a touch of melancholy. She had a deep spring of sorrow. I saw it in her eyes and the way she fought a losing battle with the strand of hair that wouldn't tuck behind her ear. "Like I said. Family. A man is meant to marry one woman. One life, one wife."

I wondered for a second if Deirdre lived in the twenty-first century, then I saw her crucifix necklace. I got it then. She was saving Jonathan's soul by serving Jessica.

"All right," I said. "I'll go say hello. You walking over there?"

"In a minute." She smiled at me. I couldn't read it. Besides the spring of sadness, I couldn't read Deirdre at all.

Jessica pretended to see me for the first time when I was halfway to her. Quelling a tidal wave of hatred that would surely overcome even the power of my customer service smile, I sat at the edge of her booth. We were equals. I wouldn't stand over her as if I was her waitress.

"Nice to see you again," I lied.

"Same here," she lied back. "You play beautifully."

"Thank you."

"And your voice is heavenly. You're an artist."

I put my elbows on the table and fondled my glass of whiskey. "Is there something you want? Being here? Because I do believe in the odd coincidence, but not this one." I was all smiles. If Rhee saw me, she'd assume I was making friends with a customer.

Jessica looked down at her own drink, a half empty clearish-brownish thing with soda and lime. "You played a song in the middle I didn't recognize. I mean, let me correct myself. I did recognize it. I asked myself many of the same questions."

"Were you as honest with yourself as you were with me?"

A smirk played at her lips. "I deserve that."

I could have pounced, but I didn't. She wasn't there to get beat up. She wasn't there to apologize, and she certainly didn't come to see me sing. She came to get Jonathan back. As far as I was concerned, I was pissed as hell at him, but I hadn't decided I was finished with him. So I stayed silent, waiting for her to explain. She didn't move a muscle unnecessarily. Her face gave away nothing. She didn't twitch or fondle a glass like I did, and she didn't have a customer service smile. She had an expression that went deeper. It was more practiced, more ingrained. She had the grace Debbie tried to instill in me. In spades.

"There will come a day when you want to talk to someone." She reached into her bag and took out a card. "Someone who knows more about who you're involved with. If you can forgive the little joke I played on you, you can contact me. We can talk."

She slid the card to me. It was a plain, matte, white business card with her name, number, and an address in the industrial part of Culver City.

It was so wildly classy I resented her all over again. I slipped it into the pocket of my dress. "If I have something to ask, I can just go to Jonathan, don't you think?"

She sipped her drink. "Has he told you about Rachel?"

"Yes."

"Everything?"

"I can't prove a negative. Neither can you. And if you think I'm repeating what he told me so that you can cross-check it... well, that says more about you than it does about me, doesn't it?"

"Your hostility does the same." I felt slapped, and I shouldn't have. She barely moved a muscle or changed her expression, adding to my feelings of inadequacy. "There are a lot of moving parts here, and if I may be honest, you're out of your depth."

I rolled my glass between my palms, cooling them, thinking of Jonathan's porch on our first night together and how he'd used his glass and the ice in it. The shot had loosened me, reducing my stress and inhibitions. I'd walked minefields like Jessica's before. Unfortunately, I always forgot my map. "So what you're telling me is you want to help me stay away from your ex-husband, whose heart you broke? No, I don't think so."

"It's not that simple."

"Oh, yes, it is."

"Things have been put in motion. I wanted to warn you away, so you don't get hurt."

I didn't like threats, especially vague ones. They implied the person making the threat didn't respect me enough to explicate, and that was guaranteed to twist my knickers in a knot. I tried to keep my game face on. "I'd understand if you just wanted him back, but you want something else."

"Right now, I'm trying to get you out of harm's way. I'll be happy to explain but not here."

Oh, that was a sneaky trick. I wouldn't touch it. Wouldn't believe it. Why would she have my best interests at heart? I thrust myself forward. She didn't balk. "He has one dick, and it can be inside one woman at a time. Nothing you say will stop me getting peeled off the ceiling every time he puts that astonishing cock in me. If you miss it badly, if you imagine it when your new man's on top of you, if you think about it when you're alone with your hands under the sheets, I understand completely. He's a monster fuck, Mrs. Drazen, and you're going to have to go through me to get him back."

Through the slight smile spread over her face, she practically whispered, "You're a class act." I tried not to react. I tried to be implacable and cold, and I knew, as sure as it never snows in Los Angeles, that I failed. My face was lemon Jell-O held up by toothpicks. Jessica pushed her glass away and stood. "I'm sure your refinement will keep the astonishing gentleman coming back for more."

Lemon Jell-O turned to cherry, and if there was a deeper shade of red to turn, I had no idea what flavor it was. She looked over my head and smiled. "Jon, how are you?"

His voice came from over my shoulder like a warm sweater, fresh from the dryer on a cold night. "Fine, Jessica."

My plan had been to rail at him, to throw rage his way. To let him know he couldn't have me watched. I had boundaries even if he didn't, and I didn't like being stalked. But when he put his hand on the back of my neck as if he owned me, I was awash in gratitude. It was the best possible comeback to Jessica's jab about my lack of refinement, and I didn't have to say a word.

Jessica said, "I was just having a word with Monica about her song. It made me think of you. Deirdre, honey, you all right?"

Deirdre had entered the circle, still tucking her stubborn red curl behind her ear. "Yeah." She turned to Jonathan and punched his arm. "Hey, man."

"I hope you're getting a lift home, Dee. Monica and I are leaving." He looked at his ex-wife. "Jess, I don't know what you were doing here, but I'm dispensing with all the niceties and saying good-bye." He squeezed my neck and looked down at me. "You ready?"

"My stuff's in the dressing room."

"Let's go, then." He held out his hand and I took it, sliding from the booth as he helped me up.

I walked to the back without saying good-bye, pulling him along. I didn't start shaking until we were both behind the dressing room door. Before I could even flick on the light, he pushed me against the wall, his mouth on mine, pressing my head to the plaster.

"Jonathan," I gasped. Didn't I want to yell at him? Wasn't I mad about something? I knew I had things to say.

He kissed my neck and stroked my breast through my dress. "The camera. Not mine. I asked Dave to keep an eye on you is all." He pressed his club of a cock against me.

Fuck it. Fuck explanations. Fuck boundaries. Whatever he said was good enough for me if it let him take me right then.

With both hands under my skirt, he kneaded my ass as he kissed me. His finger looped in the crotch of my fancy Bordelle panties and yanked them. I pulled one leg out, and he draped it over his hip, opening me to him. He taunted my nipple through my dress, drawing his thumbnail against it before putting his whole hand over my breast.

I undid his pants and released him. He put one hand on my chest, leaning into me, and he used the other to guide himself in me, which he did with a hard, fast thrust.

Eyelids half-mast with pleasure, he thrust again, even harder. I squeaked when his dick hit the end of me. He put my other leg over his hip so I was wrapped around him. He leveraged me against the wall with his body, a fulcrum where we were joined, the base of all that held us together.

I put my hands on his face, and he took them off, holding them down.

"You ready, goddess?"

"Take me."

He grunted as he pushed hard, getting so deep it hurt. Without a moment's hesitation, he pounded me again, forcing me against the wall as if he wanted to punch through it. Again and again he took me, hard and fast, pushing into a tingling warmth, forcing pleasure to current through me, the base of his cock slamming my clit over and over.

"Look at me," he demanded in a husky voice. I did, though my hair was falling into my eyes. My breath was timed to his thrusts. "You talk to me, do you understand?"

"Yes, sir." I could barely understand myself.

"Never shut me out."

"Never. Oh, God. Jonathan. My king."

"Don't come, Monica." He slowed down, angling himself differently so I felt him inside me, deep, hard, deliberate. "Don't let your emotions get the best of you. Talk. To. Me." He thrust with every word, sending me into a place where verbalization was nearly impossible.

"Yes."

"What do you want to say?" he asked.

"Let me come?"

"No. What else?" He slammed into me and ground against me, pushing all the way in, his face by mine, his scent of leather and earth and clean laundry overtaking me. "Why did you shut me out?"

"I'm scared. You scare me."

He cupped my cheek. "Why?"

The room wasn't well lit, but I saw the green in his eyes where the lights from the parking lot cut through the window blinds. "You can hurt me, Jonathan. You can do damage."

He stroked my bottom lip with his thumb. "Your honesty is beautiful." He pulled out and pushed into me again, jamming himself against my wide-open sex.

"Again, please," I begged.

He thrust into me again. And again, until I thought I'd explode from the crotch out in a spray of screams. My breath got raspy and hard, my chest hurt with the effort to move air through my body when I wanted to stop breathing completely. He put his hand over my mouth and took me fast and hard. I came, crying out into his palm. He put his chest to mine, his cheek against my face, and with a long groan, he filled me, jerking and rocking. I felt his warm breath on my neck, his hand sliding down my sweat-coated face, whispering my name. We leaned against each other for a minute, breathing together, until he kissed my cheek.

"You're staying with me tonight, at least," he said softly.

"Why?"

He kissed my mouth again and said, "Your house and your car need to be swept for cameras. I can't let you go back there until it's clean."

"What if whoever put that there was really after you? How do you know your house isn't full of cameras?"

"It's getting checked right now."

We kissed as he pulled out of me. He let my legs down. I was still short of breath, still sensitive between my thighs. My lips hurt where his late-day scruff had rubbed me, and my spine ached from being pushed into a brick wall. As usual, I felt as if I'd been beaten near death with a fuckstick.

Jonathan kneeled before me and helped me get my lacy underpants back on, kissing a trail up my leg. When he'd straightened my dress, he kissed me.

"We have to talk," I said.

"About Jessica. What did she say?"

"About that, and—"

There was a loud knock on the door. The handle jiggled. "Monica," Rhee called, "you in there?"

"Yes."

"Bernie's here." Bernie was the guy who played after me.

"Out in a second."

I hoisted my bag. Jonathan ran his fingers through his hair and took it from me. We got outside into the crisp, autumn night. The valet went for Jonathan's car. Mine was parked on the street. He walked me to it, our fingers linked. "People are waiting at your house to sweep it for cameras and mikes."

"This is so weird."

He held my chin when we stopped by my car. "It's probably nothing. We need to go there so you can let them in." He put his arms around my waist. "You, darling, will gather clothes and things. Then I shall bring you back to my bed, and I will have you again. And maybe again."

"We have to have an unpleasant conversation."

"Do you believe I'm not spying on you?"

"Yes."

"Did you fuck someone else?"

"God, no!"

"Are you leaving me because I interrupted your work?"

"No."

"Are you leaving me at all?"

"No, Jonathan, really—"

"Then I fail to see the urgency. Let's take care of business and let unpleasantness take care of itself."

CHAPTER 18

JONATHAN

I DIDN'T WANT to hear a word about what my ex-wife said. I didn't want to
navigate her labyrinth of lies and half-truths, and I didn't want to explain anything
to Monica while my mind was on Kevin and the cameras. We needed to hand off
keys, pack her for the night, and get her into my bed. Then I would explain or fuck
away whatever Jessica told her. Jessica was going to the mat. I couldn't deal with
her shit for another minute. Her worst nightmare was seeing me happy, apparently,
because I hadn't seen her as much in the past half year as I'd seen her in the
past month.

I got to Echo Park first and parked across the street from Monica's house. The
green minivan was gone, replaced by a black van. Margie's guys. I walked up to her
chain-link gate. A man greeted me. Late twenties. Suit and tie. Pinkie ring. My eyes
adjusted and I saw two others shaking the bushes.

"Jonathan Drazen?" he said, holding out his hand.

"The same." I shook it.

"Name's Will Santon. You look exactly like Margie."

"Tell her she looks younger."

He smiled at me. "This place yours?"

"Girlfriend."

"We found a wireless minicam on the porch. Not the best, but good enough.
Middle-class work."

The porch. What had we done on the porch? Anything? My mind was a blank.
I was blinded by the lights of a little black Honda tearing up the hill and into the
driveway.

"Don't tell her," I said. "Let me take care of it."

Monica got out, all legs and hair, looking like a force of nature, a wild animal entitled to her own sovereignty. Her sexuality wasn't coy or cute. She wasn't saucy; she was feral. Her very presence on the earth stirred me.

"Hi," she said, smiling.

Santon smiled back at her. "Miss, is this your house?"

"I live here."

"I'm Will Santon. I'm a licensed private investigator in the state of California." He showed her an ID card. She looked at it, back at him, and back down to the card. "I've been hired by the law firm of Bode, Drazen, and Weinstein to check your house for surveillance devices. Do I have your permission to enter?"

She glanced at me. I nodded.

"Yes." She flicked her keys and headed in. We followed her, a line of four suits. The other two fanned out, glancing at everything, as Santon gave Monica papers to sign. I stood behind her and prayed that whoever watched her did so only from the outside. If they got inside, I would have the strong urge to burn the place down.

Finished with Santon, Monica turned to me and whispered, "I'm uncomfortable."

I kissed her forehead. "Go get your toothbrush and whatever, and we'll get out of here."

CHAPTER 19

MONICA

I FOUND a bag in the closet and threw it on the bed. My drawers were a mess. My
closet was even worse. I took whatever I touched first and threw it on top of the
bag. I needed work clothes and after-work clothes. Shoes. Underwear. Lacy
Jonathan shit seemed absurd. Would his rule still stand? Garter belts and stockings
felt frivolous and ridiculous with men in my house looking for cameras and
microphones.

I threw both options on the bag. From the bathroom, I got makeup, a
hairbrush, ties for braids, and my toothbrush. I was sure I was forgetting
something, but I wanted out of there. I'd buy whatever else I needed.

I stuffed everything in the bag and picked it up. It had covered something: a
manila envelope labeled *Jonathan S Drazen III* in Sharpie. One of Gabby's files.
Darren must have found it and left it for me. I picked it up. There was enough
inside to give it some heft, but it wasn't as big as the envelopes she'd created for
people in the music industry. Twenty pages, tops. Probably a bunch of friends
highlighted in orange and family in yellow. Jessica in pink. The corners were curled
and the color faded. I almost slipped it in the bag. But no, I wouldn't bring it to his
house. That was crazy.

"How you coming?" Jonathan leaned in the doorway, his jacket falling on his
shoulders in a perfect expression of some kind of victory over gravity. Over
everything. If owning a doorway just by standing in it was possible, or beating the
shit out of a space by existing within it, he did. His concern over what was
happening in my house had a physical presence. It emanated from him in a dense

aura of worry, making him seem bigger, more present, more powerful. I was suffocating under the weight of it.

I glanced down at the envelope. His name faced down. "Thirty seconds or less," I said. He didn't move, making me nervous. "Shoo. Girl stuff."

He slipped out of the doorway, and I breathed again. I slipped the envelope into my top drawer, slung the bag over my shoulder, and walked out of my room with my head down.

CHAPTER 20

MONICA

Telling him about my conversation with Jessica, and the song, weighed heavily on me. I couldn't think about much else. I couldn't do it in a neutral space. I couldn't just tell him and walk out. It was late. My house was overrun.

Jonathan put his hand on my thigh as his other hand rested on the steering wheel. "They're going to be out of there by tonight."

"Yeah. It's a small house. Yours took how long?"

"Couple of hours."

I looked out the window. I still felt invaded. "If there's nothing there, you're in trouble for making a big deal about it."

"We'll work out a suitable punishment." He didn't look as though he expected to be punished, though. He looked as though he was placating me. I didn't care for it. I would have given anything for it to be yesterday again.

We waited as the gate opened. It seemed to take forever, rumbling and clacking in a way I didn't remember it doing before. When Jonathan took my hand and looked at me, he seemed tired. Gorgeous and powerful as always, but wrung out.

"I don't want you to worry," he said.

I squeezed his hand. "I'm fine."

"But I want you to think about who might have done this."

"Something tells me you have an idea."

He didn't say, but I knew he thought it was Kevin. The fact that Kevin had nothing to gain from watching me notwithstanding, anything evil in my life, and stalking me was truly evil, could only be one person's responsibility. Career going poorly? Kevin. Art show hits a snag? Kevin. Bad day at work? Kevin. Camera trained on my front porch? Kevin.

When we got inside, he dropped my bag and put his arms around me. I rested my head on his shoulder. We rocked together, entwined, fitting together like puzzle pieces. He kissed my cheek, my jaw. A tingle of heat pooled between my legs. I looked up, giving him access to my neck. He was going to take me again, and it would be slow and sweet and generous. His hands worked up my back, and I put my fingers in his hair as he kissed my shoulder.

My body screamed for him. Just once. Before telling him anything about Frontage. Just a little bit of comfort. Just to be enveloped inside him. I didn't need a fuck. I needed to make love, and the way he touched me showed me he understood.

"Jonathan."

"Monica."

"Wait," I groaned.

"No."

"Please."

"You're mine."

"Tangerine."

He stopped and stood back, looking me in the eye. His hair was mussed, and his eyes hooded with heat. "Okay, little goddess. What is it?"

"I have to tell you things. I can't put it off anymore."

"All right. Let's get some fresh air." He took my hand and walked me out to the backyard.

We sat on the outdoor couch, in the near dark, which I appreciated. I didn't want a bright light shining on our conversation. His hands stayed on me, stroking my palm, my thigh, soothing me.

"So, you saw Jessica there tonight," I said. "I don't have to tell you that part."

"Yes."

"And you saw us talking."

"Yes."

"She gave me her card and offered to tell me everything about you." His expression didn't change. "I said 'no, thank you, if I need to know about Jonathan, I'll ask him.'"

He squeezed my hand. "You're perfect."

"Well, maybe not. She asked if you told me about Rachel, and I said yes. She asked if you told me all of it, and I kind of went off on her."

"Really?"

"I told her I didn't know what she wanted, but she couldn't have you back because you were too good in bed."

He laughed good and hard, throwing his head back and showing the night sky his face. His laughter filled the huge yard, and even I smiled a little, because really, what man could be upset at that? I wanted to end the conversation right there. If I crawled into his lap, he'd put his arms around me, take me upstairs, and we'd make love so sweetly. Just the thought of it made my arms tingle.

"I haven't gotten to the really uncomfortable stuff yet."

He wiped the tears from his eyes and leaned back, smiling, totally relaxed, his arm draped over the back of the couch. "Go ahead, then."

"You really are good in bed, you know."

"Thank you. It takes two."

"Right. Okay. There's a song." I said the last sentence as if I'd jumped off a cliff. *There's a song.* Three words, and I was committed to finishing. I stared into my lap. I couldn't look at him. "Jessica heard it." I cleared my throat. "I wrote it after you called me submissive and before I gave you the list." I glanced at him. His smile was gone. "I recorded it as a scratch cut, which is something passed around the industry as a sample. I hadn't written a song in a while, and it was all I had. So, it came out good. One of the acquisitions guys heard it and wanted to hear me sing it. They came tonight."

"What was his name? The acquisitions guy?"

"Eddie something." Jonathan's eyes closed slowly, and his mouth shut tight. "What?" I asked.

"Let's hear it."

"Hear what?"

"The fucking song."

My heart beat so hard my ribs were going to break. My lungs quivered, filled, and seemed to empty only part way. I didn't have an instrument to hide behind or a piece of paper with my requirements for him to read. I just had two minutes of pure, raw, fucking vulnerability in his backyard while he pondered not only what he thought of the song, but me, what he felt about me, what his ex-wife heard, and what *she* thought.

"It doesn't have a title yet."

"The song, Monica." His voice was like a brick, blunt and hard, without nuance. He waited. I didn't know what he was thinking, but I realized the more time I took to start, the more crap would run through his head, and maybe that wasn't a good thing.

I sang it in my soft, jazzy voice. I didn't look at him because I didn't want to see his reaction. I just wanted to get through it. I started to crack in the last bridge, where I asked if I'd do the things to him he did to me, because the questions weren't about sex anymore. The song revealed too much. Fuck. I hated music right then, as I sang the last line. I wished I'd never heard a note.

His face was in his hands, and his elbows were on his knees. "What were you thinking?"

"About you."

He looked up. "When you *recorded* it? What the fuck were you thinking?"

I couldn't answer. I had been thinking about myself. That it could be an opportunity. That it was a good song, and once it was a song, it was mine, no matter what it was about.

Even in the dark, his face frightened me. I'd seen that expression before. On my father, just before he threw something or tore apart the living room drapes.

"I'm sorry," I whispered.

"I'm glad you're sorry. But what are you sorry for? Exactly? Are you sorry you had to tell me or sorry you were so selfish in the first place? Because it's not about you. It's about *us*, and we're not a big secret. Unless we split tomorrow, that song is about me and it will follow me wherever I go. Fuck, Monica, I know you're ambitious. I don't expect any less. What I didn't expect was that you'd do something so stupidly self-centered."

Even though we were outside, I felt as if a box closed in around me. If he'd been wrong or if I had a leg to stand on, the box might not have felt as though it was filling with water and I was three seconds from drowning. But I had done wrong. I didn't realize it when I first recorded the song, but I knew it when I played it in front of Jessica. I'd chosen my ambition over my respect for him, and there was no denying it.

His expression was impassive, walled off. The box filled further, and I felt not only trapped, but alone and scared. If he said another word, I would lose my shit.

"Okay, I get it," I said before walking back into the house.

CHAPTER 21

JONATHAN

WHEN THE SCREEN door slammed behind her, I kicked over the glass-topped
coffee table. It shattered. I considered doing more violence to the furniture, but I
wasn't angry at the furniture. I was angry at myself. I had no business feeling what
I felt for Monica. I had no business getting involved in a kinky, emotionally
charged relationship with an unpracticed submissive. Stupid. This, I'd earned.

When I'd held Jessica's hands down during sex, she told everyone I wanted to
rape her. One slap on the ass, and I was an abuser. It hurt badly enough when she
called me those things to my face. When she did it behind my back, it was worse.
Later, I realized she'd had a rough time with men before me. I should have been
more understanding, but it wasn't like I didn't have my own shit.

When Monica sang her song in the husky voice of a fallen angel, I knew her
intentions were pure. I also knew the results would suck. Enough of our social
circle hated me already. Who knew what or whom her performance would affect.
My business? My family? The possible repercussions came in flaming scenes of
scorn and derision. Lost deals. Uncomfortable dinners, come-ons from the wrong
women, bruised ribs from jocular elbows of men thinking Monica was my whore,
or worse, available to share.

Jessica had added humiliation to my confusion by confiding in our whole social
circle and enough of my family to make Easter dinner a nightmare. I never dug out
of it, and the song could just bury me further in a reputation I didn't earn and
didn't want. I didn't want an entire lifestyle of bondage. I didn't want the clubs or
the costumes. I wanted to be normal, except when I wasn't. Yet again, I'd be
branded.

I paced around the pool. Monica had to go. She and her song and her god damn artistic aspirations had to get cut out before I got infected. I had to do it quickly and move on. I had to ignore any and all pleas for forgiveness. I had to forget my feelings, how she wrapped herself around me, how she'd charmed me and disarmed me. I needed to shock her out of my system.

I stopped, and like a siren's call, the pool invited me. I kicked off my shoes and dove in. The water was cold and heavy, and my clothes only made me sink lower. I swam to the surface, and the effort brought me back to my head. The panic and worry came back, but a lower grade. The usual stuff, not the all-consuming stuff.

I navigated to the edge of the pool. I was afraid to get out because I would freeze my ass off, but mostly, I was afraid to deal with the woman on the porch, if she was even still there. I leaned my cheek on my forearm and said, "Monica, Monica, you were perfect."

I was sad to lose her, but I couldn't be seen with her if she was singing that song, and she'd made clear I wasn't to interrupt her work. I knew my little string of sadness would grow into a ball of yarn. I knew how much I wanted her, and why, and how. After knowing her only six weeks, I'd miss her.

My phone rang. It had been on the glass table I'd smashed and apparently survived. I pulled myself out of the pool and dripped my way over to it, my pant legs sticking.

It was Will Santon.

"Hi, Will."

"We found five, with mikes, all over the house. They were on wireless, and they've been disconnected. Probably after she sprayed the car outside."

"We'll need you to work on finding out who did this." I wasn't supposed to care anymore, but I found myself talking as if I did.

"Any ideas?"

"She's working with an artist, Kevin Wainwright. They have a history."

"We're on it," Santon said.

"Send my sister the bill."

"You got it."

I was about to hang up. "Santon?"

"Yeah?"

"Any in the kitchen?"

"Nope."

"Thanks," I said softly and hung up. My relief dripped off me with the cold water. None in the kitchen. What did we do in the bedroom? I'd kissed her eyelids. Not optimum, certainly. Definitely a problem to be solved, because the fact they'd gotten inside at all was bad news, but nothing kinky got on video. At least if my private life was all the buzz, her dignity might be saved.

I don't know how long I stood there holding my phone, but when my teeth chattered, I went inside.

No cameras in the kitchen. Monica's imagination had saved me a shard of embarrassment. Meanwhile, she was having a huge crisis, and I threw a temper tantrum over something she apologized for. I had been ready to abandon her when she needed me to protect her because she wasn't perfect. And why? Because I was worried about what people thought.

They didn't know what I knew. They didn't know what it was to be completely in control of a woman's body, her pleasure, her thoughts, her emotions. They didn't craft moments the way a sculptor molds clay, tapping her consciousness during the day to create anticipation for the night, pushing her, crafting our climaxes not just as a pleasurable endpoint, but as a carefully timed, deliberate *act*. The culmination of my intention was what was most gratifying, and I couldn't give up control any more than Monica could give up music.

I had tried it with other women and failed or come up short. But not Monica. It wasn't just what she allowed and how she obeyed; it was the ways she didn't. Her moments of spontaneity came not in response to a weakness on my part, but the openings for surprise that I left her. Like the kitchen. The last place I expected to find her might have been the only safe place in the house.

What we made together was greater than what I would have created myself. Monica was my perfect canvas. The rest would have to fall into place. She was mine. What we had was mine. I'd earned it.

Fuck the rest.

CHAPTER 22

MONICA

THE BLANKET I'd wrapped around myself smelled of the old Jonathan. Sage. Fog. Jessica had chosen it for him, but I buried my face in it anyway. I stared at the open gate. A cab was on its way. If he didn't show up before the cab, I would just fold myself back into the world and never see him again. It couldn't be any harder than what I'd done before.

I smelled him before I heard him. The leather-and-sawdust Jonathan. I looked back inside and saw him standing behind the chair closest to the door. His hair was wet, but his clothes were dry. He wore his trademarked mask of implacable amusement.

"You waited."

"Cab's coming."

He sat in the chair. "I'm sorry I went off on you."

"It's fine."

"I feel like I should explain."

"Look, you got mad. I know why," I said.

"No, you don't." He leaned back in the chair and crossed an ankle over his knee. "When I married Jessica, I was a nice vanilla guy. We had plenty of sex, and we thought we were just fine. We were. Except I always had this dark place because of what happened with Rachel. I was so young, and not ready. And my father... well, I couldn't look at him. I still can't. I never told anyone. No one knew about it, except Jessica. Her knowing made me happy, and being happy, well, I started getting ideas about how good it would feel to fuck her just a little harder. Hold her hands down. Tell her when to come. Slap her ass." He paused, as if remembering some specific incident. "It didn't go over well. I didn't know how to stop, and she didn't know how to shut up. All her friends were convinced I got off on beating her up. They told their husbands, and before you know it—"

"No one's talking to you at the Eclipse show."

"Right. And I lost her. When you get divorced, you don't just give up the person, you give up all the dreams you had with that person. Those are harder to let go of." He uncrossed his ankle and put his elbows on his knees. "Now I'm with someone else, and she's beautiful with me. But she sings this song, and everyone will hear it and think I'm trying to rape and abuse her. It all came back."

"I can't tell you how sorry I am."

"You should cancel that cab."

"I really want to go home."

"You're not going home tonight. They found cameras."

"Oh, God." My chest felt as if a spike went through it. That was my house. It had always been my house. I felt myself breaking down and I had to grind my teeth to keep together.

"It's clean now. And there were none in the kitchen."

I laughed with relief. The episode on the kitchen floor was the first thing I'd worried about and the one thing I tried not to consider as a possibility.

"We need to find out who did it. And now I really want to have you watched."

I shook my head. "I'll stay with Darren."

"That's not a long-term solution."

I got annoyed. He'd taken the conversation and made it his own. "Jonathan, stop it. Long-term solutions are my problem."

"How's that?"

I took a deep breath. I knew what I wanted to say, but after finding out about my house, and his story, I didn't know if I had the strength. I curled deeper in the blanket. "I'm sorry, Jonathan. What I did with the song was wrong. I'll do what damage control I can. I'll record something else and get it to Jerry. I can't make Jessica unhear it, but it's not like she didn't know about your preferences."

"I know Eddie from Carnival Records, by the way. You met him at the Loft Club. Buddy from—"

"Penn. Right. I'm sorry. I can't make him unhear it either. Maybe he'll think you're hot shit now?"

He shrugged and swung his legs over the chair's arm. He seemed really relaxed for a guy who looked about to belt me twenty minutes ago.

"I was careless with your feelings," I continued. "I should have run it by you first. Because it's your life, and you may not want your kinky shit all over. I mean, it *is* all over, but you don't need your lover confirming it. I thought about it, and I don't want that shit all over either. I could play it off as metaphor, but your rep means I can't. Then we become the couple no one can talk to because we make them giggle."

He laughed a bitter little laugh, as if he knew exactly what I was talking about. He did. I was just repeating history for him. I'd be the second woman to leave him because he was dominant. Before he came outside, I'd consoled myself with the fact that he didn't love me and we hadn't known each other that long. That seemed untrue, though. I was going to hurt him, and I was powerless to stop it.

"So," I continued, "that's when I realized if I'm going to be with you, I can't talk to anyone. I have to keep a whole part of my life locked up tight or people will look at me. I'm the submissive here. I'm the sucker getting her ass spanked. I'm the one walking around with bruises on her wrists. You're the master, and I'm under you. I mean, what the fuck am I doing? Do I not care about my life and my career? How am I supposed to get a leg up in a meeting when the guy on the other side of the desk is imagining me with a ball gag? How can I be seen as a musician who can deliver in front of a crowd if they think I'm a man's slave?"

The cab pulled into the driveway in a flash of headlights.

"I'll send him back." Jonathan swung his legs straight.

I unwrapped myself from the blanket and stood. "No, I'm going. What we have is not what I want. It's too much. I've never met a man like you, and god willing, I never will again because I don't think I could take it. I already can't imagine myself with anyone else."

He looked at me. "You're not leaving, Monica." He took my hands. His were cold, and the temptation to warm them between mine was unbearable.

I said, "I wanted you to know, before I go, that I love you. I thought I didn't want to love anyone again, and maybe I didn't. I mean, look what it comes with, right? The more I fell in love with you, the harder it got to leave you. It's the hardest thing I've ever done."

When he stood, he seemed taller, closer, more solid. "You're not going."

"I am."

"No. Don't you see how perfect we are? What you're breaking isn't some little, meaningless coupling. We aren't some casual fuck, and we never were. Not from the first night. Not from the first time I laid eyes on you. You were built for me. I denied it as long as I could, but we were meant to be together. You are the sea under my sky. We're bound at the horizon."

"Please don't make this worse." My voice cracked. I sniffled. God. Damn. Those fucking tears.

He stood and put his arms around me, engulfing me. How he fit. How his touch felt perfect on me. How I wanted him as he kissed my cheek and neck and breathed my name. "Don't go," he said softly. "I want you, little goddess. Always. Please. Tell me what you want. Tell me what I have to do."

The cab driver honked.

"Let me go, Jonathan."

"No."

I pushed him away with all the force I had, and still he held me. "Let me *go*."

He squeezed me harder. "We're not finished."

I wanted to fall into him, to acquiesce completely. Giving in to his embrace and his touch, letting him take me upstairs would have been so easy. That night would have been beautiful and tender, but what about the next day, and the next week, and the next month?

When I pushed him away again, he released me. I stepped back, almost falling. He held his hand out to help me, but I avoided him.

"Good-bye. I'm sorry," I said.

"Don't be sorry." He stood straight, his chin proud and his shoulders relaxed. "This isn't over."

I wanted to tell him I loved him again, but it would have done more harm than good. I ran down the steps. The cab was about to leave without me, but I grabbed the door handle and opened it. The driver stopped, and I got in.

With one last glance back, I saw Jonathan backlit on that magnificent porch, standing as if he had complete control of the situation, every inch a king.

PART II
BURN

CHAPTER 23

MONICA

THE NEWSPAPER WAS open to a seemingly random page toward the back, but when it caught my eye, I had to examine it further. Discreetly. Because studying such a thing would draw attention from the man I sat across from. The girl in the paper was naked, on her back, with her legs thrown over her head. The light cast the seam between her legs in shadow. Her hands were tucked behind her back, and she was gagged with black cloth. She looked uncomfortable. She looked unhappy. Worse, the picture's appeal was in her miserable expression and the pleased yet benign expressions of the men watching her.

Only when I heard metal tapping against porcelain did I return my attention to the man across the table or, at the very least, to the ring clicking against his coffee cup. He picked up a business card he'd let drop next to the creamer.

I was ambivalent about the pinkie ring.

On the one hand, it ate at my trust. Who could have confidence in a man who wore one? On the other hand, its oddness was intriguing. Will Santon's fingers slipped down his business card, pivoted it, rested it on the coffee shop table, and slid down its long side again. The fingers were thick and well-formed I imagined them sliding inside me two at a time, the ring resting against my asshole as the thumb teased my clit. I found the thought as unarousing as the woman in the paper. What normally would have sparked my desire, sparked exactly nothing. My mind was on sex all the time, but my body had taken a powder. I couldn't feel a damn thing between my legs no matter how hard I thought about fucking.

"I promise you," he said. "Your place is clean."

"I believe that you believe that." I twisted my teacup in its saucer. The pink

349

roses were worn, and the saucer didn't match. All the décor in the café was found, thrift-shopped, or rescued.

"I've been doing this a long time," he said.

How long could he have been doing it though? He was thirty-five, tops, without a grey speck in his dark hair or his two-day-old black scruff. His eyes, grey as a rainy day, looked as though they'd seen their share of nastiness. His gaze did not waver, but I knew his peripheral vision was as clear as my narrow field. His jacket fit perfectly, but it was the open shirt collar, the haircut around the ears, and the comfortable shoes that told me who he was.

"You're military," I said.

"Marines."

"Something ending in 'ops,' I bet." He didn't answer. "My dad was killed in Saudi escorting a second-rate prince to some mosque."

"I'm sorry to hear that."

"You have kids, Mr. Santon?"

"Daughter. She's four."

And no wedding ring, I noticed. "Would you let your daughter go into that house?"

His gaze slipped to his empty cup. Black coffee. He'd finished his black coffee in a single swig when it was burning hot. "I got a call from your boyfriend—"

"Ex."

"Ex-boyfriend."

"Ex-lover."

"He asked me to reassure you. I'm reassuring you."

"You know what would reassure me?"

"For us to sweep it again?" His head was cocked as if he thought that would be an acceptable answer.

"Find out who it was."

"We're working on it."

"I believe you are. And I'm sure he paid you a lot of money to come here and tell me my house was clean and you were working on it. But I'll be reassured when I know who did it, not when Jonathan Drazen says it's time to be reassured. Thanks for trying."

"He also asked me to see if you looked okay, how you sounded. He said when you're upset, it's in your voice."

I swallowed, feeling scrutinized in a way I hadn't a second earlier. My chin went up a notch, and my shoulders straightened. I couldn't help it. "I'm sure you're not supposed to tell me that."

"Do you know what I'm going to say to him?"

"No, and I don't care," I said, caring a great deal.

"You're terrified."

"I'm fine."

"I've heard terrified women. Some were scared for a moment when bad shit was happening, and others got beaten down by a daily, low-grade fear." He arched an eyebrow, as if asking me which one I thought I was.

I stood. "You can tell him whatever you like, but if you tell him I'm anything but perfectly all right, he's going to worry, and that's going to make more work for you."

"I don't need the extra work."

"Then you know what to say."

Will stood and handed me the card he'd been fingering. "If you want the place swept again, call me, and I'll have it done." When I took the card, his pinky overshot its destination and brushed mine. Though the touch surprised me, it did not rouse any feelings between my legs.

CHAPTER 24

MONICA

THE DESIRE TO BE TOUCHED, to connect, to find commonality between myself and someone else overwhelmed my common sense. It wasn't just anyone I wanted to touch. It was him.

Though I was alone by choice, I was desperately hurt. I carried around an ache in my chest and a cloying desire on my skin. I missed Jonathan. I missed his sharp tongue and his strong arms. Yes, I missed his dick and all our play, but it was the loss of his stare, the warmth of his attention, and the emotional safety of his sphere of influence made me feel unmoored.

Did I look scared? I leaned into Darren's bathroom mirror. I looked the same to me. I could call him. I could see him just one time. Maybe I would. I put my mascara down and looked at my phone.

It was 8:59 in the morning. In one minute, my phone would bloop with some short, pithy message from Jonathan. He sent me a text at nine every morning on the dot. I never texted him back, and I never told him to stop. I had two weeks' worth of pings from him, making sure that at least once a day, I thought of him. It was controlling in such a precise and unemotional way that on day four, when I realized what he was doing, I tapped him a livid response. But I never sent it. I thought of him so much more often than once a day anyway.

—Bring an umbrella. It's going
to rain—

I scrolled back. He had reports from DC:

352

—It is truly awful here—

*—Another lunch meeting. Bullshit
on the menu—*

—You belong with me—
And when he got home.

*—Debbie said you aren't living
in the house? Will Santon is
going to call you—*

—Sea and sky—
I'd replaced my beautiful platinum diamond navel ring with the fake one I'd
bought when I got the piercing. I returned Jonathan's through Yvonne, who had
spent a lunch warning me about connections between BDSM and abuse, had left it
in his office when no one was looking. The next morning, his nine a.m. text read:
—I'll hold this for you—
He was so confident I would come back, and all he had to do was wait. It made
me crazy. I wrote songs about how crazy he made me, scrawled on the backs of
napkins or on my forearm while I raced down the freeway. I wrote verses about his
eyes and choruses on his voice. I wanted to exorcise him through music, but I
feared I was doing nothing more than keeping the burn in my belly alive.

CHAPTER 25

MONICA

THE RESTAURANT SEEMED SPECIFICALLY DESIGNED to attract entertainment industry types, like an oddly shaped orchid meant for the attentions of a specific species of insect. It was packed at lunch with agents and executives in suits, feeling up writers and artists for their commerciality and ass-fuckability.

I hummed to myself in the bathroom as I looked in the mirror for something to fix. I was fine, wearing two loose braids, a black dress, big stinking shoes, mascara. I'd even filed my nails. I was there to meet Eddie Milpas, and I looked better than fine. I looked fantastic.

When I walked back into the restaurant, he was being seated. I gave him my sterling silver customer service smile and sat when the waiter moved my chair. The window by our table overlooked the marina. On that windy November day, the boats swayed as if they were on a keyboard, playing scales.

"It's nice to see you again," he said. "I ordered appetizers, The calamari is fantastic."

"That's great."

Eddie said, "So, I wanted to talk about what we're looking for and what you have for us." I nodded. "Jerry brought me your scratch cut a week ago, and I didn't listen to it until the night before I saw you at Frontage. And when I did, I couldn't believe you pulled it off. That song is a hit, Miss Faulkner. Not to be crass, but it has money written all over it."

My smile went from customer service to nervous and uncontrollable. "I'm happy you like it."

"I may need you to rerecord it with the right production value added."

"I have another song I'd like to do."

"We...meaning me and Harry Enrich, the president of Carnival...we really want that one."

Two glasses of white wine came. He looked at me over his glass as took a sip. He had nice marble green eyes and brown hair. I may have taken a second look at him ages ago, before Jonathan. But for now, I was stuck. Temporarily, I reminded myself. Other men would appear, or none. Didn't matter.

I placed my glass on the tablecloth, letting it make a wet crescent in the fabric. "Actually, that song's no longer available."

"Did you sell it?"

"No. It's just unavailable."

He tapped the edge of his glass. "This have to do with the person you were writing about?"

Eddie had seen me with Jonathan at the club. And Jonathan was aware that Eddie had heard the song. So it wasn't as general a question as it seemed.

I wasn't concerned with the existence or performance of the song. It could be played off as a metaphor or a story. Once my past with Jonathan, and his reputation, came into play, the song became about me and what I did in the bedroom. That meant that under Eddie's gaze, at a meeting about my career, I felt naked and vulnerable. I felt his eyes slipping the dress off my body and his inexpert hands experimenting with pain.

"Look," he said, "the BDSM thing is really hot right now, and we're looking to capitalize. We're going all in with the marketing. You'll be an icon. Tall, beautiful woman in black leather, belting that thing out. We have more kinky songs ready to go, but no performer with real experience who can pull it off. I mean, the whole thing will fall apart on the Today Show if our singer uses the wrong phrase, right?"

The intensity of his imagination squeezed my lungs, forcing out the air. Everything I feared was happening, right then, and I hadn't prepared myself for anxiety so strong that every coherent thought ran from my mind like brown specks running from a kicked anthill.

"The song isn't available," was all I could say.

He smiled with his perfect teeth and twinkling eyes. "You'll figure it out. When you do, I'm pretty sure we can sign you." He slipped the menus from the side of the table and handed me one. "You should try the yellowtail. It comes with artichokes that will knock your socks off."

He opened his menu and pretended to look at it, but I knew he was wondering what I looked like on my knees, bound and gagged, legs spread, cunt wet and waiting for him. I pushed the image from my mind and just ordered the yellowtail.

As if feeling my discomfort, Eddie changed the subject. We talked about my plans for my musical future. I made up a bunch of stuff. Making plans was impossible when I had to take every opportunity that presented itself. Except this one. I had to turn this boat around. I had to go from Bondage Girl to something else, but I didn't know what, and I didn't know how. He seemed damned determined to stay on uptrending sexual fetishes as my brand. The more I engaged him on it, the more he'd expect me to say yes and the more I'd convince myself I was nothing more than a bound, spread-eagled fucktoy in his mind.

I didn't want him to know I'd broken it off with Jonathan. I was unprotected without him—sexually available and emotionally vulnerable. Before Eddie had a chance to offer coffee, I used my job as an excuse to get the hell out of there.

I went through my shift at the Stock confused, panicked, and anxious. I put on my smile, made witty repartee when necessary, and delivered drinks as if I had twinkles in my toes, but I felt the rock in my chest go from still and heavy to vibrating. Not in a good way. In a painful way. The hum was the sound of regret. I had a chance at a career move, and I was going to lose it because it was the wrong one. Because I wasn't the audience's fucktoy any more than I was Jonathan's. I'd walked away from him to protect my non-existent career, and it had careened out of control.

At the end of my shift, I flipped through my tickets, closed out my money, and handed the open tables to Mandy.

"Real bitch on five," I said. "Watch the salt in her cucumber cosmos. She has a 'condition,' and her untimely death is going to become your fault. Henrietta Sevion is by the pool. She's on the phone, so just bring her wine and smile. Renaldo Rodriguez is on the corner with a fucking entourage of blondes. I have no advice."

Mandy cracked her gum one last time and gently spit it into a napkin. "You're grumpy."

Robert, who seemed to hear everything no matter who he was serving at the bar, said, "Needs a drink." He nodded to me. "Want something before you go?"

"No, thanks." His offer was tempting, but it was nine o'clock, and I still had work to do. "Where's Debbie?"

"Office." Robert flipped a bottle as a prelude to wiping it down. "Can you tell her to hurry on the schedule? I have an audition this week."

"Nope. She hates when we nag about it, so I'm not going to do it for you. I'm asking her for time off, and then I'm going home."

Mandy poured the mixers for the drinks on her tray. "Oh yeah? Going somewhere for Thanksgiving?"

"Vancouver the week after."

"Ah that thing you're doing with both your ex-boyfriends? Which you don't think is weird?"

"It's not weird unless you make it weird. The piece, you should see it. It's going to make me famous." I wagged my finger at her. The piece *had* to make me famous. I could be Art Girl instead of Bondage Girl. I could do abstraction. The Vancouver piece gave me a gem of hope in the seven acres of shit I'd slogged through with Eddie. Mandy rolled her eyes and went to serve Renaldo Rodriguez and his blonde entourage.

I'd just gotten a passport. It had just come in the mail, Kevin and Darren had to go to the B.C. Mod without me to take meetings and do the setup. Letting my passport expire was a stupid oversight on my part, and I promised I wouldn't let it happen again. I would be fully present for every step from then on.

I went into the guts of the hotel to the liquor room, where Debbie's unobtrusive little office sat. When I got to her door, I heard two voices: hers and one male, talking seriously. I knocked. Usually Sam was in there with her, as if she owned the hotel and he worked for her, not the other way around.

"Come in," called Debbie.

I opened the door and saw Debbie first, leaning on the window ledge. Then I had the wind knocked out of me.

Jonathan sat in her leather chair in his work clothes. Blue suit, striped shirt, red cufflinks. He looked at me like the first time, when I felt as if he was drinking me through the straw of his gaze. But back then, though I'd been celibate, I had something for his eyes to drink: a piqued sexuality and availability in my heart that I didn't realize existed until he'd awakened it. When I saw him in Debbie's office, I felt emotionally dehydrated and sexually bloodless.

"I'll come back later," I said and spun on my heel before I heard the answer.

He caught me in the liquor room, by a stack of boxes piled eight feet high. "Monica." His voice was so gentle I couldn't ignore it. I turned. "Hey. How are you?"

"I'm fine." My voice sounded out of tune and ill-played. He looked perfect, well rested and fed, as though my absence had had no effect on him at all.

"You look good." He stood three feet away. Why could I feel the heat from his body? How was his gaze so physical on me?

"Thanks. You too." He wasn't moving away. Just standing. I couldn't even look at him. "I get your texts," I said.

"I know," he whispered and raised his hand, his fingertip touching my sleeve. "You can go in to talk to Debbie. I'll wait out here. You're at work. I don't want you to be uncomfortable."

My laugh was a gunshot on a yesterday's bloody battlefield, so short and awkward that I cast my gaze up to see if he'd noticed. His eyes, tourmaline with blue flecks I'd see if I got close enough, had that bemused look, as though nothing happened in his purview that he hadn't predicted, and the hurt I'd caused myself was simply something I had to get control over.

Until that look, I hadn't wondered, or even thought about, who he was fucking now. But with his heat on me and under the pressure of his presence, I had to ask myself if he breathed her name at the height of his pleasure, if he touched her with all the violence and tenderness he'd touched me with.

"Thanks," I said. "I'll be out in a minute."

Debbie had moved behind her desk. She'd been looking older lately. I'd been led to believe her real age was thirty-eight, but that was never discussed. "Sit," she said.

I stood. I didn't need to stay long. I didn't want to keep Jonathan waiting outside. The thought of him existing on the other side of the wall was painful.

"I need these days off." I handed her a slip of paper. She checked it against the calendar on her desk.

"This should be fine." She looked back up at me. "How are you doing?"

"All right."

"Really?"

"Yes."

She leaned back in her chair and indicated the leather chair where Jonathan had been sitting. Anyone who hadn't been attuned to his lingering smell might have missed it. "You took it seriously, didn't you?"

I sucked my lower lip between my teeth and nodded.

"I told you not to," Debbie said.

"Yeah, I kinda forgot."

"Understandable. Just keep it together on the floor. Yes?"

"I'll be a woman of grace."

Debbie looked at the schedule again. "Thursday, Doreen needs to leave at ten. Can you do half a shift?"

"That's Thanksgiving."

"Do you have plans?"

I shrugged. "I can be here."

She scribbled my name in the schedule and dismissed me.

When I went back out into the liquor room, Jonathan was gone. I didn't know whether to be relieved or sad.

CHAPTER 26

JONATHAN

I DON'T KNOW what I must have looked like to her. She looked more feral, hungry, and proud than she ever had. On edge, too. I knew if I touched her, she'd calm down. If I put my lips on her face, her breathing would slow. If I put my body close to hers, she'd stop twitching.

But I had to wait. She had to come to me. And she would.

Even as we stood outside arm's distance of each other, I felt the space between us mold into something perfectly matched. I'd thought she was on edge, but the fact was, I hadn't felt right since she rode away in that cab. Two weeks had stretched out into an endless horizon. I was on a path getting smaller in the distance, but always staying the same in reality. She chose to walk away, and she would have to choose to come back. I was a patient man. I could wait, but I didn't have to like it.

"What are you going to do with her?" Debbie asked after I let Monica leave without seeing me again.

"Wait like a good boy."

"How long?"

"I don't know. Why?

"Because you're here, talking to me about bulk ordering liquor and borrowing staff, when you have a bar manager to liaison with me." She waved her hand dismissively. "Go run your empire."

I threw myself into the leather chair. "What if the bar manager at K is a douchebag?"

"You're saving me from a douchebag? Have we met?"

359

"In fact—"

"Did I not help you get through that nightmare with your ex-wife?"

"You were a godsend."

"So stop bullshitting me. You come during her shifts and stay with Sam and me in the back, or you come after her shifts to drink at the bar. How long are you going to wait?"

"You want an exact date?"

"I want an event. Something that has to happen."

"Fine. When I meet someone as close to perfect as she is."

"Better start looking, my friend. She's already moved on."

"What does that mean?" I leaned forward. I felt myself getting pissed as the bottom dropped out of my chest.

"It means if there's not someone else already, there will be soon. I can see it when she talks to customers."

Debbie was always right about people. Usually, that was beneficial. Today, it was a problem. Today, I wanted to hurt someone, starting with myself. I left before Sam even got there. I could drink at home.

My phone rang as I turned onto my street. Margie.

"What?"

"Good evening to you too, little brother."

"What can I do for you, Margie?"

"You have Will Santon's team flying to Vancouver to watch Kevin Wainwright?"

Before I left the Stock, I'd called Will to let him know Monica's travel dates. I had his team following Kevin, to make sure Monica was safe from him, as well as tracking the money behind the cameras in her house. He said he was close to finding out where they came from, as if I didn't already know.

"Yes?"

"Has it occurred to you I might need to use him?"

"To do what? Have some movie producer followed to his mistress's house?"

"What's the difference?"

"The difference is a few million everyone involved can afford, and someone I care about getting hurt. Physically and irrevocably hurt." I was yelling. That wasn't going to get me anywhere.

"You know, Jonny, I don't mind you getting paranoid and crazy, but you're doing it on my dime."

"You're an attorney. You're protected. If I get caught stalking, I fry. I'll write you a check if you can't afford to feed the kids this week."

"Now you're getting nasty."

"Margie, sweetheart, please."

"I gotta pull him, Jonny. I'm sorry."

"Fine. Thanks for letting me know." I hung up.

Things were not going well. My patience with Monica was wearing thin. I hadn't considered her casting around for a new lover so soon. The thought of it made my fingers go cold. Will's inability to trace the cameras before he got pulled, a mere week before Monica was going to Vancouver with that sicko, pushed me out of rational thought and into a place of frozen rage. The situation was getting more slippery than I could manage.

Then I saw Jessica's Mercedes SUV in my driveway, and I thought I might break something. Aling Mira must have let her in before retiring for the night with Danilo.

My ex-wife sat on the back patio sipping coffee from a silver pot that had been on our wedding registry. I hated that thing. I thought about packing up all the shit of ours I hated and giving it to charity.

"Jess," I said, "how are you?"

She put her hand on my shoulder and kissed my cheek. Just one cheek, not a double air kiss. Somehow, that seemed more intimate.

"I'm fine." She wore perfectly fitting blue jeans, cowboy boots, a white shirt, and a bandana around her neck. I used to find her country girl airs charming. She was raised deep in Beverly Hills, where tourists got lost looking for Olympic Boulevard. "I came to talk about something. I thought you'd be here this time of night, but well, I guess not. And my appointments keep getting pushed."

I sat down. "If you came here to fight, Jess, I don't have the time."

"No. Of course not. I, uh... There were guys doing renovations to my studio? New plumbing? And I was confused."

"There's lead in those pipes—"

"I was just worried you were getting it ready to sell it."

"I'll let you make an offer if it comes to that."

"I can't, Jon. You know that."

"You didn't sell the trees?"

"I did. I got two million each for them, and the documentation was bought by the museum. But they cost a fortune. Keeping a dead thing alive takes a lot of engineering."

I nodded. Jessica's problem had always been that the cost and ambition of her work didn't quite jibe with what she could ask for it. She didn't have Kevin Wainwright's way of turning something that didn't exist into money. Art, for her, wasn't about money, or professionalism, or business. Art was about art. I used to love the purity of her vision.

"You could make smaller things," I said. "And more of them. Just an idea."

She looked away. She didn't know what I was talking about. She said, "Remember when you first took me in *that* way? Right there, by the shed. You pulled my hair back and bent me over the wet bar. Then you yanked my pants down and hit me."

"I slapped your ass. Yes, I remember. I didn't exactly know what I was doing at that point."

"I was offended."

"You were scandalized." I was surprised to find myself smiling. Only in hindsight did how outraged she'd been seem funny. At the time, I was guilt-ridden and devastated over her reaction. "I believe you called me a pig and moved to a guest room on the other side of the house."

"And you—"

"I jerked off. Do you have a point here? We've covered this."

Her tone got hard, as if she feared I'd interrupt again. "You persisted, and I never considered your way. I never gave it a chance. Even when I was trying to reconcile, I still wouldn't try things your way. I don't think I was fair to you." She smoothed a nonexistent crease in her jeans. It was the only crack in her poise.

"This because Erik left?"

She shook her head. "He's back, sort of. We're talking, but I can't stop thinking about you... and kissing you again. You always knew how to kiss."

I leaned back. Was she really going there? Was she really going to offer me my married life back with a little kink thrown in? Did she honestly think I'd take her back? I should have kicked her out right then, but something else was in play. Some other motivation I had to tease out.

"And you're saying you want to try it my way?"

"I want to." She looked me with those big sapphire disks, wheaten lashes blinking. She was so beautiful. Angelic, even. "We'd need to set some boundaries beforehand."

Boundaries. The whole act was about tightly controlled boundaries, and she presented them as if they'd be concessions by me toward her. It was bullshit. The whole conversation. Her whole sudden pursuit of me. She was hiding something, and if she stayed tightly wrapped up, prim and proper, she'd never reveal it.

"No," I said. "My way. Right now. Then you tell me if you can take it."

She bit her lip. I didn't know what to hope for, but the longer she waited, the clearer my plan became.

"Okay," she said softly.

I didn't move. Not a blink or a hair. "That's 'okay, sir.'"

"Doesn't that seem a little silly?"

"You want to do this or not?"

"Yes, sir." A nervous smile played on her lips. Part of me would have loved to wipe it off with my dick. The rest of me didn't want to touch her.

"Stand up."

She stood, leaning on one foot and jutting her hip out, hands on her waist. All attitude. It would take some poor soul ages to train the woman.

"Unbutton your shirt."

She stuck her tongue in her cheek and swung her narrow hips, unbuttoning as though she was in a strip show.

"Stop trying to look saucy. This is a functional matter and not for your pleasure."

Oh, the look on her face. I don't think I could have forgotten it. When she told every mutual friend we had that I wanted to beat her and take away her right to say no, when she told them I had rape fantasies and that I hated women, she'd had no idea. The damage I could have done—but wouldn't have—wasn't to her body.

She unbuttoned her shirt completely and started to take it off.

"Stop."

I could have told her how I wanted her to stand, how I wanted her to look, where her hands belonged, but it would have been a waste of my time. I got behind her and untied the bandana on her neck.

"This is what it is," I whispered in her ear. "This is the kind of sex you're agreeing to."

As I slipped off the bandana, I considered binding her at the elbows like I'd done with Monica the night she got her voice back. But Monica could handle it. Even though I told Jessica I was going to show her what she was agreeing to, in all its pain and messiness, I had no intention of doing so. It would probably damage her psyche forever. Then she'd call the cops. Mostly, I really didn't want to put my dick anywhere near her. I did, however, want to figure out what she wanted.

"Put your hands behind your back."

She turned her head when she "obeyed." Jesus Christ. Two commands and she'd exasperated the hell out of me. I never would have felt an ounce of control with her.

"Face forward, Jess."

I didn't tie her at the elbows. The wrists would have to do. I moved around to face her. Her open shirt showed off her white cotton bra and flat stomach. Her shoulders drooped. I couldn't have tied her hands more comfortably, yet she looked awkward. "How does that feel?"

"Okay so far," she said. "A little weird."

"What's weird?"

"Jon, seriously? What's *not* weird? I'm standing here with my shirt open and my hands tied behind my back."

"Is your cunt wet?"

"Do you have to be vulgar?"

I stood close enough for her to feel me whisper. "Yes. It's about communication. It's about saying what you want and don't want, clearly, and sometimes with a filthy mouth. So let me get you on board with what you just agreed to." I kicked her legs open. I righted her when she almost fell, but the annoyance on her face made me want to drop her. "The answer to my question is, 'No, sir. I'm not wet. This sucks.' I'll tell you I don't care how much this sucks for you. Then I'll prove it.

"I'll undo your jeans. I'll pull them down to the middle of your thighs so it's hard to walk. You'll be uncomfortable, and that will please me. Then I'll get behind you, and I'll grab a handful of your hair at the back of your head and bend you over that table. I'll take off my belt, loop it once, and slap it across those sweet white cheeks until you're pink as a rose and your face is covered with tears. I'll stop when I can stick two fingers in your cunt and feel how sopping wet you are. Then I'll fuck you until you beg me to let you come, which I may or may not let you do. That going to work for you?"

The color had drained from her face.

"Didn't think so," I said, stepping away.

"Do it," she whispered.

"Jess, really."

"Do it! Start with the hair. Or the pants. Whatever."

"No."

"Do it!" she said.

"Stop, Jess."

"Are you a fucking *man*? Or do you just beg and cry for what you can't have? Is that how you get off?"

I threw her over the table. She fell onto it, bending at the waist with a grunt, ass out and arms bound by her own scarf. God, how many times I wanted to hear her grunt, to cut through the thick layers of refinement and find a woman past careful words. The woman I met so many years ago, before she'd built her walls.

I stuck my knee between her thighs and yanked the hair at the base of her neck. Her mouth hung open, and her chest heaved. She wasn't aroused, that I could tell, and I didn't care.

"Choose a safeword, Jessica."

"Do we need—?"

"Question me again and I'm fucking your ass so hard you won't be able to sit."

I almost heard her teeth grinding. "Declan," she said.

"Interesting choice.. Avoid it all and tell me what you really want, coming here. I'll stop for either the safeword or that, but nothing else until I'm satisfied."

I undid my belt after turning her head so she could watch me snap it out of the loops. I put her cheek to the glass. Out of the corner of my eye, I caught sight of a sharp triangle of white porcelain by the chair leg. One of the broken plates had missed the broom the morning after I made Monica recite "Invictus."

"No yelling, Jess." I shifted to her side, still holding her hair and my belt. "No crying. Do you understand?"

"Yes," she whispered so softly, she was barely audible.

I hit the edge of the table with a *smack* of my belt. She jumped at the sound.

"Yes, what?"

"God, Jon—" I hit her ass. The belt landed with a satisfying *thwack*. She stiffened and ground her teeth. "It hurts. You're hitting me."

"You asked for it, Jess." I pulled her hair in my fist. "And that's, 'It hurts, *sir*.'" I laid into her ass again, and she yanked her head, making a sound like a bad brake shoe. "Now tell me what you want."

"I want you."

"Bullshit." I whacked her again. That was three. Too many. And I wasn't holding back much. They had to hurt. "This started a month ago. You chased Erik away. Why?"

"You."

I pulled back my arm, yanking her hair She screamed.

"Fuck, Jess. Stop lying!"

I pulled her hair and looked in her face. Her cheeks were wet with streams of mascara-colored tears. Her lower lip quivered. I had been a white hot ball of anger. If I had been thinking, I would have stopped. A dom should never, ever have an ounce of anger in his heart when spanking a sub. That wasn't fun. That wasn't all right. But between losing Will's services and Debbie's advice about Monica, I wasn't functioning. I was a panting, heaving mess looking into my ex-wife's tear-filled eyes.

"You used to have such a tender heart," she said through her sobs. "Do you remember when I miscarried? You took me to the hospital, and you were joking the whole way? Trying to make me laugh. But when we got there, you were crying. And you fell asleep in the chair next to me with your head on the bed."

"What do you *want*, Jessica?"

"I want to go home."

I pulled her up and untied her. She was miserable from the experience, and so was I. She wasn't ready for something that hard, even if she'd had any proclivity in that direction, and I wasn't sexually stirred in the least.

"Go take Erik back. He's good for you." I handed her back her bandana. "You know the way out."

I didn't look back when I went through the house, bolted up the stairs, and closed my bedroom door.

My god. Three strokes. That was stupid.

CHAPTER 27

MONICA

WORKING with Kevin and Darren had been intense, and I was grateful for the distraction from my beaten wreckage of a love life. We fought. We drank. We made music and art. I brought my pain to the table, using it to color and nuance a work of art that was basically about heartbreak, loss, and grief.

When we'd had breakthroughs, I couldn't have been more content. And then, one day, we realized we'd done it. Though plenty of it could use a tweak or ten, the piece was generally finished and not a minute too soon.

Standing in the center of the draft room, listening to my viola playing Kevin's lullaby, forty some odd tracks of my voice in wordless harmony, over Darren's techno thumping, I laughed. I felt drunk, melancholy, miserable, high, blissed. For two weeks, I'd cried every night and put on a customer service smile every day, but when I worked with the guys, I was myself.

When the thing was finished and photographed, we lounged around on a circle of couches in Kevin's backyard and drank cheap beer out of the bottle. Darren and Kevin had gotten wrapped tighter than the old amp cords at the bottom of a duffel. They called each other when they weren't working. As far as I knew, Kevin was still into women, and Darren was at least marginally involved with Adam, but I often felt like a third wheel to a marriage of kindred souls.

Kevin made broad intellectual pronouncements. Darren shot him down. Kevin pulled reasoning from the rubble. Darren told him he was full of shit. Over and over. By the time we'd documented every track, sound, and scrap of material in the piece, the two of them had become white noise.

I hadn't gotten over seeing Jonathan looking so hale the other day. So polite. "I don't want you to be uncomfortable." Asshole. But my meeting with Eddie had hardened my resolve. I never, ever wanted people looking at me like that in a meeting, and the only way to change it was to lose the song and Jonathan. I had to do what I'd been trying to do for two years: focus on my career.

"Earth to Planet Mon," said Darren, waving his beer around.

"Yeah." I barely snapped out of it.

"Happy Thanksgiving."

"National Orphan Feelbad Day," I said. We clinked bottles and drank.

"Did you get a flight to BC?" Darren asked.

"Yeah," I replied. Darren and Adam were going a day early to hang out in Vancouver. "Same plane as Kev."

"And your passport?" Kevin pushed his longish black hair back for a second, lowered his hand, and it flopped below his eyes again.

"Done. Do you need me here for the breakdown and pack up tomorrow?"

"No way," Kevin said, worrying the label on his beer bottle. "Pros do that. They'll have it boxed by noon and at the B.C. Mod in a week. We just show up to put it all together and look pretty for the preview exhibit. Black tie. All rich guys. Just like you like them."

"Fuck off."

"Agreed." Darren stood and took a last swig from his beer. "I gotta blow."

"So to speak," I shot back.

"Hilarious. See you on the couch."

"You're joking," Kevin said. "You're still sleeping on this asshole's couch?"

"If it happened to you, you'd feel uncomfortable and violated too."

"The P.I. said the cameras were gone."

"But I don't know who put them there. Once I know, I'll go back."

"And how are you going to know?" Kevin asked. "I mean, you dumped the guy who hired the P.I."

They couldn't see my face go fire-engine red in the dark, which was just as well. They knew I'd split with Jonathan but not why. Kevin had a point, and Darren and I had gone over it all a hundred times. I should have told my mother to sell the place. Just pull it from under me. It wasn't like I'd ever call it home again.

"On that note—" Darren tossed his bottle in the recycling. "This city's bouncing with parties in honor of National Day After Thanksgiving Day, and I'm being dragged to the gay half of them."

"Hey, wait!" Kevin said. "You guys have to sign the copyright papers." He ran inside, and he came back out again as if they'd been right by the door. After setting a stack of papers on the crapped out old bar he'd salvaged from an empty lot, he handed Darren a pen. "Right here."

"Dude, you got me signing papers by candlelight." Darren put his face nose-close to the page, and Kevin laughed. Darren signed. I got up and did the same. I felt as though we were sealing a deal, probably because I was half tipsy, and the outdoor space, candlelit and cool, added a coat of profundity to the proceeding.

"To us—," Kevin held his beer aloft. "The Nameless Threesome." We clicked bottles to our collaborative name. We were a cooperative, the future of creation, the new trend in authorship. Collaborators. Teams. Kevin had seen the trend and made sure he was a part of it. Kevin was a visionary, even to the detriment of his own ego.

It had been fun. More fun than I'd anticipated, and for the first time in weeks, I didn't feel anxious and alone.

When Darren left, Kevin held up his bottle. "Another?"

"I have to be at work at nine-thirty."

He handed me another anyway. "This is a small show, but it was a good idea. I'm glad we did this."

"Yeah. It was good. And I've never been that far north."

"You're smart, Monica, and you get it. You get what it is to make art I've been meaning to say something to you."

"You're not going to get maudlin on me, are you?" I leaned my elbows on the bar behind me, bottle dangling from one hand. The beer was going to my head.

"I was wrong. The way I treated you. Calling you Tweety Bird. Marginalizing you. I denied the world your beauty, and it was wrong to you and the world." He stroked my cheek with his thumb. I was slow to react, and if I was being honest with myself, the human contact felt nice. He leaned in, his nose close to my cheek, and I caught his malt and chocolate smell. "You were right to leave."

"Kevin, I—"

He put his full lips to mine, and my body responded by twisting. He held me. His tongue tasted of beer. I pushed him away.

"I can't."

"Why?" His face found my neck. I recoiled, hating that I was so hungry to be touched but only by one person.

"I'm in love with someone. It wouldn't be fair to you."

He clamped both sides of my face. "I'll live with it."

When he went to kiss me again, I scrunched up my eyes and lips, shaking my head. He held me fast. I did not like it. The sweetness of being touched was gone, replaced by a feeling of violation, like control of my body was being taken from me. I panicked.

"Kevin, no!"

"Do you need a safeword?"

"*What?*" When I tried to pull away, he clamped his arms around me and shoved his knee between my legs, spreading them.

"Monica," he said with effort as I wiggled. "Calm down. What's the—"

I bit his shoulder, hard. He screamed, and when he pulled away, my teeth still had him. Skin broke. Blood soaked through his shirt. Faster than an insult, I felt a hard impact on my face, and I lost my bearings from the slap.

He wore an expression both shocked and ferocious. I swung a full bottle of beer at it. The bottle didn't break, but it hit his temple with a *thok*. I lost my grip, and inertia pulled the bottle out of my hand and onto the ground. It landed at my feet in a sunburst of suds.

Kevin was crouched, holding his bleeding head. I didn't know whether to help him or run away. I was shocked into inaction until he came at me. Then I ran.

I ran into the studio, through the kitchen and his workroom, past the installation in its finished form, down the hall, and out the door. When I got to the front, where my car was parked, the metal front door didn't slam right away. He was right behind me, his gorgeous face smeared with blood.

"Kevin. Stop!"

He didn't stop. He grabbed my arm and threw me against my Honda.

Fuck.

My keys were in the studio.

I swung. He ducked. I had my opening. I ran down the block and didn't stop until I heard music.

MONICA

LIKE ANY SELF-RESPECTING ANGELINO, I kept my phone in my pocket. The party
I'd found was hopping with kegs and disorganized bottles on a paper-covered table.
Art covered the warehouse walls, some of the silkscreens tilted from encounters
with drunken partiers.

I called work when I found a quiet corner..

"Hi, Debbie? I can't make it tonight. Something happened."

"What's 'something'?"

"It's personal."

"If you're screwing my girls over, I get to know why."

I didn't want to go through the whole thing. I'd already shown my manager
enough unprofessional behavior. "I left my car keys behind a locked door. I'm
trying to get my roommate on the phone, but he's not picking up. I don't think
he'll get here in time to get me to work."

She sighed and covered the phone to talk to one of the staff. "Where are you?
I'll send Robert."

Shit. I could feel my face throbbing where Kevin had hit me. I couldn't go to
work like that. "No, Debbie. I'm sorry. I didn't tell the whole thing. I was in a fight.
I'm not presentable."

"Stop arguing and text me where you are."

She hung up.

My face was throbbing with the bump of the music. The warehouse space had
been coopted for the night by German Benefactors, an artist's cooperative just
starting to make waves. The place was huge, and packed, and smelling of piss

where it was dark. Though two outstanding DJs had been hired, no one had thought to bring in a Port-a-Potty.

So I was forced out into the light, clutching some reddish drink, putting the cold plastic up to my face, avoiding people I might know.

Which didn't work. Ute Graden, a struggling actress of German descent with naturally white hair, found me sitting on a cinderblock wall by the street, watching my phone and the road for Robert. She and her four friends milled around, sipping, laughing, and talking about their work and dreams. They were part of my crowd. My world, and I felt so out of it.

Ute and I made small talk about our careers, where I mentioned nothing about a song I had to pull from Carnival because I'd promised my ex-lover I would.

"What happened to your face?" she asked.

"Fell on some bad sidewalk. Fucking Frogtown's falling apart."

"Looks nasty."

"Hurts, too. Hey, what ever happened with that indie film you were doing? About the prostitute with the kids?"

"Ran out of money, like, midway through. I'm 'on call' but...oh hel*lo*."

She was looking over my shoulder. I followed her gaze, and once a crowd of boys in turned caps and low-slung skinny jeans passed, I saw Jonathan across the street, waiting for cars to pass.

"Oh, fucking fuckery," I said.

"Yeah. Head to toe. That's a man."

"If nothing else." *God damn you, Debbie. You are such a yenta.* What was her deal? Was she my boss or my mother? I was going to have to have an honest, respectful, non-job-losing conversation with her.

As he strode across the street, I saw what Ute saw. He had on simple trousers and a sweater with a leather jacket. In contrast to the rest of the men at the party, who spent hours looking as though they didn't care what they wore, Jonathan looked neat and put together, as if he cared. He was tall and lean and straight, with his hair brushed back off his forehead. He owned the world and everything in it. The difficulty of staying away from him was so past his looks, so past any single physical attribute, and fell into a new, undefined category of "right."

I set my back straighter and tilted my chin up. I thought Debbie would send Robert, but instead I'd have to pretend I was fine and my face wasn't pounding.

"He's coming over here," said Ute, brushing her hair flat.

"He's my ride," I said.

Her eyebrows arched.

I paused. Jonathan liked blondes, if his wife was any indication. Ute was beautiful. She'd do well with him.

I thought about adding a short explanation. Maybe 'I'm in love with him, but I left him' or 'he was my lover, boyfriend, master, king...' None of it worked, and by the time I came up with 'we were together for a while,' he was upon us.

"Hey," he said, and that voice went right into my gut and ripped stuff out.

I stood up. "Jonathan, this is my friend, Ute." She had on a smile that wrapped around her face like a gag.

"Hi." He looked at Ute briefly, then back to me. "What happened?"

"I fell. What are you doing here? Is Debbie being a yenta?"

"I happened to be at the bar, and she couldn't spare anyone."

"On Thanksgiving? You don't have sisters to invite you to dinner?"

"Dinner ended at eight, and the kids went to bed. Where did you fall?"

"On my face." I hadn't seen a mirror yet, but his expression worried me. Was I going to the Vancouver opening with a big stinker on my cheek?

He turned to Ute. "It was nice meeting you." Nothing about his voice was nice. He put his hand on my back, between the shoulder blades, and guided me toward the street. It was a possessive gesture, and he had no business making it. When we were far enough away from the party, I shrugged off his hand.

"Sorry, Jonathan. I wish she hadn't sent you."

"Why?"

"You know why."

"Tell me about your face now. And the truth this time."

The party had street spillage, sending pockets of people onto the sidewalk and neighboring lots. The light industrial district thrived on those parties, but Jonathan and I were constantly getting bumped and shifted by gaggles of half-drunk hipsters.

"Can you just take me home?" I smelled his leather jacket, his cologne, the Jameson on his breath. He stood inches from me. If I just leaned forward, I could kiss him.

"Where's your car?" he asked.

"Kevin's."

"What happened?" His voice was tight as a bowstring, and his posture matched.

I felt the pressure of a big fat cry push out my lower lip, squeeze tears from my eyes, and steal breath from my lungs. "I hate it that I break up with you twice, and both times you show up in a crisis and I get upset."

"What happened?"

"I fell." My voice cracked mid-sob.

"You look like you fell on someone's fist."

"It was actually more of a really hard slap, but you should see him. He looks really bad."

Jonathan blinked. Slowly. "What happened?"

I didn't answer. He put his hands on my shoulders and, as if by force of will, removed all anger and judgment from his expression. It only made me cry harder.

"Fuck you."

"What happened?"

"He wanted..." I broke down. How could I tell Jonathan that I missed being touched by a man, by *him*, so I let something happen I should have stopped? Or why I was blaming myself when I hadn't done anything? "He kissed me, and I bit him. Then he hit me. I hit him with a bottle and ran, and my car and keys are at his place. And you're not supposed to be here witnessing this, so I do not feel guilty at all."

I tried to read his expression, but it was hard to see through my tears. He slipped one of those freaking hankies out of his pocket, and I snapped it away before he could tell me to blow.

"It's my fault," I said.

"Really?"

"Yeah. You said not to be alone with him, and I should have listened. You said he wanted to hurt me, and here I am. Now I don't know how I'm supposed to go to Vancouver with him."

"Where was Darren while you were getting beat up?"

"Parties. It's the biggest night of the year."

He put his arms around me, and I fell into him, putting my cheek to his shoulder, my face to his neck. He felt right. So right. So warm and gentle. That was the touch I'd wanted when I let Kevin near me. I'd gotten it so wrong. I felt a tightening on my ass, then a tickle. He'd slipped my phone from my pocket.

"What are you doing?" I grabbed for the phone, but he held it high, tapping and dragging until a map appeared. He'd found Kevin's address.

He handed me the phone. "Stay here with your friends for a minute. I'm going to get your car."

"Jonathan, just take me home. Don't get in a fight."

"A fight?" His voice was tense with control. "You think I'm going to take him behind the gym and punch him? Do I look like an adolescent?"

"No, but—"

"Stop." He put his hands on my face and got close enough to kiss. "You're mine, and I will defend you. But this isn't a movie. You don't destroy someone with a fight. And Monica, I know you walked away from me, but I am going to destroy him nonetheless."

He kissed my forehead and walked toward the studio.

CHAPTER 29

JONATHAN

I COULDN'T SAY EXACTLY how much of the situation could have been avoided if Margie hadn't pulled Will's team, but at the very least, I would have gotten a call when Monica ran out. If I hadn't been at the Stock, she'd probably be begging the bus driver for a free ride back to her hill or crossing Elysian Park to get home. Somalia was safer.

She had to come back to me. Soon. He'd had his lips on her, and I burned from the inside out. I didn't want to get upset about it in front of her. Her lips were mine. Her face was mine. I'd let her go, secure in the knowledge that she'd come back to me. But in the interim, anything could happen with either of us. Though I knew the difference between what was fake and what was real, I couldn't guarantee she made the distinction.

And also, her body was mine, regardless. Mine to kiss. Mine to fuck.

Mine to hit?

The contrast wasn't lost on me. I'd spanked her ass pink with the intention of a harder, rawer fuck. And she wanted it, begged for it. He hit her in anger, on her face, and hard. But what was the difference? When and how did she become a punching bag for the men she was involved with?

Wainwright was two blocks away. I saw her car in the front lot before I saw the building. The poor street lighting left dozens of dark corners and blind turns, but it made it very easy to see that the front door was ajar. Music came from it. A stringed instrument over a hip-hop percussion line that seemed a little bit off. It was disconcerting, all raw nerves and tension.

I pushed open the door and slipped into a narrow hall with doors on either side. Music came from the big room at the end. A voice, layered over and over, with that single stringed instrument and hard percussion. Something was off about it, but it was definitely Monica. I saw her bag half falling off a table in the big room. I grabbed it, and when I turned, I saw the piece.

It stood complete. The sections had been labeled for transport, and the wood packing boxes stood next to it. Like the coalmine, it was a freestanding room with an inside and outside.

It was cut in two by a foot-wide horizontal wound around the circumference. Shingles covered the walls, and the windows, framed in the Craftsman style and broken where the wound intersected them, were painted in gold and silver. Curious, I went inside.

From the inside, the open jaw of wood and plaster in the horizontal cut looked more evil, more hazardous. Detritus spilled everywhere. Broken cinderblocks. Gum-stuck urbanite. Grassrooted clods of parkway. All of it was anonymous, generic, unwanted, ripped out, found but not rescued. On the walls was a huge screen print of an open wound. It could have been any body part, from some ravaging knife fight or a ten-hour surgery; that didn't matter. It was three hundred sixty degrees around, and grotesque. On the other corner was an insect with a mandible and antennae that went around the walls.

Then the music made sense. Monica's voice, her words layered so many times that their syllables and meanings were lost. The strings sounded a little off key and the bass riff was half a millisecond off time, then gradually more, until the core was a disconcerting cacophony that fell back into the correct beat, looping into a false sense of a more permanent rightness. Each corner of the piece accentuated a different vocal layer, and each speaker had a different tone.

"It's good," I said. I knew he was within earshot. "Music's the same inside and out. But you hear it differently."

"Reality's the same inside and outside the relationship." He stood in the doorway, which was too tall for the room. Two people could leave at the same time, but only if one was on top of the other. "Before and after, life sucks. What are you doing here?" The left side of his face was cut and bloody. He held a red-soaked bag of ice to it.

"She did a good job on you," I said. "You deserve worse."

"Come on, man. She's a cocktease."

"Not with me."

"Fine, dude, whatever. What do you want?"

I walked past him and stopped. "Came to get the car. You let her walk out into a dark street alone. I don't know what comes over men like you."

"You know what? Fuck you. You're just another rich guy with ownership issues. Pussy like that's never owned."

I pushed him against the doorframe. The bag of ice dropped, breaking and spreading cubes and shards all over the floor. "You don't—"

He pushed me back. We were evenly matched, physically, so when I pushed him back, we ended up in a lock in a doorway designed for one person, straining against each other, unmoving for our red faces and effort.

I slipped my foot behind his ankle and yanked his leg from under him. We fell, with me on top. I got my knee in his sternum while he was still disoriented. I got lucky. I kept my head. In that millisecond, I looked at that piece of shit and thought, *One hard hit to the face, and I have him.* Then the voice of reason chimed in. I wouldn't have him. Knocking him senseless would do nothing but give him a headache in the morning. Worse, I'd lose Monica's respect. She expected better of me, and we were too precarious for me to do something temperamental and stupid.

I had to remove him from her life peacefully and permanently.

"Listen to me," I said, out of breath and knowing my upper hand wouldn't last. "I'm going with her to Vancouver. We will both act like gentlemen. You will not speak about her like that to me or anyone else. Do you understand?"

"You don't know her," he choked out.

I dug my knee in his chest. He swiped at me, catching my cheek. "Do you understand or not?" I asked.

"Fuck you."

I stood up. "I'll take that as a yes."

CHAPTER 30

MONICA

I MADE sure I was facing the block Jonathan had walked down. He was taking too long. I knew Ute's crowd by sight, name, or both, and under normal circumstances, I would have had a fine time listening to their Hollywood war stories. Broken commitments. Rich executives demanding endless hours of free work. All of the tales laced with hope hope hope.

I didn't mention my meeting with Eddie, or his insinuation that if I'd just release a single song about being a submissive under the beautiful Mr. Drazen, I'd have a deal. A real deal, with a real record label. I just smiled and accepted condolences about Gabby. I talked briefly about the B.C. Mod show as if it was some little project that may or may not actually lead to something. I kept it vague and kept Kevin out of it.

A pressure on my shoulder made me jump. I was still edgy from wrestling with Kevin, but when I turned, it was Jonathan. He had a scratch on his right cheek.

"He's left-handed," I said, pointing at the scratch on his cheek. "You said you wouldn't get physical."

"What are you...?" He touched his face and came back with blood. "Thorn bush. It's dark over there." He held out my bag. "I parked your car around the corner. I'll have Lil drop it to you tomorrow."

"Why can't I just take it?"

"Because I'm driving you home."

"No, Jonathan—"

"I want to talk to you."

He looked as though he had to tell me something, and since he'd just gotten back from Kevin's, I was pretty sure I needed to hear it. I said goodbye to everyone with Los Angeles hugs, promising calls and get togethers that I wanted from the bottom of my heart, but I would never make happen.

He walked me down the block, saying nothing until we got to the Jag. He opened the passenger door for me. I leaned on the car, not ready to commit to letting him drive me home.

"Get in."

I crossed my arms. "What happened at the studio?"

"I saw the piece."

"And?"

"You know it's phenomenal. You don't need me to tell you that. Now get in."

"I don't need to be pushed around twice in one night."

He leaned on the car, one hand on each side of me. "I need to get off this street with its four hundred drunk kids going back and forth from a party." He wasn't touching me. Not even our clothes were touching, but I felt him in a push of desire. I wanted him. My lips, my cunt, even my throbbing face wanted him. When he spoke again, his voice went from his mouth to my heart, lighting it on fire. "I need to speak to you privately."

"I don't want to speak. I want to go home and look in a mirror."

"You bruise easily. Okay? Now get in the car."

My hand went to my face. The skin was numb, with pain underneath it. "It must be awful."

He took my hand and kissed my cheek. It hurt and gave me incredible pleasure at the same time. When he moved his lips from my cheek to my neck, the hurt disappeared and the pleasure increased. "It's not," he whispered.

"Is this a ploy to get me in the car?"

He looked in my eyes, then he kissed my lips, parting them with his tongue. He paused only to say, "Yes."

I gave in to him, his arms resting on either side of my head and closing out the rest of the world. Only in that kiss did I realize how bad the last weeks had been, how much I'd missed him. Not just his physical attention, but his words and gestures, his protection and devotion.

He dragged his lips along my jawline and said, "What do you want, Monica?"

"I want you."

"You want me what?"

"To take me to bed."

"I'm not a toy." He said it while kissing my ear and touching my throat, his erection firm on my belly. He used his most tender voice. "You can't throw me away, then reel me back whenever you feel like fucking."

"Then stop touching me whenever I throw in a line."

He pulled away slowly. "You're right." His eyes scanned mine, and his expression changed, as if he'd realized something. I didn't know if I liked it.

A part of me wanted to reel him back in. It was the part of me that loved him in the first place, naturally. That part wanted to rub against him. That part had watched him walk across the street like a stranger, with all the heated possibilities that implied.

But my brain said "no." My mind was the repository of memory, and in that repository sat Eddie Milpas's suggestion that I become Bondage Girl for the masses, the symbol of their unspoken, unwanted desires. I could sing like a frog, and it wouldn't matter as long as I wore a rich man's collar.

"Let's talk in the car," I said, "but I'm taking myself home."

He paused, and I wanted to fall into his eyes, so close, so piercing. I slipped from under him and into the car.

He shut my door and walked around the front. I was so disappointed in myself. I had left him for good reason. I left him for the same reasons I left Kevin: my life, my career, my work. So how did I end up in the front seat of his car, about to talk about things I didn't want to talk about? How would I handle being in close quarters with him when all he had to do was touch me and I'd fall to pieces? I was weak, and I knew it. That was why I'd left Kevin so sharply. That was why I was celibate for so long. If being in control of my pussy wasn't an option, at least I could control who I saw and under what circumstances.

As weak as Kevin had made me, and as much as that weakness had made me run from him, it was nothing compared to what Jonathan did to me.

He got in the driver's side, and I closed my eyes. I didn't want to see him or the way the light hit his cheekbones or the taut skin of his jaw. If I could just close off my nose and ears, I'd get out of the car intact.

"Monica," he said, "are you all right?"

"It's been a long night."

"You can't go with him."

"Fuck you, it's my career."

"The masochism's not supposed to leave the bedroom."

"Go to hell." I went for the door handle. He reached across me and grabbed my wrist.

"You're not hearing me. You don't belong near him. It burns a hole in me."

I was entitled to see whomever I wanted for whatever reason I wanted. Jonathan and I were broken up. But I felt guilty for leaving him, and my guilt spoke. "Who was she? In DC? You going to tell me you don't have someone to fuck in every port of call? Tell me about her, and we'll call it even."

He leaned back, letting my wrist go. "Are you serious?"

I shouldn't have asked, because his look wasn't one of denial, but "How dare you ask?" The way he said it, I was sure he'd done some fucking in the past two weeks and it immobilized my heart. When I was a kid, a hole the size of a fist opened up in the middle of our street. Three inches of asphalt dropped into a deep nothingness. It got bigger and bigger, falling into itself until Teddy Ramirez's Toyota got stuck.

My chest had that sinkhole in it. It just fell in on itself, creating a bigger opening into nothingness and sucking the breath out of me. No. That was not good. That was the very definition of awful. I shifted and went for the door. He reached across me again and blocked the handle. "You can't run away every time something gets difficult."

"Jonathan, please, I can't bear the thought of you with someone else." His body was so close to mine, so real. That son of a bitch. Built so right for me and how many others?

"Wait. You think there was someone else?" he asked.

I bit my lip. I didn't know what I thought any more.

"Monica. There's. No. One. Else." He let the handle go and stared at me for a second. "There's only you. You think I'm stupid? You think I can create what we have with another woman? I know the world. I know the people in it. Us? What we have isn't something we made. It's something that existed before we even met."

The sinkhole in my chest reversed itself, like film run backward, from broken to whole.

"I'm sorry," I said. "I shouldn't have asked. It wasn't my business."

"Why did you walk away from me if you still care?" he asked.

"I'm human. It's a terminal condition." I wanted him to kiss me. I wanted his lips, his hands, his tongue, but I couldn't, not when there were so many sensible reasons not to. "I took a meeting with Eddie Milpas. He wants to make me a star, which I'd laugh at coming from anyone else. But it's not funny because he has the power to do it. He wants to put Carnival's muscle behind me. If he does, I'll have everything I ever wanted."

"Monica, that's—"

"He wants the song," I said. Jonathan leaned back, against the door, a rueful smile at his lips. "He's not getting it. I keep my promises, and to be honest, I wish I never wrote that thing. But that's not the rub. He has plenty of songs with kinky lyrics that'll sound great from a girl all dolled up in leather and chains. BDSM is hot right now, apparently, and I'm 'in the know,' so I can pull it off."

I paused, because the image exploded in my mind. "Fuck! I spend a few weeks with you and I'm Bondage Girl. What the fuck am I supposed to do now? Do you know how hard I've worked? Do you know what I've put into this, and to sit across from this guy, and he tells me...wait for it....he tells me that I'm perfect because I'll *know what I'm talking about*? Who am I? What the *fuck*?" I slammed the dashboard. "And Kevin, do you know why he forced himself on me? Because *he thought I liked it that way*. God damn it. Jonathan, what if those cameras were in my house because someone wanted to blackmail *you*? And I'm getting caught in that net now. This is not what I want.

"I want to sing. I want to make music. I alienated my mother, I sacrificed a hundred other careers, I lost my best friend over it, I practice and work all the time. It's all I think about. It's all I want. But I'm trapped in this kinky thing with you right when all the work could be paying off. This sucks. My career could break any minute. These should be the best days of my life, and I wish I was dead."

I had to stop or I was going to cry, which I didn't want. Crying would derail my whole point. I didn't look at Jonathan because I didn't care what he felt or thought. I didn't want to see his beautiful face because he'd turn me into mush. I looked at my hands in my lap, then out the window at the party.

"I'm sorry," he said.

"I don't blame you. You didn't intend to ruin my life. But I'd really like for it to not get any worse, if that's okay."

We sat in silence. I considered saying goodbye and opening the door, but I couldn't. I considered running before he could catch me, but I couldn't do that either. Instead, I faced him. He rubbed his chin absently and stared into the middle distance.

And then my mouth opened and words came out. "The worst part is, I miss you."

He didn't react, but I did. I turned into stone. Jesus, what was I saying? He was last thing I needed. He was trouble. Six feet two inches of life-damaging trouble in a sweet, tempting motherfucking devil of a package.

He turned to me, as if having decided something. "You and Darren take my plane up to Vancouver. Let me put you up in a hotel."

"No."

"Would you stop making me crazy?"

"You're not hearing me."

"I'm hearing a lot of pain from all quarters. It's going to get worse if you don't let me protect you. When you get back safe, we talk."

"There's nothing to talk about."

"Oh, goddess." He brushed my cheek with the backs of his fingers.

"Don't call me that."

"We have so much to talk about."

I closed my eyes. His touch felt like a boat on still water, leaving ripples in its wake. When would I stop craving him? "I don't want my life ruined."

"Neither do I. But this..." He brushed his hands over my face, bringing my skin to life. "This, I want. I've never wanted anything so badly. I feel your hands on your phone when you read my texts. I go to the Stock after your shifts just to stand where you've stood. I fall asleep on the pillow you used when you were in my bed. I need to share whatever piece of the world you're in. Tell me you don't feel the same."

"You know how I feel," I croaked.

"We can't go backward. You and I are going to figure out how to make this work."

His confidence should have made me hopeful, but it only filled me with dread.

"I want to go home now. Please."

He walked me to my car. When he handed me my keys, dangling them from his fingertips, I had the desire to do what I did when we'd met, what Will Santon had done: overshoot my grasp for a touch. Just a little. But then Jonathan spoke.

"Until we talk, and you get your head on straight, I'm not touching you. You were right. We get reeled in, you and I. We touch and we feel good, and then we land in bed and we forget the basics."

"Talking's not going to fix this."

"Neither is fucking."

I snapped the keys from him. "We can fix us, but we're not going to fix the world, Jonathan."

"The world is full of assholes." He opened the driver's door for me and closed it when I was safely in.

I lowered the window. "When I met you, I thought you were an asshole."

He smiled. "You did not."

"I did. A gorgeous asshole."

His laugh came from deep in his chest. He bit his lip and reached out to cup my cheek but fell half an inch short. "I was an asshole for making you another conquest." He put his hand in his pocket, and I missed the potential in that almost-touch. "Get out of here, goddess. Get some rest."

When I got back to Echo Park, Darren was out. My face was a little swollen. I made myself an ice pack and went to the couch. I lay there with the TV muted, remembering him. The kiss we shared. His touch, the heat. I slid my hand under my cotton panties, shuddering in anticipation. I wanted to come. I wanted to want to come. I wanted to fall into my filthiest imagination and wrap myself in sexual desire.

But when I touched my opening, I found it unprepared for attention. A little fiddling got me nowhere, and I felt as though I was trying to get music from an instrument I'd never heard of. I pulled my hand away and went into an uneasy sleep.

CHAPTER 31

JONATHAN

I'D WALKED her to the car with few words, but not because I had nothing to say. I had plenty to say. In the time it had taken for her to forgive me for destroying her career, I'd thrown a dozen mental balls in the air, and if I spoke, I would have dropped them.

I didn't have compassion for her situation. I had a raw empathy that made me want to hold her and whisper lies of comfort. But it wasn't going to be all right. Things weren't going to go back to normal. The only one way the whole thing would blow over was if she lived a life of obscurity. The recognition and success she'd earned and deserved promised to exacerbate her situation. There was absolutely no chance of people unknowing what they knew, and there was even less chance she'd drop her ambitions to protect her privacy.

If I let her go, the most likely scenario was that she'd swear off men until another dominant appeared. Then she'd fall right back into her submissive role with him.

That was not acceptable.

I had calls to Asia until well into the night. In the morning, after what felt like thirty minutes of sleep, I had Kristin find out when Eddie Milpas would be at the Loft Club. I needed to feel him out. I didn't want to take action based only on Monica's exploding imagination.

CHAPTER 32

MONICA

I woke at half past eight and stared at Darren's popcorn stucco ceiling. The vertical blinds cast stripes across it, and only when my eyes hurt from looking at their odd symmetry did I get up.

I had an email from Kevin. I was tempted to delete it without reading it, but I was curious. I read on my phone while bleary-eyed and in the bathroom.

Dear Monica,

You're not going to pick up my calls. I know you.

I feel like such a fuckup. I don't care. I'll put it all in writing.

I never knew what I did wrong. I should have damned my pride and waited on your porch until you told me why you left me. Really why. Not because of Tuesday nights. That could only be a symptom of some other disease.

I didn't know what I was doing making the coalmine piece. I just did it, and it took a year. I wasn't going to invite you. I thought if you saw it, you'd be pissed but you'd know how I felt. I figured it was the equivalent of me waiting on your porch, twenty months later.

Everyone said you were single, but you weren't were you? When I saw you go in there with another man I wanted to eat my face off. And then you were in the garden crying on his shoulder. I can only imagine it was over the piece.

Remember how we read Blake sometimes? I thought of this one—

I told my love, I told my love,

I told her all my heart,
Trembling, cold, in ghastly fears—
Ah, she doth depart.

I WENT A LITTLE CRAZY. I knew I wanted to do cooperative work before Eclipse, and you were the first person I thought of. I was just going to mention it to you later. After we talked. But the crazy took over.

We did good work together, but you wouldn't talk about what happened with us, even though it was all over the piece. I heard about your new boyfriend and the kind of shit you were into. I thought maybe that was what you needed from me and you couldn't say.

Wasn't that easy, was it?

Last night, after you left, I was pissed. And hurt. And I said a lot of shit to that dickhead about you I shouldn't have. I'm sure he repeated it to you. In the moment I meant it because my face was busted. But now I'm too embarrassed to wait on your porch. Once we get back from Vancouver, I will.

—KEV.

I SAT on the bowl and read it again. Then the Blake poem. Then the letter in full.

I was a heartless bitch, hiding behind silence and self-righteous indignation that stayed unchallenged. I thought I was taking control of my life, but I'd left a mess behind me. How many people had I done that to? My mother? She never failed to hurl some innocent-sounding cruelty at me, but I'd cut her off and call it independence.

Everything hurt. I'd woken up with no more than a dark spot under my eye, but it weighed down half my face. My back felt twisted and weak, aching as if I'd lifted a piano up the stairs. I didn't know what to do about my pain, or even if anything needed doing.

My phone blooped at nine a.m. exactly.

—How's the eye?—

I'd never answered a nine a.m. text, but after the night before, and Kevin's email, I thought I ought to.

—You should see the other guy—

There was a long pause. I imagined him reading my text, so surprised I answered he had to take a second to organize himself.

*—I feel your hands on the
phone—*

I caressed the little plastic and metal box like a lover, feeling a warmth and tingle between my legs that had been missing the night before.

—I have to go to work. Lunch shift—

—I know—
Asshole. Gorgeous asshole.

CHAPTER 33

JONATHAN

"I REALLY COULD HAVE USED you guys last night," I said, blaming Will for something that wasn't his fault. Margie, the money source, had moved his whole team onto a divorce case with triangulations from Flintridge, to Santa Monica, to Monterey Park, and back. I could have deduced who was splitting up if I cared.

Santon seemed unperturbed by what had happened to Monica. We sat at a table at the Loft Club. Santon didn't seem impressed by the club at all. A mark in his favor.

He slid his hand over his glass in a way that looked like a threat. "I can't get into the house, so even if one of my guys was there, I make no guarantee it wouldn't have gone down that way."

"Do you have anything on this guy? Or are my hands tied?"

"We found some warrants in Idaho. He led an anti-war protest outside Boise city hall and got picked up for inciting a riot. He dropped out of sight a month after he did his thirty days and no one up there actually gave a shit when he showed up down here. Parole officer my guy talked to never thought of him as a criminal. Then we found two open. One battery charge. A DUI. Different parole officers."

I scanned the club. Larry poured drinks. Guys in suits laughed at the bar. I expected Eddie soon, and I wanted to be done with Santon before he arrived.

"The cameras?" I asked. "Anything?"

"We got taken off before we found out how it was done and who ordered the job. We did track the serial numbers though. Followed the money."

387

He paused, and I rotated my hand at the wrist for him to continue. He didn't. The guy was unflappable.

"Well? Where did it come from?"

"You."

I snorted a laugh and drank the last mouthful of whiskey. "Fucking fantastic. Was it out of Ibiza?"

"Canary Islands. Someone's got their fingers in your pie."

"Apparently." I held out my hand. "I appreciate you coming here to finish this off."

Santon took it, and we shook. "Call me in a couple of weeks when things free up."

"Will do."

He left, and I went down to the locker room, chewing on what the fuck was happening with the Canary Island trust. Kevin certainly didn't have the right kind of mind or connections. It was possible I was underestimating him. It was also possible I had latched onto him because I despised him.

The club's huge lot had a driving range, tennis courts, batting cages, and a fake pitcher's mound and home plate. The owner had owned a major league team or two, and he kept baseball in the club even if the facilities weren't used much. Eddie and I used it more than any other two members. I'd set up the time with him to feel him out about Monica. Maybe I could convince him to try another marketing angle, any other angle, because I knew what he wanted to do was putting her through hell.

I rubbed the ball, scraping the fake pitcher's mound under my cleat. Eddie stood in the batter's box. Such a cocky fuck. Guy hit .209 on his best season.

"Come on, Drazen!"

I waved him off, getting ready for my pitch. Eddie's stance was as comical as it had been at Penn. "Eddie! You constipated?"

"What?"

"You're standing there with your ass out."

"Fuck you."

"No, fuck *you*." I threw. He hit it to the left field, smacking a target marked SINGLE before it puckered the nylon mesh. A minor miracle. I caught a glimpse of the speed clock to my right. Sixty-five. My shit was rusty. Or I was distracted.

After his success connecting bat to ball the first time, Eddie was back in the box, looking triumphant.

I took another ball from the bucket. "I heard you met with Monica Faulkner."

"She's a hot number." Eddie whipped the bat around before getting into constipation position. "You buy her song or you're just keeping her from singing it?"

I fingered the ball. "Why?"

"We want it, and she's not giving it up."

"It's her song."

"It's all about collaring and floor licking. Got you written all over it." He pointed the bat at me. "I want it. It's money. I think you're keeping her from releasing it."

I threw a strike. Seventy-five, but my elbow had snapped a little from the exertion. I wasn't pulling from the shoulder. "You're giving me a lot of credit."

"You're the master."

I hated it. I hated knowing the undertone of what he meant, because someone like Eddie trivialized something I took seriously.

"Doesn't work like that, douchebag," I called out.

I threw another strike, well inside the zone. Clocked at seventy-seven, but it didn't jerk my elbow.

"Then help me understand 'the point.'"

"The point is you can't trick her out like a whore and put her on stage."

"Come on, man. Give the world a taste of what you got."

When I threw the next pitch, he connected. Hard. I stuck my glove in front of me and caught it before it hit me in the nuts.

"Sorry, O'Drassen." He used my great-grandfather's name from the old country when he wanted to tease me. It bothered me in college, and he'd latched on to it. I was setting up the next pitch when Eddie stepped out of the box. "Seriously, I want her. *We* want her. She's got that thing. You know the thing. The thing I can sell. Every man in the room will want to fuck her."

"What?" I had it coming. I'd been the joker, the storyteller, the adventurer. I'd been the guy making cracks about who I fucked, and where, and how many times, over beers. Meanwhile, I'd defended Jessica from every unkind word hurled behind her back. Why should anyone think I gave a shit? "She won't fuck you, Ed."

"Why not? I'm a record executive," he joked.

Despite the fact that he was kidding, the images came to mind like a neighbor I avoided. Her eyes half closed. Eddie on top of her, pushing one of her legs up as he pumped into her, and her saying his name when she came. Over and over. Then the images came faster. Her laughing with him. Bending over for him. Holding his hand. Looking up at him with love, a smile spread across her face while he thought of using her and dumping her.

I shook it off. I was being an adolescent. "Get in the goddamn box."

"All right. Sorry, man. I didn't know she meant something to you."

When I felt the ice in my chest and my mind went completely and utterly clear, I should have known. I'd spent a long time getting my temper under control, and I knew it well. My temper wasn't a fire burning out in a confused jumble of thoughts; it was a frozen lucidity, a clarity of intention, whose sole purpose was to harm. I'd learned the warning signs, but on the mound, I fooled myself into thinking I was concentrating on the strike zone.

I threw a fastball, straight and hard. I coiled the power from my hips, up my back, and to my shoulder, pivoting my arm like a catapult. The ball landed right where I aimed: between Ed's ear and eye.

He didn't just fall. He spun around from the impact and landed on his back.

Fuck. I glanced at the speed clock. 91. That's about what it had felt like as it left my fingers. I ran up to Eddie and kneeled beside him. He was unconscious.

God damn, what the fuck *was on your mind?*

Nothing. That was the problem.

A crowd rushed over just as Eddie opened his eyes. I got him to his feet. A pretty doctor had been at the pool, and she took a look at him. He was well enough to flirt with her. It was too late to have a gentlemanly conversation about Monica and her place in the musical lexicon, of course. I could hardly say, "Listen, Ed, take the BDSM shit down a notch, and she'll sign with you."

I had to go to plan B.

CHAPTER 34

MONICA

I ALMOST DIDN'T ANSWER Kevin. Three days passed in a heat of songwriting and waitressing. When I realized I'd let the time pass, I thought that maybe I was doing the same thing I'd always done: turn my back on someone until it was too late to go back.

Kev,
*   I want you to know I got this, but I don't know how to answer it right now.*
*   See you on the plane.*
*   Mon*

THE DAY before I left for Vancouver, I stood at my locker, shoving my work shoes in and stepping into my street shoes, when Jonathan appeared like a shiny new penny.

"Your eye healed up nice."

I jumped. "Jesus, stop that. I thought you were leaving me alone until I got back."

He leaned on the locker bank, crossing his ankles. "Take my plane. Seriously."

"You came here to convince me to take a private jet to my art opening? Talk about a nice problem to have." I slammed the locker shut and locked it. He smiled at me, then for half a beat, too quickly for anyone to notice, he dropped his eyes and drank me in. I felt as though he was stroking me from toes to shoulders, and a tingle went through me.

"Great, I'll make sure it's ready."

"I didn't say I'd take it."

I brushed past him. Not because I wanted to make a threatening gesture, but because my desire to be near him made the hallway too narrow. He walked beside me as if he belonged there. As if I'd agreed to a discussion about our relationship before the appointed time, which I hadn't.

"So, what's keeping you going to LAX in traffic and getting on a coach flight with three hundred other people?"

The employee exit spit out into the parking lot, which was crowded with staff arriving, leaving, and greeting each other with laughs and short conversations.

I had to walk close to him or talk loud enough to be heard by everyone. "Look, I'll have the conversation if you think it will change something, but if I start accepting favors and gifts beforehand, it's tainted."

I approached my Honda with my key out, but as I went for it, he put his hand on the car, covering the seam between the door and the roof. That hand was right in front of me, with its spray of copper hair and fingers shaped to please. All I could think about was it running over my body, flat first, then curving to my shape. It would stop to hold and grab the parts it found, tightening on my skin, bruising me with badges of agonizing pleasure.

He said into my ear, "I admire your nobility, but the conversation's already tainted by a few dozen orgasms."

He still wasn't touching me, and he pulled his face away enough so I'd have to do just a little more than lean into him to steal a kiss. I craved the warmth of his breath and his touch. God, his touch. His body was arched and I stood straight, though the desire to fit into him like a spoon in a drawer was an almost chemical impulse.

Kiss me kiss me kiss me...

But he stood still. "You don't want to be on a flight with Kevin Wainwright any more than I want you on it."

I could have mentioned Kevin's email as proof that our encounter was a misunderstanding, but I wouldn't be an excuse maker for a guy who didn't understand the word "no." He'd ended up with a bleeding shoulder and bashed-in face for the trouble, but that was hardly the point.

"We've done everything wrong," I said. "Me, mostly. So I'm not going to walk into a conversation with you all sexed up from your money."

His smile spread, and his eyes closed a little. He bowed his head as if he didn't want me to see his amusement, but I saw his shoulders shake a little with laughter.

"The things you say," he said when he finally picked up his head.

"The things you *do*," I replied. "Can I get in, please? I have to pack."

He took his hand off the door. "You should wear that thing you wore to the Eclipse show. I know you won't let me buy you something new."

"Forget that, Drazen."

"The shoes at least." He stepped backward twice, and I couldn't help but give him the same type of look he'd given me earlier. I drank him in. His neck, his shoulders, the dark blue suit covering the body I imagined. The chest pressed against mine. The arms stretched over me, holding my hands down. The hips thrusting into me cruelly. He took another step back, and I felt as though I was being pulled forward.

Stunning creature. I wondered, like he said, God had made him for me as much as I'd been made for him. Of course, God then spitefully created a world where we couldn't be together without being puppets of other people's imaginations.

CHAPTER 35

MONICA

I STOOD on my front porch, shaking. I looked only at my keys as they slid into the lock and only at the knob as I turned it. My gaze zoomed no wider than the door as it opened. I hated acting like a toddler playing peek-a-boo, believing if I couldn't see Mommy, she couldn't see me.

The house already smelled musty. I put my head down and walked to my room. I shut out my peripheral vision because I couldn't be sure there weren't eyes in the corners. I focused on my feet as they traversed my living room rug. My kitchen floor. The wood floor of the hall.

My room.

I threw the duffel on my bed.

The closet. The dress, still in a dry cleaning bag.

The shoes, clumped on the floor.

The bathroom. My fancy makeup.

The dresser.

The top drawer.

I only had the Bordelle underwear left.

Under a manila envelope.

The bed.

The duffel bag.

The objects pushed inside.

Shoes. Dress. Underwear. Makeup. Envelope.

The zipper.

My feet on the floors. The rug.

The porch.
The door.
The key.
Click.
My breath.
Exhaled.

CHAPTER 36

MONICA

I DRIED my hair with the bathroom door open. When Darren's screen door opened, I jumped. He was on his way to Canada with Adam, and I wasn't expecting anyone. I half hoped it was Jonathan but knew it wasn't. Peeking out to the living room, I saw Darren shuffle in. I pulled a dress out of the hamper and wiggled into it so I could get to him quickly.

"What the hell are you doing here?" I asked.

He shrugged. "Men."

"Men? What's that mean?"

He grabbed a beer from the fridge and cracked it. "I mean, how the fuck do you deal with us?"

"You're cute and you have these nice dangling bits. So?"

"So, well. Adam."

"I've met him."

He rubbed the label on his bottle. "Really nice guy. Really."

"Really. So? Why aren't you at the airport?"

"I kind of freaked out on him."

I threw myself on the couch and patted the seat next to me. "Go on."

He plopped onto the chair. Somehow, the couch had become my territory. "As we were loading up a cart, I just... I don't know. There was this reflective metal panel in the wall, and I was standing next to him. I saw us in the metal panel. Foggy, but it was us. He was looking at his phone, and I was looking at the panel thinking, 'Oh fuck. This is what other people see. Is this who I am? Did I decide this? And when?' I care about him. I love being with him, but when do I start calling myself bisexual, or gay, or...who the fuck am I, Monica?"

I had plenty of platitudes. I had advice I couldn't even pretend to take myself about just being who you are and letting the world see what they wanted. Uttering those words without hurtful irony would have been obscene. "I don't think any of us know ourselves."

He rubbed his lips together, a gesture I remembered from our early days. Darren was trying not to cry. It was painful to watch.

"I've been trying not to worry about it," he said. "I've been trying to figure out if I care whether people think less of me or not, and honestly, I don't think it's that. I mean, fuck, I'm a drummer. I'm always the one standing in the back. It's just... I feel like I never had the chance to work it out and say, 'All right. This is what I'll be to the world.' I got all wrapped up in him, especially after Gabby. Am I gay without him? Or am I back to who I was? Because I never thought about it before him, so now I'm taking on this whole identity without ever deciding on it. Am I making any sense?"

"Yeah." My throat was dry. "Did you leave him at the airport? Did he get on the plane?"

"No. He followed me to the parking lot. I mean, the poor guy was so baffled. He's asking me if there's someone else, or if I'm upset about Gabs and that's causing the freak out."

"The thing about a freak out is you don't know why you're freaking out," I said, opening the fridge. "How do you feel about him?"

"I don't know."

"Ah." I cracked a beer for myself.

"I do know how I feel about missing that flight."

"How?"

"Fifteen hundred in the hole. Non-returnable flight. Whole new last minute ticket. I have seven hundred in the bank and two maxed out credit cards. I could take the car, but even if I start driving now, I'll miss the show."

I swallowed my beer, thought for a second, and said, "I think I have a solution to that part of the dilemma."

CHAPTER 37

MONICA

Darren had taken some convincing. He was obviously uncomfortable with using Jonathan's money, but he needed it. He was swayed when I assured him it would be just him and me. Jonathan wasn't coming, and I wouldn't let the plane ride color my decision to stay with him or not.

We took the bus to Santa Monica Airport to avoid parking fees. I'd explained as much of the situation to Jonathan as I thought appropriate. I left out Darren's freak out and replaced it with "he missed his flight." Jonathan didn't seem smug about winning the Great Private Jet Battle, only irritated that I insisted on taking the bus.

"It's just a waste of time," he said. I heard him tapping computer keys. Multitasking again.

"I have nothing else to do. And I like the bus. It reminds me of when I was a kid."

"Were you this worried about tainting conversations when you were a kid?"

"My spankings weren't undertaken so willingly back then."

He sighed and let it go.

Darren and I sat with our bags between our feet. He got up for women with children twice during the hour-and-a-quarter long ride. By the time we got to Sepulveda, the crowd had thinned, and he and I had stopped the seat-flip.

"Did you tell Kevin you wouldn't be on the flight?" he asked.

"Texted him."

"He told me his side of what happened the other night."

I shook my head. "I bet he did."

"Really, Monica, I've been meaning to tell you. I think you should give Kevin another chance."

I twisted around to look at him. "Are you serious? Is your mind totally poisoned?"

"He's not the same."

"No, he's worse. Let me ask you something: Were you the one who told him about me and Jonathan? Maybe you mentioned the bruises on my wrists?"

Darren pursed his lips and looked down. "He had an idea already. Geraldine Stark spent a couple of nights with Drazen and came back with some stories. To Kev, it was like a lightning bolt."

Geraldine fucking Stark. Of course. The artist who put the trompe l'oeil on the side of Kevin's building had to have been with Jonathan. She told Kevin, probably post-coital, and then Kevin went ahead and told Darren. Together, they'd strategized how to get us back together.

"It bothers me that we worked together so many hours at a stretch to make this thing, and the whole time, you and Kevin are planning a reconciliation I don't want."

"What do you want?"

"Right now? To be left alone by anyone with a dick. You're all trouble. I want to never again hear who Jonathan fucked before I met him. Even if it was the first lady or Brad Pitt, I don't want to know."

"Why not?" His tone was confrontational, as if he was daring me to give him the truth.

"You know God damn well everything about this *hurts*. So stop being a prick." I turned toward the window, shutting out further argument. We travelled in the fold of time between day and night, when headlights got turned on and the streetlights went from dead cold to humming half light.

"Did you open the envelope I left?" he asked.

"No, did you?"

"No. Is it still in the house?"

I turned away from the window to reengage our conversation. "I left it at your place."

"Not even curious?"

"It's probably a family tree."

"Then why not open it?"

"I haven't had time." I could see, from his expression, he didn't believe me. "I need to talk to him. And I need it to be clean. About us. No external shit. If there's nothing in there, it's nothing. If it's external shit, then it's not fair for me to know it."

His eyes locked onto mine, and I felt naked. "You want him back."

"I don't know what I want."

"Fuck. You want him." He shook his head in a way that indicated nothing less than disappointment and shame.

"What? Is that a problem for you?"

"I should have driven up."

"Are we back on the whore thing?"

"Don't hit me again!" He covered his cheeks with his hands. "Please. My manhood couldn't take it."

Despite the fact that I wanted to belt him, or yell at him, or even shut down and go ice cold, I laughed.

He smiled and said, "Can you tell me, do you think this is you liking to get tied up? Or are you doing it because he likes it?"

The woman in the seat in front of us turned her head a little, and I shot her a look. She had a baby on her lap and a hemp sling over her shoulders.

"Both," I said, looking straight at her because fuck her. I was ashamed and horrified, and that made me feel hostile. She turned away. "It's his reputation I don't like. And everyone knowing. That's coloring the type of attention I'm getting from the industry.

"I want to reassure you. I want to tell you this is who I am, and this is me now and forever, and I'm so happy I discovered this side of myself. But I don't know. Everything about it is wrapped up in him. I can't imagine letting anyone else touch me like that, which is not what you want to hear. I know that. You think it's a power thing, and sure, it is. Would it be with anyone else? If I met the right vanilla guy, would I go vanilla?" I shrugged and put up my palms. "It could go either way. I'd have to be in the situation to find out."

"Well, I like him because of the way he treats you. But I don't, because of the way he treats you. And I think you're missing out with Kevin. He loves you."

"Oh, please give me a break."

"Deal with it." He squeezed my hand but looked away. "This is our stop. Let's get out of here." He waved to the baby in front of us. The mother held the child tighter.

CHAPTER 38

JONATHAN

As soon as Will confirmed he couldn't send anyone to Vancouver, I knew I was going. I'd sleep even less than usual if I didn't. I arranged a revised manifest, made my calls, packed, and met them on the plane already set to leave that night.

My hope had been that she'd take the plane, I'd slip on with her, and we'd have three solid hours to sort ourselves out. Her fears about what other people thought were well-founded but meaningless. They'd think what they would. She needed to know that what we had was bigger than them and that any concerns she had about being dumped were unfounded. Sexually, she and I needed hard limits. Our discussion had to include how much control she actually exerted when we were alone. I'd gone too far with her without properly setting limits and explaining kinks she had no experience with. In my delight over her, I'd been irresponsible.

I still wasn't sure how to convince her without touching her. But I felt as though she was slipping away, and I couldn't let that happen.

I'd gone through immigration and carried my own bags. Security was non-existent. It was my own plane after all, and everyone at the airport knew me. I told them not to hassle my two passengers, and they joked about my habit of bringing women on planes and sending them back without me. I looked forward to the jokes changing. The prospect of keeping Monica was more exciting than bedding a hundred women. I rejected the offer of a ride to the plane. My legs worked, and I didn't want to announce myself so loudly.

Monica and Darren had gotten through immigration in record time, apparently, and they were already stepping up into the cabin. They were inside and out of sight before I reached the stairs. My pilots, Jacques and Petra, had been married seven years and still held hands as they waited for me.

"Jacques," I said.

"Jon. We're scheduled to wait for you. Two days," Jacques said.

Petra chimed in. "We might have to bounce back for a doctor's appointment."

"Well, I think you're going to have to come back and do a pickup anyway. I'll text you the names for the manifest when I have them." I looked them both over. They seemed nervous. "Something you want to tell me?"

Petra smirked.

"No," Jacques said. "Come on. We have a schedule to keep."

I stepped onto the plane behind the pilots.

CHAPTER 39

MONICA

THE PLANE WAS PROBABLY the nicest thing I'd ever seen. The pilots had pointed us up the little stairs embedded in the dropped-down door and into a cabin with ten cushy leather seats. Two seat banks faced each other around a gleaming lacquer table. The wood matched the liquor cabinet and the galley, which was cleaner than my kitchen had ever been.

Darren threw himself into a seat, and I sat next to him. We had work to do. We'd detected a flaw in the sound for the show. It wasn't much, but the music was meant to be loud, and the little click in one of the forty-some tracks would seriously ruin the experience. I freed my phone and headphones to start.

I smelled Jonathan. Then I saw him standing over the table. I felt like a kid caught eating her lunch before the bell.

"I had a feeling you'd show up," Darren said.

Jonathan slipped in across from us. "And you didn't bring me flowers or chocolates or anything?"

I slid toward the window, watching Darren as he said, "I didn't want you to get the wrong idea."

"Or Monica to get the wrong idea," Jonathan looked at me with that irrepressible smile. It was nice that he was smiling and nice that Darren was remembering that part of him liked the guy, but I had a mixed bag of feelings.

"This is the second time you've shown up where you weren't supposed to be," I said.

"It's my plane."

"You know what I mean."

"I do. I am going to the opening and the viewing the night before because I love art and because I'm on the finance committee at the B.C. Modern. Now. I have work to do." He put his laptop on the table and glanced at each of us expectantly. Despite the six other seats, that table was the only laptop-convenient surface. Bastard.

Darren followed suit, his Mac out in a flash. He glanced between Jonathan and me as if one of us would suddenly go into heat.

"I need to check the loops," Darren said to me, all business. "There was a weird clicking. Then I'm mixing down again." He handed me the clunky pro headphones he'd brought and looked at Jonathan. "She has a perfect ear."

"Indeed."

I put on headphones and watched Darren's computer screen, listening for a flaw that might be part of the hardware or a tiny blip on track thirty-two of forty.

The plane took off. The tiny thing felt shaky, unsure, too fast. My stomach fell between my feet, but I tried to keep a straight face, even when I gripped Darren's forearm. We had to start the loop again when the laptop slid across the table. There was no one there to tell us to put our stuff away, and it didn't seem to be a requirement anyway. Jonathan pretended to work, but I knew he was watching me.

I glued my eyes to Darren's screen when the plane evened out and I could swallow again. I'd heard the music for the B.C. Mod piece a hundred times, but in only a few minutes, I was listening with my whole brain for a click that may or may not have been there. I watched the wavy lines flow across the screen like heartbeats until my phone buzzed and lit up. A text. From the guy sitting across from me.

*—Is it hot in here? Or are you
just gorgeous?—*

He was looking at me over his computer screen, lips curled in a smile.

—That's so unpoetic. Even for you—

*—Shall I compare thee to
a summer's day?—*

*—In Los Angeles? Yuck. Is
there a shower in this tin can?—*

He leaned back, a smile creeping across his face. He ignored his computer in favor of the phone. The cold, electronic blue lit his face while the soft light from above warmed his brow and hair.

"Mon?" I barely heard Darren through my headphones. "Did you hear the click?"

"Uh, no. Can you run the loop again?"

—I feel your hands on the phone—

My heart skipped a beat. Or stopped. Or did the thing where I felt its presence in my chest.

—How, exactly?—

—As if they were on my body—

—We have a no touching rule in effect—

—Only until you commit yourself to me—

I knew where this was going, and I wanted it, dangerous as it was.

—What if I don't commit myself?—

—You will—

—Then what?—

—Then I'm going to take those touchy little hands and tie them to your knees—

—No kissing first?—

—No—

—Not even your cock?—

He pursed his lips and looked at me. His hands slid over the glass. Fuck that, he was not taking control of this conversation. I put my elbows on the table, leaning over it toward him.

—What if I crawled at your feet,
kneeled before you, looking up at
you as you pulled out that piece
of meat between your legs—

He glanced at Darren, who sat in the dark, eyes glued to his computer screen and unaware of our bloops and dings. Then Jonathan leaned forward, mirroring my position on the table, as he texted.

*—When I'm done tying your
hands, I'm going to bend you over
and press your cheek to the
mattress. Then tie your ankles to
the bed's legs, holding them spread
for me as you stand—*

*—What if I kissed the tip of your
cock? And you took me at the back
of my head while you rubbed it along
my closed lips, and I opened them—*

Our forearms rested on the table, lateral, not touching, as we watched each other and our little glowing screens. Our phones dinged and blooped and buzzed rapid fire, like electronic jumping beans.

*—I'm going to put my thumb
on your clit, then move it up to
your asshole until it's wet—*

*— In one move, you put your
whole shaft down my throat—*

*—I'll lean my wet thumb on your
asshole until it yields to me—*

*—I flatten my tongue on the base of
you as you pull out of my mouth—*

*—My thumb will enter you and
you'll groan and strain against
your ties—*

*—I look up at you and open my mouth
for you to fuck it again—*

*—I'll kneel and lick your cunt
until you beg for me to fuck you—*

*—You tighten your grip on the hair
at the back of my head—*

—I won't—

*—and press your cock into me until
my tongue touches your balls—*

*—I'll spank you until you can't do
more than sob—*

*—Cruelly, you fuck my mouth and I
love it because it pleases you—*

*—When you least expect it I
will enter you and fuck you. Hard.
Two strokes, then pull out and rub my
wet dick all over—*

*—Spit drips down my chin and onto
my chest—*

*—Your asshole will be fresh and
wet and ready for me to slide into
it. You will scream—*

—oh—

—Then you will moan—

"I heard it," I said, pulling off my headphones. "The click."

"Me too," said Darren. "Okay, all I have to do is—"

"Slide over, I have to get out." I bumped him, and when he didn't move fast enough because he was wound around the equipment, I stood on the back of his seat and climbed over him.

The bathroom was probably nicer than anything I'd ever seen, and I didn't care. I didn't have to pee. I slapped open the door and Jonathan was right behind me, closing it behind us. I put my arms around him.

"Behind your back," he growled and laced my hands behind me. My back was against some kind of counter, I felt more than saw cabinets, a toilet to my left, and a tile floor. Mostly, I saw Jonathan. His hands were on the cabinets, his face an inch from mine.

"Touch me, Jonathan. Please."

"Commit yourself to me."

"Oh, God. Don't—"

"Commit. Yourself. To. Me." He said it softly and firmly, half whisper, half scream.

"I'm yours. Touch me."

"You don't even know what you're promising."

"Yes, I—"

"I cannot watch you walk away again. If you commit yourself, you're mine. You will set your limits, and I will honor them. You will be exclusive to me. You will submit yourself to me sexually. Completely."

"Yes."

"People will know."

I thought I would have agreed to do anything for him, but that stopped me dead in my tracks. "Why can't we be discreet?"

"I want everything. I want to take you out. I want us to be tied without worrying about who sees us, and I don't want men looking at you like you're single."

"Fine, then Carnival's going to put me on stage in a collar."

He raised an eyebrow as if he found that interesting, not repulsive. "You crossed that off your list."

"Figurative collar. If everyone knows already, I might as well let them have their way and put one on me. But it won't be your collar; it'll be theirs."

"Tell them that's not acceptable."

"I'm not in a position to negotiate."

He bent his knees a little to get his face level with mine. "You don't know the power you have."

My hands were still behind my back, but my shoulders sagged. I was uncomfortably aroused, and though I was happy my pussy remembered sex fondly enough to moisten, the sweet physical desire was in opposition to the shitstink in my heart. "I just want us to be secret for a while."

"No secrets."

"Oh, you know what? Mister No-Secrets-Sir. Mister Your-Honesty-Is-Beautiful. Tell me about when you were sixteen. Westonwood Acres?"

If I'd held out any hope of him putting his hands on me, I'd dashed my chances pretty cleanly. He removed his hands from the cabinets and leaned against the opposite wall. I flushed red.

"It was Gabby," I said. "You didn't know her deal. She wanted to know everything about everyone she thought could help her. People with money or connections or both. Westonwood Acres came into my hands the day of her funeral."

"Those records were sealed."

"Everything was blacked out but the institution, your name, and the date."

He scanned my face, his eyes flicking back and forth, then he cast them downward. "I took a handful of pills. The Adderal was mine. The Oxycontin and the rest were my mother's. I don't even remember all of them."

"Why?" I reached for his hand, but he pulled it back, still obeying the rules. Damn him.

"Do I have to talk about this in the bathroom of a Gulfstream?"

"Commit, Jonathan."

"Are you sure you never considered law school?"

I could have cracked a joke, denied it, or even demanded an answer, but he was stalling. I wouldn't give him something to answer with another stall. I folded my arms.

As if understanding the gesture, his mouth curled in a wistful smirk. "Now you know why I ran to you when your friend killed herself."

"I thought it was because you cared about me."

"That too. Believe me, that too."

"What was so bad you'd try to take your own life?"

He nodded and slipped down the wall until his feet were wedged against the opposite counter. He put his hands in his pockets. "Remember Rachel?"

"I'll never forget that story." I slid down as well, leaning my feet on the opposite wall, a mirror of his posture.

"It wasn't just the once, her and I," he said. "It was a thing. I was infatuated, and she was fucked up. It was intense. All encompassing. My father wasn't in the picture then, but we snuck around. Tough to do when you're fifteen, but enough money makes it easier. I got my license and a car as soon as legally possible." He smiled as if some uncomfortable, yet pleasant memory flooded his mind. Then he shook his head. "Anyway, drunk driver. Meaningless loss. Devastation. A family I couldn't lean on or they'd know the truth. Et cetera, et cetera."

"I don't think you can 'et cetera' any of that."

His laugh was short and humorless. "No. I shouldn't." He hooked his thumbs in his pockets. "I have a big family. I know, we're loaded, so it's not like we all lived in a one-bedroom apartment, but someone was always around. It wasn't until she died that I realized I was surrounded by seven sisters and two parents and all these friends, and I was alone. Very, very alone. My dad said, 'Oh, son, by the way, I took care of her family, so don't worry.' Like that was all it was about for him. Or not. Maybe he was hurt and didn't want to show me because he was in denial? Or she really didn't mean shit to him, which disgusted me, because I knew it was true."

"Your dad sounds like a charming guy."

"You have no idea just how charming he is." He looked at his feet, then continued. "I felt like I came from shit, and that was what I was. Rachel, for what it was worth, understood the dynamic. She made me feel less isolated. And when she died, I felt worthless and alone. A handful of pills seemed like the best way to take care of it."

We watched each other for a second before I said, "I want to hold you."

"Commit yourself to me."

"Yes."

"Will you be okay with people looking at you, knowing you're submissive to me?"

I swallowed. I wasn't ready. I didn't think I'd ever be.

"From your face, I can see that's a no," he said.

A buzzing noise came from the speakers, shocking me straight and alert. Jacques's voice came soon after.

"Mister Drazen and passengers. Please buckle in. We're landing in a few minutes."

Jonathan snapped open the door and let me go out first. He pressed himself to the doorframe as I passed so our bodies did not touch.

CHAPTER 40

MONICA

WE PILED INTO THE LIMO, exhausted. Night time in Vancouver looked much like night time anywhere else. Though I was excited to be outside the U.S. for the second time in my life, my body, mind, and heart had been through too much in the last six hours.

"We're at the Travel Lodge," Darren said. "I assume you're not staying there."

"Neither are you," Jonathan said.

"Jonathan," I grumbled.

"I own a hotel practically on top of the museum. Don't be stupid. Staying in Richmond's going to waste time and money. Separate rooms, in case you're concerned."

"I'm not," I said.

"Thank you. That'll be great," Darren said.

I wanted to kick him. Why was it okay for him to accept an expensive hotel room, but whenever I accepted a gift, I was whoring myself? I tried to give him a look, but he just dicked with his phone. Then he smirked a little and glanced over at me. Then I realized that in his mind, by accepting it himself, he was saving me from doing so. Thus, I was no whore.

Men.

"Boxes arrived this afternoon," he said.

"Have you heard from Kev?" I assumed he wasn't invited to Hotel Fancypants, and he'd need to know where we were.

"Nope."

"I'll arrange food sent up to your rooms, and an early wake up call," Jonathan said. "When's the earliest you can get in for set up?"

"Seven," I said. "It's gotta be done in time for the preview at four."

"It's tight," Darren said.

"And we have zero experience doing this kind of thing, so Kevin needs a wake up call, too." I kicked Darren. "That's you."

I noticed Jonathan's silence, but I didn't look over. I didn't want to see his reaction.

Hotel C looked like all of Jonathan's hotels, a sleek, modern building no one would mistake for home. The long front drive had a marble fountain, and the entire hotel seemed to be made of glass and steel. Staff descended upon us immediately with Mister Drazen this and Ma'am and Sir that. Darren stayed outside to manage the equipment unloading. We got through the door and entered a lobby done in black and brown, wood and matte surfaces, with a cement floor and warehouse ceilings. A woman with her brown hair in a French twist and a black leather skirt handed Jonathan a clipboard. She looked lovely despite the fact that it was after ten p.m.

"Mister Drazen, happy to see you back."

"Thanks, Marsha. Can you call Kristin for tomorrow's meetings please? There were some changes."

"Of course."

"Should we go check in?" I asked Jonathan, who was signing a bunch of papers.

"Done already."

"Must be nice."

"I admit it," he said as he handed the clipboard back to Marsha with a smile. "It is. Where's Darren?"

"Getting the processor and mixer out. His life is those computers."

"Are you and I having a drink before bed?"

A drink. I'd agree to anything after a drink. I'd beg for anything, even without it, and he'd deny me just to make a point. "I'm wiped out."

"Come on then. Marsha will sort Darren out."

I looked back at my friend and found him talking to Marsha earnestly while indicating equipment. My guess was he wanted to take it up himself and sleep on top of it, and she wanted to put it in with hotel security. That argument could go on indefinitely.

A man appeared behind Jonathan. "Mister Drazen?"

"Anthony."

"Can I help you with anything? Take you up to your room? Get you a table at the bar?"

Jonathan turned to me and asked, "Do you need something to eat?"

I didn't answer right away. I don't know what my expression said, but something about it caused Jonathan to turn to Anthony and say, "We'll let you know."

"Very good, sir." He spun on his heel and walked away.

"What is it, Monica?"

"I have a problem."

"Say it."

"I know I'm tired and hungry, and I have a lot to do tomorrow. But I can't play this game with you. I'm not good at it. I want you. I want to be naked with you right now. The fact that I'm this close to you and I can smell you, feel you, hear you... Fuck, I'm going crazy."

"It's entirely reciprocated."

"You don't look like you're going nuts."

"Self-control. That's all it is."

"I can't sit across a table from you. I barely made it through the plane ride. The past few weeks have been dead for me. My body shut off. Then you came along. I want it shut off again because I'll agree to anything right now."

He leaned into me, not touching, his hands in his pockets. "I'll only let you commit to me if you mean it. I won't let you make a mistake because I won't tolerate you walking away again."

I leaned toward him a little. I felt the warmth of his breath, and his open jacket brushed my shoulder. "That first time we met, in your office, I threatened you with a lawsuit."

"You floored me."

"You handed me Sam's card. I brushed your finger with mine."

"Yes."

"I wish I hadn't done it," I said. "I wish I'd just walked out."

"It was too late way before that."

"I need to go to my room alone. And I need to not know where you are."

He smiled. "I'm right next door to you."

"I just told you not to tell me."

He chuckled and shrugged.

Darren came up to us, a valet rolling the hardcase behind him.

"I have some things to do here," Jonathan said. "I'll have Anthony show you to your rooms."

With that, he strode off to meet Marsha by the counter.

"Handsome guy, I'll admit," Darren said as we watched Jonathan move across the floor as if he owned the joint. "And not half the asshole."

"But Kevin's better?"

Darren shrugged. "Kevin's my friend at this point. And so are you. So for me, it seems natural."

"Not to me."

"I'm getting that."

CHAPTER 41

MONICA

THE ROOM WASN'T A ROOM. It was one of two suites on the top floor. I saw the skyline through the floor-to-ceiling windows in every direction. The décor matched the lobby's; matte blacks and dark matte woods with textured grains stained for contrast. I traversed the corners and expanses of the living area and bedroom, every step further proof that I was alone. The black leather couch was too big. Seating for six. Closet space for a family or clothes horse.

Something was missing. After the second time I circumnavigated the rooms, I realized that I didn't feel as though I was being watched. I hadn't realized the feeling stayed with me when I locked my door behind me, but in its absence, I grasped that it had.

I tried to call Kevin and got no answer. We were on international roaming. He'd probably off shut his phone. We needed him. He'd taken us on to energize the creative process, but the practicalities of an installation were beyond me. If he got held up too long, Darren and I would be in a world of shit.

I pulled my jacket off, and the sleeve went inside out. The poly-satin undersleeve's seam had split ages ago, but the loose threads and edges were invisible when I wore it, so I kept the thing, promising to fix it some day. Were our relationships jackets we wore? Every one was a manageable, condensed, digestible thing on the outside with a gaping wound on the inside. Then when we pulled ourselves out, they prolapsed, like a jacket sleeve, and exposed the raw, broken places we never got around to fixing?

I looked at the jacket a little too long. I was so fucking horny and pink, it was painful. Jonathan was right. We could fuck ourselves blue, but until we figured out how to be together, we were only using each other's bodies for mutual immolation.

His room was likely behind the thick wooden door with the big lock. It sat next to the empty china cabinet that would probably be filled if I called the concierge and announced I was entertaining. If Jonathan wasn't in his room already, he would be soon enough. He had to make a show of sleeping. I touched the door, trying to feel him on the other side. I lay my cheek against it. How I wanted him. If only he wasn't carrying the baggage of Bondage Girl, the looks, the smart comments, the self-defeating turning of my own brain.

What if I rejected him completely, again? Like an addiction, the bodily ache needed to be broken first, then the habit. If I made it through this trip, I might get home ready to take on something new. Maybe date? Maybe meet someone nice? Like any addict, I couldn't see a world outside the drug. But I knew there was one.

I stepped away from the door and got ready for bed in a haze. I hung up the dress and got out my work clothes for the next day. I'd done all right. My voice was an instrument for the piece. I'd recorded cleanly and done good work. I just needed to finish the job. Tomorrow. I had to focus on that.

I got into bed naked, feeling the brush of cool, hotel sheets on my skin, and immediately Jonathan was back on my mind. The drug. Putting his hands on me. Stroking my back, my ass, my thighs. He cupped my breasts, caressing them, then pinched and twisted the nipples until pleasure turned into a sharp bullet of pain. My hand followed the path my mind created for him, and I looked forward to release and rest. Arching my back into the imagined warmth of him, I spread my legs, giving my fingertips a place to land. I slipped them between my folds, pretending they were his, imitating the tenderness he showed right before the roughness took over.

I rolled over onto my stomach and slipped my fingers over my clit. I wasn't ready. How could that be? I couldn't go to bed frustrated. I wouldn't be able to sleep. My mind needed to talk some sense into my body, but apparently, they weren't on speaking terms. I put my ass up and felt a little tingle that might have been something or nothing, but I didn't touch myself. I just imagined myself in his ready position, waiting, unsure of what he'd do next. But it was too comfortable.

I slipped down to the floor.

The carpet was grey wool, rough to the touch. It dug into my knees and palms as I crawled, naked, into the living area. My arms and legs kept a midtempo rhythm, head bowed in submission to someone who wasn't in the room. Everything was taller. I was lower than the table, the couch, the chairs. My body's reaction was almost immediate. Fluids collected between my legs, lubricating them against each other.

What a repulsive creature I was, unable to find arousal without crawling on the floor. Even my self-loathing turned me on so intensely I had to stop crawling for a second to shudder at the power of it.

I was alone. I was safe. No one was watching. I could allow myself to feel it, to do it, to be however I wanted. I got to the door between my suite and his. On my hands and knees, I put my lips to it, thinking his name over and over, tasting the flat flavor of wood and dried lacquer, finding his sawdust scent inside it.

Doubts came, but I washed them away in the knowledge that no one had to know. Only a locked door kept the company of my submission. My sexual abdication. The resignation of responsibility and control.

When I moved my lips from the door, I saw myself in the window, a translucent reflection of a lone, naked woman crawling to her master's door. I fell to the carpet, put my cheek on the rough wool, and watched my reflection as I turned my back to the door, hoisted my ass up, and slid my hands between my ankles.

I was ready for him, but he wasn't coming.

I spread my knees and slipped my hand from my ankles to between my legs. I gasped, then as I pushed through the layer of thick slickness to stroke myself, I groaned.

"Jonathan," I whispered so softly I barely even heard myself, "my king."

Knowing him, knowing how he played and how he fucked, I touched myself ever so gently, around the opening, over the tip of the clit. I placed my fingers at the tip and pressed my hips into them slightly, then back, anticipation and hunger in every move. Two sides of myself warred. The side that wanted to just rub and orgasm out of myself, and the side that wanted to lie there with my cheek to the floor and milk it for every second of pleasure. I wanted the milking side to win. So I stroked my clit with a single fingertip three times, then once hard, then three times lightly, then stuck two fingers in my soaking pussy.

Repeat.

I heard sounds on the other side of the door. A shuffle. A light clicking on. A drawer opening. A voice speaking a foreign language as if it was on the phone.

Right there. He was right there on the other side of the door.

I pressed my finger against my clit and drew it down, hard. It hurt, just a little, then exploded into pleasure so deep I had to lift my cheek off the floor. I rubbed it again. I'd jumped four stages of desire right into orgasm close. My thighs warmed. My folds shuddered when I touched them, and my back straightened. My face came off the floor, and I kneeled, legs spread, fingers between my legs and rubbing in a circle. A ball of heat wound tight around itself in my pelvis. I crouched, pressing the heel of my hand against my clit, and then bent my back. I drew my wrist, then my forearm, along my wet slit until my fingertips reached my lower back. The constant, single direction of pressure broke the coil of pleasure, and when I straightened, bringing forearm, wrist, and hand back over my clit, I exhaled in a clenched groan. I did it again until my forehead was on the floor, and I pulled back, my forearm now a slick instrument. My ass and pussy clenched repeatedly as I tried not to cry out loudly enough to be heard by the king on the other side of the door.

CHAPTER 42

JONATHAN

Sometimes, talking to people in Asia was enough to make me want to do bodily harm to myself or others. I shouldn't have let that phrase enter my mind after what I'd revealed to Monica in the bathroom of the Gulfstream.

Sunshine and lollipops. I thought the words so hard I almost said them in Korean as I explained to my VP of operations that the vision for Hotel M in Seoul was exactly the same as the ones in Los Angeles, Vancouver, New York, and Chicago. The spirit of the thing was what mattered. Getting the exact same designer for Seoul as we had in New York was less important than getting the same *type* of designer.

I hung up, then looked at a calendar as if I could deny the truth.

I had to go to Asia tomorrow afternoon at the latest.

Fuck.

I wanted her so badly, and it took all my concentration not to take her too soon. I couldn't lose focus. Too much was going on. But there I was, getting Jacques on the line and telling Aling Mira to pack. I had no choice. Putting business first was a habit I couldn't break.

That was two weeks right out of the gate. Two weeks outside LA. Outside her sphere. I didn't want to go away. I was so close with her. So close to getting her commitment, her heart, her promise, then some shit across an ocean threatened to explode into a fuckstorm of red lacquer shrapnel. I dropped my laptop and phone on the table. My jacket went over the chair. My tie got yanked off as if it had offended me personally. Shoes, kicked. Cufflinks, tossed.

I hadn't intended to tell her about the suicide attempt. I didn't like talking

417

about it, and I didn't like her knowing, but, the minutes in the bathroom between deciding to tell her and actually doing it were more intimate than anything we'd experienced. She'd peeled off my skin and seen the isolation inside. She couldn't turn away from me now. Couldn't.

The door between our suites opened with a keycard, and I had it. It was mine, after all. The wood was warm to the touch, and smooth. Dry. The moldings were curved by the most perfectly even paint job money could buy. Running my finger along the seam, I imagined the little bit of air seeping through was shared between us. We were conjoined by the molecules, the scents they carried, the temperature, from her lungs to mine and back again.

I peeled off my shirt in the dining room. I didn't want to look at an empty bed, and I wanted to be close to the door for reasons that didn't have words my mind could define. I didn't want to waste the air, or something equally absurd and impossible to accept.

Wearing nothing but my briefs in a hotel dining room, next to an empty china cabinet, I put both my hands flat on the door, stroking it downward. I didn't know what was coming over me, but that door became her body, and I wanted to touch it. Needed to.

Then, through the door, I heard it. Her voice. Singing.

CHAPTER 43

MONICA

My forearm had been covered in sex fluid, and I stank of the flight and fast food. After collapsing on the hotel floor, ashamed, exhilarated, and sexually satisfied until Jonathan worked his way into my sphere again, I needed a shower.

The bathroom was black with white fixtures, and I was alone. The four showerheads were powerful, and the water was scalding hot. The frosted, glass-walled shower stall was as big as a walk-in closet. I scrubbed with over-perfumed hotel soap, and as I rinsed, I started singing a song I'd started the day before in a pencil-dulling heat. I'd memorized the words even as I wrote them. As I leaned against the glass tiles, I worked out the bridge, over and over. I felt like I had it, and it had been sticking in my craw since yesterday.

I'm scared all the time
  And I need all the time
  I'm scared all the time
  And I need all the time

I heard a click behind me, and a chemical infusion of fear made every vein in my body pulse. A man. In my shower. Uninvited. I screamed, or tried to, but because I'd forgotten to breathe, it came out a croak.

"Shhh," Jonathan said. He wore nothing but boxer briefs that showed the glory of his erection.

"You fucking fuck."

"Please." He put his hands up in a gesture meant to show me he wasn't going to touch me.

"What on earth would compel you?"

"You." He leaned forward, and I stepped against the wall. His forearms pressed against the wall on either side of my head, and he got inches from my face. Water fell on his dry hair, running dark paths to his face. It dropped off his nose, his brow, his chin. "You. Goddess."

Suddenly, the sexual satisfaction I'd achieved on my knees with the whole length of my arm was inadequate. "Take me."

"Commit yourself to me. Be mine for all the world."

"I already told you yes."

"Make me believe it." His eyes closed, slowly, as if he didn't want to see my face. He was wet, his body a waterfall. The rushes of water accentuated every curve and angle of him.

"How?"

"What was that song? I couldn't hear all of it."

"I wrote it yesterday."

He opened his eyes. "Would you sing it for me?"

His body still didn't touch mine. I felt his breath on my shoulder and the presence of his erection, and I wanted it as much as I'd ever wanted anything. He wasn't going to touch me. Not a finger. He was going to breathe on me and whisper in my ear, naked in the shower, until I burst.

"Please," he said.

A part of me wanted to tell him to fuck off, but another part wanted to be close to him so badly that a song seemed as, if not more, intimate than sex. "Are you ready?" I whispered.

"Yes."

I took a deep breath and sang for him, my voice low, much the way I sang him my song of fears in his backyard. This time, I sang without shame or contrition.

CRAVEN RUNS
Crave stays
Craven runs
Crave stays
A cold, dark stain on a hot sidewalk
From a water balloon thrown
Craven freezes
Crave ducks
And writes the sound of nothing in crimson chalk
Craven stays
Crave runs
Craven stays

Crave runs
Puzzle pieces in an open box
Find perfect fit, alone then
Crave touches
Craven sees
Pieces shifted, while five little lenses watch

I SANG the bridge a little louder looking in his jade eyes. I wanted to connect with him, to put my feelings into him so he'd understand.

I'M SCARED ALL the time
  And I need all the time
  I'm scared all the time
  And I need all the time

I STOPPED. We said nothing, our voices shushed, and the only sounds in the room were the droplets of water falling on our bodies and the whoosh of the showerheads. His eyes flicked over mine, his expression a mask. I didn't want to hear his thoughts. I didn't want to talk. I wouldn't like what I heard; I knew it.

"That one's not so revealing, I guess." I knocked the handle down to shut the water.

"More revealing, actually." His lips were at my cheek, but I didn't have the courage to turn and kiss him. "Puzzle pieces. A box full, and only one fits. And you leave me standing on my porch because you're scared."

"I was either going to stay with you because I was scared or leave you for the same reason. At least this way I'm not dragging you into my shit."

He leaned away. The tile pattern was pressed into the flesh of his arms.

"Don't," I whispered, putting my hand on his waist.

He didn't twist away, but he didn't want me to touch him. I sensed it in the way he stiffened, his sharp intake of breath, the way his eyes closed halfway. "The cameras in your house. I know who put them there."

The *plink plonk* of water dropping from the faucets and our bodies echoed like slaps on the tile. "Who?"

"Me." He opened the door with a snap.

"What?"

He stepped out and grabbed a towel, wrapping it over his shoulders. I was still naked and wet, unimpressed by towels or anything else, standing half out of the shower.

"Santon found the serial numbers and followed the money to one of my accounts."

"What does that mean?" I felt wound up, hot, heart pounding like a drum machine.

"It means someone who had access to one of my accounts had them put in. To answer your next question, yes, Jessica had access to that account. Yes, I think it was her, and no, I don't know why."

"Why?" I asked as if I hadn't heard him.

"Still don't know. What I do know is you're not ready to deal with whatever she's going to dish out."

If I had been mentally sober, I wouldn't have been so insulted, but it had been a rough ten minutes. "So basically, you burst in, mostly naked and fully hard, terrifying the hell out of me. You make me sing this heavy song in your ear, and then you tell me your ex-fucking-wife is the one who shit on my house, and for a finale, you call me *weak?*"

"I'm protecting you."

"Bullshit. How about the sadism staying in the bedroom?"

I balled my fists and stared at him, trying to transmit how offended I was. The showerhead dripped three times. *Plink plonk plink.*

He moved so fast I didn't even see it, but I felt it in the shifting of the air. I flinched as though I was about to get hit. His hands grabbed the sides of my face, and his mouth came to mine, his tongue parting my lips forcefully. I opened them once I was over the shock. His tongue touched mine. It may as well have touched my clit, my cunt, my ass, such was the intensity of the feeling. Between the song and the adrenaline rush, the chemicals in my body were set to respond, rushing blood and fluids between my legs. I put my hands on his neck, moving my face against his. He pushed me against the glass of the shower.

I pressed my pelvis against him, grinding against his dick. He felt good. Better than good. He felt right. I wanted him. I wanted his chest against mine. I wanted his hands to grip my ass. My nipples hardened for him, as if drawn millimeters closer by sheer magnetism.

Grabbing my hair as if for leverage, he pulled away. "Monica," he gasped, eyes closed, lips grazing mine.

"Jonathan, please."

"I shouldn't even be in here."

"Yes, you should. It's fine. We'll just do it now. Figure the rest out later. I'm screaming inside; you have no idea. I don't feel like myself. It's like something in me is sleeping until you show up. When you do, it turns into a wild animal in a matchstick cage."

He pulled away. "You drive me crazy."

I felt him leaving even before his body moved. "Don't make me beg."

"I won't let you." He dropped his hands. "I'm sorry. I just lost control when I heard you singing. But you can't come back to me just because we're naked in the same room. I can't..." He looked at the floor, then back at me. "Jessica's the tip of the iceberg. You being afraid—it hurts in my bones."

"I know," I said, resigned to him walking out of the bathroom without fucking me blind. "I'm the one sleeping on her best friend's couch."

I snapped the robe off the hook. It was warm, white, and plush as hell, yet when I put it on, it offered no comfort.

"Just go," I said. "I can't even look at you."

He paused, looked at the floor, then he spun on his heel and strode out without looking back.

CHAPTER 44

MONICA

No word from Kevin.

I heard not a peep from Jonathan's side of the door. I touched it once before bed. At one-thirty, I sat on the floor with my back to it, looking at the ridiculously opulent suite. Everything was done perfectly, and nothing was fixed.

I knew who'd put the cameras in the house. Maybe I could go home, or maybe knowing it was Jessica would make it worse. What the hell was she trying to do? Make a public scandal? If so, why now? Why with an anonymous waitress she'd tried to take into her confidence? Who did it and when was it done?

I wished I hadn't found out. All the questions I'd tried not to ask because they were upsetting came to me in a flood, and I couldn't sleep. I repositioned myself on the floor, pulling cushions from the couch. I was about to open a work of art in a museum, and at early o'clock in the morning, I found myself curled up in front of a locked door, my mind going in circles.

In between those questions and stumbling blocks over my house, I had to ask myself if I wanted that man in my life. Due to my prolific musical output over the past Jonathan-free weeks, I knew he was a work-stoppage waiting to happen. He knew it. That was why he'd walked out in wet underwear rather than take me right on the floor.

I really did wish I hadn't touched him that first time. I wished I hadn't taken that monkey of a bet that night at Frontage. I wished I hadn't met him at the Loft Club after his trip to Korea, and I wished I hadn't forgiven him for kissing Jessica. I had had every opportunity to take control of my life, but I didn't.

I watched the sky go from navy to royal, to cyan, to baby boy blue. I'd entered a fugue state of regret and dissatisfaction but had found no sleep. It wasn't a good day to be tired, but I had to get up and do the work.

CHAPTER 45

MONICA

"Have you heard anything?" Darren asked without a "hello" or "good morning."

"No." I peered over his shoulder at the breakfast buffet. It was ridiculously luxurious. "Nada. I called him, like, seven times." Silver chafing dishes held three different preparations of egg, sweet treats like pancakes and French toast, and breakfast meats all in a row. Or if we preferred our breakfast fresh and had a minute to spare, stations with men in chefs' hats were ready to make us an omelet or waffle. The dishes were pure white and spotless. The flatware was heavier than a clarinet. Everyone who worked there smiled in their crisp whites, and all the guests seemed perfectly comfortable with a white-linen-and-crystal breakfast.

I got a little fruit and a croissant, feeling as though I wasn't taking advantage of what was given, but I had no appetite.

"I called the hotel," Darren continued. "They can't tell me if he checked in or not. It's against some kind of law or rule or whatever." He carried his corn flakes to the table.

I grabbed tea and followed. "We should blow by the hotel."

"Yeah. Then we gotta go to the B.C. Mod and pray we can figure it out."

I shrugged. "You know he's probably there in a designer suit already, chatting up the curator about luminous banalities and cultural fetishism until she lifts her skirt."

"It's a him."

"Kev's not that picky."

"Crabby this morning. Did we fail to get Mister Drazen into bed?"

"He means nothing to me."

Darren cracked a laugh.

"Good morning," came a voice that shouldn't have surprised me at all.

"Speak of the devil," Darren said.

"Good morning," I said as Jonathan sat down. He looked well-rested and fresh as a fucking daisy. Suit pressed. Shoes shined. Hair messed up exactly enough so it looked as though he spent no time on it at all. I figured I looked pale and wrung out, dark circles and all. My body wasn't built for three hours of sleep a night, and certainly not for as little as I'd gotten in front of his motherfucking door.

"How are you guys getting around today?" he asked.

"Don't even think about it," I said.

A waitress brought Jonathan scrambled eggs, potatoes, and fruit. He didn't even have to stand at the buffet for it.

"Please," Darren said around his cereal. "Whatever you're going to offer, I'll accept. She won't take anything from you in front of me. We had this fight—"

"Shut up," I snapped.

Jonathan put sugar in his coffee, smiled at me, and turned back to Darren. "The hotel car is a blue Audi. Your driver's name is Feran. He'll take you to the museum and back, and he'll take you back for the event tonight."

"We have to make a stop," I said. "We haven't gotten in touch with Kevin, and I want to go to the Marriot and see if he's there."

"They won't tell you anything," he said. "Not even his room number. It's the law. Do you want me to find out for you?"

"You own that hotel, too?" I said.

"Yes," Darren cut in. "Can you do that please? See if he checked in? Text me if she's being a bitch."

Jonathan raised an eyebrow at Darren, seemingly offended by the name-calling. Was he seriously being protective against Darren? And this was the same guy who left me in my bathroom, fully unfucked, without looking back? This guy was bristling about me getting called a bitch by a guy who was practically my brother?

"Darren," I said, "it's cunt to you. See-yoo-en-tee."

Jonathan smiled behind his coffee cup.

Darren laughed but didn't repeat the word. "I prefer bitch, but whatever." He threw down his napkin. "I gotta arrange the equipment. When is the driver going to be around?"

"The front desk knows who you are. Have them send him when you're ready."

"This is the only way to fly, isn't it?"

"It is."

Darren kissed me on the cheek and left me with Jonathan, who looked unflustered.

"I couldn't sleep," he said.

"You don't sleep anyway. You nap."

"Three hours I need, and I didn't get them."

I leaned to the right, just to be a little closer to him. "I crashed in front of the door."

He sighed as if he got no satisfaction from the information. "I was lying on the couch not sleeping."

"My guess is it was for the same reason I was on the floor, not sleeping."

He fingered his water glass, and again I couldn't keep my eyes off his hands. His watch had a fat metal band in a blackish silver. Analog. One dial. The simplicity of it, draped on his wrist, brought out the arch of his hand, and I remembered the deep clinking sound it made when he fucked me.

"What are we doing?" he asked.

"You're trying to get me to beg for you back."

"I'm trying to get you to see that your fears are real. If we do this, if you commit yourself to me, you're going to get consumed. I think that's what you're trying to avoid."

"Yeah." I could see it. The cameras in my house were no more than a sign of worse things to come. The uncontrollable publicity that had nothing to do with my music. The implication that any success I had was because of him. The kink. The enemies. But worse, the emotional entanglement. I already felt more than I wanted to. If I actually let myself go, he would truly devour me.

I shook my head. "Can we decide when we get back? My brain's mush right now."

"Would you come to Seoul with me?"

"What? Why?"

"I'm going to have to leave as soon as I get back to L.A., and I can't wait another two weeks for us to figure this out. If I take off, I could lose you. I need to convince you, and I need it to be real. I can't fuck a commitment out of you. That'll be worthless. I have to have your heart, Monica. The real thing. Without fear."

"I can't promise I won't be ever scared."

"Of me." He put his hand over mine. He didn't touch it; he hovered as though he wanted to touch me and was as afraid of the contact as I was. "I don't feel close to anyone, except sometimes you. Sometimes I have moments with you." He took his hand away and put it back on his glass. "I want you, and I need everything from you. First, that you take me the right way. No compromises. No halfway mark."

He didn't equivocate with his gaze or posture. A part of me melted in his direction. How I wanted to yield to him, and how I wanted to run in terror. The tension between those compulsions made words as impossible as movements. I couldn't run away from him or touch him. I couldn't agree to two weeks away from L.A., the logistics of which were no small thing. I had a job and a commitment to Frontage.

"Will you come?" he asked. "I'll be working, but I can make sure you have the time of your life."

His eyes seemed bigger than they ever had. As if he really wanted me to come and would be devastated if I didn't. As if our relationship hinged on a trip to Asia.

"Monica." Darren spoke up from behind me, interrupting a gaze a hundred feet deep and a million years long. "Come on."

"We'll talk later," I said to Jonathan.

"See you tonight." He smiled as if nothing in the world was wrong.

CHAPTER 46

MONICA

FERAN, a handsome Middle Eastern guy in a black jacket and pants, was waiting in the navy blue Audi sedan. I didn't know Audis came that big, but the equipment fit in the back, with one of the back seats folded down. I told Darren to sit in the front, and we were off to the museum.

Vancouver was huge in a different way than Los Angeles, more vertical. The towering glass buildings clumped together like schoolchildren lining up for home room. The lower architecture was old, with brick brownstones backed by narrow alleys. Parking lots were few and far between. I guessed that posed a problem people were willing to live with because the streets were wall-to-wall humanity, even at eight in the morning.

About a minute passed before both my and Darren's phones dinged.

—He never checked into the Marriot—

"Shit, Darren," I said.

"Yeah, I got it. What could have happened to him?"

"Why are you asking me?" I had an unjustified defensive reaction, as if somehow it was my fault he was M.I.A. because I didn't sleep with him.

"I'm not asking you." Darren twisted to face me. "I'm asking generally. What could have happened? He doesn't *miss* shit like this."

I said what I wouldn't have said if he really had accused me. "It's not because of the other night? Do you think?"

He pulled his phone from his pocket and scrolled around. "Get over yourself.

430

Let me make some calls."

And call he did the whole way to the museum. A virtual glad-hand and polite, warm ends to conversations allowed him to make four calls in fifteen minutes.

We pulled up to the loading dock behind a blond stone building. Though the museum itself was new, the old warehouse in the center of town was a hundred years old if it was a day, gutted and repurposed to save it from extinction. That was when Darren got through to someone who knew something.

"Geraldine, hey, man," Darren said as we got out and Feran started unloading. "Have you heard from Kevin?"

I ignored the pause because I already expected the call would be a dead end.

But Darren bent his neck to the sky and closed his eyes, mumbling, "Oh fuck." Then he put his arm around my shoulders. That did not bode well. "Did you get him one?" I heard her voice through the phone, with its New Yawk twang and fast talk. "Why didn't you call us? We're sitting here—"

He obviously got cut off. Geraldine's voice came through loudly in a machine gun fire of clipped consonants. "Fine, fine. No, it's okay... We don't blame you. Can you call me if you hear anything?" He hung up soon after. "We're fucked."

"Is he okay?"

"He's alive. He called Geraldine for a lawyer since she has family in Idaho."

"He's in *Idaho*?"

"He got himself on some international watch list. When he was stopped at customs, they found out he had open warrants and shipped him to the state where the crimes were committed. Back home."

"Crimes? Watch list?"

"He was on parole. He skipped when he came to L.A. We've hit the end of my knowledge. "

I was glad he was okay, at least. Not hurt or dead. Not drunk in an alley. And though it was egotistical and narcissistic to even consider it, I was glad he didn't stay away because of what had happened between us.

"We can do it. Right?" I said, taking a box from Darren.

"He has the diagrams."

"Do you remember how it goes together?"

"I want to say yes," he said without confidence.

"Me too. We can do this."

"Yeah."

We were relieved of the boxes of equipment as soon as we got into the guts of the building. Four men in dark blue suits and badges opened the boxes, checked them, checked our ID, and asked a ton of questions.

"Unnamed Threesome. Where's the third?" asked a bald guy who looked as if he was made of lead.

"Late," I auto-lied. "We need to check on the rest of the piece? It was coming through L.A. Special Transport?"

"Do you have the tracking numbers?"

"No."

"Commercial invoice?"

"No."

"Customs transfer certificate?"

"Look," Darren cut in, "the guy with all the paperwork got held up with an immigration mix up. We have the sound equipment and specs for it, but that's it."

"Mister Rivers!" A man in a black turtleneck and wire-framed glasses approached us. He seemed to be in his mid-fifties, with a close-shorn head of grey hair. Darren recognized him. They shook hands.

"Monica, this is—"

"Samuel Kendall, your curator. You must be the lady without the passport."

"I fixed that."

"Obviously." What could have been an insult actually wasn't. He said it with a slight bow of his head and a little play of a smile. "I heard what happened to Kevin. We actually have a problem far more serious."

As if a mask had been removed without him moving a muscle or changing his expression, I saw that Mr. Kendall, under his veneer of jolly intelligence, was livid.

"How serious?" I asked.

"Career-ending serious." He smiled again in that same way. "Please, follow me."

Darren and I walked down a long hall with him. He spoke with his head half-turned, his words echoing against the cinderblocks. "We allocated space for this piece, and a ton of it. We have financiers who expect a full show, and collectors waiting to see a whole piece."

We entered a larger, unfinished space with exposed ventwork and sprinklers. Crates and boxes stood everywhere. Kendall found three crates close to the loading dock and indicated them. Two were eight-feet tall. One was as big as a kitchen table.

Kendall stood by them and smiled, tilting his head. "What the fuck is this?"

Darren picked up a clipboard from the short crate and flipped though the paperwork. I never realized how brave and unflappable he was. At least in situations that didn't involve me or his sister. Or his sexuality. He was as easy to throw as anyone, just not in matters of his career. Bless him, that was the only place I felt as though I had the wrong time signature.

"We're missing four crates." He flipped through the pages. "A page of the commercial invoice is missing."

I inspected the tall crates. They'd all been labeled and numbered to match the assembly instructions. Kevin had reviewed it with me for no other reason than to sate my curiosity.

"They're currently in customs, thank you," said Kendall. "Even if they're released immediately, they won't get here for the preview. Sir and Madame, I cannot express to you the financial impact this will have on the museum if we do not have this piece installed. Allocation of space is eighty percent of our concern, and to have a gallery empty is unacceptable."

"The gallery won't be empty," I said. "We'll have to figure out the sound system, but I think we can get this to work. It won't be a complete piece, and it won't match the catalog, but the space will have something in it."

"If it sells, there will be financial repercussions."

"If it doesn't, it'll be worse," muttered Darren. He looked up from the clipboard. "Can we get these moved?"

"Right away," Kendall replied. "We've gotten a lot of interest in this piece." Darren and I looked at each other as Kendall hailed down a guy with a forklift.

CHAPTER 47

MONICA

MY IDEA WAS SIMPLE. The installation had four walls. Two had been delivered. A bunch of carefully indexed detritus was in the kitchen table-sized box. That was enough for half a piece. If we placed it against a corner of the gallery, we would at least have four walls.

"Two of them will be plain white," Darren said. "The whole meaning of the thing was about the overwhelming nature of emotional vulnerability."

"Think about the overwhelming nature of telling *that guy* his gallery's going to be empty."

We didn't know what we were doing. We'd made something using Kevin's expertise, and though we tried to learn all we could while contributing to the visuals, Darren and I had essentially designed the sound. We placed the speakers, deciding which types to use and where. We conceptualized it, recorded it, mixed it, and made it work. We talked with Kevin about how the sound would work within the scope of the piece, but anything that could be seen was his. He had the last word.

So the assembly design had been up to him, and it concerned us only insofar as the speakers needed a place to be hidden.

The galleries were packed with artists hanging their work, and when they heard about our plight, we found volunteer helping hands and working minds who understood how to put up an installation. The front of the house, with the doorway, and the adjacent wall. The bug inside was a whole, finished asset. The thing didn't look entirely broken. Darren and I decided how to get the sound to work by using the museum's walls, which we decided to leave white. Darren could

434

have drawn something on them, but it wouldn't have matched Kevin's artistry. We placed the glass and broken cinderblock as we remembered it. When it was as good as it was going to get, with the walls stabilized, the top part hovering over the gash, and the layers of my voice filled the room, the artists that had helped us stood back and applauded themselves and us for pulling a rabbit out of a hat.

Though we'd make a success of the show if it killed us, the talk around the galleries was that Kevin's career was jeopardized. Non-delivery of work was such a dead serious infraction that even the craziest artists didn't get away with it. Non-delivery was a loss of space. It was a loss of prestige and face. It was apologies and returned money.

When he got out of whatever hole he was in back home in Idaho, Kevin would have to dig himself out of an even deeper hole in the art world. I didn't envy him. As a matter of fact, I felt very, very sorry for him.

CHAPTER 48

MONICA

WE WERE VERY close to being late. The piece had gotten up and the music turned on as the caterers finished the buffet and bar. Feran had been at our service the whole time, even shuttling Darren around to pick up a cable he needed to reconfigure the sound. He sped us through the city, around side streets and highways, and got us back to the hotel with seven minutes to spare.

"Dude," Darren said, "thanks."

They shook hands like only men can, and Darren and I ran to our rooms.

The door between our suites was open. I peeked into Jonathan's space and found him in a tuxedo shirt and tie, setting in a cufflink. Clean-shaven, hair neatened for the event, wearing a suit sexier than any lingerie, he silenced my reproaches about the open door just by looking as though he'd stepped out of a magazine.

"You look nice," I said.

"Thank you. I had some things sent from Yaletown," he said. "They're in the closet."

"I brought my Eclipse dress."

"No doubt you did." He tapped his watch. "I'm leaving. But you guys are going to be late if you don't move it."

"I have to close this." I indicated the door.

"Shoo."

As painful as it was to cut him out of my vision, I closed the door. Of course, I had no intention of wearing any dress he had sent from wherever he said they were sent from. I got out my Eclipse dress, which was the most beautiful thing I owned.

I loved it. But next to it in the closet hung a wide garment bag designed for multiple hangers. In this case, seven.

I hung the Eclipse dress in the bathroom, behind the door, so the steam would relax it, and ran the shower. As I undressed, I made it a point to not think about the seven dresses. In all likelihood, they didn't go with my shoes. I didn't have the right accessories, and looking at them would only hammer home what I already knew. The dresses had been picked out by someone who didn't know me, didn't know my taste, and obviously shopped with an eye to making that gorgeous man's female interest look like a wet dumpling.

The shower wasn't the right temperature. Not quite too cold. Maybe it was too hot. That was it. I inched the handle a quarter inch toward cold and ran to the closet as though the bag held candy and opened it so fast the zipper screamed.

"God help me," I said. "I am not made of stone."

Seven dresses. Four black. I pushed those to the side. Everyone was going to be wearing black, and time was ticking by. Darren would knock in minutes.

One tonal print. Out.

The last two fell just below the knee. A sparkly, flesh-colored halter with a handkerchief bottom, and a red, low-cut power suit that screamed *don't fuck with me*. That was it. And it went with the shoes.

I showered fast, keeping my hair dry. Quick shave. Soap all over. Dried like lightning and out to the closet.

Right. Red dress.

I pulled my underwear out of the bag, and of course, though I intended to wear my regular cottons, the lace and garter were right there. The set was white with gold hooks and clasps. The suspenders were satin with overlayed lace, and the rings holding the straps were as big as quarters. The front was held together with tiny gold hooks. Fuck it. At least I had an outside chance of getting laid in it.

When I pulled the dress out of the bag, I saw another, smaller bag was attached. I opened it to find a pair of red-soled shoes inside. Oh. Could it be?

Removing the cream halter dress, I found a pair of five-inch stilettos in a matching cream. Fuck, they all had shoes. Which meant I needed another hour. I had to look at every dress in the bag, every pair of shoes, and God help me, two of the black ones had scarves.

There was a knock at the door two rooms away.

"Mon? Come on!" It was Darren.

I ran through the bedroom, the living room, the dining area, and called through the foyer, "One second!"

Red dress.

But when I got to the closet, I realized I didn't want to look like a bitch on fire. I didn't want to be dangerously sexy. I wanted to be sweet and approachable. I slipped on the cream dress. I looked pretty. Like a woman of grace.

CHAPTER 49

JONATHAN

PLAN B WAS on his way to the museum from the airport. Petra had gone to her doctor's appointment and gleefully told me she'd have to stop flying in a few months. I envied Jacques.

I'd left Feran with Monica and Darren, sent someone else for Plan B, and drove myself to the museum. I was much more comfortable at B.C. Mod than at the Eclipse show. My wife held little sway on this side of the border, and my place on the finance committee came not through family connections but a love of art Lanie Jackson had noticed when I donated some postmodern pieces to the burgeoning museum.

It was a small space and would never be the Moma or L.A. Mod, but Vancouver didn't need a palace. It needed something intimate, like the city itself.

That night would be a smallish, boozy affair with collectors and fellow curators. It was Monica's moment, and without Kevin around to suck the wind out of her, she could enjoy it. At the entrance, a string quartet played lilting top forty classical with a pianist at a black baby grand. I said some hellos, shook some hands, laughed at a couple of stupid jokes about L.A., and got a whiskey. I eventually found the Unnamed Threesome by following the sound of Monica's voice.

It wasn't the same piece. Though her voice, layered forty times like angels singing, then screaming, then moaning, was perfect, the piece wasn't as good. Adequate. It would do. It wasn't shameful, and it didn't look wrong as much as it looked somehow aborted. I couldn't figure out if the difference was that I'd seen it in its complete state and my eye had been colored, or if it truly did have something truncated about it.

Samuel Kendall approached me, hand out, wearing the same black turtleneck he always wore. "Did you see the Simulcra Brothers piece in the West Hall?"

"Not yet." I pointed at the truncated house. "Got stopped by the voice."

"What do you think?" he asked.

"I saw it in L.A."

"Ah, so you saw it complete." He ground his teeth. He was not a happy man. "It was good. Amateur mistake." He wagged his finger at me. "Never deal with amateurs."

I swallowed my drink and smiled. "Amateur comes from the Latin agent *amatus*. To love. Never worry about love. Love delivers. It's the incompetent professionals that'll screw you."

Kendall laughed bitterly. "Every freaking time." He looked over my shoulder. "Who is that?" I followed his gaze to Plan B, who had just arrived.

"Harry Enrich, the president of Carnival Records. Great guy. I have some property for him to look at. He's thinking of opening a mini-studio up here."

"Who isn't?"

Harry came my way with his wife, Yasmine, on his arm. He was a small man with wiry hair and cheeks that were never free of late-day shadow. "Jonathan, you've met my wife?"

"Nice to see you again."

"Beautiful plane," she said.

"I'm glad you enjoyed it."

I introduced them to Kendall, and Harry didn't waste a second before asking him, "Who is this?" He pointed at the ceiling. "I know that voice."

"She just walked in," I said, knowing I was smiling.

She'd chosen the cream dress with the tiny sequins. As willful as she was, she proved she was mine with every small, seemingly inconsequential decision. She looked breathtaking, even on Darren's arm, leaning on him as if he were her brother. In my mind, he was. She waved when she saw me and made her way to the bar.

"Don't recognize her," Harry said.

"Monica Faulkner."

It rang a bell. In the tilt of his head and look in his eye, I knew Harry recognized the name. I also knew he didn't know it well enough to be attached to any notion of how she should be signed or branded. That had all been Eddie's idea.

<h1 style="text-align:center">CHAPTER 50</h1>

MONICA

I DRAGGED Darren through the lobby and into the galleries without telling him I was looking for Jonathan. I found Jonathan by our piece with three other people, including Kendall of the black turtleneck. The other man looked like Harry Enrich from Carnival, but he couldn't be. Jonathan looked more relaxed and comfortable than he had been at the Eclipse show. More affable, somehow, better in his own skin, if that was even possible.

"I need a drink," I whispered to Darren.

He nodded and pulled me back to the lobby. The string quartet and pianist, two women dressed in long black skirts and three men in tuxedos, played a Brahms' Hungarian Dance like a dirge. It somehow worked. Gabby and I had taken a ton of gigs like this through high school and college. Little parties and big events full of wealthy people trying to act wealthy. They paid crap, but we figured we would have been practicing anyway.

"What are you having?" Darren asked, somewhat less comfortable in a suit and tie than Jonathan. He cast his eyes down to his phone.

"Whiskey rocks. Who's texting? Kevin? Is he okay?"

"No." He tapped the bar then shook his head as if a fly had landed on his hair. "No, I mean it's not Kev."

"Okay?"

"Adam has landed."

"Is he coming?"

Darren rubbed his eyes. "I don't know what I want."

"Well, if he's here and he came to see you, you'd better think of something fast. Like a piece of pie or a cookie. You don't want him to waste the trip."

Our drinks came with a flirty glance from the bartender to me. He had arched eyebrows and full lips, reminding me of Kevin..

Christian Rondo, one of the artists who had helped us that afternoon, introduced us to Donna Santonini. Meeting her made me blush because not only was her work unforgettable, it was also pornographic and arousing and high-minded, all at once. I loved her, told her so, and met seven other people in the next ten minutes.

My customer service smile was getting a workout. Everyone thought I was with Darren, and we fell naturally into a brother/sister routine we'd honed since we broke up. The musicians took a break, silencing the background noise. Our klatch of artists didn't notice. We just kept talking about getting shafted, fucked, disrespected, kicked in the ass. Stuff we all had in common.

And Kevin. We talked about the missing status of Kevin Wainwright.

I felt Jonathan's hand on my back. Even through my dress, I knew his touch. His fingertips just grazed me, and I wanted to melt under them.

"That dress makes me want to destroy you," he said in my ear.

I faced him, and I noticed his hand left my back. I felt suddenly cold. "Missed your opportunity last night."

"I'll take you when you're ready and not a minute sooner." He pressed his lips together, looking at me as if he'd swallow me whole once the moment of readiness came. "I have someone here who swears he's heard your voice on some scratch cut one of his acquisitions people brought him."

I looked behind Jonathan and found the guy I thought was Harry Enrich talking to three other people I didn't recognize. "The president of Carnival records?"

"Eddie's boss."

Jonathan and I stood together, looking at each other, no words passing between us. I saw the blue flecks in his eyes and the laugh lines at their corners.

"I could introduce you," he said. "Or you could remind him of the cut he heard." He glanced at the empty piano, then back at me.

"I could prove I'm not Bondage Girl?"

He nodded. "The song can be what you want. Sing it."

"You're releasing it?"

"Yes."

"What if I sang something else?"

"Your call. I'll never hold you back again."

"Jonathan." Leaning into him with my eyes half-closed, I whispered it so softly, I doubted he even heard me.

"Go," he whispered just as softly. "Take what's yours."

He stepped back, and I felt at once totally alone and totally powerful.

Eleven steps to the piano.

I could do the new song, "Crave/n/" He'd recognize my voice, maybe, but I'd be Monica.

Six steps to the piano.

But if I did "Collared," he'd know who I was right away.

Bondage Girl.

Two steps, and limited time to get the song out before the musicians came off their break.

I slid onto the bench and started with a B-flat scale, then my fingers decided the song for me.

CHAPTER 51

MONICA

THE HOTEL CARPET silenced my feet. The sconces lining the hall cast warm light on the wainscoting, and the elevator got smaller in the distance as if it was stepping away from me. I felt as though I was walking down the center aisle of a church after receiving a benediction that actually conferred a blessing.

I touched his door when I walked past it. Just once and exactly in the center. I slid the keycard through the reader. The green light flashed, and I opened my door.

A single lamp lit the living area, and the first thing I checked was the door between our rooms. It was closed. I touched it, pressing my whole hand to the wood, then I knocked. I breathed three times before the door opened.

Jonathan stood there, jacket open, tie undone, shirt open halfway. A glass of whiskey with a single ice cube hung from his fingertips. "How did it go?"

"You left."

"It was your moment." He leaned in the doorframe, but his bare feet were still on his side. "Which song did you pick?"

"I did 'Collared,' but different. Less bondage. More sweet."

He took a sip of whiskey. "And?"

I looked for a negative reaction and saw none. "They demanded another. So I did 'Craven.' Went good. Real good. I wish you were there."

"I'm here now."

He was, in all his straight-shouldered, commanding, controlled beauty. Right there in front of me. Close enough for me to smell whiskey and leather.

443

"I'd like to go to Seoul with you," I said without thinking. Even as it came out of my mouth, I knew it was the right thing. I felt a press of tension flow out of me in a flood from the rightness of it.

Jonathan looked at the floor, and I couldn't see his face. Had he changed his mind? A little tension returned until he picked up his head and looked at me. His smile went wide, and he touched his chest.

"Goddess." He looked as though he wanted to say more but didn't have the words.

"I have to figure out what to do about work. I might lose my job."

"I can smooth it over with Debbie."

"Do *not*." I held up my finger. "It's my responsibility."

"You've made me very happy."

I had a snide response at the ready, but instead I said, "I'm glad." The ice in his glass clinked, and I looked at it wistfully. He held it out. I parted my lips, and he raised the glass to them and tipped a little liquid in, his fingertips at the bottom so they didn't touch my face. The whiskey stung my tongue and burned my throat. Hot and cold swirled in my chest at the same time.

"Thank you," I said. "I should be getting to sleep."

"Of course," he said, stepping backward into his room.

"Not like I'm tired or anything."

"Right."

"But there's this no touching rule, and if I spend another second with you, I'm going to lose my mind and try to take your clothes off. I'm tired of being the one with no self-control around here."

He just looked at me, up and down, a little smirk playing at the corners of his mouth. I knew that look; Jonathan calculating the game, imagining all of its possibilities.

"I'll tell you what," he said. "Your choice. We wait until we get back to L.A. We talk. We agree you never turn your back on me again unless I cheat on you or hurt you, neither of which will happen. We rush off to Korea, and I'll probably have you on the plane or in a car or something. I don't even know. Or the other option, and this is a terrible idea..."

He stopped.

"Go on," I said, a little excitement building between my legs.

"Right now, you agree never turn your back on me again unless I cheat on you or hurt you."

"And?"

"When this ice cube melts, the no touch rule is rescinded."

I cleared my throat and looked down. My hands were at my sides, fingers twitching as if I was playing a stringed instrument. "Jonathan."

"Monica."

"I can't imagine a situation where I'd turn my back on you again. At least, not for us being who we are. I won't deny it again. I won't pretend it's anything but what it is or that I'm not submissive to you sexually. If you fuck or even kiss someone else, we're through. And if you hurt me or if you're careless with me, I really will walk." I softened my tone and leaned towards him. "Barring that, I'm yours. You own me. You always have."

He stepped into my side of the doorway. He was so close. All I had to do was lean forward, and he'd have to catch me to keep me from falling.

"Here's how it's going to go then, Monica. Are you ready?"

"Yes."

"When this ice cube melts, I'm going to make love to you so slow, everyone in this hotel is going to know my name. It won't be play. It's going to be dead serious."

"Okay." I peered into his glass. That ice cube looked huge.

"Then it's playtime." As he'd done on our first night, he took his glass and pressed the coldest bottom part to my nipple. He didn't touch me, only the glass did. I hardened through the dress, parting my lips so the *ah* could come out. "I'm going to tie you down and take every part of your body until I'm satisfied. It will hurt, goddess, and you will beg for more."

"Promise?"

"You're not scared?"

"Actually, I'm kind of really turned on."

He drank the rest of the whiskey and lodged the ice cube in his mouth. He put down the glass and leaned toward me. The ice touched my lips, and he dragged it across them, dripping cold water down my chin. I opened my mouth and took the cube, but he didn't let go. Both of our mouths were lodged on that cube, me at six and one and him at five and two. A low groan escaped my throat. I ran my tongue along the bottom of the ice, trying to get it to melt faster. His face was so near, and the cube so cold and big between us, I felt both the closeness and distance acutely.

He yanked his jacket off, taking me with him. I grunted but didn't let go. He undid his cufflinks, tossed them aside, and went for his shirt buttons. I saw the laughter and pleasure in his eyes as I tried to twist my head to watch, but couldn't.

I undid the clasp behind my neck that would release the halter. The bodice dropped, and it was his turn to groan and try to twist his head. My turn to laugh around that god damn hateful ice cube. I unzipped the side of the skirt as he shrugged off his shirt, the yanking pulled our mouths in different directions. Our muffled laughter was a symphony.

Cold water dripped down our chins, and we sucked on that cube, willing it gone. The dress dropped to the carpet, revealing the white lace and satin garter with the big gold rings. He gasped and said something that sounded like it could have been "oh my God." He held his hands over my hips, as if he wanted to caress me, but the ice cube still existed. It was shrinking, but the no touch rule kept him inches above my skin.

His belt clanked when he undid it. His zipper buzzed. He held his head so I couldn't look down, and the cold, amused look in his eyes told me how much he enjoyed my frustration. Bastard. He leaned down to pull off his pants, and I bent with him.

He was naked. I was in garter and heels. The ice cube was half its original size.

He pushed forward, still not touching me, until I got the hint and walked backward, connected to him at the mouth. Step by backward step, through the living area and into the bedroom. I backed up to the bed, and he dropped on top of me, hands on the mattress on either side of my head. The ice cube was down to a sliver, and he slid his tongue into my mouth. I gasped, finally feeling a piece of him against a piece of me, even if the ice made him cold. I'd take it. Anything. My skin was hungry for his touch.

I don't know when the ice actually disappeared down my throat, but his mouth on mine became more of a real kiss, more a dance of breaths and movements. I dared to touch his chest. When he didn't pull away, I groaned into his mouth. His skin against my hands, the bumps of his nipples. The ribs at his sides. The hardness of his hips. The line of hair on his belly.

Before I could get my hand between his legs, he shifted down and took my nipple in his mouth, sucking it between his teeth and sending pulsing shivers down my body. I wove my fingers in his hair, pulling him to me.

"Oh, God, Jonathan. Take me. Please."

"Not yet." He moved to the other breast. "Slow. We've waited too long to rush." He slipped a finger under the garter belt, backing away to look at it. "And what you're wearing. It's magnificent."

He leaned back and drew both hands down my thighs over the belts and straps, pressing my legs apart with a gentle push. I opened for him, showing him how wet and ready I was. He kissed between my thighs. Licked. Sucked. I tried to push his head to the center, but he worked the other thigh until I was a pulsing, undulating mess. He looked up at me, pausing, his mouth hidden behind my sex.

"Yes," I whispered. "Please."

He put his tongue on me, and my back arched. He backed off until I calmed, then he licked me again in earnest.

"Fuck!" I shouted, reacting to the gunshot of pleasure in my crotch. He spread me open and lightly ran his tongue over my clit while watching me. His heat ran from my knees to my waist and was about to regroup under his tongue. "I'm going to come unless you stop."

"Come then," he said. "Won't be your last time tonight." With that, he put his thumb in my cunt and licked my clit in earnest, pressing his second finger on my ass, massaging it without entering it. He was telling me something, and I was listening. He sucked gently on my clit, and a little harder, and a little harder again until he yanked a fast, violent orgasm out of me. I pushed against his mouth, holding the back of his head.

When I was done, he kissed inside my thighs again and worked his way back up to my face.

"Thank you," I said.

"My pleasure." He took my hands and pulled them over my head, pressing down with all his weight. "Open your legs for me."

I did.

"Bend your knees."

I pulled my legs up as far as I could. He looked deeply into my eyes, nose to nose, and slid his cock into me. I was sensitive and wet, and I felt as if a lightning rod had been lodged into my pelvis. All fiery sensation, and slow. He moved as if he was underwater.

"How is that?" he asked.

"Like I'm going to come again. I feel everything. Every inch."

He pushed in, still holding my hands, rocked his hips, then pulled out. He repeated his movements at that pace until a little nugget of frustration built in my belly.

"Faster," I said. "Can you go faster?"

"You mean like this?" He pulled out and pounded me, slamming against me. Five times. I cried out, reaching the next level of pleasure.

Then he stopped, letting my hands go.

"Exactly like that," I said.

"No," he said with a smile. "Can't. Sorry."

"Oh, no. Don't be an asshole."

But his smile told me he had every intention of being an asshole, and worse. The underwater pace continued. I felt like a balloon was opening up inside me, squeezing all pleasure and sensation out, but he just moved on top of me, rocking, kissing my neck, dragging his lips across my cheek, until he gazed into my face.

"I want you to feel me," he said. "I want you to see this side of me, how I feel about you."

I touched his face. "I know."

"Goddess. You're beautiful. Let me be yours." His face lost a little of its control, tightening and loosening at the same time.

"You know I love you," I said.

"Oh, fuck. I'm there."

"Yes."

He increased the pace incrementally, but it was all I needed. The balloon expanded, and I came, pushing my hips forward and taking all of him inside me. My orgasm was slow as the fuck. I felt every second of it as the ball of fire moved from the backs of my knees to the base of my spine, collecting around his cock before it shattered. I kept my hands on his face, feeling the muscles clench as he came. We cried out together, a stream of names and curses and unspellable pulsing vowel sounds. We prayed to whatever god we believed in, because feeling like that meant that there had to be a God, and heaven, and earthly bliss. We rolled onto our sides, still pumping together, emptying the last of our orgasms inside each other.

There was only breathing for a minute after that. He kissed my fingers when I put them near his mouth. I'd wanted him for weeks, yearned for his touch even when he was miles away. Having had him, I could only say I wanted him again.

"I hope you don't think you're rolling over and going to sleep," I said.

"I have promises to keep this evening."

"Ah, the owning me."

"Every part of you."

"When do we start?"

"Give me a minute to change from vanilla guy to kinky guy."

I rolled on my back and laughed. Vanilla? Jonathan? The thought. He turned and stroked my chest, fingers reaching for a nipple. He fondled it hard, then pinched until it hurt. I gasped, and he twisted it until my face contorted and I breathed through my teeth. Then he let it go. I groaned as the blood rushed back.

"God help me," I said.

"Go run a bath, goddess."

I faced him. "Yes, sir."

The bathroom had been merely functional up until then, and the tub had been of no use to me. Though I'd appreciated its size, the curves of white porcelain should be used for sitting and soaking for hours. It had a control panel with buttons for the temperature and the chrome water jets. I ran it hot, because that was how I liked it. Steam rose and fogged up the mirrors. The hotel had provided some scented tubes. I considered each one and decided on the least flowery.

I took off the garter, dropping it on the floor in a pile of white lace and satin.

"It smells like a bordello in here," Jonathan said from the doorway.

"Do you hate it? I can start over."

"No. I like it. I want you relaxed."

I stood by the tub as it filled, the swirl of arousal between my legs matching his more visible excitement. I didn't feel relaxed, necessarily. I felt as if I was tiptoeing on the head of a pin.

"Get in," he said.

I complied. He turned the faucets off before following.

"Now," he said, putting his arms around me and pushing me against the wall of the tub. "Put your elbows here." He placed them on the marble shelf outside the tub, where one might put candles or soap if one wasn't busy giving up control of one's body. He moved his hands over my breasts, my stomach, and my thighs. He parted them until my knees were above the water, resting my feet on the ledges at each side of the tub. My hips floated, leaving my pelvis just below the surface.

Jonathan stroked between my legs, letting his thumbs course the length of my cleft and onto my clit. Then his hands moved over my sides to my breasts again, stroking my nipples with his thumbs, and back down. He repeated his movements up and down my body until I groaned.

He pressed his middle finger to my ass. "Don't clench. Easy. Relax."

I tried to think accepting thoughts as he stroked me again and slid his thumb in my pussy. I let out an *ah*. He hooked a finger in my asshole. I didn't tighten, keeping myself as loose as I could.

"How does that feel?" he asked.

"Good."

He thrust two fingers in before I'd even finished the word. I cried out. It was good. Very good. He drew them out then thrust them back.

"You're ready, and you're mine." He took out his fingers. "Flip."

His pressure on my body told me what to do. I put my hands on the ledge, and my knees on the benches. My ass and sex hitched up, my nipples touching the cold edge of the tub. The sting of his hand slapping my ass caught me by surprise, and I yipped.

"Shh. Don't make me gag you."

"Yes, sir."

I felt his mouth on my cheeks, kissing across them. Then his tongue worked its magic on my pussy, my clit. Everything tingled. He put his tongue on my asshole, and I thought I would die of pleasure.

"You're clenching." He picked up a hotel bottle of something I couldn't identify, because I dared not look around.

I felt something liquid on my back. His hand spread it over me, between my cheeks, lubricating me. When he slid two fingers in my behind that time, I didn't clench because the feeling was much different. I was aroused everywhere, and it became a wordless harmony, a counterpoint note, its existence completing the sensations in my clit.

"Better," he said. "You're doing well."

"Thank you."

He pulled his fingers out and pushed my ass down a little. I felt his dick at my crack, and his thumb dug into one ass cheek, opening me to him.

"Stay relaxed."

"Okay."

"I mean it. I have you. You don't have to worry about anything."

"I trust you." I meant it, and as if sensing my sincerity, he put the head of his cock on my ring muscle as I tried very, very hard not to reject it.

He pushed forward. I tried not to scream as the head went in. I held my voice behind my teeth, letting the rumble fill up and fall down my throat.

"Easy. Easy."

"Okay," I squeaked.

"You're in control for now. Move however you need to. Whatever pace is good. Just stay relaxed. Focus on me. Trust me." He reached around and stroked my front from neck to clit and back again. I couldn't move for fear of the pain. "Breathe. Breathe, then move."

I didn't think I'd be able to move again. He put his hands all over me, relaxing me, reminding me he was there. I thought compliant thoughts. I accepted his calm, his patience, his trust, and moved into the pain a little. I was better lubed than I realized, and he slid farther in. It didn't hurt more, which calmed me. I pushed toward him again, and he went in.

His hands stopped massaging and pressed open my cheeks. "How are you feeling?"

"It doesn't hurt as much as it did."

"In a minute, it won't hurt at all. It's going to be the complete opposite." His voice contained nothing but surety and confidence, and that made me feel safe enough to push into him again. He tensed so that he slid all the way in. He pulled out slowly, coating my ass in unexpected pleasure.

"Ah, that's good, goddess. Very good."

I pushed him back in, and I felt full, open, vulnerable, and cared for all at once. But I did not feel pain. It had gone away and been replaced by something wholly new. A harmony. The note was different, but the song was the same.

As if sensing that, Jonathan took control, pulling his cock from my ass and pushing it back in again. He waited.

"Do it," I said. "Sir. Please. Fuck me in the ass."

"Your filthy mouth," he growled. "I love it."

He slapped my ass and took complete control, thrusting against me, holding my cheeks open so he could get all the way in. I grunted. The feeling of being stretched past my limit was overwhelming, as powerful as relinquishing myself to his pace. The water splashed around us, still hot, still soapy. We leaned into it until only my ass was over the surface. He reached under the water, to my pussy, and hooked two fingers in me, using the grip as leverage. The heel of his hand rubbed my clit every time he pounded my ass.

"You've got it, Monica."

"Sir, may I come?"

"No."

"Oh, God."

"Don't you dare." He grunted it, no help as his hand kept at my pussy. I tried to think of the feeling on my asshole, the pulling and stretching. The raw sensation and the pleasure of the friction. The feeling of being full with him.

"Soon," he groaned.

I did scales on the marble, pressing the correct fingers to the counter for each note. I crossed over in my head and went back down the scale, choosing a B-flat because it always gave me trouble. Anything not to come.

"Please," I cried, "sir, god please."

"Three more."

He took me three more times and barked a "yes." I came with him, feeling my asshole pulse and clench around his cock. He filled me, and I felt him throb, emptying himself in a long, powerful groan.

Still in me, he put his arms around me and held me tight. He pulled me up until he sat on the ledge, and I was on his lap with his dick lodged in my ass. We panted together for a moment before he shifted and slipped out of me. My asshole felt uncomfortable, as if his cock was still hard and huge in me.

"Ah, that feels weird."

"It's still open. Give it a minute."

He held me still, moving my hair off my shoulder, kissing the back of my neck, while gradually I went back to normal. Sore. Fucked in ways I'd never been fucked before, but normal. Functional.

"You didn't tie me down," I said.
"You seemed too tense. I decided on the tub instead."
I twisted to face him. "You're a good listener."
"Thank you. Now, back to bed, no?"
"Yes," I said. "Yes to everything."

JONATHAN

I slept five hours.

When I woke, she was tangled in me. I lay there another forty-five minutes, just pressing my nose to her scalp and filling my head with her scent of canned peaches. As of that very minute, my job was to keep her. Make her happy. I slipped out from under her and packed my things for a trip home, then to Seoul, with her.

I ordered breakfast, and by the time it came, her eyes were open.

"Good morning," I said.

She put the pillow over her head and turned onto her side. I slowly pulled the sheets off her, revealing her perfect body. I slid my hand between her legs. It was a compulsion. Rolling her on her back, I pulled her legs apart. She grunted under the pillow.

"I didn't hear you," I said.

"I didn't brush my teeth yet."

"I won't kiss you then." My fingers found her cunt. I rubbed the moist skin in the center, and she groaned.

"You look so clean and together," she said.

"How's your ass feel?"

"Fucked."

I slapped inside her thigh. The sound was hard and final. "Wider."

She looked at me as she obeyed, spreading her legs as commanded. I didn't have a game plan. I just wanted to see her. I bent to put my face between her legs and licked her lightly. She tasted of sweat, sex, and a little of my orgasm. She whispered my name, and I picked up my head.

"Take a shower, goddess. Breakfast is here. And no touching." I gave her clit a cruel flick that made her yelp and made me smile.

She kissed me quickly before trundling off to the shower. I caught her wrist and pulled her to me, kissing her as hard and deep as she deserved.

CHAPTER 53

MONICA

DARREN WASN'T COMING BACK to L.A. with us. His return ticket was good, and he and Adam decided to head back together. I assumed my faux-brother was going home as entangled as I was.

Jonathan and I decided to leave the hotel late. Breakfast had been picked over as if attacked by a murder of crows. We sat together on the couch. Jonathan was under me, bare feet up on the cushions, and my back was to his bare chest. I still wore the robe I'd left the shower in. I had a hotel notepad on my lap, and he stroked my shoulder to the collar while kissing the back of my neck.

"If I gagged you," Jonathan said, "I'd do it in such a way that you could still say your safeword."

"Okay, so we'll put it as a yes?" I wrote down 'gag.'

"If you want. There are aspects that aren't interesting to me."

"Then why's it on the list?"

"I'll try anything you want to."

"I don't understand. I'm crossing off things left and right."

"I don't get to cross off soft limits. Hard limits, like sharing, yes. But anything that's not disgusting to me, I do it if you want to. That's my job."

I tapped the eraser on the pad. "What other aspects of gagging are you talking about? Besides that I can't talk right."

"We can do it if you want."

"No, it was just something that wasn't horrific."

He paused to run his fingertip over my shoulder. "There's an element of humiliation. Not that you can't talk at all, but you're reduced to grunts. With a ball gag, it's more pronounced, and you add drooling. It reduces the sub to her most primal, animalistic self. She relinquishes control over her voice and her spit."

It was my turn to pause. "Have you used a ball gag on someone?"

"Yes. It's not my favorite thing. I prefer when your silence and submission are a choice. And the humiliation makes me uncomfortable."

I bit my lip. "But cloth doesn't sound too bad."

"Put it on the maybe list."

I flipped pages until I found the maybe list and put *gag with cloth* at the bottom of the page. Jonathan looked at his watch. "We've been at this two hours."

I craned my neck to look at the clock. "Wow."

"You're very thorough. But we can continue this on the plane." He said it as if he was ready to go, but his hand slipped under my robe.

"Jonathan, what are you doing?"

"Adding something to the list." He undid the robe's belt. "Spread your legs. If I told you this in words, you'd say no. I want to show it to you."

"What is it?"

"Knees up. Open all the way. You have to trust me." His fingers reached between my legs, finding my cleft wet from the sex talk and stolen kisses. Gathering moisture from my hole, he ran his fingers to my clit, two fingers circling it.

"This goes on the yes list." I arched my back.

His hand came off me and back down with a solid *slap*. I cried out at the deep sting of pain, gasping. But like a firework shooting into the sky with a hard streak, the explosion afterward lit up the sky.

"Do it again," I groaned. He did, and again the pain was followed by its sister, pleasure. I'd slid all the way down and was fully supine, head in his lap.

"So this goes on the yes list?"

"Yes. Again, please."

"You're insatiable." He cupped my chin and kissed me. "Later. We have to go."

"Jonathan?" I closed my legs and shifted to look him in the eyes.

"Monica."

"Did you have anything to do with Kevin getting arrested?"

"I'm sorry?"

"He's traveled before, so it was weird he suddenly got on a watch list. And then for him to get picked up now? Those warrants have been out forever."

"It had to happen sometime."

"Yeah," I said. "But did you have anything to do with it happening *now*?"

He stroked my bottom lip pensively. "No."

CHAPTER 54

JONATHAN

I GAVE Jacques and Petra the cockpit-door-closed order, which they were more than used to, and I had Monica twice on the plane. The first time, I had her in a seat like a normal person. The next time, on the galley counter because I could.

We didn't get much further on the list, but we'd made such good progress already that I wasn't concerned about it. Her commitment opened her up to communication about what we were doing in a way that hadn't existed before. She was thoughtful and full of questions. Part of me wished we'd done it sooner, and another part was glad it had taken time.

I let her have the window as we circled Los Angeles over the miasma of smog. She leaned against me. I had my arm around her and pulled her as close as as the seat belts allowed, putting my nose in her hair.

"Last night," I said, "I told you I loved your filthy mouth."

She turned to me. "Yes?"

"I lied."

"Really? Should I say 'have intercourse with me' when I want it?"

"No. God no. What I meant was, I love your filthy mouth. And I love your mouth when it sings and jokes. I love your body, and everything it does to me. I love when you come, when you squirm under me, begging for it. I love your hands, and your eyes. I love your honor and integrity. I love your loyalty, your intelligence. I love your honesty, even when it hurts me. I've fallen in love with you, Monica. I didn't think it would happen to me again, but it did. Thank you."

She stared at me, big brown eyes wide, mouth parted just a little. I didn't think I'd scared her but shocked her. If I'd used three words to say the same thing, I

456

might not have faced the same silence, but those three words would have been inadequate.

"You're welcome," she said.

I laughed.

The intercom buzzed as Santa Monica Airport came into sight. "Sir?" came Jacques's voice. "Can you come up front?"

I kissed those parted lips and unbuckled. "Give me a sec."

"Way to kill a moment, Drazen."

I kissed her again, half standing. She put her hands on my neck so I couldn't get away and kept them there until I took her wrists and pulled them down. I walked backward to the cockpit door and opened it.

"Yes, Jacques?"

He pulled off his headphones. "Sir, I just got a call. The LAPD is waiting on the runway."

CHAPTER 55

MONICA

When he got back, his contented expression had changed to something more pensive and tense. He sat and buckled without looking at me. When I took his hand, he clasped back as if making a perfunctory gesture.

"What?" I asked.

He didn't answer.

"Jonathan. Don't shut me out."

He held my hand tight as the plane dropped down to land. "I get sued all the time. It's not even anything. I have lots of things people want. So they come after me." He looked at me finally. "I'm used to it, and I've learned to manage it. So I'm not worried about anything. But you... I'm worried about what you'll think."

"Remember the part of the trip where I committed myself to you?"

He sighed, looking resigned in a way I'd never seen. "I have no idea what this is about. But the LAPD is on the tarmac, waiting for me."

I didn't realize my mouth was hanging open until I had to close it to speak. "Why?"

"I don't know. But I want you to stay on the plane until I'm gone or until I come and get you. I'll have Lil make sure you get home. Pack. I'll call you. We may be off to Korea later then planned, but make sure you're ready."

"No."

He raised an eyebrow. "Is there a good reason you need to exit the plane immediately?"

"I want to be with you."

"Sweet, but no." He must have seen my determined look. He added, "Please."

I sat back as the wheels touched down. We held hands as the plane taxied to the gate. Two black and whites waited, lights flashing. I didn't like it. I knew plenty about cops. I knew how they stood and how they walked. Sonny Rodriguez had been shot gangland style on my corner. On the other end of my block was a narrow strip called "Ghost Alley" because of all the murders there. Those days were done in the neighborhood, but the cops, the questions, and the tension lived and breathed in my mind.

The Santa Ana winds whipped around the plane and bent every palm tree in sight. The wind sock on top of the control tower was held still and erect.

Jacques came back, not his usual polite self, and opened the door with the steps behind it. It fell with a scrape to the concrete. Jonathan stood up, and with a look back to me and a raised finger indicating I should stay put, he walked out.

I unbuckled and went to the other side of the plane, pressing my face to the window. There was talk, and four officers surrounded him, which didn't happen unless some sort of violence was involved. Weird. Unless there was a great donut shop by the airport and two extras needed an excuse to come.

My view was obscured by the wing, but it looked as if they were handcuffing Jonathan.

No.

Sorry, but no.

I don't know what I expected to do, but I ran out as he was led to the car by the stocky cop on his left. I didn't call out or demand anything because another cop stepped between us with her hands out.

"Stop. Are you Monica Faulkner?" she asked.

"Yes."

I held up my hands to show they were empty and craned my neck to see around her. I heard the stocky cop's voice uttering the words of the Miranda Act. Jonathan asked something, seeming so together and calm, a picture of control. The Santa Ana winds brought two words of the cop's answer.

Domestic violence.

Jonathan glanced at me and smiled before the cop helped him into the back seat of the cruiser.

PART III
RESIST

CHAPTER 56

MONICA

AT 11:23 A.M., I turned past the historic fig trees. The gate opened. I pulled the
Honda in and parked next to the Jag. I checked my face in the mirror and went up
to the porch. I dropped my bag and knocked. Waited. As I was about to knock
again, the gate clattered closed. The button for the gate was just behind the front
door, so he must have been there. I had no idea how long he'd make me stand
outside. Patience was always a part of his game.

The door opened. His hair was brushed back and clean, his face shaved. He
wore a tan polo that was tight in the arms, accentuating his hard, smooth biceps.
His jeans hung on his hips as though they were made for him. And the
motherfucker had the nerve to wear a belt.

"You're a sight for sore eyes," he said. His eyes, however, didn't look sore at all.
He looked as if nothing ever touched him. I had no idea how he did that.

"Are you okay?" I asked. "I was worried."

"I'm fine. It's going to be fine."

I had been waiting to hear that before I dealt with the other issue that had
kept me from eating and sleeping for two days. "Then, what the fuck?"

"What the fuck, what?"

I crossed my arms. "What. The. Fuck. Jonathan."

He put his fingertips on my jaw and slid them to the side of my neck. I sighed
at his caress. His thumb brushed my cheek, his pinkie tickling the sensitive part of
my throat. I involuntarily tilted my head into him.

"Your safe word?" he said.

"Tange-fucking-rine. Now explain—"

He grabbed the hair at the back of my head and yanked me to my knees. I lost my breath, the motion was so sharp and hard. I was kneeling in a second, and he flipped his pants open in a few swift moves. His dick was rigid and straight at my lips, glistening with a drop of liquid.

I had told him about that fantasy the night I gave him the list that became a song. He said he wouldn't fulfill it until I trusted him. I closed my mouth tight.

"Open," he commanded.

I turned my eyes to him, his cock in the foreground of my vision. His face bent toward me. He slapped his dick against my lips, twisting my hair. I opened my lips to tell him to fuck himself, but I was unprepared for the ferocity with which he jammed his cock down my throat. I choked, gagged.

He didn't stop. He grabbed my hair with his other hand and pivoted me, controlling me, owning me. I felt as if he wanted me off balance and uncomfortable, held up not by my knees, but by the knots of hair in his fists that shifted my head where his cock wanted. I opened my mouth and throat and let him take me. I made noises there were no letters for. Spit ran down my chin, and when I looked up at him, he gazed back with fierce intensity. He took his dick out of my mouth.

"You fucked her," I said.

"No, I didn't."

"You lie."

He pushed me into the house. "Hands and knees."

I fell, but I scooted myself to standing. I backed away. My breath rasped from the facefuck I'd just endured. "Say it. You and Jessica."

"I didn't do anything."

"You. Lie."

He pushed me against the wall, hard. I pushed him away.

"Pick your skirt up" he said.

"Admit it."

"Pick your skirt up, Monica."

"Admit it."

He took my shoulders and twisted me to face the wall, inches from a Mondrian. We had agreed to all of it, more or less, at the hotel in Vancouver. Hours of making that boundary list on the couch, and one scenario we embraced was that sometimes I'd fight him, and I'd use the safe word if shit got too intense or painful Right then, I wanted to fuck him as much as I wanted to resist. I'd longed for him for two days, hovering somewhere between rage and panic.

He yanked up my skirt, pushing me against the wall with his other hand. "What am I admitting?"

"The cops said you hit Jessica with a belt and fucked her."

"They lied to get you to talk."

"Fuck. You." He moved my panties aside, jammed his fingers in my cunt, and flicked my clit with his pinkie. "First chance you get, you cheat." I moaned.

"You're so fucking wet, Monica." He pulled my hair until my neck was twisted so I could face him. "You wouldn't be if you believed that."

"They didn't pick you up for nothing."

"What if I did fuck her? You left me."

The thought made me so angry I flung my arm back and hit him in the face. He threw me over the sideboard, bumping a little bronze sculpture of stacked squares and knocking over a picture of his sisters. His dick pressed against my ass, hard, hot, and ready. One of my shoes fell off.

"They said they had audio," I cried, face wet with tears. "They have pictures of her ass. It's welted. You did it. Just say it."

"It." He pulled my panties down to mid-thigh.

"You fucked her."

"I showed her what she was asking for." He slid his cock in me as if he had an engraved invitation, fucking me as though he owned me.

"God, Jonathan," I cried, tears forming. "Why? Why don't I mean anything to you?" I didn't say "no" or "stop" because even though we had a safe word, I knew him. If I told him to stop, he would, and the pounding I was getting was the pounding I wanted.

He slapped against me with every word. "I. Didn't. Touch. Her."

"Liar." I swung back, trying to hit him. My reward was having my arm twisted behind my back so I couldn't move it.

"What did you tell them, Monica? You told them I spanked you, too."

"I said it was consensual. I don't lie."

"Good for you." He let my arm go but pressed my face to the tabletop so hard I couldn't move. He changed his angle and fucked hard and slow for a few strokes, pushing me down. The lacquer bit my nostrils. Pleasure was overtaking me, overwhelming my better sense.

That was what I wanted, wasn't it? I wanted to get fucked, but I didn't want to want it. I wanted his cock, and I wanted it hard, without the responsibility of asking for explanations. He pulled my hair again, yanking my head to the side so I could see him.

"I want to see you come," he said.

"Go fuck yourself," I replied breathlessly.

"Put your hand on your cunt."

I twisted, resisting the order, and he used the torque to drag one leg out of my panties. He put that leg over his shoulder while the other stayed on the tabletop. My other shoe fell with a clop. I lay on my side while he stood, shifting to straddle the leg that wasn't over his shoulder.

"Now." He put his thumb in his mouth and made a wet, sucking pop as he pulled it out. He pressed it to my clit.

"Oh, God."

He pounded me hard. The photo bounced off the sideboard and crashed to the floor.

"I said I want to see you come," he gasped, taking my pussy with his dick.

"Fuck. I hate you, fucker." I swung at him with my free hand, but he caught it before I struck him. He pinned it to my ankle with his strong fingers. "I hate you." It sounded like a plea.

"Well," he said, a word for each stroke, "I. Love. You."

He kissed my cheek, and everything in me tightened around him as his cruel thumb pressed, twisted, rubbed my clit. He grunted against my cheek. He pinched the fleshy nub, pushing and pulling in opposite directions. I came like a gunshot, a crack of a scream exploding from my throat. I begged him to stop, but he kept rubbing, and I kept coming until my cries must have sounded far more like pain than pleasure. Jonathan pulled his face from mine, circling his hips as he groaned a long *mmm* sound.

He was coming, and I loved him. Fucker.

CHAPTER 57

MONICA

THE COPS HAD TAKEN my information and made sure Lil picked me up. They asked me nothing besides my most basic information and let me know I had to make myself available for questioning the next day. They came to my house in the morning, gently asking the most painful questions, breaking my heart with every word.

I'd cleaned every corner of my house except Gabby's room. I stayed up all night, eyes glued to the television and internet. Whatever was happening with Jonathan, it had been either unworthy of media attention or kept under a dark, wet blanket.

I had called Geraldine Stark to thank her for letting us know about Kevin. She should have told us right away, before Darren had to call randomly, but she treated the whole thing like squeaky gossip. I made excuses and hung up. I called Darren. He was with Adam and couldn't talk. I didn't tell him about Jonathan. It would have taken forever to explain that I knew nothing.

I could not have imagined more tortuous days between watching him get into the squad car and getting his text.

—Where are you?—

I'd grasped the phone, letting half the tension in my body drop out of me and onto the kitchen floor.

—Home—

I was frozen in place, looking at the ellipsis at the bottom of the screen that meant he was typing. The shelves from my fridge were dripping soap, forgotten in the sink.

—Can you play?—

Initially, my biggest fear had been that I was somehow responsible for the accusation of domestic violence. That someone had heard about us, or seen my bruises at the Eclipse show. Or that maybe Kevin had gotten a word in edgewise at the border. Because who else had he been with? Who else had he hurt?

—Fuck you—

—Be here at 11:23, exactly—

But then the police had gently questioned me. No cold room. No good cop, bad cop. Two female officers spoke in a soft voices and told me they'd protect me from the man I loved and the sex I craved. They told me Jessica had come to them for an order of protection with photos proving he'd abused her during sex. Her reputation as someone who wanted nothing to do with Jonathan's kinky side indicated she'd been the unwilling victim of abuse and possibly rape.

I had gotten through the interview by using my customer service smile, but inside, I boiled.

—You missed the fuck you part—

—No, I saw it—

At 11:22 a.m., I had sat outside his gate in my car, waiting for the time on my phone to flip. I didn't know what the exactness of the time was about. I felt as if he was taking a slice of control and connection in a situation where he felt he had none.

I didn't believe he'd raped her, because I knew him. I didn't believe he'd struck her without consent for the same reason. I was livid because during the time we'd been separated, he'd been so broken up about me he fucked around with, who else? Jessica.

At the same time, for two days, I had missed him. I worried about him. I didn't sleep enough. I went to dinner with friends but barely ate. I checked my phone so often, Yvonne had snapped it off the table and pocketed it. When he finally did text, I felt relief, and rage, and at the sight of the word *play,* I felt rushing need between my legs that only he could release.

After he took full control of my resistant body, yanking an orgasm out of me, he picked me up and got me standing. I touched the hem of my skirt, but he moved my hands away.

"What now, Jonathan?" I was emotionally frustrated, sexually satisfied, and physically exhausted.

"Let me," he said, kneeling in front of me. He held out the empty leg of my panties, and I stepped into them.

"You hurt me. And you cheated."

"Hurting you isn't my fault. It's Jessica's. And the second isn't true." He slid my panties back up my legs, running his fingers under them to get them in the right place.

"It doesn't matter that we broke up," I said.

"Yes, it would, if I'd done anything." He pulled down my skirt, caressing my ass, my thighs, and my knees as if they were precious. "She came here the day I saw you at the Stock. Debbie said you'd moved on, and I was upset."

"She said that? It wasn't true."

He looked up at me, his hands on the backs of my thighs. "I know. Debbie's a yenta. I should have known. But Jessica was here, and she goaded me. That's not an excuse, but it's what happened. She said she wanted to do it kinky just once, and even after I explained exactly what that meant, she pushed all my buttons."

"So you fucked her."

"No! Jesus, Monica." He cupped my ass as if to make me understand. "I had her unbutton her shirt, and she still wanted it. So I bent her over the table and gave her three whacks with my belt. I'm not proud of it. But everyone's clothes were on."

"Do you understand how unlikely that story sounds?"

"Yes. But you're the only one, Monica. The only one."

"I don't forgive you."

But I did, and we both knew it. I looked down at him, with his tourmaline eyes and copper hair, and believed him despite my better judgment. I forgave him despite my misgivings. I loved him just because I did. My heart wasn't sensible or guarded enough. Not by a sight. I was a walking raw nerve ending of emotion, as if the years I'd spent away from men and sex had made me more emotional, more vulnerable, more foolish. I ran my fingers through his hair, feeling like the victim of a crime of consent.

"Can you stay with me a few hours?" he asked.

"Let me clean up, then I'll let you know."

CHAPTER 58

MONICA

He was on the back patio, sock feet on the table, phone pressed to his ear. I watched him, thinking about how much had changed since the last time I watched him on that chaise, talking to Jessica on the phone. I'd left without saying goodbye. How long ago was that? A little over two months? Leaving without saying goodbye again would be unforgivable.

I slid the door, the change in pressure making a clack. He looked up, and when he saw me, he waved me outside. He'd hung up by the time I reached him.

"My lawyer slash sister," he said, holding out his hand. I took it but sat in the chair, swinging my legs over the arm.

"That sounds awkward."

He laughed. "You have no idea. And don't get too comfortable, because she wants to meet you."

"When?"

"Now."

"It's Saturday."

"Lawyers don't get weekends. She has no kids or husband, so she works."

I sighed. I wanted to spend the next hours soothing myself with his body, trying to rub away feeling manipulated and used. My disappointment must have been evident, because Jonathan pulled me up, wrapping his arms around me.

"I owe you. I know," he said.

"Fine."

Lil drove. Apparently, we were headed out to Beverly Hills. Traffic was pretty terrible, even for a weekend. Jonathan and I sat in the back seat. I had a leg

470

hitched on the seat so I could face him. He leaned in my direction but faced forward.

"Are you going to wait for your sister to debrief me? And which one is this?"

"This is Margie. She's the oldest. She's very straightforward. I think you'll like her."

"And she's going to tell me everything in legalese, because you won't say a word about getting picked up at the airport and put into a police car while smiling like your Mirandas were a big joke."

"I was smiling for your benefit." He took my hand, weaving our fingers together. "I didn't want you to worry."

"I'm worried. Very worried. I was sick to my stomach until the cops came and told me what happened."

"Which was false."

"Then I was worried about you and mad at the same time. So, fail. And stop avoiding."

He leaned his head back and looked out the window.

"Is it bad?" I asked.

"We don't know. We've got radio silence from my ex-wife." He sat up and faced me. "The prosecutor's going to want to talk to you."

"I'll tell them the same thing I told the cops."

"I don't want you to think lying's going to protect me."

We just stared at each other for a few seconds, maybe more. It felt like forever and not long enough before I had to break it. He put his fingertips to my cheek, brushing his thumb on my lower lip. His hands were magical, igniting a fire, touching a fuse that ran to the core between my legs by way of my heart.

"I know you have lying in you," I said.

"My lies are all white."

"Flake white."

"The brightest, most guilt-free of the whites."

"And the one so toxic it's illegal."

A smile curled one side of his mouth. "I'm not lying about Jessica or about anything that matters."

"Who decides what matters?"

His hand slid off my throat and down my chest, resting on my sternum. "You matter. We matter. I haven't touched another woman since I had you at the Loft Club. Monica, it's you. Being with you is all I can think about. It's all I want. We are bound. I can't be unfaithful to you any more than the sky can be unfaithful to the sea."

"Nice words."

"Your nipples are hard." He brushed them with the backs of his fingers. "Your body won't deny what your mind fights."

"If I decide to believe you, understand I know there are things you've lied about."

"Such as?" He drew a nail over my nipple, the fabric like Teflon, letting it slide across. My lips parted.

"I don't believe Kevin got picked up just because," I said.

He pinched my nipple hard, giving a little twist. My back arched.

"Who cares?" he whispered.

"I do. About the truth."

He put his hand under my skirt. I was a little sore from the hate fuck in his living room, but my wet lips fluttered under his touch.

"Open your legs."

I did, and he hitched up my dress until it gathered just under my breasts. He placed my heels on the seat until my underwear was the only thing between me and his eyes.

"The truth, Monica," he said, putting his thumb lightly on my clit, using my juices to slide over the skin. "The truth is that I love you. The rest is unnecessary complication."

"I disagree." But I was lost. It didn't matter if I agreed or not. I wanted some part of his body to rub against me. He flicked my engorged clit, and my breath hitched with the pain and pleasure.

"You won't." He took a small box from his pocket, opened it, and plucked my diamond navel bar from its velvet bed. He kissed between my legs, over my underwear, breathing on my clit to make it warm and receptive. His lips traveled to my naked navel, which he kissed gently. "You belong to me. That means I take care of you. Your body and your heart." He slid the navel bar through the piercing. "That means I'm committed to your happiness. And it means there is no other woman." He slid the smaller diamond cap on top, sealing the gem to me. "I don't share. And you don't have to either. You have to trust me."

"I can't."

"It's a choice. Make it." He slid to his knees before me and slipped his fingers under my panties. I lifted my butt, and he pulled them off. His tongue ran from my knee to my thigh. When his tongue found my folds, I thought I'd burst.

"Oh..." I put my fingers in his hair.

He looked up and said, "Hands under your ass."

I sat on them.

"Keep these legs open."

The commands turned me on, sending another wave of pleasure through me. By the time his tongue found my clit, I was non-verbal. He licked so gently, flicking it, then circling my hole, making sure every inch of me was on high alert. A little suck, a flick with his fingers. Sweet, exquisite torture. He slid those flicking fingers in me, then sucked my clit again.

"May I come, sir?" I asked in a breath.

"Maybe," he whispered. "Keep these legs spread for me." He ran his tongue over my clit again.

"Oh, God."

He slid his thumb in my cunt, and when he drew it out, he traced the line up and down me. Another flick made me bite back a scream.

"Let me come, sir."

"Say please."

"Please, I'm begging. Please."

"Are you mine?" he asked.

"I'm yours. You own me. My cunt is yours. Please let me come."

"Am I yours?"

"I own your sorry ass and everything it's attached to, please. Please."

He licked my clit again, sucked it through his teeth, and made my ass lift off the seat. He got three fingers in my cunt and hooked them, pushing into the rough spot inside me. His name left my lips over and over, and I tried to keep my legs open when they just wanted to clench around him. His tongue and teeth worked me until a tidal wave of pleasure broke through, sending shocks of fire through me. His fingers inside me did something else, blinding me with a different note, a severe release that felt sharp as a razor, strong as a sledgehammer.

I pushed into him, holding myself up on the hands he'd commanded under my ass. I hissed his name through my teeth so Lil wouldn't hear through the glass. My orgasm abated, fading like the end of a song. His tongue's ministrations slowed. My hips twitched around him.

I ran my fingers through his hair as he kissed the inside of my thighs. "Jonathan?"

"Monica."

"One day this will stop working."

"But not today."

CHAPTER 59

MONICA

WE WENT into the elevator with a man in a grey suit, putting our backs to the wall and watching the floors light up above us. Jonathan's hand hooked mine and clutched it.

He was holding my hand in an elevator. Like a normal person. I looked at him, and he turned to me.

"What?" he asked.

"Nothing."

Grey Suit got out, and the doors slid shut.

"Margie litigated my divorce," Jonathan said, still facing the doors.

"Okay?"

"We had a lot of talk about irreconcilable differences over sex. How it was had, et cetera. There were gag orders that were broken. No pun intended."

"Okay."

"My sister may look at you in that way you were afraid of. She's still curious about the whole thing."

"That's awkward."

"You have no idea."

My face hurt from holding back a nervous smile. "If she's curious, you should send Debbie at her with a riding crop."

He glanced at me, and I knew he was trying to hold back nervous laughter as much as I was. The elevator dinged, and the doors slid open. "Madame Silk would have her crawling on the floor in a second."

"I knew it!" I exclaimed.

He put his arm around me, and we walked into the hall. He opened glass doors for me. Two receptionists sat behind a stark white counter topped with red blooms. The older seemed to know him and picked up the phone when she saw him. He still had his arm around me.

"Did Madame Silk ever get her crop on you?" I whispered.

"We discussed it and decided against."

"How thoughtful and sensible of you."

He pulled me to him. "It was much, much more complex than that."

"Mister Drazen?" the receptionist called. "Come this way." We followed her past the desk and into the belly of the office. He held my hand the whole way.

Margie was almost as tall as I was, and she shook my hand like a man. She did not size me up, nor did she give me the impression she had an ounce of curiosity about what I did in bed with her brother. Either Jonathan was wrong and she didn't give a shit, or she was as in control as he was. Her sage pencil skirt and tapered jacket were tailored to exist without being noticed as anything but part of a God-created whole. I knew her age, and she wore it well. She had the alertness of a child, yet her comportment was so graceful and self-aware, she was more adult than I thought I'd ever feel.

We sat across from her desk like recalcitrant schoolchildren, facing huge windows that looked over the city. We shared small talk, a few lines about their family I didn't understand, a word or two about traffic on the 405, and a couple of innocent questions about waitressing and music.

Then Margaret Drazen put her elbows on the desk and indicated her brother while speaking to me. "So what did this one tell you?"

"He lied. As usual." I glanced at Jonathan. He leaned into the arm of his chair and rubbed his upper lip as if he was trying to hide his mouth. I knew he was biting back a smile.

"Which lie was it this time?" Margie asked me.

"The one where they both had their clothes on and there was no touching."

"This the same scene where he hit his ex-wife with a belt?"

"That one."

Margie leaned back. She looked as if she was going to fall out the window and get poured over Los Angeles. "This is so fucking fascinating. See, he tells me this story, and I'm thinking assault and battery. You hear the exact same story and think infidelity."

Jonathan broke in. "You're going off the rails, Margie."

"But, Jonny..."

"We talked about this," he said, his posture still relaxed.

"It's very simple," I said, my voice clipped and brusque. "His belt is for holding up his pants, binding me, and hurting me. His body, any part of it, is to give *me* pleasure and pain. If he gives any other woman either of those things with his body or any clothing accessory, it's cheating." I turned to him. "The fact that we were officially broken up notwithstanding."

"You said she wouldn't want to talk about it," Margie said to Jonathan.

"Apparently I was misinformed."

"You two need to talk more."

"Sorry if you're an hour behind the curve."

Margie put up her hand. "Okay, that was fun, let's move on." She turned back to me. "First. Let me tell you about the great state of California. We're a preferred arrest state. Any domestic violence accusation with some merit warrants an arrest."

"Define merit," I said.

"You're sharp. Merit means she had a recording of the incident on her phone and pictures of a reddened ass consistent with getting hit hard with a belt. Since she provided all of this to the police, the prosecutor decides how to proceed. But with the multimedia presentation available to him and the years of rumors, if he didn't arrest Jonathan for felony battery, he'd lose his job. Even if she drops the charges or recants, the prosecution still has to continue."

"Felony battery?" I said softly.

"They're required to arrest as a felony," Margie said. "The DA can bump it down to misdemeanor, but if the Ice Queen remains trenchant, a reduction's unlikely."

I couldn't look at Jonathan. It sounded so dire, and yet, what he'd done to her wasn't a fraction of what he'd done with me. "I don't understand how this will lead to getting her husband back."

"Ex-husband," Jonathan grumbled.

"Agreed," Margie said, "especially not with the mandatory order of protection."

"This is very simple." Jonathan twisted his whole body to face me. "My ex-wife doesn't want me back. At the time, I didn't know what she wanted, and I was trying to get it out of her. You don't have to like the way I did it, and if you want me to apologize again, I will."

"You can stick your apology."

"I'll be sure to do that. You and I were broken up, but I knew you were coming back." His face flashed with that cocky confidence then changed to something more sincere. "But what I wanted to tell you was that at the time, I didn't know what she wanted. Margie and I figured it out last night."

"She wants you, Jonathan," I said.

"No. She wants money. She's had trouble maintaining her lifestyle and her art at the same time. I set up a trust for her to pull from whenever she wants. It's a few million a year and I don't notice it, but that's what she uses to finance her work. We were set to renew the terms after ten years, and I cut her off."

Margie broke in. "It's a revocable trust. He can do what he wants unless he's declared incompetent. Then it automatically flips to an irrevocable trust. The terms will be reinstated. It's a stopgap against hospitalizations, drug addictions, that sort of thing."

Jonathan broke in. "She's using my kink to call my sanity into question. She pushed me into spanking her and tape recorded it to show how out of control I am."

They paused their tag-team routine, and I glanced from one to the other. Margie leaned forward with her elbows on the desk; Jonathan with his ankle crossed over his knee, leaning over the arm of the chair toward me.

"The cameras?" I said. "She was trying to get something to show you were crazy? How would it be admissible?"

"It's all back room deals," Margie said. "We think she might have counted on a little shame from you to corroborate, as well as my brother's desire to protect you. Kinky shit on tape could have served a hundred purposes."

"Fuck her."

"That's the spirit."

He took my hand. "She came to me only because the cameras were a bust."

I squeezed his hand. "I've met her. I'll tell you one thing. She'd drop everything to have you back."

"I'm spoken for."

"Regardless. She always manages to get you to do things, doesn't she?"

Silence built between us as we held hands and searched each other's faces. I examined his for understanding that what he did was wrong, and I think he searched mine for forgiveness.

Margie cleared her throat.

He and I didn't move.

"Monica," she said. "I want to tell you why you're here."

"To verify that he's telling the truth?" I said without moving my eyes from him.

"No. I need to tell you what to expect."

I moved my gaze from him to Margie and leaned back in my chair. He didn't let my hand go. She took that as her cue to continue.

"She's probably going to contact you and ask you to verify that he hits you. Just know anything you say will be twisted. She has to prove that what he's doing is impairing his ability to function. Barring that, since she's after his money, she'll threaten to go public and blackmail him."

Jonathan squeezed my hand, and I turned to him. "If I spend even thirty days in jail, we go back to the old terms of the trust and she can drain it."

"Arraignment's next week," Margie said.

I felt as if I was being played, as if those two had worked out a routine and delivered it. I couldn't tell if I was being lied to or just manipulated, but I didn't believe Jonathan gave a rat's ass about a few million a year. Something else was at stake that they weren't talking about, and I needed to shake things up.

"I think I should go see her," I said.

The air went out of the room.

"No," Jonathan said.

"I'm sorry?" Margie seemed keen for an explanation.

"Absolutely not." Jonathan's tone was definite and dominant.

"I wasn't asking permission," I replied without my submissive voice.

"Let's hear it," Margie said. "She might have something."

"The only way you're going to get an angle on what she intends is if I see her. If she makes an offer, I can take her up on it and go see her to get dirt on you. I'll tell her I'm pissed at you because you spanked her. We'll have tea and talk about what an asshole you are. I come back here and report everything."

"No."

"Are you going to the Collector's Board thing?" Margie asked Jonathan before turning to me. "She'll be there. It can be a casual conversation."

Jonathan's tone was clipped, as if he didn't even want to talk about it. "It's all Jessica's people, and they're going to be snickering about this arrest. I won't subject Monica to them, and I'm not going without her. So. Done."

"What is it?" I asked Margie. "It sounds like a great idea."

"Fifty of the city's biggest art collectors drinking and spending money," Margie said. "I went with him last year. It was like high school without the acne."

"And Jessica will be there?" I asked.

"Four artists for every collector." Margie smirked. "You never met a bigger bunch of whores in your life."

Jonathan was right, I *did* like her. "I want to go."

Jonathan stood up. "Margie, as usual, a fucking pleasure." He looked at me and held out his hand. "Let's go."

Margie pushed her chair back and stood. We were done. I got up without taking his hand.

CHAPTER 60

MONICA

I DIDN'T SPEAK until the elevator doors closed. "You know I'm right."

He was on me in a second, his tongue prying my mouth open, his hands on my face, his hard cock against my hip. I had much to say, but none of it seemed important. I was helpless. A ring of fire built between my legs at his touch, portents of pleasure pushing me forward. He hitched my leg up and did a slow grind against me.

"Jonathan. I should do it. I mean it." My words came in gasps.

"No."

"I can help you."

He smacked the red button on the control panel, and the elevator came to a halt. A bell rang in a constant clatter, but he didn't pull away. He pulled my skirt up and hooked his finger in the crotch of my panties, sliding his finger along my wet folds.

A voice came over the intercom. "What's your emergency?" It sounded automated, as if there really wasn't someone on the other end.

He turned to the panel and said something in a language I didn't understand, then put his lips on mine as if it was our last kiss.

"Can you repeat that?" asked the voice robotically.

He repeated it and undid his pants, pulling out his gorgeous cock.

"I'll have someone there in ten minutes."

"Cameras."

"It's Saturday. No one's at the desk. Whole system's probably shut down."

He fell into me, pushing me into the wall, a hand pulling the crotch of my panties away as the fingertips dug into my ass. I hitched my leg on his hips. He guided himself into me and thrust hard, shocking the breath right out of me. Bringing my other leg around him, he thrust again. And again.

"Oh, fuck," I said.

"Fuck is right." He twisted my nipple through my shirt. The exquisite pain was a direct line between my legs, making me spread them wider. He buried his face in my neck. "You are not to see her, goddess."

"Jesus. I can't think."

"Don't think." He pushed his belly on my clit, and a thousand fireworks went off between my thighs. "Just do what I ask." He rotated his hips, rubbing me sideways, then forward. He looked me in the eye, and let his hand creep up my face. He slipped a finger in my mouth. I tried to suck on it, but I couldn't keep my lips closed; I was gasping so hard. He pulled it out, dragging saliva across my cheek.

"I'm coming," I said.

"You're coming, what?"

"Sir."

He didn't withhold. He pummeled me, driving forward until I cried out through clenched teeth, pressing my legs around him, praying to a God I didn't even believe in. Jonathan's prayer was right behind mine, and he grunted it into the spot where my ear met my neck. His purposeful thrusts slowed into jerks, leaving nothing but hot breath on me. Our chests rose and fell in time, and our mouths found each other in a gentle, satisfied kiss.

The alarm suddenly seemed louder and more annoying, and the elevator cold and hard. Only Jonathan's face, as it took up the whole of my vision, was soft and inviting. He pulled himself from me and gently lowered my legs. As I straightened my skirt, he pressed the alarm button. Blissful silence followed, and the elevator jerked down.

I had about thirty seconds to say what I wanted to say, and I was not eager to do it. "I'm going. She's wanted to tell me something for a month, and it's time I heard it."

He pressed his lips together. "No."

"You have to trust me. I committed to you. That means something."

"I get it. You don't need to prove it to me."

"I'm not trying to prove anything to you. I don't have to. I dedicated myself to you. I gave my body to you. That doesn't mean I'm suddenly more compliant."

CHAPTER 61

JONATHAN

I PUT Monica in the Bentley so Lil could take her to work. I refused to hear
another word about her seeing Jessica, but I should have acted more laid back.
Such rigidity would only make her want to see my ex-wife that much more. Yet I
couldn't even pretend I would talk about it later. I had to let Monica think it was
about money, but the truth was that Jessica knew too much. "Just paying her off"
might have seemed cheap in the short run, but in the long run, it did nothing to
protect me. I had to find a better way to manage the problem, and I needed to buy
time with compliance.

My lunch with Eddie Milpas was three blocks away. I called my sister and
walked.

"So?" I said.

"She's not your type," Margie said. "She has dark hair and a brain."

"Thank you. I didn't need your approval."

"Neither did she. Which I like. I always expected your next one would be on
her hands and knees, licking a doormat. That's not what you got. You got someone
bigger than your grip. So, good luck with that."

"If they put her up on the stand, I'm worried."

"You shouldn't be. She looked me right in the eye when she made her claim on
the contents of your closet. If the truth is something you need to use, she'll tell it.
But I wouldn't count on her to lie," Margie said.

"Monica? No. I'd never ask her to. She's..." I stopped myself, wanting to use
words like *clean* and *pure*. They sounded ridiculous. "She's honorable."

"God help you, then."

"I don't want her talking to Jessica."

"What did you want me to do about that?" Margie asked as if bored, but I could tell she knew what I was going to ask.

"I want Will Santon's team back."

"You want to follow her. After she just got over surveillance equipment in her house. You're a paragon of sensitivity. Really."

I stopped outside Karen M's. I saw Eddie at a window seat. No small thing. A year ago, they would have seated him by the bathrooms. "Do *you* want her talking to Jessica? Because that woman's going to lie. She's going to turn a sexless spanking into a grudge fuck, and then I'm going to be the one licking a doormat."

Margie sighed. "I gotta tell you, little brother, on the rare occasions you feel something, you go deep."

"And with respect to that, I'd appreciate your indulgence."

"Take Santon. But on a personal note…"

"Yeah?"

"Don't get caught. In case you haven't noticed, you're on thin ice already."

We hung up. Sheila was my favorite sister, but Margie was always a voice of sanity when things got chaotic.

I sat across from Eddie. The window looked over a line of tall bamboo meant to block the sight of Wilshire Boulevard traffic. Eddie looked at the menu, then at me, then back at the menu, as if he didn't know exactly what was on it.

"Nice tie," I said as an opener.

"Thanks." His tone was clipped and quiet. I knew the guy. He was a percolating case of verbal diarrhea unless he was pissed off.

"I hear they've changed to locally grown tomatoes," I said, "so avoid the caprese."

"I heard the same."

"There's a shitstain on your cuff," I said. He glanced at me, then away. "Are we dating, Ed? Did I just fuck your best friend or get you the wrong birthday gift or something?"

Eddie, reengaged in the conversation, leaned on the window, spreading his arm over the table so he could fuss with a matchbook. "My boss gets back from a trip Friday. Some last minute thing to look at property up north, and he saw the girl I've been pushing. But according to him, I've been doing it wrong. My whole marketing strategy? Wrong. So *he's* managing her. *He's* signing her. Personally. Harry Enrich hasn't personally managed talent in fifteen years."

"She'll be happy to hear it."

"She shouldn't be. It's not all skinny ties and burning CDs any more. He hasn't caught up to MySpace falling apart. She'll be on his learning curve when he doesn't even know he has one. That leather corset's gonna start looking real comfy."

The waiter came. We ordered quickly. That had apparently been bothering him, and I needed to clear it up. He was burned. The collection of talent was his job, and a singular voice had been pulled from under him. In a city full of hopeful musicians, voices like Monica's were impossible to come by. Needles in haystacks. Finding another voice he could use could take him a year or a lifetime.

"Ed, listen. I don't want any hard feelings. But it wasn't happening your way. I could have gotten Randy from Vintage Records up there just as easy."

"Randy Rothstein? Please."

"But I kept it at Carnival out of respect for you."

He laughed. I admit I smiled as well. The notion was ridiculous. He was up a creek and had a right to be angry. I had the right to not care.

"You went over my head less than a week after you beaned me," he said. "I had a headache for a day and a half."

"I apologized."

Eddie pushed his drink aside as if it was an actual obstacle. "Listen, asshole. If you had a problem with me signing your girlfriend, you could have told me."

"So you could what? Tell me to go fuck myself? She wasn't signing with you anyway. Not all decked out in leather and chains."

"You don't know that."

"Ed. She was walking. Who's going to know it better than me? I saved your ass and hers. Now you can all make money together."

"I got nothing. Enrich can have her. Without a marketing angle, she can sing like a mermaid and it wouldn't matter."

"Mermaids don't sing. You're thinking of sirens."

He shook his head and smirked. "You need to go out and find me another girl who likes to get tied up."

"I have one for you." I lowered my voice and leaned in. "Nice voice, but she comes with an angle. Might not be as hot as what you had in mind, but it's like a slot and a tab. She's got something already going."

"I swear to god. Where do you find the time?"

"She's an artist," I said. "Think Laurie Anderson but drop dead gorgeous. Plays everything. She can play the spoons and bring you to tears. Has the chops for installation and performance work, knows the art scene."

"Not as commercial," he said.

"It's what I have."

"You got a name?"

The waiter came with lunch, and I wrote the name on a napkin.

CHAPTER 62

MONICA

I HEADED down Echo Park Avenue on foot, phone to my ear.

"Are you in the house?" I asked as I pushed the gate open.

"Just got dressed," Darren said.

"I'm on my way. No, wait, I'm on your patio. Are you alone?"

He opened the door in jeans and his red Music Store polo. "Yes. How was the trip home?"

"I really, really like that plane." I pocketed my phone.

He stepped aside, and I entered. My stuff was all over the living room, neatly piled, but the room still looked as if someone had been crashing on his couch without paying rent.

"Did the police question you?" he asked.

I was a little taken aback, and it must have been all over my face. "How did you know?"

"It's all over the society pages. And the *LA Times*, you know... It's news if it's about rich people beating their wives."

"She's not his wife, and he didn't beat her." I defended him and his word, knowing that the truth and Jonathan had a passing, convenient acquaintance.

"Not in the conventional sense." He placed his laptop on the kitchen bar and spun it so I could see the screen. Then he set about making coffee as if he didn't want to look at my reaction.

The Celebrity section. A section I ignored because Gabby had always read, assimilated, and digested the entire thing every morning, distilling it for me over breakfast. I was grateful I wasn't in the habit of looking at it because the day after

484

Jonathan was arrested at Santa Monica airport, a picture of him and his *ex*-wife appeared in Rumors Bureau column. It was the only mention of his arrest anywhere in the news, and it was short, with little but a wedding picture of two people happy to commit to each other. The burning jealousy that bubbled from my gut left an awful taste on the back of my tongue. He was mine. I owned him. Those pictures were lies.

"Monica?" Darren watched me as he filled the pot with water.

"What?"

"Are you okay?"

"It barely says anything. Arrested at the airport on domestic abuse charges brought by his ex-wife. History of kinky activity. Wife declines comment because she's 'too upset,' Oh, and I'm an unidentified female passenger. His little trick fuck whore. Remind me never to look at the internet again." I pushed the laptop away and turned to my pile of crap. I could have stalled and pretended to rummage through my stuff, but I knew exactly where that manila envelope was. I ran my hands over it, the aged edges, the curled flap.

"That what I think it is?" Darren asked.

"Yeah. Did you open it?"

"It's long and involved, so I just put it back." He looked at me over the edge of his coffee cup.

"Great. Long and involved." I slid out the contents. Eight and a half by eleven printed pages, stapled. About twenty pages, pure text. Double-spaced with wide margins. Markings all over it in red pencil. Lines. Scribblings. Hash marks. Slashes. Across the top: *Lloyd Willman/Evert Toth, ed.*

"It looks like someone's term paper."

He looked over my shoulder. "I think the ed. means *editor*. My first assumption was that it was a newspaper article."

"Fan-freaking-tastic."

"And unpublished, looks like. Or it wouldn't look like something someone handed in for eleventh grade finals. My sister was a scary girl. I think digging dirt on people was more fun for her than actually trying to get them to sign her."

"When do you have to leave?" I asked.

"Fifteen minutes."

I threw myself on the couch. I flipped through. All words and marks. I looked up at Darren, who was wiping down the counter. I cleared my throat.

He didn't look up when he said, "You're stalling."

"Why would I stall?"

"You tell me."

I had a hundred answers.

Because I know half-truths and pieces of a story.

Because I'm committed to a man who is still a mystery to me.

Because I love him, and I will stand by him, no matter what the papers say.

Because Jonathan lies.

So I didn't answer but tilted my head down and read.

CHAPTER 63

MONICA

THE STAR of the article was the rain.

There had been a winter of storms. I was nine. Dad was away, as usual. Christmas sucked because we were broke and the crawlspace flooded. Pebbles from the driveway of what became the Montessori school came in on a tide of floodwater, pecking the north side of the house for hours.

I hadn't done the math before. Why would I? Why would I remind myself that I was in third grade when he was busy having sex and falling in love? But that was the year I learned multiplication and long division and the year Jonathan lost Rachel.

The story wasn't much different than I'd imagined. A party had started out as a family affair for Sheila Drazen, and it became wilder and more drug-infused once the adults left and the kids arrived. The police found a bong containing chartreuse absinthe, the remnants of White Widow bud, and sixteen-year-old Jonathan S. Drazen III's DNA.

What happened after was the stuff of police procedurals, but according to witnesses, Jonathan argued with his girlfriend, Rachel Demarest. She grabbed his keys and ran into the rain. Everyone assumed she was keeping his fucked-up ass from driving. The next morning, Jonathan was found passed out on the muddy front lawn of a house a quarter mile off, and his waterlogged car was found on the beach three miles south with no girlfriend in it. A day and a half later, he was committed to Westonwood after an almost successful suicide attempt. It wasn't a half-hearted cry for help; he did almost die of heart failure.

Three months in Westonwood. The place was known for its lockdown: no phone, no radio. Nothing. A prison for the rich and disturbed.

But while he was away, his world was not quiet. What had happened during the rains had rippled outward in those months, and the Drazens had deflected and shrouded all of it.

Rachel's body wasn't found, and her death dissolved an already troubled family. The police had been to the Demarest house for over a dozen domestic disturbances over six years. Neighbors told stories of sexual abuse by her biological father, and near constant yelling and fighting after her stepdad moved in. Rachel had found solace in her classmate Theresa, who opened the Drazen home to her for study.

In the months before the accident, according to Rachel's mother, Rachel started coming home with gifts. Pearl earrings. Gold bracelet. A new laptop. She became closed and distant. When police questioned Mrs. Demarest about the gifts, she threw around accusations. She didn't believe her daughter had had an accident. She wanted the matter looked into because Rachel had been intonating that the Drazen family wasn't all they were cracked up to be. She called the *LA Times*, who interviewed her and dismissed her as a crackpot, and the *LA Voice*, which seemed to be the paper the article was written for.

Suddenly, she didn't want to talk to anyone. She called everything off and became non-responsive to further investigation. No interviews, and only the required police depositions, which she attended with a very expensive lawyer.

The Demarests had been paid off, that much was clear, and the article ended right there, mid-sentence.

"What the fuck?" I said. "Even this thing is half a fucking story."

Darren stepped into his shoe. "What's it say?"

"His girlfriend from sixteen years ago died under suspicious circumstances, and the family paid off anyone associated with it. Or got them fired. For all I know, the rest of the article is about who they killed."

"You gonna tell him?"

I slid the papers back in the envelope. "How can I? I don't know if any of this is true. It could be someone's idea of a short story. He's got enough shit going on without me coming to him with this....this.... I don't even know what this is."

"Gabby's causing trouble from the grave." He shrugged on his jacket. "I like that."

"You would. Can I use your computer? I want to look up some of this."

"Yeah. Not that I care, but will you be here when I get back? You look like you got your walking shoes on."

"I'm going home today." I glanced at my pile of crap, wondering if I could make it on one trip.

"I'm thinking about Gabby's room."

"Move in."

"Did you ask?"

I rolled my eyes. "Fine. I'll ask daddy if it's ok if a boy lives with me."

I thought that was hilarious. Darren didn't.

CHAPTER 64

MONICA

THE ALL-KNOWING INTERNET revealed a big fat goose egg, but I was never much of a researcher. I did find Evert Toth, who had a masthead listing as managing editor of *elLAy Rag*, a local left-wing free paper picked up in coffee shops all over the city. Though one might assume such a paper was trash from front to porn-filled back, it wasn't. Some of the biggest exposes, blown whistles, and no-bullshit journalism happened inside. I called the paper, got routed all over the place, and finally ended up on voice mail. I left a message.

I walked home, phone in hand, unwilling to put it in my pocket. I had something else to do. Someone else to call.

I was many things. I was submissive. I was masochistic. I was trusting. I was a sexual slave. But obedient?

Not as much.

I rooted around my bag and found a matte white card. I stopped at the corner because if I waited until I got home, I might change my mind. I dialed the number. The voice that came over was silky smooth, betraying nothing, giving nothing.

Hello, you've reached the workshop of Jessica Carnes. Please leave a message after the tone, and I'll get back to you as soon as possible. If you are a curator calling to schedule a studio visit, please press five.

I choked a little. I knew what I wanted. I wanted to probe her plans. I wanted to represent myself as her friend and ally to bring back information to Jonathan, but I suddenly felt highly unqualified to protect him.

I almost hung up, but her caller ID would reveal who I was, and if I hung up,

488

I'd look weak and manipulative. She wouldn't trust me. She'd use me. I needed her to respect me if I wanted her to attempt to partner with me.

"Hi, Jessica. This is Monica Faulkner. I'd like to take you up on your offer to talk if it's still on the table. Thanks."

I hung up before I could say something stupid or laugh nervously.

Fuck.

What did I just do?

CHAPTER 65

MONICA

THE STOCK WAS BUSY. Super busy. Wall-of-drunk busy. Ass-pinched-turn-around-and-I-can't-tell-who-did-it busy, especially considering rain threatened on the horizon. I put on a happy face, but my preoccupation reduced the power of my customer-service smile. I couldn't check my phone while I was working, and I needed to know if Jessica had called me back. I wanted to see Jonathan's texts, because I was sure there was at least one.

I barely had time for a break, but I ran to the bathroom. On the way out, I saw Debbie.

"I'm going at midnight," she said. "Robert's handling the tips."

My disappointment must have shown on my face. Not about Robert managing the tips. The system for their division was fool-proof, which was good since Robert needed a system with exactly that name.

"What?" she asked.

"I wanted to talk to you after the shift."

She looked at her watch. "You have four minutes."

"I don't want to say it so fast I offend you and lose my job."

"So don't."

I'd rehearsed it a billion times, but there was no neutral way to ask. "You told me I shouldn't have taken Jonathan seriously, and you told him I'd moved on."

"Yes."

"Why?"

"I don't understand the question. He's not usually serious. It looked to me like you'd moved on." She shrugged as if everything had been on the up and up.

I started to feel like maybe it had been, and I was the one who had the problem. "I'm sorry to be blunt, but it gave me the impression, well...that it was..." I stopped. How had I painted myself into such a corner?

Debbie just waited for me to get myself out. She didn't say a word or look impatient.

"Why do you want us together?" I asked. I managed to not use the word *manipulative*.

"You think I'm motivated by something other than friendship?"

"I don't pretend to know." Another wait. I felt as if I could hear the seconds go by.

Debbie didn't look at her watch, and there was no clock in the hall, but when she straightened a fraction and said, "Time's up," I knew she was right to within the second.

Break over. Time to get back on the floor. The second half of my shift passed painfully but quickly. Every douchebag with a Hugo Boss suit or Audi keys made me want to scream. The intensity must have served me well, because my tips were more than I'd ever seen. I started to think about putting some cash away in my dwindling savings account or buying myself more pretty things to wear under my dresses.

I was snapping my locker closed when Robert came up, a little self-important swagger in his gait.

"Someone's here for you."

I didn't want to smile, but I did. Jonathan had come, obviously. "I'll be right up."

He turned and walked off, calling behind him, "She's by the bar."

"Ok, thanks."

She?

CHAPTER 66

MONICA

I WENT upstairs with less anticipation, less heightened awareness than I would have if I thought I was meeting Jonathan. It was probably Yvonne or some random friend who was passing by and wanted to hit an after-hours.

Seeing a bar after closing, with the lights on and the music off, is much like seeing a beautiful woman without makeup. All the parts are there but made unappealing. Glasses thunk against bus trays, squeaky-wheeled press buckets make their way across the floor behind the slap and swoosh of grey-fringed mops. The staff laughs at each other's jokes, which are invariably on customers. Guests lingered, mostly in earnest conversations about the next destination for drinking or fucking. Some clung by their fingernails, as if a change of venue would break a spell.

In the case of the Stock, the city had darkened beneath us as much as it ever would, and the sky was a burnt orange with reflected light. It was one fifteen in the morning. I had a pocket full of cash. Maybe I'd go the hell out and talk to people. Maybe I'd cling to a venue until four a.m. to avoid sleeping in my house for the first time in weeks.

But I wasn't going out. I wasn't getting drunk, and I wasn't reacquainting myself with anyone. Only one woman was at the bar. It was Jessica, and she was not alone. Jonathan stood over her, and they were arguing fiercely. They looked like a married couple on the verge of a blowout, talking over each other, tense hands in front of them. I didn't want to approach them. But something else took over.

She wasn't supposed to talk to him. She wasn't supposed to be in fifty feet of him. He was mine. I had a reaction that could only be described as biological. Rage filled my blood from some angry gland until my fingertips clenched and my teeth ground together.

Jonathan looked up. As soon as he saw me, he came my way like a torpedo.

"What the fuck?" I said.

He gripped my shoulder and spun me around. "Walk."

"No." He pushed me toward the back room. I shrugged him off. "I want to talk to her. That's why she's here." He took my bicep and yanked me off the floor. "Get off me."

He didn't listen. He pulled me through the halls, past the few coworkers left, along the concrete floors of the back hallways. His face was stern and blank, a fixed mask of intention. He pushed me into the break room, locked the door, and drew shades over the window to the hall. When he finally faced me again, I pushed him away.

"Don't you *ever* do anything like that again," I said.

He pressed me against the wall and put his face to mine in a punishing kiss. I gave in to the heat, the urgency of his mouth on mine, his tongue demanding response, his hands still pushing my shoulders. I groaned into him, my voice a breath I had no choice but to take.

"I told you not to meet with her," he said, face near enough to kiss me again.

"You're not the boss of me."

"Oh no?"

"Dragging me away from a conversation, trying to isolate me, you're giving her quite a case."

"Pick up your skirt."

"Using sex to control me..."

"Show me your cunt, Monica."

I felt a pool of arousal below my waist at the command. Though Jonathan didn't hold my arms, his grip on my shoulders made skidding my hands over my skirt uncomfortable and awkward. I pinched the fabric and bent my wrists, hiking up the skirt one inch, then two. I got a fistful of cotton and yanked. The whole thing rode up as our eyes met, our breath mingling.

"So, what? You going to fuck me now?"

"I am."

"You think that's going to stop me?"

He put a hand at my throat, fingertips at the base of my jaw, forcing me to look at the ceiling. The restriction and posture sent a tidal wave of desire between my legs. I wanted to wrap them around him and take him inside me.

"I've never punished you, goddess. But I will."

"Go on. I'm not scared of you."

He looped his fingers in my panties and drove his fingers along my wet cleft. I gasped and moaned when he thrust two fingers in me. When he pulled them out, I felt their loss. I wanted to be filled with him, despite the fact that he was pissing me off, or because of it. Pressing his torso to mine and keeping his hand on my jaw, he put his wet fingers in my mouth.

"This mouth is mine," he said. "It doesn't talk unless I tell it to."

The taste of my sex filled my mouth as he drove his fingers down my throat. I sucked them clean to please him, to please myself. The sensations caused by his forcefulness were overpowering.

He took his hand off my throat and ran it along my belly, to my thighs, inside them. He found the crotch of my panties and pulled them off. Then, without a pause, he pushed me onto the lunch table. The metal legs scraped the linoleum as he slid me back and bent my legs so my sopping pussy lay before him.

"You're not fucking my decision out of me."

Standing between my legs, he unbuckled his belt. "Don't make me gag you."

I held up my middle finger. He smiled as if he couldn't help it then grabbed my hand and held it down, hard. His thumb dug into my wrist, and I knew my expression broadcast pain. My legs tightened and closed, but he pushed them apart.

"I'm going to fuck you, and you're going to shut the hell up for the fucking duration." He drove into me without an ounce more warning. He fucked me as if he owned me, my body bent, powerless, exposed.

He told me to take it, but he was the one who was doing the taking. He held the meat of my thighs, spreading my legs. The pain of his hands digging into my skin, his banging cock, him standing over me in dominion. I'd never look at those humming fluorescent lights without feeling a buzz in my cunt again.

I got up on my elbows, and he pushed me back down. "Don't move unless I tell you to."

"I'm going to—"

"You are not."

I *was* going to come. A tsunami of pleasure rushed over the horizon, rising waters pooled at my feet, ankles, knees. I had another half a minute to complete oblivion. But his eyes shut and he grunted, then moaned, pushing into me slowly. He was coming, motherfucker, and he'd never just come because he couldn't help it. Outside the first time he fucked me without a condom, he never lost control. Jonathan's orgasms always had a purpose.

Taking his hands off my thighs, he leaned in. "Give me a number between one and ten."

"Two."

"Forget that, then. Between five and ten."

"Seven."

"That's how many times you're coming before sunrise. But you have to come home with me."

"You son of a bitch. We're playing orgasm games again?" I asked.

"You're being a poor sport."

I got up on my elbows, feeling done with that conversation already. "Tomorrow's my day off, and I want to work on some songs."

"I have a piano."

"All my staff pads are at home. All my notes. Forget it."

He picked me up gently by my biceps, but his fingertips sent bolts of not-so-sexy pain through them. He must have seen me flinch. "Are you all right?"

"I'm fine."

"I'll come to your place. Let me drive. Please. Give me a couple of hours to do nothing but make you squirm." He tugged at my skirt, and I hoisted myself up so he could get it back in place.

I put my arms over his shoulders and kissed him. I couldn't help it. I had absolutely no choice. His lips sat so close to mine, and they were so responsive. His tongue ignited the smoldering fire between my legs. I wrapped my legs around him, letting his mouth take mine.

"My place until sunrise," I said as he kissed my jaw, then my neck. "Then you get the hell out so I can get to work."

"To write," he whispered.

"Yes."

"You promise?"

I pulled away. "I might also go to the bathroom once or twice. Do I need to fill out a form or call you first?"

A smile drew across his lips. A joke was incoming, but there was a click as the door was unlocked from the outside. Jonathan got his dick back in his pants before the cleaning crew swung the door open.

CHAPTER 67

MONICA

"Saying I don't know what I'm dealing with is plain insulting."

We were on the matte black rocket, which I loved because I had my arms around him, inside his jacket, and I could feel the angles and bumps of his body. I'd tucked my skirt around my thighs to his satisfaction so I wouldn't expose my pantie-less glory to Los Angeles. Once that was settled, he'd put my helmet on me as if to cut off any further discussion. Talking to him when he was a disembodied voice was hard. I didn't want to wait until we got to my house to talk to him because we'd be in a private place and he'd try to shut me up with sex again. It would work, for the hundredth time.

"I'm not insulting you. I'm telling the truth. Jessica can teach Machiavelli a few things," he said through the speaker in my helmet.

"I need to see your face."

"You'll see plenty."

"Stop the bike."

We were on Sunset, by the Junction, the one neighborhood where people gathered on the street, walking from bar, to restaurant, to bar, to home.

"We'll be to your house in eight minutes."

"Now."

He stopped at a light and pulled off his helmet. His hair spiked and curled with the disruption, and when he turned to me, incredulity was in his eyes. I couldn't hear what he said, and I folded my arms. I meant what I said, no matter his unheard response.

He held the corner of the helmet to his lips, and his voice came through my helmet. "You don't get to give orders."

I pulled off my helmet. I could only imagine what it did to my hair, but I was past giving a shit. I put the helmet on the seat and slid off the bike.

"Monica."

"Jonathan."

The light changed. Horns shrieked. Curses cut the night. Jonathan and I stared at each other as our lane slowly sifted around us.

"What's the problem?" he asked, paying the flipped birds around us no mind.

"I want to talk, and I want to do it somewhere you can't fuck me."

"You think dragging me into a coffee shop is going to stop me from fucking you? Shit, if I want you in the middle of this intersection, I'll take you."

He would, too. But also, he wouldn't.

I stepped away from the bike. A dented Acura came to a screeching halt inches from me.

"Fuck!" Jonathan shouted, swinging his leg over the seat as if he was about to cradle my broken body in his arms.

The Acura's driver cried obscenities. Something about me being a stupid fucking bitch. Blah blah. I'd been called worse on a random Tuesday night at the bar. I flipped him off without even looking, walking backward, drawing Jonathan out of the street.

But what I considered a meaningless gesture, the driver considered a call to arms. He leaned so far out of the car I had no idea how his foot stayed on the brake. "Get your big flapping twat outta the street, you bitch whore!"

Jonathan put the kickstand down on the bike, which I didn't understand. Why on earth would he park it in the middle of the street? The light had turned red again, but obviously that was temporary. The guy in the Acura flung some more curses my way. Apparently, he didn't see the guy with the stone-cold expression heading for him. If he did, he might have stopped calling me a fucking skank and started getting into a defensive posture.

Shit.

I darted in front of Jonathan, but he was moving so fast, I had almost no time to get between them. My ass pressed against the door of the car, and Jonathan was nearly there. I held up my hand. "Stop."

"Get out of the way."

"Hey, bitchface!" said the guy behind me.

"Get the bike, please," I said to Jonathan.

"Get out of the way."

"Are you a fucking adolescent? You're going to get into a fight on Sunset Boulevard? What the fuck? Please, bend me over in the intersection instead."

"You people are fucking crazy!" said the driver the second before the light changed. Despite the fact that I was practically leaning on his car, he took off.

More honking as Jonathan and I stared each other down in the middle of the street. More cursing as his bike sat in the middle of the center lane. We had to yell to be heard over the noise.

"Why can't I meet with Jessica?" I demanded. "Why is it so important to you?"

"You're asking me *here?*"

"If you can fuck me in the intersection, I can ask questions." He grabbed my arm. I shook it off.

"You don't know her! This is a game, and you don't know the rules. If she gave you her number, it's because whatever she's trying to do to me, she's going to use you for."

"So you're protecting yourself," I said.

"And you."

"I don't need protecting," I yelled. A delivery truck missed me by inches as it tried to make the light. The wind shear thrust me forward a few inches.

"Goddess," he said, pulling me to him for safety, "you are a shitload of trouble."

"You sorry you wanted a commitment?" Cars whipped around us at the green, horns screaming again.

"No. You've turned my existence into a life."

An SUV swerved, but we held our gaze. "I'm about to turn it into your death."

As if daring L.A. drivers to hit a couple in the middle of the street on a Saturday night, he leaned over and kissed me. I kissed him back. It's not every day you get to flip off a whole city.

CHAPTER 68

MONICA

I DIDN'T TELL Jonathan my phone had started buzzing while we were in the street. As I dismounted in my driveway, I glanced at it.

Jessica.

As if sensing something was amiss, Jonathan took hold of my wrist. He saw the screen display his ex-wife's phone number in brilliant backlit blue and white. His eyes flicked up to mine, the phone lighting his face from beneath, as the phone purred in my hand like a kitten. His lips tightened.

"What?" I asked.

"You know what."

"I'm not convinced I'm a tool for your destruction. I might be a tool for your salvation. Have you thought of that?"

"What if she told you I fucked her?"

"Did you?"

"No."

"Then what's the problem?"

"You'll believe her. And even if you don't, a part of you will always wonder. She'll alienate us from each other," he said.

"I'm insulted by the notion that I'm going to be used to hurt you. I'm not so weak-willed. Not with her or you. I'm going to see her. I'm going to let her think she's using me, and I'm going to find out what she wants. I'm going to let her think I'm on her side."

He gritted his teeth. "This is not a woman you take on a fishing expedition."

"You may not love her any more, but you respect her. Which is more than I can say for how you feel about me." I walked toward my house. I felt him reach for me, but I was too fast. I jangled my keys and approached my door.

Jonathan came up behind me, pressing his front to my back. "I'm sorry." He nuzzled my ear.

"No, you're not." I turned the key.

"I am."

"Good. I'll let you know how it goes."

He reached around and pushed the door open. "My apology doesn't mean I'm letting you go."

"I'm going."

He pushed me in and slammed the door behind him. He reached for my clothes, attacking my mouth with his, lips churning, tongue probing, hands yanking. My hands explored him as well, taking the edges of his clothing and unbuttoning, unzipping, unfolding, exposing whatever piece of skin I could find. He pushed me back into the bedroom, kissing me as he went, stripping my shirt. He thrust me against the doorframe and lifted my bra, exposing my hard nipples. His tongue found them, then his teeth. I held the back of his head as his hand found my other breast and twisted the nipple he wasn't sucking. My fingers ran through his hair, and my legs wrapped around him. I felt his erection, hard and hot, pressing into me as he shifted and dropped me through the doorway. We fell onto my bed.

He pulled his shirt over his head, exposing his tight, lean frame. I reached for his chest, but he held my hands down and kissed my neck then my breasts, biting where curve met plane.

"Oh! Yes."

"Hurt?"

"Yes," I said, my voice husky with lust. "Again."

He did, biting and sucking the skin of my neck and breasts. I thought I'd explode. The pain was alive, coursing through my body, a sensation like pleasure but hard, cruel, heated. He opened my legs while sucking the skin of my shoulder. My pussy was ready for him. He put his head between my legs, kissing me from knee to the curve where thigh met pelvis.

"Ah, yes," I cried.

He slapped inside my thigh, and the sting went right to my pussy. When he leaned in and bit where he'd slapped, gently, then harder, I uttered affirmations. I didn't want him to stop. I wanted to feel it. All of it. His tongue slid over my clit while he bent my legs to my chest, his teeth on my wet cleft. His fingers scratched my skin and landed in my hole, thrusting inside. It felt, raw, passionate, all-consuming.

He sucked my clit, and the pain made bookends for the pleasure, heightening it. Reaching with his other hand, he put three fingers in my mouth, and I felt bound and helpless, like a hooked fish. The pain was my only companion as the flood of pleasure came. I screamed into his fingers, arching my back and ass off the mattress.

He kept me immobile with his teeth, fingers, and tongue, licking and sucking until even the pleasure was pain, and tears streamed down my face. He picked up his face, kissing inside my thighs, my belly, licking the diamond navel ring that came to signify his ownership of me. I breathed heavily, eyes half-closed in post-orgasmic rapture.

"I'm going to be sore all over tomorrow."

He kissed my cheek, pulling one knee back up to my chest, gently pushing my calf until it rested over his shoulder. "You have no idea how sore you're going to be."

I was so wet from his mouth and my own arousal that he slid all the way into me in one stroke.

"Do it." I gasped. "Make me sore. Make it hurt again."

"I can make it hurt. You know your safe word?" He fucked me slowly, knees under him, my leg over his shoulder.

"Small, orange fruit." I felt another orgasm scratching and mewling at the door. It wanted in, but Jonathan had to turn the handle.

"I need you to promise me something," he said.

"Anything."

"You'll let me take care of my business." He fucked me harder, leveraging himself by gripping my bicep.

"Yes."

"You won't interfere." He went deep into a thudding pain inside.

"Yes, sir."

"Say it."

"Sir. I won't interfere. Just do it. Please." He slapped my breast, then grabbed it painfully before he slapped it again. "Yes!" I cried.

He continued, hurting me just enough to heighten sensitivity, hitting me with exuberance as I cried *yes, yes* so he wouldn't stop. He hit my breasts, my ass, my inner thighs without humiliation or punishment. Only joy. He did it because I liked it, and he liked it. Together, we were red-faced, near laughing, sometimes screaming, twisting, begging, fucking deep and hard, shamelessly gratifying each other's most secret needs.

And when the thunderclouds gathered, coalescing into a solid wall of sensation, blocking out the sun and sky, I had his name on my lips. Pain and pleasure became indistinguishable, and I shut down into a clenching ball of *now*. His face was close to mine. I was twisted in a knot from the pressure he put on my knees and elbows and exposed sensitivities. I caught the last of his orgasm as my sky cleared and I could see the firmament again. He dropped his head in the crook of my neck and bit. The pain brought me back to myself, like a wakeup call from a dead sleep.

When his mouth slackened and his groans stopped, I said, "Ouch."

"Sorry."

I turned my head toward him and laughed at the absurdity of it. He caught on and laughed with me, holding my head close as we kissed, smiling. I untwisted myself and lay flat, joints and muscles loosened. I knew I'd suffer tomorrow from our fucking, as well as the promise I had no intention of keeping.

CHAPTER 69

JONATHAN

I ORDERED breakfast from the diner around the corner, and when the delivery guy rang the doorbell, I was on the patio setting out plates. I heard the bathroom door shut. She was awake.

What Monica didn't know, and what helped me sleep, was that her house had been swept twice for cameras while she'd spent weeks crashing on her friend's couch. The place was clean, so I felt fine about giving her the roughest fuck I'd given anyone in my life. Even with Sharon, who'd suffered getting shit beaten out of her to the point of an emotional breakdown, I'd been more careful. She was breakable. Others had done a good job of proving that.

Monica, on the other hand, was made of tough stuff. That toughness was showing in her insistence on seeing my ex-wife. I had a gut feeling that by seeing Jessica on her terms and her turf, Monica would be walking into more than she could handle. She thought they would have a conversation, but it would be a game. The end result would be us separated by my ex-wife's casual half-truths and outright lies.

The idea that I could keep tabs on Monica until the whole thing went away looked more and more impossible. I couldn't suddenly restrict her. She was used to being her own woman. She had to work, and she had to play music. I couldn't put a team of people on her when she'd just gotten over the cameras in the house. I had to make her not *want* to see Jessica, and the only way to do that was to make the trouble she was causing seem unimportant. It was a good strategy, and I was failing at it.

She came out as I finished putting out her tea. She wore a long-sleeved, black turtleneck and skinny jeans. She walked stiffly, but her smile was loose and relaxed.

"Good morning," I said.

"The king sets the table."

"He's hungry." I put my hands at her neck and kissed her. Her lips tightened. I pulled back and saw what had made her flinch—a tiny smear of reddish-grey where my fingertip had touched her jaw. Stroking her collar away, I saw that her neck was covered in bite marks and bruises. "Jesus Christ."

She refolded the collar until her neck was covered. "I didn't know whether to show you or not."

"Up." I tugged at the hem of her sweater. She bit her lip. "Come on."

"The last time I looked like this, you felt too bad about it to fuck me."

I pulled up the shirt. She lifted her arms, her face contorted in pain. I pulled the sweater off completely, and she tucked her head so the collar would expand around her. She stood before me, naked from the waist up, looking as though she'd been beaten in a back alley. The curves under her breasts were deep red where blood vessels had broken under my teeth, and the mounds themselves were bruised. The bend of her neck had the same beaten mottle. Her biceps were blackened in fingertip shapes. I touched them lightly, drawing my fingers down to the striated ligature marks on her elbows.

"Your knees?"

"Yeah," she said. "Matching marks on those. You tied me really tight."

"You said it felt okay."

"It did."

"Your thighs? Your ass?"

"I'm fine." She put her hand on my face, but I didn't want to be comforted. I unbuttoned her pants.

"Come on," I said. "Let me see."

She slid her pants down, pain on her face. She'd have to put them back on and that would hurt, but it was too late to undo the order. I kneeled, sliding the jeans over her legs. Her thighs were a mess, and her knees did indeed have matching marks from when I'd tied the joints together with an extension cord.

"Don't be sorry," she said, stroking my hair as I kissed her bruised legs.

"I am."

"I said not to be."

"I don't take orders."

"You should try it. It's amazing."

From my kneeling position, I eased her into a chair and spread her legs, kissing the devastation inside them. I didn't have a mother's healing kiss on a scratched knee, but I had no other way to show her the pain in my heart at seeing her hurt and knowing that I'd done it and I'd do it again and again.

"You only came six times last night," I said. "I promised seven."

"I couldn't take another."

I probed her folds with my tongue. "Take it now."

"I need my tea," she groaned, running her fingers through my hair. I didn't touch her with anything but my mouth. My hands had done enough damage. Though pain had been welcome a few hours earlier, the aftermath would be straight pain, without the accompaniment of pleasure. I wove my arms around her until her hands found mine, and I clasped them as my mouth worked in service to her. Gently. Without urgency. Her sweet, sore cunt tasted coppery, like raw flesh but got wet and responsive, her clit filling into a hard, slick pebble under me.

She groaned as I worked her with my tongue and lips, teeth tucked safely away. I looked up at the broken skin of her chest, making eye contact as her lips whispered my name, and I prayed to whatever deity would listen to please, please not take her away. She arched, clenched, gasped like the beautiful kitten she was. When I leaned up to her, fresh cunt on my lips, my phone dinged.

"You gonna get that?" she asked.

"When I'm done kissing you." I put my hands on the arms of her chair and slowly put my lips on hers. I wanted an unrushed moment of forgiveness and gentleness.

"Can you make love to me?" she asked.

"No."

"Why not?" She drew her legs around me. I knew it hurt.

"I'm flattered, but I'm simply not attracted to you."

She had her hand on my erection before I could back away. "Really?" She smiled, kissing me, stroking me.

"That? That's nothing. Something I left in my pocket." She could stroke my dick all day, but there was no way I was taking her in the condition she was in.

"Please? I'll beg."

"Tempting offer. But I'm hungry." I pulled away. As I went to sit down for breakfast, my phone dinged again, then rang.

"You'd better check it," Monica said, pulling her sweater back over her head. "Could be a towering inferno at Hotel K and you didn't know about it because you were eating eggs."

I checked. Margie. And it was Sunday. I looked at Monica then pocketed the phone.

"Jonathan, I see your face. Take the call, would you?" She stepped into her jeans gingerly, eyes like chocolate coins, looking at me as if I was being serious over nothing.

"Save me some," I said as I started to step away from the table.

"You got enough for an infield and everyone in the dugout."

I slipped my phone out of my pocket and walked down the stairs to the driveway. With one look back at my goddess buttoning her pants, I answered the phone. "Margie. Working on the Lord's day?"

"Your problems never rest, Jonny. Your beautiful and talented ex-wife wants a meeting."

"Today?" I climbed up to Monica's front porch, noticing the cracked, slipping foundation still hadn't gotten fixed.

"Tuesday. And in other bad news, are you sitting?"

"Out with it." I sat on the porch swing. It creaked.

Margie took a deep sigh of a breath, which she never did, because she was utterly unflappable.

"Come on. Speak. I'm sitting."

"It's Rachel."

My brain stopped functioning.

"Jonny?"

"Can you be more specific?"

"Why did you move her a month ago?"

I heard Monica getting plates and silverware together. If I could hear her, she could hear me unless I was careful. Even if I remained cryptic, Monica had enough intellectual curiosity to connect the dots into the shape of a web of lies.

"I moved her to protect someone."

"Monica? Or yourself?"

"Yes. I'm a selfish prick. I have someone I don't want to lose, and I needed to protect that. If I left her where she was, Jessica could have shown Monica where she was. I needed to maintain a little plausible deniability."

I had panicked very badly when Debbie called six weeks ago and said Jessica had shown up at the Stock and said something so upsetting to Monica that she was visibly shaken. I'd been convinced Jessica insinuated things about Rachel. Because everyone in the world who had cared about her, and there were painfully few, thought she was dead.

She wasn't. Not quite.

Jessica knew everything. At our engagement party, I'd been hypnotized as a party joke and remembered what the whiskey had blacked out. Rachel had survived the crash. She didn't walk away. But on the night of the Christmas rains, she'd been pulled out of the ocean with a part of her brain intact. Jessica had helped me find Rachel and helped me move her. She'd helped me fail in finding her family. Mother dead. Father disappeared. Her stepfather had never been worthy of her. Jessica, by my side, had reminded me to man up and take responsibility for my part in her condition.

"Okay, I know you did your best," Margie said, her tone promising bad news. "But people in vegetative states don't travel well. I just got word from the new facility that she has pneumonia."

"She's had it before."

"She's dying, little brother. I'm sorry."

CHAPTER 70

MONICA

JONATHAN LEFT me with a lot of breakfast.

He'd come back without any color in his face, looking as if he was miles away. With no chance in hell of talking him into a good-bye screw, I walked him out.

"I'm going to be gone for a few days," he said. "I'm sorry."

"We talked about this. You travel. It's fine."

He stood half on the porch, half on the steps when he turned back to me. "You promised you wouldn't see my ex-wife."

That was a hard comment to answer. If I told him I had every intention of seeing Jessica, he'd worry needlessly. If I said otherwise, I'd be lying. "Jonathan, honestly, promises made while I'm in a submissive posture shouldn't count."

He paused, looking at our clasped hands. "Probably not."

Even though it hurt to lift my arms, I put my palms on his cheeks. He did not look well. His skin was cold. There really must have been a towering inferno at Hotel K.

"I have a meeting with her on Tuesday," he said. "Can you wait until after that?"

"I don't see why not."

My sneaky non-promise must have been completely transparent to him. There was a pretty good chance the only time I'd get to see her was when he was out of town and unable to use his dick to lure me away. He knew it. I knew it. Pretending otherwise was absurd. Yet we did. Somehow, he was willing to take the chance and walk down the steps to his bike after a deep, soulful goodbye kiss that let me know he was still my master and king.

I cleaned up breakfast and dressed to rehearse. I had a lot to say about pain and its relationship to desire, glory, satisfaction. Maybe I had too much to say, because I wrote a seven-page ramble of a song with three alternating choruses and verses up the wazoo. I still felt as though I hadn't scratched the surface.

My body ached. I was tired. I felt isolated. Jonathan's touch stayed on me in the soreness between my legs, the rawness of my lips, the sharp bite of pain when I moved my arms. I pulled my collar up over my face to see if his smell lingered. It did, if only slightly, and I kept the collar up even though it increased the heat of my longing with every breath.

A couple of days. How could I last that long? How would I think about anything else? And what would happen on the next two-week trip? Did he think I would agree to come with him every time?

When I realized I'd been staring at the piano keys for twelve minutes, I shut off the metronome and crawled into bed. Our scents lingered on the sheets like the twin deities, pain and pleasure, lulling me to sleep with thoughts of their harmonized perfection.

CHAPTER 71

MONICA

I woke when the sky was melting from light to dark, and the nest of crickets outside my window started screaming their mating call. Every living thing was trying to fuck, except me. My aches took on a new level of sharpness after a decent rest, and the smell of sex exhausted me. I stripped the bed.

I'd brought piles of clothes back from Darren's. I hadn't done laundry in his building unless it was absolutely necessary, but I was home now. The sheets needed doing, and the towels, and my clothes, obviously. The Bordelle underthings I hand-washed lovingly, caressing them the way he did.

I passed Gabby's closed door a dozen times. That part of the house was as much mine as it ever was, but I still couldn't go in without Darren. I still braided my hair for her. I still kept what little music she'd written to integrate into my mine, to save her name and her legacy.

The battery on my phone had died, so I plugged it in and went about cleaning my bathrooms, mopping the kitchen floor, doing all the things I'd neglected while I was away. In my mind, the metronome ticked in four-four time. A song was bubbling up, and my verbal mind waited patiently while my non-verbal brain processed the point and purpose of it.

I was on the porch shaking the dust out of the couch throws when the phone blooped. It must be Jonathan saying something that would make me smile. I ran to it.

—*Are you there?*—

—Yes—

*—I feel your hands on the
phone—*

*—I miss you already. Can we
have a call—*

*—Can't. Just checking
in. I feel good knowing you're
there, and mine—*

The subtext was he felt good knowing I was there and doing what he told me. Which meant, no Jessica. He either thought very little of me believing I was obedient, or a lot believing I'd get the right message from so few words. Or maybe I should just take it at face value.

Bored, I checked my email from the phone. I hadn't set up digital roaming while out of the country, and then the phone died, and the fact was, email wasn't my thing. Most of my social interactions were local and done with a phone call or text.

But that couldn't be said for everyone. I'd given Harry Enrich my information after the B.C. Mod show, and shockingly, he'd used it, sending me a personal note early Friday.

MS. FAULKNER,

IT WAS a pleasure to hear your work tonight. I understand Eddie Milpas has been working to sign you on with us. Why don't you come by our offices Tuesday to discuss further?

BEST,

HARRY

PS – Do you have representation?

EDDIE HAD BEEN WORKING to sign me? Sounded like he was trying to put a collar on my neck and shackle me to a display case, but who was I to question?

My phone rang while it was still in my hand. I didn't usually answer numbers I didn't recognize, but the green button was a reflex, and I put the phone to my ear. "Hello?"

"Hello." The voice was female and tight as a drum. Pleasant, but not effusive. Welcoming, but not warm. "This is Jessica Carnes. Am I speaking with Monica?"

"Yes." I sat on the piano bench, willing myself not to shake. All of Jonathan's warnings and the events of my two prior meetings with Jessica blew out my nerves. I had to remind myself to channel him, his utter dedication to self-management no matter his feelings.

"How are you?" she asked.

I had no answer prepared. No story to tell to get what I wanted. "I'm fine. You?"

"Very well, thank you," she said. I didn't think I had another nicety left in me, and she saved me from having to come up with another. "You left me a message?"

Oh, she was going to make me ask. She wasn't giving me an inch or admitting she had made first contact at Frontage. She wasn't going to admit she'd shown up at my job at whatever o'clock in the morning. "I thought I'd take you up on that offer to meet."

"Things have gotten a little more complicated since we spoke last."

"Yes...I...I guess you're right. I thought you came to see me last night. Never mind."

After saying that, I felt a sense of relief. I was avoiding immediate repercussions from seeing Jessica, and it wasn't even my fault. Coward. Yes, that was the craven woman. I wasn't her any more. But I couldn't push Jessica. If she wanted to wiggle out she would, no matter what.

"If you feel differently at some point, I would like to meet. We can do it under your terms and talk about whatever you like," I said.

"Why the change of heart?"

"Things got more complicated, like you said. I feel like I can't see the whole picture." That was probably too specific and would leave me little room to flip my story around if I needed, but that was it. I said it, and it was very close to the truth.

"Can you get to Venice in the morning?"

"Yes." A lump rose in my throat. I was doing it. I was going directly against Jonathan's wishes. I had to remind myself that I wasn't trying to hurt him. I was trying to help him.

"I'll text you the address."

"Okay. Thanks." I had nothing else to say, so I hung up.

I'd started an evil thing and had to go through with it because I wouldn't stand by and watch him get run over. Maybe I was going out on a limb, and maybe I'd make it worse, but how could I sit still while someone was trying to hurt him?

"Fuck," I whispered. My car was at the Stock.

CHAPTER 72

MONICA

A BLACK CORVETTE pulled up in front of the house, taking the downhill nice and slow. Robert cared about his ride the way most people cared about living things. I skipped down the porch and met him at the curb.

"Thanks," I said, getting in. I was more or less on the way from the valley, but it was still an inconvenience for him.

"Fucking hill, man." He put the car in gear and inched downward.

"When I was a kid, I rode my bike down it, no hands."

"Bet you did." He paused briefly. "So, car's at work, huh?"

"Yeah."

"You went home with the guy from Hotel K? Sam and Debbie's friend?"

"You got a problem with it?"

"Naw, man. Just curious what his deal is."

I didn't know what he meant, and I didn't want to know what he meant, either. I just wanted to get my car. I didn't want to hear about anything Robert might have seen or heard. Nothing. Not a word.

We sat in silence down Temple, to Hill, around the block a few times or ten until we stopped at a light a block from the hotel. It was the same light Jonathan had stopped at when he met me after work and told me he'd always love his ex-wife.

"What did you *think* his deal was?" I asked.

Robert snapped out of some sort of reverie. "Huh? Who?"

"Jonathan, the guy from Hotel K?"

512

"Shit, I don't know. He was there that time you couldn't talk, then gone, then....coupla weeks, he was in the corner yacking with Debbie and Sam all the time. But not when you were there. Shows up last night, you're there. I dunno. Just asking."

"Asking what?"

"Is it serious or what?"

"Yes. It's serious," I said.

"All right. Thanks for letting a guy know."

The light changed, and I laughed to myself.

"What?" He turned into the lot.

"I thought you were going to tell me that you saw him with other women."

He looked at me and smiled, turning into the employee level. "Guys don't rat on other guys."

"Robert! Don't even—"

"But there was nothing to rat. Seriously. Stop with the girl style. It don't suit you." He pulled in next to my little black Honda.

"Fine. I wouldn't have believed you anyway." I blooped my car and got out.

Robert cut the engine and pulled his small black duffel from the back. "You think I'd lie?" He slung the duffel over his muscular shoulder. "I'm not saying I woulda minded getting with you for a night, but I wouldn't lie to do it."

"I don't think you'd lie," I said, getting in my car. "I think you could misunderstand."

"That's where you're wrong."

"Oh really?"

"Yeah. If I saw him with someone, and it was something, I'd know."

I looked him up and down. "You know what? I believe you." I turned the ignition. Nothing happened. Just one click. "Uh oh. Do you have time to give me a jump?"

"Turn it again."

I did. One click, then nothing.

"It's your starter." He walked to the front of the car and knocked on the hood. "Pop it."

I did. He lifted the hood and chocked it up with the metal brace.

"Should I turn it again?"

"Yeah."

I did. Same. I got out and stood next to Robert as he shone his phone's light at the engine, analyzing the mass of wires, compartments, and hoses. I knew what most of it was but not how to fix it.

"All right. If you got a bad starter, I can bang it while you kick it over. Sometimes that kinda gets it going. But you need a new one, probably."

"Shit."

"Yeah, except... It should be right there. Just back of the battery and down, past these wires that serve the electricity. But there's bolt holes. No starter."

"What do you mean?"

He looked more closely then got under the car. I leaned down, amazed at how he would just crawl under a chassis out of curiosity.

"Do you want a proper flashlight?" I asked. "I think I have one in the trunk."

"Nope. I'm telling you. There's no fucking starter on this car. It got jacked."

"My *starter*? Are they expensive?"

"Three hundred. Two? Look, I know it's weird but..." He shrugged.

"Oh my God," I said, realizing who would do the surgery required to remove a starter from a twelve-year-old Japanese car. "Fucking Jonathan. Son of a goddamn bitch."

He'd stranded me. I couldn't get out to Venice without a car. A cab would cost a fortune, and if a bus that far out of town even existed, it would take hours one way. I couldn't get the car fixed in time for a meeting in Culver City in the morning. That was why he'd left so easily. He walked away accepting that I had no intention of keeping any promise I made while my legs were spread. I should have known better.

"I gotta get to work," said Robert. "You wanna call a tow?"

"Nope. I'll figure it out."

"How you getting home?"

"I'm not. I'm going to go upstairs and get a whiskey. Then I'm going out. If I can't drive, I can drink."

"Debbie's gonna make you pay for it."

"Fine. I'm not too broke for a little alcohol." I took out my phone when we got to the back hall and scrolled to Jessica's last text. I didn't want to talk to her. The ice in her voice put me on edge. I had no idea how I would handle our conversation tomorrow.

"You can get some guy at the bar to buy you a few," Robert said, stopping by the lockers.

"No way."

> *—Sorry. Can't make it out to Venice tomorrow. Maybe somewhere more east?—*

"Why not? It's just a drink."

"It's cheating."

"Girls are crazy. I'm tellin' you, if I were a girl and I had a nice pair, I'd never pay for a drink."

> *—My studio in Culver City, then?—*

I loved how she managed to keep it on her turf. If I asked her for an Echo Park location, she'd probably manage to find a place she rented, owned, or regularly patronized.

"If you were a girl with a nice pair," I said, "you'd be the one all the guys wanted to fuck but hated. You'd have a string of one-night or one-week stands until the guy saw you letting someone else buy you drinks. Then you'd only attract the guys looking to spend a little money and put their dicks somewhere comfortable. You'd wake up one morning at fifty years old with a pair that wasn't so nice any more, and you'd wish you'd bought your own."

—Great. Thanks for the change.
See you at ten?—

Robert and I walked up together. "You don't know nothing about men. Sure, we might get a drink for a girl like you to get laid. But being seen with you? That's what gets *other* girls. See what I'm sayin'?"

"No. I'm still buying my own drinks."

"Whatever."

I sat in the corner in the same spot Jonathan had been known to occupy and tried to arrange a car for the next morning. Darren had work the next day, but once he found out what I was doing, he refused to let me drop him off in the morning and borrow his car, texting me like he was my fucking therapist:

—You have a way of sabotaging
your own happiness. I'm opting out—

A guy with glittering dark brown eyes, messy black hair, and a mouth like a movie star leaned on the bar next to me. "What are you drinking?"

"Piss and vinegar." I was busy answering Darren's accusation in a flurry.

"That a new thing?" he asked. "What's in it?"

I pulled my eyes away from my phone for a second. "Piss. Also, vinegar."

He laughed. Ignoring my bludgeon of a hint, he leaned toward me. "Let me get you your next one. I'll piss in it myself."

I slugged the dregs of my whiskey, letting the ice cube linger on my lips. I parted them to touch my tongue to it, reminding me of Jonathan, the master of melting ice. I slid the glass to Mister Eyes and said, "Piss your little heart out."

He looked at the empty glass then back at me. I turned to my phone. I should have known better than to be a total bitch, because in L.A. you never knew who you were speaking to, but I missed Jonathan. I was angry at him and I was trying to avoid lashing out.

—Nice try with the car. I'm not Kevin.
You can't orchestrate my demise—

—Lil can take you anywhere
you want to go—

"Someone break your heart today?" Mister Eyes asked.

"No, but really," I said, "it's not personal. I'm sure you're awesome. But there are a hundred girls in here right now who are available. Okay?"

515

—Except where I want—

—Please wait until I get back. We
can talk—

—I am officially done talking—

I slipped my phone into my pocket. When I looked up, Debbie was watching me. That alone was not abnormal, but I felt as if they were Jonathan's eyes watching me talk to a handsome man, and I was suddenly uncomfortable.

I texted around and got some responses. A party in Koreatown. A show in Silver Lake. Nothing appealed. Fuck going out. I walked out to catch one of the cabs that usually waited outside the hotel. If I was seeing Jessica, I'd need a good night's sleep.

CHAPTER 73

JONATHAN

THE MACHINES BEEPED AND SIGHED, blinking like the dashboard on a 747. The room smelled of rubbing alcohol and dying flesh, and in the darkness laid a once beautiful, intelligent woman who had been reduced, by me, to a pile of idly reproducing cells. I'd been driving that night. Drunk. Stoned. Stupid. Then I passively let my family cover it up while I sat in a padded room feeling sorry for myself.

Sixteen years, a dark room, and maybe she would finally get what she'd always wanted. She'd wanted to be free of her family, and by the time Jessica and I had found her, they were dead or missing. She'd wanted to be free of hunger and pain, and she'd gotten just that. But I didn't think this was what she'd had in mind.

I'd gone from her lover to her guardian because no one else cared. She'd been forgotten, and I was the carrier of her memory. The man who broke her became her keeper. When she'd "died," everyone felt sorry for me. Even though I had no memory of what happened, I knew something was wrong. I knew there was a debt to be paid. When Jessica and I found out she was alive and we'd sent a team of smart men and woman to find her, I'd hoped she'd be in some suburban house with two kids and a dog. But the trail had led us to an expensive, secret facility for people who couldn't move. Fuck, how I'd cried and thanked God and the saints for Jessica's shoulder.

A million years before, we'd lain on our backs on the grass of Elysian Park, where my family would never find us. Rachel liked to wonder what it was like to be me. She thought I had not a worry in the world. Yes, my father was a fucking sociopath, but he didn't stick his fingers inside me like hers had, and he didn't scream and hit me and lock me in the house like her stepfather had. Whatever I endured would end when my trust fund spread its legs at twenty-one. For her, the light at the end of the tunnel had not appeared.

"Do you wish for things you can't buy?" she'd asked.

I'd looked over at her. Blades of grass sat in the foreground of my vision, slashing her face, which was turned to me. Her eyes were tobacco brown, wide and light with sun inside them. "You're fascinated with money," I said.

"I think I am." She'd smiled. "It's made you different, you know. You're fearless. It's exciting, kind of. Watching you is like watching someone who's really, truly free."

I'd laughed. I never felt free in my life. "What do you wish for? Besides money."

"You make me sound like a gold digger."

"You are, but you're terrible at it. I think a few more years and you'll be sleeping with the right guy."

She'd flung herself on top of me and pinched my sides. I laughed and rolled her over until I had her pinned.

"Tell me what you wish for, and if it's any part of my body, your wish will come true at the Regency Hotel in forty minutes."

She'd giggled and turned her face to the sunlight. "Free, Jonathan. I wish to be free."

I'd unpinned one of her shoulders to pluck a seeded dandelion out of the grass. "Blow." I held the white puffball in front of her.

She'd blown hard, and the seeds went into my face. We laughed, and blew the rest of the seeds off together, wishing her free from the constraints of her family and her scarcity. They floated away on their sinuous parachutes, like little messengers to God, saying *take me, take me, take me. Set me free.*

CHAPTER 74

MONICA

THE BUS. West on Sunset. South on La Cienega. Hour and a half. A cab ride from
my house to Jessica's studio was fifty bucks one way. I wished I could have taken
the hundred for a round-trip cab out of Jonathan's ass, but that would have to wait
for another day.

I wore three-quarter sleeves and long pants. I wrapped a scarf with a spider
web pattern around my neck to cover the bruises. I felt lucky it was getting cold,
but I had no idea how I'd hide the roughness of my private life in the summer.

The walk was a quarter mile, but it was cool, and I'd worn comfortable shoes.
Jonathan hadn't texted me back the night before, nor had I received a nine a.m.
ding. Was he angry? Was he shutting me out because I hadn't fallen for the busted
starter trick? Or was the emergency that pulled him away so dire he couldn't
answer me? Both concerned me. I had a gnawing anxiety that grew worse with
every step toward Jessica's studio.

Up ahead, a big white truck was parked and running outside a light industrial
building. The building was painted west-side tasteful—charcoal, with white trim
and a chartreuse door—and guys in bunny suits trotted in and out with six-inch
diameter hoses. I checked the address, and I was sure I had the right one.

A guy in a polo shirt put orange cones on the sidewalk, stopping me. "Street's
closed."

"Is that twelve thirty-eight?"

"Sure is."

"I have an appointment here."

"Not today, you don't. Got a lead and asbestos removal team coming in. It's a hazard, so you're going to have to go around the block if you want to pass."

I pulled out my phone. No message. Crossing the street, I craned my neck around the truck and saw Jessica in the side alley, arguing with a guy holding a clipboard. Her smooth veneer was slipping, just a little. It seemed to be as much of a surprise to her as it was to me.

Of course.

Jonathan.

Well. Didn't that just suck ass.

I started calling him and thought better of it. I texted him and deleted the whole thing. I'd already thrown out one unfounded accusation and gotten no reply. A string of them would do no more than make me look psychotic.

I walked to Washington Boulevard, where I'd at least be able to find a café where I could sit down and blow my cab money. I found a purple building housing a tea shop called Yellow Threat. I got something hot and herbal and sat down on the outdoor patio.

She texted me soon after.

—So sorry. I'll be held up 30 min—

I felt like her co-conspirator at that point. Jessica and me against Jonathan. I was determined to understand the situation so I could help him. His ex-wife, perfectly content with his broken heart until she saw him with me, was hell-bent on destroying him for money and spite. She wanted to meet so she could use me, and Jonathan wanted to prevent that so I didn't hurt myself or him. Both of them underestimated me.

They forgot I was a musician, that I'd gone to a performing arts school and been the victim of manipulation and backstabbing. I'd already opened my case and found my strings cut and my staff notes swapped. I'd already been given the wrong time for auditions. I couldn't come out of that world without learning a thing or two.

—I'll be at Yellow Threat for an hour
if you want to come by—

Jessica and I, working against Jonathan to see each other. Ridiculous, yet somehow inevitable.

I checked my watch. I'd definitely lost a writing day. I wasn't happy about it, but there was nothing I could do but warm my hands on my tea. The sidewalk made the block walkable, but it was empty. The light industrial street had been taken over by architects and production companies at the turn of the twenty-first century, and they'd painted everything in bright colors and edgy murals. I noticed one of Geraldine's half a block away. She'd painted the side of the building to look as if I could see through it to the highway, as if she wanted to negate whatever happened inside.

I saw him walking across the crosswalk in a dark suit with a blue shirt open at the collar. His black hair caught the wind, and his eyes scanned every plane and surface.

"Mr. Santon," I said when he reached me, "what a coincidence."

"You believe in those?" He sat down.

"No. I'm assuming my lover sent you to talk me out of seeing his ex-wife?"

"Close. But no. I can't tell you what he hired me to do, except I'm not supposed to be sitting at a table with you."

"You must have put your own cameras in the house. If you know where I've been, I don't know how. I haven't seen you."

"That was off the table, obviously. We're not watching you. We're watching the other one. And you'll never see us, Ms. Faulkner. Any trace of us is gone before we even are."

"Big scary ops guys. My dad always said he could take any of you in a brawl."

"The idea is to avoid the brawl in the first place. Knowing what I know, which is too much, everyone involved wants to avoid a clusterfuck. Except you and Ms. Carnes. So I am going to sit here and enjoy a cup of tea, until night if necessary. If anyone joins you, I'll be right here. Then I am going to drive you home."

I leaned forward, elbows on the table. "How do I shake an ops guy?"

"Guys. Plural." He glanced at a guy on a cell phone halfway down the block. He gestured and spoke loudly to make himself just another piece of furniture. Someone standing quietly with a phone to his ear would attract notice. Then Santon glanced at a black Toyota at the light and waved to the driver with a flick of his wrist. The driver flicked back and drove off when the light changed.

Great. Even if I ran away and jumped in a cab, I'd have to shake the other two. "He needs to trust my loyalty."

"That's between you and him." He twisted around, hailing a waitress. "Personally, I don't give a shit."

The waitress came, and he ordered himself a cup of coffee and a muffin. She flirted with him, a nervous grin crossing her face. He was a nice-looking guy. I'd forgotten to notice.

"What's with the pinkie ring?" I asked when the waitress left.

He held up the simple gold band always present on his pinkie, not an affectation or accessory as I'd assumed. "My wife's."

"She wearing yours?"

"Around her neck, with her dog tags. We swapped when we re-upped. Weren't there four weeks when she took sniper fire half a mile from the Green Zone."

"I'm sorry."

"It was messy. Death always is."

"You understand, I'm just trying to protect him."

"I'm just trying to do my job."

I sipped my tea, and we sat in silence as his coffee was brought. A black Mercedes stopped at the light. A blonde driving. Jessica. The parking lot was around the corner, and her blinker flashed for the turn.

I looked at Santon, and though his eyes appeared to be on the scalding black coffee he was about to swallow in a single gulp, he gazed in the halfway point between the table and the street. Blank sidewalk, but Jessica and I would be in his peripheral vision.

Jessica saw me, and I shook my head. She nodded and turned off her blinker. Will Santon could take me home. Motherfucker.

CHAPTER 75

MONICA

I KNEW Will wasn't gone for good. I had a gig at Frontage that was well-attended, including a table of five guys in agent-gear by the warm speakers. I greeted them, played, and said goodbye with a stinker of a smile, but my heart felt made of lead. Jonathan hadn't called, texted, written. No contact besides Will Santon's unwelcome presence.

Could he be that mad?

Was that *how* he got mad? Falling off the face of the earth? How was I supposed to react?

Irrelevant questions. What I needed to ask myself was how I *wanted* to react. So I called him. It went to voice mail, which I didn't want. There would be no angry, terse, or blustery messages. I texted.

—Are you shutting me out? WTF?—

I had friends who had given men their hearts only to find them turned to ice directly after. Or slept with them after declarations of indefinite amounts of attraction, but the indefinite amounts lasted no more than a week. I wondered if that was what I was dealing with. Had my commitment to him chased him away? Or did he expect my submission to be an abdication of control over my decisions? Was obedience required inside and outside the bedroom? Had I missed that point on the list?

I couldn't have. I never would have allowed it, and neither would he.

I had just gotten home when my phone blooped. I dug around my bag and

523

found it, hoping against hope that it was Jonathan. An outsized level of disappointment flooded me. It was Jessica.

—I'm at Make on Echo Park
and Baxter. I believe you're nearby?—

That presented a problem. It was a block and a half away, but I had to get there. I believed Santon when he said I wasn't being watched, but Jessica was. That meant something or someone would stop us from meeting in that block and a half.

Fuck it.

I looked out the back door. My house was built on a lot that was nearly vertical toward the rear. A retaining wall of cinderblock held the hill at bay, barely. Behind it, untouched chaparral stretched five hundred feet to a walkable dirt alley kids used to get into trouble. The whole stretch was unlandscapable without a bunch of money, which Dr. Thorensen had, apparently. His plot was terraced into vegetable gardens, private spaces, and a little utility area with a shed. My part of the hill, naturally, had fallen to scrub and brush. A hundred-year-old ficus with exposed roots was on the downslope, and wildflowers bloomed in spring. In the first weeks of December, dead thorns twisted around the trees, weeds turned to sticks, and brown was the new black.

I'd have to go through that to get to the path, then get spit out onto Echo Park Avenue. Of course, it wouldn't work. I'd get bitten by a rattlesnake or something. Worse, Santon, who'd probably taken a vow to never sleep again, would be waiting for me on the street.

I dug my old cowboy boots out of the back of the closet, and a pair of jeans I didn't care about. I'd spent the whole day trying to get this done, and I wasn't giving up yet.

My yard needed some love. I hadn't trimmed anything at the end of summer, so the flagstones and garden patches were covered in dead leaves and detritus. I tossed the pink and orange balls back over the fence to the Montessori school and made for Dad's tangerine tree. He'd planted it for me before he and Mom moved away, saying it would feed me if I got hungry. It just kept growing and was high enough to hug the spaghetti of power lines crisscrossing the sky. I used it as leverage to climb the wall onto the overgrown slope.

It was pitch dark back there. The path was no more than a right-of-way between the backs of houses. Echo Park and Silver Lake were full of untended spaces. Staircases built during the Depression, forgotten paths that were never lit or patrolled that were taken over by residents for extra garden space or burial grounds for unwanted cars.

I grabbed saplings and vines to pull myself up the hill. There was garbage everywhere. Just as I was thinking about how I had to get up there in the daytime with a few plastic bags and clean it out, I was pushed into the ficus.

"Where are you going, goddess?" His voice came from behind me.

His breath in my ear, his scent in my nose, the feel of his chest on my back, the way he fit like a puzzle piece... I didn't even want to ask him what the fuck he was doing in the woody part of my backyard.

"You didn't call." I leaned my head back and exposed my throat. He made me forget everything when he unlooped my scarf and put his mouth on my neck, his lips a lightning rod for the electricity to my core.

"I was busy. I'm sorry." His teeth found the place where my neck met my shoulder, and he gifted me a little crush of pain that translated directly to pleasure. I sucked in my breath. He ran his hands down my arms, to my hands.

"Apology rejected. Return to sender."

Knotting his palms to the backs of my hands, he pressed them to the tree trunk.

"Spread your legs," he said in my ear. I wasn't fast enough. He kicked them apart. He was so fucking rough, and the precarious feeling of not knowing what he'd do next sent a gush of moisture between my legs.

How long would Jessica wait? Until tomorrow. Because Jonathan had appeared, and his hands were on my stomach, pushing up my bra. He pressed my bruised places gently while finding the untouched spots and pushing his hands against them until I groaned.

"You want something?" he asked.

"I missed you."

"I missed you, too." His voice softened as if he meant it, and his hands drifted down to my waistband.

"Are you going to fuck me?"

He unbuttoned my jeans and unzipped without answering, pressing his cock against my ass. I ground against him. "God, I want to." He took my right hand from the tree trunk and, still pressing my left to the tree, he slid it down my pants. "But it looks like you're going somewhere?"

"Yes."

"You wet?"

I ran my finger to my hole and felt the sopping, slick mass under it. "Yes."

He removed his hands from mine but curved his body around me, his front to my back, his voice in my ear. "How wet?"

"Fuck-me-now wet."

"Touch your clit. Do it so it feels good."

I rubbed my engorged member with one finger, circling it, pushing myself into him.

"Two fingers," he said, pulling away just a little. "Use two fingers on it, letting the center fall in the crease between them."

I moaned.

"Feel good, goddess?"

"Yes."

"How good?"

"Not as good as you fucking me."

"Good answer. Hook your fingers. Put them in your cunt. Then drag them back out to your clit. Rub with the very tips."

"Oh, Jonathan, please. Please fuck me."

"Don't you like this?" There was something in his voice, some sarcasm. As though this wasn't foreplay, but him making an argument. I stopped and started to pull my hand out of my pants, but he grabbed my bruised elbow, making me flinch. "Don't stop. Make yourself come."

"I don't—"

"Do it."

I couldn't stop. I couldn't demand he explain what the fuck he thought he was doing because when he said *do it*, I wanted to. I wanted to please him, to submit, to *be his*. I was more than a submissive because submission implied a choice. I was his slave.

I rubbed my clit, gathering fluids, juice flooding between my fingers. I let out a high-pitched *ah* then choked it off.

"Let's hear it, Monica."

"Oh, God," I whispered.

He moved to my side, crouching so his breath was on my cheek. I turned to face him, eye to eye, my legs spread, my left hand on the tree, my right hand in my pants. He still didn't touch me, just breathed with me as my lower lip dropped and my lids hooded.

"You like it."

"I like you better." My breaths got shorter and hitched. My cunt was hot under my fingers, twitching, engorged, soaking.

"I bet," he said.

"Take me."

"Come."

"Yes."

The tingle ran from my knees to my waist, and my ass bucked as if Jonathan was still behind me. I cried out loud enough for the neighbors to hear, driving my hips into the tree as if I was fucking it. My chest rose and fell against the white bark, my cheek feeling its rough winter texture as I looked at him, just a shape in the darkness.

"That was okay?" Jonathan asked.

"More, please." I took my hand from my pants.

"You're insatiable." He kissed my wet fingers. "I'm glad you like it, because that's your life if I go to jail. I'm not one of those nice guys who will tell you to date other men. I'm the guy who owns you whether I'm in jail or not."

"Tell me what you think she's going to say."

He leaned on the tree and put my index finger in his mouth, sucking it clean. "Is it so wrong to want to keep you away from the ugliest parts of my life?"

"Yes." The feel of his tongue as he sucked my fingers was arousing me again. I leaned my shoulder against the tree, bracing myself against the drop down the hill with my boot heel.

"It's wrong to want to protect you? To keep you above my shit? A goddess?"

"Yes. It is wrong. It can't last. If you make me into some perfect thing that's separate from your life, we're going to disappoint each other. And that'll be it. We'll be over."

"I don't think so." He finished with my fingers and knotted our hands together.

"Yes, Jonathan, yes. We'll be over. I love you. I love your past, no matter what it was. I love your present, and I want to be your future. But lying will break us. One day you'll wake up and realize I don't really know you, and it'll be too late to bring me close. That'll be it, whether you leave me or not. We'll be over."

"My secrets might be out for public consumption very soon. So let's have *now*, before you run away."

"I want to hear it from you."

"No."

"Then I have to go meet someone." I dropped my hands and grabbed a branch, hoisting myself up the hill.

He put his hands on my biceps and pulled me back. "Don't. Just give me time."

"No."

I said it, twisting a little to face him, and lost my balance. I fell back, my weight on him. He lost his footing, and we tumbled down the hill, all elbows and feet, complete with *oofs* and screams and the sounds of cracking, rustling brush. My world blurred into a spinning, dark vortex before I landed in a heap at the top of the retaining wall. Jonathan fell onto the flagstones in the backyard, his back slamming against the low wall bordering the tangerine tree.

"Oh!" I shouted, scrambling up. "Jonathan!" I jumped the wall and landed by him.

"Are you okay?" he asked, though I was standing and he was prone.

"I'm fine. I've fallen down that hill a hundred times." I pulled him up. He cringed.

"Are you sure?" He picked a twig from my T-shirt, and I brushed his collar. He turned his head and grimaced.

"Could I be any more bruised than I am already?"

He smiled, then I smiled, and we laughed. He put his hands on my cheek, and we kissed through our laughter. He bent his neck and drew a long breath.

"I think you twisted your neck good," I said. "You should have just let me go meet her."

"Never." He kissed me again, keeping his neck straight. I kissed him back, deeply, because I was about to disappoint him.

"Now," I said. "And if not now, tomorrow."

"I'll take you to bed."

"I thought I was too beat up to fuck?"

"I'll make it work."

"Every day between now and when you're ready to talk to me? Your whole plan for dealing with Jessica can't be to keep me in the dark? She's going to get you declared incompetent. This is all right with you?"

He went to put his right arm around my shoulders and stopped himself, groaning.

"What?" I asked.

"Nothing."

"You're hurt."

"I'm fine. It's not that big a hill."

"But you fell on a bunch of pavestones." I put my arm around his waist and helped him to the back door. "And you're not that young any more, you know."

"Oh, you are getting such a spanking for that."

"Not if you can't lift your arm."

"I'll spank you with my dick."

He barely got through the sentence before he started laughing. I joined in because the visual was so close to a pornographic Monty Python skit that we couldn't hold it in our heads without laughing. We were still cracking up when I sat him in a kitchen chair.

"Ow!" he complained between laughs. I kneeled in front of him and unbuttoned his shirt. "Not now, baby. I'm too tired."

I pushed the shirt as far over his shoulders as I could. "Can you get out of this?"

"Are you making a pass at me? Because I'm already taken by a brown-eyed goddess."

"Can you just do it, please? My God, you are a pain in the ass."

He leaned forward, and I helped get his shirt off. The left sleeve was the hardest on him. Even though he smiled through it, his arm was stiff and he moved gingerly. The T-shirt under the button down was easier. I pulled out the good right arm, stretched it over his head, then dropped the whole thing over the stiff left arm. His bicep was swollen and red, and his shoulder blade had a red bump the size of an egg growing on it. He bent his arm.

"Not broken," he said, grimacing.

"But you're going to have some nice bruising from your neck to your elbow. Welcome to my world."

"Mine don't come with the memories."

I kissed him. He put his right hand on my cheek, and I put my arms around him, still treating him tenderly. I opened my eyes while I kissed him because I wanted to see his eyes closed in surrender to me, and I had that blissful sight. Jonathan, enjoying my kiss, in that slight abdication, made my heart flutter. I sighed. Then his eyes opened just a little, as if he wanted to see the same thing, and we smiled.

"Sit still. Let me get some ice." I stepped to the freezer where Gabby and I had kept compresses for fingers and arms that ached after hours of practice.

"Why don't you just take me to bed?" he said as I put compresses on his neck and arm.

"Not a bad idea. Get up."

We walked to the bedroom, and I propped him up on pillows, happy that I'd changed the sheets. His arm was getting stiffer, and by the time I'd set up the compresses, he could barely move it at all.

"Guess who's not driving tonight," I said, holding out my hand. "Give me your keys so I can put your car in the driveway. There's alternate side parking tomorrow."

"I can afford a ticket."

"But if the car blocking the sweeper in the morning is my guest's, Roger across the street puts all the garbage in *my* front yard. He did it with Darren, like, a hundred times."

He reached into his right pocket and pulled out his key. "You need to move to a better neighborhood."

"I know what you're thinking"—I swiped the key—"and forget it. I'm not a kept woman."

"We'll see about that."

I pocketed the key and went to my bathroom. Stepping onto the toilet, I reached the top of the vanity where I kept bottles of pills hidden from Gabby: painkillers I'd been prescribed for an extracted tooth, muscle relaxants for painful menstruation, and Xanax a friend had given me for a short bout of insomnia. I took them to Jonathan, who was dicking with his phone with his good hand.

"I have painkillers."

"Why? You in pain without me?"

"Let me get you some water."

"Monica"—he looked me with dead seriousness—"no painkillers."

I put the bottle of Oxycontin on the dresser. "How about some Tylenol and a muscle relaxant?"

"Deal."

I took the bottles to the kitchen, and as I poured a glass of water, I considered what I had in front of me, what I wanted to do, and what was keeping me from doing it. As I poured the pills in my hand, I reconsidered then went back to the bedroom. "All right. This is the Tylenol. This is the muscle relaxant. Go."

He popped them in his mouth and swallowed, then drank the water. "You're a good nurse."

I put my knee on the bed and swung myself to a straddling position. "I'm not done nursing you." I undid his pants.

"Oh, really? What nursing school is this?"

I pulled out his dick. It was half hard already, and when I kissed it, it stood at full attention. "I have no clever answer." I licked the length of his shaft with the flat of my tongue.

"Hell is freezing over," he groaned, putting his right hand on my head and running his fingers in my hair. I opened my mouth and let him put pressure on the back of my head, slowly pushing his cock into my mouth, past my tongue, and down my throat. He kept the pressure, and I breathed calmly through my nose, my eyes locked on his. When he eased up, I drew my head back, sucking him on the way out. He sighed, and a look of pure, relaxed pleasure overcame his face. A line of saliva connected my mouth to his cock. I licked my lips.

"You never let me use my hands," I said.

He blinked, as if thinking about all the times his dick was in my mouth, counting off instances and places. "Total oversight on my part."

"You like control."

"Guilty as charged."

"Let me have you," I said. "Give yourself to me."

"Submission's not fun for me."

Hands behind my back, I took him again, all the way down, tasting sharp sweat and a drop of salt as I sucked him on the way out. "Let me please you, sir. Let me give you my best."

"When you put it that way..."

I placed one hand at the base of his cock, and with the other, I cupped his sack. I took him completely, trying to keep submission on my mind and in my attitude as I controlled what he felt. The pace was mine. The intensity was mine. When he put his hands on me, it was with affection, not control, and when he came, filling my throat and closing his eyes, I maintained that attitude of gratitude and abdication, licking him clean.

"Thank you," he whispered.

"How is your arm?" It hung at his side, unused during the whole episode.

"Feels stiff but okay." His eyelids drooped as he watched me. He stroked my hair and cheek, and I kissed his fingers.

I kneeled and pulled him gently from the waist. "If you scoot down, I'll rearrange the compresses."

He did. I put a pillow under his head, elevated the sore arm, put him under the blankets, and drew them up. I shut the light and curled up next to him. Seconds later, his breathing slowed, and I slipped away.

CHAPTER 76

—*I went home*—

The content of Jessica's text didn't surprise me. The fact that she'd bothered to send it did. She was desperate for contact.

Jonathan's car was parked right out front. I'd never actually driven a Jaguar, but as soon as I turned the key, I understood the difference between it and my Civic. It was smooth everywhere. The seams didn't rattle. No crumbs were in the corners, as if one simply ate more neatly, or not at all, in such a car. It went from park to drive as if by the power of thought, and the dashboard lights didn't glare or ask me to read them. They existed to be understood in a hueless grey and whispered information urgently. *Half full. Forty thousand RPM. Seventy-five miles per hour.*

What heaven, driving a black Jaguar on PCH at midnight.

I enjoyed the ride so much, I hadn't even thought to turn on the radio, and when a classical station came on, I woke up to the complications of being in Jonathan's car. She had an order of protection. If his car pulled up to Jessica's place, alarms would be raised. Possibly by Jessica, the police, Santon's team—wherever they may be. Whatever the case, once she saw the car, I couldn't pretend we had broken up and I was looking for vengeance. I was going in as the loyal girlfriend, and my leverage would decrease. I passed her house. Lights out. Car in driveway. It was midnight on a Monday, after all. I spun around the corner, wound up all turned around because the streets weren't on a grid, came back to the beach side of the street, over shot the house by two blocks, and parked. I needed all my options, and that meant walking in as if I'd taken a cab.

The modernist house sat on an incline with twisting stairs to the top and desert flowers on the way up. I slipped up the concrete steps quickly and inconspicuously, hoping the crickets and ocean waves covered my footfall. The door was huge, heavy, and red with a knob in the center. The front of the house had small plate windows since they faced the street. The back would be made of glass from floor to twelve-foot ceiling, since it faced the ocean.

I stood on my toes and peeked. Lights were on farther back in the house, and I saw the blue flicker of a TV. The bell was the light-up kind. I put my finger over it and held my breath.

Then I pressed it.

Ring and run! Ring and run!

When I was a kid in the EP, as we called it, we'd ring bells and run away, hiding behind parked cars or a hedge, just for the joy of watching as someone came to the door. No game was more infantile, yet I was tempted to play it.

Ring and run! Ring and run!

She wasn't coming. I had enough time to run away and get back in the car. Take PCH to the 10 to the 110 and get off at Stadium Way. Take a leisurely drive through Solano Canyon in Jonathan's car. Pull the sleek machine into the drive. Crawl back into bed with the love of my life and make him breakfast in the morning like I oughta. Explain I was moving the car and had to take it for a spin. He'd love to hear that. Delight him. That was my job.

Ring and run! Ring and run!

A light flicked somewhere in the house, sending wide bands of dim light across the concrete path. I had a meeting tomorrow with the president of Carnival Records, and my voice would be hoarse and I'd have bags under my eyes. I had to go home and rest. Go immediately. I had a career. I'd worked hard. Jonathan could take care of himself. He was a big boy. Sing. I wanted to sing.

The front light flicked on, and the big knob flicked and twisted. I stepped back. One step.

Run!

The door swung open as I stepped down. She was dressed in slacks and a button-down shirt. She looked as if she'd just walked out of a soap ad. How did Jonathan ever fuck her? Did she sweat? Did she groan? Did a tear of post-orgasmic joy ever drop down her cheek?

"Hello, Monica," she said. "Finally."

"Hello, Jessica."

"Won't you come in?" She stepped out of the way, and I walked into her house.

CHAPTER 77

MONICA

THE UGLIEST LAMP in the world illuminated the room in warm light. It was gold with a parchment shade and a neck shaped like seven tennis balls stacked on top of one another. Everything else was impeccable. Somehow, though, a mark of impermanence stained the décor. Nothing looked settled or important. The corners were visible. The surfaces were without tchotchke or photo. The art was original but marginal. I had been right about the back wall. The windows stretched corner to corner, exposing a lit up pool and a view that was pure blackness at night, but in the day would be clear to the horizon, where sky met sea.

"Would you like a cup of coffee?" Jessica asked.

"More of a tea person."

Jessica made a *mmm* sound, as if my choice of hot beverage spoke volumes about my worth as a human being. Of course, that was my imagination. Her face betrayed nothing. "I'll have some made. Decaf? It's late."

She'll have some made? Did the staff not get time off? Did they work in shifts? Well, if that was my new life, if those were the entitlements one was to expect, then I was going to be as considerate as possible.

"Caffeinated is fine. Doesn't bother me. And green, if you have it."

"Would you like to sit outside?" She indicated the back.

"Sure."

She opened the sliding door to a patio and flipped a switch. Heating torches went up, lights went on. I nodded and walked out. I sat on a chair, listening to the ocean I knew was there but couldn't see. I had trouble imagining having access to such a patio every night and being at anything but complete peace. Or was that

533

what she feared? That losing the money to maintain the patio, the house, the studio meant she couldn't be at peace? I imagined the level of anxiety I'd face if the things that kept me sane were taken away. My voice. My ears. Even my piano, with its broken pedal, was a rock I held tight when I felt anxious. Jonathan removing that much of her income had thrown her off a cliff, made her panic. Cornered her. Poorly thought out for a man who controlled everything at all times.

Even with the torches, it was chilly. I realized then, too late, that I didn't have my scarf. The crew neck on my tee was relatively tight, but my bruises were visible with even the most minor inspection.

It was darker at the chair across from me. But Jessica was coming. She'd see me move to a darker corner.

I reminded myself to always remember the rules about Jessica, especially rule number one. Fuck her. It wasn't about her. It was about protecting Jonathan from her little rat eyes.

I moved to the dark corner.

"So," Jessica said as she closed the door, cradling a manila envelope.

I looked at her linen slacks and button-down white shirt again. Maybe she'd just gotten back from somewhere, or maybe she and Jonathan were partners in their sleep habits, hanging out until all hours and waking up after what most people would consider a nap. Maybe they used to stay up all night giggling and sharing stories, all dressed to the nines, not a hair out of place.

I had to shake myself out of my thoughts. "I'm sorry to come so late, but it seemed like everything was conspiring against us meeting."

"'Everything' being Jonathan?"

"I don't know."

"Did you ask him?"

"No." Her question had been so direct and her tone so kind, yet condescending that I started to understand why Jonathan didn't want me near her.

An older woman in a black dress came out with a tea tray and left silently. Jessica poured tea into two white cups that were so plain, they must have cost a fortune.

"I understand why you don't want to ask him. He can be intimidating."

I didn't answer. I still didn't know if I was playing rabbit-in-the-woods or qualified-to-kink, so I just poured myself tea. "I'm sorry I was rude to you when I saw you last."

She waved it away. "I understand. I came on too strong. I assumed you were naturally curious."

I consciously, and with great effort, let the insult slide. I'd asked for it, considering I hadn't asked him the details of blocking me from seeing her and I had aggressively avoided Jonathan-bashing at Frontage. "This is a very nice house. The view must be incredible in the daytime."

"It is. You can see all the way to the horizon. It's cooler too, with the breeze coming in."

"Have you lived here long?"

She smiled a little, and I wondered if she could see that I was feeling her out. "Erik and I moved here after I left Jonathan. It was far away from him. That was the best thing about it."

"And Erik? Is he still here? It's a big house to live in alone."

"Moved on." Turning the line of questioning over to her life was obviously not on her agenda because she changed the subject back to me. "So, why the change of heart? You wanted nothing to do with anything I had to say."

It was time to pick what and who I was going to be. "When he got arrested, I got... Well you used the word curious. I felt like there were things I needed to know, and you were trying to tell them to me, but I wouldn't let you."

"And you figured you'd get them out of me so you could go back and tell him?"

I held my breath. I'd failed somehow, because she jumped on my motivations so quickly. I must have looked like a deer in headlights and turned shades of pink, even in the dark corner. "I don't know what I'm going to do." My voice crackled like a piece of paper being thrown in the trash.

"You're going to tell him everything I said. And he'll rebut me. Like my wrist, which I'm sure he denied breaking during sex. And beating me in his backyard. What did he tell you about that? Did he tell you I told everyone he wanted to rape me and hurt me? But he didn't, of course, says *he*? Do you have any other source of information?"

I didn't, but I said nothing.

"My lawyer says you found surveillance devices in your house, and he's saying it was me. Is that what he told you? That I did it?"

"Yes."

"I'm not the one with the sick fantasies. Why would I do that?"

How could I answer? How could I say, "So you could try to prove he was an abuser. To shame him. To get him declared incompetent." I wouldn't tip Jonathan's hand. I gazed down at my palms in my lap and tried to think of some rebuttal that made sense, but I had nothing.

She took my silence as permission to continue, her words measured and careful. "Every piece of information you have comes from him. Let me tell you something. He has control fantasies. If cameras were in your house, you have no farther to look than the man next to you. If a woman says he broke her wrist because he was holding them behind her back during sex, believe her."

"You said you were joking."

"I shouldn't have told you when you were working. That was the joke. It wasn't funny, but I don't lie. Jonathan does. You know that, right? You know he lies."

I took a deep breath. How could I admit that without betraying him? To sit there and say I believed everything he'd ever said would earn me nothing but her laughter. I felt cornered, hateful. Jonathan was right. I shouldn't have come.

"His father ruined my family. Did he tell you that? He killed Daddy. Broke his heart with some sneaky business deal. I didn't know when I met Jonathan. I had been protected. Daddy never even told me he'd lost nearly everything until I introduced them, and by then, it was too late. I loved him, and I fought for him.

Just like you're doing. His whole family ruins people." Jessica leaned forward and put her hand over mine. "I know he didn't tell you about Rachel either. What he did to her."

My eyes shot to hers. My breathing picked up. "What?"

"You have bruises on your neck," she said.

I impulsively touched the bend where shoulder and neck met, as if to hide them or make sure they were still there. "What did he do?"

"He killed her."

He killed her. Had I known that, somewhere deep in my gut? Had I been avoiding it? Lying to myself, as I often did? Or were there more lies on top of those?

I felt trapped. Months ago, I'd been flying, my own buzz filling my ears, with a destination in mind but a path not mapped. I had a job and friends and hope. One night, I spilled a drink. I touched a man's hand, and I let him kiss me on the hood of his car. Some time after, I don't know when, I fell into a web of lies and deceit. The harder I struggled, the more trapped I became. But who was the spider? Was it Jonathan? Or Jessica? And how could I get out of their fucking web?

I glanced around, feeling the wetness in my eyes. God, one blink and I'd be a mess. I sniffed and took a napkin from the tray. I saw the manila envelope she'd brought out sitting on the low table. On top of it, face down, sat her phone.

"I'm scared," I said. She squeezed my hand. "He is rough. He…" I trailed off.

"Go on."

"He calls me names, and…" I put my hands to my neck and looked into the distance.

"Does he choke you?"

"He calls me whore. Did he say those things to you?"

"Well, no."

I started to get up "Never mind."

She took my hand and squeezed it, pushing me back down. "It was just different for me. For me it was bitch and slut. Humiliating women is part of his sickness."

I looked away. I needed to keep the pain on my face. I touched my neck again and whispered, very low, "He hurts me."

"I'm sorry," Jessica said, "I can't hear you?"

I looked back at her, finding the tears of a minute ago were still available. I blinked them out, and they dropped like stars.

"Does he choke you, Monica?"

I nodded.

"He does? He chokes you?"

I shook my head. She looked confused. I cleared my throat and eyed my bag. "I think I should go."

"He choked me," she said. "I had bruises just like yours. I thought I was going to die. That's the turn-on for these men. Watching your pain and fear."

"These? Bruises like these?" I said, touching my neck.

"Yes."

"I fell down a hill."

"You don't have to lie to protect him. I've been in your shoes."

I squeezed her hand. Her French manicure was perfect on all of her fingers but the right thumb, which was cracked. "Can I have a glass of water?"

"Sure." She craned her neck to see in the house. "She's gone to bed. God. Couldn't wait another half an hour." She slid the manila envelope from under her phone and handed it to me. "This is for you. There's nothing in there Jonathan doesn't know, and it's everything he won't tell you. I know everything, and that scares him." She patted my head as if I was a terrier. "Do you want ice?"

"Yes, please."

She squeezed my hand one last time and got up, closing the door behind her.

The temptation to open the envelope was intense, but I had very little time. I hugged it to my chest, unopened, and snatched Jessica's phone. I slipped through the sliding glass doors and out the front. The phone was recording a voice memo. I shut it down as soon as I hit the street. If she tried to chase me, she'd be looking for my car. I still walked behind hedges and in the darkest parts of the street until I got to the Jag. I sped away as fast as the car and common sense allowed.

On the drive home, I considered that I'd done something really stupid. I didn't know which stupid thing I'd done. A string of things had seemed right at the time and could still be right. The phone, which wasn't getting signal and would be untrackable until it was turned on again, frowned at me like a hostage. I could turn it on and quickly put it into airplane mode. I could pop the SIM card. I could hear everything if I really wanted to.

"Fuck off," I said to the black rectangle on the passenger seat. "You're full of shit."

I giggled at my double entendre that recognized the recording of Jonathan's spanking was inside. Then I laughed because my brain emptied of everything but the one thing that mattered. I trusted him. He hadn't earned it and he certainly had pushed my limits, but deep in my heart, I didn't need to hear the recording. I believed him. I always had.

When I realized I was going ninety-five, I pulled over. I rubbed the tears from my eyes, got my breathing to a normal rate, and turned on the overhead light. Once I got back, I wouldn't be able to open the envelope because Jonathan would be there. Whatever was in there needed to be read furtively, in the dark of night, alone. It would be evil and ugly, written with the silk of a spider's web.

CHAPTER 78

MONICA

MY FEET DRAGGED up the steps, boots clopping on the wood. I was fucking tired.
I should never stay up late the night before any meeting, but especially not *that*
meeting. I was going to crawl under the sheets with Jonathan, curl up next to his
beautiful, warm body, and sleep.

Except he was sitting on the porch. He did not look happy.

His jacket was slung over the back of the porch swing. He wore his pants,
fastened, his shirt, unbuttoned thrice, and his shoes. The shoes bothered me. He
could walk away any second. He held out his hand. I dropped his car keys in it.

"I shouldn't have to tell you," he said, "but don't do that again."

"Do what? Steal the car? Or drug you?"

"See my ex-wife."

"That's the one thing I won't apologize for."

I put the envelope and phone next to him then leaned on the porch railing. He
didn't even look at them but kept his eyes on mine and his foot braced on the table
in front of him. We regarded each other in silence for a second.

"Have you put the starter back in my car?" I asked.

"Yes."

"I'll get over there later."

"Lil will take you."

"I'll take the bus," I said.

"No, you won't."

"Go to hell, Jonathan."

"*I* should go to hell? I? Me? I should go to hell?"

"Yes, you. You have felony charges against you, and you spend all your time finding ways to keep me from helping you. What was your plan for dealing with her? You gonna just let her blackmail you because you have the money lying around?"

"No, Monica, I had a plan. But I spent all my time making sure you didn't fuck it up."

I sat back on the railing and crossed my arms, locking my feet against the vertical rails so I didn't fall over. "You could have just told me."

"I don't tell people things like that. It's not my way."

I rocked back on my feet. The railing had held for a hundred years and would hold for a hundred more, but Jonathan didn't know that. He stiffened when it looked like I'd fall.

"Did I fuck it up?" I asked.

"No. You just fucked *me* up. I couldn't think. I knew all the things Jessica would say to you, and I thought she would drive you away. Whatever you needed to hear, and I thought the worst, she'd say it. Then this time, you'd be gone for good."

If touching him would have been appropriate, I would have stroked his cheek and kissed his mouth. I would have held his hands, warning them against the late November chill. I would have whispered my love in his ear in the cadence of his laughter. But we had too much of the last two days between us to make any of that meaningful.

"I am very sorry about the sleeping pills," I said. "I didn't think until after that you need your self-control, and I took it away. That was wrong and a breach of trust. I'm sorry." When he didn't answer, I continued. "I may steal your car again, though."

"Take it." He waved his hand as though he was giving me the last bite of dessert. "Can you tell me what she said?"

"Apparently, you killed your first love. She made it out like cold-blooded murder."

The anger drained from his face, replaced by the flatness of fear.

"Don't look like that," I said. "I love you."

"But I did it."

"I know."

We regarded each other for what seemed like a long time.

"That envelope, right there, she gave it to me. It's a draft of an article written for *eLA Rag*. I already have a piece of it that Gabby got her hands on, don't ask me how. They suggest that you were driving the car Rachel was in when she drowned. You saved yourself and let her die. Jessica said you're aware that she knows all this."

"I am."

"Can I hear the whole story from your lips, please?"

"No, Monica. No. A thousand times, no."

"All I got from her was the goddamn envelope before I took her phone. So I can go back and—"

"This is *her* phone?" He pointed to the black rectangle on top of the envelope.

"Yes."

He picked it up. "You stole her phone."

"I prefer the term *lifted*," I said. "In any case, if she did 'ask for it' like you said, the raw audio might be on there."

"You *stole her phone*." He cradled in the space between his palms, as if he didn't want too much of it touching his skin. "Did you listen?"

"No. That's all you. Figure it out."

"You don't want to know how far I went with her?"

"You told me how far you went."

"You are so strange, Monica."

"I never made the decision to love you. But I decided to trust you. That was a choice."

He fingered the phone, flipping it over as if contemplating a greater meaning. "If the whole scene is on this phone, its best use may be to go public."

"Whatever you want."

"People will know." He looked at me with meaning, as if trying to impart a few volumes of knowledge.

I knew exactly what he meant. They'd know how we were together. They'd talk, and they'd look at me in a way I didn't want to be seen. "Fuck people and fuck what they know. Do what you have to."

He held out his hand, and I took it, letting him pull me onto his lap. His arms wrapped around me and pulled my legs to one side. I put my fingertips on his cheeks, letting the rough stubble scratch them. I traced his jaw, the angular line, the hardness of it, and his lips, source of so much pleasure, their softness on my fingers as I imagined them between my legs. I shuddered a little and rested my head on his chest, losing myself in his leathery scent. *God, please let me not be confusing love and beauty. Let this be as real as it feels, not some imaginary thing.*

"Why did you want to see her?" he whispered.

"To try to lift her phone. But if I told you that, you'd just say no. And if I failed, you would have thought I was incompetent."

He kissed my forehead, my cheeks. "You're not leaving me?"

"No."

"But you haven't heard everything."

"I don't want a reporter's research. I don't want Jessica's lies. I want it from your mouth. I chose to trust you, and I want you to choose to talk to me."

CHAPTER 79

JONATHAN

I HELD her silently for a long time, wondering if she could keep her promise to stay with me. I'd become so attached to that woman that her presence, somewhere in the world, comforted me. The connection, once I'd admitted it was there, was palpable, a rope of energy between us. Knowing what she was doing at any given moment was an almost religious experience, specific to her, and almost sexual in its purity. I knew she felt too, but she was a wild card. Her reactions never fit my expectations.

If she was going to leave me because of things I'd done, she would have done it already. The effects of unburdening myself could last indefinitely and affect me the way they'd affected me with Jessica, in well-timed words and the sense that I was trapped by her knowledge. But it didn't matter any more. As of last night, I'd done enough to alienate Monica from me and more to bring her close. The tension between the two had to break.

So I formulated a way to express the narrative. It didn't run in a straight line. It started on a rainy December night, took a left when I was twenty-three, came around the bend a year later, switched gears the previous month, and only began the previous night, with a death.

"Rachel died last night," I said. She pulled away to look me in the eye. Even in the dark, I saw her confusion. "Well, I lied."

I wanted to see her face, so I pulled her up to a straddling position. Her shoulders slouched. I brushed her hair from her shoulders. It was too dark to see her face clearly, but I knew I wouldn't like what I saw.

"I'm sorry. There's more. Do you want me to come clean?" I asked.

She put her hands on my shoulders. "Ok, go ahead."

"Rachel required constant care. The accident left her in a vegetative state. She wasn't even herself anymore, so little of her brain was functioning. She could have lived forever, except that when Jessica first met you at the Stock, the day with the cast on her arm, I panicked. I thought she'd tell you everything. I didn't know why, and mostly, I didn't know why I cared so much, but I knew I did. I needed time to think, so I moved her to another facility. She never fully recovered."

"I'm sorry," Monica said. "Are you sad about it?"

I felt myself smile, because that would be the question Monica would ask, not the thousand others. "Yes, but other things too. It's complicated. I'd assumed she was dead between the accident and when I was about twenty-three. I'd done my share of grieving over it. But I found out she was alive, and Jessica and I found her and moved her."

"Okay, wait—"

"Hold on, Mon—"

"You found her? Who was keeping her?"

"I said hold on, goddess, please."

"Have mercy on me, Jonathan. I thought she was dead until a minute ago. You have no idea what's been going through my head."

"What?"

She put her forehead to my shoulder. "You killed her during sexual asphyxiation and covered it up with the accident."

"You have a very vivid imagination."

"So, that's not what happened?"

"You know that's not my kink. I mean... Jesus, I should have explained this sooner." I pulled her up again and took her face in my hands. She looked very tired. I had no idea how to make this any shorter, but I knew we had to finish it, if she could stay awake for it. "I have to stop and tell you about my father."

"The passive drunk you told me about?"

"One of the many lies I tell about him."

"The one who seduced Rachel first."

"Not a lie. That was the beginning of me learning the truth of who I am. He's a sociopath. Clinical. He has no empathy. He only finds things interesting or not interesting, and hurting people is interesting. Young girls are interesting. Seeing my mother scream during childbirth? Same. My sister Carrie is a psychologist, and once she realized it, realized all the shit he'd done over the years, she moved to Italy. Swear to god. I see that look on your face. It's not genetic."

"I didn't think you were a sociopath."

"No, but I'm a sexual sadist." Saying those words was hard, even though I knew how true they were. As much as Debbie had tried to remove all of my negative connotations from them, I still felt a pang of self-loathing. Monica didn't seem perturbed, probably because it was just us on her porch. I knew that her shame was in how she was seen by strangers, not what we called each other when we were alone. "I thought for a long time that made me like him. That we were the same because I enjoy that look on a woman's face when I squeeze a little too hard, or that I like to make her uncomfortable. I thought it was a part of him inside me."

"And it's not?"

"It is. But even he's capable of doing good things. He was the one who rescued Rachel from the car and put her into a facility."

She leaned back as if stunned. "Why?"

"She was about to blackmail him. She was going to expose that he had been with her when she was sixteen. You don't blackmail J. Declan Drazen. He doesn't appreciate it, let's say."

"Why didn't he just let her die?"

"I don't know. He has a thing about not shitting where you eat, so if he thought she was within his circle, he wouldn't have hurt her. But he was secretive. We found out everything about the accident the hard way. When I went to him about it, he literally laughed. I found out I was driving when some reporter came sniffing around, probably this guy." I tapped the envelope. "I found out she was alive right after that. It was, let's say, overwhelming."

"You felt like a fly caught in a web."

She'd captured that feeling exactly. What she didn't capture was the feeling that if I got free of it, I'd be less human for letting go of the grief and guilt. It was mine. I owned it. If I unburdened myself, what would I become? An animal who stopped caring about the things I'd done? I couldn't allow that. My shame was made me a moral person, even if it crippled me emotionally.

She snapped up the envelope and pressed it to my chest. "You should read this."

"I don't need to."

"It says you were soaked in salt water. Has it occurred to you that *you* rescued her?"

"I dove in, but I was too drunk to rescue anyone," I said. "Probably nearly drowned myself."

"They got your medical records. The skin on your hands was totally fucked up. You were banged to shit. Like you wrestled with the ocean pulling someone out of it."

I remembered that. In my sequestered hospital room, my mother had been at my side, smelling of whiskey, and she claimed ignorance about that and everything. Dad spoke to me after, describing Rachel's death by drowning, the body's absence, the car "she stole" floating into the Pacific with the tide. He'd get me another. Not to worry.

I'd been so shredded about Rachel, I'd paid no mind to my bruises or the skin missing from my hands. I figured that in my blacked-out stupor, I'd fallen. Repeatedly.

Maybe Monica was right. Maybe I hadn't been such a passive player. Or maybe it didn't matter anymore, because Monica's big brown eyes looked at me for answers as if I had any. She looked at me as if she was on a starting block, waiting to win the race to forgiveness. I could tell her anything. I could tell her I'd strangled Rachel and buried the body, and she'd forgive me. God damn. I had done something truly evil in letting the woman love me.

"We ruined her family," I said. "Not that it was worth much."

"You know, I think—"

I didn't let her finish. "Jessica's family, too. My father put hers in his grave. And when I married her, she was cut off. Then she became this *thing* that tries to squeeze me."

"Jonathan, listen—"

"And Kevin. I mean douchebag, yes. I had my chance to hit him on the head with a cinderblock, but that somehow wasn't permanent enough. I needed him wiped off the map of Los Angeles. So I had his warrants checked at the border. I needed his career with you to be over, so I made sure the last page of the commercial invoice was missing."

The look of shock on her face, the feel of her limbs tightening made me want to reassure her at the same time as it strengthened my resolve. "I mean, look at you. You're surprised. You can't believe I'd do something like that, right? You knew it was true, but you can't believe it. Say it."

"I believe it." Her voice was soft and low, as if she was telling herself more than me.

"And you still love me? Because you believe in my innate *goodness?*"

She rolled off my lap and sat next to me, looking into the empty, diagonal street. "You hurt me too, when you did that. With the invoice. Any box could have been held up. I might not have been able to figure it out."

"I didn't care. Don't you get it? I wanted to possess you, and I didn't want Kevin in my way. And you love me, Monica? Do you still love me? Are you that naïve?"

"I still love you."

"You have no idea what you're talking about. Look what I've done to you already. You're stealing things and drugging me. What are you turning into?"

"You're turning into a dick."

"I'm not turning into anything. What I am now, I've always been. I can't believe you can hear this story and sit there as if it's nothing."

"It's not nothing." She pulled her knees up to her chin, a defensive posture if I ever saw one. "Did you want me to judge you?"

"Why wouldn't you? Don't martyr yourself to me."

"Jesus Christ! What is *wrong* with you?"

"Your decency is endearing, but it's already dying." I stood up, my course of action set. I felt that tightness in my chest again but ignored it. "At least with Jessica, she knew what she was getting, and she could handle it. I can't say the same for you."

That hurt her, as it was meant to. The urge to gather her in my arms and say I was sorry was overwhelming. I had a moment where I could have done that, explained it all away, but that would be an act of a cowardice. I refused to allow another woman to be ruined because of me.

"Get out," she said, feet on the swing, curled and tangled at the ankles. "Just go."

"Your car is fixed," I said, scooping Jessica's phone and envelope.

I walked off the porch without looking back. The slap of the car door seemed final. The roar of the engine and backing onto her sheer drop of a street seemed like continued punctuations in an ever long sentence. I rounded the corner, then another, up a hill, until I was at the top of hers again. If I went back around and she was still on the porch, I'd grovel. I'd pour my heart out to her. If I told her I was afraid of corrupting her, exposing her to my family, turning her into an unscrupulous monster, killing her, maybe she'd prove me wrong.

But she was gone. Part of me was glad she was protected from truths that could be used to draw forgiveness and love from her. But the rest of me felt cracked down the middle.

I parked the car at the side of the road by the freeway entrance because the crack had opened into a void, and I was falling into it. I couldn't drive. I knew I'd done what I had to. I knew I'd been a man. Done it right. Taken responsibility. I vowed that my single life wasn't going to be what it had been before. I wasn't going to bed whoever caught my fancy. I would play it straight. No looking. No dating. No casual fucking.

Because who else did I want? Who else fit so right? Who else could heal me? Who else could I damage as deeply, hurt as fully? Who needed more protection from me?

Right there, in my car, I said good-bye to a piece of myself. I gave up on it because doing so saved Monica from being the third in line for ruination. Saving her was a dark glow at the edge of the void, and that void... My God, that void was endless, lonely, black with loathing, and I clutched the wheel, white-knuckled, as I fell down it.

CHAPTER 80

MONICA

THAT WAS BULLSHIT.

That was a guy who felt responsible for his first love dying.

The choice was clear. I could get upset or not. I could disregard everything we'd been through already and write him off, or I could do him the favor he did me when I walked away and be ready for his return.

I opened my text messenger to let him know I was there for him when he came to his senses. I didn't hit send. The send button would deliver an immediate *ding* across the city, and he'd answer it (or not) and then we'd bounce texts (or not) but nothing would be solved. I'd prolong whatever agony he was going through.

I was fully awake, and though my second wind would be short, I had enough in me to give him something with the ghost of a chance of truly comforting him. I wanted to sing him a song. Make him music, and one *ding* wouldn't cut it. He needed more *dings*. A chorus of them. A symphony. His phone needed to light up and make music.

I crawled out of bed and got my metronome. After placing it on the night table and setting it mid-tempo, I broke down a song into the beats of a send button without sending it.

I__A
  m__b
   er
   e__und

*er_*
the
_r
ains

547

IF EACH LETTER became the tap of a beat, time taken, and the send button punctuated each line, assuming the network functioned properly, his phone should ding to the rhythms of my hurt and my steadfast concern.

Three/three/two/five/three. Sixteen beats. Four measures. No downbeats or dynamics with a phone ding, but I could play with the timing and give every fourth a dotted quarter for *umph* if I needed it.

I set the metronome and practiced tapping into my phone. I used the enter key instead of the send button. An hour later, I felt like I'd nailed it, and my second wind was wearing down. Now or never. I cracked my knuckles and began.

CHAPTER 81

JONATHAN

Two in the morning. Still raining. I could have called any Asia office and caught them in time for a good balling-out over whatever. God help them if they called me with some crap they could manage themselves.

I wanted her already. Her body under mine. Her voice saying my name. Her all-consuming hunger for life. The first months would be the hardest. I knew that from losing Jessica. How could I compare the blip that was Monica to the ten years I'd spent with my bitch of a wife?

Even if I hadn't believed it at the time, Jessica had run her course. That was the difference. My time with Monica had been cut off at the knees.

I already wanted to know what she was doing. Instead, I went into the shower and tried to scald the thought of her from me. I undressed in the bathroom, leaving my clothes on the floor like a slob.

My phone dinged once, then again. It was in my jacket pocket, draped over the vanity. Fucking Asia. The whole continent should fall into the sea, and by the urgency of the dinging, it sounded as if it was. By the time I got there, it had gone off another ten times, and a rhythm was appearing. The texts were coming furiously. The thing must be broken or stuck.

I finally got it out of my pocket.

The
  _sk
  *y_*

split
_ap
art
_t
*ears_*
fal
lin
*g_*
*into_*
the
_un

IT WENT ON. And on. It was Monica, singing me a song. I sat on the toilet,
dripping, staring at my dinging, buzzing phone, and the seeming nonsense
streaming across my screen. I could put it together if I concentrated. The effect
was hypnotic.

The dinging stopped, then something came in a full sentence.

*I_AM_HERE_UNDER_THE_RAINS_THE_SKY_SPLIT_APART_TEARS_FALLING_INTO_THE_UNBREAKABLE_*

A FIST GRIPPED MY CHEST, tightening when I thought about what to do next. My
neck and arms hurt as if the nerves were being squeezed. I broke out in a sweat.
Ridiculous. I tried to get control of myself, but it was hard to breathe. I leaned
back again. I must have been coming down with something.

I did the only right thing and blocked her number.

CHAPTER 82

MONICA

I DIDN'T HEAR BACK.

How long had he waited for me? Two weeks or more? I felt as though that would kill me, but I'd do what I had to, even if it meant I didn't sleep the night before a huge meeting and I felt like hell. I checked my phone constantly. Nothing. I had to remind myself to breathe.

That was why I'd been celibate, to avoid staying up all night before meetings. Of course the meetings had come just as I was getting more drama than I could handle without a therapist.

I am music.

I am music.

I am music.

In a sense, I was a wreck. The night was emotionally devastating. I never heard from him after my song. I believed I'd have him back, eventually, if he didn't find someone else in the meantime, but I was upset. I'd never been dumped, and the powerlessness and vulnerability was physical. My veins felt sucked dry, and my rib cage seemed to have shrunk too small to contain my lungs.

A good cry might release some of my anxiety, and I'd been tempted to let it come, but I didn't want to risk being unable to stop. I put all of my emotions in a box and taped it shut with words.

I'm fine.

I'm fine.

I'm fine.

I couldn't play my viola. Much as I tried to keep the notes strong, the dynamics kept dragging toward sad. I had better luck with the piano, pounding the keys until I was sure the cops would come.

I got control of myself. I didn't know how long it would last, but if I could keep myself together through the meeting with Carnival, I'd be satisfied.

A text came through. I jumped, anxiety flowing out of me in a torrent and sucking back in when I realized it was Darren.

—*Are you guys decent?*—

—*No, but I'm dressed and alone*—

A knock on the door was the response. I opened it to a perfect, clear fall morning, and Darren with his laptop.

He jerked his finger toward my driveway. "He left his car?"

"No, I—" I noticed a note on the porch swing.

MONICA:

Please know I'd arranged for this replacement before last night. Just take it, and we can call it even.

-Jonathan

I had an old black Civic with more dings than a bell choir rendition of "Deck the Halls," and what sat in my driveway was a pristine white Jaguar roadster. Convertible. Top down.

"Asshole," I said.

"Dr. Thorensen's parking in your driveway again?"

I reached in my mailbox and found a navy blue Harry Winston box tied with a white ribbon.

"You are fucking kidding me," Darren said, plopping into the porch swing.

I opened the box. Inside was a heart-shaped silver key ring and a white car key. "I don't think I am."

"That for the hickeys all over your neck?"

"I should buy *him* a car for these hickeys." I pressed the button. The lights flashed, and a soft *pip* emanated from the car. Darren left his laptop on the swing and stood next to me, looking at the thing over the porch rail. "It's gorgeous. Too bad it's going back."

"What? That car—"

"We broke up."

"Again?"

I sighed. "He feels so right. When we're together, everything is perfect. But his past, it's ugly. It messes him up. I don't know how to get him out of it."

"Probably not your job."

"Yeah." I sat next to him, and he put his arm around me. "I don't know what to do."

Darren didn't say anything but pulled me closer. I felt exhaustion in my bones and a deep pit of sadness in my chest. I wanted to cry so badly, but I couldn't go to my meeting at Carnival puffy eyed and dehydrated. If I accepted Darren's comfort, I didn't stand a chance of keeping my shit together. I stood up.

"Let's go on Mulholland," he said. "Or hit the 405 at, like, noon."

"I have a meeting in Beverly Hills in an hour and a half, and I think I should leave early in case I wreck on the way. I've never driven anything like this before."

"Can I sit in it for ten minutes? Come on, don't hold out on a guy."

Men, even cute, sensitive, bisexual ones, were still men, and cars and guns were somehow hardwired next to sex and food.

"Whoa, Monica!" Dr. Thorensen leaned over the fence, staring at my car. "Take out a HELOC?" He raised an eyebrow at me, smirking. A lock of light brown hair fell in his eyes. He was in his late thirties and looked as though he was in his late twenties. Single. Straight. My friends melted whenever they saw him walk down his driveway.

"Dr. Nordicgod speaks," Darren whispered, obviously not immune to the good doctor's charms.

"It's a loaner," I called out.

"If you're taking it for a spin, I'll come along."

"I can't. I have somewhere to be, then I have to return it."

He whistled. "Sweet ride. Come over and tell me how you liked it. I might take one for a test drive soon."

"Will do."

He waved and went inside.

"Fucking Echo Park," I grumbled, turning to Darren. "What brings you anyway? New car smell wafting around the corner?"

"My wi fi died, and I didn't want to have to get a four-dollar coffee to use the signal at Make."

"All yours."

"I was going to go through Gabby's room." He looked at me as though he expected me to deny him access.

"No problem. And please raid my refrigerator. It's stuffed."

JONATHAN

"ARE you taking Monica to the Collector's Board thing?" Margie asked outside the conference room. Her office buzzed with activity, but no one approached her when she was about to go into a meeting.

"Not going."

"Good. I don't want to get dragged. Dee and Emm are going." Dee and Emm was code for Dad and Mom. The worst thing wouldn't have been taking Margie but Monica.

"All the better." I couldn't tell her I'd walked off Monica's porch with no intention of seeing her again. My sister liked her, and I didn't want to disappoint her or explain my failings.

"You sleep at all?" she asked.

"Same as always," I lied. I'd slept about three hours less than usual.

"You need to rest before you open your mouth in front of her lawyers. I can't believe I have to tell you this again." Her annoyance was a show. We needed to appear to be having an animated discussion when Jessica and her lawyers turned the corner. Margie and I had been in the same room since five in the morning when I drove to her house.

The car had smelled like Monica, and the mirrors were set to accommodate the angle of her beautiful neck. She'd put the seat too far forward and left the wheel turned too far to the left. Still, I wished I could lend her the car another hundred times, just not to see Jessica.

My ex-wife turned the corner, lawyers flanking her. Ryan Myers, who had overseen the divorce, was in his fifties, in a brown suit that matched his fake tan. He'd been ready to tell the neighborhood I beat Jessica for kicks. The other guy was in his thirties and wore a grey pinstripe three-button job with a magenta tie. I didn't recognize him. Margie filled in the blanks without me needing to ask.

"Bennet Rinaldo. Litigator. Ass pain."

"Why do they have three people and we have two?"

"Because you're the aggressor, Jonny. You have to walk in here undermanned or you look like a bully."

"She asked for it."

"Say that any louder and you're on your own."

Polite smiles were exchanged between the five of us. We were having an informal meeting, yet no handshakes were exchanged. Margie held out her hand to indicate they should go in first.

The conference room had windows on two sides and a large wooden table in the center. Coffee and fruit had been laid out on the sideboard. Jessica found her place between her lawyers, and Margie and I sat opposite them.

Jessica was beautiful, and exactly what I'd needed when I was with her. She was sharp, and cold, and in control. I never thought I'd need anything else from a woman because I hadn't yet become a man. I'd changed, but she hadn't. She sat in the clear sunlight, hands folded in front of her. For the first time, she awakened not an ounce of longing, anger, or regret in me. I was glad she was out of my house, out of my bed, out of my daily concern. I wasn't even pissed at her anymore. I didn't think she could get me to hit her again because, somewhere in the past weeks, I'd let her go more completely than I'd imagined possible. A relieved smile crawled across my face, and she saw it before I could wipe it away.

"Gentlemen and lady," Margie said, sitting, "good morning. I understand an order of protection has been filed against my client and is waived temporarily because the plaintiff's lawyers are present."

Legal formality and boring. I tried to keep my eyes off my ex-wife, but she looked like a stranger, and that fascinated me. Had I kissed her lips while she slept? Had I stroked her body languidly while the breeze came through our open window? Had I confessed everything to her in a heat of intimacy or brought her to orgasm with loving care and tenderness?

I couldn't attach any feeling to the events I knew had occurred. I was sure they happened. I'd held her hand when her father died and wiped her tears away with my lips. We'd argued about silly things, like everyone, and we'd argued about serious things. I'd panicked when she told everyone about my kink because I thought I'd lose her. I remembered the fear, and when she told me she was leaving, everything that I was afraid of actually happened. I begged, on my knees, I'd begged her to stay. I remembered all of it as if I watched it on television or read about it in the paper, as if it was someone else's story.

There was a sharp pain in my calf that felt suspiciously like Margie's heel.

"Can you answer the question, Mr. Drazen?" said Rinaldo, the litigator, with a shitheel, superior tone that made me want to punch him.

I leaned forward. "You're going to need to rephrase that." I had no idea what the question was, and I needed him to repeat it.

"On November the twenty-fourth, what were your intentions when you met your ex-wife, Jessica Carnes, at your house?"

"My intentions? My intention was to go home and get some work done before a dinner meeting. She was already there."

"You're stating you did not expect her?"

"Yes."

"Can you describe your frame of mind?"

"No."

"Mr. Drazen—"

"I have to agree," Margie said. "You haven't even filed civil charges, and you want to go into discovery? Or was there something else?"

Myers cut in. "There are circumstances under which we can drop civil actions, which would give the state prosecutor little to go on. We can advocate for thirty-days probation and a standing order of protection."

"Describe the circumstances," Margie said.

"All financial channels between Mr. Drazen and Ms. Carnes can be reopened, permanently."

I looked at my gorgeous ex-wife, whose need for money must be deeply shameful to her. She didn't look at me but kept her back straight, her shoulders relaxed, and her eyes on her lawyer.

"No," I said before Margie, and I felt her heel again.

That was apparently exactly what Rinaldo wanted to hear. He opened a folder with full-color photographs that made me want to avert my gaze. My ex-wife's welted behind, three red slashes across it. I had no idea I'd hit her that hard. I had been pissed off, and it was difficult to feel how hard I was swinging through a haze of rage.

"You admit to giving her those?" Rinaldo seemed to be in charge of the uncomfortable questions.

"I do."

"Why?"

"We agreed to it beforehand," I said.

"Are you saying she asked for it?"

"Not in those words."

"And in the month previous, you broke her wrist during sex."

"She fell."

"Yes, I understand that's the story. You left her in the emergency room as well, so you wouldn't be questioned," Rinaldo said.

"I left her because I had a plane to catch and her boyfriend showed up."

"Your current girlfriend was seen last night with bruises. Did she 'ask for it' as well?"

I glanced at Jessica. Her eyes were in her lap. "You must really want this money," I said.

"Your comment has been noted, Mr. Drazen."

"Monica and I fell down a hill last night. I'd laugh about it if I wasn't so banged up myself."

"Bruises at the base of her neck are not consistent with a fall."

Margie clicked her pen to get everyone's attention and spoke in a tone that stopped Rinaldo and Myers in their tracks. "Thank you, Doctor. Unless you can produce photographs of these alleged bruises, I couldn't care less about them."

Rinaldo listened, then smirked. "We can send a forensic photographer to her right now. The State of California doesn't need her to accuse him of anything."

"The State of California cannot compel a woman to use her body as evidence in a prosecution. Do you have anything else?" Margie demanded. "Because I'm seeing precious little."

Myers nodded to Rinaldo, and the young litigator's shit-eating grin returned. "Ms. Carnes's phone turned itself on to record when you threw her against the table." He pressed a button on his phone.

It started with a scream when I pulled her hair. What a convenient starting point. I looked at Jessica again, and her eyes were glued to the phone. I felt her desire to look at me as her screams echoed through the room.

I demanded a safe word. She questioned its necessity, and I said,

"QUESTION ME AGAIN, *and I'm fucking your ass so hard you won't be able to sit.*"

IT SOUNDED BAD. Really bad. As if she didn't know what a safe word was or why one was necessary, and I'd interrupted her with a threat.

"*IT HURTS. YOU'RE HITTING ME.*"

CALCULATED. So calculated. Somewhere in my mind, I admired her. She would have made a truly impressive partner if she wasn't such a cunt.

The clacking of my belt opening sounded filthy and violent, and my telling her not to yell when I hit her couldn't have sounded more like abuse. Listening to the scene play out was as uncomfortable as it should have been. And it was quite possible a judge would hear it. The recording could fry me.

"Wait," Margie interrupted. "Can you pause that a second?"

Rinaldo paused it, but the violence of the encounter lingered in the room.

"Where did that start again?" Margie asked.

"With a scream." Rinaldo had a wonderful shit-eating grin on his face that would look great once it was wiped off.

"Funny," Margie said. "I heard this one this morning. It starts much earlier." She pressed her own phone. My voice came through.

"Jess, how are you?"

A vanilla conversation progressed into the lead in the pipes of her studio, her hurt for money, our history.

"And you're saying you want to try it my way?"
"I want to. We'd need to set some boundaries beforehand."
"No, my way. Right now. Then you tell me if you can take it."

"Stop," said Jessica. "This is fake."
"No," I said. "It's exactly what happened. I'd swear to it."

"Okay." Jessica's voice, soft and audible.
"That's 'okay, sir.'"
"Doesn't that seem a little silly?"
"You want to do this or not?"
"Yes, sir."
"Stand up."

"I don't want to hear this," Jessica whispered to Myers.
He whispered *shhh* and patted her hand as my voice came through again.

"Stop trying to look saucy. This is a functional matter and not for your pleasure."

The next part was hard to hear, but Margie turned it up.

"This is what it is, this is the kind of sex you're agreeing to."

I commanded her to put her hands behind her back and face forward, then I checked on her, asking if she was all right.
    I watched her reaction across the table. Her face flushed, and her jaw set. I

hadn't seen her blush since the first time I'd kissed her. The red deepened for the next part, which Margie turned up.

"I'll undo your jeans. I'll pull them down to the middle of your thighs so it's hard to walk. You'll be uncomfortable, and that will please me. Then I'll get behind you, and I'll grab a handful of your hair at the back of your head and bend you over that table. I'll take off my belt, loop it once, and slap it across those sweet white cheeks until you're pink as a rose and your face is covered with tears. I'll stop when I can stick two fingers in your cunt and feel how sopping wet you are. Then I'll fuck you until you beg me to let you come, which I may or may not let you do. That going to work for you? Didn't think so."

"Do it."

I NOTICED for the first time how shrill and desperate her voice was. At the time, it had sounded like a controlled whisper. On the recording, it sounded like a child's whine.

"Jess, really."

"Do it! Start with the hair. Or the pants. Whatever."

"No."

"Do it!"

"Stop, Jess."

"Are you a fucking man? Or do you just beg and cry for what you can't have? Is that how you get off?"

THEN THE CRASH.

Margie paused it. "We've heard the rest."

"Where did you get that garbage?" Rinaldo asked.

"You Tube," Margie said. "It had seven hundred views this morning. But let me refresh. Huh. Got about forty-two hundred now. Funny what people find entertaining, isn't it?"

"A woman asking for it," I muttered. Margie shot me a look, but I was spared the heel.

"She stole my phone." Jessica's eyes bore into me.

"I have no idea what you're talking about."

"The singer."

"Go near her again, and I'll kill you."

Margie's heel drew blood. I would have to buy her flats for our next meeting.

"Like you did Rachel," Jessica said through her teeth. "Took sixteen years. But there's no statute of limitation on murder, even manslaughter, Jon."

Ryan Myers stood, closing his files. "We're done here. Ms. Drazen, you and your client can consider our offer. Get back to me when you have an answer. The photographs still stand, as well as the possible pattern of abuse with his current girlfriend, which we'll be sure to mention to the prosecutor."

"Thanks for the warning." Margie stood and shook his hand. Meeting over and, as usual, only the lawyers walked away unscathed.

CHAPTER 84

MONICA

I wore bruise-hiding clothes for the meeting, but as I wrapped my scarf around my neck, I wondered if Jonathan would come back to me before or after they were gone. My eyes welled, but I choked it back. Self-control. A woman of grace. I had to be that. I could crash after the meeting.

The car was, in a word, themostfantasticthingever. Fuck Jonathan. I got to the meeting feeling as though I was the architect of a major planetary takeover. I would return the car as soon as I was done there, but until then, it was like a space pod in a science fiction movie. Up the elevator, I told myself the usual. *My name is Monica. I stand six feet tall in heels. I am descended from one of the greatest writers of the twentieth century. I sing like an angel and growl like a lion. I am music. I am a goddess.* I choked on the last word because it was his, but I believed it. I didn't think I ever had before.

I expected to be awed by the size of the lobby or the glass-enclosed conference room, but I wasn't. The dark wood floors, the receptionists' desk that put their heads six inches above the person they were talking to, the marble staircase to the executive offices, all of it would have given me an anxiety attack six months earlier. But on the day I actually had a meeting that would have sent my friends into fits of envy-laced congratulations, I felt not a bit of tension or worry. Everything was in its box. Every emotion, positive or negative, was put away.

I understood what Jonathan found so appealing about self-control. I was the master of my body, my feelings, my words. I was fully in the moment, keeping my shit together. I was unattached to the results of the meeting. I was only concerned with being *in* it.

I'd heard those sentiments before, but I only realized that I had internalized them as I waited to be brought to a meeting where I was but a single, struggling singer in a room full of people who could make my dreams reality. I had what they needed. I had the music.

Carnival Records didn't have a cutting edge reputation. They weren't "street." They recorded gangsters and drug addicts, same as anyone, but internally, they were old school and buttoned-up. The office was all business. They weren't there to create or be part of an arts community. They took care of business. That was all. So though I'd worn a yellow dress with cream shoes, a cream scarf to cover Jonathan's marks, my hair in braids, and red lipstick bright enough to stop traffic, the employees kept the colors toned down, the lipstick nude, and the arty affectation to a minimum.

I wasn't waiting long before the receptionist brought me up the stairs, her ass swaying like a pendulum in her Robert Rodriguez skirt, big cloppy shoes silent from practice. She led me into the conference room. "Would you like some coffee?"

Again, Los Angeles was spread before me from Wilshire to the haze of the horizon. "Tea would be great. Just plain."

She smiled and left. I didn't sit but looked out the window onto the city of Los Angeles and the miasma of smog over the east side. Windows looked out into the hallway and all the blinds were up, so everyone in the office could see where Harry was and who he was talking to. He came into my sight, flanked by an entourage, mid-conversation. He smiled and waved through the window to me, stopping to finish talking to Eddie Milpas and an older woman who had a very important point to make, apparently. Two younger women flanked with notebooks and smart suits. A young man with three days of facial growth and a plaid shirt with slacks, an intern from the looks of him, opened the door when Eddie pointed to it. The gaggle of them strolled in.

"Ms. Faulkner," Harry said.

We had handshakes and introductions. Eddie and I exchanged a meaningful look that acknowledged we'd already met. I tried to put an innocuous expression on my face to tell him I wasn't going to wrestle with him over Bondage Girl in front of his boss. Everyone sat.

We had almost exactly the same small talk as every other meeting I'd attended. Traffic first. Los Angeles neighborhoods next. Some personal family stuff from Harry about his kid's Little League. I avoided a conversation about baseball that could have gone on for days.

"Well," Harry said as if he was cutting in on his own conversation, "it was something else to hear you perform last week. Wasn't what I expected to see when I came out there."

"I'm glad you enjoyed it."

Jerry, the producer who first recorded me playing "Collared" with a theremin, blasted in wearing a navy jacket and a windowpane shirt with the top three buttons undone "Sorry, sorry." He winked at me.

Harry gave him a smile that could have been swapped for a glare with no change in the message, then turned back to me. "Everyone in this room has seen you play."

I hadn't expected that. I thought they might have all heard Jerry's recording, but apparently, they all stopped by Frontage at some point. Of course, Harry had heard me play the B.C. Modern.

"We're all very impressed," he said. "Eddie and I have been discussing some marketing strategies, and he's come up with some ideas that are out of the park."

Customer service smile.

If it was Bondage Girl, we were going to have a very short meeting.

If it was me pretending I was some sort of expert in the art of submission, I was taking my little F-type Jaguar home, picking up Darren, and going up and down Mulholland until I needed to hit a gas station. Then I would bring it right back to Griffith Park with an empty tank.

"Out of the park, huh?" I said. "I'm excited to hear it."

"Were you considering doing more work like you did at the B.C. Mod show?"

Without Kevin?

Could I? I wasn't visual. I had taste, I could put stuff together, but I didn't have what Kevin had. "I'd like to, but it's complicated. That was a one-off."

He waved his hand. "It's an attitude. The work will follow, if that's what you want. We want to brand you something like a Laurie Anderson. An all-around package. A musician, yes, but also an artist."

"We want to introduce you around to some of L.A.'s art patrons," Eddie broke in. He seemed on board with the new strategy. I hoped he'd thought of it, because if he was just along for the ride, it would be half-assed. "There's an event Thursday night at L.A. Mod. The Collector's Board gala. Very big thing."

"It's short notice," I said. I had work, but I could switch a shift. Work wouldn't stop me. Jonathan had been clear he wasn't going, but maybe that had changed. I didn't know how I felt about seeing him under those circumstances.

Harry picked up the thread. "It's very short notice, but this event is only once a year. Next year, it'll be too late. We want your face there, photographed with Carnival Records." He indicated Eddie. "An artistic partnership."

I don't know what expression I wore, but I wore it long enough for Eddie to break the silence.

"What do you think?" he asked.

"Can I get back to you on Thursday night?"

"No problem," Eddie said with the same tone he'd used the last time we met, as if *maybe* really meant *yes*. He held out his hand to one of the assistants, and she handed him a piece of paper. He passed it to me. "These are the terms we're offering."

I looked at the paper, but the words and numbers swam before my eyes. I bit my lips between my teeth to keep from smiling.

CHAPTER 85

MONICA

I COULDN'T DRIVE. I kept hitting the gas pedal too hard and taking unbelievable risks because that fucking car moved like a Serengeti cat. I had a heart-lightening exuberance I hadn't felt since, well....ever.

I needed a lawyer. The problem was artists didn't hire entertainment lawyers. I couldn't call someone out of the phone book or get a recommendation from a friend and hire an entertainment lawyer for a ridiculous hourly rate. Entertainment lawyers took on clients they believed in and either charged seven-fifty per billable hour or took a percentage of the contract's value. They didn't just look over a contract; they negotiated it, and negotiated hard. The big ones were picky. They weren't wasting their time on a negotiation where their client had no leverage.

I pulled over, parking by a meter on LaBrea. I called Jonathan but got a recorded message in a soothing female voice telling me the subscriber wasn't available. I'd never heard that one. I didn't go to voice mail. Just nothing. Fuck it. I played with my phone until the web told me the number I was looking for.

"Hi," I said when I got a pick up. "This is Monica Faulkner. I'm looking for Margaret Drazen."

"Hold please."

I waited. I was sure I'd be sitting at the side of the road in my white convertible for a good long time. Her firm was huge, her name was on the door, and I wasn't even a client.

"This is Margaret," Margie said.

I sat straighter, pausing because I didn't expect her to pick up. "Hi, uhm, this is

563

Monica. Jonathan's..." I paused again because I didn't know how to describe myself.

"Yes. Hello. Nice to hear from you. How are you?"

"I'm fine. I really hate to do this. I feel like I'm imposing on you."

"You don't need me to help you move or anything, do you?"

"No. I need a lawyer."

"Fancy that," Margie said. "I'm a lawyer, and I got a staff of them running around here."

"I know, but I need an entertainment lawyer. I don't want you to think I'm trying to use Jonathan to get ahead. I'm just in a bit of...well, a great position, actually. And I need help with some contract negotiations. So I'm sorry, but—"

"My dear," Margie said, her voice warm and comforting, "don't you realize? You've turned my brother around. You may live to regret this, but you're one of the family now."

She seemed so happy, I couldn't tell her about the previous night.

CHAPTER 86

JONATHAN

"That's Steinbeck country," I said, watching the waitresses work the floor.

"Yeah," said the blonde in the blue dress. Her friends were ten feet away. "They made us read all that in school. I'm more of a Heinlein, Ellison girl myself. You?"

She was lovely. The perfect vision of womanhood in a simple, short blue dress and heels. Not slutty. Fair hair twisted up. Warm smile through pink lips. Fingertips at the wine glass she sipped from. She was smart, and we were both sober, which was also nice.

"Modernists, I guess. Pynchon, that kinda thing. Ever read *Mason & Dixon*? It's hilarious."

"None of that stuff in the Salinas library," she smiled. "Sheriff Traulich would burn it himself."

I normally wouldn't talk to a woman at my own bar, and I'd promised myself I wouldn't sleep around. But that morning, I'd run over a silver heart Harry Winston keychain as I pulled out. Since it felt insignificant, like an out-of-place stone, I opened the gate and continued. I almost hit the white Jaguar parked across the driveway on the street.

The return of my gift had hurt, even though it shouldn't have. I should have expected it. Of course Monica wouldn't accept it after what happened. She was still honorable. I'd managed to leave that intact. I looked in the glove compartment for the navel ring and didn't find it. I was sure it would turn up on my desk.

But it didn't, and that confused me. I'd gone up to the bar to verbally pistol-whip Freddie about hiring a sixteen-year-old to carry drinks, and to think about not thinking about Monica. The first got done, the second was interrupted by the blonde in the blue dress.

"...and they all play country music," she said.

I'd missed something, and I didn't care. I'd never actually needed to care before, but that had changed. The woman in a blue dress was a nice person, by all accounts, but I had no interest in sleeping with her.

I couldn't hear my phone over the music, but I felt it buzz in my pocket. My first thought was the memory of Monica's song, but I'd blocked her. There would be no more songs. It was Eddie.

—Cancel Thursday night. I
have to go to the Collectors
thing. You going?—

"Hang on a second," I said. "Let me take this." The woman in the blue dress nodded. She wasn't boring or easy. She was fine, but she wasn't a goddess.

—Nope—

—Ok. Monica said you weren't
going. Just checking.—

I dialed his number and walked to the hall with my finger pressing my free ear closed. "What does Monica have to do with it?"

"Carnival is sending her with me. Why? You don't trust me?"

"No, I don't. You're a lousy driver."

"She's driving herself. See, I knew you'd flip out."

"I'm not flipping out."

"You are flipping out," he said. I got into the elevator. "It's business. I'm not touching her, okay? Harry would have my ass, and God only knows you'd bean me in my sleep or something."

"I apologized."

"Whatever. I knew I had to explicitly say something, and that's what I'm doing. Don't flip out."

"Okay, Ed," I said as I walked into the hotel lobby. Michelle, the rooms manager, tried to stop me with something I was sure I didn't care about. I waved her off and headed for the exit. It was pouring rain, and I had no umbrella.

I was flipping out.

CHAPTER 87

MONICA

DARREN WAVED from the Frontage bar. It was crowded. I did some meet and greet before I made my way to him and Adam.

"Thank you," I said when he handed me the keys to my Honda. When Jonathan had said he'd replaced the starter, he obviously meant "with a new car" because the Honda had still been missing a piece.

"Came to three-twenty-five," he said.

"I'll have it for you tomorrow."

"Damn right you will. Because you owe him." He indicated Adam, who put his arm around my waist.

"I'm taking it out in kisses." He planted his mouth on my cheek, and I squealed. He held me harder and I laughed louder, playfully punching his shoulder and forgetting Jonathan for half a second. Adam was a good guy. I owed him and Darren for towing my Honda from the Stock parking lot to a repair shop, paying for the work, and driving it to me. Kisses and a few hundred bucks were the least I could do.

"It's in the lot," Darren said once Adam let me go before I got cooties.

"Where are you guys off to?"

"Loft party at the Family Four. You coming? Dizzy Roth wanted to talk about the B.C. Mod piece."

That sounded like the best offer I would get. "I'll meet you there."

567

CHAPTER 88

JONATHAN

I'D TRIED to let the world spin on its usual course for two days. I tried to see what would happen if I just worked, stared at the ceiling, and avoided Monica. I didn't ask Eddie if he was *really* going with her, and I didn't ask Margie about Dad's attendance. That lasted twenty-four hours. I found myself in the pouring rain at Frontage, watching at her through the window.

She was smiling. Darren was there, but he didn't concern me. The other guy kissed her cheek, and she laughed. I stepped out from the bus shelter, into the rain. He touched her waist, and she permitted it.

I don't know what brought the clarity. It could have been the kiss. It could have been the touching. But the laughter put me over the edge. Seeing her with her friends, as free of me as I'd made her, without all the destruction I'd brought. Happy, while I could barely have a straight thought without her voice invading.

I had wanted to talk to her. That was it. Just tell her I didn't want her to go to the Collector's Board thing because my father would be there, and I simply didn't want her near him. I was soaking wet in the middle of Santa Monica Boulevard, wondering if I should hurl myself through the window or the door, as if those were the only rational choices.

I was on my way to the door when they were on their way out. I moved fast. That was always my advantage, not strength but speed and agility. I had the guy against the wall, crushed against the umbrella he'd started to open, before he'd even seen me.

"What the—"

"Jonathan!" Her voice. It sounded very far away. I had the guy's eyes on mine. He looked confused, and I wanted to kill him for not knowing what had upset me.

Monica. Even with the rain in her hair and in her eyes while she was snarling like a lion, I wanted her. What the fuck had I been thinking?

"God damn it. What is *wrong* with you?" She pushed me off the guy who had kissed her, then pushed me again. "You are fucked, you know that?"

I stepped back. She stood between him and me, hands out, ready to take me on. I couldn't get to him without knocking her over. "Move. Just move."

"Are you serious?"

"You're mine. No one puts his hands on you. No one."

The three of them stared at me for a second, then Monica jerked out her thumb. "This guy?"

"That guy."

"Okay, besides the fact that you walked out on me—"

"Enough!"

The voice that cut the rain was near as powerful as anything I'd heard. Had a car alarm gone off from the vibrations, I would not have been surprised. It was Darren. Little pipsqueak snapped me right out of it. I went from rage to shame before he was finished with the last syllable.

"I have *had it* with the two of you," Darren shouted. "I am sick and tired of the whining from you"—he pointed at Monica—"and the psychotic behavior from you." He pointed at me. "Stop acting like a dick and throwing money at her. Stop breaking up. Just stop. The next time I hear you two broke up, I'm sending out wedding invitations."

I was struck silent. A part of me smiled, but it wasn't my mouth.

Darren took the hand of the guy who had kissed Monica and pulled him away. Of course, the coupling had never been Monica and him but Darren and him. I opened my mouth to apologize, but Darren wasn't facing me. Rain soaked my shirt, dripping under my collar. I'd never felt so ridiculous. Losing my temper never had good results. Monica hugged them both and came back to me. Her skirt stuck to her legs and her shoes sloshed, but she took her time.

"Do you feel like an ass?" she said.

"Yeah," I said. "How did you get here?"

"Little black Honda."

"Can I walk you?"

"Did you bring an umbrella? Because you broke mine."

I took my leather jacket off and held it over her head.

"Chivalry will get you nowhere," she said.

I sensed she meant it. A drop of water fell from her nose to her lower lip, and I had to swallow the desire to kiss it away. "I need to talk to you."

"Really?" Sarcasm dripped from her.

She started walking, and I followed her. She kept too far away for my jacket, so I just rolled it over my arm. We walked down the block, getting ever more wet with each step.

CHAPTER 89

MONICA

THE NEIGHBORHOOD WAS RESIDENTIAL, lined with single-family houses and the occasional apartment building. Wet, brown leaves covered every car, curb, and grassy patch. We said nothing the entire walk to my car. I was getting wet, but he was soaked. His hair was dark brown with water, and his eyelashes stuck together in points of four or five. He looked down, hands in his pockets. He must have been freezing.

I stopped by my car. "This is me. Thanks for walking me."

"You could have kept the car I got you." He put his hand on the wet bark of the parkway tree.

"I know. I drove it to my meeting because this one wasn't fixed yet. So, thanks for the loaner."

"I don't like us when we're formal. All please and thank you."

"What do you want then?" I crossed my arms.

He pursed his lips and looked at my feet, then back up to my face. "I want you to be real with me."

"You want me to be real?"

"Yeah."

"Real. You want real?"

"Real, goddess."

"You *blocked* me, you motherfucker!" I pushed his shoulders, and he stepped back into the tree trunk. "I wrote you that song, and you were so disgusted, you blocked me." I pushed him again, but he had nowhere to go.

"I had to."

"Oh, let's hear about that."

"If you kept sending me shit like that, I was going to come back to you."

"As opposed to what? This?" I spread my arms to indicate the block, the rain, our bodies almost touching, the fight over who was allowed to kiss me.

"I knew if I saw you again, I'd want you." He was pleading, leaning forward, hands out as if passing me a basketball pumped full of pain. "That fucking mouth. As soon as it opened, I knew I'd want to kiss you. And those wet clothes sticking to you. And the hair plastered to your face. You're custom made for me to hurt. Do you understand?"

I understood all too well. "Hurt me."

"Monica, that's not what I mean."

"Ruin me."

"Stop."

I stepped forward. "Destroy me, Jonathan."

He cursed under his breath and pushed his lips to mine. His movements were fierce, his tongue invading my mouth, his arms circling me. He tasted of fennel toothpaste and whiskey, the same as the first time I'd kissed him. The memories went down the curve in my back and settled between my legs. He pushed me into the car, pressing his erection into me, and I pushed back, letting his hardness find my cleft. I groaned into his mouth.

"God," he said, "I have to have you."

"Take me. Own me. Use me. Pick a verb. Just, please."

"Fuck you. I'm going to fuck you. That's my verb."

He pushed his hips into me hard, and I bent my neck in response. My legs wrapped around him, grinding. Water dripped from his forehead onto mine as he kissed me. The rain had gone from a heavy mist to a driving torrent. He straightened and pulled me off the car.

"Take me home," I practically had to shout over the weather.

He pushed me against the car and kissed me in the rain one more time.

CHAPTER 90

MONICA

WE FUMBLED up the steps with lips attached, past the porch swing where he'd tried and failed to break my heart, into the living room, where we dripped little pools of water like a reverse archipelago behind us. I took his hand and walked him into the laundry room.

The laundry room was a foul, filthy place, and I was immediately ashamed of it. When I cleaned the house, the laundry room was the last floor to get a mop-over and the last sink to get wiped clean. So nine times out of ten, I just didn't bother. And there I was, with a guy who had a team of people clean his corners with Q-tips, dripping onto gross, 1980s-era linoleum. It was the first water that floor had seen in months.

"It's a mess in here," I said, turning away from the towels I had strung up to dry, weeks ago.

He put his arms behind me and unzipped my dress. I noticed his chattering jaw and the ice of his fingertips as they grazed my spine.

"What does that have to do with me fucking you?" He peeled off my dress. My bra cups were heavy, soaked, hanging off me, and he slipped the straps off my shoulders, easily releasing me. I was down to panties and shoes, and he was still freezing in wet clothes.

Pushing him against the dryer, I unbuttoned his shirt, kissing down the center of his torso as I went. He was damp, and I warmed him with my mouth, licking his hard, tight, nipples. His arms came out of his sleeves like a molting caterpillar. I threw his shirt on top of my dress on the floor and worked on his pants while he kissed me.

572

"On your knees," he said.

I got down, eye-level to his crotch, and opened his pants. The zipper didn't work well wet, but I got it down. I hooked my fingers in the waistband and took his briefs down with the pants, arcing the elastic over his erection. He stepped out of the legs, kicking off his shoes while he did, and held up a foot. I peeled off his sock, then did the same with the other foot. He was naked. Perfect. I gazed up at him, his perfect, lean body with its cut lines and furrows making a triangle from his hips to the beauty between his legs.

I took his cock in my mouth, licking every surface as if to warm it. He put his hands in my hair and groaned.

"Let me feel you."

He held my head still and pushed his cock all the way down my throat, balls-deep. I breathed through my nose, the aroma of his wet skin filling me. He held me still, and when I looked up at him, he was watching me. He slid out slowly. I put my tongue against him as he did.

"Have I mentioned you're very good at this?" he asked.

"Yes."

"Stand up."

When I did, he gathered up the clothes and put them in the dryer. He stared at the buttons and smiled.

"You have no idea how to use this, do you?" I asked.

"Not the knobs, no."

I turned the machine on. Jonathan picked me up by the waist and put me on top of it. The dryer shook and rattled under me.

"Lean back," he said, "and spread those knees for me." He slid a finger under the crotch of my panties. I drew in a breath. His fingers moved from my entrance to my clit. "You're wet." He slid his fingers in me. They were cold.

"God, yes."

He pushed my knees farther apart with his free hand. "Tell me what you want."

"I want you."

"You want me, what?"

I wanted his cock in me. I wanted to come. I wanted him to do whatever he wanted to make me scream and beg for him. I looked at him, his perfect skin mottled with goose bumps, his nipples hard with cold, hair still wet. For the first time, I noticed the blue tinge around his lips. "I want you to dry off. You look hypothermic."

I snapped a towel off the line and put it over his head, leaning forward to dry his hair. He let me, drawing me closer as I caressed his head more slowly and gently as he got drier. I hopped off the dryer and ran the towel all over him, chest to back to glorious butt to muscular legs and the tops of his perfect feet. Wrapping the towel around his shoulders, I kissed him.

"I feel better already," he said.

"You need something warm to drink. I have tea."

"You? Tea?"

"You can pick a flavor. Come on."

He picked me up as if he was carrying me over a threshold, brought me to the kitchen, naked but for my underpants, and deposited me on the counter. I leaned to the shelf and got my teapot, then leaned the other way and filled it. I gave it to him, and he put it on the stove.

"The tea's on the shelf above," I said. "I have some assortment thingie in the back."

"Assortment thingie. Let me see." He found the box and brought it back, but he didn't open it. I put my legs around his hips, drawing him to me. He stroked my eyebrow with his thumb. "I'm sorry. I was cruel last night. I said terrible things."

"Yes, you did."

"And I blocked you. I knew it would hurt you, and I did it anyway. What you sent made me question my actions. I wasn't ready to question them. I thought I'd done the right thing, protecting you from me. I'm still not convinced otherwise."

"Does that mean you're going to leave me again? Because Darren's going to shit if you do."

"Fuck Darren."

"Don't leave me to protect me, Jonathan. I'm a grown woman, and I'm perfectly capable of ruining my life without your help."

"Yes, Mistress." A smile stretched across his face as he chose a black tea and held out the box for me.

"Not kidding." I snapped out a chamomile. "I mean it. I had to hold my shit together for a meeting the next day, and it was the hardest thing I ever did."

"But you did it."

"Yeah, but—"

"I'm proud of you." He put his hand on my cheek, and we kissed until the teapot whistled. He shrugged his towel tighter and poured the steaming water into two cups, dropping in the teabags.

"I called Margie," I said, crossing my legs and waiting for my tea to cool. "She's getting an entertainment lawyer from her firm to work with me. I'm sorry if that was wrong."

"It's fine. She likes you. You're the eighth sister she never had."

I cleared my throat. "And you know that thing? That collector's party?"

He glanced up at me, head bent toward his tea. "The Collector's Board at L.A. Mod. Of course."

"Carnival is a donor, so they're sending Eddie. They want me to go with him. It's part of presenting me as an artist." I saw him tense, changing the angle of the towel draped on his shoulders. "It's business."

"Absolutely not."

I was silent as I stared at him over the rim of my cup.

"Monica?"

"Jonathan."

"He wants to fuck you."

"I don't think you're actually threatened by Eddie Milpas."

He rubbed his eyes. "I'll tell you what. You'll go with me."

"Really?"

"Really."

"Oh, Jonathan, I'd so much rather go with you."

"I want you to be warned it's all Jessica's crowd. They're nasty. They're bored and rich. If you're with me, you're a target for their boredom."

"I don't care."

He put his face to mine. I smelled the tea on his breath. "They'll whisper about you."

"Fuck them."

"We found the whole audio on her phone, and we posted it online. It's gone crazy. Everyone knows."

I got closer, put my nose next to his, and whispered, "What part of 'fuck them' was unclear?"

"That's my goddess." He pressed his face to mine, his mouth open only enough to move them in time with me, giving me a kiss made purely of lips and skin. There was sex in the kiss, but only the wafting hint of his breathing. Then he slipped his tongue between my lips, and my spine tingled as if some unholy spirit used my vertebrae as piano keys.

I groaned. My mouth accepted his darting tongue, the command of his lips. I arched when his hand slipped down to my breast, grazing the back of his hand against my hard nipple.

"Take me," I whispered into his mouth.

"I'll do as I like," he said into mine, and I felt the force of his words in the pressure between my legs. The personality change that accompanied play was so stark that the first utterance in his stern, serious voice, made my cleft quiver like a plucked string. "Hands behind you on the counter. One on top of the other."

I did it. He put his hand at the small of my back and pressed upward until I was arched and facing the ceiling.

"You need to go back to Bordelle." He pulled my knees apart roughly. "This cotton shit is unworthy." Opening two drawers, he placed my feet on the edges so my legs stayed open. I heard the clink of silverware. "This thing," he said before I heard the soft crunch of fabric being cut. He'd sheared my panties with a steak knife. "It offends me."

"Yes, sir."

He ran his hand over me. I couldn't see what he was doing. I felt his dry skin awaken nerve endings, grazing over my breasts, belly, thighs. Even the slightest pressure sent shards of pain at the black-and-blue base of my rib cage and the soft meat between my legs, a punctuation for the pleasure of his touch.

"You're still bruised," he said. "That'll take time to heal."

"Don't stop."

"I'm going to be gentle where you're hurt," he said. "But everywhere else is mine."

"Yes."

"Now, you want your tea?"

"Yes, sir." Though my body was awake with desire, my voice was husky with heat and exhaustion. My vocal cords hadn't forgotten that it was close to midnight.

He pressed my mouth open with his thumb and forefinger, as if I was a kitten taking medicine. The teabag hovered over my face, dripping hot liquid over my mouth. I felt hot fluid on my lip and the dry, waxen taste of chamomile tea on my tongue. It traveled down my chin and my throat. I swallowed it like an offering of communion.

"Thank you, sir."

I closed my eyes, feeling the warmth of dripping tea down my chest. He must have dipped the bag back into the cup because the heat renewed on my nipples. Lines of molten liquid dripped down around my ribs to my back. I gasped when he put the bag on my belly and dragged it down to the edge of my triangle. I quivered in anticipation. That hot thing, on me. Soft and pliant, yet firm in its burning intensity. But he didn't. He leaned over, kissing and licking the tea from me. He sucked my nipple gently as his hand stayed on the teabag, which felt as though it was cooling too fast.

I groaned. I had never thought to put a hot teabag on my clit, but it was all I could think about. He had to do it. Had to. Before it got cold.

When he moved his mouth to the other nipple, cleaning it with his tongue and lips, he slid the bag down, pressing it against my clit with the heel of his hand while putting two fingers in me. I yelled. Hot. Not straight-from-the-pot hot, but hot enough. Ten times hotter on my clit than anywhere else, and the fire added exponentially to my desire. Hot tea dripped down my cleft. I shuddered everywhere, spreading my legs wider, pushing into his fingers. His tongue was still at my nipple, and I was bruised, yes, but I wanted him to bite it. I wanted him to hurt me. I was addicted to it.

He pushed his hand against me, heel on hot teabag on clit, fingers in cunt, and he rubbed them in circles. My pussy drank it. The bag got drier as the tea was squeezed out of it, making it rougher, like crackling leaves in the fall. The little scratches from hot, sticklike herbs drove me to the edge.

"I want to come," I cried.

"No."

"I can't." I opened my eyes to find him looking down at me.

"You're mine. No matter what happens. Your pleasure and pain. Your skin. Your lips. Your cunt."

He pushed the bag and his fingers into me. "Jonathan. You own me. I am yours. God, who else? Fuck. Please. My king. Please let me—"

"Come."

With a sharp movement, he brought me to orgasm in my kitchen again. I thrust against his hand, screaming, back twisting. He put his other hand behind my head so I didn't bang it on the cabinet, and when I found myself winding around to the point where I almost kicked out a drawer, he caught me, panting and naked.

"Thank you," was all I could say.

"You're welcome."

"God, I love you."

"And I, you," he said softly. "You still want tea?"

"It's cold," I said into his ear. "I don't like it cold."

"You have it all over you. Let me get you in the shower."

He took me to my bathroom and got me into the tub. I stood under the water, letting it run where the tea had.

Jonathan got in, exquisitely naked, taut, lean, skin over muscle over bone in perfect proportion. I didn't know if he worked out. I didn't know where he'd find the time. He could just be the way he was with no effort whatsoever, and that was all right with me.

"You just dried off," I said. "And I'm making you get wet again." I put the bar of soap to his chest and rubbed, working over his shoulders slowly, and back to his nipples, to his tight stomach. His erection was huge, waiting, a sign of things to come. I stroked it with the soap. I didn't want to rush. I wanted to take him in fully, in all his beauty, touch every surface, feel every bump and curve.

His eyes went over my body as I washed him. I cleaned his back by putting my arms around him, feeling his dick press against me. He took me by my hair and pulled my head back. The water got in my face, and I smiled. He wet my hair as he kissed my neck. He squeezed too much shampoo into my hair and massaged my scalp. The suds were everywhere. I laughed when they went into my eyes, and he laughed too, pressing his thumbs to my eyes to stroke the suds away. I was covered in shampoo, and Jonathan used it to bathe me, sliding his hands where the tea had gone. He went gently where I was hurt, roughly where I wasn't, until he got to where the teabag had made me come, and I groaned.

"Ah, goddess...." He slid his hand under my ass, his fingertips slipping into my folds. They were wet but not from the shower.

"Again, please."

"Put your hands up to the showerhead." I did, and his followed the line of my arms, cupping his hands over mine, sliding them to the pipe that held the shower head. "Hold that."

My arms up as if tied, he pushed me against the tiles and put one of my legs around his waist. The head of his cock sat at my entrance, waiting. I pushed against him, and where his member touched me, my body responded in waves of pleasure. He kissed me, hands at my ass, spreading me apart with his fingers.

"Please," I said. "I want you."

"I'm yours." He thrust into me. It felt like an electric shock through my body, pulsing as he thrust, every inch adding to the pressure. I was full, engorged, all surface area for him. "Look at me."

I opened my eyes. His hair was soaked. Rivulets of water dripped down the angles of his cheeks and neck as his hips worked into me. He pulled my ass open and slipped in a finger. Just a finger. Exquisite. The pleasure with none of the pain. I clenched around him.

"Soon, when you're healed, I'm taking this ass again," he said.

"It's yours."

He pushed another finger in, and his eyelids dropped a little. I groaned, feeling stretched and possessed, as though every part of me was under his control and protection.

"Look at me when you come," he said.

"I'm close." My arms ached, but I didn't move them, just held the pipe above me because he commanded it.

"Yes." He went faster, pushing into me. He used the fingers in my asshole to draw our bodies together fast and hard as he slapped against me.

My clit filled, my cunt opened with sensation, my ass sucked him in. "Oh, God Jonathan. Jonathan." I looked in his eyes, holding his face still in my vision.

"Come with me."

"Yes."

I released. The effort of keeping my face to his while I came prolonged the orgasm that washed over me. My arms were frozen. I couldn't arch or close my eyes. I just exploded in a controlled way, toes curling, my hands gripping the pipe. My cries echoed against the tile walls. My vision blurred. His mouth opened, and he grunted a long slow vibration, slowing, pulsing in a different rhythm. His eyes and mine watched each other, locked in pleasure, above and below.

CHAPTER 91

JONATHAN

THE HOUSE WAS AS DARK, and the rain and cloud cover had darkened it further.
We tucked each other into bed, and I curled against her. I shifted her T-shirt and
kissed her shoulder, moving my lips across it. She tasted of warm milk and canned
peaches.

"My Jonathan," she groaned.

"I'm not making a pass at you."

She turned to face me. "Like hell."

"I think you'll help me sleep."

"You never sleep much."

"Well, I've been sleeping less, and I don't feel right. Not since the arrest. And
since Rachel." I cleared my throat when I choked on her name. My neck and arms
hurt as if the nerves were being squeezed. I broke out in a sweat. Ridiculous. I
tried to get control of myself, but it was hard to breathe. I must have been coming
down with something.

She turned around to face me. "You ever going to forgive yourself for that?"

"I'll get around to it."

"You're going to give yourself ulcers."

I didn't answer. Talking about my irrational emotional issues wouldn't get
either one of us to sleep, and we both needed it. I stroked her eyebrows as I'd done
before, getting her eyes to flutter closed. She sighed and let me touch her, relaxing.
Our legs got heavy together as she released the spring of tension binding them. She
seemed on the edge of sleep, breathing regularly and softly. Her eyes stayed closed
when I stroked her hair. Then she opened them.

579

"You're wide awake," she said.

"It's all right."

She sat up. "No, it's not."

I tried to sit up with her, but she pushed me down. I was stronger, of course, but I let her press my shoulders to the mattress.

"Stay here," she said.

She rolled off the bed and padded away. I didn't know where she was going or what she intended, but I hoped it didn't involve Xanax or alcohol. I didn't want to fight about that or anything. She came back with a viola and bow slung over her shoulder like a batter coming off the on-deck circle. If I'd ever seen anything as sexy as Monica Faulkner in a stretched-out T-shirt and wielding a stringed instrument, I'd be at pains to remember it.

"You going to knock me unconscious with that thing?"

"One way or the other." She crawled on the bed, leaving one foot on the floor and stretching her body so the instrument fit under her chin. She drew the bow across, making it hum, then turned a knob at the top of the neck. I slipped closer until my lips touched her thigh. "Any requests?"

"Something bombastic. With percussion."

She laughed and played a measure. I recognized it right away as Mendelssohn's "Evening Song." She was all right, my woman. What she was trying wouldn't work, but the honest attempt wouldn't go unappreciated. I stroked her knee with my thumb as she played and rocked her body with the slow rhythm of the song. The piece was short, and when it ended, she riffed on the melody, smoothing it further. Her hips rocked the mattress like waves on the ocean. I stroked her knee, then stopped, placing my hand on her leg.

I listened with my eyes closed, feeling her sway, hearing her music, as it got farther and farther away. The sounds of the ocean outside the window grew louder, and the water rose, coming over the sill and flowing onto her floor. She must not have noticed the flood or care about the fact that her house would probably float right down the hill, because she kept playing and rocking. I was too heavy, too weak, too contented, to stop her.

The rain got louder and harder, dropping into my eyes, blinding me. My stomach was in complete upheaval, and my head swam as the waves pulled me out to sea. I had a dead weight dragging down my right arm. It was a person. A woman. Monica? I'd let her face go under while I fought the tide. I pulled her up, the effort twisting my stomach. Her mouth was full of water, and her eyes were glassed over.

The scene was mine. I'd been blacked out from half a bottle of whiskey, but things had happened, and my brain had stored them deep.

"Rachel, baby, come on!" But even saying the words took more energy than I had.

I looked upward, to safety, and saw only sheer cliffs between us and the street above. The beach had drowned under forty nights of rain, and we were about to as well. No one knew we were there. Most of the population of Palos Verdes was away for Christmas.

So it was on me. All I had to do was keep our heads over the water and not drift too far out, a simple task that became more difficult as the minutes wore on. The car drifted away, the headlights getting dimmer as it drifted out to sea. I'd been thrown clear, saved by inertia and a body limber and pain free from conspicuous alcohol consumption. Rachel was sober and stuck, but somehow, I'd jumped in and pulled her from the car.

I looked up the cliff again, the rain dropping in my eyes. It was a black edge, cutting the starry sky in half. Hopeless. Going down had been as easy as a running jump. Getting back up would be impossible. I tried to keep our heads above water, and failed, and tried again, and failed again.

A light.

Two lights.

A car parked right at the edge of the cliff. I tried to cry out, but I had nothing left. The noise of the ocean and the rain would have drowned out even the most powerful scream. All I had was my body and my last bits of strength. I swam toward the lights, pushing against the current, and saw that the driver had found a way to crawl down.

The driver was my father.

He wore the khaki trench coat I'd looked for at Sheila's house. I'd wanted his keys so I could chase Rachel. I'd seen him out the window, going after her, and run out. That's how he knew we were there. Thank God for him. I'd never been grateful for my father before. I looked at Rachel. She'd become a dead weight in my arms, but I pulled her up. A wave caught us. A lucky break. I smacked against the rocks, managing to put myself between them and Rachel. My father got thigh deep in the water, grabbed my collar, and pulled me onto the ledge. I climbed with him, pulling Rachel. Dad grabbed her and helped us up. I collapsed at the top.

"This is going to cost me, son." My father's voice. "It's going to *cost*."

The world swam as if I was riding the teacups at Disney. I opened my eyes. In front of me, so close I had no context but a few blades of grass, the dark, rainy night, and my own nausea, was Rachel's face. She too had her cheek to the grass. Her eyes glazed over. Her mouth hung open. Her hair stuck to her face. She blinked, and a tear fell over the bridge of her nose.

She faded, like a movie going to black, and the sound of the rain in Echo Park replaced the sixteen-year-old remembrance. Monica breathed in my ear in the rhythms of sleep. Outside, I heard traffic, a bus on Echo Park Avenue, and the children playing in the Montessori school yard. I opened my eyes, as if waking not from a dream but a resurrected memory.

It was morning, and finally, Rachel was free.

CHAPTER 92

MONICA

I WORE one of the dresses he'd bought me in Vancouver, sleeveless black one with a skirt that fell half an inch from the floor. The neckline so low it required a special bra that had been hanging with it. He requested I wear it, and it was magnificent.

I covered the yellowing bruises with a little makeup, draping hair, and whatever accessories I could gather. I wouldn't stand up to a forensics team, but at night, in a dark party, maybe I wouldn't have to crack a joke or tell a lie.

I'd wanted to take my own car, but Jonathan insisted on letting Lil drive, so I waited on my porch for the Bentley. It was exactly on time. Lil let Jonathan out the back. He wore a navy suit and a tie of darkest pink. His shirt was white and pressed, and he was perfect. I started down the porch steps, and he held up his hand.

"Come on, Monica. Give a guy a chance to get you at the door."

I stopped and waited. He opened the chain-link fence that seemed cheap and worn next to his cleanly pressed self. He walked up the short, cracked concrete that led to my broken wooden steps.

"Are you ready?" he asked, taking my hand.

"It's just a party."

"No, it's going to be ugly."

I kissed him once on the lips. "I've been to high school."

"The stakes are higher."

"I'm not staying home. I got all dressed up."

"Ah, speaking of..." He removed a long, thin box from his pocket. I recognized the Harry Winston dark blue.

"Jesus, Jonathan, you're going overboard."

"Yes. I am. I don't have a viola." I took the box. Cursing him out while I was smiling would be hard. I undid the ribbon. He took it and rolled it around his fingers. When I looked at him quizzically, he said, "Might need this later."

"If the ribbon is the real gift, you could save a ton of money by just getting me empty boxes."

I lifted the top. Inside the box, a flat platinum chain curled around itself. I pulled it out. It wasn't a loop connected at the end but a long strand. It had to be five feet long, with jewel-encrusted drops the size of blackberries. One sparkled with sapphires, the other, emeralds.

"A lariat," I said. "My God, it's beautiful. Can you put it on me?"

He looped the strand around my neck once, draping it so the jeweled drops fell just below my breasts. "Green emeralds for sea. Blue sapphires for sky."

"Thank you." I kissed him. "It's perfect."

"I'm glad you like it."

"You're going to make it tough for me at Christmas."

"We'll figure out some kind of trade."

"And don't think I don't see what you're doing." I pulled the strand on one side, looped it around my neck a second time, and pulled tight. The smooth, flat links clicked against one another, easily tightening around my throat. "Makes a lovely collar."

He laughed. Taking the blue drop, he unlooped it and rearranged the necklace until it was loose. "Let's not rush." He took my hand, and we went to the car.

<h1 style="text-align:center">CHAPTER 93</h1>

MONICA

He got a call on the way. He mumbled a few syllables and relaxed visibly. When he hung up, he squeezed my hand.

"What?" I asked.

"My mother isn't *feeling well*," he said, the last two words emphasized as if it was some sort of code. "We may actually have a good time if I keep you away from the harpies."

"I can handle harpies and your family."

"I'm not keeping any secrets about my parents that you don't already know. But I'd like you to be unsullied as long as possible."

"I won't think less of you because of them."

"Give me some time."

He didn't try to fuck me on the way, though our lips met so often that I had to reapply lipstick when we arrived. We stood in the parking lot as Lil drove away. Other sleek cars discharged people in expensive shoes and suits. The lights glared as I used the valet window as a mirror, lipstick hovering. Jonathan snapped the tube from my hand before it touched my face and kissed me again.

"'Soul meets soul on lovers' lips.'" He kissed me, then put his mouth to my cheek, and back to my ear. "Except when wax and pigment come between them."

"Barrett Browning?"

"Percy Shelley."

"And the second part?"

He turned my lipstick tube until the brand was visible. "Lancome, apparently." He fondled the emerald end of my lariat as if it was part of my body. "I can't wait

584

for this circus to be over." He shifted closer and whispered, "I'm taking you home, and I'm going to tie your wrists to the banister. I'm going to blindfold you, then I'm going to undress you slowly. I'll put my lips all over you until you beg me to take you, which I may or may not do."

"Jonathan," I whispered, his name a white flag of surrender.

"Did you just shudder, or is it cold in this parking lot?"

"Was there anyone before you?"

"You might have thought so at the time."

"I feel like no one's ever loved me before."

"I'm sure they did their best, but you always belonged to me."

The parking lot's lights were fluorescent and cold, but his gaze was more than warm—it was hot and fixed. I did indeed feel as though I'd never been loved before. At least not correctly. Not with purpose.

He broke our connection to glance over my shoulder, then back to my face. "Vipers descending."

I looked back. Jessica, wearing purple and cream, walked with a crowd, her hand clutching the arm of a man with an athletic build. I nodded at her. She did not nod back. She looked away to make conversation with a ruddy-cheeked man rather than engage me at all. A face I knew stood out from the crowd.

"Geraldine," I said. "Wow. Hi."

Trompe l'oile street artist Geraldine Stark looked at me, then Jonathan, and smiled. She'd let her curly brown hair go wild and wove sparkled strands through it. Her dress was a macramé shift of a thousand colors over a black satin slip. She gave me a Los Angeles hug, but I felt her eyes on Jonathan, who kept his hand on my back.

"Oh my God," she said. "Did you hear about Kevin?"

"No, I—"

To my side, Jonathan greeted Mr. Athletic. They shared words I couldn't concentrate on. As the crowd moved toward the elevators, I heard Jessica laugh behind me. Her voice was caught in the lilt of small talk and joyful greetings.

"He's stuck in Boise," Geraldine hissed. "Three years."

"What? Why?"

"His parole is real strict. He gets actual jail time. They're *pissed*. So..." She glanced at Jonathan, then back at me as we stepped into the elevator. She thought I didn't know she'd been with him. She thought she would surprise me for dramatic effect. She thought wrong. Looking meaningfully at me, then at Jonathan, who spoke to the blond guy, she muttered, "Have you heard about your date? It's all over town."

"The thing about Kevin is terrible. Honestly." The news shook me. I didn't care if she'd fucked Jonathan a couple of nights back when I didn't know he existed. I didn't care if she wanted to rub my face in it for fun. Jesus Christ, I knew the guy wasn't a virgin. A hundred women in the city could commiserate on my lover's prowess if I were the commiserating type. Which I wasn't. I was the type who got upset when her ex-boyfriend went to jail. "It's awful."

Geraldine looked away. I hoped she was ashamed.

"We incorporated light into the design," Jessica said to someone I couldn't see. "The right temperature of light was the hardest to achieve. We wound up finding old tungsten bulbs in a warehouse in Torrance."

The doors opened onto the patio at L.A. Mod, which had been decked out in hanging lanterns and silver streamers. The effect was beautiful, incandescent, as if a few dozen artists had collaborated on the décor.

"Five minutes," Jonathan said in my ear as the crowd filed out. "Stay in my sight."

Geraldine's date pulled her with the tide out toward the patio, but not before she grabbed my hand and said "*Do it...*" She laughed as she disappeared into the throng.

Photographers and reporters waited, and the flashing lights made me wince. I waved to her quickly to say good-bye, and she waved back. I wished she'd stayed, even to talk about sex or prison time, because I was alone. Jonathan was ten feet away by a serving stand, talking in serious tones to the light-haired guy. Jessica was surrounded by a gaggle of people, all laughing as if they didn't have a care in the world. Jonathan and the big guy looked as though they were going to come to blows. He glanced at me and held out his hand in a slight gesture that meant "stay away."

The elevator doors slid open and another group got out. I heard the phrase again, though Geraldine was far from me.

Do it...

It sounded recorded. I looked behind me. Two girls stared at a phone, the light glowing on their faces.

Do it...

One pocketed the phone when they stepped onto the patio, giggling.

Jonathan's conversation wasn't going well. I couldn't stand there. I just couldn't. I walked over.

"Hi," I said. Jonathan slipped his hand over my shoulder. "I'm Monica." I held out my hand. The blond guy didn't take it.

"You stole something from my house."

Jonathan pulled me closer. I felt his body inching between the other man and me. "This conversation is over."

"It hasn't started. I've got a lawyer."

He seemed aggressive and off-kilter. As big as he was, he was so non-threatening, I couldn't be scared. He was handsome and looked fine in his tuxedo, but he wasn't wearing it...it was wearing *him*. He had no presence, no voice, no significance. Then I realized who he was. Erik. The man Jessica left Jonathan for.

That woman needed a cunt transplant.

"All these phones look alike," I said. "It was dark. I thought it was mine." I pursed my lips, trying to keep my mouth in some kind of line that didn't resemble a smile. But I failed on some level. He didn't believe me. A four-year-old wouldn't have believed me.

"You know what he did?" Erik said. "To her?" He jerked his thumb in the general direction of where Jessica may have been standing.

"I hear she was asking for it." The elevator dinged behind me.

"You're both sick," Erik said.

"O'Drassen!" A voice came from behind us, at the elevator. Jonathan turned me around and led me toward Eddie. He wore a white jacket and black tie, his hair combed into a pompadour.

"Ed," Jonathan said, "take care of her." He pushed me toward the guy he'd objected to taking me to the event in the first place.

"No problem," Eddie replied. "And I'm doing great, by the way. Thanks for asking."

"I mean it. Not out of your sight."

Some guy thing happened between them, because Eddie stuck out his hand and Jonathan shook it, taking him by the bicep. Then he kissed me. "Be good." He turned back to Erik, who had been joined by a man with darker hair and ruddy cheeks.

"I feel like I'm stranded in Manland," I said to Eddie.

"You are."

As we went into the throng of photographers, I glanced back to find Jonathan and Erik talking heatedly as if I hadn't even interrupted.

"You ready to be Carnival's newest face?" asked Eddie.

"Unless you try to put me in a leather mask."

"Yeah, well that's off the table. Coulda made a lot of money. This new idea's a clunker."

"You could drop me."

"And let some douchebag from Vintage pick you up? Hell, no."

The flashing lights were blinding. Between the women in sequins and the men wearing black, it was a high-contrast world. I heard laughter and chirpy voices. I heard clearly one phrase had caught on. It was whispered and shouted and giggled over.

Do it...

I had my customer service smile ready. My hand was on Eddie's arm, but I kept my body far from his. I didn't want to embarrass Jonathan, and I didn't want to appear weak and needy. Those pictures would end up in music and art trades. If I acted like a piece of arm candy for a record executive, I'd have to explain, then prove that I wasn't.

The cocktail hour was a whirlwind of drinks, cameras, and questions. Who was I? Why was I there? I talked about the B.C. Mod show with Unnamed Trio, which brought Kevin to mind. I tried not to think about him. I talked about my gigs at Frontage, the possibility of a contract, and my education. There were no softball questions about music. The reporters were from art trades, so there was no talk of art itself, only the business of art. I brushed shoulders with Jessica once. We glanced at each other and moved on. It was business.

Eddie and I milled with the guests outside a huge pair of wooden doors. A woman in a red jacket had come by with a man behind her. He carried a silver tray filled with metal lapel pins. Gold, silver, and rhinestone. She asked our names, then selected a gold pin from her assistant's tray and gave it to Eddie. She gave me a rhinestone. I had no idea what it meant. Glancing around, I could easily tell the artists from the collectors. They were different from their postures to the make of the clothing. The colors, accessories, shoes, all spoke to social class. I caught Geraldine Stark's eye. She wore a silver lapel pin. My eyes found Jessica. She looked nervous and unhappy, tucking her hair behind her ear. She also wore a silver pin. Artists must get silver, except I had rhinestone.

A couple behind me said, "*Do it...*" together before giggling.

"We're sitting down in five," Eddie muttered. "I'll pass you back to your date."

"Thanks. That was fun."

"Get used to it."

"I thought we were all going to go broke because I didn't want to carry a riding crop."

"Not quite *broke*." He smirked at me and patted my arm.

The doors opened, and the crowd flowed into a huge room overlooking Los Angeles on three sides. Tables had been set in rows with white tablecloths and shining silverware. A longer table sat in front, by the window, Jonathan wasn't there. Chairs scraped. Voices bounced off the high ceiling. I could sit and start a conversation, but he'd been gone too long. Way too long.

Eddie and I held an animated conversation about the future of streaming with two men he introduced as website developers. I saw Erik talking to Jessica. I scanned the room. No sign of Jonathan. Between his hair and his height, he was a hard guy to miss. Seats were being taken, and the wait staff came out with water pitchers and wine. I slipped away from Eddie as he was making a point about subscription rates on internet radio, and I went out the big wooden doors back to the patio.

The staff had already started breaking down, and the area looked inelegant at best. The floodlights had been removed from the photographers' area already, making it appear flat and littered. Jonathan was nowhere to be found. The cameras had missed him entirely. I wondered if that was his plan from the beginning.

A man walked toward me with intention. He as tall, maybe six-four, and wore a black cashmere coat and scarf. He was in his sixties but well-worn, taut in the neck and jaw. He had sparkling turquoise eyes and white hair. "Have they gone in?"

"Yeah. The ladies in the red jackets give you your seat. You get one of these pins." I indicated my rhinestone, and he looked at it appreciatively.

"God forbid we should walk around without a status symbol," he said.

"Yeah. It's like a nametag but not as personal."

"Like you're only as good as the money you spend."

His voice sounded eerily like Jonathan's but wasn't. I must have looked worried because he put his hand on my shoulder. It wasn't an uncomfortable touch, just comforting. "Are you all right?"

"I'm fine, thanks."

He took his hand off me and straightened, pulling a silk handkerchief from his pocket. "You should wipe your eyes, then."

"I wasn't crying," I said, more in surprise than denial. I put my fingers to my face, but he put out his hand before I touched it. He pressed the handkerchief under my eyes. I let him. I didn't know why. He seemed nice enough.

"You're smudged, nonetheless. It wouldn't be right to have such a lovely woman look like a raccoon."

I put my hands on his and pressed the hankie down,. He brought his hand away.

"Thanks," I said.

"You look familiar," he said. "Did you come to this circus last year?"

"No."

"My God. You should have seen the place. It was a Damien Hirst homage with decapitated heads for centerpieces."

"Sounds awful."

"The forks had these hands already attached to them. With veins and nerves. I almost didn't come tonight. I was afraid they were going to try to top themselves." He wrinkled his nose, and I smiled. "Well, I'm glad you weren't here. Maybe I know you from somewhere else."

I looked up at him as if for the first time, trying to see if I could place his features. There was something about the shape of his eyes, the angle of his jaw, the way he tilted his head when he spoke.

Jessica burst out the big doors, on the phone. I angled myself behind the man in the cashmere coat. "Deny it," she said into the phone in clipped syllables. "It's not my voice. Just say no comment."

She stopped in the middle of the patio, still on her call, and stared at her shoes, then out over the mezzanine onto Wilshire Boulevard. The flights of stone steps on each side framed her perfectly, yet she still looked lost. If I felt sorry for her for half a second, the image of Jonathan getting put into a police car at Santa Monica Airport dismissed my compassion and replaced it with something much fiercer.

Jessica glanced at the wood doors then turned on her heel and went down a hall. Once she was far enough away, I handed the man his handkerchief. His back had been to her, and he didn't look around.

"Thanks," I said.

"Keep it." He smiled and went toward the wooden doors. I saw inside when he opened them. The room was crowded, and everyone was sitting. I checked my phone. Nothing from Jonathan. If he was sitting at our table, getting pissed, he would have texted me.

I went down the hall. I'd come to look for Jonathan, but I thought I might hear another snippet of phone call. I was sure he was fine. Just being mysterious, as usual. I followed Jessica into the ladies room. It was a standard museum bathroom. Clean, white and blue, with midlevel fixtures and flat, warm, white lighting. My shoes echoed on the tile. If she'd been on the call in the bathroom, she either stopped talking when I entered or she'd cut the call already.

The door opened behind me, and I heard Jonathan's voice, but it wasn't him.

"—my belt, loop it once, and slap it across those sweet white cheeks until you're pink as a rose and your face is covered with tears. I'll stop when I can stick two fingers in your cunt and feel how sopping wet you are."

I froze. It was undoubtedly him, from the floral metaphor, to the word cunt, to the dominant voice. Three women came in and stopped dead in their tracks when they saw me. The young woman with the phone in her hand had her hair done up like Audrey Hepburn, right down to the tiara. The second was tall and matronly with a sweater, flat shoes, and lines of disappointment permanently etched on her face. They both wore silver pins.

The third woman was Geraldine Stark.

The recording continued.

"Then I'll fuck you until you beg me to let you come, which I may or may not let you do. That going to work for you? Didn't think so."

"Do it."

The voice was shrill and desperate and definitely Jessica's. That must be it. The voice memo from her stolen phone.

Audrey Hepburn fumbled with the phone, shutting it.

"I want to hear it," I said. "From the beginning, if you don't mind."

She hesitated.

"I was telling them," Geraldine said, "he's really like this, and it's hot. Don't you think?" She raised an eyebrow. I didn't answer but stared down Audrey Hepburn. She was a nervous kitten, breakable and easily bossed.

"Do it," I said, my voice the exact opposite of Jessica's whine.

She shrugged as if she wasn't giving in as much as bored by the prospect of not continuing. "It's only really good when he starts this."

"I'll undo your jeans. I'll pull them down to the middle of your thighs so it's hard to walk. You'll be uncomfortable, and that will please me. Then I'll get behind you, and I'll grab a handful of your hair at the back of your head and bend you over that table. I'll take off my belt, loop it once, and slap it across those sweet white cheeks until you're pink as a rose and your face is covered with tears. I'll stop when I can stick two fingers in your cunt and feel how sopping wet you are. Then I'll fuck you until you beg me to let you come, which I may or may not let you do. That going to work for you? Didn't think so."

"Do it."

"Jess, really."

"Do it! Start with the hair. Or the pants. Whatever."

"No."

"Do it!"

Audrey cut it off. I knew what the joke was. The desperation. The pitch. An actress couldn't have reproduced something so raw. I pressed my lips between my teeth. We all knew who it was, and as it turned out, we all thought the idea of her desperately begging for a spanking was hilariously funny.

Geraldine snickered first. Then Audrey. Matronly looked as if she ate a lemon, and the crinkles in her brow sent me over the edge into laughter. Then we all broke up. Between peals of hilarity, someone would shout *do it!* in a shrill, pleading whine, and we'd laugh again.

"Do you want to hear the rest?" Audrey asked.

"No, thanks," I said. "I'll have plenty of the real thing later. Without the *do it!*" I shrieked the last two words, and we laughed again.

I checked my face in the mirror, stood up straight, and arranged my lariat. "I'll see you back in there." I looked at each of them in the mirror. "Thanks for the entertainment."

When I got back onto the patio, I stopped at the big wooden doors and turned around, stepping behind a partition. Despite the cool, collected person who had shown up in the bathroom, I was upset at hearing Jonathan promising sex to another woman. And I was upset that everyone knew. They wouldn't see him as mine. They'd look at me and either feel sorry for poor cheated-on girl or assume I shared him with other women.

"Stop it, Monica," I whispered to myself. "Stop caring." I clenched my fists.

The three artists left the bathroom, giggling and commiserating. Matronly opened one of the big wooden doors, and they were gone. Were they laughing at me? Was Geraldine talking about her nights with Jonathan, taking bets on when he'd dump me?

My name is Monica. I sing like an angel and roar like a lion. I am the owner and ruler of my mind. I keep my own counsel. I decide how I feel. I answer to no one.

I didn't realize my eyes were closed until I heard a sob and the scuffle of feet on carpet. Jessica ran out of the bathroom, crying. She stopped, and I ducked farther behind the partition. She fiddled with her phone, but she was upset and couldn't seem to get it to do what she wanted. She tossed it in her bag and rooted around in the purse, pressing it to herself so she could dig in the bottom.

For the second time, I felt pity, but I was overwhelmed. I'd known exactly what I was doing in the bathroom. I knew she was behind a stall or a wall, yet I'd egged the girls on because I could. For what? To hurt her feelings? Wasn't I better than that? I stepped out from behind the partition. "Jessica?"

She spun and saw me. "Get away from me." She used her *do it* tone. I didn't think she could even hear it.

"Are you ok?"

She ran, still clutching her open bag, heading for the stone steps. I went to the mezzanine railing and watched her go, feet shuffling. She lost her balance and the contents of her bag scattered. Papers and receipts fluttered down into the courtyard, lipsticks and pens clicked. A notebook opened like a butterfly three steps beneath her. She stopped and scooped up her things. Her sobs echoed off the granite walls, even as far away as she was.

"What happened to Eddie?" Jonathan stepped up behind me. "He was supposed to watch you." I put my hand on his face. He was cold and damp.

Jessica looked up, and seeing us both looking down at her, she left half her bag's contents and ran away them. She tripped, skidded, righted herself, and ran onto Wilshire without looking back.

"What happened?" he asked with short breaths.

"That recording." I didn't want to describe the bathroom scene. I didn't care anymore. He looked like shit, and Mister Drazen never looked like shit. "Are you all right? Where were you?"

"Looking for someone." He crunched his eyes shut.

"Who?"

"I haven't been feeling…" He leaned on the railing. "My back hurts and…" His knees bent. I took him by the arms and looked in his green eyes. He wasn't all right; he was panicking. No. That was wrong. I took out the handkerchief the man in the cashmere coat had given me and patted his face.

"You look like hell. You need to sit down." The nearest bench was a mile away, or four steps.

He took the handkerchief. "Where did you get this?" His breath heaved as if it hurt him.

"Some guy. Tall guy, it's fine."

It dropped from his fingers, and I saw the black and blue embroidered letters: JDD. It all came to me. The voice, the way he had looked and walked. It had been Jonathan's father. I was about to confirm that, but Jonathan put his head on my shoulder. I put my arms under his, and before long, I was holding him up.

"Jonathan!" I cried for help, the sounds shrieking and echoing off the granite walls.

He fell, sliding down my body. I bent over him, rolling him onto his back. I didn't know what to do. His face told me he was in pain, his hands reached for me, clutching my arms, keeping me from moving. All I could do was shout his name.

Why was no one coming?

My phone. I had to get my phone.

I dumped the contents of my bag onto the floor, searching through the contents. I looked at him, the love of my life, finally found, finally recognized, finally embraced, with his eyes toward the sky in surrender. I turned back to my pile of crap and found my phone through a curtain of tears. "Okay, I'm calling someone. Please just…"

His eyes closed.

"No! You shit!" I screamed his name and slapped his face.

His eyes moved under the lids.

I slapped him again.

People came.

I hit him harder.

I felt hands on me, clenching hard on the bruised parts of my arms.

I couldn't slap him if they held me.

So I fought, and they pulled me away.

I didn't remember anything after that.

～

CONNECTION

PART I
SING

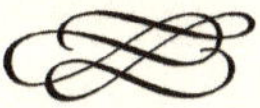

Take my hand, my love
On sinews of air we tread
Aught but distance our guide
With no tempo to our gait
No endpoint drawn
Neither plot nor plan
By the thorns of a compass rose
We bound toward the horizon

CHAPTER 1

MONICA

Dr. Thorensen had put up his Christmas lights on December first, two weeks ago, decorating his wood detailing and redwood fence with tiny multicolored dots. No fat inflatable snowmen. No Santas. No elves. Just classy little spots hanging around the edges of his property like a joyful fucking aura.

It was too early to ring Dr. Thorensen's bell. He was a single guy in his mid-thirties, and it was Tuesday morning. He was probably at his office or the hospital. Maybe nuzzling one of the women I saw come around periodically. But I was losing my shit. I couldn't wait another minute, and I'd noticed he kept odd hours. I saw him through the glass in a polo and jeans, carrying a coffee cup. When the door opened, he looked grave.

"Monica, am I blocking your driveway?" Then he looked at me. I must have been a sight. "Are you okay?"

"Not really."

"What happened?"

I felt silly, as if I'd become a story he'd tell his friends. I'd become the annoying girl next door. He'd told me once that he didn't put an MD license plate on his car because he wanted to avoid random advice-seekers and neighbors with a sniffle. I laughed with him over the story of the Montessori mother two doors down who wanted him to look at her son's scraped knee. So I'd avoided ringing his bell for five long, lonely, friendless days.

But he was a cardiologist, and when Santa brought me a gift, I figured I shouldn't try to cram it back up the chimney. One long sentence poured out. "I didn't want to bother you—I mean, it's not like he can't afford the best doctors in the world—but I'm afraid to tell them what I think or that I'll look crazy, so I was wondering if you had privileges at Sequoia Hospital?"

"I do." I feared his next words would be something like, "Sorry, I'm not working right now. I deserve to be at home in peace as much as the next person, and the fact that I spent a quarter million dollars on school doesn't make me public property." But he stepped aside and said, "Come in."

I'd never been inside his house. Though I'd always been curious about it, when I finally did see it, I barely noticed anything. I'd been blind to details for a week. My brain had somehow narrowed down to what it thought were the only important things: breathing, worrying about Jonathan, and desire to kill Jessica. But when I passed the living room, flashing lights caught my eye. Three huge flatscreen TVs were up with a leather chair set positioned to see all of them. I recognized the steampunk settings and those particular burnished brass and wood finishes from a party I'd attended before Jonathan. In another life.

"You play *City of Dis?*" I asked. The online multiplayer game was highly competitive, complex to a fault, and if a player had the brainpower to keep up with it, more addictive than crack.

"Yeah." He seemed a little embarrassed. "Need to wind down sometimes, you know."

"I know this guy who wears Depends when he plays so he doesn't have to get up to go to the bathroom."

"I'm potty trained, even in character. Coffee?"

I followed him to the marble and glass kitchen. "No, thanks. I'm more of a tea person."

"So," he refreshed his cup, "if it's not the driveway, and you're asking about Sequoia, must be a medical call?"

"I'm so sorry to bother you."

"You're fine. Sit." He pulled out a tall chair by the marble kitchen bar.

I sat, feet wrapped around the legs, a coiled tension in my hips. "You did the place nice. It's probably the best house on the block."

"It's an investment." He put a pot of water on the stove. "Could have gotten something in Beverly Hills or Palisades for twice the price and half the aggravation, but where's the fun in that?"

"It's quieter and cleaner?"

"No potential, though. Nowhere to go but down. This neighborhood's going to be Beverly Hills in ten years, and I get to live next to people like you. Interesting people. It's all lawyers over there." He glanced at me as if checking on me. "So what brings you?"

"You're a cardiologist. I'm sorry, but—"

"Stop apologizing."

"My...I guess you'd call him a boyfriend? He's at Sequoia."

"A patient, I assume."

"They say he has a heart problem. That he damaged his valves when he was younger and he..." Was I betraying a confidence? People had been talking of his suicide attempt so often that it seemed like old news, but the talk had been within the confines of his family and doctors. Dr. Thorensen waited, leaning on the counter, his cup warming his hands. "He took too much Adderall once when he was a teenager."

"This is Jonathan Drazen?"

I felt a tingle of shock, like an adrenaline rush. He knew, and he mentioned his name right there in the kitchen, as if Jonathan's condition and how he came to be so sick was public knowledge.

He must have seen the confirmation on my face. He put down his cup and opened a chrome canister on the counter. It was full of teabags. "That explains the car."

Was I just being sensitive? It sounded as though he thought I couldn't possibly have bought a Jaguar without fucking someone. I didn't have time to decide if I was mad because Dr. Thorensen continued as if he knew he'd implied something that could twist my knickers and wanted me to forget it.

"We have a weekly meeting on the high-risk cardiology patients," he said. "Just to check diagnoses and make sure we're on the same page about treatment. I've seen him." He held up a hand as if to reassure me. "I'm not his doctor or anything. Dr. Emerson is with him. He's highly qualified."

"And you agreed a sixteen-year-old overdose gave him a heart attack? That makes no sense."

"Adderall is basically legalized speed. Taking a fistful will damage your valves, and the slightest blockage will give you a heart attack. No question. It's a miracle he made it this far."

He handed me my cup. I didn't want it but found my hands clasping it anyway. "Are you sure?" I asked. He raised an eyebrow but said nothing. "I don't mean to question you. I'm sorry. I didn't go to medical school. But before it happened, we were at a party, and he was gone a long time. I think..." I felt so stupid even saying it. I'd told Margie my theory, and she'd dismissed it. "I think he was poisoned." I stared into my teacup.

"That's a pretty broad accusation." He said it softly and kindly, but under it all was a hint of condescension, as if what he really wanted to say was that I was crazy.

"He has enemies," I said.

"Yes."

"His ex-wife was mad at him."

"Okay."

"He was fine just before."

"No, he wasn't."

"I was there, you weren't. I'm sorry, but he was fine."

He put his cup down, and I felt the weight of my intrusion. He was playing a video game at eight in the morning, getting a moment's peace from a high pressure job, and I was dragging his work into his kitchen. And he didn't believe me. I wanted him to believe me, even though I felt crazier and crazier.

He said, "There was nothing on his tox screen. I sat with his attending for two hours looking at EKGs. He had a massive coronary event. There's a pretty good chance he'd been having small heart attacks in the days previous. His valves are shot." He stopped his sentence as if catching himself. He'd been talking about a man's heart like it was a carburetor.

"I should go."

"He has a very good prognosis."

"Thanks for the tea." I put it on the counter.

"Monica, listen—"

"Dr. Thorensen—"

"I'm Brad."

"Brad, it's been a rough five days. He's got seven sisters and a mother and they...most of them...act like I'm no one to him. I'm on his list, so I'm told everything, but I'm surrounded by strangers. Seeing him like that, with the IV and the tubes and just waiting to get cut open... Everyone's worried, and no one wants to listen."

"I understand the desire to blame someone, but he wasn't poisoned. I promise you," he said.

There had been no evidence of poisoning, and Jessica had been in my sights, or in the bathroom, most of the time. I was looking for a ten-second interval where she could have...What? Fed him something? Slyly injected him? Did I think I was living in an Agatha Christie novel where conceptual artists moonlit as chemists?

"Yeah," I said, "I guess."

"Tell you what. Why don't you play *City of Dis* with me for a little while? I'm in the eighth circle. I'll build you a character from my profile. You won't get an opportunity to play at that level anywhere else. All your problems go away." He snapped his fingers. "Magic. Come on."

"I can't."

"An hour."

"I haven't done laundry in two weeks, and I have to go to work."

He put down his cup. "Rain check?"

"Yes, and thank you, Brad." His short name sounded both overly familiar and coldly detached in my mouth.

"Any time."

He walked me out, and I went home to wrestle the laundry. Maybe I'd hang out a Christmas light myself. I found a letter taped to my screen door. No envelope, just an open sheet.

NOTICE OF PUBLIC AUCTION

The rest was legal bullshit, but I scanned the page for the handwritten parts. My address. Thirty days. Non-payment.

"Shit." I looked at my house as I might find an answer there, but it was just a dark wooden box with a crumbling foundation. I still hadn't gotten the papers signed to fix it, but if the permits had been opened, my mother had gotten the notice in the mail. So she knew something was going down. The notice must have been the result of my failure to send her a check two months running.

I had to call her.

I didn't want to call her.

I stared at my phone. The number was right there. I'd missed rent twice before, once when Kevin and I broke up, and once when Gabby had tried to commit suicide. Both times, I'd sent two months' rent in an envelope with a thank you note. So when Gabby died and I was short, I just figured I'd make it up. I could have, except I was in Vancouver December first and forgot. Then I stopped working when Jonathan collapsed. Honestly, even if I'd had the cash, I was too preoccupied to manage any practical aspect of my life.

That's what I got for living in her house. Really, how long could I mooch off someone I wasn't speaking to anyway? How old was I? I hit her number while I unlocked my front door. It was easier to do difficult things if I multitasked through them.

My house was exactly the same every time I went into it to shower or grab something. Nothing moved. The blanket on the couch was rumpled in the shape of an opening rose. The curtains draped over the back of the chair like perfectly-trimmed bangs. The dishes in the rack were filed and waiting for archiving in the cabinets.

The phone stopped ringing, and there was a click. Mom's voice still had the slight Brazilian accent that had been carefully chipped away but never smoothed off. My heart skipped a beat, an adrenaline rush in preparation for the confrontation. It was her voice mail.

"Hi, Mom. I got a notice the bank is auctioning off the house? Should we talk about it?"

God, that was stupid. I hung up. Should've paid the fucking rent. Should've called her to let her know I was in a pinch. Should've had Darren move in. One more stupid shit thing in a long line of other stupid shit things. I folded the notice and wedged it into the corner of my notebook. Fuck the Christmas lights.

CHAPTER 2

MONICA

I WAS NEARLY OUT of gas. I had five dollars in my pocket, one maxed out credit card, and a checking account dangerously close to scraped clean. I could get to work and make some cash, but without that eighth of a tank, I'd be taking the bus to the hospital and paying the fare with change found between couch cushions.

I didn't dare tell Jonathan things had gotten that bad. I went to him every night with sunshine in my voice and rainbows in my pocket. When I wasn't at Sequoia, I let the panic come. Slamming my locker closed, I painted on a customer service smile for no one in particular.

"Monica?" Andrea came up behind me, her hair dyed blue. It was always a new color with her, and I seemed to have missed that change. The color was already fading back to green.

"Hey, how are you? Love the color."

"What are you doing here?" she asked.

"It's my shift."

She rolled her eyes and twisted her mouth. "Uhm, we're kinda in the habit of swapping you out. So I'm working."

"No," I heard the squeak in my voice, "I need the cash." God, I hated sounding like that. I hated whining about money. She shrugged and walked out to the floor. I went to Debbie's office.

"Come in," she said after I knocked. She was alone, behind her desk and shuffling through God-only-knows. She looked up as if she was pleased to see me. She stood and put her arms out for a hug. "Monica. How are you?"

"I'm fine. I came to work, but Andrea says she's got my shift?"

"You've missed five shifts. And you were out the week before. I need to run the floor."

"I need my shift."

She put her hand under my chin. "You're in no condition to work. You lost weight. You have circles. A little lipstick?"

"Please."

"What's happening? Sit. Tell me."

I lowered myself into the leather chair. Debbie sat on the arm of the one next to it. The nightly mist that descended on Los Angeles dotted the window. It was the wettest year in history. The bar would be slow and tips scarce. Just tourists who had nowhere else to go and regulars who came out of habit. The Hollywood hitters would be in clubs downtown or Silver Lake venues.

"They're trying to stabilize him so they can do a valve transplant and open up his arteries," I said. She looked at me blankly, as if she was waiting to understand. "He damaged his heart when he was sixteen—" I stopped abruptly. I knew Debbie and Jonathan had been close, but I couldn't be sure he'd told her about the fistful of drugs he'd taken. He hadn't known he was broken until the stress of the past weeks broke him.

"Here," Debbie said, handing me a tissue. "Go ahead."

"They have to replace parts of his heart." I felt strongly that I didn't know what I was talking about because I didn't. "He hasn't been stable enough for the surgery." I pressed the tissue to my eyes. It came back with blobs of mascara. I really couldn't work the floor. "I go in every night and talk to him, but I need to work tonight."

"No, you need to go in to him."

"I need the money. I'm sorry. I know it seems gross."

"He can't give you money?" She seemed shocked, as if he *wouldn't*, which wasn't the case. Asking for money would sully the sunshine and rainbows.

"I don't want him to worry."

"What about his family?"

"Outside of Margie, they tolerate my existence. Which is fine. But I'm not asking."

"He hasn't given you something you can sell?"

The title for the Jag, which was my only transportation, had been in the glove compartment when Lil drove it to me. The platinum lariat that symbolized our bond twisted around itself on my dresser, binding sea and sky. The diamond navel bar was where he'd put it when he committed to me. "No. I have nothing to sell."

Debbie got up and walked behind her desk. Bending at the waist, she opened a drawer and pulled out her wallet. "I don't usually do this."

"Don't. I'll manage."

She took a pile of bills out and folded them once, coming around the desk. "We can cover your shifts another couple of days before we have to put you on personal leave. That's unpaid." She picked up my hand and slapped the bills into it. "Figure it out."

I squeezed the money. I couldn't refuse it. Taking it meant I could see Jonathan. "You're very nice to me."

"Jonathan helped a friend of mine through a rough time. You make him happy. So helping you is helping him. Now go. I have work to do."

CHAPTER 3

MONICA

ONE HUNDRED FIFTY-SEVEN dollars in smallish bills. God bless Debbie. I loved her. I put gas in the car. Then I bought a container of cubed cantaloupe at Ralph's for dinner. I parked three blocks away so I wouldn't have to pay for the lot and walked. Night was falling, and it was getting cold. I was bundled in a scarf and light coat, having forgotten a hat in my rush to get to work.

Sequoia was huge. Half the babies in L.A. were born there, and everyone else managed to die there. The charge nurse in the cardiac unit knew me by sight and nodded at me and my cantaloupe.

"Hi," I said when I walked into Jonathan's room of bland pinks, beiges, hard edges, and the smell of sickness and alcohol. I'd gotten him a little light-up Christmas tree for the table by the bed, and every night, he made sure it was on.

"I thought you were working tonight." Jonathan was sitting up, reading by a single lamp. I'd seen him in that bed every night for the past week and a half, and he'd gotten better and better. I couldn't believe they wouldn't let him just walk out.

"It's raining. Debbie didn't need me." I sat on the edge of his bed and took his hand while trying not to disturb the IV in it. Machines beeped and hummed. A stylus scratched on paper, tracing the lines of his heartbeat. "How are you feeling?"

"Like I want to punch someone. You?"

I smiled. "The contracts are signed. Margie was a hero. Seriously, I couldn't have done it without her. I'm finalized to record tomorrow. I'm singing 'Collared' with full production value."

He took the cantaloupe container from me. "They're getting the L.A. Phil in?"

"I know you're joking," I said, compulsively starting to help him open the

607

container. But in the past couple of days, he hadn't needed me, so I pulled back my hands. "But yeah. Fifteen pieces. String-heavy. Like, real. Next week, we're doing 'Craven.' I laid down some scratch on a few others, and they're going to pick two more for an EP."

He plucked out a piece of melon and held it up. I leaned forward and opened my mouth. He brushed the juice on my bottom lip before letting it touch my tongue. "Orchestras cost a lot of money," he said. "They must believe in you."

I took the cantaloupe gently and closed my lips around it, catching his fingers and sucking them on the way out. "We'll see."

"Is this what you brought for dinner?"

"I ate stuff at home," I lied. If he knew my fridge was empty and I didn't want to spend Debbie's money getting takeout, he'd worry. Or he'd lose his shit all over the hospital room. He'd already had a Code Blue over his mother trying to shut me out.

"You're supposed to have dinner with *me*." He wasn't mad or scolding. During the day when his family visited, I hung around in the shadows. That was the deal. I didn't have to be front and center with his sisters and mother, but I came to him at night, alone.

"What did the doctors say? Will you be out for Christmas?" I changed the subject away from dinner, which would lead to talk of my financial distress. "I have no idea what to get you, by the way." He paused, picking through the fruit, eyes cast down. "Well?"

"Not yet." He held up some cantaloupe. I took it, but I sensed he was hiding something. I chewed slowly. As if sensing my recalcitrance, he said, "I'm strong enough, but the arrhythmia's still there."

"It was gone yesterday!"

He shrugged. "Eat. I want that body ready for me when I get the hell out of here."

That was Jonathan. Focused on getting the hell out of what he perceived as a prison.

"This body's always ready for you." I parted my lips for his fingers.

He pulled the fruit back an inch, and I followed. He let it touch my tongue, then pulled it back. We played cat and mouse with the melon until he popped it in his mouth, grabbed me by the back of the head, and kissed me. Our tongues tasted of cold fruit. I kissed him as if I'd almost lost him. I pushed into him as if he was a delicate creature living only by the grace of God and modern medicine. His tongue wove around mine as if he was as healthy as ever. As if an elevated heart rate wouldn't kill him or, at the very least, send nurses running in with paddles and carts of beige machines. He could deny what was happening all he wanted. He was getting stronger, but if his doctors were to be believed, every day without that surgery brought him closer to another heart failure.

"Goddess," he whispered, "I have to have you."

"No fucking way." We'd tried two nights previous, and the word "disaster" would be used if we were underplaying the results. I'd gotten an earful from Nurse Irene and had cried for hours from the stress and the scolding.

He pushed his finger under my waistband. "Undo these."

"No."

"Open your jeans and pull them down." He spoke as if I hadn't just refused him, and the command sent waves of lust through me. "I swear to God I won't get my heart rate up."

"I'm scared."

"I'm not. Come on. Trust me." His face was inches from mine, his hand on my cheek and stroking my lower lip. Every night, I curled up next to him and slept for a few hours before I was asked to get in my chair. Every night I wanted him, and every night I worried. He'd gone from distraught, to annoyed, to depressed, to this. He felt as though he'd lost control, and he was using me to feel as though he had it back for a minute. I just didn't know if I could trust him to take care of himself.

I unbuttoned my pants. He sighed and put the container on the table. His eyes stayed locked on mine as I straightened my hips, put a knee on the bed, and pulled down my pants.

"Straddle me."

I was restricted by the waistband, but I got a leg out and wiggled around the instruments and tubes to get myself on either side of him. I made no move to shift the sheets away or touch him. I only did what I was told. "The door's ajar."

"The curtain's closed," he whispered, feeling my ass. "You're wearing this cotton shit again." His left hand, the one without the IV, stroked my lower back and found its way under my panties.

"It feels silly to waste the good stuff when you won't see it."

"You miss the point." He pulled me forward. "Put your hands behind me." I placed them on the wall behind him. With his left hand, he reached between my legs, caressing me through the fabric of my underpants. "The idea is that during the day, I'm present where no one can see. You dress for the world, but under that, you dress for me. I own your softest places, and what touches them is mine."

"How can I think about that when you're sick?"

"I need you to. Knowing I own you even from here is the only thing that gets me through the day. Can you do something for me tomorrow?"

"Anything."

"At three o'clock, when you're in the studio, at exactly three, put your fingers on your lips and think of me."

"Yes. I can do that."

He brushed his thumbnail over the crotch of my panties. My clit throbbed, and I gasped.

"Remember the office?" he whispered. "On the desk?"

"How could I forget? You were cruel."

He stroked four fingernails over the cotton he so hated. It was damp already. "I wanted you so badly."

"You could have had me."

"Anyone else, I would have just fucked. Not you." He brushed one finger under my panties, stroking my opening. "You were so wet. So responsive. A quickie on a desk would have been such a waste."

His finger ran circles around my wettest part, and his thumb touched my clit gently. When I thrust forward, he pulled it back.

"You were a bastard." I spoke through gasps as he teased me. "You could have let me come and fucked me later." He pushed two fingers in me. I closed my eyes and groaned.

"Look at me," he said. I put my nose to his and tried to keep my eyes open. "I wanted you before my trip. I needed you motivated. I had to have you."

"Have me," I gasped as he put only the lightest pressure on his thumb while rotating his fingers in my hole.

"You were fantastic that first night. Unforgettable." Pulling his fingers out, he slipped them up my cleft, stroking my clit slowly, barely moving. Every millimeter of movement sent a shot of sensation from my cunt to my knees and waist.

"Oh, God."

His right hand went to the back of my head. I knew he had his IV in that hand, but I wasn't thinking about that. I only thought about the excruciatingly unhurried motion of his fingers. "Do you want to come, Monica?"

"Please let me come. I want to."

He grabbed my hair. "I don't believe you."

"Please. Jonathan, please. Don't let me walk away like this. Let me come for you." My begging could not have been more sincere. The pleasure and tension between my legs was so intense, so heavy, it was almost painful.

"No." He dragged his fingers over my clit then lodged them back in me. He pulled them out, rolled around the outside, and then pushed them back in again. All the while, he kept my head still by holding a fistful of my hair.

"Please," I whispered.

"Why should I?"

"You love me."

"I do." But he didn't say anything more.

"And I love you."

"So?"

"I miss your body. I want to come for you. Please."

He pulled the tips of his fingers over my clit. It was just enough to take me to the next level. I couldn't speak as the pleasure soaked my body, yet it wasn't a full release. "When you sing tomorrow, wear something that reminds you of me."

"Yes." I would have promised him the World Series, but that, I meant. Under my clothes, he owned me. "Please."

Rubbing my clit in earnest, he held my face close to his. "Who do you belong to?" Like a glass of water on a hot day, my cunt drank him in. I was getting what I had craved, every inch of wet skin receiving the touch it wanted like the answer to a prayer.

"You. I am yours. Oh. I'm—"

"Come, darling."

I bit back a cry as the orgasm ripped through me like a fire hose had been turned on. My hips thrust forward and bullets of pleasure shot through my nervous system, squeezing the air from my lungs, shutting out every sense except the sensation of his fingers between my legs, his breath on my face, his eyes on mine.

He slowed but kept his hand on me, stroking me down until I felt as though I could think again. "Again, goddess. And quietly." He pushed in me, gathering juices, and put his fingers to my clit again. The waters rose like a flash flood.

"Fuck." I groaned, clenching and thrusting. A grunt stopped in my throat as I came for him again. My eyes closed involuntarily as I released, the fireworks between my legs taking up every sensory input.

A machine beeped. We froze. It double-beeped once, twice, then stopped. He patted my ass, and I knew what that meant. I scurried off him and pulled up my pants. I got them buttoned just as Irene Maslov, RN opened the door.

"Mister Drazen," she said in her thick Russian accent, "you are okay?"

"We're fine."

"I didn't know if I should be getting the crash cart again," she joked, shuffling in on her clunky padded shoes. Her hands, like risen dough, pulled Jonathan to a sitting position so she could mess with his pillows. Her grey hair was cut short, and her lower lip seemed to extend a good seven inches from her face.

"For two beeps?" Jonathan said. "I'm going to start thinking you want me to live."

"When I started to nurse, we had rules. No girlfriends in the room alone with door closed. Now patients can make request. Request is like *law*, so I have machines beeping twice all night."

"I don't think it'll beep again," I said meekly.

She went to the computer and tapped away at it with two lightning-fast fingers. "You ready for tomorrow, Mister Drazen?"

"Like any other day in paradise, Irene."

She took his blood pressure, and I sat by and held his other hand. "What's tomorrow?"

"Wednesday," he whispered back.

Irene snapped the belt off his arm. "Okay." She tapped his IV bags. "You're fine." She looked at me over her plastic trifocals. "You be a good girl."

"Yes, ma'am." She scuttled out. "I love how it was my fault."

Jonathan shrugged and held out his left hand. His left side didn't have IVs or tubes, and it was the side I'd slept on since the third night of his stay. I slipped onto the mattress next to him. I couldn't move much, but I didn't want to. He turned the light out, and I rested my head on his shoulder.

"I'm selling my house," he said.

"Why?"

"I bought it with Jessica. It's not relevant anymore."

"I have some nice memories of that house."

Curled up against him, I felt his smile. "Me too," he said, voice heavy with those same memories. "We'll make new ones somewhere else."

"Where were you thinking?"

"I don't know. Where would you like to go?"

The machines whispered dreams of a future I'd given little thought to, blinking lights of hope and trepidation. "I live in Echo Park. If you stayed close, I'd like that."

He turned his head, pressing his lips to my hair. "I'll stay in the basin. More or less. Not the west side. Too many people I know, and it's far from you."

I didn't think he could get up and walk me down the hall without collapsing, but he still managed to make me feel protected. That hospital room, that bed, his body next to mine had become my world. I came at night, and when he turned off the light, he was my beautiful, healthy Jonathan again, and I his goddess. The troubles of the day melted away.

Over the past week, with only the light pollution of Los Angeles coming in through the windows, he'd told me about a losing game he'd pitched at Penn, walking in a run in the ninth. He'd told me about the out-of-control years before his suicide attempt, about his friends and him drifting their cars on rainy nights in the Valley, breaking into schooners on the piers of Seal Beach. He'd told me about Westonwood, where he got into a fistfight over a French fry his first night and, over the next months, learned to maintain the tight control over himself he still exhibited. I exchanged stories of my father, who couldn't play a note but made sure I had everything I needed to make music, his gardening, his lust for life, and my mother.

"Why don't you talk to her?" he'd asked.

"She doesn't approve of me, and I won't change into something I'm not, to please her."

"You live in her house. You could say hello."

"It was by default. I was already there when she called Kevin a seducer and a slimeball. I just kept paying the rent, and she kept cashing the checks."

"It's unlike you to be so passive." Every word expressed in that bed was said and heard without judgment, an unspoken rule I'd been able to obey without trouble until Jonathan implied I should see my mother. He'd felt me stiffen and tightened his arm around me. "It's true." Back then, just a few days before, his voice had been weak and breathy. He'd had oxygen tubes in his nose, and talking was difficult.

He sounded so much better now. Almost like his old self. Soon, they'd give him the surgery he needed, and he'd walk out with a healthy heart. I could go back to work. He'd fuck me blind as often as I let him. Our nightmare would be over.

CHAPTER 4

MONICA

ANOTHER NURSE CAME at the two a.m. shift change. She took Jonathan's blood
pressure and tapped on the computer. That happened every night, as if he didn't
need a full night's rest. I slid off the bed, kissed him good-bye, and left.

My studio time started at eleven a.m., and I wanted to be fresh. I tried to pick
up another hour of sleep, but I only succeeded in two things: worrying about
Jonathan's arrhythmia, which would postpone his surgery yet again; and thinking
of new ways to add percussion to "Collared." It needed some kind of thump with
the stringed hum. So freshness was a fail, but punctuality didn't have to be. I
decided to conserve the gas by getting ready early and taking the bus.

That was considered a major faux pas, unheard of and even shocking to most of
my friends. One simply didn't *take the bus*. But it was a straight shot across Sunset,
and I found looking out the window while someone else drove meditative enough
to make it worth my while. It wasn't rush hour, so I wouldn't be late. I didn't need
to bring anything but my vocal chords and my viola. Just me, and my thoughts, and
Los Angeles lumbering by my window.

I imagined Jonathan naked as I tapped my thumb to a song without words. The
tempo was an expression of his curves and edges, the notes colored by the flavors
of his skin, and the dynamics became his voice when he commanded me for his
pleasure. My mind curled into itself, conjuring a song as the bus lurched and
heaved to its own time, drawing me into a state of melancholy contentment.

My phone rang. I considered letting it vibrate until it went to voice mail, but it
kept ringing. The protective coil around my song shattered, leaving me with the
music but not the mood. Might as well answer. It was Margie. Up until the day

before, I didn't know if she was calling about my contract with Carnival or Jonathan. I spoke to her more often than I spoke to myself.

"Hi," I said.

"Where are you?"

"Santa Monica and Canon."

"I'm sorry." Her voice was taut. "Did you guys discuss you not coming or something?"

I sat upright. "What's going on?"

"He's in surgery today, and I thought you might want to be here when he got out. Unless something changed with you two."

"No!" Fuck. I rang the bell to get off at the next stop. If I picked up a connection, I could make it in an hour.

"What was that?" Margie asked. "Are you on the *bus?*"

In my haste to get off the bus, I dropped the viola case. It popped open next to the driver, who yelled at me. I scrambled to get it together before my viola got stepped on, while the phone was pressed between my jaw and shoulder. I didn't have a free hand to pick it up, so I had to listen to Margie have a fit over my location and circumstance, which irritated me enough to shoot back at her. "Lot parking is fifteen dollars and it's permit parking on the street over there at this hour. I don't need to blow gas money when the bus is fine." The bus dumped me in front of the Beverly Hills Police Station. I headed across Santa Monica, scuttling to make the light.

"Wait," Margie said, and I regretted blowing off steam at her. "Did you know about the surgery today or not?"

"I was on my way to the studio, but I can make it there in an hour if I get the Rapid at Beverly."

"Stay where you are. Lil is coming for you."

CHAPTER 5

MONICA

I SAT in the back of the Bentley, wanting to absolutely die. The idea of being in the studio when Jonathan got out of surgery was unacceptable, yet the thought of not showing up to sing for any sickness besides my own seemed ridiculous. Cancelling studio time would cost Carnival a fortune. Everyone would still have to be paid. An orchestra full of people. Assistants. Session guys. Whatever executive felt like showing up to see Miss Taking-The-Bus cut her debut EP. I was a complete career fuckup. Who would set up another session after this bullshit?

Margie met me in the hallway as soon as I got out of the elevator. "They just wheeled him into the OR. He didn't ask for you which tells me he knew you weren't coming." She walked me down the empty corridor.

"I told him I was laying something down for Carnival this afternoon. He knew if he told me he was going under the knife today, I'd cancel."

"Is it important? The studio thing?"

"Not as important as being here."

"Spare me the emotional comparisons." Her impatience was a sign of how tightly wound she was. Her words were clipped, and her intent unmistakable. I felt compelled to give her any answer she asked for. She must have been a magician in a courtroom.

"It's going to make my career," I said. "But not today."

"First of all, you don't ask my brother ever again about his condition. He's a notorious liar of convenience."

"No shit."

"Secondly"—she stopped and stood in front of me—"how broke are you?"

"I'm fine."

"You two are so sweet together. Really. He lies so you'll go to the studio, and you omit your destitution so he won't worry about you. It breaks my fucking heart to see this level of well-meaning duplicity."

We stared at each other for what seemed like a minute and a half. She had that Drazen thing where she looked perfectly put together even though her family and her work were eating her alive. Her hair sat up in a copper bun, her skin was luminescent, and her lavender business suit looked as if it should still be in the dry cleaning bag.

"How broke?" Margie asked.

I took a deep breath. I didn't want to tell her. It was shameful, but I couldn't avoid it any longer. "I haven't had a roommate in months. I haven't worked since before I left for Vancouver. I bought clothes I shouldn't have. I fixed a car I didn't need to. Here I am."

"Is he not taking care of you?"

"I'm not his whore." I said it in a sotto whisper, but it seemed to amplify and echo against the hard walls and floor. Margie took me by the bicep and pulled me into an empty room. I followed because I didn't want to make a scene, but by the time she closed the door, I was livid. "Is bossiness a Drazen thing?"

She held up her finger. "Don't posture with me. No one who ever saw you together would call you his whore, so stop it. How much do you need?"

I held up my hands. Taking gifts from Jonathan was one thing; having his sister write me a check was viscerally offensive. "I'll figure it out."

"How? What's your plan to stay with him and go to work at the same time?"

I didn't have one, except closing my eyes and hoping I'd wake up at the end of it with a healthy Jonathan and an undamaged career. The signs did not appear to be in my favor. I was pretty sure I'd wind up unemployed, ten pounds lighter, and evicted by my own mother. My EP wouldn't get cut, and I'd have a reputation as a flake.

"I'm going to be there for him," I said. "If it makes me broke and ruins my career, that's the deal. I'm not taking a dime from you or anyone else. If you have a problem with that, you can take it up with him when he comes around."

"You're a real pain in the ass."

"Don't hold back. Tell me how you really feel."

"Welcome to the family," she said, as if I'd ever been welcomed. "Speaking of, we have good attendance today."

"Can I have a roll call?" I leaned on the foot of the empty bed.

"Theresa's calling, but she can't come in. Deirdre's in chapel. Leanne is here but running off to some Asia backwater in three minutes. Fiona's in and out with her entourage. Sheila's ripping paper. Carrie's still not coming."

"And your mother?"

"Fully medicated. I spoke to her."

From what I could see, Margie and her mother had a sisterly relationship. The elder Drazen was only fifteen and a half years older. "I spoke to her" meant Margie had reprimanded her own mother over how she'd treated me, which included stone cold silences, saccharine kindness, and blatant disregard when she was tired.

I nodded. "Will she ever say more than two words to me?"

"She and Deirdre love Jessica. That's not going to change."

"I don't expect it to."

"Good. There's something else." She glanced at the door as if making sure it was still closed. "Jonathan hasn't spoken to our father in fifteen years. He's here. You might not see him, he and Mom are on the outs, but he's in the building. If he meets you, whatever he tells you, grain of salt, okay?"

"I don't know what he'd have to lie to me about."

"He'd say something just to see how you react. My brother thinks it's evil. I think it's just a shitty hobby."

"Can we go?" I collected my things and stood up straight, ready for the door.

"I'm not done. About the money—"

"You're done."

CHAPTER 6

JONATHAN

When I first felt as if I was dying, I stood in a doorway at the L.A. Mod for half an hour, trying to control the tightness in my chest. I focused on my breathing, sat down, tried to think about anything else, but it kept getting worse. I kept sitting there, thinking I had to get to Monica before my father did, and I really started panicking. It had tumbled down from there to that ridiculously long hospital stay, to getting wheeled into an operating room for surgery at thirty-two.

When I woke up, I had the feeling something had gone terribly wrong. I swam to consciousness feeling as if I was being choked. I panicked the same panic I had felt in that doorway. I couldn't control my sensations, my body, my thoughts. I couldn't see clearly. I couldn't move my arms. I was bound like a prisoner. My voice was dead. My face itched. Was I warned it would feel like that?

Or was I dead and in the hell of everything I'd ever done to every woman I'd tied down and fucked? I thought of Dante. His hells were the excess of our desires and, in the deepest circles, the pain of our victims. There I was. Fuck. I was terrified. I didn't think I could stand it for eternity. The blackness, the crippling paralysis. No control. Utter submission to emptiness. I was breathing, but the pressure on my throat was enormous. I'd never choked a sex partner because I never believed I could control the results. How could my hell include that? I never believed life was fair, but was God so unjust?

"Jonathan."

A voice. Female. I recognized it as Sheila's. She always had a way about her that seemed as though she'd given birth to the world and loved it to maturity, even when her words cut deep and rage twisted her mouth.

I realized I could open my eyes if I chose to. The whisper and beep of machines broke the silence of my anxiety. Okay. Not hell. Not dead. But the choking feeling was real, and I panicked again.

Sheila's face blocked out the light. "You're intubated. The machine is breathing for you. Keep still. It's okay."

I chose to believe her. I waited. It was five minutes to three. I couldn't speak to ask her to unbind my wrists, so I stared at the clock. At three o'clock, I closed my eyes and imagined I could touch my lips.

CHAPTER 7

MONICA

THREE P.M. came unexpectedly. I figured it would, since I was supposed to be in the studio, so I'd set my phone alarm to remind me. It dinged as I listened to Eddie launch into a diatribe. I closed my eyes, shut out Eddie's aggravation, and touched my lips, thinking of nothing but Jonathan. The warmth in my chest and the smile on my face didn't last.

His voice was tight enough to shatter my reverie. "Are you fucking with me?"

"He's your friend too. It's not like you can pretend to think I'm lying." I was in the third floor stairwell, avoiding the mob in the waiting room. It was nice that Jonathan had so many family members who cared about him, it was also overwhelming.

"We got the contract signed in a week," he said.

"I know."

The fourth floor door smacked open, and Leanne Drazen tore down the stairs. Theresa's Irish twin, she was two years and ten months older than Jonathan, but she looked and acted as if she was in her mid-twenties. A tote bag flew behind her, and her red cowboy boots clopped down the steps. She looked tattered and slovenly, strawberry-blond hair falling out of a ponytail and her bag open.

"That's fucking unheard of," Eddie said. "We had to send twenty-two people home. Do you know what we paid to get them in there on two day's notice?"

"No."

Leanne grabbed the bannister and swung around, inertia and centripetal force taking her to the top of the next set of stairs. She grabbed my shoulders.

"He's out!"

"A fucking *lot*," Eddie said into my ear.

I put my hand over the receiver. "How does he look?" She put her thumb up and smiled then took off down the stairs with a wave. Sweet girl. Too bad she was never around. "I have to be here, Ed." I bounded up to the fourth floor.

"I'm not saying I don't understand. I was at the show. I saw it. What I'm saying is, I don't know if I can herd these cats again."

"Tell me what hoop I have to jump through to get a reschedule, and I'll jump it." I strode through the waiting room, past two sisters and a mother. Margie indicated a room, and I went in. Sheila, the most vulnerable-seeming of the bunch, was with him. With wild, wheaten hair and four children born close together, she was the one most visibly upset about her brother. Jonathan was there, lying on his back arms on top of the blankets and tubes everywhere.

"When can you do it?" Eddie asked.

"Next week. I think he'll be better then."

"I need a guarantee."

I touched his arm, and Jonathan opened his eyes. When he saw me, he winked. "Guaranteed." I hung up the phone. To Sheila, I said, "Well? It went okay?"

"Yeah. They just pulled a tube out of his throat and unstrapped him."

Jonathan picked up his hand and flicked his fingers to Sheila. The international sign for *shoo*. She started to object, but Margie grabbed her arm.

"Come on. The kids need you," Margie said.

"Onna has them."

Margie pulled her out, but Eileen, Jonathan's mother, strode in. "Ma," Margie said, "you were just here."

But Eileen ignored her. "Jon, how are you feeling?"

"Tired."

"Should we go?" She put her hand on my arm as if I was going out with her.

"Yes. I mean, let me talk to Monica for a minute."

She smiled the biggest, fakest thing I'd ever seen in my life. "Of course."

"Oh, ma?"

"Yes?"

He pointed at me. "Spot for Christmas Eve. Okay? Don't forget."

"Of course." Eileen looked at me. "You're free?"

"You bet." I put on my customer service smile. Once she was out, I sat next to him. I didn't say anything, but somehow he intuited what I was thinking.

"That's just how she is."

He looked as pale as death, and his body was flat under the sheets as if he could have just sunk into them. His face looked slack, inactive. His eyes were unfocused, and the lids didn't want to stay open. That wasn't Jonathan. He was some other, powerless man who didn't yank my head back by my hair as he pounded me from behind. Someone who didn't fuck me in such a slow, controlled way I felt every inch of my orgasm. He wasn't the man whose name I'd cried into the night; the man to whom I entrusted control, to whose dominance I submitted. He was another man entirely, and I loved him.

I took his hand. "You look like shit."

"You look like an angel." His voice crunched like gravel under a tire.

"I should tie your elbows behind your back with a belt and spank you until you scream. To get your voice back. Works every time."

A smile curled the side of his mouth. He croaked so low I had to put my ear to his mouth to hear him. "A week. I'm going to do unspeakable things to your body."

"Really?" I kept my face to his and my voice low. "Like what?"

I realized I'd asked too much of him when he licked his lips, paused, and said, "Secret." He'd love to tell me, I knew that, but between having his chest cracked open and the tube down his throat, it probably hurt to speak.

"I know already," I said. He raised an eyebrow. "I can read your mind."

"Not this. It's filthy."

I reached over until my body bridged his and touched his ear with my lips. "The great and powerful Madame Monica will predict the future with utmost certainty. Are you ready to hear your destiny, young man?" I was so close to him that when I looked into his eyes, I could see the blue flecks.

"What's this gonna cost me?"

"Everything."

"Worth it."

～

WE'RE IN YOUR HOUSE. The living room. I'm naked from the waist up, and you're in jeans and a polo shirt. You're looking at me like you want to eat me alive, but you don't. Yet. You're waiting. You're thinking. You're constructing the next minutes of my life like a movie director blocks a scene.

You tell me to take off my pants, and I do. You watch. You like my body. The way my breasts hang when I bend over to release my feet. My ass when I bend at the waist.

When I step out of my jeans, you step toward me in your bare feet. I look nervous. You tell me to stop my hands from twitching, and when I cast my eyes down and say 'yes, sir,' you feel power surge in you. Everything's under control. Everything's going to be all right, unless it's not. What you have planned can go terribly wrong. The worry bothers you.

You ask me my safe word, and I tell you to shut up and fuck me.

'Oh, goddess,' you say. Then you take the hair at the back of my neck and pull until I'm looking at the ceiling. My lips part, and I sigh.

'Say it. Or you can put those jeans back on and go home.'

I mouth 'tangerine' but don't use my voice.

You look down at me and you say, 'Say it.'

I whisper it so softly you can barely hear it. You spin me around and shove me into the kitchen. I start to turn back, but you bend me over the butcher block. You're sharp and violent, and when you see me cringe, your dick gets hard. You want to see me scream. You need it.

You.

Need.

It.

Your dick is out, a throbbing piece of meat aimed between my legs. There's wetness emanating from me. It would slide in so easily. You'd be sucked into my cunt so fast, and you'd forget everything.

'Say it, or you go home.' You feel me quiver under you. You think you might just have me put my jeans on and leave. That would be the right punishment for making you uneasy. You slap my ass, and I yelp as if I didn't expect it. Your hand stings, and you're poised to do it again when I speak up.

'Tangerine.'

The word is barely out of my mouth, and you're fucking me, pressing my cheek to the butcher block. Thrust after thrust...you know you're pushing the countertop against the sensitive part of my hip. I'm yours to hurt, and you know it. The things on the counter rattle as you fuck me. Salt and pepper grinders. A canister of utensils. Fancy bottles of condiments. You pull my ass cheeks apart with your free hand so you can go deeper, gripping hard enough to bruise, watching how your fingers indent my skin. My feet come off the floor, you're pounding me so hard. I gasp and grunt.

You take a bottle of olive oil and smack it against the edge of the counter, breaking the neck. I'm startled, but you push my head down hard. The glass is everywhere. Oil splashes on the floor. You run your hand down my back as you fuck me. Slowly, you pour oil on my back. You rub it all over me then pour more until a river of oil falls into the crack of my ass. You feel it on your cock. You pull out then slide in again. Hard. Once. Twice. Olive oil coats us. You slap my butt again and again. I cry out in pleasure, your name on my lips.

Then without breaking your rhythm, you jam your cock in my ass.

I scream.

You're halfway in, and you feel two things at once. You're incredibly aroused...aroused enough to lose control. But there's also the worry that in losing control, you'll hurt me. You ask me how I am.

I say through my teeth, 'Is that all you got, Drazen?' My face is red. My fingers are clutching the edge of the butcher block.

You put down the bottle and take my jaw, turning it until I'm facing you. You bend until you're so close you can smell green tea on my breath. Then you push the rest of the way into me, the skin of your dick sliding against the olive oil, stretching me without friction as a barrier.

I grunt. You know it hurts, you see it in my eyes. But you don't stop. You whisper words of encouragement, pulling out, then slamming into me. We're mouth to mouth as I whimper and you fuck my ass. Sliding in and out with the olive oil. Balls deep. I'm tight. You're getting squeezed. I'm getting ripped apart.

But my whimpering is turning into gasps and moans. I'm looking at you now with something besides agony. You go faster, pounding. Pushing deeper with every stroke. You pull me up until we're both standing. You slide your hand across my breasts and down my stomach. There's oil everywhere. Your fingers go between my legs and find my clit right away. It's hard to the touch. When you circle it, you slow your thrusts. You slip over it, reaching for my hole. Then you drag four fingers over my clit. You do this over and over, until I beg.

'Let me come. Please.'

You want me to come while you're in my ass. You want me to want it after it hurts me. That's the victory, to have us both love my pain.

I'm whispering 'please' like a chant. Your fingers move in the same circles. You have me at the edge. You own me. 'Please, please, please, please.'

You say, 'Come."

I thrust my hips into you, burying you in me. There's a moment of nothing, then you feel my orgasm on your dick, pulsing around you. Gripping you. Milking your cock until the fullness in you is too much to bear, and you have to let it go. You slam into me and come. You lose control, forgetting your hand is gripping my cunt. You bite my shoulder, and I scream for the second time. You lose yourself. You forget everything.

CHAPTER 8

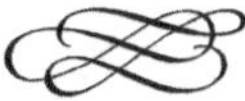

JONATHAN

I felt her.

We spoke. I wanted to possess her, but I couldn't find the strength to move my arms. I smelled her canned peaches scent and heard the warm caramel of her voice. I answered her in short sentences, because I felt as if I'd gulped a handful of driveway and forgot how to swallow.

She tapped my arm as she described what I would do to her. Even in my state, I got hard because it was an epic fuck coming from her sweet mouth. I didn't even know if she noticed, but with that tapping finger, she was keeping a rhythm as she told the story. I strained to listen as unconsciousness tried to invade again. I heard her words, but what I felt when she talked about me hurting her was the connection created when her pain turns to pleasure, and she is under me, a piece of the world I control completely.

"You're good at this," I said. "I'm taking mental notes."

"When did the doctor say you could enslave me again?"

"As soon as I was up to it."

"I predict day after tomorrow."

"You're selling me short."

"I'll be at your service tomorrow if you want. But you're in here for five days, and you need to be alone tonight."

I grumbled deep in my throat. She was right, of course. The drugs hadn't even worn off. I had no idea how I would feel about sex once the pain kicked in. All I knew was I wanted to be inside her. "Go sleep in your bed tonight, then."

"If I'm up at three a.m., I'll think of you." She stood straight and got her bag. "Actually, if I'm awake any time, I'll think of you." She leaned down to kiss me, and I touched her lips.

CHAPTER 9

MONICA

On my way out, a song hit me. I ran into the cafeteria to write it down. I texted Lil and asked her to meet me out front in fifteen minutes, and I got myself tea.

I'd been in that fucking hospital forever. What had looked sparkling clean the first day looked dingy, dirty, and worthless on day four. I spotted the black scratches on the pink cafeteria tabletops instantly and the little dust bombs sticking to the legs of the chairs. I hated the tea. It was too hot, the Styrofoam made the liquid acerbic, and Jonathan was sick. I hated the greasy eggs and potatoes. I hated the stink of vinegar that seemed to be on everything. I hated being kicked out of Jonathan's room because too many people were in it.

But on the day of the surgery, the cafeteria sparkled again. The Christmas lights were the most cheerful shades, the tinsel and garland was festive and joyous, and the fake tree in the corner, with toys for sick kids under it, made my heart swell with pride for human generosity.

My god, what do you get a man like Jonathan for Christmas?

I got into the chair I always sat in, and I took out my little notebook and clicky pencil. Everything about the hospital had sucked, but I was writing. A lot. I didn't even know if half of them were songs or opera or part of something so much bigger, but I couldn't stop the verses or the tapping of my foot as I laid them down. In the days I'd been at the hospital, waiting for the hours I could see Jonathan, my tea usually went cold before I gulped it down.

I moved the Notice of Public Auction to the front of my notebook so it wouldn't be in my way, and I wrote. Another Styrofoam cup appeared at my side when I was still neck deep in a song about an imaginary ass-fuck that was disguised

627

as a poem about something else entirely. I looked up at a six foot four man who had hit his sixties in a movie-star kind of way.

He smiled at me. "We meet again."

"I'm sorry?"

He held out his hand, and I knew that even though I didn't know him, I did. "My daughter told me my son's girlfriend was often down here. I thought it might be you."

J. Declan. Shit. Jonathan wouldn't like me being with him. And just when I was getting used to that hateful table. I shook his hand briefly then stood. "Yeah. I was just going."

He sat down. "Looks like you were in the middle of something. Can you just ignore me? There are no other seats."

I looked around. Every other table was full. I was a single person taking up a four-seater. In the middle of writing, I hadn't even noticed. "I'll make room for the rest of the family."

He laughed to himself. A silent chuckle. No more than a breath.

"What?" I asked.

"If my boy is the sun, I'm Pluto. Smallest. Farthest. Still in orbit, however. Have you seen him?"

"Yes."

"How does he seem?"

"The same."

"And his mood?"

"Hard to tell through the wisecracks."

He nodded, looking around the cafeteria. Kids screamed. Mothers yelled. A mop slapped against the edge of a yellow bucket. To our right, a man wept while a much younger woman comforted him. I glanced at Declan. He looked far away, and I felt sorry for him.

"You should talk to him," I said. I hadn't seen the outside world in too many hours, and Lil would be outside in a red zone in four minutes.

"I should," he said in a way that implied that he would if it were an option. I wanted to say more, but I remembered what Jonathan had told me and what Margie had said about his shitty hobbies. I excused myself to go home to try to manage my life.

CHAPTER 10

MONICA

IT WAS night by the time the Bentley made its way slowly down my hill. I'd called Debbie to let her know Jonathan was okay, and I told her if any shifts opened up, I'd fill in. Then I left a message with Darren, who had offered me the moon and stars, the food in his kitchen, the gas in his car, and the surface area of his shoulder should I need it. But unless I asked for something specific or called during an unpredictable sliver of time, he was unavailable. I had no idea what he was doing. When I did catch him long enough to ask after him, his "fines" and "greats" seemed sincere. So I left him alone.

"What time are you going in tomorrow, miss?" asked Lil as she opened the back door for me.

"I'm hoping for an afternoon shift," I said. "Can I call you?"

She stepped aside as I got out. "I expect you to. I don't mean to be disrespectful, but it's my job to drive. I don't want to hear about you taking the bus again." She slammed the door.

"I'm a poor girl. It's not a big deal to take the bus."

"To me it is. No more." She wagged her finger once and walked around to her side. When she opened her door, she waved, dismissing me.

I fingered the extra bus token in my pocket, went through my gate, and ascended my porch steps. There was no notice on the door, which reminded me I hadn't heard from Mom. I checked my phone. Nope. Nothing.

"Hey, Monica," Dr. Thorensen called over the fence.

"Hi."

"You all right?" He blooped his car. The lights flashed.

"Sure."

"Because you're standing on your porch staring at your phone. Is your boyfriend all right? Did the surgery go okay?"

"Yeah."

He didn't move. He just looked at me under my shitty porch light, which would be auctioned off with the rest of my house. Except my stuff. The bank couldn't auction what was mine. I'd take the light bulbs, the furniture, the fixtures, and anything that could be unscrewed, unbolted, or pulled off.

"Dad's tangerine tree," I said out loud. I didn't mean to do that.

"Excuse me?" Dr. Thorensen asked.

"Nothing. Just thinking out loud." I snapped my keys out of their little pocket.

"Have you eaten?"

I hadn't expected an actual question, so I answered honestly. "No."

"I have some pad thai from last night. It reheats like a solid brick, and I don't want to suffer alone."

I wanted to slip in during the dead after hours and fall asleep next to Jonathan again, but if there was one night I should let him rest, that was probably it. A twisting disappointment pinched my chest when I realized I wouldn't go see him. I'd have to sleep alone in my stupid shit bed. But though I could be lonely and depressed and worried, I didn't have to be hungry. "How are you reheating it?"

"I put the cardboard box in the microwave. It ain't open heart surgery."

"You have to heat it covered with a little water." I put my keys back in my bag, glad to be of use to someone. "A glass container is best. Let me show you."

CHAPTER 11

MONICA

"Magic" was too mild a word for *City of Dis* as Dr. Brad Thorensen played it. Extreme might be better. Intense. Powerful.

The idea was the player was in hell. Not just a block character of pixels. Not some person the player made up from die rolls and categories, but...*you*.

Meaning, the player created a character based on himself. Plenty of people created characters whole cloth, but the point was to create their own personal self and send it through hell. The player struggled to exit each circle, but he knew the next one would be worse, the stakes would be higher, and his missions would be harder. That being the case, when he stopped, he found his sin. His flaw. He discovered what would send him into the inferno.

Dr. Thorensen taught me how to use the controllers then went to reheat the pad thai as I instructed. The game started with a fifteen-minute questionnaire. Except it should have been a two-hour questionnaire. It should have required thought and rumination. The basics—gender, age, education, family structure— came slowly. Then deeply personal questions had to be answered so quickly I didn't have a second to think twice. Multiple choice. Choose the closest answer. Rapid fire.

—do you cook your own dinner how long does it take you to eat it how long do you chat with friends after dinner do you have a mirror in your room do you wear makeup every day is your nose big are you fat do you have enough money how much does a pound of feathers weigh where was your car made price of the most expensive bag you ever bought if you found a wallet what would you do someone hits your car on the freeway what do you do how often do you shop do you reconcile your checkbook does your thumb hurt right now how many cups of coffee or tea do you drink a day how many moving violations have you gotten what color is the red hat when was your last felony arrest did your parents spank you are you worthless what is your political affiliation do you believe in legal abortion are you on birth control how many sexual partners have you had this month how much is too much are you hungry right now do you own a firearm are people generally bad or generally good what time do you eat dinner what time do you go to bed do you dream—

PLEASE BE PATIENT WHILE WE CREATE YOUR AVATAR

"It'll take a few minutes," Dr. Thorensen said.

"I need a nap after that."

"You walked in here looking like you needed a nap." He put down two plates of moist, delicious pad thai that had been reheated to perfection. I felt a mentally overwhelming need to eat it. I sat at the kitchen bar and placed a napkin over my knee. When was the last time I'd eaten a hot meal? Days ago? I would take those noodles slow. I would make love to each one as if it was the first time.

"I'll try not to be offended by that," I said. He offered chopsticks and a fork. I could use chopsticks, but my hands had started shaking, so I took the fork.

"I see a lot of people who don't take care of themselves when a loved one is sick." He said it in a doctor voice, as if it was a professional opinion, and thus something that could not cause offense.

I wondered what it would be like to date a doctor and deal with that voice all the time. Did he use it when he wanted to tell a woman she needed to pay attention to his feelings, or she shouldn't rehearse on Tuesday nights? Was he a professional when complaining about the in-laws?

"Yeah, well," I said, spooling a single noodle onto my fork, "he's going to be out soon. Then I'm going to be fat and happy."

"I peeked in on his surgery. Everything seemed to be going fine. He's young. You guys will be tooling around in your new Jaguar in no time."

I think I turned a little red. "I just want to get back to work. They feed us. Nothing like a free lunch."

"He doesn't take care of you?"

I must have burned black, smoking holes in his face because he pursed his lips shut and looked at his plate as if he'd just stepped in my personal daisy patch. "I will allow you to take that back," I said. "A show of gratitude for the thai."

He laughed, and it didn't sound professional. Thank god. "I'm sorry. I take it back. I shouldn't have assumed."

"Got that right, doctor."

"Brad."

"Fine."

A singsong bell rang from the stereo speakers. Naturally, an audio monolith had been connected to the system to make *City of Dis* a three-dimensional aural experience.

"Your avatar's ready," Brad said. "I'm dying of curiosity."

I swallowed the last noodle and bean sprout and went to find out who the game thought I was.

CHAPTER 12

MONICA

I PULLED A LAST-MINUTE BRUNCH SHIFT, which was such a relief I think I giggled all the way through it. I'd played *City of Dis* with Brad until midnight, so I was tired which made me punchier. The game was all-encompassing. He'd started me on the eighth circle, where he was, and we cycled around to see if I'd get caught in the trap of my invisible sins. We solved puzzles, interacted with hellions, ate virtual food, and imbibed radioactive-colored drinks that made the screens blurry and shaky. The game was alternately frightening, sweet, intense, dramatic, and funny. I actually forgot about Jonathan for seconds at a time.

The call from Debbie that morning was like the clouds opening up to heavenly light. I'd texted Margie that I wouldn't be in to see Jonathan until after my shift. She responded right away.

*—He looks better. Already
demanding your presence. I
told him to hold his horses.—*

*—Do NOT tell him I need the
money you'll give him another
heart attack—*

At break time, I rummaged through my bag for my phone and found my mother had called me. Funny how I'd forgotten all about that. Not ha-ha funny, but you-are-a-pussy funny. I had ten minutes left of my break, so I had a time limit

634

to how long the pain could last. I stood in front of my locker and dialed my mother's number. Eight minutes of break left.

"Hello?"

It was amazing how her voice could sound so familiar and so strange at the same time. "Hi, mom. It's me. I've been calling."

"Are you all right?" She broadcast panic, and the rawness of her emotion sent a welling in my chest and brought moisture to my eyes.

I hadn't shed a tear of stress or worry over Jonathan because I wanted to be strong. I didn't want to show weakness in front of his family. They were all so freaking stoic. But with my mother's tone telling me that *Hi, mom. It's me* was enough to panic her, I almost lost my shit. I remembered my mom then. I remembered the things that put me over the edge, the drama, the constant emotional storms. One such storm had led her to fling names at Kevin and me, sending me out the door permanently, my viola forgotten in his trunk.

"I'm fine. I'm sorry I missed the rent twice." Silence. "Mom?" Sigh. "I got an auction notice on the door."

"Oh, I've been meaning to call you." I heard the rustle of sheets, and I looked at my watch. It was noon, and to all indications, she was still in bed. Fuck. "It wasn't just that. There were other things. I talked to the bank. They don't care about your problems. All they care about is money."

"They're banks, mom." I rubbed my eyes. "How long has it been since you paid the mortgage?"

"Oh, I don't know. I should ask how *you* are."

"It's complicated. I have only a minute left. What should I do about the auction? Should I move?"

"If you want."

"Okay, then. I'd better get going."

"Can you come up some time? I'd like to see you."

I cringed. I didn't want to see her. I knew something bad was going on out there, and whether I'd spoken to her in years or not, I was obligated to at least figure out why she wasn't paying the mortgage. But another responsibility was the last thing I needed. I tried to remove the dread from my voice. "Sure."

"I'm free most days. Today, even."

"I'll let you know."

In typical Los Angeles fashion, I left the call without making any definitive plans.

CHAPTER 13

MONICA

"I HATE you seeing me like this." Jonathan's voice had a little less gravel, but he sounded as if the effort involved in speaking was unbearable.

I wasn't allowed to sit on the edge of the bed, so I sat in the chair next to him and put my elbows on the railing. "Then you shouldn't let me in here."

"I need you. Deal with it."

"Okay, well, I'm not going anywhere."

"You look thinner."

"These are my skinny pants. You like them?" I was sitting. He couldn't even see my pants.

"I can see your cheekbones."

I touched his face, stroked the stubble on his chin, and brushed his lip, dry yet yielding under my touch. Was it wrong to want him even in that horrible place with him cut open? Was it wrong to want his arms around me when he could barely lift them? I wasn't feeling lustful but greedy, ravenous, ardent. He took my hand away and held it. Obviously, he wasn't *that* weak.

"Let me ask you a question," I said. "If I was in a hospital bed for a week waiting for open heart surgery, how much would you eat? How well would you sleep? I'm not complaining. I'm just saying don't try to deflect away from what you need by making yourself worry about me. I'm fine."

"When I can get up—"

"You can give me the spanking I so richly deserve. Until then, I'll be the one doing all the legwork around here."

"Tell me about it."

"Oh, I will."

~

THERE'S *a chair in your bedroom.*

It has red leather cushions on the seat, back, and arms. It looks antique and probably is, now that I'm thinking of it. You tied my ankles to the place where the arms meet the seat. You tied me gently, stroking between my thighs, kissing my legs, but in the end, I'm naked and spread-eagled, tied to your antique chair. Though your hands were gentle, the binds are tight. I can't move.

Then you tied my hands above my head, looping the leather straps around the sconce above me. You kiss my breasts until my nipples are so hard they're the size of dimes. You make sure I feel safe and loved. You don't want me to be scared. I'm not scared. I'm so turned on I'm pretty sure I'd come if you breathed on me.

Then you undress. You do it slowly, not sexy and camp, but methodically. You put your things away and spend a minute in the bathroom. You don't let me speak. You threaten to gag me if I make another joke. You need control over me. This is how you feel safe.

So I wait, my cunt getting wetter every second. I feel it dripping down the crack of my ass. Then you're naked and magnificent. Jonathan, darling, you are utterly spectacular. But you don't want to hear that.

You look at me. Your eyes eat me alive. I feel you between my legs even though you're half a room away. If I could draw you closer with my desire, you'd be on me. I'm hungry for you.

You step toward me and put your hands on the back of the chair, leaning over it. My arms stretch above me. You put the tip of your tongue inside my elbow then draw your tongue down until your lips touch my breast. You circle my nipple, caressing it with your lips. It's so hard, pointing up like it wants to be millimeters closer to you. You kiss it, making it wet, then release. I feel the cold air. It's so sensitive, and you glance at me like you know it. You suck it again and release it to the cold.

Then you warm it with your mouth, and you bite. I arch my back. I thrust my hips into you. I moan your name.

'Behave,' you say, pushing my chin up so I can only see the ceiling. 'Don't move.'

You roll the wet nipple under your fingers, then move to the other and do the same. Suck, release. Suck, release. Suck, bite. I'm on fire.

You kiss my belly, my legs, and I feel your fingers inside my thigh. You're brushing your fingers toward my cunt. It quivers. You flick my clit like it's a crumb on your pant leg. You do it hard, and I bite my lip. It stings. Then it fills up with pleasure.

You do it again and again while kissing inside my thighs. I'm trying not to wiggle, but everything in my body wants to arch toward you. You hurt me with your fingers then stroke. I burn with the pain, but it only makes the pleasure more unbearable. It's not enough to make me come.

I want to beg, but you told me not to speak. I'd take you anyway you'd give yourself. I'd have you in my mouth, my ass. I'd crawl on the floor to have you. You're barely even touching me, but you have complete control over me. Just with your fingertips.

And when you draw your tongue over my cunt, my toes, eyes, and fingernails feel it.

Then you do that thing. With a flick of your wrist, you undo the knots at my ankles. You stand up and tell me to get my clothes on. We're going out.

~

"You're fucking with me," he said.

"Turnabout's fair play."

He smiled then caught his lips between his teeth. "It hurts when I laugh."

"I wasn't joking."

He put his hand on my cheek, brushing the skin. Even sick as he was, the feel of his body on mine was electric. "Can you stay?"

"I have something to tell you."

"You love me."

"My God, Jonathan, I'm crazy with loving you."

"Feeling's mutual. Now, what were you going to tell me?"

"I need to go see my mother. In Castaic. I'll be back late, but I'll come right here." I wrinkled my nose to let him know the trip wasn't a vacation away from him or his hospital room.

"Lil can drive you."

"You bought me a car."

"Let me take care of you. You can rest in the back. Put your feet on the seats."

I turned and put my lips to his palm. "Go to sleep, darling."

"It's a long drive." I kissed his mouth. His lips were dry but responsive, and his face scratched mine. He put his hands on my face and pulled me close. "You trying to shut me up?"

"Yes."

"I hate being like this."

"You can boss me around when you're better."

I put my head on the mattress next to him, and he stroked my hair. I watched the clouds move across the sky, humming a tune that may or may not have been "Collared." When I knew he was sleeping, I slipped away.

CHAPTER 14

MONICA

I TOOK a white-knuckled drive up the 5 freeway past all signs of civilization, past subdivisions, up a bifurcated mountain and back down it. The bestfuckingthingever drank gas like a frat boy drank beer at a kegger. Everything was dead, flat, dry. Then it hit. Castaic.

All the garage doors faced the street like mouths stretched into a closed grimace. Front yards that had not been flattened by concrete were neglected and brown or tamed and green with sad blowup snowmen and fat, jolly Santas. Everything in the unforgiving landscape was scorched by the sun. Even the mountains ringing the town looked compacted under the weight of the sky. Or maybe that was just me.

Big girl pants.

Maria Souza-Faulkner had two settings: Park—which meant she was passive, sweet, and slept seventeen hours a day—and fourth gear—which meant she was in full-on rage with an eye to wiping the world of sin. Kevin had suggested she was bipolar. I'd laughed not because he was wrong, but because she'd never do something as sensible as see a doctor to figure out why she was crazy. Dad had loved her through all of it, so obviously she saw no need to fix what was functioning just fine.

Her house, a one-story beige box with a two-car garage and a front door set back twenty feet behind it, had fallen out of repair. Dad wouldn't have allowed that. He'd spent his time in the States painting, plastering, and gardening. The young citrus he planted had a few leaves on the twiggy branches, and the front lawn looked like an infield. I didn't know how long she'd been stuck in park, but judging from the look of the place, it had been at least through the beginning of the summer.

My mother answered the door in a long polyester thing that fell over her curves in a way that was modest but sexual. Like me, she had a body that was hard to hide, and unlike me, she kept trying. She was a Brazilian beauty my dad had met on some unholy peacetime mission. She was five eleven, in her early fifties, and she had darker skin than mine but the same dark eyes and hair. She was Catholic as only a South American girl could be, and that was the rub. She believed in the infallibility of the Pope and the virginity of Mary long after anyone else with a brain had moved on.

"Hi, ma."

She hugged me, and after a second, I hugged her back. She held on longer than I thought she would. Maybe the visit wouldn't be so bad. We'd just forgive each other. She moved out of the way, and I stepped inside.

She saw the car. My immediate reaction was to make excuses for it. It was borrowed. I was returning it. I didn't ask for it. Then I decided to shut up. I didn't come to fight, and I didn't come to lie. She closed the door without saying anything.

The house was hermetically sealed against the desert heat and dust, and the artificially cooled air was stale and thin. Everything was beige. Dad had hated beige, but my mother insisted. When she insisted, she got what she wanted.

Well, everything *permanent* was beige. Whatever had been moved in was a color, and a bright one. African masks and Mexican blankets. A hand-carved teak partition blocked a window draped in Ikat fabric. Stacks of travel books stood in front of the stuffed bookcases. It looked as if my mother had gotten the shit stamped out of her passport.

"You came," she said.

"Yeah." The couch had a pillow on one end with a case that matched the bed sheet balled up at the other end. She was sleeping on it, probably regularly.

"I don't think we can save the house," she said.

I had a speech prepared, so I spit it out. "I didn't come because of the house. It's not that I can't move or get an apartment or whatever. I just find it hard to believe you'd let the place go. I got worried about you."

"Oh, Monya," she said, calling me by my grandmother's name. "All this way for nothing." She put her hand on the doorknob.

That was her. She'd kick me out and waste away rather than admit there was a problem. Though she seemed healthy, if older, I could tell sunshine and butterflies weren't the order of the day. "Come on, Mom. I'm here. Make me some tea."

Her hand slipped from the knob. She glanced out the window at the white Jaguar as if she didn't trust it and didn't like it. As she walked me to the kitchen, I saw more third world knicknackery and clean, beige rectangles spotting the walls as if old pictures had been removed.

It wasn't until she indicated my seat that I realized what those rectangles represented. They were where the pictures of Dad had been. She'd kept them up after he died three years before, but now they were gone.

As she put a copper pot on the stove and got out a mug with I LOST MY HEART IN BELIZE scripted across it, everything became clear. The tchotchke. The missing pictures of Dad. The depression. The multiple mortgages.

"Still waitressing?" she asked.

"Yep. You still doing the books for the church?"

"What's his name?" she asked, not answering my question. "You didn't buy that car on a waitress's salary."

"I don't make a salary. I make tips." What kind of answer was that? That was the answer of a woman ashamed of who she was, and I'd given that up. "His name is Jonathan. I hope we're not going to argue about it."

"As long as it's not that other guy. I didn't like him."

"Does yours have a name?" She didn't answer, just dicked with some floral canisters that may or may not have been full of expired tea. "Mom, is there anyone out here you can talk to? The priest? Someone in the choir?"

"It's not that easy."

"Is it the rector that dumped you?"

"For the love of all that is holy, Monya, that is—"

"A totally reasonable assumption. Except for the obvious world travel that's happening. You're sleeping until after noon, so I know you're not working for him. You can't talk to anyone, and all your friends are there."

"I don't want to." The teapot whistled.

"I'll be gone in a few hours. So you might as well tell me."

She put the mug of hot liquid in front of me and left the room. I started to follow, but I saw her open a door in the china cabinet. She crouched down, rummaging through old dishes and cookbooks, until she came up with a brown paper expanding file. I sat back down, and she slapped it in front of me.

She said, "This is what you came for. All my paperwork. Take it. No, I don't want to lose the house. I love that house as much as you do. If I didn't love it, I would have sold it and kicked you to the street for being an insolent, disrespectful bitch two years ago."

"Don't hold back, ma. Tell me how you really feel."

She didn't say anything else, but she didn't laugh and forgive me either. That was it. That was what she'd wanted to say. It wasn't as bad as I'd feared. I didn't get crushed under the weight of her disapproval. But she was right. Despite my initial protestations, I wanted to save the house.

"I'm sorry about whatever-his-name-is," I said. "It looks like you guys had a good time together."

"I don't want to talk about it."

"Okay." I unspooled the string from the felt disk and flipped open the envelope. I don't know anything about finance. Numbers only interested me insofar as they related to sound vibrations, but once I spread the papers across the table and stacked them into a narrative I could get my head around, one thing was abundantly clear.

My mother had blown about three quarters of a million dollars traveling the globe.

The house I lived in had been purchased for ninety-five thousand in the mid-nineties and paid in full twenty years later with my dad's life insurance. But Echo Park had been in the nascent stages of a renaissance when my parents bought it. Since then, more and more people like Dr. Thorensen had moved in next to artists, Hispanic families, and gang members.

According to a bank located in Colorado, my little house on a hill was worth six hundred fifty thousand dollars. I knew that because my mother had cashed out every dime, and then some, piggy-backing mortgages and loans. She'd attempted to squeeze almost another hundred grand in equity out of the thing when I'd had those permits opened. As if there would be actual improvements.

She'd bailed on her job in February. She'd been at that church since I was in high school and had a salary good enough to cover all her obligations. Without that job, it had all tumbled on her. I imagined the gentleman in question was the cause of her slide.

"You're a goddamn genius, ma."

"Watch your mouth."

"You know you'll never pay this back?"

"They won't miss it. It's a bank," she said.

"It's about four banks. Mom, Christ—"

"Mouth."

"I can't even get my head around what to do." I collected the papers. I wanted to slam and bang them to illustrate my annoyance, but they only made shuffling sounds. "Can you just tell me what happened? You didn't raise me to do stuff like this."

She put her fists on her hips. "Like what?"

"Stealing. This is stealing."

"Not if I let them have that house."

"It's not worth seven hundred thousand dollars."

"The appraisers said it was, so it is. Things are worth what experts say they're worth. People like us, we're nothing. Our opinions don't mean anything. And you agree. In your heart, you know it. You think the house isn't worth anything because you love it, and if you love it, it's garbage, right? Well, how much would you pay for it? Huh? How much for your father's trees? How much for the porch your father and I sat on after you were in bed?"

"Mom—"

"How much for the kitchen where I cooked for you? How much for the side door you snuck into after curfew as if I didn't know? Or the bathroom where I miscarried two babies? How much is it worth, Monya? Even that cracked foundation your father promised to fix a hundred times before he shipped himself across the world. That house was where I waited for him. Where he *wasn't* when I found out I had cancer. How much would a stranger pay for those years? If my life there wasn't worth seven hundred thousand dollars, what was my life worth?"

I couldn't take it any more. Her face was red and strained. Her voice hit a crescendo, and I had been a neglectful, insolent bitch. I bolted from the chair, put my arms around her, and let her cry. "It's okay, ma. We'll fix it."

"I can't. I tried everything."

"I have friends who are lawyers. I can—" I stopped myself. I could have them look at the paperwork, maybe explain the situation. But Jonathan would offer to buy the house, no doubt, and I didn't want him to. I didn't want to go down a road where he bailed out my family, then my friends. I didn't want him to trade Jessica's financial distress for mine. I could soothe my mother for the moment, but in the end, we'd have to let the house go. I'd tell Jonathan I was okay with it, pretend as though it wasn't a big deal.

A call came in. Still holding my mother, I slipped the phone out of my pocket. Margie. I missed it by a second and put it back in my pocket while it went to voice mail. "Let me see what I can do."

She sniffed and stood up straight. "There's nothing to do. I'm sorry you have to move."

"I'll live." I waved it off, but I knew I wasn't convincing. "I should have been here for you. Come around more often."

"Yes. You should have."

"I'm sorry." A text blooped on my phone. My mother and I looked at each other.

"This the man with the car?" Her tone did not bode well for an intelligent conversation. If I had just learned to stop calling myself a whore, my mother hadn't. She was in park, but that could change on a dime.

"No, it's his sister, probably." I looked. It was a text from Margie, as I expected.

—Where the fuck are you?—

The next one came immediately after.

—He's bleeding into his chest.
Bad suture ripped tissue—

It took me sixty seconds to say good-bye to my mother, promise I'd do my best for her, scoop up the papers, and get in the car.

CHAPTER 15

MONICA

I texted Margie that I'd be there in two hours. It was getting dark already, and I'd hit Los Angeles right around rush hour. That would literally double the time it would take me to get to Sequoia. The hospital was inside a knot of traffic arteries that made it hard to move toward or away from during peak hours. It was poor planning for the sake of the ambulances and women in labor, but for a central, urban hospital accessible from the five points of L.A., it was prime real estate.

Jonathan was in the middle of the best cardiac unit in the country, if the internet was to be believed. Whatever happened, I was sure it would be rectified in no time at all. I worried that he might face unpleasantness and that I wouldn't be there for him, but he'd be fine. I was sure, positive as a matter of fact, that it wasn't a big deal.

I finally got into the waiting room at seven p.m. and was redirected to intensive care. I didn't shake, nor did I panic, because in ten years, the visit would be funny. When I got to intensive care, it didn't look as though anyone was laughing.

Fiona blew past me without greeting. Deirdre smiled at me, but she couldn't hide her concern like the rest of them. Sheila, who always came off as motherly and kind, was talking to Margie as if she wanted to bite off her head. Doing my own roll call, I counted off. Carrie wasn't coming. Leanne was in Asia. Theresa hadn't been around in days. Eileen stood by Margie, twisting her diamond ring. Her pumps had been traded for sneakers days ago when her medication was upped. She waved to me but didn't call me over. Margie's presence made me bold. I walked forward.

"This is unacceptable." Sheila spoke in clipped vowels and hard consonants, her finger pointed at Margie's throat. "And you treat it like another day in the park. This hospital fucked up. They as good as killed him."

I gasped, and the three of them paused, glanced, ignored.

"Thanks for the drama," Margie said to Sheila. "It's exactly what we need."

"You need to start filing a malpractice suit immediately."

"Like hell."

"You're losing your guts."

"I want us focusing on Jonathan. Not legal battles. Let them do an inquiry—" Margie said.

"And start the cover-up."

"This is not TV—"

"I'll hire my own counsel."

"Exactly what he needs."

"You—"

"I agree with Margie," I said. Six light eyes turned toward me, and I got my first ever case of stage fright. "It's going to take years to sue. A week won't make a difference."

Sheila turned her head but didn't commit the rest of her body to face me. She'd been kind to me from the minute I met her, but I had the feeling that was about to change. "Who are you?" She knew goddamn well who I was. Nobody.

I walked away and wasn't followed. Good. Fucking Drazens, all of them. Except the one. I didn't know the nurses in the ICU, so I put a harmless look on my face as I approached the dark-skinned woman with an armful of charts. "Hi, I'm looking for Jonathan Drazen's room?"

"He's down in X-ray. Come back in an hour."

I had two choices: Go back and try to find out what I needed from the Family Drazen or wait in the cafeteria until Jonathan came back. I knew Margie would tell me everything once she shook Sheila, and Sheila might even calm down enough to be nice to me. But I saw no reason to stand there and be abused while I waited.

As I walked into the cafeteria, I saw Daddy Drazen sitting with a long-haired man in sandals who had a toddler on his knee. The man was talking fast with his head down. Declan leaned in to hear and put his hand on the man's shoulder. Declan didn't seem like a sociopath, which didn't mean much of anything. I wasn't an expert on either Declan or abnormal psychology.

I got in line for a cup of tea. A song percolated in my head. I went to get my notebook, but dig as I might, it wasn't in my bag. I must have left it at home. Damn it. I took out a Sharpie and got ready to write it on my arm.

"Monica?"

I heard my name as I spaced out to the music in my head, trying to get words and rhythm to match. "Dr. Thorensen. I mean, Brad. Hi." He had a white lab coat over his suit with a nametag clipped to the lapel. "I've never seen you at work before."

"What are you doing down here?"

"Getting something to eat. I just got in." He took me by the elbow and sat me down at an empty table. "What?"

"I just had to open a transplant assessment of Mr. Drazen."

I don't know what I must have looked like. Maybe blank, because a sort of vacuity took hold of me. Or maybe I looked puzzled. "I don't understand. It was a bad suture. I know Sheila's pissed, but..." But I'd assumed she was flying off the handle. But I thought he got X-rays all the time. But I thought it was a complication, not ruination. But I was hanging on to my optimism because I missed it.

He glanced around then back at me.

"Say it," I said. "I don't want to hear it from anyone else."

"It was a suture inside his heart. The tearing's very bad. He's bleeding faster than they can pump it out. If they go in and patch him up... Well, they can't. There's no room. And the tear has moved into his left ventricle."

"Are you going to fix it?" I panicked the panic of someone whose anxiety was a show because I knew everything would be okay. For sure, there was an easy fix for all this, and Jonathan and I would soon laugh about how silly I was to worry so much. I couldn't wait for that laughter. I told the story in my head over an imaginary Thanksgiving dinner, describing the goose bumps on my arms, the dry feeling in my mouth, the sudden breathlessness in my lungs. I'd wax dramatic about holding back tears, and Jonathan would laugh that laugh from deep in his chest, and tears would stream down his face.

"I don't know," Brad said.

"What do you mean you don't know?"

"We're still doing the assessment. I have a lot of forms to fill out. I have to talk to the rest of the cardiac team. It's tricky."

"What's fucking tricky? You're either fixing it, or you're filling out fucking paperwork."

"Take it easy."

"I'm not taking it easy. I will burn your fucking house down if you don't tell me right now why you assholes can't fix it immediately."

He took my wrists and held me in place. I knew he wouldn't have done that unless he knew me. The privilege of whatever information I'd already gotten was courtesy of a few hours of *City of Dis*. "There's a good chance, and I don't know for sure because I need to review everything with the committee, but I'm pretty sure he'll need a transplant."

"Okay." I breathed, which I'd forgotten to do. That was a thing. It was a course of action. "Then give him one."

"We need a heart, and his blood type? AB negative? It's rare. He needs to get on the list. Monica, I hope I'm wrong. If the surgical team believes they can go back in and fix it, then this whole conversation is moot." His eyes, deep blue and a little bloodshot, as if he'd been up too many hours, did not waver from mine. He had the confidence of a man who had held a human heart and made it beat again.

He had made life and death happen, and Jonathan was just another patient, another puzzle to solve, another career challenge.

I slipped my hands down to hold his hands. I squeezed them and closed my eyes. "I want you to understand something. That man? He's not some boyfriend in a line of them. He is my alpha and omega. He is the sky over me. Without him, I'm lost. There's no one else, no one whose soul balances mine the way his does. I've waited my life for him, and when he came, I didn't recognize him. Not until recently. If I lose him, I swear, as God is my witness, I will be alone. No man can match him."

When I opened my eyes, Brad was looking at our clasped hands, head down. "I didn't know."

"I only live next door."

He looked back up. "I'll do my best. I can't promise anything. If he needs a new heart, I want you to be ready for a rough time. He doesn't have forever to bleed into himself, and healthy hearts don't come all that often. You need to sleep and eat and live your life while you wait."

I smirked. "My life is with him. That's how I live it. The rest is unnecessary complication." I felt like Jonathan was there with me when I quoted him. We sat like that for a few seconds, and I tried to transmit my seriousness. It felt good to just sit with someone and *be,* even if it couldn't last.

His cell phone beeped. He didn't look at it but let go of my hands. "That's my office. I have to go."

"Will you let me know?"

"You'll know, Monica. You'll know." He stood. "Just the sleeping and eating. Do those. Okay?"

My tea was cold. My granola bar looked more and more like a slab of pressed shit. "After I see him. Then I'll go home and go to bed."

He looked at his watch. "Come with me. Hurry." He waved and walked off, hand in his pocket for his phone before he'd even turned around completely. I scuttled behind.

Examination rooms inside offices inside suites inside wards, around corners and up secret stairs, I followed Brad to X-ray. While texting, he spoke to a lady in a pink smock, and Pink Smock gave him the name of yet another space I never would have found on my own. In that space was a gurney. On it was Jonathan.

I assumed Brad said good-bye, because by the time I was standing over my lover, Brad was gone. Jonathan was either sleeping or unconscious, pale as death, an altar to IV tower gods. I took his hand, pressing my palm to his. He didn't respond. It was just warm enough to indicate he wasn't lost. I stayed until Pink Smock and an orderly came to push him away. I went with them, just to make sure he was okay.

CHAPTER 16

MONICA

I SLEPT in a random waiting room despite promising Brad I'd go home. I woke up aching everywhere, went to the cafeteria, and wrote a song on a napkin. Something moved on the table. I snapped out of it. My notebook, with the NOPA inside, slid toward me. Declan stood over the table.

"I thought you might want this," he said. "You left it here the other day."

"Thanks." I stuffed it in my bag. "You're like a regular here these days. Piece of furniture."

"Like fiberglass and cheap chrome?"

"The Drazen sense of humor is genetic, apparently."

He sat down. "Not so apparent. I haven't heard my boy crack a joke in twenty years."

"He's funny." My voice cracked. I put my head down. I couldn't look at him because I had been about to say "he *was* funny." My eyes stung, and my face got red. I didn't want a man made of fiberglass and chrome to see me cry over his prodigal son.

"Margaret told me," he said.

I sniffed and tried to get my shit together. I clutched my tea, letting it heat up my icy hands. "Why aren't you ever upstairs with them?"

"This is as close as I'm allowed. They don't want me there. My wife, at least. We sleep on opposite sides of the house. Decades of neglect will do that."

"I'm sure it was purely benign." My raw emotions made my feelings hard to hide, and in that unguarded moment, my voice dripped with inappropriately rude sarcasm. I wasn't being a woman of grace.

648

But he seemed to take it in stride. "I had a very, shall we say, *intense* mid-life crisis."

"You shared a mistress with your son. Pretty intense."

"Is that what he told you? I guess he could have seen it that way. She was a manipulative girl, but yes, I did plenty I was pleased with at the time, but now... Well, now I need a golf cart to get to my wife's bedroom and my son won't see me." He massaged his coffee. "Would he be upset if he knew you were at a table with me?"

"Yeah." I felt guilty for being there. Jonathan wouldn't like it. Not one bit. If he was going to get well, he needed to know I was safe, and I was sure he didn't think of me as safe around his father. I put the granola bar in my bag. "I should go upstairs. It was nice talking to you."

"Yes, it was."

CHAPTER 17

JONATHAN

I'D ALREADY TRIED to take the fucking little tubes out of my fucking nose. The room lit up like Griffith Park at Christmas, and it was Jingle Bells all over again. I'd be okay with it if I never got defibrillated again. Odds were not in my favor.

I had a hard time staying awake for long. My exhaustion came from lack of oxygen and a body worn out working for nothing. It pumped blood that went down a tube and sucked up more blood from a bag. There was medicine too. Bags of it going into my hand. And a bag of blood that kept getting replaced like a pot of coffee.

I remember one of them saying I was a lucky man. I had no idea what he was talking about, but I thought it didn't have a damn thing to do with my health. He was blond, Nordic looking, and I asked him what he meant. He just went on with another battery of questions that seemed like every other battery of questions every other white lab coat had asked me or the person next to them. If I had a dime for every doctor who walked in and talked about me as if I wasn't there, I could buy and sell myself. The non-entity of me. The skin bag of pain and discomfort. I didn't feel as though I owned my body any more. I felt like a piece of meat being kept alive until something happened. Some miracle. Or some news.

"I'm not here to make you upset."

I felt lucid when Margie said that, my brain snapping to attention at the thought that there was something I should, but shouldn't, be upset about. "Oh, good. You're here to tap dance."

"I love that you have the energy to joke but not give a shit about your condition."

"I give a shit." The effort speaking took was monumental, but contact with someone wearing real clothes and not wielding a needle was too welcome to not answer in full. "Guy came and told me I'm in a world of trouble. There's just nothing I can do about it."

"They called us into a meeting. This must be what it's about. What did they say?"

"Let them do their jobs. I can't..." I drifted off. I couldn't repeat what the guy with the silver hair had said. Dr. Emerson. Like the poet.

As if understanding, she put her hand on my shoulder. "I took care of something while you were down. It's going to create drama."

"Okay."

"Okay, you have no problem with it?"

"Okay, tell me what it is."

"Monica's broke. She hasn't been going to work because she's been hanging around Sequoia Hospital like she works here."

"Fuck." My life spinning out of control was bad enough, but I was taking Monica with me.

"I'm giving her money and saying it's from you. You're going to back me up."

"Yes."

"Good."

"Margie?" I raised my hand a little, and she took it, coming closer so she could hear me.

"What?"

"You're my new favorite. Thank you."

"I'm keeping tabs on every dime because you're going to get better, you little fuck. I don't know how, but this isn't how it ends. Do you understand me? It's not ending like this."

CHAPTER 18

MONICA

THE CLOSER I got to Jonathan's family, the more I understood where he came from. His ability to laugh through anger and tears, the happy face he put on over his worries, and the Oscar-worthy show of confidence came from his mother. The deft manipulations of people and situations, the sadism, the raw hunger, and the social charm came from his father. The passion and protectiveness were learned through his sisters.

Margie had handed me five thousand dollars in an envelope and told me if I didn't take it, she would tell Jonathan. That would upset him enough to give him another heart attack. She was exaggerating, but I got the point. He'd arranged money and refusing it would cause him stress.

"I told you not to tell him," I'd said, holding on to a shred of pride even as I clutched the envelope.

"I ignored you. Tough."

"I hate this."

"Take it up with God."

"Well, thank you," I said. "I don't want you to think I don't appreciate it."

I needed the money. Badly. After spending a morning on the phone, I found I had long odds of saving the house. I could rescue my mother's finances by arranging a short sale, but I'd still have to move. One of the banks was adamant about the current resident vacating the premises. I could have waited for an eviction and then fought it, but I had too many balls in the air already. I needed to find a place to live and a place to store my stuff. I needed to rent a truck and pay a security deposit and first month's rent. Five thousand would just about cut it.

I had other business to attend to, as well. Accepting five grand from my lover's sister was something I never thought I'd do. The day would be a day of firsts. I dialed Eddie's cell phone. He picked up. Oh, the privilege of being me. Six months ago, he wouldn't have returned a voice mail from me, much less taken a call on the second ring.

"What's happening, princess?" he answered over a wave of ambient noise. I didn't like the nickname. It was too close in concept to "flake."

"I can't do a session," I said. "Jonathan... He's...it's bad. I need to be here."

"How bad?" The ambient noise disappeared as if he'd closed a window.

"Something went wrong. He's bleeding. He needs a transplant. Maybe. Probably."

"*What?*"

"If you have a heart lying around in the next few days..."

"*Days?*"

My head was screwed up. I was a monster. I'd thought Eddie would care that I was cancelling my recording session, but Jonathan was his friend. Why the hell would Eddie care about my fucking EP? "You should come and see him."

"Fuck."

"Are you all right? I'm sorry. I've been dealing with this for days. I should have broken it to you better."

He didn't answer right away. I thought I'd lost the connection, and then he spoke up. "When I banged up my dad's Maz, Jonathan took me all over L.A. to get it fixed. We got it home before my parents got back from Maui by, like, minutes. He drove like such a dick."

I sniffed. "Don't eulogize yet, please." I had the sudden need to see Jonathan, to stop wasting time in a cold stairway when I could be taking up space with him. I pushed through the stair doors into the hall.

"Sorry, I..." Eddie caught himself. "Tell him he's an asshole for me. All right?"

"Sure thing." The elevator dinged as I hung up, and I blocked traffic by standing there looking at my phone. I wondered why I didn't give a shit about the blown opportunity.

"Monica," came a voice in the crowd.

I turned to the source. "Jessica."

"I'd like to speak with you."

"Sure."

We stepped into a corner by a six-foot tall potted plant that looked too fake to be real, or too real to be fake.

"What?" I said.

She raised her eyebrows. "You've got no business being sharp with me."

"Thanks for letting me know my business."

"I didn't come here to fight with you. I came to see him."

"Why? To upset him? I'm sick of this. I've never seen anyone crush a man so hard then try to get him back like it was her job. For Chrissakes, I wish he'd just give you your money so you'd leave him the fuck alone."

"He will." Her face darkened like a desert under rare clouds. "This is a long-term hospitalization. The trust will move to irrevocable in a week. He'll be here."

It hit me then, her motivation for being there. It was sick. Unbelievably venal. "Unless he's dead, right? If he dies while the trust is revocable, you lose." I started to walk away, but she grabbed my elbow. I looked at where her fingers dented the fabric of my shirt then at her.

"You listen to me," she said through her teeth, "I loved him. Make no mistake. He wasn't for me, but I loved him. That doesn't go away."

"He. Is. Mine."

"Under the circumstances, he's everyone's. He needs all of us. We can have this fight now or after he's dead. Would that suit you?"

Something seethed in me. Something hot and black and angry, bubbling to the surface and settling in.

Before Los Angeles was a place, it had a tar pit. I'd gone on three field trips to the La Brea tar pits. In prehistory, an animal got stuck in it, and a predator came to eat the animal. The predator, even as he ate, got stuck. Carrion came to feast on the weakened bodies, and all were stuck. The number multiplied as more, driven by instinct and hunger, fell into the trap. Masses of mammals, winged creatures, and crustaceans came to feast. The black goo pulled them down to their deaths in a years-long chain of seething, building, predatory hunger. Ripping throats, blood-covered-fur, a routine orgy of violence and death, multiplied by an order of fear, melted into the tar and added to the organic mass of boiling, black pitch.

On La Brea Avenue, there's a park. In the park, the tar pits bubble underground, leaving puddles of sticky black goop in the grass. They come up where they want, and everything sinks into them.

When Jessica suggested Jonathan would die, I wanted to claw out her eyes and pull out her hair at the roots like one of those animals. I felt as if I'd put a lawn of sweet words over an aquifer of tar-sticky rage, and her presence had triggered a bubbling geyser of anger. I wasn't angry at Jessica, and I wasn't angry that she had the gall to bring death into the conversation like a threat.

I was angry at death. I was angry that it dared to black the light from the window, that it should come between Jonathan and me. We'd overcome so much together. What did it want? What was I supposed to do? And life? How dare life bring him to me just to take him away.

The elevator doors opened with a *ding*, but Jessica and I stared at each other as if guns were drawn.

"It's nice you kids are getting along," Margie's voice cut in.

Jessica let go of my arm. When she did, I realized something. I didn't like her. I didn't trust her. But I couldn't pretend I was angry at her. As if shunned, Jessica ran into the elevator at the last second.

"Cute, you two," Margie said. "Almost like you could stand being in the same room together."

"She's just going to upset Jonathan."

"No, she's not. He refused to see her. She's a little pissed off." Margie headed down the hall, her gait quick and sure.

I chased after her. "You look pretty pissed yourself."

"I got big news from the Department of Bad Shit. They can't get in to fix the suture. It's a transplant or nothing."

CHAPTER 19

MONICA

HE WAS LUCID. I knew because he smiled when he saw me.

"Goddess."

"Sir."

"I'm very upset with you."

"I'll skip the spanking joke."

"You need to ask for what you need." He was talking about the money.

"Thank you," I said. "But I couldn't ask."

"I can't read your mind."

"Can we have this discussion when you're better?"

"Did anyone explain the odds of that to you yet? Because—"

"Stop it." I held up both hands, and he took one.

He was going to talk. He was going to tell me what I already knew from Margie and Brad and any doctor I happened upon in the halls. But I didn't want to hear it. I especially didn't want it from him because he would be Mr. Control. Hearing it from him in that measured, shredded voice would make me either scream or run out.

"Tell me what's happening with you," he whispered. "I hear about me all day."

"Eddie asked about you."

"Tell him he's a douchebag for me."

"I will," I said.

"Did he get you a new date to record?"

"Not yet. Christmas is coming, so it's dead."

My face was close to his. He was close enough to own my attention, shutting out the scritch of the stylus and the hissing of the oxygen tubes. Close enough for him to look at me long and deep and see the contents of my heart.

"Don't lie, goddess."

"Carnival has to wait. A four-song session will take all day. If something happens, I need to be here."

A machine beeped. He pressed his lips between his teeth. He'd used that expression when he was healthy, and it made me want to beg him to take me.

"I need you to do your work," he said.

"I won't do it right if I'm worrying about you."

I felt his hand on my waist, a light touch through my shirt. It slid up to my rib cage, bringing memories of everything we'd been together when his hands were forceful and cruel, responsive to desires I didn't even know I had. He fingered the black Bordelle bra I'd worn at his command.

"You've come so far," he said. "You're not the same woman I met. You have control. You can take it and channel it into the work. If I promise you that, would you believe me?"

"I can't."

"You don't know your own power. Please. Go sing. Sheila will watch me."

"I'll think about it."

He nodded as much has he could, and I pressed my lips to his. I kissed him like I kissed him every time since he fell into my arms—like it might be the last

CHAPTER 20

MONICA

I'D GONE home to shower and rest. I shouldn't have. The Drazens had a suite at the hotel across from the hospital, and I should have eaten humble pie and gone there. But I couldn't ask Sheila for the key. I didn't have a change of clothes or the resources to buy new. Fucking pride. Now I was stuck in traffic ten blocks from the goddamn hospital. Another hour lost.

Sitting in traffic in thebestfuckingthingever was far better than sitting in traffic in the Honda. It beat the bus by a mile. But traffic was traffic, and sitting still in a Jaguar while helicopters beat the air was infuriating. Having grown up in Echo Park—before it was a real estate investment opportunity waiting to happen—I was familiar with that situation. The police were sealing off a perimeter so every car could be checked. Usually, a cop-killing created that kind of chaos. Or a gang assassination. Maybe a child abduction. I ticked off the list then closed the windows and sang a couple of the songs I'd prepared for the EP. I belted them out in the shitty acoustics of the car.

I flipped on the news. Music was just messing up the rhythm in my head, which I needed. Talk talk talk, and I half listened to the clipped chat about a mob shooting outside the golf course. No child abduction but a typical drive-by. I felt as though I knew the details without even hearing them, and I internally restated my belief that penalties should be harsher for crimes committed during rush hour. I would be there a while. I sang to the leather dash, letting the news drift away.

Yea, though he stands in the fear of the dark

658

I shall walk at his right hand
I have drawn rod and cudgel
In his defense
I shall lead him to the gate
And if he seeks his end
My heart shall keep him safe

I can walk
Without it
I can work
Without it
I can sing
Half a woman

Surely goodness and mercy
Prevail in a city of sin
As barter for a life
Beats for beat
Breaths for breaths
Trade a heart for what's mine

I can breathe
Without it
I can see
Without it
I can sing
Half a woman

I WAS LEANING my forehead on the steering wheel when I finished. I couldn't get out the rest of the song. I couldn't breathe. I couldn't see through my tears. He didn't have long. I saw it in the doctors' faces when they spoke as if their careers were on the line. The inconvenience of his death would be epic for them.

Meanwhile, I'd die with him.

The phone rang. Fuck it. It wasn't as if I was moving. I picked up Margie's call.

"Hello?" I realized how snotty and blubbery I sounded when the last vowel came out in a froggy croak.

"Are you okay?"

"The love of my life is dying, so no."

"Well, I called with a little something. Some mafia kingpin just came in with half a brain and a working heart. We're fighting our way up the list, and they're checking for a match. But he's the same blood type."

"Oh, God. Really?" My face exploded in prickly happiness, and tears sprung into my eyes.

"Top secret, okay? This is not public knowledge, as a matter of fact, me knowing is illegal. But don't get your hopes up. The guy's family's going to be an obstacle. Donor cards don't mean anything without a living will, and his family has more hope than Jonathan has time."

"Is it evil to hope he dies?"

"Yes. You and I both."

"See you in hell," I said, with a little less despair in my voice.

"I'll buy the hand basket."

The traffic broke, and I was waved through the blockade on Beverly and Rossmore.

CHAPTER 21

MONICA

"I sold the house. Thank God, Monya. Cash. At market price."

My mother had called just as I stepped into the elevator with nine other people. I was about to tell her I hadn't made any headway, nor had I found an opportune time to ask for Margie's help, when she blurted out her news like a kid blowing the date of a surprise party.

"That's great, ma," I whispered so I wouldn't annoy the three people pressed up against me. "Did they say when they were moving in?" I was happy for her. I really was. But the bank would have to put all my stuff in a Dumpster because I couldn't leave Jonathan long enough to move out.

"That's the good news! They're okay with a tenant. Okay with your rent and everything. You have to make your checks out to an investment company. ODRSN Partners. The address is 147—"

"Can I get it later? I'm in an elevator. I'll call you back."

We hung up, and I molted a few layers of anxiety. I must have bounced into Jonathan's room because he smiled when he saw me. The oxygen tubes were gone from his nose. The sun shone through the window. Yes, he had that auto-squeeze thing on his arm, and yes, he was in that god damn hospital bed, and yes, his heart was ripped up, but he was in a half sitting position and he looked as glad to see me as I was to see him.

"I don't have to move!" I announced, kissing him.

"Good?"

"Oh God, you missed the whole thing!" I blabbered. "My mom put the house into foreclosure. I thought I was going to have to move out really fast, which is

661

impossible—hello, I have twenty years of stuff in that house—but some investor bought it."

"Ah, who beat me out?"

"Crap, she told me." I wrestled with the granola bar until he took it from me and got it open in one move—with a bad heart and IVs sticking out of him. "It's such a load off. I can't even tell you."

He broke off a piece of the bar and held it. "Was it Ganten Investments?"

I took the piece in my mouth. "No, it was a bunch of letters, like DRM... But five letters and not that. I made it into a word in my head, but I can't think of it."

"Doesn't matter, I guess."

"You have to move faster next time if you want property in Echo Park." I took another chunk of granola bar from his fingers. I felt light as a feather, waving at him to indicate I wanted another piece. "Oh my God, this thing tastes so bad. It's, like, stinky."

"Stinky?"

"With a touch of dredgy." Then I remembered, as I chewed, the rhythm of the letters. The taste of the stale barley malt brought it to me. "ODRSN. That was it. It sounded like odorous. ODRSN Partners."

He was looking at the bar, breaking another smelly piece, when he froze. "Did you say ODRSN?"

"Yep."

"Are you sure?"

"Yeah, why? Is that the competition or something?"

He put the bar on the side table then closed his eyes and took a deep breath. It wasn't deep at all though. He breathed as if he didn't have room for air in his lungs.

I took his hands. "Jonathan? Should I call someone?"

He shook his head, but I didn't believe him. I believed the machines, which were silent. But for how long? He was struggling, if not with his breath or his heart, then with his mind.

"I need you to marry me," he said.

"What?"

"Marry me."

"Are you insane?"

"If anything happens to me, I want to make sure you're taken care of," he said.

"I refuse to believe you're going to die. My God, we've maybe been together a few months."

"These are extenuating circumstances. I could leave you swinging in the wind."

"No." I shook my head as if I was trying to get a fly out of my hair. "This is crazy. This is not how I want it. I don't want you to get better then regret it. It's not your job to make sure I'm financially stable. What's come over you?"

Midway through my little speech, stuff started beeping and lighting up. By the time I was done, I was being pushed out by a woman in a blue facemask and gloves. I landed in the hall, back against the wall, trying to stay out of the way.

"What happened?" Eileen asked, standing close to Theresa as if her daughter held her up.

"I don't know," I said. "We were talking about something."

He asked me to marry him and I said no. I put my hands over my mouth when I realized what had happened, and I ran down the hall without looking back. Even when I passed the cafeteria and saw Declan in his usual spot talking to Jessica, I didn't stop. I just kept running.

CHAPTER 22

JONATHAN

That went poorly.

I hadn't intended to ask for her hand, but then she said the name of my father's investment shell. He'd bought her house to save her when I couldn't or wouldn't. Whichever. I simply *didn't,* and the reason I didn't was I didn't know she was in that kind of trouble. I could only know and see what she brought to me. If she chose to protect me, I was impotent to protect her. I was stuck inside four walls with things sticking out of me, tied to a bed as much as I'd tied her.

By the time the smoke cleared, she was gone, and I couldn't explain. I didn't want to talk on the phone. I couldn't, actually. My body betrayed me with exhaustion, long breaths, and lost consciousness. I needed to be in her visual field to see what I was too tired to intuit. She needed to experience the long spaces between sentences that would seem like anger or petulant silence on the phone but were just me trying to breathe around my goddamn damaged heart.

I loved her. I wanted her. She felt right in ways no other woman ever had. Of course I was going to marry her one day, when I was out of that shitbox and untied from that bed. After more dinners and late nights. After more boundary leaping and fighting. More touching, kissing, laughing.

Just not now.

Except that it had to be now. I felt myself failing. My dips into unconsciousness came with less warning. The effort to exist was such a task, I couldn't imagine surviving. Was I scared? Fuck yes, I was terrified. The only thing that kept it at bay was the thought that I could make her life better than it had been, that I could save her from her chronic penury, keep her safe from the manipulations of men like my father. If I could die knowing I'd saved her, maybe I would have served my purpose. It wasn't like my money had anywhere useful to go, anyway.

Theresa sat in the chair Monica usually occupied, leaning forward with her fingers knit together. I wanted to explain all of it to her, but I didn't have the wherewithal to do it right. I had to explain my fear, my need to know Monica was all right, to keep a slice of control. I gave her the shortest version I had.

"I don't blame her for saying no," she said. "You need to get better first."

"What if I don't get better?"

"She'll be a widow."

At twenty-five. When was her birthday? She'd told me she was a Cancer, but if she told me the exact date, I couldn't recall it. I realized we'd never celebrated a birthday together, neither mine nor hers. I wanted to get her something extravagant six months early to make up for the time we'd never have. And Christmas, of course.

"What's today?" I asked Theresa.

"The nineteenth."

"Merry Christmas."

"What do you want under the tree? Besides a 'yes'?"

"I want her," I whispered. "I asked for the wrong reasons, but I want her."

She put her elbows on the bed and her hand on my shoulder. "Do it for the right reasons. Don't do it because it's convenient. Don't do it because you're scared. Marry her because you love her and your life wouldn't add up without her. Can you do that? Can you promise me you're not forcing it? It would break my heart to see you propose because you wanted to give yourself a reason to live."

I rarely saw Theresa so impassioned. She was more like Jessica in her refinement and grace than any of my sisters. She seemed broken down that day, slightly shattered and holding herself together with chicken wire.

"What's wrong, Tee?"

"I don't think love should be taken for granted, and I don't think you should keep on a path of least resistance."

"This is hardly—"

"Can you honestly say that if you were healthy, you'd marry her?"

"Yes. But we'd have a proper engagement." I thought about all Jessica and I had had together, and I wanted to give it to Monica but couldn't. A party, a ring, a wedding. I wanted to see her smiling as she came down the aisle toward me for the last time before we folded into each other's lives forever.

Theresa pressed something into my palm. It was hard and scratchy and oddly shaped. "Give it back when you can buy her her own."

I lifted my hand. It was her engagement ring, a two-carat sapphire cut that was totally Theresa and utterly wrong for Monica. "Daniel won't be happy."

"He'll tell himself he cares. But we cancel each other out. We add up to nothing. Trust me when I say I'd rather break up for the right reasons than get married for the wrong ones."

"I'm sorry."

"Don't be. I can't explain why I feel okay about it, but I do."

I held the ring in my fist as if I was afraid to lose it. "Thank you."

"I'll try to come back, but you might not see me for a while." She kissed my forehead and left.

I fell asleep with the ring in my hand.

CHAPTER 23

MONICA

JONATHAN WAS out of his room. More tests, more prep. More shit piled on top of shit. A hundred thousand checklists to make sure he was worthy of whatever heart came in. My mother texted me the address to send the rent check, and a quick internet search revealed J. Declan Drazen owned ODRSN Partners. Anger and gratitude swirled together inside me like a marble cake.

Dr. Thorensen was in his office looking at four computer screens. "Monica, come in." He stood. "Close the door."

"Thanks. I got your text, but I was driving."

"Sit." He stood in front of a little counter with a sink and poured water into a pot, leaving his screens unattended.

"You're playing *City of Dis*, aren't you? Where do you find the time?"

"This job doesn't afford the time for a dazzling social life, so video games it is. I have UNOS up on a screen right here." As if responding to what must have been my baffled look, he continued. "The transplant list."

"Ah. I heard someone came in…" I didn't know if I should continue. It was surely privileged information, yet once I started talking, I could hardly stop. "He's brain dead is what I heard. I don't mean to be creepy, but—"

"I think that's going to be a no-go."

"You telling me more or Jonathan getting the heart?"

"Yes."

I looked at my lap. Margie's text had given me enough hope to get in the door. When it dropped out of me, nothing replaced it. We were back where we had been that morning, except I was one day closer to the end.

667

"How are you holding up?" Brad asked.

I shrugged. "I guess I'm all right."

"You're never home."

"Doctor, my presence at home is hardly under your purview."

"I'm not asking as a doctor. I'm asking as your friend. How are you doing?"

"Fine. I feel like I'm waiting for him to either die or be saved, so the regular events of my life aren't so interesting right now."

He leaned back in his chair, eyes glowing in the screens' light. "I've lived next door to you for a couple of years."

"Three, I think."

"I wish I'd gone to your door with something besides the leaves falling on my car or the new fence. I should have known you better, sooner." His hands were folded over his tie, and his feet pushed his office chair back until the corners of his white lab coat dragged on the floor. Besides the hands, it was an exposed position. Even if he didn't intend to send the message he did, I understood the meaning in his heart.

"I'm too upset to give you a thoughtful response. I'm sorry."

"I understand. If you want to go up, he should be back any minute. Irene's at the desk. Check with her if he's okay to see. I'm watching this screen."

I stood up and touched the doorknob. "I'd give him my own heart if I could."

He sat up straight and put his hand on the mouse. "I hear that all the time." He glanced at me, his expression sucking the sarcasm out of the comment. He was just stating a fact. Death was hard, and people loved one another.

CHAPTER 24

MONICA

POLICE MILLED around the hallways with radios squawking, belts laden with black leather geometry, swaying hips from the weight of the instrumentation. I leaned on the nurse's desk, peering at Irene's Russian newspaper.

"Hi," I said. "What are all the cops about?"

She waved her meaty hand and shook her head. "Security. You feel safe? I feel safe. Like in middle of street."

"I'm going in." I stepped away.

"No, you don't." She picked up the phone and hit one of the buttons on the bottom of the keypad. "Wait." The person on the other side must have answered because she muttered something in Russian, listened, and hung up. "Come with me."

She shuffled from behind the desk and went toward Jonathan's room. I didn't know why I needed her to guide me. My world revolved around that room and going to and from it. The door was closed. She knocked. A deep, powerful voice that couldn't have been Jonathan's made some sort of affirmative noise. Irene opened the door.

One lamp was on, a warm one I hadn't seen before. The room smelled nice, like salty sea air and clear water. I located a squat blue candle burning on the windowsill that must have been the source of the scent. A huge bald man stood by the doorway—one of the regular orderlies who didn't talk much. His nametag said Gregory. Irene babbled something, and he babbled back in the same language. He stepped out of the way.

Jonathan sat on the edge of the bed. I hadn't seen him actually sit up since the

669

Collector's Board show, and I must have gasped a little. He wore a suit jacket over his hospital gown. He also had on pants and shoes. Tubes stuck out of his sleeves, and the effort it took for him to sit up was visible once I got over the initial shock.

"Jonathan," I said. "I—"

"You sit," Gregory interrupted, pointing at a red antique chair in front of Jonathan that I recognized from his bedroom. I'd described that chair and its place under a sconce one night, back when I thought I'd have him back. I glanced from Gregory to Irene, and then to my lover, who waited patiently.

I sat. "What's this about?"

No one answered. Gregory and Irene stood on either side of Jonathan, facing me.

"You ready, Mister Drazen?" Irene asked.

"For a long time now."

They did something that made me hold my breath and clutch the arms of the chair. They put their hands under Jonathan's arms, slid him off the bed, and lowered him to the floor.

"What—?" When they let him go, I was too stunned to finish the sentence. He kneeled before me. I heard his labored breathing, the rattle of the IV pole, and glanced at Irene and Gregory. "What are you doing? This is crazy."

I was ignored. Gregory said something to Jonathan in Russian, and he answered in kind, along with a wave of his hand that indicated, "I got it."

Jonathan, with great effort, pulled up a knee until he was on just one and glanced at me. "I'm going to lean on you a little."

"Sure?" He put a forearm on my knee and reached into his jacket pocket, pulling out a small black box. "Oh, Jonathan..."

He opened the box and handed it to me. It had a ridiculously huge square-cut diamond. "Thank Theresa if you see her. I'll get you one that suits you when we're up to it."

"You don't have to do this," I said.

"Shh. Behave, would you? For once?"

I pressed my lips together to keep from laughing. One side of his mouth curled in a smile, and then he laughed gingerly. I wanted to kiss him deeply and for a long time. I wanted to breathe him into me, but I knew he didn't have the breath to spare. I settled for a fraction of the kiss I wanted, just brushing my lips against his. The softest parts of our faces melted together for a second, half a gasp, a tease of desire.

"Goddess," he said, his breath on my mouth, "have me, please. I was wrong. You're not the sea under my sky. You are the sun I revolve around, the stars that mark me, the moon rising through me. I'm lost without you. If you won't have me, I'll break, I swear to God. I know it's selfish, and I'm sorry. Let me serve you. Have me as yours. Let me live under you."

I held his face, running my fingers over his stubble, his jaw in the heel of my hand. I felt him leaning into me as if this had taken everything out of him. What could I say? What could I say to being loved enough for that monumental an effort? Did I ever, in my wildest imaginings, think I deserved that level of devotion after I'd rejected him the first time?

After I'd left him, cursed him, and denied him? After lying to him, drugging him, disobeying him, using him, could I justify letting him make such a mistake even if it was the last mistake he made? I was ambitious, venal, antagonistic, impoverished, and arrogant. I was unworthy by a mile and overcome by the circumstances that would lead such a man to beg to be bound to such a woman.

So I said the only thing I could.

"Yes."

CHAPTER 25

JONATHAN

HER HAIR FELL across our fists, which were balled together around a found box holding my sister's ring. My hands shook as I removed the ring. My rib cage ached as if it was being stretched by an ever-expanding balloon. With the tube out my chest, it was filling with blood, drop by drop. I was sure the feeling of expansion was air or my imagination, but fear made it hard to get the garish thing on her finger. The size was right, but the stone was wrong. All wrong. I wanted something else for her, something more original, a ring that could only belong to a goddess.

"I won't disappoint you," I said.

"I'm not worried about you being the disappointment."

Irene's voice cut in. "I declare you engaged. Time to go." She put her hand on my shoulder.

"I want to tell you what you do to me the night I agree to marry you," Monica whispered.

"They have to put me back in. I don't want you to see it."

"Jonathan, please—"

"Time to go," Irene said more firmly.

"Go," I said to my fiancée. "Please. Come back in an hour. Then you can tell me about our wedding night."

Her head tilted a little, and her eyes widened. Yes, it was quick, but wasn't that the point? She kissed me a second too long. When we ended, I was grimacing. She must have known it wasn't about her because she got up and walked out without looking back. Good woman.

I submitted myself to Irene and Gregory, who had broken a hundred rules or

672

more to give me five minutes to ask properly for Monica's hand. Rules were good. They were there for a reason. I couldn't handle five minutes of kneeling. I felt as if I'd just run a marathon that ended in a dark alley where I'd been beaten with baseball bats and cut into small pieces with a serrated knife. Or something that made me too weak, too pained, too outside myself to manage my own body.

They got me out of my clothes, then reinserted, realigned, and recalibrated the devices attached to me. They accepted my gratitude for as long as I had the wherewithal to express it, which was an eternity but probably about five minutes in the real world. Then I fell off the cliff of consciousness. It might have been because of the drugs or just my body giving out like it did a few times a day. Even then, I didn't have the energy to feel angry, though there was a cord of that in my spine. Mostly, I felt fear. I was responsible for her now. Though the unknown was bad enough to face alone, in the dark and unprepared, I felt as though I had something to live for tomorrow.

CHAPTER 26

MONICA

I crouched on the stairwell. It was late. Jonathan couldn't see me for an hour after he'd given me the ring, or the hour after that. Sheila had come and gone, her lips pressed together in a line of rage. Eileen called to see if I was there, and if I was, was he lucid enough to see anyone. I didn't tell her we'd gotten engaged. I figured if Jonathan had wanted his family involved, they would have been involved.

I called Darren. "Do you have something blue?"

"Technically, yes." He stepped out of the studio to finish the sentence, and I heard the rain and traffic behind him.

"Something pretty and blue?"

"Okay, what the fuck?"

"I'm getting married, and I have this ring that's borrowed and this belt is, like, a hundred years old."

"What?"

"Can you just bring me something blue, please?" I asked. He started a sentence but didn't finish it. He took a breath, started to say something else, and stopped again. "Darren?"

"Jesus. I didn't...I don't know what to say. I haven't been there for you, have I?"

"Be here for me tonight. Something reasonably attractive. And blue. And new, if possible. I'm stretching the definition with what I have here."

CHAPTER 27

MONICA

DARREN ARRIVED JUST as Irene was telling me to do something with my hair then
come in. He handed me a CVS bag with four blue hair clips.

"Thank you," I said. He grabbed me and hugged me. It was the only real hug I'd
gotten all week. It was warm and perfect, without expectation or promise. I chose
a little rhinestone hairpin the color of the autumn sky and let Darren put it in.
"You're the maid of honor and the best man."

"I'm not making a toast."

"He won't have the energy. He barely had it in him to ask me to marry him in
the first place." We walked down the hall.

"I wish you'd told me...asked me for something," he said.

"You never pick up. I feel like I'm bothering you."

He shrugged, and we turned into Jonathan's room. It was lit only by the reading
lamp over his bed. I felt Darren stiffen. Jonathan was halfway sitting up but
bedridden and pale, connected to machines and IV bags of medicine and blood.
The last time they'd seen each other, Jonathan was hale and Darren was
threatening to send out wedding invitations if we had another breakup.

"Hi," Darren said. Jonathan held his hand up in greeting. "You look like fucking
hell, man."

"Darren!" I cried.

"And I can still get a knockout wife," Jonathan said.

"Tough to be you," Darren said.

People came in behind me. I didn't see them; I only saw Jonathan. I kissed his
lips for the last time as his lover and turned around. Irene and Gregory were at the

675

foot of the bed. On the opposite side of the bed from me, in the chair I usually occupied, was a short woman in horn-rimmed glasses and clerical collar. She was a few years older than me and had a mop of curly hair held in place with a vintage clip. Darren stood behind her.

"Hi," she said brightly.

"Hi," Jonathan and I chanted. I straightened and held his hand. It was cold.

"My name is Sona, and let me tell you, this is not the kind of call I usually get when I do the hospital chaplaincy. I had to dig around for the right prayer book. But happy occasions are worth the trouble. So what do we have? Both Catholic, I hear?"

"Kind of," I said.

"I hear the groom has a big family? They aren't here?"

"I'll tell them tomorrow," Jonathan said. My sigh of relief must have been audible because he squeezed my hand.

"Sona," I said, "Jonathan isn't up for anything long and involved if that's okay. I don't mean to be disrespectful."

"Nope!" She smiled with big, white teeth. "You have rings?"

"Crap." I didn't. I glanced at Darren. He shrugged, holding up his palms.

"Can we make do with something?" she asked. "People do like the rings."

"Yes! I have it." I rummaged through my bag and came up with my keys. Car. House. Front gate. Locker at work. I clicked through them.

"Clever goddess," he said. "I owe your fingers some jewelry."

My eyes hurt again. The odds of him repaying that debt got smaller with each day. I focused on loosening as many keys as possible into the bottom of my bag.

"Let's do some paperwork while Monica does that, okay?" Sona smiled again, extracting a little clipboard from a leather case. She asked our full names, dates of birth, addresses, and had us sign on the dotted lines while I untwisted as many silver rings as I could. Darren showed his ID and cracked a joke about being licensed to witness weddings. By the time she was done, I'd released two smallish key rings. I adjusted one for Jonathan's hand and found another for myself. I pressed it into his palm.

"Okay," said Sona, standing. She was all enthusiasm and light as if our wedding wasn't the most depressing situation ever. "Groom goes first. You ready?"

"Yes," he said and pulled me toward him.

"Can you repeat after me?" she asked.

"I got this." He was talking to Sona but looking at me. His big, tired green eyes were serious, committed. I hoped to God he lived even if it meant he lived to regret it. "I, Jonathan Drazen, take you, Monica Faulkner, to be my lawfully wedded wife." He paused.

"You sure you want to do this?" I asked. "You can back out. I'll still love you."

"Shh. Behave." He smirked at me and took a deep breath. "Left hand, goddess."

I held it out, and he continued as he slipped the key ring on my finger. "To have and to hold, for better or worse, for richer or poorer, in sickness and in health, to love, cherish, honor, and worship all the days of my life."

"Excellent!" Sona said. "Monica? You want to do it the same? Or do you want to repeat after me?"

I didn't want to repeat anything. I wanted to spill my guts onto the sheets. I wanted to take my heart out and put it into his chest. If there was ever a time to hold anything back, it wasn't then.

"Jonathan Drazen," I said, squeezing his hand, "you're a manipulative bastard, a brazen liar, and a sadist. You've brought me to my knees. You've dominated me. You've told me who I am and then challenged me to be it. If you made me strong enough to stand up to the world, let me stand by you. If you completed the woman I am, let me be that woman in your honor. Every part in my body is dedicated to you. Every note I sing. Every breath in my lungs. My pleasure and pain. Take me. Let me serve you. Let me be yours."

He put my hand to his cheek. I was going to kiss him before I was told because it seemed as though it was taking Sona forever. When I looked from Jonathan to her, she was holding her phone.

"Sorry," she said, pocketing it, her good mood gone. "Gotta go do a 'Last Rites'." She cleared her throat and held up her hand. "You have declared your consent before the Church. May the Lord in his goodness strengthen your consent and fill you both with his blessings. What God has joined, let no one tear asunder. I now pronounce you husband and wife."

Irene and Gregory clapped a little, but I didn't pay attention to how wan they sounded. I was kissing my husband.

CHAPTER 28

MONICA

SONA and the staff had cleared out. Darren hugged and congratulated me. He fist-bumped Jonathan, promising him a wild night of beer-slinging and barhopping in Silver Lake. He kissed me on the cheek and left, promising he'd call.

Irene had warned me, while ignoring Jonathan, that nothing was to go on behind the closed door that might bring a heart rate up. Just in case I didn't know, he was being monitored from the nurse's station, so no "funny business."

We laughed when the door closed. I wanted to lie on top of him, press my thighs to his, and tuck my head into the crook of his neck, but that was impossible. I sat in the adjacent chair and kissed his cheek.

"Do you regret it?" I said.

"I feel relieved."

"I'm glad."

He said, "I wish I could give you a wedding night. Throw you over my shoulder, dress and all, and carry you over the threshold. We wouldn't even make it up the stairs."

I made a satisfied purr. "I can just imagine it. Whose house?"

"Our house."

"Is there a porch?"

"More than one. I'll have you on all of them, regularly. Breakfast in the back. Lunch on the side. After dinner, we'll drink wine on the front porch, and I'll make love to you in the night air."

"Can I still call you sir?"

"I expect no less."

"Thank you, sir." I kissed his hand, letting my lips linger on his skin.

"Here we are," he said, "married, and we've never even talked about children."

"Can we pretend we had them?"

"Four," he said with a slight smile.

"Don't be greedy."

"Three. Can we settle on three?"

I should have agreed to ten children because there would be exactly none. There would be no house, no porches, no family.

"Can I admit something to you, my beautiful wife?"

"Yes."

"I'm scared."

I squeezed his hand and laid my head next to him. That was when the machine's beeping was replaced with a high, constant whine.

CHAPTER 29

MONICA

I STOOD in the hall staring at his door.

They'd done CPR. Changed the tube. Pumped more drugs into him. Assured me there wasn't a spare heart with his blood type anywhere but Paulie Patalano's chest.

What the hell were we made of? Sausage casings and prime cuts to be wrapped up and swapped out as needed. I felt ill. The twisting in my gut told me to run to the bathroom and bend over the toilet, but nothing came up because I hadn't eaten in Lord knew how long. When I returned, panicking, he was alive, stable, and unconscious.

All the wrong things seemed definite and secure. I knew he loved me. I knew he was right in my life. But the life that fit mine so perfectly was going to end soon. Tomorrow. The next day. Didn't matter. Too soon. The house of our love would crumble under a cracked foundation.

I found myself outside Dr. Thorensen's office. He'd have answers, or at least different questions. "You're here," I said.

He was in the dark again, shades drawn, screens flashing. "Come in. Wanna play?"

"I can't believe you get away with this."

"I'm waiting to hear about something."

"Jonathan?"

"Sit."

"Is there a heart somewhere?"

He sighed. "I'm getting him put on the emergency list. I'm pretty sure it'll go through in an hour, but I don't want to leave until I see it. Come on. Sit. Your avatar's on the cloud. We can start you from the beginning." I hesitated. He patted the seat of the couch behind him. "Come."

"Fine." I sat, kicking off my shoes and tucking my feet under me. He rolled his chair back until the back of it pressed against the couch. The cushion was already indented from his hours of play.

He said, "You ready? There you are. I made you look like you."

"Jesus, I don't look like that." My avatar was ravishing.

"Yeah, you do. Okay, so we start out in the woods. Forest all over, and we're lost. We have to solve this puzzle before our guide comes. Hold on there! Get them!"

We shot down a leopard, a lion, and a wolf. We avoided shooting a blind guy. As a reward, he set us a puzzle to solve. We had that sorted out in no time, and I saw something I recognized.

ABANDON ALL HOPE, YE WHO ENTER HERE

"Such a cheerful game, Brad. Don't you have something with bunnies?"

"You can come over and play that next week."

There won't be a next week, Dr. Thorensen... I had no time to make that into a joke. We had to navigate a parade, and a flag, right, left, left, right, and still get to our destination, a boat on a black river.

"Tell me something," I said. "What are the odds of him getting a heart in time?"

"Can't say. Hit left, left. Nice."

"Do I duck the guy in the Pope hat?"

"God, yes."

"Can't or won't?"

"Can't or won't what? Just don't let him touch you."

"Can't or won't say about the heart. Fuck."

"Oh! Nice move. Both. His blood type's rare, so a good heart is hard enough but...okay, see that opening right there? Hit your blue button and the joystick at the same time."

"Is there any way to speed it up? The heart thing? Shit! Wait..."

"You got it... No, only what I'm doing—pushing him up the list." His shoulders slumped. "We're in. River Acheron. Good job. You earned the coins, so give one to the guy in the hood."

I clicked my buttons. "He won't take it."

"That's weird." He took the controller.

"What about the mafia guy? The brain dead one? If he died, would Jonathan get his heart?"

Brad was focused on the controls. "I can't promise anything. Crap. I heard this happens sometimes."

"What?"

"You're stuck in the vestibule. That's your sin. Wow. I guess we can make you a new avatar."

"My sin?" I asked. "Which one?"

He threw down the controller and kicked his feet up on the couch. "The vestibule is where you go when you don't take sides on an issue. Like when you could have taken action but didn't. Or, look, I'm not going to pretend to be a philosopher. You were probably just feeling passive when you answered the questions. Wanna do it again?"

I thought for a second. Did I want to sit in Brad's tiny office until sunrise, waiting for Jonathan to get bumped up a list, or did I want to make a decision about helping him? "I'm going to brush my teeth and find an empty waiting room couch."

"Suit yourself."

"When you know something, can you tell me?"

"I will. You tell me if you need anything, okay?" he said.

"Sure, and thanks." I was pretty sure he didn't know what I was thanking him for.

CHAPTER 30

MONICA

JONATHAN WAS STILL SLEEPING when I got back. I sat in the chair by his bed and looked at his hand in the moonlight and the little light-up Christmas tree. His fingers were set in a relaxed curl, the key ring wedding band half falling off. I knew those hands. They were strong. They were his instruments. I couldn't see past his elbows, but I knew the rest of him. I read his body like a book. The velvet of his skin. His scent when his cologne had worn off. The warmth of his touch, its perfect pressure on me. The tones and cadences of his voice, rising and falling, clipped to command, breathy to soothe, chopped fine to laugh.

I put my palm on his cheek, and in my mind, his eyes close for a second before he turns his head and kisses my hand, my wrist, the inside of my forearm. His stubble scratches, lips awakening, tongue taunting, fingers closed on my wrist like a vise. I feel bound, secure, safe. My tingling body is an exploding cage of sin.

~

HE IS BEFORE ME, dressed in his business clothes, and I'm naked. We're in the hotel room where he spanked me the first time, the night I tried to hide my navel from him, and he gave me back my voice. He'd told me to be naked, and this is how I imagine it would have gone if I had been obedient.

He tells me to put my hands behind my back then kicks my legs open. He tells me that he won't fuck me until he hears my voice, and I whisper my doubts that it will work. He smirks in that way he does and runs his fingertips across my shoulder and down my chest to my

683

nipple. He strokes it until it's hard. He bends it down, then circles it. He switches on the light and turns me toward the windows.

It's night. We're on a high floor, and Los Angeles is covered in a blanket of lights. I see myself naked, reflected in the windows, a ghost over the city.

"Put your hands on the glass," he says. I do. The basin is spread before me, a checkerboard of pinpricks, exactly as Mondrian had envisioned. Squares of light, blinking signs of life create a haze in the distance. Above it all, my body, leaning into the window, stretched across miles of Los Angeles, bent at the waist as if I was about to fuck it.

"Anything that sounds like 'no' or 'stop' is effective. But you have to say it." He draws his palm across my ass in a hard slap. At that point, he hadn't spanked me yet, so my surprise overwhelms the arousal. I am immediately angry and defensive. "You have to use your voice. Do you understand?"

He puts his left hand on my rib cage, fingertips brushing my breast, and slaps me again. I'm not surprised the second time, nor am I angry. The raw tingle is arousing, as is the stroke and grab that follow. But what really arouses me is letting him do it. I submitted to it, making myself beneath him, under his command and control. I want it. I want every sting, every brush of his fingers against my sensitive skin. He slaps the back of my thighs, and I gasp.

"Monica, was that you?" he asks. I see him in the window, just behind me, his dark suit nearly invisible. I want him to take me, use me, fuck me like a whore. He reaches between my legs and jams two fingers in my cunt. My knees nearly buckle under the weight of my arousal. "You're wet."

"Yes," I whisper.

"You want me to fuck you?" He slaps my ass again, hard.

"Yes, please," I reply in breaths.

"Say it."

I can't. I can't engage my vocal cords. I can't make sounds. My voice kills people, I am convinced of it.

He takes his belt off and loops it once. "You don't know the power you have." He whacks me with the belt. God, it hurts. I'm more aware of the presence and place of my cunt. I feel it hanging between the raw singe of my ass cheeks. It's heavy, bloated, engorged with desire. He hits me again, lower, the leather kissing my wet opening. "Say it."

"Please fuck me."

"With your voice." Whack. The sting is definite, lingering, burning as if I'd sat on a hot stove. "You don't know the power you have." He hits me repeatedly on the word power until my ass is on fire. My clit is so engorged the belt touches it when it snaps, and I scream.

"Monica, was that you?" He's breathless himself.

I can't make the noise again until he drops the belt and slaps my cunt twice, hard and fast. The sting then the rush of pleasure pulls one long vowel sound from my throat.

"There it is. That beautiful voice." Behind me, he takes out his cock and places it at my opening. "Say it."

"Fuck me. Fuck me please." The air from my lungs vibrates my vocal cords, and I hear myself cry out as he rams into me. His hips touch my raw behind, making me feel every thrust as pleasure and pain. I'm filled with the spectrum of sensations, every thought, every cell, every warp of my soul feels him move inside me.

He pulls me up. My hands leave the cold glass, and I stand again, draped over the city, Jonathan fucking me from behind. I see him in the window, and he knows I'm looking at my giant self over the basin.

He whispers in my ear, "You're not the same woman I met. You have control."

I realize I'm hearing him say it the way he said it to me yesterday when he was trying to convince me to cut that EP. That same weak, enervated voice that I'd infused with muscle in my mind. I had stolen it and pasted it into the scene like a collage.

His fingers slip between my legs. I'm sopping for him, my clit a hard knob under his touch, and I watch my face in the window as I open my mouth to yell with pleasure as he whispers in my ear.

"You don't know your own power."

～

I PUT my head by his shoulder and fell asleep for a few hours.

CHAPTER 31

MONICA

I WENT to the cafeteria aching from sleeping like a pretzel. I felt like the ghoul of Sequoia whenever I walked in there—until I saw Declan. He was the ghoul, of course. I was an amateur.

He sat with a young woman who was twisting her long dark hair, making a single, lacquered curl. They spoke earnestly, emotionally, much as he and Jessica had spoken the other day. To be more accurate, she was talking and he was nodding in the way a therapist might. He understood. He heard every word. He had answers posed as questions. He'd go home and forget it all.

I sat at my usual table. I could have gone back up to Jonathan, but I had business in the cafeteria. I was perfectly willing to sit and work on a song until that business came to me.

Take these rolling hills
Shorn grass and dewy mornings
Dump a street on them
Shove a house, then ten times ten

Take this starry night
Clean air and sparkling skies
Spray paint it with poison
Send up bleating sirens

I'm gonna rise through

My jawbone on your throat
Gonna get black tarred again
My heels dug in

Feasting under the surface
Death on life, me on you
Claws dig, teeth cut
Locked in a forever fuck

I WAS CONSIDERING CHANGING the last verse to a chorus when I felt someone above me. I knew who it was without looking up. "Mister Drazen."

"Miss Faulkner, or should I call you by your new name?"

"How do you know my last name?" I leaned away from my notebook, closing it so he wouldn't see my anger spit up on the page.

"I could start with you next to my son at the Eclipse show. The journalists had you figured out by publication. My daughter Theresa still speaks to me sometimes. She told me about you. May I sit?"

"Sure. Could it have been the notice you pulled out of my notebook?"

"Shouldn't leave it lying around if you don't want people to see it."

"You bought my mother's house," I said.

"Both of them. I didn't actually want property in Castaic, but—"

"You almost sent Jonathan over the edge."

He folded his lips between his teeth, a move so like my lover's I had a quick vision of what Jonathan would look like if he was ever allowed to age. "That wasn't my intention."

"Maybe." I paused, dunking my teabag repeatedly. It had no effect, but it gave me something to do with my hands. "What do you do down here all the time? You're a fourth-generation billionaire, for Chrissakes. Can't you pay someone to wait around here for you?"

He laughed. I didn't know what it was with the Drazen men. Every time I mentioned their money, they thought it was hilarious. He twisted and put his back to the wall, stretching out his feet. It was a gesture for a younger man, a man who wanted to take up a lot of room. "It's always amazing to me not what people do for money or revenge, but what they do for love. That woman I was just talking to?"

"Yeah."

"Her husband just got beaten nearly to death in a parking lot two blocks away. They wanted his car, but he had worked for it, so he wouldn't give it up. She said they only got the keys away from him when they threatened to rape her."

"That's awful."

"It wasn't even that nice a car," he mumbled, flicking a crumb off the table.

"But why's she down here talking to you?"

"That's the interesting thing. See, he was in surgery, getting his internal

687

bleeding sewn up. But it was so bad, and it was taking too long. Two doctors came out to talk to her every hour." He held up two fingers to make his point. "They said, 'We're working on it. He's stable.' Then, on the fourth hour, three doctors come out." He held up three fingers that time. "She knows, from when her father had cancer, that three doctors coming out after surgery means bad news. If one doctor is attacked by a violent family member, the other is there to hold him down and the third is to call security. So she saw three and ran down here before they spoke to her."

"And like a shepherd with a lost lamb, you found her."

"If my son won't see me, at least I can do some good down here."

"Like buying my mother's house," I said.

"You're getting the idea."

I didn't trust him, not one bit. I didn't believe he stayed in the cafeteria to be in the same sphere as his estranged child. I didn't believe Jonathan had misconstrued a lifetime of manipulation and bad deeds. The facts didn't drive my mistrust; it was simply that I had to pick someone to believe. I chose my husband. Yet, if I was going to do what needed to be done, I would have to trust him enough to keep his word.

"He's dying. That suture tears a little more each day. He's bleeding into himself. A couple of days is all he's got. Tell me you're down here to do some good, and we can talk about something."

He shifted in his seat until he faced me, elbows on the table. "Go on."

"I'm a distraught wife. I might just suggest things I shouldn't."

"Grain of salt taken. Congratulations, by the way."

I ignored his glance at the borrowed ring. "There's a heart with the right blood type in this hospital. It's connected to a dead fucking brain. I want it."

"The Italian. Patalano, I believe? Paulie Patalano?"

"He filled out a donor card, but there's no living will. His family's keeping him alive with machines and prayer. It's time for the machines to give the prayers a chance to work."

"And?"

He wasn't going to give me anything. If he intuited what I was asking, he wouldn't step up and verbalize it. I had to do all the heavy lifting.

"And I think that if someone could arrange an opening in security, that heart could be available real soon."

He studied me as if seeing me for the first time. The depth of his stare made me uncomfortable, as if fingers were rooting around my insides, knocking around corners and dark places. I stayed still. Let the fucker try to figure me out. I didn't have all that many corners, and at that point, I didn't care what he turned up.

"Who would go through the opening?" he asked, an eyebrow lifted.

"Me." I said it without question or lilt in my voice.

"I admit, I thought he cared about you because you were beautiful," Declan said. "But I was wrong. You're loyal to the point of martyrdom."

"I'm tired of praying for miracles."

"You might need a miracle after the deed is done."

"I'll take my chances with him alive," I said.

He smirked, and I saw Jonathan's face in his one-sided grin. "You think because Patalano's brain dead already, you can get off. If you play the distressed woman, of course. Who would doubt you? As his wife, you have more to gain from him dying than living. And with the Drazen machine behind you? How could any judge even send it to a jury, much less convict?"

Murder. It was the word he'd avoided.

Despite the conversation, I was struck by a thought I couldn't get out of my head. I hadn't even wanted to date Jonathan, and there I was ready to commit murder for him. "I'm sure it won't be that easy. For you, maybe. You're Teflon."

"More well-seasoned cast iron," he joked. "What's in it for me?"

"There's nothing I can offer you but Jonathan's life."

He nodded. With a slight twitch of his hand, he indicated the entirety of the cafeteria. That twitch told me that Jonathan's life simply spared wasn't enough. He would still be relegated to the cafeteria at Sequoia Hospital. "I'm no martyr. My relationship with some of my family is painful. I don't want any of them leaving this world a stranger."

"I don't know if anything I can say will change his mind."

"Let me know when you figure it out."

That was it. That was the deal I was offered. Get Declan in to see Jonathan, and give him a heart attack that'll kill him. Don't get Declan in, and watch Jonathan die while some brainless mobster down the hall kept a heart alive for someone else.

CHAPTER 32

MONICA

I STOOD outside Jonathan's door, listening to the symphony of instruments that kept him alive. I hated them. They intruded, bullying me into remembering my place when we were alone together. He faced away from the door, the tendons of his neck and the line of his jaw pale in the morning light. He turned when I tiptoed in, and he held his hand out for me. I kissed it, then his lips.

"Goddess." His voice was shredded, his breathing audible. I'd die if I had to watch him deteriorate.

"How do you feel?"

"With you here?" He touched my cheek. His fingertips were electric on my face, even in his condition. "Like fucking, but that's probably a bad idea."

"I have a headache anyway."

"How does it feel to be Mrs. Drazen?"

"You didn't need to marry me to protect me from your father."

"He's destroyed everything of mine he's ever touched. And look, he's already stepped in to get control of you."

How could I bring up seeing Declan? He'd be convinced his father was a puppet-master pulling my strings. "I married you for the right reasons. Not out of desperation," I said.

"Desperation's all I have. There's something unfinished in my life, and it's us. I needed you bound to me in front of heaven and earth. I'm glad we did it."

"I'm afraid I gave you permission to die."

"I don't need your permission." He seemed so collected when he said that, as if

690

he was totally okay with leaving me, and marrying me was just him tidying up his affairs.

I felt a spark of rage and clenched my teeth. As his thumb stroked my jaw, the anger melted into irritation, then mild annoyance, and then into a liquid place that had been the base coat of my anger all day. The rush of sadness felt physical as it washed over me, pulling me into an undertow of grief. He was dead already. He knew it. It was a simple fact I hadn't come to terms with, holding out ridiculous hope. A dead man stroked my cheek, and the awakening between my legs from that touch was a ghastly perversion. I wanted a corpse. He looked ready for a coffin, peaceful at last, hands crossed over his chest, left ring finger bulging and swollen around his key ring band.

I broke as if an egg had been cracked behind my face, leaking yolk and clear albumin. My eyes fell apart under the weight of my tears. My nose clogged, lungs kicking air in hitched gulps. He touched my tears, but couldn't do anything else. He could barely lift his own head. I turned my wet, ugly, twisted face onto his palm and let him feel my sobbing contortions.

"Goddess, please," he said.

I was past the point of reason. "I'd kill for you, Jonathan. If I could—"

"Shh. That's enough."

I couldn't finish speaking anyway, my breathing was so charged with sobs. I swallowed a pint of gunk that had collected in my throat and squeezed my eyes shut until I'd stopped crying long enough to get out a sentence. "If I can, I will. You mark my words."

"Okay. Just hush."

"I'm going to suggest something. I don't want you to have a heart attack over it." I snapped up tissues and wiped my face. My eyes felt swollen and pained.

"Funny girl."

"Your father has been in the cafeteria for a week to be near you."

"Fuck, Monica. No. What did he say to you?"

I put my hands on either side of him and leaned over his face, blocking the light from the window. "I'll make a deal with the devil to save you."

"Don't. Whatever it is, don't do it."

"I'm giving you a reason to live."

He swallowed hard and stared past me at the ceiling. "*You* are my reason to live. Fuck." His lips moved in a litany of *fucks* that had no sound. They were made of breath and panic. I glanced at the machines. They seemed okay, not that I knew what that meant. They weren't beeping or honking. The stylus that kept track of his heartbeat was making the same scritchy noise it always did.

"It's okay," I said. But was it? I had no guarantee I wasn't being royally fucked with. I had no idea who I was dealing with. Declan seemed to be a different person to everyone who spoke about him. Who was he to me? Would I find out the hard way?

"I'm stuck here," he said. "I can't do anything but trust you, can I?"

"No. You can't. I love you, you have to know that."

"I know it. But your decision-making..."

"I decided to wait you out when you left me. I decided to ask you for exclusivity. I decided to let you kiss me on Mulholland Drive. I could go on."

"Maybe later," he said weakly.

"Will you do it for me? See your father?" I put everything into the question, and that was a mistake. He shouldn't see any emotion from me with regard to Declan. I should have played blithe or irritated. But I played it honest. I didn't realize my error until the machines whined and Jonathan's eyes closed.

CHAPTER 33

JONATHAN

FIONA HAD GOTTEN KICKED in the chest once at the riding academy when she was making a token attempt to learn to check a hoof for splits. The thoroughbred had gotten annoyed, and Fiona, who never listened to a damn thing anyone said, had been sitting in the wrong spot. She went flying. Two broken ribs and a bruised ego later, she quit riding. I'd probably never see Fiona again to tell her getting defibrillated repeatedly felt the same as getting kicked in the chest by a horse looked.

Monica stood in the corner, wringing her hands as if she wanted to break a bone. She was terrified. I must have gone into arrest at some point in our conversation. I forgot what I'd said.

"How are you feeling, Mister Drazen?" asked the doctor, a young guy I'd seen a couple of times. He looked at his chart and barked orders after the question. The number of people in the room had doubled in the minute I was unconscious.

"Like a newlywed."

"Congratulations." He listened to my heart, eyes on an instrument panel. "You've taken quite a beating. I don't know how many more times we can do this."

"What's the world record? I want to break it."

"Stop trying to be funny," Monica said from her corner.

"Joking in this situation is common, miss," the doctor said as he scribbled something on the chart. He spoke medicalese to the nurse before and after his statement.

"What situation is that?" My wife was about to verbally cross-check the doctor,

693

I saw it in the fact that she wouldn't look at me. She only had laser-hot eyes for the guy in the scrubs.

As if he could feel her seething, he stopped mumbling nonsense to the nurse and turned to her. "He needs a heart, miss."

"Or what?"

I could see the thrust of the conversation a mile away, even while feeling like a bag of shit with the hiss of oxygen tubes drowning out much of what was being said. If the doctor mentioned, implied, or thought about my death, she would go ballistic and get escorted out. I didn't want her to have to negotiate reentry. Every minute without her was a minute wasted.

"Goddess?" She didn't answer. "Monica." I tried to put dominance in my voice, and I know I came up short. As if hearing the intention and not the result, she turned toward me. "Go get my father for me, would you?"

CHAPTER 34

MONICA

ANY SHADOW of a feeling resembling doubt left my mind when those machines went crazy. I was in empty panic when they all rushed in. When they put the paddles on his chest and he convulsed, the empty panic turned to something else. Something like... When I felt pressure in my bladder, I went to the bathroom. I may stop and do other things, but my ultimate goal at some point was to release that pressure. Everything else is either a distraction or a means to an end.

When I walked out of Jonathan's room to get his father, I had absolutely nothing on my mind but making sure some motherfucker put a new heart in him. I did not ever want to see that again. I never, ever wanted to get used to it. If I went to jail for killing someone who was already pretty much dead, fuck it. I could be cool with that.

Declan paced the lobby, phone pressed to his ear. Even as exhausted as he must have been, he looked clean, energetic, and calm. That must be a Drazen thing. Only Leanne in her general slovenliness and Sheila in her constant backbitten rage ever seemed a tick to the left of perfect. Theresa, who looked buffed and polished when I'd met her, had looked as if she'd run a marathon in pumps when she came to the hospital. Maybe they were all human after all.

Except Declan of course. He had been described as less than human, yet somehow he had only shown me a vulnerable face. He saw me and held up a finger. I didn't have time for him. I scribbled—*Room 7719 NOW*—on one of the last blank pages in my notebook. I tore it out, slapped it in his hand, and walked away before he had a chance to answer. I had to assume he'd go up. I didn't have time to baby him, and I certainly didn't want a verbal cat and mouse.

I took the stairs to the fourth floor and strode to Dr. Thorensen's office. He would assure me Jonathan was at the top of that list, and I wanted an update on Paulie Patalano's health. A cleaning cart stood outside the open door. He wasn't in his office, but his screens were flashing and blazing some twisted circle in the *City of Dis.* It was frozen, characters halted mid-action, a puzzle half-done. On the smallest screen, off to the right, was a blinking text box with nothing in it. Above that was a list.

I couldn't help myself. I looked. Each item on the list was the word PATIENT followed by a long string of letters and numbers. A location. A gender. A blood type. A colored box. Red. Orange. Yellow. It was all red at the top of the list, and the number two patient was in Los Angeles, California. He had AB negative blood. Jonathan. A fucking alphabet soup string with a red box at the end. My lover. My husband. Patient KJE873BP7988. M. LA, CA. AB-. Code red.

"Excuse me?" A short lady in soft shoes and maintenance gear stood in the doorway. Her hair was pulled back in a tight ponytail, and her hands were covered in yellow plastic gloves.

I didn't belong there. "Sorry. I was just leaving."

I walked past her before she could ask me what new horror I'd seen.

CHAPTER 35

MONICA

BRAD WAS HOME. What a nerve. Sitting in his house on a hill with his manicured garden of native plants and refinished wood porch. He'd been sorry he hadn't gotten close to me sooner? Well, let's just see how he felt about meeting me at all. I banged on his door with both fists, not caring if I woke him from a dead sleep or mid-video.

"Monica," he said when he opened the door in sweatpants and a T-shirt.

"Is he going to die?" I demanded.

"Can you come in?"

"No. Tell me. Is he getting a heart or not?"

"I have no way of knowing that."

"Why is he second on the list?"

He held up his hands as if he was fending off an attack. "What are you talking about?"

"I went to your office and saw the list. He's second. Which means he gets the second heart that comes."

"First of all—"

"Yes, I'm sorry I went into your office. I was looking for you, but to be honest? Not sorry."

He stiffened as if he'd been hit. "It's Sunday. You can call my Doheny office after nine a.m. to make an appointment, but I'm booked until January."

He didn't exactly slam the door, but he closed it. I looked through the leaded glass windows and saw him go out to the backyard. I stood still for a second,

697

maybe ten, before I walked over to my house. Not my house. Not my mother's house. Not the bank's house. J. Declan Drazen's house.

It looked as though I would have to move anyway. If I lost Jonathan, and that looked more likely with every passing hour, I couldn't stay. He'd married me so I'd have the means to avoid his father. The foolish manipulations of a sick man.

I passed my car and walked up to my porch. I didn't go in the house, though I could have used a shower and the love of a toothbrush. I walked the floorboards where we'd stood as he put his pussy-soaked fingers in my mouth. I sat on the swing where he'd left me to protect me from ruination. Looking into the street, I thought only of what I had to do next. Jonathan was talking to Declan, a stressful situation I'd put him in. Then Declan would create an opening for me to murder Paulie Patalano. But what was the use if he was second on the list? If they were shipping that bloody muscle mass to someone else, what was the point of committing murder to save the wrong man?

I could have implored Brad to do something, anything, pull a string or ten, but I'd invaded his privacy. I should have known better. My own heart pounded as I wondered which of my fuckups would kill Jonathan. I played with the rings on my finger, both heavy with commitment to my course and my love.

A curtain moved in Brad's house. He could see me, I knew that much. I also knew I didn't want to be seen. I was thinking evil things. I might as well have been naked and in ready position on the porch. I was thinking evil, desperate thoughts, and I knew they were all over my face. If Paulie's heart went to someone else, at least I'd move Jonathan to the top.

I got in my car as Brad opened his front door, taking off before he could catch me.

CHAPTER 36

JONATHAN

I FELT him come into the room. Even through the doctors and nurses running around, poking, squeezing, and barking orders at one another, his presence was a needle at the base of my spine.

"Son," he said.

"What do you want?" I didn't look over. My scenery was the ceiling. If I lived, I would start a fund to put art on hospital ceilings for patients who were too fucked up to turn their head. No one should die looking at crusty paint and vinyl venting.

"I wanted to talk to you. To, ah, how do I say it?"

"Before I die. You want to live in peace."

"Am I that selfish?"

I swallowed. I felt myself slipping into the shattered state of semi-consciousness that so often overtook me. Getting married had required more energy than my body had reserved. The last thing I should be doing was speaking to my father. I guessed if I got to complete one act as Monica's husband, it should be to make her happy. I wished she'd picked something easier. Like swallowing an elephant.

The room quieted, and a nurse whose voice I recognized said, "We're monitoring you closely, Mister Drazen. Is there anything you need?"

"No."

"We'll be in and out." She patted my shoulder before leaving me alone with my father for the first time in ten years.

"Mom's going to be here soon," I said.

"That was what I wanted to bring up."

"Do it quick."

He sat in Monica's chair, and I didn't have the energy to tell him to get the fuck up. "I know what you and Carrie think of me. I know you think I'm a monster. Maybe, I don't know, maybe I am. I've always known I was different, but I want you to consider this. I've never done anything in a rage. I've never been ruled by what I don't understand. I've never deceived myself into thinking my actions were anything but self-serving. However, I do *want* things. I do *need* things."

I reacted. It was half laugh, half groan. I was so focused on staying together I thought nothing showed on my face. But everything must have been there. Disdain. Disbelief. Disgust.

"You don't believe me," he said.

"Oh, I believe you."

"In my life, I know I've done everything I could to keep this family together. Nothing is as important to me. When I see it breaking, it...troubles me." Even dad had a safe place, apparently.

I knew I smiled at the thought, but I felt out of myself. "And me here reminds you of how you fucked it all up?"

"Not exactly."

Lettie bustled in, checked my tubes. "You have visitors. Do you want to see them?"

"Five minutes."

She took her time, tapping into a computer, taking notes. When a man came in —doctor or nurse, I couldn't tell—they spoke briefly in medicalese, the one language I didn't know. They left soon after.

"You're close to the end, you know," dad said.

"See you in hell." I was being obstructive because it was easy.

"You're making this hard for me."

"Just tell me what you want."

I heard him shift, a flash of movement from the corner of my eye. "I want your mother. She's entrenched in her position. She can't forget the past. I need what's left of this family to work before...well, before."

"Your philandering isn't her fault."

"I need you to talk to her. She won't ignore your request."

I wanted something from him, something big, but I had nothing to threaten him with. I had nothing to ensure he'd keep his promises. What was I supposed to do? Plead? I was already flat on my back. "Stay away from my wife."

"I don't know what you mean."

"Sell that house. Hello and good-bye. That's it." I couldn't go into longer explanations of all the things I didn't want him to do. Touch her. Tell her jokes. Communicate with her unsupervised. Entangle her business. Go to her second wedding. Breathe her air. Exist on her planet. "Promise it." I felt the futility of my demand. What would I do? Hold my pinkie out for a good twist or make him swear on a stack of Bibles? What was the devil's promise worth without a blood guarantee?

"You'll speak to your mother?"

"Yes."

"If you convince her, you have a deal."

"If not?" I asked.

"Then not. I'm sorry. My promise is contingent on the actions of a third party."

"I despise you."

"What if I told you I loved you?"

"You don't have the capacity." I may have said that or something else. The space around me fell into a dream of disembodied voices and floating lights. Just a touch of pain kept me from sleep.

CHAPTER 37

MONICA

I waited in the cafeteria alone. I wrote a little, some verses about murder that could probably be used against me in court, with the judge unmoved toward leniency by the fact that they were atrocious, puerile, on-the-nose.

Whatever was going on, it was taking too long. I went up to Jonathan's floor and found Deirdre staring at a magazine that couldn't have been of interest to her. Sheila was pacing as if she wanted to carve a ditch in the floor. His mother stood, as usual, next to the chair closest to the hall leading to his room. She was the closest to the elevator, so she caught me first. I thought of something I hadn't before. She was my mother in-law. I wasn't calling her mom. No way.

"Hi, Eileen."

She smiled a smile so fake I could have bought it at Nordstrom's on the sale rack. "Monica. I hear congratulations are in order." She indicated my left hand with its borrowed engagement ring and jury-rigged wedding band.

"Thanks. How is he?"

Her face darkened. "They're constantly in there…" Her eyes got wet. The coldness of her expression had hidden the fact that she was breaking apart. She cleared her throat and straightened her neck. "A heart will come. I know it. I can feel it."

"I can too."

Her hand slipped into mine, and I squeezed it. All our bullshit fell away for a second. He was her son. We loved the same person. She wouldn't be easy to deal with, but we were bound by him whether we liked it or not. Then she smiled a couture smile; it was even kind of warmish, as if something had happened between us that had meaning to her.

I promised myself to never again forget that her goal was to protect him. That was worth something. I gave her hand a squeeze and sat next to Deirdre. "Hi."

"Hi," she replied. "You got married last night."

"Yeah."

She nodded.

"I would have married him anyway, you know."

She flipped through her magazine. "I do."

"I think your mother's pissed about it."

"There wasn't a pre-nup. Jonathan doesn't believe in them. Neither do I."

"Ah, I hadn't thought about that."

She shrugged, still mindlessly going through the magazine. "Neither does God."

I'd never engaged Deirdre for such a non-antagonistic string of sentences, but that was all I was getting from her. She settled on an article and, for all intents and purposes, read it. I cupped my tea and gave the television my attention.

It was set too low to hear, but the talking head with perfect hair had a floating box next to him. In it was Paulie Patalano—mob boss, philanthropist, and murderer—drinking wine with his wife in a picture captured in happier days. The ticker described him as brain dead, as if I needed the reminder, and placed him in an unknown location. The picture flipped to three mug shots. I recognized one face, the brown-eyed man who had come in with Theresa. Even in the mug shot, he was handsome, angry, with a knowing grin that frightened me.

My newly minted mother-in-law didn't see the television. Her gaze stayed in the middle distance. Sheila was on the phone threatening someone, and Deirdre was into her magazine. Declan was either seeing Jonathan or making arrangements for me to kill someone. I'd need to be ready. It was time for me to see Paulie Patalano in his undisclosed location.

I excused myself and took the elevator to the second floor. I scoped out the stairwell, wondering if I should take it next time. Then more complications presented themselves. First being, how would I find him? How would I do it once I got there? How could I be sure Declan's job was done? Who did I think I was?

In pacing and beating the hell out of myself, I rounded a few corners, trying to look for something I'd never defined. I only found ignorance and a lack of expertise in the simple skill of murder. I had a scattered entry plan and a slight hope I'd only get caught when it was too late to do anything but harvest Patalano's organs. After that, I'd just confess and let Jonathan's family talk him into annulling our marriage. But he'd be alive. I could deal with the rest if he lived.

The squawk of a police radio made me look up before I crashed into the uniformed cop. He was in his thirties and seemed to take up more space than humanly possible. A female counterpart stood nearby.

"Staff only," he said, blocking my way to the narrow hall.

"Uh, okay?" I peered past him. The hall looked like every other one except for the lack of flitting staff and the presence of three old Italian women in black. That was the hall. I made note of the location and walked away.

I knew Brad had said he'd be in his Doheny office, but I checked anyway. He was just my neighbor and he meant nothing to me, but I'd stepped on him in a way guaranteed to offend him. I didn't want to leave things like that. He was on his way out the door, clipboard in hand. He slowed when he saw me, which I took as a good sign.

"I know you're busy," I said. "I just wanted to apologize."

He kept walking. "I want to explain how serious what you did is, but I have a meeting."

"I know. I have reasons but not excuses."

He pulled me to the side, out of the hall traffic. "I only have a second. I don't want to make you feel better because I'm still pissed off. But first of all, the list doesn't work the way you think. Geography is important. The state of the patient. The gender. It's not like a line for coffee. But second, you're not getting away with it. When this is over, you're sitting down with me and I'm explaining to you the ten ways you fucked up." He was taller than me and used to being in charge. He had the arrogance of a cardiologist and the authority of a man not called by his first name. But when he looked at me, I knew he wasn't half as pissed as his words let on.

"All right."

"Over dinner." He must have seen me turn to ice. "Platonic. If you knew me better, this wouldn't have happened. That's all I want."

"I guess I owe you."

"You do." He walked away. Had he just asked me out? Yes and no. Jonathan wouldn't be thrilled, but Brad didn't expect Jonathan to be around, did he?

CHAPTER 38

MONICA

I HAD to see him once again before I did it and they dragged me away. I just had to put my fingers on his lips before I faced what I had to face. I wouldn't tell him what I was doing because he'd be an accessory if he didn't stop me and suicidal if he did. I would stand with him clean, as his mate, if even for an hour.

I got out of the elevator on Jonathan's floor and made a right instead of a left to check the placement of the stairwell closest to Patalano's room. I stopped at the turn as if a brick wall was in my way.

Margie and Will Santon stood in a corner, too close for friendship, too far for intimacy. Their hands were up, Margie pointing and accusing, Will in supplication. Their words were inaudible, but their faces shouted rage, hurt, and frustration. I'd have to check the placement of the stairs on the little map by the elevator because I couldn't just stroll past them. I turned and walked away.

I got two steps before I felt a hand on my arm. Margie slowed me down. She looked drawn and upset. Though I didn't know her well, I was sure she didn't want me to ask her what was going on with Will.

"I was just—" I started to explain exactly nothing and was grateful for her interruption.

"Forget it."

"Where have you been?"

She said, "This family's a full-time fucking job. Congratulations, by the way. Well done. One less pre-nup to argue over."

"It didn't even occur to me."

"Him either, I'm sure. But I want to tell you, if he doesn't make it through tonight, I have your back. I'll do what my brother wanted."

"He's not dead yet."

She grabbed my shoulders and put her eyes square with mine as if she wanted to tell me something, something critical and painful. Instead, she threw her arms around me and held me so tightly I thought my ribs would break.

"I envy you," she said. "You know that?"

"If something goes bad, like if I do something wrong, would you represent me? No matter what?"

She pushed me away, holding me by the shoulders. "What are you talking about?"

"Stuff. Life. Say yes."

"Fine." I saw Will out of the corner of my eye. Her gaze flicked to him then back to me. "Go see him. I'll be there in a minute."

CHAPTER 39

MONICA

THERE WERE doctors and nurses everywhere. Clean white sheets and sage scrubs. Trays of uneaten food and plastic detritus in soothing, meaningless colors. The lights were pinpoint and dull as if that would help him sleep with all the human traffic in the room. The doctor wasn't much older than I was, but I knew her from the way she asked questions instead of answered them.

"Hi," I said.

"You're the wife?"

The title still hit me like a bag of flour. "Yeah. I'd like... I don't know. Time. A little."

"You got it."

She hustled everyone out, and it was just me and him. He looked as if someone had painted him white. If I thought it was hard to see him after his disastrous operation, well, that was worse. That night came down to me accepting the situation for what it was or me living in a fucking illusion.

"Good evening, sir," I said.

"Get over here." His voice was no better than a whisper breaking through a stone wall. It took too much effort, as if he carried me uphill.

I put my elbows on either side of his head and touched my nose to his. "Jonathan, I—"

"If you have never seen beauty in a moment of suffering—"

"Oh, I remember how that goes. Schiller was the poet. I looked it up."

"I always thought it was the object's suffering. But I think it was the viewer's, now. I think seeing you, I've seen beauty for the first time."

707

"You've made me so happy. I wanted to tell you that."

"I played with you in the beginning. I wasted too much time lying to you."

"That's over now."

"Actually…" He paused, and I knew why.

"You're kidding," I said.

"The night of the Eclipse show, when I went to Jessica's—"

"La la la, I don't hear you."

"There was more than kissing."

I let my neck release the weight of my head. My forehead dropped to his shoulder. "Go ahead."

"Second base."

From the way he stroked my arm and nuzzled my hair, he must have thought my shaking shoulders and hitched breaths were signs that I was crying. But when I picked my head back up and he saw that I was laughing, he smiled.

"So it's okay?" he asked.

"Yes, it's okay. Is there anything else? I mean, seriously. Something that matters?"

"No. But my brain's not working well. So something might come up later." I put my cheek to his because he spoke about later as if it would happen. He felt cold already. "You never told me about our wedding night. I carry you into our house over my shoulder."

I bite my lip. He doesn't want sad. He wants to have a life in his mind. I could give that to him. "I'm laughing because Lil can see us, and the whole caveman thing is hilarious. I know you have something planned, but I have no idea what. The house is on a hill in Beechwood Canyon. Can we do Beechwood Canyon?"

"For the sake of this conversation."

"It's a modernist masterpiece in the hills with walls of windows looking over the city. You close the door and carry me through the dark house out to the backyard. It's lit with tea lights, and the pool has lights in it. Everything shimmers like it's under water. You get me to my feet, and say, 'Take your hair down.'

"I raise my arms to pull a hundred pins and braids out of my hair. My arms are out of the way, and you use the opening to kiss my cheek, my neck. Your hands follow, landing on my collarbone. You drag your thumb across it and down. You find the zipper to my wedding dress on the side and pull it. I'm still not done with my hair. I admit I'm going super slow, but it's falling out of its arrangement. You pull the dress down until it pools at my feet. Your hands find the edges of my underwear. It's all straps and rings. My hair falls totally. You step back and look at me. I feel beautiful. You've made me feel like that all day, looking at me like that in your black tux. I say, 'What do you want, sir?' And you say—"

"I say this," he interrupted. Even with his rasp of a voice, I stopped. "I say, 'Tomorrow I'm going to destroy you. I'm going to mark your body and ruin your mind. By noon, you won't know whether to laugh or cry. But tonight? Tonight, I will revere you. I will build an altar of myself. I will frame you in stars.'"

"God, you make me crazy when you talk like that."

"There's a blanket on the grass. I lead you to it. You lie down."

"The night is clear. The stars are out."

"My lips on your body trace the story of my love."

My eyelashes fluttered on his cheek. "I try to touch you, but you won't let me. God, you're still in that tuxedo."

"I took it off."

"When?"

"When I say, goddess."

I sighed, going with him. "You're perfect. Shaped for me."

He swallowed thickly. "I kiss your ankles. Pull your legs apart. I draw a map to your sex with my tongue. I feel overtaken. In my guts, I need to yank you, pound you with my dick, make you scream and beg. But I hold back. I kiss behind your knees. I control myself for you."

"I want you. You're all I can think about."

"I'm losing steam."

His eyes filled my vision, red rims and pale skin. He was soaked in exhaustion, but he needed me to create the story for him, for us. I took a deep breath and kissed his cheek, letting my lips linger on him. "Your lips inside my thighs. Your tongue finding its way to me. You kiss my clit. You finger my nipples. You're touching me just enough to drive me crazy. Your mouth works between my legs, sucking and twitching. I arch my back. I'm so close when you stop, and you know it too. You pull me to you. We kiss. I taste my pussy on you."

"Wait."

"What?"

"I turn you around. We're both on our knees. Your back is against me. I push you up, spread you. I put my dick in you, and you push down."

"You're so hard, and I'm so wet. It's so easy isn't it? Wasn't it always so easy for you to put your cock in me? Like you were meant to be there."

"I pull your head back until you're looking at the sky. I hold your face up. My hand is on your throat."

"Your other hand slips between my legs. You touch where we're joined."

"I look at the stars with you."

"I move with you. I'm safe under the sky. I feel you everywhere on me. I'm filled with you. I tell you I'm coming."

"I say, 'yes.'"

We stayed silent for a minute, deeply joined as if he were inside me, expanding together, into each other, fully unified, merged, consciousness where our bodies should have been.

"I love you," I whispered.

"Please stay with me."

I didn't answer for a long time. I kept my face buried in his neck and listened to his breathing. At some point, I would have to leave and meet with Declan. If not to get the whens and wherefores, then to kick his ass for not holding up his end of the deal. "Your family's going to want to see you."

"You ever want sisters?" he asked.

"Always."

"You're welcome."

I laughed. He smiled. "They're outside. I'm going to take care of some business and come back, okay?"

"Stay."

I kissed his cheek. It felt warmer than it did before our pretend wedding night, and I lingered there. "I'll be back."

"Stay."

"I can't. I promise—"

"Stay."

I backed up and let his hand slip from mine.

CHAPTER 40

MONICA

WHEN I WALKED OUT, I must have been a sight. The bright hall lights hurt my
eyes, and my hair was a rat's nest pressed in the shape of Jonathan's fingers.

Eileen approached. "How is he?"

I didn't say anything. Doctors would report facts to her. All I could say was
something like, "He can barely tell me how he's going to fuck me because he's
dying." But that wouldn't be helpful, least of all to me. Eileen passed me, then
Sheila, then Margie and Deirdre. Leanne in Asia. Carrie far away. Theresa in some
kind of trouble. Fiona, entourage-free for once, scuttled down the hall and blew
past me.

Declan drew up the rear and whispered in my ear, "Fifteen minutes to a fire
drill on the second floor. They don't move brain dead patients for drills. He'll be
alone. Staff's been arranged. Cops are a wild card. Good luck." He winked at me
with real élan, as if the situation was just delicious. As much as I'd doubted
Jonathan's fear and hatred of his father, in that moment, I knew it wasn't
completely unfounded.

CHAPTER 41

MONICA

I HAD FIFTEEN MINUTES.

I felt far away, my body a borrowed suit, my mind a blunt instrument, my soul in a room full of family curled up next to a dying man. Fifteen minutes to kill. I couldn't sit still. I went to the vending machines and stared at cheerful paper packets of synthetics, crisp under the unappetizing blue light. At a refrigerator-sized box of cola containers, eleven buttons all yielding the same drink, I felt like an alien standing in front of something new and unknown. People about to commit murder in movies seemed so sharp and aware. They could kick and punch with lightning reflexes. I didn't feel like that at all. I felt more as if I was walking under water.

Ten minutes.

More than anything, I wanted to rest. The thought of finding a waiting room and falling asleep on a couch seemed appealing. I'd sleep through my opportunity, and none of it would be my fault. Jonathan would die tomorrow or the next day, but I'd be okay. I'd go to work on Tuesday, and go on like I had before. Except for never touching him again, or hearing his voice, or kneeling before him like the slave I was. All the other chunks of my life would be the same.

Ultimately, I was being selfish. I wanted him to live for my sake. Because knowing he was there soothed me. Because I didn't truly believe I had any control over myself or my life if he wasn't there. Because without him, things were *wrong*. The wrongness was my perception. The world would be fine without him. Really. He wasn't Mother Theresa.

Five minutes.

Are you talking yourself out of this?

CALM YET SOMEHOW PANICKED, like a wheel moving so fast it appeared to be still, I went up the stairs. I knew where I had to go physically, but mentally, I felt as if I'd painted the floor from door to corner in blood. I pushed open the door with my fist and walked into the second floor. It was after two a.m. Skeleton crew. No visitors. I made eye contact with the cop reading the paper because anything less would make me out to be suspicious before I did this thing. And this thing needed doing.

Three minutes.

I went to the bathroom. The mirrors were streaked with cheap cleaning fluid, and my face looked poorly-wiped, tired, too fucking thin by a lot. I didn't look strong enough to do it. I looked like a wax doll.

One minute.

No. I couldn't do it. I would have to just deal with life without him and everything we could have been to each other. I would have to let him die. I couldn't rescue him. I wasn't strong enough. It wasn't the consequences that would break me but the act itself. I didn't have the spine for brutality. I was a child in over her head. A spineless coward, and an exhausted, hungry, stupid child.

A light flashed, and a squeal cut the air.

I would stay in the bathroom and watch myself fail. When they came to evacuate me for the drill, I'd run out with the crowd in a nice, orderly, single-file line.

I wasn't going to do it.

CHAPTER 42

MONICA

People in movies, apparently, obtain reflexes in moments of stress that the rest of us dream will happen to us. We dream that when we're at the edge of the cliff, we can jump to safety or to rescue, magically stronger and faster than we'd been an hour earlier. We're entertained by the idea that we could be that capable when it's necessary, and our daily incompetence is simply due to the fact that we're not challenged enough.

That never happens, of course, because life doesn't happen on the edges of cliffs. It happens in bathrooms and hallways. It happens when a fire alarm goes off, and all the avoidance slips away like a silk nightgown. For me, it happened by the second whoop of the siren when everything clicked together.

Go time.

Every choice I'd made had led me there. If I denied it, I'd be the walking dead.

Humanity scurrying and shouting. Parts of a machine spinning and thrusting. Patients wheeled down the hall. A nurse demanding I go left, me doing it, then flipping back as soon as she turned away. A security guard shouted to me. I gave him a thumbs up and continued. I grabbed some coat slung over a chair as if I'd turned to retrieve my things, and again, I turned another corner when his attention shifted.

There would be cameras, and they'd see me. I didn't waste my time trying to dodge them. I would get caught, and I would take my lumps. Shame. Prison. A destroyed career.

Patalano's hallway was clear. Declan must have taken care of that. A fire drill was a diversion so obvious that the police would have planned for it. Even the stupidest mobster would have dismissed it, yet they were gone.

I walked into his room. It was dark, and he was alone, lying on his back. Everything was exactly what I expected, as if I was walking into a familiar place. The whoosh and hum of the machines was drowned out by the siren. The machines were bigger than the ones in Jonathan's room, with more dials and gauges. Patalano's face was hidden by tubes going down his throat and a bandage on his head. His neck was kept stable by a plastic apparatus, and the eyes taped shut.

I waved my hand in front of him. Nothing happened. I don't know what I was checking for or what about that mattered. He was brain dead. His body was a life system for a functioning heart muscle. End of story. I focused on the machines. There had to be a switch or a plug. Right?

There were switches and plugs everywhere and nowhere. All the wires ran behind a two-ton apparatus and disappeared. Fuck. Why did I think it would be simple? I flipped any switch I could get my hand on. Though the thing whined, I had no way to tell if what I was doing was having the necessary effect.

"That does absolutely nothing," came a voice behind me. I recognized it immediately. Jessica.

"Get out," I said.

In two steps, she was at the machines, flipping everything back to the way it was. "You don't move a girl in a vegetative state and care for her for ten years without learning something."

"Get out!" I shouted.

"Listen," she shouted back. Our voices were covered by the fire alarm, but for how much longer? "Find his catheter."

I froze for a second, battling everything I believed about Jessica and analyzing what I saw in front of me. She was trying to help me. Was it love? Or was she saving the goose and the golden eggs? Did it matter? I found the tube coming from the center of the bed and ending in a sealed bag under it.

She saw me look at it. "Put a kink in it. It'll back up, and he'll die of septic shock in an hour."

A few drops of yellow liquid flowed through the tube. Jessica put her hand on my arm. She wasn't going to do it. It was all me.

He loved me because he thought I was *good*. Would he love me if I ruined myself for him?

The fire alarm stopped. The silence was overwhelming. I heard the forced breaths, and if I listened closely, I heard the fluid running through the catheter and the beating of a superfluous heart.

"Do it," Jessica whispered.

Do it and risk my own life. Do it, recognizing that Jonathan hadn't done it to Rachel because he must have believed something bigger, deeper, more spiritual lived in our bodies. Do it, and lose Jonathan even if he lived.

With a bend of my knee and a twist of my wrist, I kinked that thing, and the fluid running through it stopped.

"Run," Jessica said and was gone.

I became aware of voices, the squeak of gurneys, the rustle of human activity. I backed out of the room, watching that tube fill up. In my ignorance, I hadn't silenced my phone. When the *bloop* of a message came in, I jumped to turn the thing off. When I did, I saw it was from Brad.

—We have a heart. Coming from
Ojai. One hour.—

Like a kid diving for the piñata candy, I went for that kinked catheter and smoothed it until the liquid flowed. I ran out as though I was coming back from a fire drill, slapped open the stairwell door, which was packed with people coming back from the drill, and backed into a corner, breathing in gasps as if my soul had been saved at a minute's notice. I waved away anyone who looked concerned. I just needed a moment to collect myself. Breathe. That was the scariest thing I had ever done.

"Ma'am?" Two police officers, the woman and man I'd seen outside Patalano's hall, approached me.

"Yes?" I answered.

"Can you come with us?" the lady cop asked.

My heart sank. They'd come for me. Despite unkinking the catheter, I'd tried it. Attempted murder. Someone had seen me and pointed me out. When they unraveled everything, they'd see my prints all over the place. The video. My seemingly meaningless appearance in the hall the previous night. Of course.

I was finished.

CHAPTER 43

JONATHAN

I HEARD A FIRE ALARM, but apparently it was on a lower floor. Nothing to panic about. My family laughed with relief, even my father, who I believed didn't actually understand levity. I stayed still and silent because I didn't have the wherewithal to do anything else. A room crowded with people who loved me, and I'd never felt so alone. I wanted Monica to come back. I felt childish wanting her so badly, but I felt scraped down to a nub without habit or discipline, no expectations or social cues. Just the core wants and revulsions unfiltered by a personality built up by half a lifetime's worth of experiences.

I was scared to die.

My body was uncomfortable.

I wanted Monica.

Past those three overwhelming sensations, I had only sensory inputs and petty feelings. Even the slight excitement that followed the end of the fire drill didn't move me. There was some happy news amongst my family, like an unlikely Dodger win or an upcoming wedding. People scurried in wearing sage green and pink, shouting orders. My mother came to me, smiling, and kissed my cheek. She stroked it until Dr. Emerson, the silver-haired one who came in and out of my room seventeen times a day, pulled her away. Her face was replaced with his.

"We have a heart. It's a match. We're prepping you for surgery."

They handled my body like a jacket they were mending, and I felt humiliated and shut down but hopeful.

"Monica." I choked the word out to a nurse I didn't recognize. She looked up and past me to someone I couldn't see. There was a conversation I couldn't make out.

She said to me in a voice designed for clarity, "We'll let her know."

"Where is she?"

"We don't know. Just keep still now." She lifted my head and strung something around my neck. It was happening too fast. I'd already let Monica walk out of the room. I'd let it happen because I was weak, and now I'd lost control of the situation entirely. That couldn't happen. They couldn't wheel me away and cut me open again without me seeing her. They'd done it last time, and look what happened.

"No!" I swung my arm. It must have been truly pathetic because they just strapped it down as easily as if I was made of bone and rag. I said her name to myself over and over, but she didn't appear.

CHAPTER 44

MONICA

I TRIED NOT to fidget even after they took my phone.

I was raised to think cops believed fidgeting meant lying. I wasn't lying much. I wasn't with the mob or associated with any kind of underground business, which was what they kept implying. I didn't know anyone they asked about. I was just me. One of the thousands of tall, skinny, struggling artists in that intestinal tract of a city.

"I wanted to look at him," I said. The guy cop tip-tapped into a laptop, and the lady cop leaned her elbows on the table. The break room stank of stale coffee, non-dairy creamer, and sugar glaze.

"Why?" she asked.

"Because my husband's up on four waiting for a heart transplant. This guy's brain dead with this nice heart, and I just wanted to say a prayer that he died. I know that makes me a bad person." I left it there. That was about as much lying as I thought I could get away with. I could have told the truth, but they weren't looking for someone who'd screwed with his catheter. Their questions told me they were looking for a true assassin.

"That your ring?" she asked.

I held out my hand. "The diamond is his sister's."

"The other one's unusual."

"Quickie marriage to a dying man who I'd really like to see."

"Wait outside, please." They led me to a row of chairs they'd set up for people they were questioning. A stocky guy with black hair went in next. Fuck, how long could it take? I couldn't stop fidgeting. After twenty minutes, I looked at the clock.

719

Ten minutes to three a.m. Did the morning count? I waited for ten minutes, hands still, suddenly not fidgety at all. When the second and minute hands hit the twelve, I closed my eyes and put my fingertips to my lips. I don't know how long I held them there. They pressed my skin until the lady cop came out and handed me my phone and ID.

"You can go."

I ran like hell.

CHAPTER 45

JONATHAN

It was bright. The voices around me spoke like robots to each other and with fake kindness to me. They narrated what they were doing, but all I knew was I was strapped to a gurney, staring at the ceiling, with no way to see what was happening around me.

"Okay," said a man somewhere behind me. "I'm Doctor Chen. How are we doing today?"

"Ask yourself half the answer."

"Right. Okay. I'm going to put this mask over your face. You need to just breathe and count backwards from ten."

"Wait." He bent over to look at me. Asian guy. Mid thirties. Cap. Hissing gas mask in his gloved hand. "What time is it?"

"Uhm..." He seemed put-upon by the question. "Three."

"Exactly three?"

"One minute til." He started to lower the mask again.

"Wait." I looked around the room as far as my position would let me. Five people stood around me wearing the light blue uniform of doctors and nurses, hands up with their palms facing toward their shoulders. More scuttled in the background. I didn't think I could be loud enough to be heard over the ambient noise. "Unstrap me. One hand."

Dr. Chen cleared his throat and exchanged some silent communication with the other doctors. "Mister Drazen—"

"Please."

"You shouldn't be moving now—"

"Please!" The plea came louder than I thought I was capable of.

Dead silence followed. The clock ticked, and though I couldn't hear or see it, I was aware of it in the beating of my fucked up heart. I had maybe thirty-five seconds.

"Mister Drazen," said Dr. Emerson, "you need to calm down."

"I'll calm down. Just do it. Please. Half a minute."

I couldn't see his face past the mask, but his eyes stilled. He glanced at an instrument before turning back to me. "No flailing."

"No. No flailing."

He nodded to someone, and I felt movement at my left wrist. I didn't realize how tense I was until they let it go. Overwhelming gratitude flooded me, and a helix of fear unwound from my torso, though my limbs. When it reached my fingertips, I slowly raised my hand.

"Can you tell me when it's exactly three?" I asked Dr. Chen.

He looked at the wall clock, and I noticed the rest of them standing, in silence, all looking in the same direction. Chen counted down. "In four, three, two..."

I put my fingertips to my lips.

CHAPTER 46

MONICA

I COULDN'T SIT in that room anymore. I was used to dealing with pain and worry by myself; I wasn't accustomed to group stress. When Dad died, Mom withdrew, aunts and uncles took off, and I basically dealt with it alone. Having sisters who were mine only by dint of a forced union wasn't the dream come true I'd imagined. They had personalities and needs I didn't know how to meet. I didn't know how to ask them for what I needed because what I needed was to be alone.

So I quietly withdrew. Declan wasn't in the cafeteria anymore. He was upstairs with the women, sitting by his wife but not touching her. They spoke sweetly to one another which, all things considered, was an improvement.

I felt hopeful. They did nine of these a year. That was good. It was a lot, apparently. He would walk out of that hospital, and we'd figure out what to do. I walked into the back parking lot, just seeking an open space under the sky, with a spring in my step. I was a little dreamy, hoping he'd want to stay married and move into a house with me. The heart would last ten years, but maybe we could squeeze in another two. Or maybe another one would come and buy us twenty years together. It seemed like forever. I saw Jessica's Mercedes then her, lowering the trunk lid. She saw me and waved but went for the driver's door. The wave was all I would get. I got to her just as she was pulling out.

"Hey!" I tapped on the window.

She lowered it. "Yes?"

"Thanks." Thanking her for telling me how to kill someone felt ridiculous. "For helping." Still ridiculous. "I got a call on the way out, and I put the tube back the way it was."

She just looked at me as though I was nuts. "He have a heart or not?"

"He's in surgery. Do you want to stay? I mean, not for me, Lord knows. The family? They kinda consider you one of them."

"No, but thank you." The window crawled up, and I stepped back as she pulled out.

I heard the squawk of police radios behind me, shocking me out of my reverie. Close. Coming for me. I turned around and found three uniformed cops running toward me, fists on holsters.

I put up my hands.

A black and white came for me, sirens on. I put my palms on my head and got on my knees. Okay, they knew. I'd tried to kill Paulie Patalano. Fuck. Okay. Okayokayokay. Just submit. Just shut up and let them take you in and call Margie and let her work on it.

The car stopped, and the three cops blew past me, practically knocking me over. I cringed. There was yelling. *Get out of the car.*

I wasn't in a car. Obviously. I took my hands off my head and opened my eyes.

One cop had his gun trained on the driver's seat of Jessica's Mercedes. Another opened the door. More stood behind car doors.

The woman who had guarded Paulie Patalano's hallway stood over me. "Not today, girlie."

"I was just—"

"Save it. Nothing to see here." She shooed me.

I got up and backed away. Walking fast, head down, I navigated a newly formed crowd until I ran into a man who grabbed my biceps.

"What was that about?" Will Santon asked. "You kneeling."

I didn't want to tell him. I wanted what I almost did in that room to disappear forever. "I grew up in the ghetto. That's what you do when the cops run after you." He seemed to accept that and released my arms. "But it was Jessica. What could she have done? My God."

Maybe they thought *she'd* been the one who twisted the catheter then fixed it. Maybe she was going to take an attempted murder rap for me. That made no sense. I had to consider for a moment if I would let her.

"We've been working on this for weeks," he whispered and smiled. "Once we stopped having to follow *you* around."

"It wasn't her," I whispered back.

"Yes, it was," he said with satisfaction all over his face. "She killed Rachel Demarest."

"But..."

"Play with enough tubes, and someone in that condition's getting pneumonia. Trust me. We've been chasing her for weeks."

I watched as Jessica had her hands cuffed behind her.

CHAPTER 47

MONICA

More waiting. I felt as though I'd spent the past weeks doing nothing but waiting.

The cafeteria was quiet for once. I stared at my tea, trying to absorb Jessica's arrest. That had been Jonathan's plan. It had been what my curiosity had kept him from executing. I seemed so petty now. I looked at my watch, checked my texts for word from Margie, and took out my notebook.

I opened it to the last page, the only one left blank. Much of what I had in the notebook wasn't suitable to be put to music. I had drawings and staff notes, compositions for multiple instruments with no idea if there was even a possibility of matching words.

"Monica." Brad sat across from me with a prepackaged yogurt cup and plastic-wrapped toast.

"Brad." I closed my notebook. "Thank you for that text. It was...it saved my life."

"I'm sure you're exaggerating." He unwrapped his toast. "You're off the hook for dinner, you know. But I hope we can still be friends?"

"Of course. You still need to yell at me for what I did."

"I'll give you an earful." He bit the toast, wrinkled his nose, and went for the yogurt. "What are you doing here?"

"Margie said she'd text me when he got out." I looked at my phone, checking to make sure it was on for the hundredth time.

"How long has it been?"

"Six hours, give or take."

He stirred his yogurt. "That's long."

I took a second to absorb what he said then snapped up my phone and texted Margie.

—any word?—

"If she forgot to text me, I'm going to beat her senseless," I said more to myself than Brad.

A text came back.

*—Dr came out an hour ago. Issues with
the aortic valve. Clusterfuck—*

"Fuck." I didn't say good-bye to Brad.

CHAPTER 48

MONICA

THAT FUCKING WAITING ROOM, the same as every other I'd seen when they
wheeled him from unit to unit. As I exited the elevator, I realized what a home
they had become with their greyed colors and worn seats. I knew that no matter
what happened, that would likely be the last day I spent in a waiting room
worrying about Jonathan.

They were all there, like a red-haired baseball team. Even Fiona had stopped
blowing by long enough to hold her mother's hand. They looked at me, eyes
shaded from green to blue and back, as I stood by Margie's seat.

"Sorry I didn't text you," she said. "I have other things."

"Don't worry about it. Did you hear about Jessica?"

"Yeah." She waved it away as if she couldn't care less. Her mouth was tight, and
she looked drawn and panicked. I never thought I'd see Margie so flustered.

Next to her, Deirdre stood. They all stood and looked at a set of swinging
doors. Through the window, I saw an older doctor with silver hair take off his cap
and pull down his mask. He turned to another doctor, a woman, and opened the
swinging doors. Another followed. An Asian man, snapping off his gloves.

Three of them. One. Two. Three.

They came to us, and the older doctor put his hand on the woman's shoulder in
a gesture of...what? Condolences? Professional commiseration? The Asian guy
cleared his throat. What was that? Gathering strength?

Hope dropped out of me and flowed down an emotional drain, leaving black
despair in its wake. Shit. Three doctors. If one took a blow, the other held the
family member down, and the third called security.

Wasn't that how it was? I glanced at Declan. He must have seen the panic on my face because he smiled. Then I became that sister.

---TWO YEARS LATER---

729

CHAPTER 49

MONICA

The crowd wasn't for me that night. There was a relief in that. No pressure. I fluffed my dress and tucked my hair into place, fixing the web of pins and curls. The lights on either side of the mirror washed out my face, but I noticed it was rounder, healthier, happier than even that morning.

The dressing room at the Wiltern Theater wasn't the cleanest I'd been in during the previous months, hardly the most glamorous. The table was new but had the same half-eaten fast food crap that I'd known musicians to eat my whole life. The couch was worn but not ripped, the mirror was clean, and the counter had been wiped and replaced some time in the last decade. But I wasn't there for the dressing room. Darren blew in, sweating and panting.

"What the fuck?" I shouted. "You're in the middle of a show!"

"We're between sets. I had to make sure you were here." He pinched half a dozen French fries and stuffed them in his mouth.

"I'm here. I'll be out to do your encore with you, then I'm outtie."

"Is that what you're wearing?" He pointed at my wedding dress, a sleeveless silk and satin number that hugged me on top and went wild on the bottom, folding in on itself in twenty yards of lace and polish.

"It's dramatic. Everyone knows I got married today. When I get up on that stage—"

"They'll think you're nuts for doing a song between your reception and your honeymoon."

"I am. And I love you. It'll be a show that lives in infamy. Get out," I said.

"Your husband's roaming the halls looking for you."

"Get out!"

He grabbed his burger and kissed my cheek before slipping out. The door didn't click closed, and I rolled my eyes. Boys, even the sweet, bisexual ones, were careless. I took a deep breath and closed my eyes.

My name is Monica. I stand almost six feet tall. I walk like an ocean wave, and I sing like a storm. My voice is a force of its own, and I let it loose like a hurricane. I am safe. I own what I make. I am a creator. I am an artist.

I FELT movement behind me and knew from the scent it was my husband. He put his hands on my neck, where every nerve ending in my body was now located, following his touch as he stroked me, like the little magnet shavings under plastic I'd played with as a kid. When the pen moved, the shavings moved, and I arched my neck to feel more of him.

He kissed me at the base of my neck. His lips were full and soft, more than lips; they were the physical manifestation of every taste of longing, every tingle of desire, every scorch of ambition.

"We said we weren't going to do this until we were out of the country," I said.

"Do what, goddess?" he whispered, and I groaned in response, opening my eyes to watch him in the mirror as his mouth caressed my neck and shoulder. "No one knew where you were until I asked for Monica Faulkner."

"You have to give the name change a little time." It was a lame excuse. The fact was I'd been too busy touring, recording, and taking interviews to do simple tasks like changing my name. I could have done it at any time, and he knew it. We'd stayed married in the eyes of the law, but to us and the world, that day was the day. Next came the name change. We finally could call each other husband and wife in public.

"Take your hair down," he said.

I smirked. "I don't think we have time."

"I won't wait."

Demanding Jonathan.

He'd left that operating room a different man. A person doesn't just walk away from a heart transplant and continue as before. He was confused about who he was. He was vulnerable, testy, physically weak, and overly cautious. He was also sexually vanilla, which I tried to accept. I didn't think it would last, but with each passing day, I feared my kinky Jonathan would never return. I stood by him, helping him manage his recovery. I loved him. I hated him. I wanted to beat and kiss him. But I needed him as much as he needed me.

Though we'd agreed our union wasn't genuine because of the circumstances surrounding it, we never suggested our love was anything but real. I renovated my place on the second steepest hill in Los Angeles and rented it out to one of Brad's colleagues. Jonathan bought a house in the Hollywood Hills, and we moved into it. Two years, we said. If we could live together for two years, we'd get married for real. If we couldn't, I was taking my ass back to Echo Park.

I inhaled deeply and put my hands in my hair, lifting my arms out of the way. He slowly unzipped the back of my dress, touching my spine as he went.

Six months after the transplant, Jonathan had roared back like a lion. Almost overnight, he became more aggressive, more demanding, more kinky, and more dominant than he'd ever been. A year later, he got me an engagement ring of my own, a round canary diamond the circumference of a nickel. He'd gotten on one knee all over again, and I realized the reason he'd returned to sexual ferocity was because he was happy.

I unpinned my hair, leaving in the one, pencil-thin braid I'd demanded. As it fell over my back, my dress slipped off.

"You're magnificent," he said, twisting my hair in his fingers. We faced the mirror, him in the blue shirt and tie he'd changed into after the reception, and I bare-breasted with a white lace garter. "All day, I wanted you."

"I am yours."

"Apparently not, *Ms. Faulkner*." He loosened his tie, snapping it through the collar. "Hands behind your back." He must have seen me glance at the clock. "I have control of the time. Just do what I ask."

"Yes, sir." I cast my eyes down, submitting completely, and put my hands behind my back. Already a rush of fluid surged between my legs.

I would sing at Darren's encore and help his career, but if I had to be late, I would be late. Jonathan wasn't half as busy as me. He'd sold a bunch of assets, more than I could count, and started the Drazen Foundation for Arts Education. It took up about as much time out of his week as a typical DMV job. My co-chair duties took up a few minutes every morning, usually while I was tied to the bed.

My husband clamped my arms together hard enough to make me gasp and wrapped his tie around the elbows. "Look at yourself." He pulled my hair back until my head faced forward. Tying my arms at the elbows had the effect of jutting my tits forward. The nipples were tight and erect. The garter had tiny blue bows at the suspenders, my "something blue" for the occasion. "What you see is mine. Do we understand each other?"

"Yes, sir."

"I don't think you do." He held me at the bicep. "Step out."

I stepped out of my wedding gown, and he picked me up and carried me to the couch, placing me so my head was over the arm, my arms draped below, and my lower back was on the seat. He opened my legs and unsnapped the crotch of the garter. Then he stood back and observed his handiwork.

I'd really thought he was dead. When those three doctors came out, I wasn't ready for them to say everything was fine. After what I'd been through, bottling it all up to keep enough control to kill Paulie Patalano, I lost it. They really had needed a third doctor to call security. Declan thought he'd played the funniest joke on me. Shitty hobby, as Margie said. When I had explained it to Jonathan, he bought my house from Declan and cut him out all over again. But the transplant put his father back in the good graces of the rest of the family.

With my pussy on display, tits sticking out, and my head facing the ceiling, I saw Jonathan in my peripheral vision. He picked up a cup of fast food-approved carbonated beverage. He peeled the plastic top off, straw and all, and peeked inside.

"Jesus fucking Christ. What's the world coming to?" He shook the cup. I heard the contents swish around. Crushed ice. Bane of my husband's existence. He put it down and picked up something off my makeup table. Then he came to the couch, pants open, dick out, and kneeled between my legs with a tube of lipstick jammed between his teeth like a cigar. He pulled it out, leaving the cap in his teeth. He spit it on the floor like a watermelon seed.

"I'm going to write something down so you remember it, goddess. I know you're busy being a superstar, and you forget." He put the stage-red lipstick to my left breast and dragged it across, then between them, then moved it over the right.

Carefully, he wrote on my rib cage, wearing the lipstick down to nothing. When he was done, he checked his handiwork. I glanced as far as I could to the mirror and saw what was written on me.

Jonathan crouched over me, smiling, then put a hand on the arm of the couch, leaning over me. "Got it?"

"Yes, sir," I whispered.

"That's *your* name." His gaze was meaningful, harking back to old conversations about the last woman to carry that name. Jessica was serving time for a murder she'd tried to pin on Jonathan. I hadn't wanted her name, but he'd convinced me that the name was *his* and now was *ours*.

"I'm sorry, sir." I tilted my hips so that his erection touched my wetness. He moved slightly until the head of his dick touched my opening just enough to make me ache for it.

"Those crowds out there, they don't own you. I do. I marked you with my name. This is who you are now." He moved so his dick rubbed my clit ever so slightly. I jerked to feel more of him. "No, no. Don't make me pull up the extension cords and tie you down tighter. I'm not done explaining." He put his face to my cheek and ran his open mouth along my jaw. "That name is your bond to me. It's your collar."

"I'm sorry, I—"

"Shh. Tell me who you are."

"Mrs. Drazen."

His cock pushed into me, sliding in with no resistance, every surface of my body a firing bed of sensation. All the way, until his body slammed against my clit, moved, and pulled out. "Who are you?"

"Your wife."

He went in again harder. Then again, grunting with the effort. He fucked the breath right out of me then stopped. "What's your name?"

"Oh, Jonathan."

"Nope. That's *my* name."

"Mrs. Drazen."

He slammed into me. "I don't think you believe it."

"My name is—"

He fucked me for real then, putting a hand on either side of my head and taking my cunt repeatedly. He pressed his face to mine, rocking. I was close, so close he could sense it. As was his way, he slowed down, dangling me over an ocean. And I let him, because he owned me.

"Look at me."

I did. His hips stroked me, stretching me, the friction between us a white heat. I was so close. I felt the undertow of my orgasm on my legs. I wanted to get pulled under, I wanted to drown in it, but he was holding me back, a life vest I didn't want.

"What's your name?" he whispered.

I gasped a few times, lost in the sensation between my legs. "I forget."

"Perfect."

He moved once, twice, three times, and I exploded, sucked down by the undertow, pulled out to the never-ending sea. I clenched him as if my body wanted to break him and fit the whole of him inside me.

"Ah, Monica." He came right after, growling my name then grunting as he never had before the surgery. I loved seeing him in those moments, overcome with his own pleasure, his connection to me complete and unbreakable.

"I love you," I said.

"And I you."

"Can you untie me?"

He reached around me and loosened the knot. "First you decide to work on our wedding night, and now you nag me to untie you."

"You're a horrible brute," I said, feigning offense. "I'm staying at my mother's."

He leaned up, and I stood. My new name was smudged on the bottom. Jonathan helped me back into my dress. My hair was a wreck, and my makeup was worn off.

"Shit," I grumbled.

"You look beautiful."

"You have lipstick all over your shirt."

He looked down at himself. "I look like I've been shot."

"By the cheerleading squad."

He laughed. "It's dark on the plane, and I'm going to be naked and fucking most of the way to Paris anyway."

"Really? What if I have a headache?"

"I'll fuck it right out of you." He buttoned his jacket, covering the lipstick stain.

There was a knock at the door. My assistant, Ned, a huge guy there more for my protection than assistance, said, "Ms. Faulkner?"

I pressed my lips between my teeth.

"Who?" asked Jonathan. "No one by that name anymore, Ned."

"Monica?" Ned called. "You're on, whoever you are. Three minutes."

"Coming!" I straightened myself, rubbed mascara from under my eyes, and fingerbrushed the bird's nest on my head as Jonathan watched. It was hopeless. I looked as if someone had just fucked the shit out of me.

"I brought this for you," he said.

He pulled a long chain from his jacket pocket. My lariat. I hadn't worn it because it didn't make sense for a wedding. But as it stretched across his hands, drooping between them, the encrusted berries on either side swinging and sparkling in blue and green, I wanted it around my neck.

"Thank you." I looked at the ceiling, exposing my throat. He reached up, looping it around me not once, but twice. When I looked at him, he pulled the jewels, snapping it tight around my neck.

"You ready?" he asked.

"Yes." I kissed him as if for the first time—his lips the symbol of vulnerability in safety, pain and pleasure, passion and contentment—until Ned banged on the door and called me by my first name.

Jonathan and I smiled as he opened the door. We walked through the cinderblock-lined hallways with Ned in the lead, another security guy in back. Strangers who didn't expect me, techies and runners, roadies and Darren's klatch of fans, all stopped and stared for a second. I smiled at them because they'd made me who I was, and I held my husband's hand behind me.

Darren stood out there with his band, sweating in the spotlights, his sticks twirling in his fingers. It was hot, and I felt the lipstick inside the bodice of my gown reminding me of my name. I went out when called to sing with them.

Each breath, each note, each word, no matter the song, was about one thing only.

Jonathan.

Jonathan.

Jonathan.

PART II
CODA

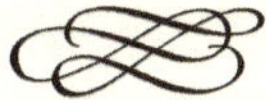

In the timeline, *Coda* begins soon after surgery—before the wedding in the previous chapter.

It's not optimum, but because of the way this story was originally structured and released, it was unavoidable.

CHAPTER 50

JONATHAN

I BRUSHED my thumb against her nipple, bending it, then I leaned down to suck it. She wove her fingers through my hair. I tasted the shower water on her, the tinge of soap. Steam still fogged the room.

"Jonathan," she whispered, "I'll miss the plane."

"No, you won't."

I drew my tongue down her belly, flat and tight, stopping at the navel bar she still wore for me, then traveled down between her legs. I bent one of her knees and put it over my shoulder, giving my mouth access to her.

"I haven't packed yet," she said, but I knew I had her.

I opened her lips with my thumbs and licked her clit slowly, tip to taint and back again, tasting the fresh, clean skin and clear, rushing fluids.

"Pack fast," I said. She'd be gone for a week. I wanted her before she left.

"I have to pack the Theremin, and it's oh, God." She moaned when I sucked her, hitching her other leg over my shoulder. "Delicate. Jesus, what is with you lately?"

I stood and wiped my mouth with my hand. She sat spread-eagled on the bathroom vanity, wet and ready. She was mine, and I loved her.

"What's with me lately?" I was in my underwear, which I didn't bother taking off as I pulled out my dick. "Maybe I'm bored."

"You could work again."

"I could." I slid in nice and easy.

As I fucked her on the vanity, I had a feeling that something wasn't quite right.

Something was missing. She was wet. I was hard. Her tits bounced when I thrust, and there was enough nudity between us to get my dick inside her.

But her arms. I didn't know where they would go next. She moved in unexpected ways. I put my arms around her, holding her together, and I leaned in close to kiss her, dragging my stubble over her cheek and the sensitive part of her neck.

She whispered, "Ouch."

I felt powerful. I'd been fucking her for months with this borrowed thing in my chest, but when she said ouch, I wanted to more than fuck her. I wanted to tear her apart. I lost my shit at the thought of it, coming in her the way I had been since the hospital, without control or intent, just because I was ready.

Monica came a second after I started, and we gripped each other, quivering. The steam had barely cleared from the mirrors when I kissed her shoulder and realized I had a problem in my arms.

I STRETCHED out in the sun, with my scarred chest to the sky, and felt that thing beating. The July heat baked me, muggy and sticky. I was sharing sweat with a stranger's tissue and grateful to be alive, yet I was in a state of constant bewilderment, thinking, *How the fuck was I pulled from death for this?*

And who was I? I'd eaten and enjoyed blowtorch-spicy food, but suddenly I found it intolerable. I felt a new pull to run that I knew, intuitively, came from the same place. I jogged in the morning, and if Monica was away, I jogged at night. I loved it. I loved the burn in my throat and the fully energized exhaustion when I'd pushed myself too hard and too long. But I'd never wanted to run before. The desire wasn't mine; it belonged to the heart, which had grown in someone else. Was I still wholly me? I pondered it too often and for too long.

"Hey," Monica said, stepping into my sunlight. She wore a pale blue dress and clunky bracelets. "I'm going."

I patted a place for her to sit next to me.

"I can't," she said. "Lil's waiting."

I flipped my sunglasses up so I could look her in the eye, and with that gaze, I let her know I was entitled to a minute of her time. "Goddess."

"I'll call you when I land." She bent to kiss me, and when her lips hit mine, I held her head there an extra few seconds. She smiled and trotted away.

I had a problem. She was going to Caracas for three days to open two shows with some madhouse band, and I wasn't going with her because of doctor's orders. The impulsive side of me wanted to follow her and let the team of highly-paid specialists kiss my ass, but I stayed behind. There was no need to rush. Three days wouldn't change anything.

When I'd met Monica, I'd known what I was. Who I was. I knew what I was made of, and I knew how to get what I wanted. I'd still been in love with my idea of my ex-wife, but my goddess had cured me of that. I'd thought being happy was what had made me demand control in the bedroom, but I was wrong, or at least only partly right. All the soul-searching in the world had led me to a false conclusion.

I'd been dominant because I knew myself. In knowing myself, I had the confidence to bind and hit and hurt, because I'd know when to stop.

When we got home from the hospital, Monica and I eventually made love again. Still, I wasn't myself. I was mostly me and partly someone else. An alien piece of meat had been lodged in me, and I didn't know what it would do. Would it beat right for me or for the person it was meant for? Would it skip a beat at the sight of some strange woman? Would it break over a different past or a lost present? I kept imagining it jumping out of me like a frog from a frying pan, slapping on the kitchen floor with a *splat*, and beating on the tiles while squirting yellow plasma. Once, I dreamed it bounced out of me and landed in the pool to swim with Sheila in a trail of curly red blood. I laughed in my dream, but when I woke up, I ran to the bathroom mirror to make sure I had a scar instead of a hole.

I'd felt like a foreigner in my own skin, dragging around a sack of muscle and bone held together with medicine. Even after the doctor appointments dwindled and life returned to something that looked like normal, I hadn't adjusted to being two people in one body, and my wife knew it. She was drifting away like a bottle bobbing in the surf, tide by tide. She wasn't Jessica. She'd never leave for someone else, but she'd leave with distraction and indifference. At the thought of the lost intimacy, I felt a blade of ice cold rage so thick, I had no room for a reaction or an emotion. My head was clear. The anger had pushed out all the clutter. She was mine to lose, but she was mine.

CHAPTER 51

MONICA

I MISSED TWO THINGS.

I missed my freedom, and I missed slavery.

I was caught in a nether region where I couldn't come and go as I pleased, and I didn't feel protected.

I was being unfair, and I knew it. What man could be expected to keep up Jonathan's intensity for any length of time? No human could be a raging lion after having their heart ripped out.

So though we burdened each other with many things, I never burdened him with my longing for my dominant Jonathan. That man was gone, so I loved the man who'd replaced him. He was everything I'd almost lost in that fucking nightmare of a hospital. He was funny and thoughtful, gracious and wise. He was still the best lover I'd ever laid my hands on.

"Hello?" Jonathan's voice was thick with sleep. The sun was just coming up over Caracas, tainting the sky brown.

"I'm coming back early," I said as I walked across the tarmac toward the Gulfstream.

Jacques waved. His copilot for the day took my rolling suitcase and stowed it underneath the plane.

"Really?" Jonathan sounded as awake as if he'd had a gallon of coffee. "I have something for you."

"But I have to go right into the studio," I said. "Jerry wants me to work on 'Forever' for this sampler idea he's—"

"I'm sorry?"

742

"I'll walk in the door the same time as if I'd stayed here. I just wanted you to know what I'm doing with your plane."

"Well, thank you."

"Don't be mad."

"Goddess," he said, and I heard something in his voice I hadn't heard in half a year. It stopped me on the steps up to the fuselage door.

"Yes?" I was shocked by the small sound of my own voice.

"I don't give a fuck about the plane."

"It'll be fast. I'll be home by lunch."

"Text me where you're going to be."

"Why?"

"What?"

Fuck. I'd promised myself I'd never forget what Jessica had done to him, yet there I was, serial-bailing and giving him attitude about it. "It's the same place as always," I said, backpedalling as I snapped my seat belt. "I'm fine."

"Maybe you are," he said, then his tone changed to sound more pensive. "Maybe you are."

He hung up, and I was left with an oddly shaped emptiness.

Jonathan loved me. I never questioned that. His love was in everything he did. I heard it in his voice and felt it when he fucked me. Even when he took me like a stranger and reveled in hurting me, there was love in his abandon.

I also didn't question his commitment in what he'd thought were the last moments of his life. I was worthy of his love. I'd earned it, and he'd earned mine. We'd earned the easy part and the hard part. Most couples don't face life-and-death tests of their love until they're old and grey, or until they had children in middle school, but he and I had been put through the fire unprepared and come out stronger.

Yet we'd missed the basics, and they weighed on me. I constantly forgot that we loved each other because of the daily misunderstandings and confusions.

Like buying our house, which had been a series of misspoken desires, concessions, and bitter words left unspoken. Like water flowing downhill, it had been chosen via the path of least resistance. I didn't even remember choosing our real estate agent. I just remembered her showing up.

"So," she had said pertly. Her name was Wendy. It suited her. "I understand you want to get moving on this before Mrs. Drazen goes to Paris?"

I sat next to Jonathan on his couch, frozen in shock. "Paris? I didn't say I was going."

"You're going. It's a huge opportunity." He'd turned back to the agent, who wore a decal of a smile. "She's the opening act for—"

"Nobody," I interrupted. "I'm not going. So anyway, no."

Like any real estate agent in Los Angeles, Wendy had been perky, perfect coiffed, and blandly unthreatening. She'd come highly recommended for her discretion, her taste, and her ability to seamlessly manage massive amounts of money.

"What kind of house are you looking for?" she asked.

"Kind of house?" I asked, stalling.

Jonathan had been out of the hospital for a month, and we'd spent it managing a heart transplant. Appointments. Doctors. Medical procedures I didn't understand. Big pills in little boxes. A diet and exercise regimen that made me shudder. And Jonathan himself, my husband, felt shaky and unsure. I woke up most mornings feeling unqualified to live my life.

"Era," Jonathan said impatiently. I heard the rasp in his breath. It was late afternoon, and he needed to rest. "Something modern. Fifties. I'm sick of leaded glass."

"I, uh—"

"Did you have a neighborhood in mind?" Wendy interrupted me, making eye contact with Jonathan.

"The hills," Jonathan said. "Beechwood, maybe."

"Really, I think the ocean—"

"Great. How many bedrooms? Or do you want to go by square feet?"

"Big," Jonathan told her. "This house is cramped."

"Cramped?" I interjected. I thought his house was palatial, but I'd grown up with eleven hundred square feet, and I didn't like being bulldozed.

They both looked at me, and I felt ashamed. Then I felt ashamed for feeling ashamed. I wasn't embarrassed because Jonathan and I disagreed on the style or size of the house; I was embarrassed because we hadn't discussed it.

"Wendy, I'm sorry," I said, standing. "We're obviously not ready to discuss this. Can we get you to come back some other time?"

"Of course!" she'd chirped and was gone in a flutter.

"What was that?" Jonathan asked.

"We weren't ready to meet with someone about this. Not until we can agree on the basics. I didn't..." I drifted a little then came to the truth. "I've never bought a house before. I've never met with an agent. I didn't know what was expected."

He'd looked tired, as usual. He'd always looked tired in those first months, which was why I didn't talk to him about anything important. I'd tried harder after the non-meeting with Wendy. I agreed to stuff and put my foot down on others, and we bought a big fat compromise of a house that I lived in but didn't love.

I hadn't wanted to exhaust him. I thought it was the best way to help him get better. I hadn't had a period in months from the combination of anxiety and Depo-Provera. But when I got sick and thought I might be pregnant, I didn't tell him because I didn't want to start an argument about children. No stress. That was all I wanted.

When he'd gotten back from the hospital, he couldn't really walk. He just didn't have it in him. He had a staff of people and a huge family, so he didn't need me, yet I'd been surprised by how much he did need me. He needed to talk, and in those conversations, he laid out our future like architectural plans, pointing at the lines and angles I needed to see. I rarely disagreed with him. He was prone to frustration with his body and the exhaustion of small tasks, and I was still in a stunned state. I was functional, competent, and emotionally broken. But I'd thought I was handling our situation well. I was the picture of maturity and capability. I even laughed sometimes, when it seemed appropriate.

"Children," he'd said one night, on his back in the bed. The lights were out, and the flat latte color of the Los Angeles night sky lit the room. "When can we start?"

"You mean start having sex again? Your doctor said anytime." I leaned over him, half-sitting. His bandage had just been taken off, and the scar on his chest was still pink.

"Fucking with intention."

"I've never known you to fuck without it."

He smiled and touched my lower lip. "When does that shot wear off?"

My Depo-Provera shots rendered me infertile and nearly menstruation free for two to four months at a time. "Right after Valentine's Day, I guess."

"No more shots."

"Jonathan, I... I think we should talk about that again."

His expression became wary.

I froze, afraid of upsetting him. "I want children. You have to understand it's... this is hard to say." I touched his chest, brushing my fingers over the scar. "Everything seems so precarious."

"You'll stop feeling like that once I can walk more than ten fucking feet. Soon."

"Let's revisit this then. Please. I just need to know you're strong enough to handle running out in the middle of the night for chili chocolate ice cream."

"Who makes that? It sounds disgusting."

"It's delicious."

He pulled me to him, and I laid my head just below his chest. His heart beat in my ear. It sounded perfectly normal, a functioning organ capable of sustaining his body until something else broke. But it wasn't beating with life. It was a ticking clock, and it would stop too soon.

I'd gotten another shot in early February. I reasoned that he didn't need to know. I'd put him off. I couldn't do it much longer, but we were taking it one day, and one white lie, at a time. I'd need the next in June or so, and we could revisit then. Or not.

But it always came up, even when it didn't. When we talked about the house, we needed a bigger room just for the elephant, and after I dismissed Wendy the realtor, the animal only got bigger.

He'd leaned on the arm of the couch and crossed his ankles, the same posture as the first night I'd gone to see him at his office, when I threatened him with a lawsuit. "Whatever we get should be the exact opposite of what I had before you were in my life."

"I think that's reactionary."

"That's a big word that means nothing."

"Don't build us on top of what you did or didn't do before. How's that for a definition?"

Who were we, standing half a room apart with our limbs crossed? How did any of this matter? How had it become important? If he wanted to pass the next ten years in a big modern house overlooking Los Angeles, who was I to say otherwise? Wasn't that a small price to pay to be with him?

"I want you to go to Paris," he said. "You've never been."

"Who's going to watch you if I go? Who will make sure you don't forget to do what you're supposed to?"

"If you want children to take care of, that can be arranged."

"I don't."

"Then you don't need to baby me."

And that had been that. We got a house by default. The style he wanted and the location I wanted, because on paper, it seemed like a compromise. It had been more of a treaty.

CHAPTER 52

MONICA

I ATE a lunch of chicken fingers and half a radicchio salad in the engineering room. I shot the shit with Jerry and Deshawn. We talked about promoting the sampler, getting beer thrown at me in Caracas as a sign of respect, the roaches in the hotel, the excellent food. Half an hour later, we were back to work. Executives drifted in and out to listen to me. Eddie even showed up for fifteen minutes.

My phone was facedown on the baby grand piano; its sheen let me know when the glass lit up with a call or text. But I couldn't take a text. We were trying to get the last two words of the song right. *Forever fuck.* It had to sound like a powerful curse but be muddled, and on key, and gravelly and transcendent, all at the same time. My feet hurt, and my brain and eyes were so exhausted, the foam egg-carton pattern on the walls seemed inverted.

I couldn't possibly take a text, even from my husband.

Only when I was done did I check it.

—I want to see you—

The text had come twenty minutes earlier, while I was in the middle of recording "Forever." The song was based on a poem I'd written while Jonathan was in the hospital, and I had been so angry, I imagined myself in an eternal, raging battle with death.

—Where are you?—

Ten minutes later.

*—You were supposed to be out two
hours ago—*

I scrolled through Jonathan's texts. Jerry and the sound team packed up. I was going to have to deal with my husband. I had my career, and he knew what it entailed. He didn't have the right to harass me while I was recording.

I took a deep breath and called him from outside. "Hi." The parking lot behind the studio smelled like sweaty asshole and stale cigarettes.

"You're out?" Jonathan asked.

"Just finished up."

"I have a surprise for you when you get home."

Home. A house on the beach that already had too many painful memories. Medications. Falls. Fights. He'd been sick and pissed. I loved him. I'd never leave him, but some days, I felt as though we were coming apart at the seams.

"The guys are going to dinner. I'm a little hungry," I said. The silence seemed eternal, and though I imagined him staring into space with the phone at his ear, when I heard a car door slam, I knew he hadn't been inactive. "Jonathan, it's—"

"Stay there."

"Not tonight, I—"

"This sounds to me like you're telling me no." The calm, arrogant dominance in his voice was like a slap on the ass, because I hadn't heard it in six months. "For the sake of clarity, goddess, when it comes to me, that's not in your vocabulary. I don't hear it."

I said, "Yes, sir," with all the sarcasm of a spoiled adolescent and immediately regretted it. Luckily, my husband had already hung up.

CHAPTER 53

JONATHAN

This shit stopped tonight.

I parked in the back and went into the building. A couple of doors were ajar, and I could hear the laughter and mumblings of men. I heard her three doors down, her voice humming, piano strings getting hammered one by one, slowly.

I slipped into the engineering room and looked at her through the window.

She sat at the keyboard, scribbling in a notebook, then considering the keys again. Her back was straight, neck as long and white as a swan's, her ebony hair braided and twisted onto the top of her head. A goddess. She'd waited. I didn't know what would have happened with us if she hadn't.

The engineering booth was empty and dark, and I watched her like a movie. I saw her bite a fingernail. Close her eyes. Tap a finger then burst out with a word in one long note. It was *you*. She hit three keys, then three different keys, sang the word again in a different register, and wrote it down.

I felt as if I hadn't seen the length of her neck in months, nor the delicacy of her wrists. I knew every inch of her skin, every curve of her body, yet that day, when she'd said *no* to me, I anticipated the prospect of showing her why that wouldn't wash any longer with no little delight.

I went back into the hall, closing the engineering room door.

CHAPTER 54

MONICA

HIS SCENT CUT through the dank musk of the studio before the sound of the door closing reached my ears.

"Hi," I said without looking up from my notes. "Can we go meet those guys? Jerry wants to lay out a plan for Wednesday." His fingertips grazed the back of my neck, and I shuddered, closing my eyes halfway.

"No," he whispered.

"I'll meet you at home later if you want."

"Stand up."

I looked up. He stood over me, hand at the back of my neck, face broaching no arguments. I didn't know what my expression said, but my mind went utterly dark for a second. I stood, reaching for my bag. He gently took it and laid it back down. I started to object but didn't get past the first syllable before he had his fingers to my lips.

"Unbutton your shirt," he said.

We gazed deeply at each other for longer than usual, and I knew even before my fingers touched my shirt that he wasn't interested in a standard sweet encounter. He brushed his thumb over my lips, across my jaw, and lodged it under my chin, forcing me to look at the dusty fluorescent lights. I undid my buttons in a businesslike fashion while he spoke.

"I haven't told you this in a long time, so I want to remind you. You are mine. Any time. Any place. Without questions. You get on your knees when I say. You spread your legs when I say. You open your mouth and take whatever I put in it. Do you understand?"

He must have felt me swallow against the heel of his hand. He was back. I didn't know when or how, but this wasn't the sick Jonathan who got pissed at his handful of pills. This wasn't the guy who let me top him, or the man who made love to me fearfully and gently. That man was a good husband. He was difficult, because he felt as if his body wasn't his own, but a good life mate by any standard.

But for as long as I'd been married, I hadn't felt safe. Until then, staring at the ceiling, unprepared to hear the voice of my king again. My insides vibrated like a piano string, and I shut my eyes tight against tears.

"Yes, sir," I said.

"Pull your pants down."

I worried about the door. Was it open? And the door to the engineering room. Anyone could walk in.

This was a simple matter of trust, which I'd forgotten how to do. *Trust him. You're safe with him.*

I opened my pants and wiggled them down. I wore lace and garters, which felt scratchy and uncomfortable under jeans, but I wore them because I'd promised I would, even if I'd promised a different man. He slipped his finger under the straps. His touch had gone electric, exactly right, like when we first met. I felt it through layers of skin and muscle, down to my bones.

"All the way off."

I stepped out of my pants.

"Why are you crying, goddess?"

"I don't know."

"What's your safe word?"

I blurted a laugh to the ceiling. "Fuck. I forgot."

"Do you want a new one?" He slid his finger under my bra, pushing it up and releasing my breasts. My nipples were hard candies, ready for him.

"Yes, sir."

"Your choice."

"*Invictus.*"

He pinched a nipple and pulled it to the point of delicious pain. "'Out of the night that covers me, black as the pit from pole to pole, I thank whatever gods may be, for my unconquerable soul.'"

"Jonathan..." His name was a prayer.

"Turn around."

I faced the piano, putting my back to him. He slid his hands over my neck and under my shirt collar, pulling the shirt down my arms and drawing his hands over my skin.

"I'm going to ask you something," he said, pulling my long sleeves halfway off. He twisted the sleeves around my arms, wrapping them and tying them tightly at the elbows.

He paused long enough for me to say, "Sir?"

"Are you happy?" he asked.

I heard the distinct clack of his belt buckle. I didn't answer. He slid his belt out of his pants with a *whook*.

"I asked you a question."

"Yes, sir."

"Is that the answer?" He gripped the back of my neck.

"It's confirmation that I heard you."

With a sharp push, he pinned my face to the shiny black piano. "Are you happy?"

"Can you be more specific?"

"Sure."

With a thwack that was as hard as it was unexpected, he slapped my ass with his belt. I screamed.

"Too hard?"

"No, sir."

It was. A fierce burn settled where he'd hit me, and I already wanted more. I wanted him to tear me apart. In the breath's worth of time it took for my body to register pain, I cracked. I didn't want to go to dinner with Jerry and the guys, and I didn't want to go home. I wanted to hurt, and hurt deeply. I wanted to feel pain, and safety, and surrender; to lose myself and my will. I'd forgotten how much I needed that, but like a woman waking from a dreamless sleep, the reality of who I was came back to me. I swore I wouldn't say my safe word until I was near death.

"Behave then, before I gag you." He whacked me again and again.

I grunted but didn't cry out, even when he hit the sensitive area at the backs of my thighs.

"Now"—his breath rasped with effort—"tell me, goddess, are you happy?"

His last stroke was so hard it felt like a blowtorch on my ass. He fisted the hair on the back of my head and brought his face close to mine. "To avoid misunderstandings. Are you *happily married*?"

I swallowed. He put his belt down in front of my face and squeezed my ass. The pain was overwhelming. I could barely see through it, nor could I form words past the gushing arousal between my legs.

"Answer me," he said. "And the truth. Are you happy?"

His face was foggy through my tears, but his voice was clear enough to focus on.

"No," I said. "I'm not."

As much as I broke down into tears and hitched sobs, he seemed unfazed by the news, as if he'd already known. And as if he didn't give a shit about my happiness. He brought his hand over my burning cheeks and laced a finger in the crack, down to my opening.

I was soaked. Dripping. Gushing readiness for him. I wished he'd asked me for the truth after he'd fucked me, because how could he now? I told him I'm miserable and expected a body-ripping, passionate screw? Crazy, magical thinking.

He slipped a finger inside me. I'd fucked him a hundred times in the past six months, but that finger cruelly jamming into me, his palm lying against my scalding ass, was the best thing I'd had in half a year.

"Thank you for telling me the truth," he said. "But you're wet. And crying."

"I'm sorry, sir."

"Poor goddess." He pulled his finger out and slipped it onto the hard nodule of my clit. My eyes shut. My mouth opened. My cunt was awake with anticipation as he continued. "Even in love, you need pain."

"I love you," I whispered.

He drew his hand back and slapped my ass with full force. I bit back a cry.

"Don't talk," he growled. "There's been wholly too much talking between us, and not nearly enough."

I nodded.

He folded the belt in two and said, "Open your mouth." When I did, he put the belt in it. "Bite."

I bit the leather. It was still warm from hitting me. Had he ever been this cruel and hard? Had he ever been this *dominant*? I couldn't remember. I couldn't think.

Then Jonathan put his hands on my hips and let his cock touch where I was wet. I bit the belt as if I wanted to swallow it. He didn't ask for permission to jam his dick into me in one stroke, making me grunt into the tanned skin. He didn't ask if my happiness was required. He just fucked me. He fucked me as if I wasn't even there, slapping himself against my burning ass cheeks, a frame of pain for the pleasure between my legs. He pulled my cheeks apart, stretching them, pain everywhere, and drove into me with everything he had, using me mercilessly. I lost myself in him, in the hurt, in the rising tide of my emotions. I'd told him I was unhappy, and the weight of the misery fell off, leaving an empty place for him to fill with his cock and his searing belt.

I grunted with every thrust. It was coming, the rush of pleasure.

My grunts turned to squeals, and he slowed to barely moving. "I didn't say you could come."

I hadn't had to ask permission for an orgasm in six months. I hadn't even thought of it. He removed the belt.

"I'm sorry, sir," I gasped. "May I come?"

"When?"

"Now?" I paused for a hitched breath. "And later, if it pleases you."

"No." He slowed, letting me feel every inch of him. He opened my cheeks again, right where my legs met my ass.

I was red and sore, getting his whole length. I choked out a half sob, half moan.

"No," he said, slapping my ass. "The answer is still no."

"I don't think I can stop it."

He pulled out. I gasped. As much as I expected him to continue fucking me, I didn't expect what him to quickly guide himself into my asshole and mercilessly push forward.

"No!" I shouted.

He yanked my head back by the hair. "What?"

I couldn't repeat it. Safe word or no, he'd stop, and I knew, more than anything, that I didn't want him to stop. "Nothing. Please, go on."

He pushed the rest of his cock into my ass without preamble.

My soft weeping turned into face-soaking sobs. "God, oh God, it hurts."

"Pain is the point, isn't it?"

"Yes, sir."

"Your ass is mine, whether I warn you or not. Do you understand?"

"Yes."

He yanked my hair again, pulling back until I faced him. "Yes, what?"

"Yes, sir."

The first few strokes were murder. I felt torn apart, ripped from the inside. We'd done some gentle, well-lubricated anal in the past few months, but not like this. Not as a beating.

"You've been a bitch, goddess. That's over. From now on, you step when I say walk. You eat when I feed you. You come when I allow it. If I so much as look at your knees, you get on them and open your fucking mouth."

I grunted. He reached around me and put his palm on my throat. He pulled me back, and though I felt as though I was falling, I trusted him and put weight on my aching legs, shifting backward. He sat on the piano bench, and with my back to his front and his cock in my ass, I sat into him.

"Spread your legs." Not giving me a chance to obey, he yanked my legs apart, squeezing my ass cheeks together and tightening me around his cock. "All the way. I want your cunt out."

I bit back a cry of pain. I spread my knees, on tiptoes to the floor, fighting for balance. My elbows were still tied behind my back, and when it looked as if I'd fall, he pulled me upright.

"Reach back," he said. "Spread those gorgeous cheeks apart."

I did, fighting the constraints of my knotted shirt, cursing the stinging skin on my ass as much as I blessed it.

"Now come down, all the way. All the way. That's it. Bury me in you." He reached around me and slipped his middle finger in my cunt, gathering wetness, and dragged it to my clit. "You're not coming until I say. You're going to hold back by concentrating on one thing and one thing only."

"What, sir?" I groaned, the pleasure in my clit pushing against the pain behind it.

"Pleasing me. So fuck. And fuck hard. Go."

I moved up his length and back down, his shaft sliding against my anus, friction hot against the dry muscle.

"Faster."

His cock beat my insides, shredded me, while his fingers took my cunt three at a time. The heel of his hand kept a constant pressure on my clit.

"Come on, goddess. I'm not pleased."

I pulled my cheeks wider and slammed down on him harder, my knees aching, my arms on fire, and my ass beyond pain. Yet the pleasure between my legs grew, pressing against the agony and winning.

"That's good," he growled. "Very good."

"Thank you." I gasped, relieved, relaxed now because he was content.

I heard his breaths getting shorter. I was close, but I didn't care. I wanted him to have what he wanted. I wanted him to be satisfied. I beat down on his cock, mindless of what I was doing to myself.

"I'm going to come," he said.

"Thank you," I squeaked, more tears streaming.

"Come with me."

"Yes. Oh, yes."

He grunted, but it was more than a grunt. In the second before I lost myself in pleasure, I noted how vocal he was. More than ever. He released, truly, fully, losing control, pulling my hair until I thought he'd tear it out. I was washed away in the pleasure of his hand on my clit, the torture in my ass as my orgasm clenched it around his cock in an undulating rhythm. I came forever, lost in it, in him, his satisfaction, in the pain. I was gone, my identity washed away in complete submission to his pleasure and his will; without ambition or desire of my own, I was simply enslaved, caged, collared. Nothing. No one. Not a feeling of dissatisfaction in my belly, only humility and a feeling of complete, overwhelming gratitude.

"Goddess?" he whispered when I stopped twitching.

I tried to answer, but I was blubbering. I took a few breaths to calm down. "Yes, sir?"

"Are you okay?"

"Thank you."

He untied me. I put my aching arms on my knees, and he pushed me gently forward, his dick slipping out of my ass. I sucked in a breath.

He pulled me into his lap and kissed the tears running down my cheeks. I held him and wept fully. The emotional release poured out of me as he rubbed my back and kissed my face and neck. My awareness of the world around me—my body, the chair, the room, the building, the time of day—was brought about by the softness of his lips and the way he whispered, "Goddess, goddess, goddess."

"I haven't been what you need," he said softly.

"You couldn't be. I understand."

"That's over now."

"Thank you."

He put his hands on my cheeks and brushed my lashes with his thumbs. I let my eyes flutter closed.

"You can't leave me until I destroy you," he said.

"If you destroy me, I'll never leave."

"Regularly." He took out a monogrammed hankie and held it up. "Blow."

I blew my nose. He pinched and wiped for me, as if I were a child. He kissed my lips, owning them with tenderness and confidence. I let his tongue into my mouth, its soothing warmth exploring me as if for the first time. The tenderness with which he kissed me was in such contrast to the beating I'd just received that I broke down in tears again. He held me and rocked me in the soundproof studio for what seemed like hours, saying sweet things in my ear. I felt so good, so calm, so loved.

"You'd better cancel dinner," he said. "You're going to need some serious aftercare."

"You think the guys would notice if I ate standing up?"

"Come home, and I'll feed you in bed."

"Yes, Jonathan. Yes to everything."

"And you shall have everything."

CHAPTER 55

MONICA

Sometimes, I felt as though I wasn't in love with a man. Sometimes when things were tense, or we fought, or we made love, or I was away for too long or in the house for too many weeks, or even when he kissed me on the back patio, I stopped seeing him as a man. I stopped seeing him as even human. I felt as though I'd married a time bomb.

I thought once, as my plane crept down a runway away from some dipshit town, that he was more human in that ticking time bombness than he'd been as a normal man with a normal heart. More human in his mortality, his vulnerability, his lack of control.

Wives care for sick husbands who come back from war. Husbands stand beside wives with illnesses that deteriorate their bodies and minds. We read about their strength and dedication, their stand-by-your-manness. But no one talks about the adjustments and the sacrifices. Grieving for the husband who doesn't exist anymore isn't feel-good news. We're supposed to be chipper and upbeat and never admit to a single soul that we miss the men we thought we'd married.

I felt like a piece of shit for missing the hard, bruising sex. It was different with Gabby. When I'd wanted to go out but had to watch her, I'd felt burdened. I admitted it to myself but did what I had to do anyway. I always felt like shit about that too. But with Jonathan, I so ecstatic he was alive that I didn't even realize how much I'd missed him until he asked me if I was happy.

"What's wrong?" Jonathan asked in the back of the Bentley.

He'd just fucked my ass raw in the studio, just hurt me badly, and I'd begged him for every stroke. I'd never felt closer to him than in those minutes of pain. But

757

on the way back, after I came down from my high and we had a bathroom break, I remembered why the last six months had been so hard.

"Nothing."

He stroked my arm with his fingertips. Perfect pressure for the gathering of electricity, as always. "Nothing?"

I shook my head, more at myself than at his disbelief. Nothing, my ass. Something. Everything. "That was a lot of exertion back there."

Exertion wasn't just a word but a keyword. Code for unreasonable fear. Secret speak for death. Terror in a few breaths of syllables and the tongue rubbing on the back of the teeth.

"You've been told a hundred times—"

"I know, please." I dismissed him. "I know."

He grabbed a fistful of my hair and turned me to face him, and my scalp became a center of pleasure. "You're shutting down."

I couldn't deny the truth. Not after he'd torn me open. For those minutes in the studio, when he commanded me, I'd forgotten to worry about him, and he was again my master and king. When he pulled my hair, I wanted to be ripped apart again, just for the release from thinking about him dying.

"I'm not," I said. "I'm just—"

"Open your legs."

I was pissed he'd ask at a time like this, and relieved. I spread my legs across the leather seat. Not far enough for him apparently, because he pulled my head back and yanked my knees farther apart. I gasped when a bullet of arousal shot through me.

He pressed four fingers between my legs, where the panels of my jeans met. "I am not going to die fucking you." He scratched the fabric, and I felt the tease through the layers.

Was this the time to answer honestly? Shouldn't we talk over dinner or in bed? Or across a desk surrounded by pens and blotters and serious things?

"You might. You could."

"I won't." He pushed against my crotch, and I pushed back as if I had no control over my body.

"You might," I gasped when he undid my jeans. "And you deny it, and it's a lie you tell yourself. I'm tired of walking around and pretending it's not a problem, because it is. It's a big problem. It's all I think about."

He slid his hand past my waistband until the tip of his middle finger reached my

clit. He barely pressed on it, just rotated around the slip of skin at the top. "You never told me that."

"I have to be strong for you. You chase me out of the house to work, and I think it's because you don't want me to see you weak. And, oh God, Jonathan, I'm going to come."

"No, you're not." He reduced the pressure and intensity until I could only feel the outer edge of his hand's heat. "Pull your shirt up. Let me see your tits."

I yanked up my shirt and bra, and he leaned down and sucked on a nipple so hard and fast, it hurt like hell. I bucked under him.

"I'm going to die before you," he said, taking a last nip before putting his face to mine. "Way before you. You want to spend the time worrying? Or fucking?"

Which? Was that the only choice: this dichotomy of soul-eating pain or soul-revealing pleasure? I waited too long to answer apparently, because he circled his fingertip over my clit again, barely touching it. I groaned. I wanted to say fucking, to tell him what he wanted to hear, but when he had me like this, I couldn't tell one of the thousand untruths about my feelings. I couldn't say what would make him happy for the sake of saving him from stress.

"Which is it, goddess?"

"I'm going to come."

He brought his finger down my folds, to where I was wettest, leaving my clit kissed by nothing but the damp air in my jeans as he brought the rest of me to life. His outer fingers touched the welts he'd left earlier, setting them on fire.

"Which is it?" he asked.

"Fuck me or let me come," I whispered.

He pulled his hand out of my pants. The loss was painful.

"You are not stopping," I groaned. "Don't even—"

He held my face, putting his nose to mine. "You only talk when your cunt lets you. From now on, I control when you talk. And today, you talk."

The car stopped in front of our house, and the gate clanged closed behind us.

"You're a son of a bitch." My body arched toward him, making a lie of my words.

"Before I was in the hospital, you could hold yourself together. Now you're calling me a son of a bitch for doing what it's my right to do."

I glared at him, hating him and loving him at the same time, pain and pleasure always hand-in-hand with my king.

"Button up," he said, pulling my shirt down.

I closed the fly on my jeans, and he opened the door. The late afternoon sun blasted my face, turning Lil's form into a rectangular silhouette.

We didn't speak as we walked to the house. A modest thing by Drazen standards, it had a private beach in the back and the whole of Malibu in front. It was an old house built at the crest of the modern era by an ambitious architect who was way ahead of his time. It didn't have a porch, but a small overhang shaded the wide front door. He disabled the security system and put his hand on the knob but didn't turn it. Lil drove away, the sound of the engine giving way to the evensong birds and the breath of the freeways below.

I started to think about everything I could be doing. Over the past six months, my brain chemistry had changed so that when I was upset, my thoughts went to music and the business of making it. One ass fuck in the studio wouldn't change that.

"Come on. I have things to do," I said, knowing that wouldn't go over well. I reveled in my defiance. Fuck him with his new heart and old ways. If he wanted to talk, he could take me to dinner.

He swung the door open but didn't leave room for me to pass. I crossed my arms. He smirked. I felt the tightening of my cheeks as I almost smirked with him. What game was I playing? I wanted to get to work, and I wanted him to fuck me.

No, I didn't want him to fuck me. I wanted him to either rip me apart or let me make music mourning the loss of my wounds. If this defaulted to a vanilla middle ground because he thought he'd made his point, I would lose my shit.

"Take your clothes off. All of them."

I rolled my eyes. Lightning quick, like a man who had done nothing but work on his reflexes for the past six months, he grabbed my hair and dragged me to my knees. My safe word was *Invictus* and I probably still had a tangerine option, but the insides of my thighs tingled when he leaned down and growled in my ear.

"Unbutton your shirt."

I reached for my placket and carefully, without fumbling, undid the buttons one by one.

"I'll do what I have to to get you to talk to me. So first..." He yanked my hair, and I gasped. "Take it off. And the bra."

I shook both off until I was bare-breasted at the front door. How would he get my pants off? What did he intend?

He let go of my hair. "Stand up."

I got on my feet. He stood in the doorway, framed by a house I'd agreed to with a shrug, his hands at his sides. One of his fingers twitched.

I crossed my arms. "Are we going in or not?" I leaned on one hip, breasts out as if I didn't give a shit one way or the other how naked I was. "I'm tired, and my ass hurts. Can we just—"

"You're really pushing it."

I tapped a single finger on my bicep, a tic of impatience. Even though his beautiful green eyes didn't leave mine, I knew he saw it, and even if his mouth didn't smile, I knew I was pleasing him. We needed this, and we needed it to go down exactly the way it was going to go down.

He put a finger on my lower lip. "Open your mouth."

I didn't.

With his other hand, he cupped my jaw and exerted pressure, slowly opening my mouth. God, I wanted his cock in it. I wanted to taste the soft skin as it slid to the back of my throat. I relaxed my mouth, and he put his fingers in. First one, then four, pressing my tongue down.

He pulled me to him, speaking softly and firmly into my face. "I don't mind repeating myself. This is my mouth, and when I say open it, it opens."

I couldn't speak, but my eyes agreed. I was putty in his hands.

"Get your pants off while I explain my position."

I unbuttoned and unzipped while he held my jaw open. I couldn't swallow, and drool formed over his fingers.

"Do you remember the hospital? The week before the first surgery?"

Remember? How could I forget? I got heart palpitations thinking about it. Any time I smelled alcohol or something beeped, my chest felt as if it had been encased in a clenched fist.

"That week, we had rules," he said. "Should I remind you?"

I nodded as much as I could.

"Get your pants down." I wiggled to slide them down while he spoke. "The rules were: only the truth, even if it hurt. We would never protect each other from each other. And no judgment."

I got my pants down to my knees. I was twisted, fighting the tight jeans, the pressure of his fingers, and the memory of lying next to him in the never-dark Sequoia Hospital.

He removed his hand, which was wet with spit that dripped down his arm to the elbow. "All the way off."

I leaned to get my shoes off. He held my elbow when I almost fell then resumed watching my clumsy and twisted operation until I was completely naked before him. He was perfectly calm, perfectly commanding. Only the huge bulge in his pants indicated how involved he was in what was happening.

I stood with my hands at my sides. "I remember."

"I want that again."

"It's hard when you're telling me to get my clothes off."

"You know what, Monica, you don't even know yourself. Look at you. I haven't seen you this relaxed in months. The only time you let your worry go is when you give me control. And your worry is what keeps you from being honest."

I swallowed. Blinked. A torrent of wetness welled behind my eyes. "I don't want to break the scene."

"Stay still. Stay naked. Speak your mind."

"I almost died with you a hundred times. That recovery room, they had you in this induced coma, and you looked dead. There were bags of blood. Bags hanging over you, and you were all opened up. And, I'm sorry, I haven't said this because you're the one who went through it." I swallowed a gallon of tears. "I don't want to see you like that again. But I think about it all the time. I dream about it. I see it when I close my eyes. I want you to live, so I do what I think will make you happy, and I always get it wrong. Stay or go. I give you attention or none. It's always wrong."

"What about your happiness?"

"It doesn't matter. Not as much as yours. It's not life or death."

"It is, Monica. It is."

I shook my head. "You can't convince me of that. We can do this hurtful honesty thing all day. You're the priority, and I'm okay with that. Deal with it."

He nodded, looking down for a blink, then at me. He reached for my wrists. "These go behind your back."

I did as instructed.

"Now get on your knees."

I bent them. With my hands behind my back, it was hard to balance.

"Do you need some help?" he asked.

"Yes."

I thought he'd take me gently by the elbow, but he dragged me down. He was right. I was relaxed, totally submitting and trusting him, loving every bit of discomfort he dished out.

"Spread your knees apart."

I did, too slowly for him. He kicked them wide.

"Do you remember your safe word?" he asked, unbuckling his belt.

"Yes." A tingling rush went down my spine with the promise of his dominance and the way it made me forget how fragile he really was.

His cock was out in the next second. "Open. Your. Mouth."

I parted my lips enough to breathe, and before I could open my throat or prepare, he put his cock between them and pushed my head into him. I choked on the mass of his dick, but the scent of his soap, the taste of his skin, the shape and thrust of him brought a wave of pleasure and a strong desire to please him.

"Take it, goddess. Take it all. Not one inch should be left."

He pushed forward again, fucking my face mercilessly. He pulled out, letting me breathe and making eye contact with me. Checking on me. I was safe. I gasped, chest heaving, and opened my mouth again.

"I want you to think about something. While I take your mouth, I want you to think about how its purpose is my pleasure. To fuck." He stuck his dick down my throat, all of it in one stroke, and pulled it out as violently as he'd put it in. "To talk." He jammed it in again before I could utter a word. "Whatever I say."

He began in earnest, treating my throat the way he'd treated my ass an hour before—as a receptacle for his soap-scented cock. He moved my head by my hair, pulling out to let me breathe but no longer than necessary. My hands were behind me, so I couldn't wipe the drool off my chin or move my hair from my face.

"I'm going to come down your throat." He was so strong, so solid, so commanding with a wisp of hair over his forehead, his monster cock dripping with my spit, hanging in the foreground of my vision. "You're going to swallow every fucking drop. Do you understand?"

I opened my mouth as wide as I could, looking up at him through my hair. I wanted to tell him to fuck me anywhere he wanted. To make it hurt. Make it uncomfortable. I wanted to forget everything in our way. The hurt, the stress, the worry. I wanted to break the cycle again, and be nothing more than under him.

But he didn't give me a chance to beg for it. He cupped my jaw in his other hand and stuck his wet cock in my waiting mouth to fuck my throat. He could live forever. He could pound my face like this in an eternal grind, never sick, never dying, never at risk. No. This dominant beast was built to fuck and to hurt and to live.

He pulled out long enough to let me breathe then shoved it back in, coming with a bark, his balls pulsing against my lower lip. His hair-pulling violence turned to stroking and caressing as he filled my throat, slipping out for a breath, and sliding in again.

"Goddess," he whispered. "Mine mine mine..."

My arms and knees ached. My throat was sore. Thank god I didn't have to sing the next day. Not that he'd care. Not this Jonathan, my Jonathan, with his come coating my throat as I swallowed, looking up at him. He smiled at me, and when he picked me up and carried me though the door, I forgot to worry about him at all.

<h1 style="text-align:center">CHAPTER 56</h1>

JONATHAN

I COULD SEE this would take some time. It had taken me months to figure out we even had a problem; it wouldn't take me that much less to solve.

The flip side of the loyalty I loved was her stubbornness. She'd fully engaged in her submission when we started out because it was new and exciting. She'd discovered things she didn't know about herself, and she'd watched me discover my own boundaries as well as hers. Then I got sick, and her world flipped. She had become distrustful, and to her, the stakes were life and death.

All that made me want to fuck her harder, to drive submission back into her. While my dick was out, she was obedient and subservient, perfect as usual. In the doorway of our house, her mouth open, her chin slick with spit, waiting for me to come down her throat, she was a goddess. But once it was over, she would close her mouth and not talk about what was bothering her. She was going to simmer and worry and seethe, holding it all inside in an effort to protect me.

It was cute. Sweet, even. In a way, her protectiveness made me love her more than I'd thought I could love anyone. She was a mother lion, even with her hands behind her back and her mascara running down her cheeks.

And as if cued, as I carried her, I had a vision in four-dimension Technicolor, clear as reality and sharper than the truth: my heart blew through the scar in my chest, and I dropped her. The vision went *whoosh* when the heart flew out of me, *thup* when it landed on the floor, and *clonk* when I dropped her. I didn't hear myself fall, because I was dead.

This had to stop, but I didn't know how to do it. I didn't know how to shut it down. I shook myself free of the afterburn as I laid her on the bed. It faced the

Pacific ocean, and the constant crash of the waves would make a nice backdrop over her screams of pleasure. She'd wanted to live on the beach, and I'd given her that, but I'd never given her myself. That was going to change. I couldn't live like this.

"I missed you," she said, and I knew what she meant.

"You barely knew me." I rolled her onto her stomach. I wanted to tie her up, but I couldn't. I had in the studio, but I'd kept thinking as I stroked her back, *what if the heart rejects me and she's tied down?*

She tucked her hands under her thighs. "How much do I need to know you to love you?"

"Put your hands on the headboard," I said, pulling her hair from her face.

She stretched her arms and turned to face the big glass doors onto the patio. The beach on the other side was private, and that slice of sunset was ours alone. Her eyes were blasted light brown in the dying sun, and they followed me as I stepped back and looked at her.

She was long and beautiful, with hair like a turbulent ocean. She was my songbird, my goddess, my slice of control in a world of chaos.

Ten years with her was better than sixty with anyone less.

I picked her legs up by the ankles and bent the knees, spreading them apart. Her cunt was wet, and her ass was welted pink. I looked back up at her face. Her eyes were closed tightly, wrinkles in the skin around her wet lashes, and I remembered how hard I'd hit her. Six months' worth of frustration. I'd never hit her out of anger, only arousal, but maybe the two had gotten mixed up somewhere.

"This hurts," I said, hovering my hand over her ass.

"Yes," she said, eyes open into the sun again. "Thank you."

She wasn't trained to thank me for spankings. No one had told her it was how a submissive was supposed to please their master. She simply thanked me because she'd gotten something from me she couldn't give to herself. How could I not love her?

"Wait here." I kissed her cheek and went to the bathroom.

I snapped open the medicine cabinet. I had a shaving salve and a lubricant. Abandoned hair things. Toothpaste. Band-Aids. Monica had a pale pink box of who-even-knew under the sink. The movers had taken everything and brought it from my house to this new house, and my wife and I had been too distracted and too vanilla to note where we kept the salves for her poor, welted ass. I'd been a sorry excuse of a dominant.

I laughed at myself and put the lubricant back. That wouldn't work.

I snapped it open. Little half-used tubes of whatnot clacked around. Perfumey stuff that would burn. Zinc oxide would be fine for a small area, but her whole bottom needed attention. I clicked open a smaller box. Ah. Sunburn ointment and Neosporin. Perfect.

I checked a little velvet bag with a drawstring. I didn't know what I was hoping for, maybe the home-run of ass lotions or a magic unguent that would make her able to sit for more than five minutes without flinching. I just opened it and slid out a white plastic stick. A pregnancy test.

The nerve to my heart had been cut during the transplant, so I couldn't feel it stop and seize up. Couldn't feel the squeeze in my chest. But I knew it was there.

I turned the plastic wand. Not breathing. Not thinking about the fact that I'd been snooping into something that had been inside a bag, inside a box, inside a cabinet.

Not pregnant.

I wasn't relieved. I wasn't disappointed. I just realized how much I wanted a different result and how little control I had over it.

I slapped everything back in its place and went into the bedroom. She was still there, facedown, hands touching the headboard, bathed in the sunset. It would be dark in a few minutes, so I turned on the little lamp by the bed.

"I found these in your stuff," I said, holding out the tubes.

"I think the Neosporin's expired."

I flipped the tube. "Next month."

"Yes, sir."

I sat on the edge of the bed. "Ass up."

She shifted, arching just enough to get her pelvis off the bed.

"Goddess, when I say ass up, I mean ass up." I put my hand under her and jacked her up until her ass was in the air.

She groaned. I spread her legs under her and pressed down on her lower back. Perfect. I kissed a raw welt, and she squeaked in pain.

"None of that." Though my words were cruel, I didn't want her to hurt right then. She'd earned her pleasure.

I squeezed a lump of the sunburn cream onto my finger. It was cool to the touch, and when I put it on the pink skin, she breathed easily.

"Now," I said, "we have a problem. Fucking you in the ass isn't going to solve it."

"Yes, sir."

"First off, we need to drop the sirs and thank yous and all that shit until I say otherwise. We're off scene. Verbally. But the ass stays up, or I'll welt your welts."

"Fine."

"I want you to talk to me." I dragged a mound of clear cream over the curve of her ass, watching it get smaller in the seam between her and me, disappearing into a cool coat.

"I'm fine," she said. "Everything is fine. I think, just... I think I needed this. What you're giving me now."

I ran my fingers on the inside of her thigh until there was no cream on them, and I slipped my middle finger between her legs. Her eyes fluttered closed.

"You're not fine. You're wet as fuck." I put my fingertip on her clit. "You're so close I shouldn't even touch you. But fine? You're not fine."

"I am. I—"

"You don't tell your husband you're not happy and an hour later tell him you're fine because he fucked you hard enough."

I slid two fingers inside her. Wet didn't describe her. She tightened around me, and my dick stretched my pants. I pulled my hand out and ran it over her clit again, front to back, touching every surface, waking it up.

"Jonathan, I can't talk to you like this."

"You don't talk to me, period."

"I want to come."

"You'll come." I gingerly spread her ass cheeks. She looked as if she'd been fucked by a battering ram. Bruises were rising already, and she was deep red around the edges. I'd need to leave that part of her alone for a while. "Tell me." I kissed her lower back while stroking between her legs. "Tell me how it's been for you."

"I don't want to. I don't want to upset you. I just want you to be okay."

"I am okay, except that you've been closed to me." I put three fingers in her, and she bucked. "Stay still. You can take your hands off the headboard."

She tucked them under her.

I slowly removed my fingers. "Tell me one thing you think of that makes you worry."

She sighed.

I put my hands on her thighs and kissed her clit. "Tell me."

"I love you."

"That's not what I asked."

She paused. "And I wonder if you've taken your rejection meds."

"I know you've been checking the bottles."

"When I'm here."

"Exactly." I gave her a long stroke with my tongue.

She groaned but stayed still. Such a good woman. "I told you I'd stop traveling if you wanted."

"I don't want."

"Why?"

I sucked her clit because it tasted good and because I wanted to please her, but mostly because I didn't know how to answer her question. She'd just accepted my encouragement and never asked why it was there. I felt the muscles of her thighs tremble and tighten.

As if she spoke best on the edge of orgasm, she continued. "You throw me away. We have such a short time together, and you kick me out. Jonathan, if you don't want me, let me go. Don't stay out of obligation. Not for ten years of misery with me."

I pulled my face away. "Oh God, Monica. You can't mean that."

I'd intended to torment her for as long as it took, then bring her to orgasm with my tongue until she begged me to stop. But she broke me with those words, and I changed the plan. I got on my knees and pushed her onto her back. Her hair made a ladder across her face, and I brushed it away. Her eyes were wet, and her face was creased from being pressed to the sheets.

"I mean it," she said. "That heart has ten years in it, and you can't spend them with the wrong person just because you got married under pressure. It's wrong."

"Would you have married me if I'd asked you under any other circumstances? If I'd taken you up to Mulholland and asked you under the stars, with a ring and a few nice words?"

"I would have said yes."

"Why?"

"I love you is why. But that doesn't mean you're obligated to stay now. Because you wouldn't have asked. Not for a while." I must have had a look on my face or made a sound that hit a button, because she blinked, and tears ran down the side of her face. "I'm not trying to make it about me, and I'm not looking for reassurance. But if you deny it..."

"I'm not denying it. I would have asked you... I don't know when. After a few birthdays. There are no rules for the way it happened."

"I want you to think about it," she said.

"About what?"

"About if this is what you really want." Her voice was sober and cold. "If I'm who you really want to be married to."

"Goddess..."

"No, I mean it. If you want to be together but not married. I just want you to have what you want. I want you to be sure."

I almost answered. I almost reassured her and told her how I felt about her. I almost made metaphors with the sky and stars, weaving threads of certainty into a gauze of confidence. But even if I got her to believe it for a second, she'd wake up wondering if I'd lied to appease her.

So I kissed her cheek. "Will you stay?"

She nodded, and I felt the insecurity in it. She'd never been insecure with me, and it unmoored me at the same time it filled me with a feeling I hadn't had in a long time.

I unbuttoned my shirt. She reached up and helped me, pulling it off and throwing it across the room. I got my pants off and stood over her naked body. Her magnificent tits were goose bumped, nipples hard, skin golden in the lamplight.

"Spread your legs for me."

She did it, hitching up her knees. There was so much between us. I would have married her in an instant, under any circumstances, and as I wedged myself between her legs, I knew my job wasn't to reassure her with pretty words or gifts but with actions. She'd believe it, or I'd die trying.

I put her hands over her head and leaned on them. "Look at me."

Her eyes went wide, looking up at me. "May I come?"

I pushed against her with the rhythm of slow torture. "Quiet now, goddess. Don't ask again."

Her face went from pleasure to constricted concentration as she tried not to come. I fucked her harder. She pleaded with me without saying a word. Her face begged for release, her beauty crunched into pain.

"Say my name," I said.

"Jonathan."

"Monica."

"Jonathan." She cried it, sobbed, breaking herself into pieces to say it.

"Come, my wife. Come for me."

She came in two strokes, arching and twisting. I held myself back until she'd finished, and I drank in every cry, every moment, every shudder.

My purpose in life had been simple up until then. Live. Just live. Now I had a resolution. Love her until she believed it.

CHAPTER 57

MONICA

LOVE WAS EASY. Love, the way everyone else defined it, was the fun part. But every hell, every conflict, every bit of miserable anxiety in those first six months had been born of nothing but love. I'd thought that was my new life. Ten years of it at least, until his heart gave out and he had to find another. Then another ten. Or more. Or less. Or not. Or maybe. I was playing Russian roulette with God by being away so much, but I thought he wanted me away, and he thought I wanted to be away. I didn't know whether to jump or crawl those first six months, then he came to the studio and fucked me like an animal.

The morning after he'd reclaimed me, with my ass aching and my cunt as sore as it had ever been, I woke up forgetting to wonder about his pills and his life. Just for a second. In that crack in my wall of concern bled something else I hadn't thought about since Sequoia. It had needled me every time I saw Declan and disappeared behind the buzz of death seconds after Jonathan's father left the room. Now that I thought of it, while in Jonathan's arms with the sound of the ocean outside, I couldn't go another second without telling him, even if it meant it was our last together.

His eyes were closed, light lashes casting darker shadows. His chest rose and fell under me, and his scar was hard white beneath my hand.

"Jonathan," I whispered, hoping he was asleep.

"Yes," he answered, eyes still shut, as if he was wide awake and had been listening to my thoughts.

I got my knees under me, the pain of every movement reminding me of how many times he'd brutalized me and how consistently I'd begged for it. "I need to tell you something."

He opened his eyes. Had they always been that green? Or was it a trick of the light and my fear of losing him?

"Okay, go ahead." He stroked the top of my breast.

I pulled his hand away and held it in my lap. I paused. A hundred years passed, and he said nothing. Not a word of encouragement or doubt. I could have hanged myself in the amount of time he'd wait. As always, he was a patient man in all things.

"When you were... I mean, you weren't yourself," I started, "and you were dying right in front of me. I thought you were second on the list for a transplant. It was like... I thought that was it."

His brow creased as if he didn't understand what I was talking about. God, there were so many little details, and I wanted to tell this story fast and dirty so I could get it over with.

"You hate your father already, so it's not like this will make it worse. I went to him because I wanted something."

"What did he want in exchange?" His voice was hard and cold, and the implications of his assumptions justified the tone.

"Forgiveness from you. Enough to get your mother back to him."

He put his hand over his face and rubbed his eyes. "That's what that whole thing was about. I barely remember it. I was in and out of consciousness ten times in a minute." He patted my hand then rubbed my fingers. "What did you want?"

I balled my hand into a fist. I didn't want his affection. I couldn't bear to feel it stop when I put the pieces together for him. "So I saw Brad's list. I didn't understand how it worked. So I thought what I was seeing was... you were second, and I thought it meant you were going to die. It seemed like a guarantee. And Paulie Patalano was brain-dead and right on the fourth floor." Unable to stand the weight of his gaze, I looked in my lap, where his hand rested in mine, our fourth fingers still circled by the cheap silver key rings. "I thought your father could get me access to Paulie's room."

He moved his hand away, placing it at his side. I wished he'd slapped me in the face. It would have been somehow kinder.

"Did he?"

"He did. He's very clever. And everything you said about him is probably right. But I was the one who went in Paulie's room. I was going to do it. I was going to end him so you could get his heart." I didn't mention Jessica's part. What I'd done was my choice and my responsibility. Now wasn't the time to diffuse it with Jessica-shaped shadow play. "I knew what it meant. I knew that if my plan worked, you'd have a heart that you thought was stolen. You never would have felt right about yourself. I knew I was condemning you, in a way. And us. I knew you wouldn't forgive me. I was ending us. And I should say I'm sorry, but I'd do it again if I thought it would save your life."

"You didn't do it though."

"Brad texted me while I was in the room. He had a heart from that poor guy in Ojai. The one who jogs and hates spicy food apparently. So I didn't have to go through with it."

He took my hand again and rubbed each finger as if considering their ability to do harm. "God saved you."

"You believe in God? You believe he'd step in and save me? And he'd kill someone to do it?"

"God was in Brad's text. I believe that. But swear to me, I mean, I don't think that circumstance will recur, but swear to me you won't ever consider something like that again."

"I won't let you die if I can prevent it. I don't feel right about it, and I won't pretend I do, but it's like how a soldier must feel when he kills the enemy. I'm sure it doesn't feel good, but there wasn't a choice. And if it comes to me not having a choice again, I'll do it again."

I searched his face for distaste or foul rancor, and I found none. Then I looked for disquiet or emotional blankness, and I found none of that either. I couldn't read him, even when he took my arms and pulled me forward onto him. I rested my head on his chest.

"I have to tell you," he said, "I'm scared of death. But you? You put death to shame."

"Do you still love me?"

"Yes."

"Are you going to leave me?"

"No."

"Do you forgive me?"

He took a long time to answer. I told myself it didn't matter, that his forgiveness was beside the point when I had his love.

"I fear you. I am in awe of you. I can't forgive you for something you didn't do."

I'd thought I was committed to him before. I'd thought I'd given him my whole heart and that I owned him completely. But I hadn't. Maybe I'd spend the rest of his life realizing I'd never owned him, loved him, or committed to him fully. Maybe it was a matter of the changing acoustics of an ever-expanding heart.

I kissed his scar, and he stroked my hair. I worked down his body and took his cock in my mouth. I wanted to eat him alive, swallow his forgiveness, absorb his compassion. I wanted to become him, to own his pain and kindness, his sadism and his maturity, holding it to myself in a drum-tight skin of gratitude.

CHAPTER 58

MONICA

I usually had a dream. I was in Sequoia, but it wasn't Sequoia. The hallways
were narrower, the lights dimmer or blindingly bright—endlessly white and long.
Doors everywhere, some locked and some ajar. In my right hand beat a throbbing,
pulsing heart, dropping blood on the bleached linoleum. I only had as much time
as the blood in the heart, and I needed to get to Jonathan's room with it or he
would die. Sometimes the hospital was empty, and I couldn't find the room.
Sometimes it was populated with people who didn't know what the hell I was
talking about or where I should go. Once, I dreamed the halls were lined with
chicken coops, and Dr. Brad sent me in the wrong direction on purpose.

Jonathan always died. I always woke up in a state of grief and misery, and he
was either next to me or I was in an empty bed, looking for a way to call him
without worrying him.

The night after he reclaimed me in the studio, with every inch of my body
stinging and alive, I expected to have that same dream, as surprising and terrifying
as it always was. But it didn't come. And not the night after, when he made me wait
twelve minutes before touching me. Nor over the next week as he broke me,
pushed me, hurt me until I was a puddle of emotional satisfaction. I never had that
dream again, as if my subconscious was suddenly okay with the whole arrangement
of my life and my conscious brain was the only troublemaker.

He hurt me, but he didn't bind me. When I asked him to, he spanked me for
questioning him, but he still didn't tie me up.

I mistrusted this in quiet moments, but I let it go. He was too good, the same
man he had been. Still wise and kind, still generous and funny, but with an added

helping of scorching cruelty in bed. He'd scared the dreams away, and I was safe at night, but in the day, I still carried my anxieties. Even when I forgot to worry, I reminded myself that I hated grey and pale pink, that copper and blood had the same smell, and that the heart machine in the hospital made the same beep as the timer in the coffee shop. My brain did its due diligence, creating panic as insurance against death.

Jonathan had been more productive. Six weeks after he returned from the hospital, he started forgetting his anti-rejection meds because of the complexities of dosing, and his immune system started slipping because he wasn't getting enough nutrients. Shortly after Valentine's Day, he found out I'd been staying home to watch him. He'd sliced the air with his hand and said simply, "No."

He hired help.

Laurelin was a nurse, which I normally wouldn't hold against her. But I wasn't behaving normally. She came to the house to interview in the afternoon, after a long line of women and men who'd spoken to Jonathan about what he expected, what he needed, and what they could do. They'd all smelled sanitized. I couldn't sit in the interviews, because the hospital stink caused me so much anxiety I wanted to throw up. I told Jonathan I had to practice, but I peeked in on every interview, and every time he said one of them was no good, I felt relieved.

But Laurelin didn't smell like a hospital. Nothing about her reminded me of Sequoia. Her hair was the color of scrambled eggs, and her belly was rounded with the beginnings of her second trimester. She'd worked in the infectious diseases unit at Hollywood Methodist but couldn't continue while pregnant. She smiled a lot, which they all did, but she seemed to be made of sunshine and she smelled of rosewater. When I met her, I felt as if a blanket had been thrown over me on a cold night, and I couldn't imagine she would let anything happen to my husband.

"Her," I'd said. "You need to hire her."

"Really? Why is that?"

"She's pregnant. She's going to take good care of you. I can feel it."

"What does taking care of me feel like?"

"It feels like the only right and good thing. And she smells nice. And you like her, I can tell," I said.

"I think she might be bossy."

"I'll take that as a yes."

So she was hired, and she'd been the bulwark against my needling that she was supposed to be. I could travel and work without worrying, and without Jonathan worrying that I was worrying. Maybe it had been a bad idea. Maybe Laurelin had made our need to communicate less urgent.

Four months after she'd been hired, and two weeks after Jonathan reclaimed me, Laurelin shuffled in wearing jeans and a sweatshirt even in the late June warmth. Her code for the front gate worked three mornings a week.

Jonathan had left his little blue book on the counter for her. It was pliable leather with ruled cream pages and a black ribbon marker. In it, he kept notes about his diet, his exercise, and if he was late or early taking his rejection meds.

"Hi, Laurelin! How are you feeling?" I asked.

"Not bad." She pulled Jonathan's blue book and box of meds toward her. "I've skipped just about every complication I could." She put on a glitter face, swinging her blond ponytail from one side to the other, then popped open the box of pills that had a day of the week and a time of day in each compartment.

"How much longer?"

"Seven weeks," she said, brows knotted about what she saw in Jonathan's little pill box. "What's this?"

"What's what?" I didn't look at her, just the teapot as I filled it.

She looked at her watch. "It's ten, and he hasn't taken his morning treatment."

I didn't say anything.

"Monica?"

"Yeah?"

"Where is he?" She flipped to the last page of the book.

"He's on a run."

She snapped the book closed. "Well, we're going to have to have a little talk, the three of us."

I felt chastened. I shouldn't have. She worked for Jonathan, and thus, she worked for me, and it wasn't as if I were the one who had missed a handful of pills. That had been my husband, wanting one more tumble before his run, then breakfast, then his cubicle of meds.

Laurelin hummed and pulled the blender to her. She had packets of vitamin powders and access to the fridge, so she set up his Shit Shake for that day and the two following.

I felt as if I'd been let off the hook. I hadn't been able to resist him that morning. He wanted a tumble. No pain, no scene, no demands, just a one-two-three bite of vanilla cake. Delicious. Not something I wanted every day, but a good interlude between the usual screaming, bruising games we played. I must have been smiling, because when I looked up, Laurelin was staring at me and smirking.

"I know you're still newlyweds—"

I slapped my hands over my ears. "La la la! Stop it, Laurelin!"

She ripped open a packet of powder and dumped it in the blender. "You can get on with it after he takes his meds."

"You know how responsible he is," I said.

"Generally."

"Can you not give him a hard time? I'll take care of it from now on."

She poured milk in the blender and shook it, peeking in the top. "You're away too often to keep that promise."

She was right. But I knew when I was away, he was perfect. When I was around, he let things slip.

"Well, consider me chastened. I'm going to lunch. You can berate my husband when he gets back." I kissed her on the cheek and ran out.

∼

I spotted Darren halfway down the block from Terra Café. He looked taller by a few inches, possibly because Adam, who walked beside him, was only five eight. Darren keened a little to the left, bumping his boyfriend affectionately, and Adam nudged Darren with his elbow.

"You're late," I said.

"Oh, Miss Hotshot's on a schedule." Darren gave me jazz hands while Adam kissed my cheek.

"The line in this place is nuts. So this five minutes counts." I wagged my finger at him as if I meant it, which I didn't. Not even a little. I couldn't have cared less if he was late.

"Did you finish the EP?" Darren asked.

"Yesterday. It was great. I mean, all of it. Every track I feel good about."

"How many?"

"Six."

"Nice." He looked at the menu. Organic fair trade lunch, gourmet cakes and pies, vegan, free-range, grass-fed, gluten-free, cruelty-free, flavor-challenged, and the descriptions of what wasn't added, wasn't done, or wasn't offered took up half the board.

"You look different," Adam said, looking me up and down. He'd really grown on me with his sharp mouth and cutting sense of humor. If you could take a joke, he was the guy to hang around, and if you beat him to the punch, even better. Thin-skinned weeping willows need not apply.

"I'm the same."

"Just richer," Adam snapped. Darren elbowed him, and Adam laughed.

I shrugged. "There's that. But you're still buying your own lunch."

"But no," Adam continued, "seriously, something's changed since the last time I saw you."

Darren cut in. "The last time you saw her, she was in a hospital cafeteria. She hadn't eaten in weeks. It was a fucking nightmare."

They'd come to visit a few days after Jonathan had his transplant. I barely remembered it. No, I did remember it. It was Christmas. Darren had brought me a piece of holiday cake, and I'd eaten it down to the last scrapings of frosting. The cake I remembered, the conversation, which probably centered around physical damage and medical procedures, was lost.

We sat at a cramped spot by the window and put our number on the table. I'd seen Darren a lot since the hospital. He was the only one I'd told about the horrors of Sequoia. The recurrent dreams. The heart-gripping fear whenever I heard a machine beep or saw an innocuous color combination. I told him about how I went miles out of my way to avoid the hospital compound and turned off any TV show with scenes in a medical facility. I even refused to use white sheets in the house because the sheets in the hospital were white.

He'd been there for me in the middle of the night when the door alarm beeped and I freaked out because it sounded like a heart monitor. He gave me directions when I got lost in West Hollywood because I couldn't find a way to get where I was going without passing Sequoia. He'd heard about all the dreams of endless hospital hallways while Jonathan died in a room I couldn't find.

"When is Jonathan going back to work?" Adam asked. He traded real estate insurance products, so anything that happened in real estate was hugely interesting to him. I always had to make sure to only tell him things that had been announced publicly.

"He's selling most everything," I said.

"Really?" He considered his iced green tea latte. "He need more money?"

"Shut up." I flicked a few drops of condensation from my cup at him.

"Sorry."

"I mean, who wants to run an empire on borrowed time?" I said. "At this point, it's either sell it all or go back to working like a dog. And that's all you're getting out of me, Mister Corporate Raider."

Adam rolled his eyes. "You going to tell her?" he asked Darren, biting the straw of his emerald-color latte.

"Tell me what?"

Darren pressed his fingers into his eyes as if he still had sleep in them.

"You are an unbelievable chickenshit," Adam mumbled.

"Fuck off."

"Okay." I held up my hands. "Listen, this is cute, but if you guys haven't talked about this already, I'd be happy to step outside while you—"

"Easy, it's not a big deal," Darren said.

"Really?" Adam seemed put off.

"I'm moving out of Echo Park."

"You're moving in together!" I squealed joyfully. "That's awesome!"

"Yes, but that's not it. We did something impulsive, and we're just sticking with it before some asshole makes it illegal again," Darren said.

I heard something about assholes at the end, but not really, because I'd scraped my chair back to run around the table. I plopped right in Darren's lap and hugged him. Adam got in on the action until we were a pile of happy limbs.

"Just say it so I know I'm not hugging you for buying a pot farm," I said.

"We got married!" Adam said.

Three tables of people twisted around to look at us then broke into applause. I stood and clapped too, and Adam pushed his lips onto Darren's cheek. My ex-boyfriend blushed. I sat when the applause died and our food arrived.

"So," I said, "why now? Or then? Or when?"

"Yesterday," Darren answered. "The deal was, when I had a foothold as a musician—"

Adam interrupted between taps on his phone. "And I was not holding my breath—"

"Oh, fuck you."

"It's got nothing to do with your talent, and you know that, honey."

"Whatever. That was the deal. I've been working at Redlight Studios pretty regularly, and Harry and I have been working on some really broad, commercial stuff."

"Yeah," I said. "I know all this. Why are you stalling?"

"I don't want you to compare this to what you get, because you, I mean you're getting a different kind of deal."

"Oh. My. God. You got signed."

"It's nothing," he said. "It's music for a video game. *City of Dis*, if you've heard of it."

"I have."

"Well, it's a good gig and good money. And I didn't even mention it because who cares? But it just got us noticed enough that we're getting signed by Beowolf Records for a really small thing—"

Adam dropped his phone on the table. "And this is why I said, 'Marry me now, or I'm done with you.' Nothing is a big enough deal for him. He'd accept my proposal after his fifth Grammy, maybe."

"Are you guys having a party or something? I want to give gifts and get drunk. You owe me that."

"When we get a place not in the slums of Los Angeles, so sorry," Adam said. "Something nice on the west side with a big enough yard for a reception."

The look on Darren's face told me there had been some contention over either the size or the location, but I said nothing. I'd get it out of him later.

My phone rang.

"Let me get this." I slid the phone off the table and walked outside.

Jonathan and I had made a new deal after he reclaimed me. If he called, any time, any place, I picked up. If he called during a show, I had to pick up in front of the audience. The only way to avoid that was to tell him when I would be on stage and when I would be in the studio, then he'd only call if it was an emergency.

"Hello, goddess," he said.

"Hi." I felt warm and giddy.

"I think we should cancel on Sheila tomorrow."

"Why?"

"I noticed you were walking straight. Can't have that."

As appealing as the thought of him making it hard for me to walk was, he needed to be at Sheila's tomorrow. "We can work around it."

"Since when are you so eager to see my family?"

The rule of never lying to save each other pain was still in effect. I couldn't travel thinking he wanted me gone, and he couldn't chase me out to save me from being around him. We were to be direct in our insecurities and our desires, even if they would hurt.

"I want to go," I said, telling the truth but keeping a tiny lie to myself. "I happen to love almost all of your sisters as much as Margie."

"Truth?"

"Truth."

"Come home."

"May I finish lunch?"

"Hurry. I want to fuck you blind."

Fluid rushed between my legs. I almost buckled at the knees. We hung up, and I dialed Margie while leaning against a parking meter.

"Yes?" she snapped.

"He's trying to wiggle out of tomorrow."

"You have one job, Monica. One job."

"I can do my best, but—"

"For the tenth time, he is not going to have a heart attack when we yell 'surprise.' You're going to give yourself an ulcer," she said.

"The doctor said no stress. That's stressful."

"Is he taking all his rejection meds?"

"Yes."

"Eating right?"

"Yes."

"Is he exercising?"

I sighed, frustrated. She was building a case, and the jury would find in her favor. "Jogs miles and miles a day."

"Is he not taking care of himself in any way possible?"

"He's a model citizen."

"So what's the problem?"

"I love him, and I don't want to lose him. That's the problem. When are you going to tell him about the Swiss thing?"

"Tomorrow I'm going over to your place to get some things signed. I'll bring it up then. Be scarce."

"Okay." What I said with that "okay" was that she'd better do it or I would blurt something out in the bedroom. We'd agreed that it should be presented as business, and Margie was business, but after one more day, it would feel like withholding.

"What did you get him for his birthday?" Margie changed the subject.

"I wrote him a song." As soon as I said it, I knew the song was wrong. It was about a flat compromise over a house. I'd written it before he'd reclaimed me, and I suddenly hated it.

Margie's sigh was audible over the traffic. "You're a good wife. It's almost sickening."

CHAPTER 59

MONICA

THE MORNING of Jonathan's birthday, I woke him by putting his cock in my mouth, and he twisted me around and put his mouth on me at the same time. He didn't even say good morning before I came, groaning with his dick down my throat.

"Monica, you didn't ask."

"But, wait, we're in scene?"

"Get up and stand by the window."

I had to write him a new song, and dinner was at five. I was already cutting it close. I wasn't a particularly quick songwriter. Since we'd both collapsed without fucking the night before, this could go on for hours.

But I couldn't hesitate. I wasn't afraid he'd beat me harder. I was afraid he'd think I didn't want to play. So I stood, already naked, and faced the back patio. I wanted to do this and do it hard, then write the song, because I had no idea what I wanted to write. I had no idea what to say except everything.

"Put your hands on the glass."

I leaned forward and put my fingertips on the back doors. Behind me, I heard his belt buckle clink and his fly zip as he put on his pants.

"Whole hand. Come on, Monica. Commit." He spanked my ass playfully.

I put my whole palm on the glass and stretched my back.

"Open those legs." I did, and he pressed on my lower back until my ass was all the way up. "Good."

"Thank you."

He nonchalantly went out the back door and looked out over the ocean. The salt breeze blew his hair back. Then, as if noticing something for the first time, he played with the bamboo stalks in the patio's stone planter as if they were strings on a harp. Then he stood in front of a pot of rattan. It looked just like any other potted palm in Los Angeles. He'd had it brought in a few days ago to block a sliver of view from the beach. He'd insisted on rattan, and from what I'd heard on the phone, he had to go see it personally. I'd had no idea what his problem was. I didn't know if it was some obsessive pickiness he'd inherited from his new heart that hadn't yet had the opportunity to show itself or if it was something I simply had never known about him.

But my king wasn't impulsive. He bent one of the leaves and snapped out his pocketknife, which also just happened to be in his jeans. He cut off a branch and stripped off the leaves.

He stood right in front of me on the other side of the glass door, as if he were in a different room, as if I couldn't see him. He rolled the cane around in his hands, then across them, inspecting it for I didn't even know what.

He walked back in the house with the switch. "Now," he said from behind me, "I think we've talked about your orgasms before, and who owns them."

"You do." I looked out the window. Without him in front of me, I felt exposed, my breasts hanging, ass up.

"No one can see you." He slapped my ass.

"Yes, sir."

"Do you believe me?"

"I want to."

He swatted me with the rattan switch, lightly, as if testing. Then he did it harder. It was no thicker than a pinky, and that second time, it made a whipping sound before it landed with a *crack*. Then he did it a little harder.

I sucked in my breath.

"How is that?" he asked.

"Good, sir."

He cracked it again, at the topmost fleshy part of my ass. The sting was incredible, searing me. I felt as if my flesh was opening. Then he did it again, an inch or so below the last stroke. I let out an *mmm* sound, biting my lips. And he did it again. There was a rhythm to it, a slow build as he worked his way down to my knees, searing pain leaving blossoming pleasure in its wake. Two taps to aim, one to awaken the skin, and one to make me scream in pain, and it went *thwap thwap* thwap THWAP. *thwap thwap* thwap THWAP. *thwap thwap* thwap THWAP.

IN THE LITTLE studio in the guest house, the piano keys went *tap tap* tap TAP. *tap tap* tap TAP as I searched for the notes. I shifted in my seat. Jonathan had given my ass and thighs plenty of aftercare, but I wouldn't be comfortable for a couple of days. I'd think of him and his mastery of me whenever I sat or walked, which was the point.

I had only a few hours, and I was slow. Slow with words and clunky with melody. I missed Gabby. She made things work in minutes. I'd write a poem to the snap of my fingers, and she would tap out the rhythm and embellish it until we had a song. Not every song was good, but at least I knew what I was dealing with before ten minutes had passed.

But by myself, I had a hard time. I thought the work was good in the end, but I wasn't producing well under pressure. I didn't even know what the song was about, except time.

Ten years. It had been impossible to talk about that length of time without impaling myself on it. It was so far off, and tomorrow. It was a lie, because it could be so much more if he took care of himself and played by the rules. Even after his heart gave out, if the doctors saw he ate right and took his medicine, he'd get another heart if it came available. It had been done. And was it really ten? Because there was a very healthy guy in Wyoming who had had his for a record-breaking twenty-five years, and there were new advances in anti-rejection meds every day and and and... .

None of that would matter if he was dead. So I'd planned for that eventuality by girding myself, day after day. It would hurt. I would be in the hospital again, crying over him, alone, vulnerable, and scared. A shaft of ice already stabbed my spine whenever I passed Sequoia Hospital, and the knowledge that one day soon, I would go back for the same reason froze me in panic.

All I did was pray for him. The first six months of our marriage had been one big prayer without end, amen.

I couldn't get control of it by running or staying, and he wanted children. Children. I'd lost my father, and it had crushed me. But Jonathan wanted to have children and disappear when the oldest was nine. Or eight. Or who even knew. Left with a hopeless mother who had lost the love of her life. No amount of money could cure that.

And now, six months later, with his breath in my ear and his sexual dominance reestablished, was anything solved? No. Nothing was. But God damn if I was going to sing him a birthday song about a house because it was the only thing we could agree on.

He was better than that.

We were better than that.

I had a few hours to write him a new song. Not about how much time we had. Not about all our failings, but about what we meant to each other. About how fulfilling and worthwhile those ten years could be, if I stopped squinting into the distance at the end of them.

Tap tap tap TAP. *tap tap* tap TAP.

CHAPTER 60

JONATHAN

JOGGING. Herbal tea. Rabbit food. Jesus Christ, how had I survived six months without making my wife beg for mercy? I stood in the driveway, looking at our house from the street, for the hundredth time. It was deep in and behind a wall of roses, but who could see? From what angle? If I fucked her on the back patio, were her shaking tits visible from the public part of the beach? Could they hear her scream next door?

The low-slung, mid-century glass box was so well-designed and so well-placed that unless we kept the lights on and fucked against the window in a certain part of the bedroom at night, we couldn't be seen. I'd known that from the second day. But it *felt* as if we were exposed, and she liked that.

That morning, before she'd slinked off to the guest house to tap on the practice piano, I'd taken her against that window. Her handprints were still on it, like two frosted starfish. She'd put her hands against the glass when I told her to, ass out, legs spread almost but not quite wide enough. I'd stuck my fingers in her.

"No one can see you," I'd said then slapped her ass.

"Yes, sir."

"Do you believe me?"

"I want to."

I'd caned her hard and thoroughly until my arm ached and she was a groaning mess. It was her way of telling me she trusted me but needed that shade of doubt. It brought her so close to orgasm, I barely had to touch her with my dick before she came.

I might even learn to like this house.

"What are you doing in the middle of the street?" said a voice from behind me.

I didn't turn around. I knew my sister's voice better than I knew my mother's. "You should call before you show up."

Margie was hanging half out of the window of her Mercedes and waving for me to get out of her way into the driveway.

"I'm a newlywed, you know," I said.

"We had an appointment." She pulled in, and I followed on foot, letting the gate close behind me.

I opened the door for her when she stopped. "We did. I forgot."

She got out, yanking her briefcase free of the passenger seat floor. "You shouldn't have fired your assistant before you were finished with your business."

"I'm sick of calendars and commitments."

She made a thick sound that could have been interpreted as a *harrumph*, except that was too passive-aggressive for my sister. If she had something to say, she'd never let a vocal tic replace a well-placed barb. I led her inside.

"You want something?" I asked, opening the fridge.

"Nice place," she said, putting her briefcase on the island bar. "I almost went to the old one. Up in the hills." She snapped the briefcase open.

I got her a glass of water with no ice, and she thanked me as if she'd actually asked for it. But she didn't have to. I knew her at least that well. I opened a bottle of water for myself. I was off Perrier. Carbonation was on the No Intake list.

"Is it what you expected?" I asked.

"I expected a house cut in half with masking tape," she answered, taking papers out and laying them in neat piles on the granite.

"Did I make it sound that bad?" I had leaned on Margie the most since the surgery. I'd never talked about my emotional life before, but I had to now or I'd break. Margie was my valve, because she was honest and straight, and she knew when to shut the hell up.

"For two people suffering from post-traumatic stress? I think you're doing great. Not that I have anything healthy to compare you to." She clicked a pen and handed it to me. "Sign where I put yellow tabs. Initial on the purple."

I started from left to right, signing away about ten years of my life. The business I'd rebuilt for Dad in repayment for silence over Rachel. Twenty-two to thirty-two—over a billion and a quarter in assets in a managed trust. He could have it. Sale of the hotels, except K, where I met Monica. I wasn't ready to let that go. Another half a billion in real estate to a trust Margie would manage and share. After all the sales, my responsibility would be to do nothing but take care of myself.

"You think you might get bored?" Margie asked when I was halfway through the stacks.

"Yes. But I don't know what to do about it."

"There's this thing I heard about. You might be interested. Could kill some time. Definitely burn through some cash."

"Go on."

"In Switzerland. They're really close on an artificial heart."

"No."

"It's made from tissue. It doesn't need an external battery," she said.

"No."

"They need a lot of money for development, but you have it."

"Am I speaking the wrong language? No."

"Why?"

"I don't like the Swiss. The cheese offends me."

"Nice answer. Got a reason that makes sense?"

I put down the pen. I knew my mouth was set because I felt the tension in my jaw. "What would be the point? To get my wife's hopes up when it won't work? Then I die anyway? The sooner she starts coping with it, the better."

She pushed the pen toward me. "Finish up."

I got back to signing at the tabs. Full signature for yellow. Initials at purple. "I have the Arts Foundation to run. That'll keep me busy."

"Yeah. And you don't have to waste your time hoping for anything. You don't have to build a future."

"I'm the one who wants kids."

"That's not a future if you're dead. That's called a legacy."

I checked the details and flopped the last contract closed. "Just like a lawyer to get hung up on semantics."

"Just like a man." She restacked her papers, clacking them against the counter. "You just want to piss on the world one last time like it's a fire hydrant you'll never see again. I don't blame her for holding out on you."

Coming from anyone else, I would have been enraged. But Margie's love was so unconditional, I didn't know if she could ever say anything to make me truly angry.

"You know this is not about legacy," I said.

"Not consciously."

"It's about Monica."

"The everlasting gift of your DNA? Way to woo a girl."

I laughed. I had nothing else for her. I couldn't even explain myself to myself.

"It's nice to see you laugh, little brother. I thought they'd transplanted your sense of humor there for a while."

"Are you staying for lunch? I could stand to be insulted for another hour."

"Sorry." She plopped the papers in her briefcase. "Some of us have to work."

"I have a thing," I said. "For the birthday dinner later. I need you and Sheila to help."

She raised an eyebrow at me while she snapped the case closed. "A thing?"

"You'll like it. It involves jewelry."

"I hate jewelry."

"You'll like this."

CHAPTER 61

MONICA

I EXITED the studio in the mid-afternoon, completely unsatisfied with my work. I went into the kitchen and, seeing as Jonathan wasn't around, reached for his box of pills.

I didn't know where I'd picked up the habit of thinking it was all right to count someone's meds. From living with Gabby, maybe. Jonathan had Laurelin to monitor him, make sure his medication was taken, and help him mind his Ps and Qs. That didn't stop me from peeking in his little plastic box with the days of the week on it.

Too many sets and subsets of pills. No wonder he needed a medical professional.

"Stop it," I told myself, snapping the box shut.

I pushed it back into the corner between the toaster and the fridge, but it was too late. The medicines had a smell, and they brought it all back. The inevitable images of him dying in that fucking hospital, his heart breaking right out of his chest. The colors of the hospital lounge carpet, the paint, the cafeteria, the recovery room, all of it flashed before me. I closed my eyes as if that would block out the smells and colors of those weeks.

"He's fine," I said to myself. "Stop it."

"Stop what?" Jonathan came in from the patio, slick with sweat and ocean water. He'd been jogging.

"Stop tracking sand all over the floor. Look at this mess!"

"Why?" He grabbed my waist and pulled me into him. "Afraid it'll scratch your back?" He pushed me into the kitchen island and bit my neck at the curve.

"Don't leave a mark!" I pushed him away, not that it did anything. "We're going to Sheila's and—" I couldn't finish when he stuck his hand between my legs and yanked my pants down by the crotch. "We just did it," I groaned. I could have ended the California drought with what flowed between my legs.

"Define 'just.'" He unceremoniously pulled up my shirt and grabbed a nipple. My body went on high alert.

"I'm still sore."

"That's how I like you."

I pushed him away for real. "I don't want to use my safe word for stupid bullshit, Drazen, but back off. I'm making a snack. What do you want?"

He smiled, taking the hint but not believing me. "You, with butter and jelly."

"I have a baguette left from last night."

"Fine." He pulled my shirt down.

"You should have protein. An egg or something."

"There's enough protein in my morning shake to create an entire mammalian species."

I kissed him gently. "You should try the bread with the chimichuri."

"Hell, no." He opened the fridge and leaned into where the condiments hung out. His running pants hung low on his hips. "I see you looking at me," he said, still rooting around the back.

"You've gained weight."

"These are my fat pants." He smiled, shutting the door and putting the goods on the counter.

I unscrewed the cap on the hot sauce and ripped off a piece of baguette. "Try." I dipped the bread into the sauce, but I got as little as possible. I wanted my husband to get over the spicy food thing. I knew it embarrassed him. I held it up. "Come on, I made this with my own hands, with my mother. Think of the generations of women who have perfected it for the sake of this one moment in time."

"Not to be dramatic."

"I'll get a samba band in here if you like. *Cha cha chadda.*" I swung my hips to the rhythm, with my piece of bread out.

He grabbed my wrist and held it still. I froze. Had I insulted his masculinity or something?

He locked eyes with me then tore them away. He kissed down the inside of my arm, my wrist, and took the bread in his mouth. He chewed. I waited. He had zero change of expression, and I smiled a little.

He swallowed. "I feel like my face is burning from the inside."

"Well, you look gorgeous."

He let my hand go and screwed the top back on the chimichuri. "You're just seeing a free man."

"Oh, right, Margie came today. Did you get rid of everything?"

"I gave up every hotel from A to J. I kept the one where I met you. I'm sentimental like that."

"Did she tell you about the Swiss thing?"

He froze. I swallowed. Was it more complicated than I thought? Was it too expensive an investment?

"Yes," he said.

"And?"

"I'll think about it."

"Really?"

"I—"

I had an explosion I couldn't control or foresee. All my pent-up feelings went off like controlled detonation, except the building didn't collapse but took off like a rocket. I threw my arms around his neck, wrapping my legs around his waist.

He was thrown back a step catching me. "Jesus, Monica."

"Happy birthday, baby." I kissed him seven times. I couldn't stop, but then I had to talk. "They're so close they just need a push. I know it's a lot of money but it's worth it when they figure out the rejection thing it needs its own special rejection meds which they're also developing and then a healthy testsubjectwhois—"

"Whoa whoa."

"Young, with no secondary problems."

"Monica."

"It's you. You. Especially if you fund it, then they have to make it you. And it lasts forever. You'll have to get hit by a bus when you're a hundred and ten."

He loosened his grip until my feet hit the floor. "Do you know what the odds are of it working?"

"Great!" I stuffed the bread back into the bag. "The odds are great. I mean, I don't know. I didn't ask. But the odds of the one you have lasting even twenty years are worse, since they're, like, zero."

I felt like a giddy schoolgirl. I wanted to sing and dance, and my smile was totally involuntary. I could barely contain myself. I felt as if the past seven months might be erased, put away in some jar in the china cabinet where we could ogle how cute and silly it all had been.

Jonathan leaned against the counter, clicking the ice in his water glass and staring into it as if it were a problem. I felt crazy and childish in comparison. I cleared my throat, choking back the relief and trying to find that worry again. But it wouldn't go away. I was over the moon, and he was still on the earth.

I breathed deeply, trying to calm down. I was overreacting for sure, but it was his heart, his life, his chest. If he was somber over it, then I could take it down a notch. I moved the bread bag three inches. I touched a pan, shifting it on the stove. I smiled as I turned a knickknack a quarter way around. My mother had given it to me. It said BELIZE.

"I thought you were going to eat something," Jonathan said.

"Fuck it." I stood in front of him. "I want you for a snack." I dropped to my knees and yanked down his sweatpants.

"Okay, Monica—"

I gave him big eyes from below. "You don't want me to suck your cock?" I felt him harden in my hand.

"I'd love a blowjob, thank you. I have to take a handful of pills. Then I'm going to shower. So I need you to go upstairs, take your clothes off, and be ready for a quick go before we leave. And when I say ready, I mean mouth open and hands behind your back."

"Yes, sir," I said through a smile.

"Your legs should be open all the way this time. I mean it. We're on a tight clock."

"Yes."

"Have I mentioned how much I love being married to you?"

"Not today."

"Let me finish up here, and I'll show you."

CHAPTER 62

JONATHAN

I LOVED BEING MARRIED to Monica—at least, I did once we had reestablished full participation by both parties. The weeks following my visit to the studio, minus the constant medication, had been exactly what I'd wanted from the honeymoon we never had.

Things would get back to normal soon, whatever that was. I still couldn't find a taste for the food I used to like. Anything spicy tasted like poison, and I craved sour foods as if I were pregnant. I thought less and less about having a strange piece of meat inside me. My chest didn't feel as heavy with attention as often. I was in a routine with Laurelin, the medicine, the nutrition, and my odd addiction to jogging which made the team of doctors happy.

Normal. For somebody.

But at least I could still make plans for Monica's body and execute them. If I couldn't eat the spicy chimichuri, which we apparently had a never-ending supply of, at least I could spoon-feed her while she was on her hands and knees.

I'd overheard her fielding calls from the people she worked with, putting them off, apologizing. She was an artist, and she'd need to get back to it soon. We still hadn't talked about how to manage that part of our lives because when we did, I'd have to admit for the first time that I didn't want her to travel so much. I didn't know what to do about that.

The visions of my heart leaving my body persisted. Sometimes it flopped around the floor and squirted blood; sometimes it only came halfway out; and sometimes, when I scratched the itchy scar, my fingers went through the soft tissue and touched the foreign, beating thing, and in response, it detached and slid into my palm.

Monica was always there in those waking dreams. In the easiest ones, she was simply horrified. In the worst of them, I was driving and killed her when I died at the wheel. But traveling? I was convinced the heart would stay on the ground if I flew, as if it weren't tethered to my body but to the state of California. I'd ruin her trip and probably her life. I was never scared of my own death. I'd dealt with that already, but its effect on Monica would be shattering.

None of it was rational. None of it made sense. And my nearly physical ache for children made the least sense of all the crazy nonsense I believed. Knowing that didn't shake the fear or the longing away.

I'd managed to wiggle out of traveling until we drove down to Sheila's place in Palos Verdes. The June sunset left the sky palette-knifed in orange and navy, and the temperature hung between inoffensively cold and completely generic. With the top down and Monica next to me in the Jag, twisted in her seat, the weather was perfect.

"Are you going to sit like that in front of my sisters?" I asked.

"Hey, if you wanted me to sit straight, you should have been a little gentler."

"You didn't marry me for my gentle ways."

She poked me in the ribs and I laughed, but she sat straighter.

"Is there any country in the world you haven't been to?" she asked.

"Probably."

"Any one you want to go to?"

"Iceland. But I'm not cleared yet."

"Yes, you are. You haven't asked Dr. Solis at all. We could send a bunch of shit shakes ahead and make sure whatever cardiac unit there was knew you were coming."

I didn't answer right away. We were communicating, but I shouldn't answer rashly. I pulled off the 110, slowing my car and my thoughts. "The thought of it is…" I knew what the honest answer was, but it was hard to speak aloud.

"We can do everything to make it less scary—"

"I didn't say I was scared."

"Well, I am." She took my hand, looking out her side of the car. "Anyway. The food's really bland there. You should like it."

I reached under her arm and tickled her. She squealed and twisted away. What was I going to do with her? Besides spank her raw and love her senseless? At some point, I would keep our honesty promise and break it to her that even if I funded the artificial heart, I wouldn't test it. But her relief and happiness were too precious and delicate. I hoped some other obstacle would present itself in the meantime. Blood type, body size, anything.

I went through the gate and parked in front of Sheila's house, pulling the emergency brake. "About the Swiss thing…"

"Yeah?"

"If it's not what you think or if it doesn't work out, you're going to be disappointed."

"It'll work out. I know it."

She didn't wait for me to come around. She just opened the door and got out, bouncing as if it were someone's birthday.

CHAPTER 63

MONICA

JONATHAN FOLLOWED ME, flipping his keys in his palm, spinning them around a finger, flipping again. Spin. Flip. Spin. Flip. All in the rhythm of his gait, like a perfectly tuned instrument of movement and sound. He wore a white shirt open at the collar, sleeves rolled to the elbow, and jeans that fit as if custom built for him. Jogging miles every morning had toned his legs and added grace to his gait.

I rang Sheila's bell. The door was wide enough to fit two adults walking abreast, so I didn't know how he was supposed to get in without seeing everyone. But it hadn't been my job to hide everyone. It had been my job to get him there on time.

He slipped his hand across my bare shoulder and grasped me by the back of the neck, saying nothing and owning me completely. I relaxed right into the warmth of his hand.

The door opened. Sheila wore a pair of skinny jeans and a lavender hoodie. Bare feet. Hair brushed for a change. "Happy birthday!"

"Thanks." He kissed her on the cheek, leaving his other hand on me as if I'd run away.

Was the party off? Had something happened? Where was the big opening salvo? Sheila stepped out of the way. Jonathan guided me in the door, and I greeted her. Looking over her shoulder, I caught sight of the buffet and felt more than saw the presence of other people.

After Jonathan stepped in and the door closed behind him, the shout of "Surprise!" came all at once, at incredible volume, from an impossible number of people. They appeared from the hall, behind the couch, the patio, as if a switch had been flicked.

Jonathan stood in the doorway a second then clutched his chest and stepped back. Mouth open, eyes wide, as if in shock and surprise at the pain.

I went blind, reaching for him, everything shut out but the sounds of the beeping machines, the stench of alcohol, the shadowed lines of the blinds falling across his white face in the afternoon.

Hands on me. Strong arms, and the sounds of the room pierced the veil of terror.

Laughter. A few dozen people laughing hysterically, and a collective *awwww*.

Jonathan held me up, looking at me with a smile.

"You asshole!" I said.

"Come on," he said. "It was funny."

"No, it wasn't," I whispered softly so he'd know I was serious. I dropped my register and changed my inflection to sound like him when he didn't want an argument. "Don't ever do that to me again."

"I think it was that bite of chimichuri." He rubbed his stomach and smiled.

I didn't laugh. Didn't smile. Didn't give him anything but ice cold anger.

He looked pensively at me, pressing his lips together, before he said, "I'm sorry."

I was still shaken. I couldn't forgive him. Not yet, and luckily I didn't have to, because Leanne put a drink in my hand.

"Thanks," I said.

"He's a fucker." For a fashion designer, Leanne usually dressed in clothes that were no more exciting than the average plain Jane's, and to be honest, she was kind of a slob. But that day, her jeans were rippling with shades of blue and the creases in her hands were deep indigo.

I swished the drink. It was a yellow, juicy thing with ice. Behind me, Jonathan gladhanded and laughed.

"What happened to your hands?" I asked.

"We're doing denim tie-dye in India." She indicated her jeans, which went from deepest indigo to pale sky in irregular patterns.

"Hm," was all I said.

"Not perfected yet, obviously. And it's messing with the sideseams." She grabbed her belt loops and yanked up her pants.

"God, I wish you'd brush your hair," Margie said to Leanne from behind me.

Leanne's bracelets jangled when she extended her silver-ringed middle finger at her sister. They tormented each other for a few more seconds, Drazen-style, and I twisted around to look for Jonathan. I found him chatting with Eddie and another guy, perfectly happy, no chest pain, arms gesturing without stiffness. He wasn't having a heart attack.

As if summoned by my attention, he looked at me through the crowd and winked.

Asshole.

Gorgeous asshole.

I excused myself and went to the kitchen. Staff buzzed around, slapping the oven open and shut, speaking the language of waitstaff I knew all too well. Eileen Drazen stood by the sink in sensible tan pants and a jacket, throwing her head back as if she'd just taken a pill. She sipped whiskey and turned around.

"Hey," I said. "How are you doing?"

I reached in the cabinet for a glass. She and I had met under terrible circumstances, and once I understood that, and she understood that I wasn't after her son's money, she was still made of ice. But at least she was only cold, rather than cold and dismissive.

"Fine. You?"

"I'm getting over the psychotic break I nearly had a few minutes ago." I filled the glass from the fridge door.

"Yes. On the scale of inappropriate jokes, that was deep in the red. You should make him suffer for it."

"Where's Declan?" I wanted to avoid him. He'd laughed off the three-doctors incident as simple misinformation, and I didn't have a fact to hold against him. Sure, he *could have* innocently told me three doctors exiting the operating room meant the patient had died because he'd thought it was the case. To a certain extent, it was true. But it had been two doctors and a patient advocate. So that was explainable. And he *might have* not known that the anesthesiologist was expected to sit through the entire transplant to manage the induced coma and, thus, would exit with the other doctors. Sure. It was all plausible. But his smile of satisfaction when I dropped? That was totally subjective and completely real.

So like the rest of his children, I simply didn't trust him.

"My husband's around." Eileen waved her ring-thick hand. "Everyone is here somewhere. I lose count of all of them."

"Have you seen Leanne's jeans?"

I said it to get a reaction, and she shuddered as if it was scandalous. My mother-in-law was such a backward prude that sometimes I wondered if it was all an act to protect a burning sexuality.

"I think they're cute," I said, sipping my water.

"You would," she said without reproach. "I've learned to stop concerning myself with my children's tastes. They get away, and then, poof, they're not your responsibility. They're just people who invite you over for holidays."

I nodded.

"How many does he want?" Eileen asked.

"Ten or more," I said, putting my empty glass in the grey bus pan.

Eileen barked a little laugh. "Men."

"Yeah."

"They figure if they have the money for a staff, they can breed to their heart's content."

"You didn't want eight kids?"

"I wanted seven. Though the eighth?" She shrugged with a smile. "He'll do. It was nice to have a boy. Broke up the catfights over who used the last of the conditioner."

I laughed. "Really? With all your staff? You ran out of conditioner?"

"Your husband was pouring it down the sink," she said. "The joker. No matter how much Delilah bought, he dumped it or hid it."

I caught sight of Eddie in a tan suit and red tie.

"Ed," Eileen said. "Nice to see you." They double-kissed.

"You too, Mrs. Drazen."

I rarely saw Eddie Milpas in his social setting. He knew Jonathan from college, but to me, he was the guy in the engineering room who made everyone else nervous. So I nearly burst out laughing when he called Eileen Mrs. Drazen.

"Come to check on the catering?" Eileen asked.

"Came to steal away this lady," he replied, cocking his head toward me.

"Do we have to talk about business?" I asked.

"If you'd call me back—"

"My cue to leave," Eileen said. Without another word, she was gone, leaving me with Eddie and the constantly moving catering staff.

"I'm sorry," I said. "I was going to call you on Monday."

"Which Monday, exactly?"

"This coming—"

"Look, I know you have other things on your mind. So I'm not going to sit here and watch you fidget."

I crossed my arms. "I'm not fidgeting."

"Can I give you a piece of friendly advice?"

"No."

"Professional advice then. One hundred percent free. Get yourself an agent to filter your damn calls."

I laughed softly at the irony. That was exactly what I'd been trying to do when I met Jonathan.

Eddie continued, "If I wasn't friends with your boyfriend—"

"Husband."

"You'd miss out on the opportunity of a lifetime if I didn't happen to be at this party."

"Okay, you've got my attention."

"Your EP is releasing in a few weeks. Right about then, Quentin Marshall is doing another charity song. Single cut. Wide distribution. Like the Christmas one for the drought in Australia. Everyone's on it."

"Everyone?"

"Everyone. Omar. Brad Frasier. The Glocks. Benita. The list will knock you over. They have a space for a girl act like you, but here's the thing."

My heart pounded. That did sound like something groundbreaking for my career. Being associated with big names like that could get my name out to people who had never heard of me. It could give me credibility and standing. And if it was a little after the EP came out, even better.

"Okay," I said. "Tell me the thing."

"They have to herd all these cats, and that means it could record on a dime any time between the fifteenth and the thirtieth, and the big names? Well, they call the shots. They get there when they get there. The less-established artists have to be ready to go."

"I'm ready."

"Can you fly to New York tomorrow?"

"Tomorrow? New York?"

"Quentin Marshall? Hello?"

My throat went dry. I wanted to go. I wanted to get on a plane immediately and sit in the studio waiting for The Glocks to show up. I wanted to hear Omar sing in a studio. I could learn so much from that guy. He had a sound no one could emulate. If I could watch him, I was sure I'd pick up some tips.

"I don't know," I said.

"You don't know?"

"I have to ask Jonathan."

He put up his hands. "Fine. You have until tomorrow."

"Tomorrow is Sunday."

"Music doesn't take the weekend off."

"Okay. I'll call you by tomorrow night."

"Noon. That's the best you get. I have a line of people who would scratch your eyes out for this opportunity."

"Monica," Margie said, poking her head in. "We need you at the piano."

I glanced at the counter before following Margie. The catering staff hovered over a cake, lighting thirty-three candles. It seemed like enough fire to burn the house down, but that was the point. A man who almost died at thirty-two deserved every single flame.

Stop.

I needed to stop obsessing over the transplant. I'd given my worry a wide berth, as if it was insurance against something bad happening, but I'd let a healthy concern metastasize into a cancer. I had been perfectly happy letting it take over my life until I dreaded singing "Happy Birthday" because it sounded like a dirge.

I knew where the piano was from my last visit, when Sheila had insisted I play. I'd thought she was trotting me out like a trained monkey, which I resented for a few seconds, but once my fingers hit the keys, I realized what she'd done. I'd played "Wade in the Water" for his family, and music did what music does: it brought us together and gave us something to talk about. It was a way into our shared humanity. I'd loved music before I loved my husband, and it would outlast the two of us.

As I stroked out a scale in the parlor with thirty people in attendance, I let myself love it again. I caught Jonathan's eye across the room. He was fingering an apple with his nephew David. I knew the positioning. Split-fingered fastball. David, at ten, was too young for that. I shook my head at Jonathan and took my hand from the keys long enough to wave my finger "no no" at him. He smiled, winked, and showed David the whipping motion that would get the ball to split, along with his nephew's young tendons.

He's not teaching our kids that.

"Up tempo, people!" I cried just as the cake appeared.

"Happy Birthday"—well, there's not much you can do with it when everyone's singing and not listening to the piano. I smiled. Fuck it. I gleefully let everyone else set the tempo, and I sang along in the dragged out rhythm. No one knew why I was smiling, not even Jonathan, who came up and leaned on the piano.

Sheila brought out the blazing white confection and placed it on the piano as we sang, "*yooooooooouuuu!*"

His face lit golden and his smile a true thing, from his beautiful candlelit green eyes to his borrowed heart, he blew out his candles. Or tried. No one could blow out thirty-three candles (and one for good luck) in one breath.

"Nice effort," I said, standing.

He put his arm around me, and we blew together. I clapped and faced him. I wanted a kiss, but he glanced at the cake, then at me, then back at the cake, then at me, as if he was trying to tell me something. I looked down at it, thinking we'd missed a candle.

And we had. One little bugger was still bopping along, but I didn't blow it, because inside the ring of candles sat an open, frosting-caked velvet box, and inside the box was a ring.

"Jonathan?"

He plucked the candle out of the cake. "That was the candle I hold for you." He blew it, and the flame popped up again.

Thirty people and ten kids said, "*Awwww.*"

He pursed his lips in a smile. "I didn't know there would be so many people here."

Margie took the candle from his fingers. It still burned. It must have been one of those parlor trick candles, and it was sweet.

"What are you doing?" I asked, still confused. He guided me back onto the piano stool, and I sat. "We're already married."

"Not properly," he said, picking the ring out of the box. "Not on my own power and not for the right reasons."

Were there dozens of people in the room? I couldn't hear them. I couldn't see them. Only this man, this king, getting on his knee in front of me.

"Jonathan, you don't have to. I…"

"You going to give me your hand or not?"

"I can't." I put them in the corners of my eyes as if to press the tears away. "I'm using them. Hang on."

"Get on with it!" a male voice called from the crowd.

"Shut the fuck up, Pat!" someone else said.

Jonathan touched my left wrist, and I brought my hand down. I didn't wear the borrowed diamond anymore. Just the key ring wedding band.

"Will you marry me, Monica?" I sniffed back a bunch of tears, and before I could answer, he continued, looking at me. "Will you have a normal engagement with me? Will you get to know me on any given Tuesday?" He shook his head quickly, as if making it all up on the spot and discarding an idea. "Can we plan a real wedding and argue over seating arrangements? Can we find the things we agree on naturally? Flowers. Invitations. Whatever is important to *us*. I want us to be right with the world. I want us to take our time, because you're worth it. We are worth it. Nothing skimped or rushed. You deserve all of it. Everything."

Doing it all over. A second chance at a mask of normalcy. He wasn't rethinking or going backward. He was giving me a gift.

"I love you," I whispered through my tears. "I want you. Everything."

He slipped the ring on my finger. The diamond was huge and the color of sunshine.

"A canary diamond," he said. "For my songbird."

"Gross, Uncle Jon!"

Jonathan turned around toward David, who had a face like kneaded dough at the thought of icky grown-up love.

"Yeah, gross," a laughing, adult voice called out.

Jonathan glanced at me for half a second, and I saw mischief in those eyes. I didn't have a moment to tell him not to do whatever it was he was about to do, before he scooped up a swipe of white frosting from his cake and flung it at his tormentor.

"Quiet, Patrick!" Jonathan said.

Impulse moved my arm. I scooped up another bunch of frosting and flung it at my husband and fiancé, coating the bottom half of his face in a buttercream goatee. "Be nice to the guests!"

He blew, spraying me in vanilla, and everyone laughed and clapped. David, seeing the world as only a ten-year-old could, recognized an opportunity when he saw one. He mashed his hand in the cake then flung it at both of us. Jonathan, not to be out-immatured by a ten-year-old, whipped around and threw a mess of it at his nephew, with half of it getting on Eddie.

"Hey, asshole!" Eddie shouted.

"Language!" Sheila called, too late.

Her son threw another handful of cake at her. The young pitcher had great aim, getting his mother in the face with white confection.

"You!" Sheila said with a pointed finger.

I shut the cover over the piano keys just in time, because all hell broke loose. Cake flew everywhere. Laughter. Squeals. My god, the cake must have been huge. I was covered. Jonathan was covered. Everyone I could hit with a lump of cake was covered, and we were all laughing through beards of white frosting and fruit filling. The kids were licking the floor. Eileen slipped on a wad of cake and laughed, and her granddaughter put a handful down Eileen's shirt. Leanne fell when she tried to help Eileen up, and Jonathan, my beautiful king, put his arms around me and kissed cake off my lips.

"Goddess," he whispered, even though in the chaos, he didn't have to. No one was paying attention to us.

"Yes, Jonathan. Yes. I'll marry you."

"Let's take our time." He kissed my cheek, sucking frosting off.

Our time.

He was giving me permission to stop counting the months and years. Permission to let it happen as it would, to stop using worry as a paper-thin bulwark against the tides of fate. This was our time. However long it was, it belonged to us.

~

THE STAFF HAD MADE short work of the mess. Clothing had been stripped off, some laundered, some left in bags, some rinsed and worn wet. Sheila had loaned me a pair of pale blue velour sweatpants and a white shirt with a neck so wide it fell off my shoulder. It was probably the best party I'd been to in my life.

"I love this on you," Jonathan said, pressing his lips to my bare shoulder. We sat at the piano in the empty parlor as I played a soft jazzy thing.

"It doesn't go with the ring."

"I can't wait to see how that looks on you naked."

"It's beautiful. I love it." I did. I had a hard time keeping my eyes off it.

"I'm not trying to take away our marriage, goddess. You need to know that."

"I know."

"But it was hasty."

I sighed. Yes, it had been hasty, and for all the wrong reasons, but I hadn't thought about it that deeply. I hadn't thought about anything deeply in the past six months, because it hurt. I had the feeling I wouldn't be able to avoid it anymore.

"I got you a birthday present," I said.

"What do you get the guy who has everything?" He brushed his lips on my shoulder and drew his fingertips along the back of my neck.

I smiled, and a ball of hitched breaths gathered in my throat. He thought he had everything. I had no idea I'd married such an optimist. "I was supposed to play this for you in front of everyone, but you stole my limelight with this big stinking rock."

"They had a bigger one, but it was imperfect."

"It's not the size of the boat."

"Yes, it is. It's a buoyancy thing, see." He motioned with the flat of his hand, swaying it. "Too small and it sinks."

I laughed, and he laughed with me.

"Do you want to hear your song or not?"

"More than anything."

I took a deep breath. "I want you to know, I wrote one before, and it was all about what we've been through in the past six months. And I hate it. It was... I don't know. It was ugly, and it dwelled on things that weren't important."

"Can I hear it?"

"No." I hit the first notes definitively and found my opening tempo. "It's short."

"Sing it twice."

"You ready, Drazen?"

"I'm ready, Drazen."

I sang it quietly for an audience of one. I wasn't confident enough that it would survive me belting it out. Not until I did a few hundred rewrites.

How fragile it is
    And how real it all feels
    I can touch it, taste it
    Hold it like a baby forever
    But that's not the deal

I am your ever
    You are my after
    I am your altar
    You are my prayer

Where do I end
    And you begin
    Because I'm untied sometimes
    And we're a dandelion seed in the wind
    I'm a seed or a flower.
    Or I'm a breath or a wish

I am your heart
    You are my beat
    And I am your voice
    And you are my song

"Happy birthday," I said, letting my hands slip off the keys. "Many more. Many, many more."

He kissed me, then I kissed him. His skin smelled like cake, and his tongue tasted of salt water. We wrapped our arms around each other, connected at the mouth, as if we were passing a common soul between us.

CHAPTER 64

MONICA

She was most perfect in nudity. I left her standing there, hands at her sides, in front of my chair so I wouldn't have to move to watch her change. I put my elbows on my knees and folded my hands together, leaning forward. She was an arm's length away, but I didn't reach for her.

"Look straight ahead, Monica."

I knew what it did to her when I kept her in stasis. I'd known the first night when I'd sent her upstairs naked, and I knew now, after my birthday party, with the canary diamond heavy on her finger, that her body was changing before my eyes. In trying to stand still, she was acutely aware of my gaze on her. If she stood still and I kept my concentration, she'd be soaking wet and very close before I even touched her.

Her nipples hardened in the cool night air. The triangle between her legs was a promise of compliance and unyielding pleasure. The ocean outside the open balcony door would be the background noise to the melody of her cries.

Slowly, I reached my hand forward and touched her belly. It quivered like the undulating ocean behind me. I drew the finger down between her legs and stroked inside her thigh. Her body reacted involuntarily, and I took my hand back.

"I'm not going to fuck you," I said. "You're already bruised everywhere I want to put my dick." I kissed her navel then pulled away.

"My mouth is in great shape," she said.

"So is mine." I stroked her gently, awakening her nipples. "What if I laid you on that bed and pulled your legs apart. Just the tip of my tongue on your cunt. If I was gentle, would you come, do you think?"

"Yes. I would."

"Do you like your ring?"

"I love it."

I stood and wedged my foot between hers, pushing her legs apart. She was used to it and spread them without a stumble. I went behind her. She was framed by the ocean, the curves of her ass blue and black in the evening light. I got on my knees, close to her so she could feel my breath. I waited until the tension was so taut it felt as if it would break like rock candy.

I brushed my finger inside her thigh. She was painted in angry bruises there too. I'd stopped feeling guilty about inflicting damage; I knew the difference between hurt and harm.

"I'm sorry about the party. About worrying you. I was joking, not thinking."

"I'll die if you do that again."

I brushed my fingers over her soft wet lips, slightly touching the dampness.

"I just..."

"Go ahead," I said.

"That hospital. The smells. The colors. You. It claws at me. In my sleep, I hear the doctors whispering. I dream you're dying in a room I can't find. When I think of it, I just think of you in pain. It hurt me. And I'm sorry I'm being self-involved."

"You're not being self-involved." I kissed the small of her back.

"I dread it. I know I'm going to have to go back there with you, and the dread hangs on me."

I rested my cheek against the curve of her spine and put my arms around her waist. She didn't move her hands, ever obedient when in scene. I could hear her lungs through her rib cage as they let out short, sharp breaths.

"I didn't give you permission to cry," I said gently.

"I'm sorry."

I pulled away from her and stood. "On the bed, goddess. Facedown. Hands under your thighs. And face the window."

She did it, and when she automatically put her ass up in ready position, my dick went completely rigid. I pressed her ass down until she was totally flat against the bed. She watched me peel off my clothes. I put pajama bottoms on so I wouldn't distract her.

"Wait here."

I went into the bathroom for lotion. The last time I'd done that, I'd seen her negative pregnancy test. I thought about that thing every time I went in there. The burden of it was so heavy that I often went down the hall to piss.

"Are we still in scene?" she asked when I sat at the edge of the bed.

"No." I put a blob of lotion in my hand and closed it into a fist to warm the lotion.

"I want you to fuck me."

"Nope."

"Why not?"

"Because it's my birthday, and I can do whatever I want." I put the lotion on her back and slowly dragged my hands down from her shoulder blades to her waist.

Her eyes fluttered closed. I put more weight on the heels of my hands and moved them back up to her shoulders. She groaned.

"What were you and Eddie talking about?" I asked. She stiffened. "Relax. It's just a question. Did he upset you?" I worked my hands over her shoulders and down her biceps.

"No. But there's a thing in New York. I don't think I can make it."

"No?"

She made a noise in her throat that was a cross between "no" and "that feels nice."

"The last two weeks have been good, goddess. Really good." I focused on her shoulders for a second then moved back down her body. I stopped at her ass, which, in all its beauty, was welted and tender. I pressed my thumbs into the sides of her spine and moved back up.

"Mmm."

"You are everything. My everything. There's nothing I'd change about you. And that includes your talent and ambition."

"I don't want to be away from you," she grumbled.

"I'm bound to you wherever you are. You know that, right?"

She opened her eyes and looked at me through the web of hair. "Come with me."

"No. I have things to do here."

"Like what?"

"Hush." I moved the hair away and kissed her cheek, then I grabbed the lotion and moved to the end of the bed. "You need to make your life happen. If I hadn't been sick, you'd come and go as you pleased. As *we* pleased. That's what I want for you."

The insides and backs of her thighs couldn't be touched. Her ass either. What a gorgeous mess. I'd planted that rattan thinking I might use it, but I had no idea how effective it was. I gave her feet and calves attention, rubbing away her worry and stress.

"We need to live fully, goddess. We both need to live as if we could die tomorrow, and we have to plan for a future where you're a hundred and ten."

She moaned. I'd promised her my mouth, and my dick wanted hers, but when I finished rubbing her feet, she was fast asleep.

CHAPTER 65

MONICA

I CALLED Eddie from the back deck while Jonathan had his run, and I told him I was going to New York. Laurelin dropped into the lounge chair next to me in her sensible little sneakers and zip-up purple fleece.

"You're going again?" she asked.

"Yeah. New York. It's a big deal, kind of. Why?"

"I have a week away coming. Jerry is taking me to—"

"You can't!" I sat up straight in my chair, tingling with adrenaline. "No, I mean. You can but not now. Please!"

"Don't worry." She put her hand on my shoulder. "I'll set him up. He'll be fine."

I wanted to support her, and I wanted her to have a nice time. I wanted Jonathan to be fine. But the reality of him being alone wasn't making it from my brain to my mouth. No, worry was taking a detour through my heart instead.

"You know what?" I said, leaning back in my chair. "I'll just stay home. It's not that big a deal."

Laurelin leaned back and put her foot on the little glass-and-metal table. She must have thought I was schizophrenic. "You know, if this was my house, I'd never want to leave either. I'd just sit here and gestate all day."

I laughed, and she smiled at me.

"I think you can go," she said after a minute.

"Nah."

"I think you *should* go." I didn't answer, just tilted my head a little, and she continued. "I'm not going to be here forever, and you all need to learn how to function. I mean, these issues? The pills and the way he has to log everything?

They aren't going anywhere. It'll always be this way. And you hovering over him because you're scared, I get it. But at some point, you have to let go."

I set my jaw. "I'm not letting him go."

"You know what I mean."

I did. I knew she meant I had to stop mothering him, but I'd taken it the exact wrong way because it served my immediate purpose. If I acknowledged that I knew what she meant and that I'd heard it, I'd have to admit she was right.

CHAPTER 66

JONATHAN

I RAN FAR AWAY. Far enough to be out of Monica's earshot and then some. I made
it to the crowded part of the beach and trotted to the street, trying to shake a
feeling that if Monica went to New York, things would get disorganized and
neglected.

I'd had a mitt when I was about eleven. It was a Rawlings Gold. The best. And
I wore it in just the way I liked it. One spring afternoon, I was dicking around with
my cousins in the yard, tossing the ball around and trying out new curse words. We
went inside to play video games, and I left my glove in the grass as I'd done dozens
of times.

It never rains in Los Angeles, unless you leave your glove out. Then it pours,
and the leather hardens. Stupid negligence can turn into disaster. I got another
glove, but it was never the same. My hand grew before I could wear it in right, and
I always felt an acute loss I couldn't explain.

I didn't want to treat Monica like a baseball glove. I didn't want it to rain on
her while my back was turned.

"Quentin?" I said when I got through to my friend. A dozen seagulls screamed
at me when I interrupted them on a bench.

Quentin Marshall answered in his Aussie clip. He was a rock star specializing in
charity work, and I'd written his foundation a few checks over the years. "Drazen!
How are you doing? I heard about the heart, mate. That's tough stuff."

"It keeps life interesting."

"Bet it does."

He paused, and I heard a siren in the distance and the belch of a city bus. Typical New York ambient noise.

"So what can I do for you?" he asked.

"You invited my wife to sing with you for something?"

"Yeah, I hope that's all right? She's got a great set of pipes. And the cause could use your help as well. There are kids dying of dehydration every day."

"You can always count on my help. But if Monica decides to go, I want you to do something for me."

"Just say it, and you got it."

How was I supposed to phrase this without sounding like a sicko stalker? I meant no harm by it, of course, and it wasn't as though she hadn't traveled before, but I felt differently than I did months ago, even weeks ago. "If there's anything she needs, or if there's something special you think she might need, even if she doesn't know what it is—can you make sure she gets it? I want her taken care of."

"That's it?"

"That's it."

"Mate, I will treat her like a precious flower. On my honor."

"Thank you."

"My pleasure."

We hung up. The ocean pounded the edges of the rocks into smooth stones, a millennias-long process I witnessed for a few minutes before I got up and continued my run.

CHAPTER 67

MONICA

I'D BEEN AWAY from post-surgery Jonathan before. I'd flown to places I'd never been to and experienced them through hollow eyes and a worn-down heart. I couldn't say my trip to New York was any different. I was still worn out; I was still dragged home by tight-twisted strands. I was still worried. But something had changed. The worry wasn't colored a dark grey, and my thoughts of Jonathan weren't painful. I didn't feel guilty. I felt alive, vibrating, humming with potential, and I missed him. I missed his company, his laugh, his touch. I missed his enfolding presence beside me. The guilt left a vacuum in its absence, and nature, in its abhorrence, filled it with hope.

I flew commercial. I wanted to be surrounded by people. I wanted to feel the hum of life in the comings and goings of people: the babies crying; the pilots and stewardesses in their neat little packs, rolling suitcases whirring behind; the bright colors of the snack stand in the artificial lights; and the carpets worn where people walked.

I didn't make up a story when I told Jonathan I didn't need his plane. Instead of saying something facile about scheduling, I tried to express my need, as intangible as it was, and he understood, and agreed, and asked if I was going to fly coach.

That didn't seem necessary. Marrying a Drazen had its privileges.

He'd laughed and held me, offering his team to set up the flights. As close as we'd been in bed, or at play, or when he was rubbing my back and telling me how much he loved me, when I explained why I wanted to fly commercial and he understood, I felt truly married. He understood me. I could tell him even the worst nonsense, and he did more than agree. He became a part of me, tapped into my thoughts, a partner.

I'd thought I knew what that meant, but I didn't.

I was so high, I chatted incessantly with the guy next to me about music and dance. He was a French choreographer, and of course he gave me a definite "I'd be happy to fuck you" vibe even after seeing my ring. But I didn't care. I wasn't sleeping with him. I could still enjoy the conversation. I was married to a king, after all. I didn't have to concern myself with what other people wanted from me.

A bodybuilder in a suit waited for me at the gate with a handwritten sign that said "Mrs. O'Drassen."

"Hi," I said. "Are you Dean?"

"Yes, ma'am." He took my bag. "I'll drive you to the hotel to drop your things. I'm hired out for as long as you need me, so you can call any time."

"Great. There's a dinner tonight. In Hell's Kitchen. Can you take me there?"

"Absolutely."

I'd never been to New York, and I couldn't believe how crowded, tight, old, and yet shiny, spacious, and vibrant it was. And this was just from the window of a silver Rolls Royce.

Jonathan had set me up at the Stock New York, the sister hotel of the one I used to work at, citing the hotel he'd just sold as "too grubby." Everything was perfect. The room was huge, slick, with precisely designed proportions and windows that let onto a little patio that I wanted to sit on with my husband.

Jonathan was in the process of transferring his hotel on the Lower East Side. Hotel D, on Avenue D. His fourth and a huge risk. He shook his head whenever he talked about it. He'd said it was too small for me. Too old, too trendy, too loud—he had a million reasons why I should stay at the Stock. After few minutes of listening to him, I knew why he was keeping me away from D. He didn't think it was safe. Who even knew why. He'd been known for putting beautiful hotels in up-and-coming neighborhoods like canaries in a coal mine. Maybe this little bird hadn't gotten out.

The Stock had every imaginable trend-forward trapping. Wool rugs with barely discernible patterns that looked as if they'd been through a war zone in exactly the right places. Maple and mahogany paneling. Blackened brass chandeliers with frosted glass shades that curved in ways that were surprising and yet inevitable. Good-looking staff in sharp uniforms.

I was wrung out from the flight, but I shook it off by taking a coldish shower, and I left before I missed Jonathan more.

"Ah, I know your face!" Omar said when I showed up for the pre-studio dinner.

Hartley Yallow and the Trudy Crestley were already there, and the table was huge.

"I know yours too," I said. Everyone knew Omar's face. He had classic South American good looks that came from an Argentinian mother and an Italian father. His voice, however, was something no genetic pairing could predictably create.

I sat down, and we ordered. More people came. I could hardly keep up with the names, because even though I knew them all, I was overwhelmed and in love with that moment. Ivan Braf showed up with his wife, and I envied her presence. I wanted Jonathan next to me, even if he didn't say a word. It wasn't that I wanted to steal moments before his death; I wanted this moment to be complete, and without him, it wasn't.

But it was good. Very good.

Quentin Marshall showed up with the guys from The Breakfront. "Monica Faulkner," Quentin said in his thick Aussie accent. "So happy you could come. Now we all have to take our game up a notch." He wagged his finger around the table.

"Oh, I don't think—"

"We need her on the chorus," Omar said, pointing his fork. "Flat out."

"*You* were on the chorus," Quentin replied.

"I—" I couldn't finish a denial.

"There's no point having her here unless you showcase her voice," Omar argued.

"That's true," Quentin replied.

"Hang on!" I said, putting my fist down. I didn't watch for their reaction, because I knew I didn't have a second before they'd interrupt. "Even if all this is true, it's irrelevant. My name won't sell the record, and the point is to *sell the record*. Nobody knows me, so showcasing me gets you nowhere."

"She has a point," Trudy said.

I nodded to her, and she nodded back.

"Fine!" Quentin proclaimed. "We rehearse tomorrow and try it out. Once Victory Spontaine gets in, whenever that is, we decide once and for all." He clacked the ice at the bottom of his glass. "My drink is empty." He twisted in his seat to look for a waiter.

I hadn't realized until that moment that the rest of the restaurant found our gathering very interesting. Black rectangles hovered over heads, and little phone flashes went off. The dinner was publicity. I hadn't thought of that. I wished I'd worn lipstick or done something with my hair.

Omar, who was next to me, leaned close. "I'm fighting for you to get the chorus."

"Why?"

"Because you have the most unique voice I've ever heard."

I swallowed. "Well, my point stands."

"If we want to sell the record, it has to be a *great record*. That's the number one priority."

I couldn't believe he was saying that to me. Omar D'Alessio. Holy shit. I couldn't believe he was even talking to me.

"You're pretty great, Omar."

"I never said I wasn't." He put his arm around me. "But there's room for another."

He kissed my cheek, and I felt accepted as a musician and artist. Jonathan was the only thing missing from that moment. I wished he could have seen it.

CHAPTER 68

JONATHAN

Laurelin puttered around the kitchen, putting ingredients into two blender jars that were meant to hold me for two days. She put measured portions of vitamins, greens, milk, powdered puke, and dried shit into a healthful grotesquerie of layers that would be in the fridge for my reluctant consumption.

I didn't have to think about it. I just had to blend it and choke on it. She'd already taken my blood pressure (one-ten over seventy), drawn blood (a monthly task), and hooked me up to an EKG (looked good). The meds for the week were set out so I didn't have to count them. The privilege of money. I could pay someone to keep me from the mundanities of my illness.

"Where's he taking you?" I asked.

"We're driving up to Monterey," she replied in a singsong voice. "Donny is staying with Grandma, so it's kind of a last hurrah before I get huge."

"Good for him."

"I have everything you need here until Wednesday. Then you follow this list on the fridge to make new. I'd make them for you for the whole ten days, but the ingredients are perishable."

"I wish they'd perish," I said in passing just to make a joke. I was looking at the news on a tablet and was on humor autopilot.

"Oh stop. Be cheerful." I looked up at her to see her holding up her finger. "Twenty years ago, you'd be the one who perished. And when you complain, people think you won't do with you're supposed to when they're gone." She winked and went back to arranging my fridge.

"Are you trying to tell me something?"

"Attitude is everything." More lilting vowels to express something serious. "You missed a few days in your log." She flicked her wrist at my little blue leather book. "You need to take it with you everywhere. Even if you're going to a restaurant."

I rolled my eyes and immediately felt like an adolescent or worse. I ran through the international news as if the tablet was on fire, trying to not feel over-mothered. I hired her to do this. I couldn't get mad about it. "Okay," was all I could get out.

"What is this?" She took a plastic container out of the crisper and held it at my eye level.

I looked at it then back at the tablet. "Monica's Brazilian chimichuri. Her mother was over the other night. The two of them ate it like... I don't know." I waved my hand. "They slather it on everything like they're trying to scald their faces. It's blowtorch-hot."

"Oh, that sounds good."

"Does spicy food bother you? With the pregnancy?"

"Nope."

"Take it then." I scrolled through the financials. "We have two."

"Really?" She peeled the top off and took a whiff. "Oh my God, this smells so good." She put it under my nose, and I pushed her away. "Oh, I forgot. Well, I understand. Donny doesn't like spicy food either." She put the container in her bag of medicinal crap.

"Donny's three," I said.

Laurelin shrugged. "He's a good boy." She patted my shoulder. "Like you."

I didn't want to fuck my nurse at all. Not even a little. But I wanted to spank her. Hard.

I turned back to my tablet and tapped the local news, missed, and hit entertainment, which I couldn't care less about. But I let it load, and probably because Monica's name was associated with my account, or the wifi, or because it was the top entertainment story of the minute to people who weren't married to her, her picture was front and center.

Her and some swarthy guy. His arm was around her. He was kissing her cheek at a restaurant, and she was smiling, looking at the ceiling. She looked happy and carefree. In her element. And on his face? That was a simple prelude to fucking her. I couldn't take my eyes off the picture and that look in his eye. His fingertip was on her shoulder as if testing his right to touch her.

I knew my wife didn't have cheating in her heart. But I also knew men, and that asshole had her body on his mind. He wanted to fuck her. My wife. Mine. I wanted to take his skin and peel it off him. Rip him apart.

"Mister Drazen?"

Laurelin's voice sounded a million miles away.

"What?"

"Are you all right?"

I tore my face from the screen and looked at her. Her brow was knit, and she was packed to go.

"I'm fine."

"I think I should take your BP again."

"No, no. I'm fine. Let me walk you out." I smiled, but I knew no joy reached my eyes. I hustled her to the front door.

"Mister Drazen," she said when we got there, "really, you need to avoid stress."

"Stress is part of life. Don't worry. I'm good."

She left. I went upstairs and paced. Looked at my watch. Did some math. I couldn't keep Monica enclosed. I couldn't keep men from wanting her. She only got more beautiful every day, and men were disgusting creatures who cared for nothing but the daily mounting pressure in their ball sacks.

I trusted her. With every cell in my body, I trusted her. But when I thought about how I'd almost lost her, how she hadn't been happy and I'd just kept letting shit slide, I wondered what would have happened if I hadn't gone to the studio that day and reasserted myself.

She could be away. She could travel. Her career was necessary to her happiness, and more than anything, I wanted her to be happy.

So why did that picture bother me? We'd reestablished ourselves. I trusted her. She needed to do her job and make her art. What was the problem?

The problem was that we had a disconnect, and that disconnect was me. She'd come back to me fully, but I hadn't broached my side of the distance. I hadn't gone to her with an open heart the way she'd come to me.

That was going to change.

CHAPTER 69

MONICA

THE BALCONY HAD room for two, maybe three if everyone liked each other. It overlooked a tiny cobblestone street in Chinatown and onto the tops of the beat-down signs in Cantonese. Manhattan had many of the same structures as Los Angeles. They were straight up from the ground at ninety degrees, had corners, straight walls, windows, and roofs. Some buildings were made well and some were sad. But the whole proportion of the place was different. It couldn't be absorbed by car; it could only be experienced on foot or bike. Then the flower boxes, cornerstones, and cobbled streets took on their natural life.

I had no business being on the balcony off the studio, since Omar and Trudy were smoking and I wasn't about to even try it.

"It gives me my edge," Omar said. "Biggest secret in music is how many of us smoke."

"The other type of smoke, not such a secret," Trudy said.

She was a guitarist and could smoke her brains out for all I cared. From Omar, well, I admitted to being a little disappointed. I took so much care with my vocal chords. I could tell when there was a forest fire in Flintridge based on how my throat felt.

"Does he do this all the time?" I jerked my head toward the inside, where Hartley had abandoned his drums to throw up last night's party.

Trudy smashed her cigarette underfoot and blew a cloud carelessly. It landed in my face, and I resisted the urge to wave my hand in front of me.

"Constantly," she said. "But he never pukes. I think it's a flu or something."

"Oh." I tried to not look more worried than any normal person would. Normal people got the flu and just suffered through it. But I had a husband on immunosuppressants, and a flu could kill him.

"Quentin's looking for another drummer." Omar shrugged. "Or Franco can do it."

"Nope," Trudy said. "He's down with it too."

"What is it? A percussionist's strain?" I joked.

"All those guys hang out together. It's like incest without the sex."

I didn't know what came over me, but the words shot out of my mouth before I'd even thought about the logistics. "I know one. He can be here tomorrow. He has something today. He's really good."

"Do I know him?"

"He's from LA originally. So probably not. He's super-hot in indie circles."

"Not that husband of yours, is it?" Omar smiled a half moon of perfect white piano keys. It was the third time he'd mentioned Jonathan that day, as if he was trying to gauge my reactions.

"The only instrument Jonathan plays is me."

"That can be good or bad."

"He's a maestro, trust me."

I went inside. I'd wanted to learn from Omar, and he'd taught me a few things, but I was starting to feel as if it all came with a price. Maybe that price was simple flirtation and attention or maybe he expected more, but I was getting irritated with his off-color comments and sultry eyeballing.

Everyone was filing back into the studio. There were fifteen actual musicians. Some kept klatches of preeners and hangers-on. Others traveled alone. Add to that the engineers, press, security, and agents, and the room was as hot as a sweatbox and smelled only ten percent better.

I couldn't believe there wasn't a drummer among us, but it was worth a try. I found Quentin in the middle of eating a slab of crunchy fried fish, surrounded by people I didn't know.

"Hey," I said, trying to slink into the tiny room unobtrusively and failing.

"Faulkner! Everyone out!" He made shoo-shoo motions with his fingers, and everyone shooed. He closed the door behind them.

I hoped I wasn't stepping out of the frying pan with Omar and into the fire with Quentin.

"Sorry," he said, rooting around his leather messenger bag. "Not a big deal, but I didn't know what this was, so I didn't want to give it to you in front of everyone." He handed me a long, blue velvet box. "This was at reception with your name on it."

"Thank you," I said, taking it.

He slung the bag over his shoulder. "I have to find a drummer."

"No one in this building can do percussion? It's a house full of musicians."

"You have no idea how hard it is to find a good one."

"I kind of do."

"Evan Arden's in the bathroom puking his guts out, and he's on bass. If I can't find someone within the hour, we're all going home for the day." He made motions to leave but was so slow about it. He glanced at the velvet box then back at me. "Sorry, not trying to be nosy."

"Not trying?"

"Even straight guys like a little sparkle. Come on. Don't hold out."

I smiled. What could it be? Jonathan never disappointed me, but I was afraid it was a diamond-studded leather collar or a bracelet with the word SLAVE in emeralds. That might require a little more explaining than I was willing to do.

I held the box at my eye level and cracked it open so only I could see. Whatever it was, it didn't sparkle. I didn't know if that excited me or scared me. But it looked harmless enough. I opened it all the way.

"What is it?" he said, hand on the doorknob.

"It's a Sharpie." I turned it toward him. Indeed, right inside the bracelet box lay a black Sharpie. I could see from his expression that he was disappointed, as if he'd expected an actual bracelet in the bracelet box.

"What's it for?"

"I have no idea." I opened the little card that had been folded inside the lid. It was typed.

*Keep this with you, **goddess**.*

I closed it slowly.

"He's more of a romantic than I thought," Quentin said.

"You know him?"

"We have a long history of feeding children together."

"Is that why you hired me?" I said before I could catch it. That was a completely unprofessional thing to ask, and it made me look like an insecure ingrate.

"I hired you because Dionne Harber couldn't make it. I don't regret it." He winked at me and got away with it.

"Thanks. And I'm sorry, I didn't mean to imply my spot was bought."

"It wasn't. Trust me."

He left with a smile. I opened the velvet box again. Shook it. Looked under it. Turned the card over. Nothing special. I got my stuff ready to go.

Typically when I traveled, Jonathan and I spoke once a day, and our conversations were short and mostly about his medicines and appointments. But that was the old us. The miserable us. The couple treading water in a sea of doubt and unsaid truths. I didn't know or understand the couple we'd become, and I didn't think there was much precedent for it.

So I didn't know what he intended with the permanent marker, and I didn't know enough to be excited or anxious. I was only curious as we laid down some tracks, and I played my theremin for everyone in the studio while we waited for two other people to decide if they were too sick to continue.

"We're doing a small thing at a club after," Omar whispered in the hall outside the bathrooms. "You're invited."

"Thank you. I think I'm just going to bed."

"Alone? I bet we have the day off tomorrow." He put his hand on my wrist.

"You know I'm married, right, Omar?"

"Where is he?" He spread his arms, indicating the whole of the studio, New York, the world about us, where Jonathan wasn't.

Was he drunk? Who would make such an implication? What person in their right mind would assume my husband's presence was required for my fidelity?

The answer came to me in the tightness of Omar's jaw and the tension in his fingers. He was on something. Some white substance whispered in his ear that he was a god and entitled to whatever he felt like having.

I sighed. I'd really admired him. He sang like an angel, but he'd just been in the studio thirty minutes ago. I recalled the moments of inappropriate laughter and long space-outs when I'd thought he was preparing, but he'd been stoned the whole time. I knew how many artists worked stoned. I'd always told myself it was their thing and not my business, but suddenly I felt as if it was most certainly my business.

"My husband's home," I said, "waiting for me to call."

He looked at me as if he didn't believe me.

"Look," I continued, "I know what you've probably heard about me, and it may be all true. But this scene, the drugs, and the other shit? The partying until all hours? The fucking around? It's not my thing. And if that means I'll always be small time, well, it's okay."

He didn't move, as if stuck in that moment. "You think I got where I am because I party?"

"No, I—"

"No?"

I didn't think he'd coasted. Not at all. But he wasn't interested in hearing it. I'd insulted his talent and his manhood, and he was walking away with at least one intact.

"Break it down," he said firmly, his jaw still grinding. "You just said you'd be small time if you didn't party. You know what, girl? I've done everything I could to support you. I lifted you up the minute you got here. And this is the attitude you throw me? You think your pussy is dipped in gold? Well, fuck you."

He turned on his heel and went down the hall just as Rob Devon cut the turn and ran into the men's room as if his belly were on fire. In seconds, the hallway was silent again.

I dragged myself out the door, and Dean waited for me in the Rolls. I'd walked into the studio wrapped in confidence and love, and I was walking out feeling as if my expensive ride was an ugly appendage, a street sign pointing at my gold-plated cunt. God, I must make such a scene with this stupid car.

"Mrs. Drazen," Dean said by way of greeting.

"Hi, Dean."

"Back to the hotel?" He opened the back door.

"Yes, thanks."

I slid into the pristine comfort of the Rolls. It envelops you, that luxury. The money. The sense of well-being. That was the point, wasn't it? When the car started, there was no jolt, no rumble, just movement.

I called Jonathan as the streetlights streaked across the night sky, then stopped seamlessly at a stop sign, then started again.

"Hello, Monica," he said, and I wanted to cry.

"Hi."

"I see you're on your way back to the hotel?"

"Is this Dean telling you everything, or do you have a tracking device on me?"

"Yes to both. How are you?"

"Do you know the Rolls doesn't even obey the law of inertia? Like when Dean stops at the light, my body doesn't go forward a little. and when he starts again, I can feel it moving, but it's not like I feel my back against the seat. Did you know that?"

"I never noticed."

We went through a busy part of town, and I curled into the seat, watching the Saturday night crowds walk the streets. People crossing stared at the car, big packs and smaller groups, dressed for big things and made up for the lights and sounds, a single wave in an ocean of revelry.

"Did you get my present?" he said.

"Yes. I love it. How did you know I needed to write my name on all my tags?"

"Are you all right?"

"What time is it there?" I asked.

"Sun's just thinking about setting."

"Is it hot? Is it gloomy? Tell me things."

"It's nice. It's mid-June. Same as always. The marine layer burned off, and I can see... let me look... one two three four five clouds out the kitchen window. One is shaped like a rabbit. One is shaped like a guitar. It makes me think of you."

"What about the other three? What are they shaped like?"

"Big white turds."

I laughed. "Did you take your medicine?"

"Yes, Mom."

"And drink your shit shake?"

"Yes."

"And did you go for a run?"

"Yes. You never answered my question. Are you all right?"

I sighed. I knew he could hear it. I wanted him to. "I feel, I guess, not lonely. Not alone. Just separate. Separate from you, and separate from everyone here. It's... I can't pin it down. I guess it's not a bad feeling as much as it's a weird, disconnected feeling. Uncomfortable. I don't know."

I could hear him breathing, and the lawn mower outside our house, and the birds in Los Angeles.

"Would you believe me if I said I know how you feel?"

"Yeah."

Dean pulled up to the hotel. A doorman in a snazzy uniform was ready to open the door before the car stopped without a jolt. The inside of the hotel looked gilded and soft through the glass windows, as if the lights were colored gold.

"Do you have your marker?" Jonathan asked.

"Of course. I'll treasure it always."

"Hang up with me then and call back on the tablet. I want to see you."

Dean opened the door for me, and I hung up.

CHAPTER 70

MONICA

I'D KICKED my shoes off and dropped my bag before calling Jonathan from the iPad. He picked up on the first ring.

"How is the hotel?" he asked.

"It's a parody of itself." In the screen of the tablet, I saw he'd moved out to the side patio that overlooked the twinkling grid of the city. "Or a farce. I can't decide which." I pouted at him from the edge of the bed.

"I'll tell Sam you said so."

"I wanted to stay in D." I snapped the drapes open. Manhattan was dark and vibrant and closed tight in a granite-and-clay-brick embrace.

"It's in Alphabet City. There's piss in the doorways from the seventies. I already don't like you spending days in a studio in Chinatown."

"A little grit's kind of nice."

"Nice?" He leaned forward in his seat.

"Yeah, nice." I opened the patio door, holding my tablet out so he could see me.

"Turn the camera around," he said. "Show me the view."

I did, then I showed him the street below and the building across Lexington. "Not much to speak of," I said. "Except, yeah, New York's kind of fabulous."

"Go back inside."

I turned the tablet and looked at him in his dying-daylight rectangle. He was looking directly into the lens, which was right above the screen, and though the mic was tiny and tinny, I knew I was hearing his dominant voice.

"Put the tablet on the desk so I can see you."

I leaned it against the lamp. Seeing him inside that rectangle with our backyard behind him was somehow ridiculous. In the top right corner of the screen, a small box showed what he saw as I stood there. My face was off screen. I was only visible from neck to knees.

"Take your clothes off," he said casually yet firmly, as if asking me to pass the salt. As if it was no more than a courtesy to ask for what should be available to him without question.

I pulled my T-shirt over my head and watched myself take off my bra. My breasts bounced out, and I saw my hard nipples in the screen. Jonathan was impassive, tapping his thumbs together as if keeping a rhythm. I peeled off my pants, down to the lace thong I wore for him in his absence. I let him see it for a second, but he twisted his hand at the wrist in a "get on with it" motion. I got my thong off and stood before the tablet, naked neck to knees.

"Are you wet?" he asked.

"Yes."

"Check for me."

I put my hand between my legs. I saw it slipping down my belly in the screen, saw the way my knees bent a little when I spread my legs to accept my fingers.

"I'm wet," I said.

"Put your fingers in your mouth. And let me see."

I bent to look at him, lips puckered around my fingers, tongue curled around them. The pungent, sordid, sexy taste of my cunt filled my mouth. His eyes warmed with arousal.

"Go get the pen," he said.

I plucked it off the desk and showed him.

"Put the pen in your mouth. Get the desk chair. Sit in it, and put your feet on the desk. I want to see your beautiful cunt."

I wheeled the chair over, placing it in front of the desk. He waited, fingers laced together on the iPad screen. He was casual and intense at the same time, as if he didn't have to worry about me doing what he asked. He was just going to wait.

I put my feet up on the desk, exposing myself to him. I could see myself on the little corner of the screen, the soft part of me, the place where I was split in two, the fold of sensation between the smooth mass of skin, and I was shocked by the sight of it.

"That's mine," he said. "You understand, my wife, that everything I see there is mine?"

"Yes."

"You're wet, and that's mine too. No matter where you are, I own your cunt."

"It's yours. It's only for you. It's so wet for you."

"Mark it," he said.

It took me a second to understand, even with the Sharpie in my teeth. Then, seeing my thighs against the wet flesh between them, I knew what he meant. I popped the base free of the cap and leaned over, pressing the pen tip to my left inner thigh. I glanced up at him.

He gave a slight shake of his head. "You start on your right, at the knee."

I switched and pulled the skin to make it taut for the marker. Like his fingers, the Sharpie was firm and purposeful; like his tongue, it was damp and warm.

"Wherever you are," he said low and steady as I wrote his name, knee to crotch, "I own you. I own your filthy mouth. I own your dirty mind. When you get wet thinking about fucking, it's mine. Every drop from you. I own your every thought. You are my property."

I looked back at him. My breath was short. When I saw myself, the flesh between my legs was now exposed, wet, and swollen. "Jonathan's" marked my inner thigh, and a bolt of pleasure ran through me.

"This is crazy," I gasped. "I'm going to come."

"Not until you finish the other side."

"Okay." I didn't know if I would make it.

"No touching."

What was I supposed to put on the other side? I couldn't think. I glanced at him. A shadow of a smirk crossed his lips.

I started with the letter "P" a few inches from my center, the pen tip becoming him, his body, his intention, his attention. The tingling was a wall of sensation as I spelled "Property" down my leg. As I put the leg on the Y, the pressure had built up so much, I knew I didn't have long.

"Look at yourself," he said.

"I'll come if I do."

"No, you won't. Not until I say."

But I didn't. I just looked at the marks between my legs. I was owned. Property. Without desire or ambition, a slave without responsibility or longing. Free.

"Look, Monica," he said sternly, and I looked.

Jonathan's Property.

"Yes," I said, flooded with a tsunami of an orgasm that pushed at the walls of my control. "You own me. I am your subject." I could barely speak through the throb. "You are my master."

"I'm going to put my cock inside you, everywhere, and I'm not going to ask first. You're going to spread your legs and submit yourself. Your mouth. Your cunt. Your tight little ass. I'm going to hurt you. I'm going to crack you open and suck you dry."

"Oh, god, when you talk like that." Every word rushed me to orgasm, but like the door at the end of the hall in a movie, it got closer and farther at the same time. Juice dripped over my ass. How long would he do this? "I am yours," I said, because I wanted to say, "Let me come."

"Put your fingers inside yourself."

I slid two fingers in me and groaned.

"Shh. Over your clit. But don't come yet."

I didn't know how it would be possible. My clit was swollen and soaked. I touched it gently.

"Would you like to come?" he asked.

"Yes, please."

"Move your fingers very slowly, and don't make a sound. I want to see how your body moves."

I moved my finger in circles.

"Slower, not enough to come. Not yet."

But it didn't matter. I was on the edge. The dam burst, and I came, first bending over, mouth open, face rigid, then arching my back until I was leveraged on the edge of the desk and thrusting my pussy at the camera. When I came down, looking at him with my hair disheveled and my hand cupping the throbbing mass between my legs, I smiled.

He shook his head. "You are in so much trouble."

"I'm sorry, I couldn't—"

"No talking. When I see you, be ready for the spanking of your young life."

He winked and cut the call. I was left staring at a dead iPad.

I wanted to go home. I wanted his arms around me, his sharp scent, his cruel hands, and his unforgiving mouth. I held my phone as if I was testing its weight. I could book a flight right now and show up naked on our doorstep.

But what if the tightness in my stomach was the flu? Everyone was getting it. But it didn't feel like any flu I'd ever had, because it was just tight. No more, no less. Like a butterfly's torn ligament. But if I had it, I couldn't go home.

Between my legs, the words *Jonathan's Property* was scrawled in Sharpie. I was his, and I wanted to go home to him. Could I go home the day after tomorrow for a weekend? And if so, should I? I could have the flu. I could be carrying it. No, I couldn't go. I couldn't risk his health, because complications were a cotton candy funnel rolling around the edge of the drum. It looked like nothing, then not too much, then an insane cloud of pink sugar before you even blinked, and we were back to dying at Sequoia.

I couldn't go home if I was sick.

The phone buzzed in my hand. It was Quentin.

—Omar's got it. We're off for a week—

I could go now. Tomorrow.

—Ok got it—

I tapped the phone to my upper lip, looking out over Lexington Avenue. So many people everywhere, in a city that never sleeps.

*—Do you have the number for
a doctor who keeps late hours?—*

—Sure. You all right?—

<blockquote>
—I'm fine just want to see if I have
this flu thing. I want to go home and
can't be sick. Pls don't tell Jonathan…
it's a surprise if I'm home early—
</blockquote>

An address and number came through. I believed I was being diligent about my husband's health, but I knew that no matter what the doctor said, I was going home. I'd rather talk to Jonathan through a wall than a phone line.

CHAPTER 71

JONATHAN

I CUT the call because I was frustrated and I couldn't show it. Watching her come thousands of miles away wasn't good enough. Her willful obedience drove me to distraction, and her accidental disobedience made my palms sting with the longing for her ass under them. I wanted to mark her with my own hand. Make her come with my body. Fill her with myself, and there I was in my kitchen, with a dick hard enough to crack the granite countertop.

This wasn't working. A thousand times this wasn't working.

And why? Because I didn't want to travel. Because the thought of being too far from Sequoia froze me solid. And a plane? I couldn't get the image of my heart jumping from my chest out of my mind, and the thought of isolating myself on a plane made that image play and replay until the organ squeaked out a puddle of blood in the leather seat.

But being away from her wasn't working either. She was getting recognized for her talent, and that meant she was becoming desirable to a certain kind of asshole. She was trustworthy. I didn't have to assert myself. I didn't have to lay claim on her. I was an intelligent man with a wife who had laid down her life for him. I knew she'd never betray me. I could feel the fidelity in her heart.

But I did need to assert myself, and the thought of men who wanted to fuck her breathing the same air as her made me boil. I was a child. An unreasonable, hateful brat.

All true. And so what?

I was hungry, and the fridge was empty of anything I wanted. I snapped out my box of pills and the last jar of chimichuri.

If staying close to her and keeping those men off her meant I got on a plane and went where she went and did what she did, then my anxieties about traveling would have to just shut the fuck up. I took a handful of pills and choked them down with warm tap water. Then another, swallowing more frustration than vitamins, more anger than medicine. My body was going to reject this heart just because my mind was rejecting everything I'd held on to for months.

That picture with Omar. If I trusted her, why had it burned me? Why did it feel like a punch in the gut?

Because I'd left her alone. I'd deserted her. She didn't need a leash. She didn't need a reminder of her vows or commitments, but I'd assumed she didn't need or want my presence. I'd accepted that because it was convenient for me. I didn't have to go anywhere if I made it her fault I wasn't going. I'd been responsible for that picture and the state of our current discontent.

I ripped open a bag of bread and jammed a piece in the chimichuri. The oil and flakes of parsley dripped off it. The peppers were invisibly green in the mix, and I didn't give a fuck. I ate it. Cringed. God, that chemical burn. How could I have eaten stuff this hot and not needed a skin graft after? How could this not be damaging tissue? I smelled flesh burning and knew it was in my mind. I curled up the bread and scooped out more, eating it before the burn from the last bite had dissipated.

I didn't swallow. I kept it in my mouth, nurturing it, letting it hurt me, rejecting whatever weakness this new heart had brought, because they were reactions to something that had happened to someone else. They weren't me. I had the opportunity and responsibility to reject the changes I didn't want, and goddamnit, this was excellent chimichuri.

I ate it, leaning over the counter, until the last flake of parsley was gone and my eyes ran with tears. And as if all the new traits I'd gained feared I'd leave, I had the desire to go for a run.

"That, I'm keeping," I said as I dropped the empty jar into the sink. "I like it."

I laced up my sneakers and took my phone, because this run had a purpose. I had no more excuses. In the middle of the run, as I was whipping wet sand, I slowed to a walk and called Dr. Solis.

"He's with a patient," his assistant said. "Should he call you back?"

She'd presented me with the perfect opportunity to bail. His call back might not go through, or maybe I wouldn't pick up. If he called back late enough, I wouldn't be able to get Jacques online for a flight plan.

"I'll wait."

"Is this an emergency, Mr. Drazen?"

"No. Yes, but no."

I faced the darkening ocean, watching the last of the sun dip into the horizon. I heard the birds overhead and had a flash of my heart jumping out onto the wet sand before a wave came in. The weight of the heart was enough to dig it into the sand and create a wake of ripples as it fought, still beating, to stay on the beach against the pressure of the water. I stared at the spot, feeling an emptiness in my chest as two seagulls came down and plucked up my heart, fighting for the fresh meat.

"Fuck you," I said. "You're not real."

"Jon? What's the trouble?" Dr. Solis said, jarring me.

"I need to travel."

"So?"

"Cross country."

"Tell Patty the city. She'll notify the nearest cardiac unit and text you a number. Is that what this was about?"

I swallowed. No, that wasn't what it was about. It was about a paralyzing fear that I didn't recognize because it was so foreign. It was about my wife and how I'd abandoned her because of that fear. It was about regret, and forgiveness, and worthiness.

"Yeah," I said. "That was it."

"Good," he said and hung up.

Damned doctors. Hold a human heart in your hand and the everyday courtesies go out the window. I laughed to myself. I was going to New York.

MONICA

"Can you explain this one more time?" the old doctor asked with an accent so deeply New Yawk, he sounded like an old Irish cop in a black-and-white movie.

The office was in the eighties and Seventh Avenue, with old cabinets, ancient metal and glass syringes in frames, and photos of a family, then a family's family. The certificates and diplomas, if observed closely, were from the fifties.

I sat on the leather-surfaced examining table with my hands folded in my lap. "My husband is immunosuppressed—"

"I got that part." The doctor moved his half-moon glasses to the top of his bald head. "I'll be happy to help you, but if you're not actually sick…" He pivoted his hand at the wrist.

"I can't bring the flu home."

"Do you have any symptoms?"

"My stomach is a little ishy."

"Vomiting? Diarrhea?"

"No."

"So go home."

I made a face and twisted my shoulders. I don't know what I was trying to express but discomfort and awkwardness.

"Do you not want to go home? Does he beat you?"

"No!" He did, of course, but that wasn't what the good doctor meant. "I'm worried. If I get him sick, it's not like a normal person getting sick. He had a heart transplant."

The doctor up held his hand. It was surprisingly big, like a wrinkled leather dinner plate. "I'll tell you what. You're a nervous wreck. I can see that. And your blood pressure's through the roof. You gave Bernice a urine sample when you came in?"

"No, I—"

"Do that then. We'll check your sugar. Check for antibodies. If there's anything irregular, I'll let you know. You might be carrying a virus, and you might not. There's not much more I can do."

"That's fine. It's great. Thank you!"

"You're very cute, young lady. If I were about sixty years younger, I'd be the older man in your life."

I laughed, and he helped me off the table with his dinner-plate hands.

I gave my sample and waited.

What would I do if my results came back with some sign that something wasn't a hundred percent? Like elevated blood sugar? That could mean my body was fighting something, or it could mean I ate too much bread with lunch. Would I stay in New York to keep Jonathan safe? Or would I go home and tell him to stay away from me?

I'd been sick only once since the surgery, at the end of February. A cold had kept me out of the studio, and as frustrating as that was, it also meant I was relegated to another bedroom until Laurelin cleared me to touch my husband. I cursed her. I yelled at her. I told her that I was leaving for Corfu in three days and I was entitled to see Jonathan before then.

And she reminded me that by infecting him with a cold, I'd send him back to Sequoia Hospital faster than if I hit him over the head with a two-by-four.

That shut me up.

I was smiling about it when the good doctor appeared from behind his shellacked wood door.

"Mrs. Faulkner?"

I didn't correct him. "Yes?"

"Congratulations. We've found the source of your ishy stomach."

CHAPTER 73

JONATHAN

THE NIGHT I decided to shed the yoke of love I carried for my ex-wife, I'd felt so unburdened, I laughed. When I let go of my fear of traveling, I didn't laugh quite as hard, but I walked home quickly, smiling the whole way.

"Mira!" I said when I saw her. "Pack me some things, would you?"

"Sure, sure. How long for?"

"Few days." If I stayed longer, I could have the hotel launder them or buy new. It didn't matter. Nothing mattered but getting out of this old skin of a house and into my wife's arms.

"Business or pleasure?"

"Pleasure! A little chilly. Los Angeles in November-ish."

She smiled widely. "Yes, sir. When are you leaving?"

"Immediately. Go. Jeans and shirts. Two sweaters. Go." Ailing Mira trotted upstairs as I remembered something. "Mira!"

She leaned over the banister. "Sir?"

"Two leather belts. One narrow, one wide."

"What color?"

"Doesn't matter."

She nodded and went upstairs.

I got on the phone. "Jacques?"

"Hello, Mister Drazen."

"I need to go to New York."

"When?"

"Now."

I was greeted by an unusual pause.

"What?" I said.

"I'm calculating how long it will take to get there."

"From where?"

"We just got into Chicago."

"With the plane?" I started my own calculations.

"For the Prima Culture conference. You—"

"Signed off. Shit." I stood in the middle of the living room and rubbed my eyes.

When I'd stopped flying, I'd freely loaned the plane to anyone on my staff who needed it for business, and months ago, my executive group had requested it. So the Gulfstream was in Chicago, which was three flying hours away. An hour getting a flight plan approved, half an hour prep. Three hours in the air. Redoing it all once he hit Santa Monica, and the last, most unmovable of obstacles was pilot exhaustion. If he flew into Chicago today and came right back, he wouldn't be able to legally pilot the plane to New York.

"I can get back, but then I can't take you," he said.

When did I decide to start hiring such law-abiding staff? Was I going to have to jog to New York? "Is Petra with you?"

"She's with the baby."

I'd hit some nerve; I heard it in the edge in his voice. Petra had given birth to their little boy, Claude, weeks ago. Jacques had been manning the plane on his own, which was completely legal and fine up until then. At that moment, it had become a pain in the ass.

"Do you have a nanny?" I asked, knowing the answer.

"She's breastfeeding, Mister Drazen. I'm sorry. She can't pilot to New York and back without feeding him."

I thought there might be answers that had to do with latex nipples and breast pumps, but I knew nothing about them. Jacques probably would have suggested it if it had been a possibility.

And did I need to go, really? What would happen if I waited a day? Exactly nothing. No lives or livelihoods were at stake. But having decided I wasn't afraid, that I was ready to go anywhere with her, I couldn't wait another second.

"Listen," I said, "I'm being a nightmare of a boss, and the fact that I admit it isn't going to soften this. I need you to get home, and I need Petra to fly that plane. Get a freelance copilot or a nanny, on me, but I need to go."

"Mister Drazen. We won't hire a nanny. That's not how we do it."

What I enjoyed about Jacques was that he'd never asked me why I suddenly had to go anywhere. He just flew the damned plane. In return, I couldn't ask him what kind of stupid fucking rule prevented him from taking care of his son while Petra sat in the cockpit.

I plopped back on the couch, and put my feet on the coffee table, stretching my legs, tensing and releasing.

"How long in the air between here and New York?" I said. "Five hours? Six?"
"Yes. But—"
"I have an idea. Just hear me out."

CHAPTER 74

MONICA

I SNAPPED the hotel room door shut and ran to the bathroom, stripping as I went. The mirror in the deluxe suite went from floor to ceiling seamlessly, and it made me look sickly skinny. So when I got in front of it and turned to the side, I felt the same, or worse, because I was knocked up, and to me, I still looked like bag of bones.

"You have to start eating," I reprimanded myself. "Someone else is counting on you."

I surprised myself. What was I doing? I didn't want a baby. I just wanted to make Jonathan as comfortable and happy as possible for however long he had. That was it. Not raise children into orphanhood.

I breathed heavily and tilted one leg. Inside the thigh, the word *Jonathan's* became visible. I was marked, written on, branded with his name. I closed my eyes and asked myself what I wanted to pray for.

Was I relieved? Disappointed? What would change? Would I throw caution to the wind and let my sons and daughters go through puberty with a brave and dead father? What was I agreeing to?

I didn't know. But I knew things were going to change. If we were having a baby, then fuck it, I'd just deal with it.

A smile stretched across my face as if it were someone else's face. I felt the muscles tense and expand, felt the swelling in my heart one felt when one smiled with joy. I felt as if deciding to deal with it had cracked open part of me, and that smile spilled out.

I opened my eyes. This was awesome. When did it get awesome? Had I been holding on to the desire for his children without realizing it? Had it crept under the covers with me? Had it been in my diet? The air I breathed? When had this glee snuck into my heart?

I pressed my eyes shut against tears. I didn't want to cry. I didn't want my body to have any confusion. The burst of emotion came from a place I didn't know existed. Some string of code in my DNA, some hormonal rush that was more biological than logical.

I was overjoyed. Thrilled to bursting. I jumped up and, still naked, ran to the tablet. I couldn't wait to tell him. The metal and plastic were cold in my hand as I woke the device, then I stopped. I wanted to hold him. I wanted his reaction to myself, to own it the way he owned my orgasms. I wanted to feel his strength and his warmth around me when he found out.

Instead of calling him, I made reservations to go home.

When I put the tablet down, I saw the Sharpie on the desk. I picked it up, went to the bathroom, and stood in front of the mirror. My body looked the same to me. I turned every which way and saw no difference. His name between my legs was barely visible when I stood, just a few unreadable hashes of black. I popped the cap off the marker and pressed the tip to the skin below my navel.

"Upside down and backward," I said. I looked in the mirror. That just confused things.

Right is left and up is down. I drew a J with my right hand and, convinced I was doing it correctly, continued until I'd written *Jonathan's baby* across my abdomen.

Then I laughed so hard I lay on the bed and cried with joy.

CHAPTER 75

MONICA

I COULDN'T CONTAIN MYSELF. It was twenty minutes to boarding, and I fidgeted around the terminal, wishing I'd taken the Gulfstream. I picked up the phone. As much as I wanted to call Jonathan... I didn't. Not yet. I wanted to see his face and hear his breath. I wanted him to hold me so close I could feel that motherfucking heartbeat.

"Mom?"

"Monica, are you all right?"

She was wide awake, and it was four in the morning in Los Angeles. If I'd called at noon, she would have been sleeping. That was Mom. I'd learned to accept it.

To say my mother's attitude about me had changed after I'd married Jonathan would be a gross understatement. And now she'd be the first person to hear the news from my lips.

"I'm pregnant." Silence. I didn't realize how quickly I'd been circumnavigating the terminal until I slowed down. "Mom?"

A woman rolled over my foot with her square bag and gave me a dirty look. Fuck her.

"Monya."

"Are you all right?"

"Am I all right? Are you asking if I'm all right? My only daughter marries a dying man in the hospital, nurses him back to health, and gets pregnant with his baby, and you ask if I'm all right?" I started to reply, but she cut me off. "How can I not be all right? I'm so happy I cannot even speak. My God, a baby. A *baby*."

"Thanks, Mom." I was glad I'd told her, but I didn't feel the explosion of joy I'd hoped for. The reveal was kind of a letdown. It needed to be Jonathan, but in front of me.

"Where are you?" she asked. "How far along? Do you have the sickness?"

"I have no idea, but I had kind of a little period a couple of months ago, so the doctor figures two months. And I'm not sick at all. I mean, there was a little flu going around, so—"

"Do you have it? You can't catch anything."

Between the worry in her voice and my flight number being called, I lost track of the conversation. "I know, I know. My plane's boarding. Just don't say anything to anyone. I haven't told Jonathan yet."

"You can't tell him."

"What? Why?"

"Anything can happen." Her voice took on that mysterious, awed tone it got when she talked about the inscrutabilities of God. "You have to wait until you're twelve weeks. You don't want to disappoint him."

"Disa—"

I realized what she meant in the middle of the word. She'd miscarried a few times and had just bled the babies away without ever bothering my father with the gory details. She was who she was. The fact that I was a different person completely, healthy and young with every reason to carry a baby to term, didn't matter. She would worry about stuff because that was what she did.

"Okay, Mom. I won't tell." I painted the lie white and called it a day. "I have to go."

"Call me when you get back."

"Will do."

I walked up to the gate and boarded the plane, a little disconcerted. I'd dreamed of doing things like flying first class from New York to LA, booking at the last minute without a thought to the extra cost. But once I could, I didn't give it a second thought. Taking money for granted seemed to be an unavoidable symptom of actually having money.

I got the window and leaned my head into it as soon as I sat. I watched New York get as small as a Lego set, with pieces scattered around the outer boroughs and stacked beautifully on the erection-shaped island in the middle. The evening air was crystal clear, even on a weekday. I'd been shocked at how little pollution there was, and as we flew away, chasing the setting sun, I prepared myself for the soup-thick air of my home.

Should we bring up a baby there? Los Angeles, with all of its silicone reality and blind eyes to real problems? The poverty we swept under the rug, the crumbling school system, the undercurrent of violence and ferocity that coexisted with my little hipster world and was completely foreign to Jonathan's. Should we go somewhere cleaner? More real? More wholesome? More sincere?

I didn't even know what I wanted from having children. I didn't know what questions to ask. I needed Jonathan to even continue thinking about it. Past his excitement, the happiness I knew my news would inspire, he'd have ideas. I wanted to hear them, all of them. I wanted to hear his dreams for the future, and I wanted him to talk far ahead. Ten years. Twenty. Thirty, even. Because I was having his baby, and goddamnit, by hook or crook, he was going to live.

CHAPTER 76

JONATHAN

PETRA STOOD in front of my plane in her uniform, carrying a bundle of navy blankets. Both my pilots were complete professionals, but Petra made most professionals look like part-timers. Jacques stood next to her, also in uniform, but tired, as if he were the one who had been nursing a newborn.

"You flying?" I said to him after Lil let me out of the car and handed me my bag. "You look too tired to drive. Can Lil give you a lift?"

"He'll take you up on that," Petra said with a smile as she handed me the bundle she carried.

"Claude," I said as I held him. He still had the squishy pink look of a newborn. He looked angelic in the mid-morning light. "Nice-looking kid, Jacques. Lucky thing your wife has strong genes."

Petra pressed her lips together as if she was trying not to smile. "If he roots, come and get me."

"Roots?" I asked.

Claude waved his hands around, not knowing what they were for or if they were even his. I gave him my finger, and he clutched it.

"Tries to latch on to your breast."

"Ah. I'm sure I have a bad joke somewhere, but it flew out of my head."

"That happens." Jacques picked up my bag. "I'll help you up. Lange's gonna copilot. He's running through the terminal as we speak."

"I owe you for this." Worse than owing him, having that baby in my arms made me feel like a petulant, spoiled ass who couldn't wait a day to see his wife.

840

Jacques shrugged. "You're usually pretty easy. And you know, it's nice to see you getting around again."

I would have questioned him on how obvious it was to everyone that I wasn't myself, but it didn't matter. The baby wiped it all away. I picked a piece of crud from his eye, and when I pulled my arm back, Petra put the diaper bag around my shoulder.

"He needs to be changed fifteen minutes after a feeding. I nursed him in the car, so you'd better get to it," she said. "You know how to change a diaper?"

"I did it for my nephew once."

"Great. If he cries, you swaddle him tight. I'll show you how. He doesn't use a pacifier, but you might let him suck on your finger for a minute when he's wrapped. And you hold him and bounce him. Not much rocking, just bouncing. The noise of the plane will probably put him to sleep, but if not, he'll scream. That's on you, sir. I can't come out of the cockpit for fussy. Only hungry."

"Were you saying something? I was distracted." I smiled at her to let her know I was kidding.

"We have half an hour or so of flight prep. If you play your cards right, he'll sleep through it."

Jacques started up the stairs and indicated I should follow.

This would be the longest flight of my life, and I was ready for it.

CHAPTER 77

MONICA

I slept a little, all wrapped up in my first-class-approved blanket. I woke close to landing at the same time of day as I left, chasing the sky from blue to yellow. The city below was grey, blanketed in thick brown smog, and we were descending right into it.

I hadn't been dreaming, but when I woke, my mind was in mid-question. What would it be like to be pregnant? Would I be sick? Active? What could I eat? Could I fly? Could I fuck? I didn't even have a doctor. I'd just run to the clinic for my last Depo shot. No way I could do that for this pregnancy. Jonathan wouldn't allow it, and I didn't want to. I wanted the best, even if I didn't know what that meant yet.

I hustled through baggage and to a taxi stand. If I knew Jonathan, he'd be in bed still, but I wouldn't make it home before his run. I sat in the back of the cab, tapping my fingers and wondering how much of a surprise I wanted to deliver. I'd snuck back without using any of his staff, so he had no way of knowing I was home. It could be too much of a surprise. Not quite thirty people jumping out from behind the couch and yelling "Happy Birthday!" but not a stress-free event either.

Stop worrying. Just stop it.

I turned on my phone. I could call him. But what if he came home from his run, and I was just there in a total non-shocking kind of way? Then I could tell him. I ran alternate scenarios through my head. In bed, naked. In the kitchen, making eggs. I could write him a note and leave it on the banister. I could call first and tell him to wait somewhere in the house. I considered everything as the cab slid onto the 105 freeway toward home.

CHAPTER 78

JONATHAN

I'D GOTTEN the baby to sleep without much trouble. He'd sucked on my finger while I sang him a few off-key verses of "Collared." Thankfully Petra couldn't hear me give her son evil ideas, and he couldn't understand a word of it. They only spoke French to him anyway.

The plane started down the runway. I put my feet on the seat across from me and slipped out my phone. I wanted everything to be perfect when I landed. I needed to know where she was, who she'd be with, and how close she would be to the hotel.

"Quentin?" I said when he answered.

He was somewhere loud, a club or restaurant, and I couldn't yell with a sleeping baby in my arms. I just hung up and texted him.

—Is Monica with you?—

—I have no idea where she's off to—

—You were supposed to watch her—

—Sorry, man. Didn't work out
that way. Haven't seen her
since last night. The sessions broke
down. Starting up again on Tuesday—

843

Damnit. I couldn't hold Quentin responsible, and that was the problem. He owed me nothing, and now Monica was MIA. How did I know she wasn't being attacked by that singer? Or dead in a ditch? Or getting roofied in some dirtshit club?

I should have hired someone to watch her. I should have sent drones or bugged her purse. I had been so busy proving what a nice, reasonable guy I was that I walked right into this. Fuck that. Never again. I was neither nice nor reasonable when it came to Monica. The next time she went anywhere without me, I was planting a locator chip under her scalp.

I called my wife. She wasn't dead.

"Jonathan? Where are you?"

Would I blow the surprise? I had to think fast. "I'm on a plane. I'll be back in a few days. Where are you?"

"No! Oh, Jonathan! I'm home. In the house."

"No!" I immediately looked at the baby. He was sleeping like a doll. "Don't move!" I hung up. "Petra!"

Calling to her from the seat wouldn't work, and it would wake the baby. I reached for the intercom. Couldn't get it. Shifted. The plane sped up. It was going to take off in seconds. I couldn't reach, nor could I put the baby down. I hit the intercom button with my foot.

"Mister Drazen?" Petra asked. "We're taking off—"

"No. Stop. No take off. I'm going home."

"Oh, *merde*!"

I'd never heard her swear before. It was cute, and I braced myself for what was about to happen. The plane slowed down. I leaned my head back, and Claude rolled his eyes open then screamed. After the plane stopped, the cockpit door clicked open.

Petra peeked out. She was back to her normal level of professionalism. "Everything all right?"

"Yeah, I just… don't need to go anymore." I found myself yelling over the baby. I stood and rocked him.

"You need help with Claude?"

"No, I got it. I owe you for stopping the plane."

"My pleasure. I'd rather go home."

"Me too."

CHAPTER 79

MONICA

I RAN to the door when I saw the Bentley across the drive. He got out with a bag, leaving Lil half out of the car when he said something to her with a wave. She got back in and drove off.

He turned to the door, jacket under his arm and bag over his shoulder. His hair was a little disheveled, and his cheeks were scrubby with two days of beard. His shirt was open to the second button, and his sleeves were rolled to the elbow, revealing his taut forearms and strong wrists. And his hands. Those hands. Like the marble statue of David, he was an altar to the aesthetics of perfect proportions.

"Hi," I said as he strode to me.

"What's this about?" He looked stern, but under it, he was pleased to see me.

"You were supposed to be home."

"I was. But let's cut the supposed to's. If you came home to get laid, you shouldn't be wearing clothes. So let's fix that."

He reached for me, just touching the red scarf around my neck, but I backed up.

"I want to try something different."

"Really?" He stepped forward again. One more step, and we'd be in the house.

"I want you to do what I tell you," I said.

He stepped forward again. I backed up, and we were inside.

"Like how?" He slammed the door shut.

"Like I'm in charge."

He dropped his bag and jacket with a thud. "I told you I don't bottom." His arm shot out and grabbed me by the waist.

845

I pushed him away. "Today, I'm the boss."

"You want to start a limits list? We won't get laid for a month."

"You have to just trust me." I pushed him backward, and he fell into a chair.

"Monica"—his voice got serious—"really. This is not going to work."

I put my hands on the arms of the chair and leaned forward until my nose was an inch from his. "You smell like baby powder."

"And you smell like you want to piss me off."

"Trust me." I placed his hands on the arms of the chair, laying them flat. "I won't tie you up or hurt you. That's mine. But I want you to stay still. That's all." I pulled my scarf off.

"Better watch it with that thing," he said. "I know how to use it."

I got behind him and tied it around his eyes.

"Monica?"

"Jonathan?"

"I'm not turned on."

"You will be."

I peeled my clothes off quickly. I'd showered but taken no effort to scrub off the Sharpie. I was still marked with his name and the location of his baby. I took a deep breath. He tapped his finger, mouth set in a tight line. Not turned on. Almost frightening in his stress. He really didn't like taking orders. But he would love this. I turned my naked back to him, facing the Mondrian over the fireplace, and crossed my arms over my abdomen. I didn't know how long I would last. I felt like a bottle of soda someone had shaken but left sealed.

"Take the blindfold off," I said. I heard a rustle behind me.

"You have a great ass."

I turned, fully nude, and after half a second, I moved my arms to my sides. His eyes worked their way from my face, to my tits, hardening them without even touching them, and down my body until he stopped where I'd written *Jonathan's baby*.

"Really?" he said.

"Really."

He laughed. Not a laugh of humor or derision, just delight. Pure, childlike delight. I had to laugh with him. I got on my knees and crawled to him, still laughing, and he kissed me all over: my cheeks, my forehead, my neck. His hands went everywhere, as if touching all the parts he loved, then he kissed my mouth, long, hard, and deep.

"Thank you," he said, breaking the kiss for half a second before putting his lips on me again.

"No problem." It was the least I could say, a joke of miniature proportions.

"You know you wrote it backward, right?"

I leaned back and looked at my abdomen.

"Is it because you have your doubts?" he asked.

"No. I did it in the mirror."

He pushed against me until my back was on the wool rug, and he was over me like an unclouded sky.

"Are you happy?" he asked.

I put my hands on his cheeks. "I didn't think I would be. But I don't know. I'm just elated. I feel like I'm walking on air."

He put my hands over my head and kissed me. "I want to say thank you over and over. I find myself at a loss for words otherwise."

"Don't speak. Just fuck me."

"I want you, I love you, you're mine." He said it all in a string, as if it was one thought. "Do we need a bigger house?"

"This is plenty of space."

"We have to ask Sheila what schools to apply to."

"We can worry about that later."

"The wait lists for preschools are four years long."

"That's obscene."

"I have to set up a trust and fund it. Tomorrow I'll call Margie and have it done."

My face wasn't supposed to tighten, but I feared it did, so I just spoke my mind. "The Swiss thing. You need to promise me you're going to fund that. Before the trusts."

"The trust is easier."

"I don't care if the kid grows up poor. I care that it has a father."

"Hope is deadly."

"Maybe. But tell me you don't have a little bit now? Or some reason to hope you're not taking a bunch of pills just so you can fuck me harder and more often? Don't you want to try? I mean, look, think of it this way. Maybe you'll save someone else."

"Monica, you don't know what this does to me. The idea of leaving you alone. I've been, I think, afraid to make you happy because of what we both know is coming."

I brushed my finger across the scruff on his cheek, this living man, blood beating through him as he scratched and clawed to be reasonable, sensible, and mature while still living life corner to corner. I'd thought I understood his struggle, but I didn't. I thought he just wanted to live or die. I thought he just wanted to be in the moment and not worry, but he'd carried the weight of his own life alongside the weight of mine.

"All I want is for you to try," I said. "Let me and the baby know we're worth you fighting for your life."

He smiled ruefully. "You make compelling arguments. When we met, I thought you were studying law."

"Because I threatened to sue you?"

"It was cute. You were so sexy, the way you tried to back me into a corner. I wanted to bend you over that desk and spank you raw. The minute I laid eyes on you, I wanted to fuck you until you begged."

"Do it now."

He kissed the space between my breasts. "You came when you weren't supposed to. I had plans, but I don't think I can follow through on them."

"Don't you dare."

He put his ear between *Jonathan's* and *baby*. "I can't hear anything. When is he coming?"

"She's coming in late January. And I'm coming today. I'm still me. Do everything. Don't make me beg. Or make me beg. Whichever. Just make me."

He got on his knees and pulled my legs apart. His name was still visible, and Jonathan looked at me everywhere, as if searching for something inside himself, bathing me in the scalding water of his gaze.

He smirked and put his eyes on mine. "I'm thinking. Can I destroy you when you're carrying my baby?"

"Yes, you can."

He slapped the inside of my thigh. It stung like hell because it was unexpected. I gasped and bit my lip.

"I'll decide what I can and can't do," he said. "And I'll decide what you can do. Do you understand?"

"Hurt me," I whispered.

He slapped the inside of my other thigh, and yes, it hurt. And yes, it was demeaning, and yes, I pulled away. I thought I might come from that alone.

"No more demands, goddess. I have ways to hurt you that aren't as much fun." He pulled the red scarf off the arm of the chair. "No talking. No whimpering. No crying. Not a peep out of you. Just yes and no."

"Yes." I couldn't imagine, as he kneeled above me, his knees keeping mine apart, that the word *no* would exit my lips.

"Put your hands over your head and grab the table leg."

I did it, stretching to reach the leg of the heavy sideboard.

"I haven't tied you up since the surgery. You've noticed?"

"Yes."

He leaned over me and wrapped the scarf around my wrists, attaching it to the sideboard as he spoke. "I was nervous. I kept dreaming the heart would leave me. Probably all the talk of rejection going to my head. But I worried that it would happen while you were tied up, and you'd be trapped until someone came." He leaned back and checked his work by pulling me toward him until my arms were completely extended. "I know it wasn't sensible. But it was there." He stood and reached for something in the bag he had been about to take on the plane. His blue book. "You got away with a lot in the meantime."

"Yes," I said.

"Open your mouth." I did, and he put the book in it. "Hold this for me."

I bit down on the leather. He stepped back, and the book blocked my view of him. I heard the clink of his belt and the rustle of clothes, but I couldn't see him. I could only see the damn book.

"The rules—and you can tell me what you object to when I take the book out of your mouth—the rules are this. I'm going to do what I want to your body. You're going to have your safe words. If you worry about the baby for one second, you use them. And if I worry, I'm stopping the scene. It doesn't matter if those worries make sense. And when you start showing, we're renegotiating."

He pulled my legs up and bent my knees until my ass was off the rug, then he took the book out of my mouth. He was naked and perfect from his scar to his huge cock. Lithe and strong. Nimble and taut.

"Yes or no, Monica." He slapped the book on his palm.

"Yes, sir."

"Good." The book landed on my ass with a *thwack*. I chirped and held my cry. He paused then smacked me again. Paused, letting me feel the delicious sting. "Yesterday, you forgot that I own your orgasms. That means I say how and when you come." *Thwack.* "Every time." *Thwack.*

"Sorry."

"You don't sound sorry."

"I'm not."

"You were getting three. Now you're getting four for lying. Count with me."

The book landed between my legs, flat on my engorged clit, and I bit back a scream. It hurt, stung, burned in the opening notes, and the echo was pure pleasure.

"How many is that?" he asked.

"One."

He smacked it again, and I twisted away at the same time as I wanted it again. He straightened me and spread my legs, exposing me to him.

"Count."

"Two."

"You okay?" he asked.

"Yes."

Thwap. Harder than the others. I held back a scream.

"Breathe," he demanded.

"Three!"

"Last one."

He did it again, and it hurt bad, but it left a rush of warm, pre-orgasm quiver in its wake. How had I ever lived without that? How had I ever had an orgasm without the counterpoint of pain?

"Four," I said through my teeth.

He put the book aside and slid his fingers in me. "You're soaked." He drew his wet fingers over my clit, and it burned. That burn, not his touch on me, nearly put me over the edge into orgasm. "And you're close. What am I going to do with you?"

Begging him to fuck me might cause an indefinite delay as I was told to think about what it meant to make demands out of turn, so I said nothing. He moved his hand over me, setting my soreness on fire.

He leaned over and slid his dick into me. I gasped from the pain and the rawness, which had brought every nerve ending into high alert. I was sensitive at every range of the spectrum, and he was stretching me open, putting his whole length into me. I strained against the ties from the pain and the pleasure.

I expected him to take me like an animal. But he didn't. He shifted slowly, making sure I felt every inch. He pushed against my clit, angling himself so he rubbed against it, slowly, slowly, in a tortuous rhythm.

"Please," I whispered.

"You wanted something?"

"Faster."

He didn't go faster. If I'd had a metronome to count by, my bet would be on slower.

"Why?" he asked.

"I want to come."

"Really?"

"Please."

He pressed into me, breathing the words into my cheek. "You are so good. But you have to wait."

"I can't."

"Do you know what happens when you rush? Things don't go right. They're not full. Not complete. If I let you come now, you'll be conscious. You'll say thank you and start thinking about music before you even close your legs."

He pulled out slowly and pushed back in. I moved my hips into him to speed it up, but he adjusted and made it worse. I groaned.

"If I let you come now," he continued, "you'll be satisfied. But you deserve better than that. You deserve to have your mind erased."

"I have a snappy comeback. But I can't breathe."

He moved as if we were underwater. The pressure built, and stayed, and built again, never breaking. What should have taken a second took several. My brain told me I was coming, but I didn't. I stayed in the netherworld between knowing I was going to come and actually doing it. The ultimate mix of pain and pleasure. A tug-of-war between two matched opponents.

CHAPTER 80

JONATHAN

IF I'D TOLD her to add two and two, I didn't think she could have answered. It did occur to me to ask for a little simple math, but we were treading a wire-thin path as it was. If I pulled her back too far, I'd confuse her body and ruin the orgasm. She wouldn't be able to have a good one until her body came down fully and her over-stimulated nerves recovered, which could take hours. That was never fun. It made everyone cranky.

But I wanted to see how far I could go and how much pain this caused, because there would be a time, soon, when the bruises and contusions wouldn't wash, and I would derive no pleasure from hurting her. It was one thing to break and push a consenting adult. It was another thing to spank and grab a pregnant woman until she was black and blue. I would have to find other ways to dominate her or we would both wind up unsatisfied and discontented. Controlling her orgasms to the point of pain was a possibility. She was suffering, and she loved it almost as much as I did.

She was giving herself to me in that microcosm of her pleasure, and especially her pain, because in the macrocosm of her love, she was giving me what I wanted most: a family, a home, roots that were mine completely. Nothing borrowed. Nothing temporary. Through all her doubts and legitimate fears, she was taking a leap of faith into the net of my happiness.

I would live for her, for the family she was about to give me, for the home she'd agreed to create. My orbit around her was going to get tighter and tighter until, for better or worse, we fused into a single sun.

A tear dropped from the corner of her left eye, and I kissed it, still shifting with a slow, grinding rhythm. I had to pull her over the edge. It was the perfect time. Another second would be too late. I gave her no permission to come but got up on my knees and thrust deep and hard. Her eyes opened wide and rolled back with the second thrust.

I had complete control over her.

What that did for me, there were no words. Just a peace. A sloughing off of life and its pressures and worries. I existed only in this corner of the world, and it was mine, fully under my purview. The rush of euphoria that followed was submission in itself, to the act, to her, to the power she'd given me.

"May I come?" she whimpered.

"Yes."

I took her. Made her mine. I saw the tide coming in her, and I encouraged it. When she was midway, I'd slow down to make it last, then I'd let go and fill her with me.

It was a good plan. But I looked down as she started to cry my name.

I didn't know what I was looking for. Maybe I wanted to see our connection point when I came or see her cunt pulsing around me. But that's not what I saw.

I shriveled up. Stopped moving.

My name rang in my ears as I looked at my dick, seeing something horrifying, like the death of joy, and I couldn't hear my name anymore. Maybe she was screaming in her orgasm, or in pain, or in blame, I didn't know, but I couldn't form a sentence or command.

The streak of blood on my dick was unmistakable.

I only had one word in my head.

"Tangerine."

CHAPTER 81

MONICA

"What?"

I was pulled so far out of my orgasm that my body went rigid and my mind was soaked in adrenaline. He might as well have screamed *Stop* in my ear. I yanked my hands against the ties with a motion so violent, I heard stuff clatter and clunk as it fell. He got up on his knees, and I saw the fullness of him.

His cock was streaked in red. It wasn't supposed to be. Not unless something was broken, and we weren't doing broken. We were doing celebration. This was wrong. Everything was wrong. I pulled again, even as he reached up to get the scarf undone.

"Monica! Stay still. Give me a second."

But all my yanking and pulling had tightened the knot, and he growled as he tried to pick it loose and failed.

"Say it's from hitting me," I begged. "Please say it's from—"

"I don't know what it's from. Just stay still."

I couldn't. I had no control over my body. I yanked and pulled, trying to slip free, but my husband knew knots like he knew ice cubes and sore bottoms. If he'd set up the knot to keep me from slipping out, I wasn't slipping out.

"Jonathan," I said without anything else to say. Him, I just wanted him. I wanted to say his name to gather strength. He got up, and I had a full view of his beautiful, bloodied cock. "Don't leave me."

"I'm not." He walked away.

"Don't leave me here!"

853

But he did. He walked away, and I didn't know why I felt so bereft. Some need to run away, coupled with the inability to even lower my arms, made me panic. I could feel something dripping down my leg. And he wasn't there. He was going to the fucking kitchen.

Then I heard knives clack and his footsteps coming back toward me. I calmed. Barely. He came back a bread knife and leaned over my hands.

"Stay still," he said. "Please. I don't want to cut you." He put the knife to the scarf.

"What's happening?" I asked.

"I don't know." His concentration stayed on my bound wrists.

"I don't want to lose it."

"Me neither."

"It's from spanking me. That's all. You hurt me worse than I thought. Let's not do that again, okay?"

"Sure." He laid his hands on my wrists, pressing them apart and making the fabric between them taut. He sliced the scarf open with a *snap*.

I got my arms under me and started to get up, but Jonathan pushed me down. I resisted. He pushed harder.

"Hold on. Gravity," he said.

"That doesn't even make sense."

"I know, I know."

He put his arms under my shoulders and my knees and carried me to the couch. I was sore where he'd hit me. That was the reason for the blood, but he seemed worried, and I wanted to respect that. I didn't want to be dismissive or call him silly, but his knotted brow and the taut line of his jaw made me want to stroke away his fear.

He leaned over me and caressed my cheeks. "Can you wait here while I get dressed and get you some clothes?"

"Why?"

He got up and plucked his clothes off the floor. "We're going to the hospital."

I got my elbows under me to sit up, and with only one arm in his shirt, he rushed to push me down.

"It's nothing, Jonathan. I'm sure of it." I said it to calm him, but I wasn't sure if I believed it out of anything but necessity.

"Then humor me. Lie back."

I did, and when he saw I'd obeyed, he trotted upstairs. I looked down at his name inside my thighs. I was drawn on like a cinderblock wall in gangland. Jonathan's dominion over me was written in black Sharpie, his territory marked in permanent ink.

Was I losing the baby? And so what if I was? What was the big deal? I didn't even want to have children right now. I wanted nothing to do with it. Jonathan was going to die after a tortuous wait for a second heart before the kid was in high school. What kind of selfish bitch creates a child to go through that?

All I had to do was go back to the me of a few days ago. Nothing had changed.

Except everything. Having carried that baby knowingly for two days, I'd had a cellular alchemy. The shape of my brain and my heart had shifted, grown. I wasn't the same person. I wanted that baby. I wanted it so badly, and I didn't even know it.

I wanted this to be nothing, an embarrassing symptom of rough sex play, but the twitch in my abdomen, the tightness told me otherwise.

Jonathan came down the stairs dressed, with a dress over his arm.

"Do you think they can save it?" I asked, my voice breaking on "save."

"I don't know." He sat on the edge of the couch. "Arms up."

I raised my arms, and he put the long, modest dress over me. He snapped out a pair of simple cotton underwear and slipped them over my ankles then drew them up my legs and over me.

"I was supposed to get rid of all that underwear," I said.

"Sometimes you need it." He stood beside the couch.

I heard the crunch of tires on pebbles outside. "Is it Lil?"

"Yes. I texted her." He put his arms under me and picked me up, carrying me toward the door. "I don't think I can drive."

"Thank God for her." I looped my arms around his neck, and he carried me out.

"Sir," Lil said as she opened the back door. "Mrs. Drazen, I hope you're all right."

"I'm sure it's nothing." I didn't know why I said that. As the minutes passed, I started to think that was some whitewash of hope on a steaming pile of tragedy.

Jonathan held me tight and somehow got me in the car without putting me down. I shifted down and put my head on his lap.

Lil looked into the back. "Sequoia?"

"Yes."

"No!" I said, rigid. I looked up at Jonathan. "No. Anywhere but there. Please. I can't."

"It's the best obstetrics unit in the world, Monica."

"I don't care. I can't go back there. I can't. Let's go to Hollywood Methodist."

"It's a different ward entirely."

"Do you know how far out of my way I go to not drive past it? And it's on Beverly, so yeah, I'd rather be late than see it. I'd rather go to the urgent care clinic on Sunset. I'd rather see the witch doctor in Silver Lake than go anywhere near that hospital. It smells like death. It's hell. Nine stories of fucking hell, and I won't go."

Jonathan looked at me for a second then back at Lil. "Drive."

"Jonathan!" I said as Lil closed the door. I tried to get up, but he pulled me down.

"Listen to me," he said. "I know how you feel. Believe me, I get it. But that was enough blood to scare the hell out of me, and it wasn't enough to convince me this is completely over. If we lose this baby because we went to a second-rate hospital or nowhere at all, because we were scared... well, I'd like to know how you're going to forgive yourself. Because you're going to have to teach me."

I looked away from him. His gaze was going to break me. It was a wall of resolve. He was doing what he wanted to do, and I had to go along. From my angle on his lap, all I could see was the grey-blue glass of the sky, streetlights, and telephone poles zipping by. A speck of bird or plane.

He was right.

Fear was fungible, and death was forever. Overcome one to face the other. Blah blah. I didn't want him to be right. I wanted to fall down a hole of despair or climb a pillar of hope, and reason and rationality were distractions from the choice.

Reaching for the hope, I touched his face. "I'm sure it's fine. We're just overreacting."

"I hope so."

"Didn't Jessica miscarry? What happened?"

He turned toward the window. "We were throwing an event at the house. Some fundraiser for the artist co-op she was in. She just takes my hand and brings me into the house. Doesn't break a beat. I'm following her, and I can see the blood inside her stockings. I picked her up and carried her to the car, but it was too late. It was a mess before we even got there. So much blood. I never saw her cry except in the front seat of my car. The pain was so bad, and you know, I asked her how long it had hurt before she told me."

"Could they have saved it?"

"The doctor wouldn't guarantee anything, but just said that next time we should come right away."

I relaxed into that, watching the fancy streetlights of Santa Monica turn into the more urban, less fussy designs of the west side of LA. "I had pain yesterday, but I thought I had the flu."

"Let's see what happens."

"If we lose it, do we try again?"

"I don't know."

That didn't help. If he pulled back from getting what he wanted most, what he'd *always* wanted most, then I didn't know who he was anymore.

"Did you try again with Jessica?" I flinched from my own question. It sounded petty and mean. Our situations couldn't have been more different. But I wanted to know what to expect from him. Did he give up or truck on?

If he heard the question as cutting, he didn't show it. "We both got checked out. I was fine, but her uterus had a shape that made it hard for her to go to term. We were fine, but it never took again. In a way, it improved things between us for a while."

I cupped his face in my hands, and he looked down at me then leaned over and kissed me.

"This won't end us," he said. "I swear, if it's the last thing I do, I'm keeping you."

The car stopped.

"I'm ready," I said. "If you stay by me. I'm ready."

Lil opened the door, and Jonathan carried me through the sliding glass doors into Sequoia Hospital. Hell on earth. I closed my eyes, but the smell was still there, and the ambient noise. When something somewhere beeped, I clung to him.

CHAPTER 82

JONATHAN

I'D CALLED AHEAD while gathering our clothes, and I was able to carry her right up to the second floor. We were offered a gurney outside the elevator, and I put her on it, insisting even when she clutched me. She weighed nothing to me. I could have carried her ten more miles, but I knew hospitals better than I wanted to, and she needed to be on the gurney.

We exited onto the maternity ward. The first thing I heard was people laughing, and I looked down at Monica to see if she heard it. I thought it would relax her. Maternity wards were gentle places with better results than the parts of the hospital she'd been stuck in for weeks.

Her eyes were clamped shut, as if she were a child who didn't want to see anything scary. I was about to make some wisecrack about ocean views and a full buffet. Describe the dancing girls and rare art she was missing. Anything to calm her down. A chuckle. Even if she slapped me and told me to shut up, it would have been preferable to seeing her coiled in dread.

"Mister Drazen," a young woman in blue scrubs said.

"Are you Dr. Blakely?" I asked. It had taken Dr. Solis seconds to recommend this young woman with the flat brown ponytail above all others.

"Yes. Dr. Solis told me you'd be coming." She looked at Monica. "How are you feeling?"

"Fine," my wife lied.

"This way, then."

The nurse, a muscular woman in her forties with a military cut, asked a battery of stupid questions. Monica answered them with her eyes closed.

858

"Mister Drazen," Blakely said as she stepped into the exam room in front of the gurney, "Dr. Solis says you're immunosuppressed?"

"Yes?"

"You shouldn't be in a hospital."

Monica opened her eyes. "Go."

"I'll text you our findings," Blakely said as they moved Monica from the gurney to the table.

Monica seemed so helpless, so separate from her mind and will, so corporeal as she stretched across the table. Her dress hitched above her knees, and I saw the Sharpie script of *Jo* and *erty*.

I wasn't abdicating responsibility. Not the medical part. I knew my limitations, but I wasn't turning my back on her. I wouldn't let her sit, alone and hurt, while I protected my immune system. "I'll stay, thank you."

"Jonathan, please," Monica said. "She's right. I'll be okay if you keep your phone on. Really, I'm not freaked out. You need to go."

But she was freaked out. From the ends of her hair, through the writing on her thighs, to the tips of her toenails, she was terrified. I hadn't known her that long and I had plenty to learn about her, but I knew goddamn well when she was lying about her comfort to protect me. We'd both done that enough to get PhDs in it.

"I'm not going," I said then turned to Dr. Blakely. "This is my wife, and she needs me. I don't want to hear, from either of you, that I should go home and live in a bubble and wait for a fucking text telling me what's happening with my family." I sat in the seat next to the table and held Monica's hand.

"He can wear a mask outside maternity," the nurse suggested as she tapped on a computer keyboard.

"Will you?" asked Monica.

"Fine."

Dr. Blakely sat on a stool at the end of the table. "You're not my patient. Dr. Solis will chew you out if you get sick. Let's get these underpants off."

Monica picked up her butt, and the doctor helped her slide out of them. The nurse started to pick up Monica's dress but glanced at me once she saw the words *Jonathan's Property*. I wanted to mention it or make a tension-splitting joke, but I didn't want to embarrass Monica. The nurse put crinkled paper over Monica's abdomen. The doctor spread Monica's legs, and I thanked God Solis had recommended a woman.

"Well, no question of paternity," she said, looking over the paper. "The baby has to work on his handwriting though."

The joke wasn't that good, but I was glad she'd made it. The tension fell off my wife as she laughed.

"All right." The doctor smiled behind her mask. "Let's see what we have here."

Monica cringed, and I heard a squishing noise. I squeezed her hand.

"Plug is in place."

More tension dropped off Monica. Maybe she was right. Maybe the book had been the wrong tool. Maybe I would have to start getting proper toys. I had to stop using whatever was on hand if it made her bleed.

The doctor put the sheet back and put her Monica's legs down. The nurse wheeled a cart over.

"I'm supposed to tell you jokes," I said to Monica. "Something clever and funny to take the edge off."

Blakely and the nurse said things I didn't understand, and they exposed Monica's abdomen. So much like my own experience as a patient. Experts talking about me as if I wasn't there, huddling together before approaching me with an approved line of bullshit.

Blakely squeezed clear gel on Monica's abdomen as if every patient had the baby's ownership scrawled backward on the mother.

"I'm waiting," Monica said. "I know you have a few thousand jokes in there."

"Knock, knock."

She laughed as if that were the entire joke, which it was. I didn't know any knock, knock jokes.

The ultrasound screen went live as if it had been fingerpainted in shades of grey. We watched as if it were the seventh game of the world series, but we had no idea of what we were seeing.

Silence. Too long. Shouldn't we be hearing a heartbeat? I'd had sonograms when I was in the hospital, and I always heard whooshing. I squeezed her hand. The doctor slid the wand over Monica's abdomen while tapping keys.

"Okay," Blakely said. "Well, that explains it." She pointed at a black oval. "This is the ovum, and typically we have a little peanut-shaped blur in there, and there isn't. It's empty."

"What does that mean?" Monica asked.

"Well, it's a blighted ovum. Meaning the egg was fertilized and made it to the uterus, but the cells stopped dividing. Either the cells were reproducing incorrectly or there was some other technical malfunction. Your body kept doing its job though, so you have an ovum and the beginnings of a placenta." Blakely shut off the machine.

Monica went white, and something in me did too. I wanted to throttle this young doctor. I wanted to choke her until she admitted she was wrong, that she'd misread the images. It was all a big mistake. There was a baby in there, right as rain and thriving.

"I was traveling," Monica said. "Did that do it?"

"Probably not."

"We're rough in bed, the two of us." Monica was past sense. Her hand had gone cold, and she was babbling. "I shouldn't say this, but you're a doctor, right? I mean, sometimes, it's just, well, like I said we get rough and—"

"I saw the bruising, and no, that wouldn't cause this. I'm sorry. The good news is, you're in perfect shape. You should be able to conceive again without a problem."

I stood. "Thank you, Doctor." I held out my hand. Those people had to leave immediately. I got it. I'd heard it. I needed to be alone with my wife.

"Not so fast," she said. "Let me give you a quick rundown, then I'll leave you alone. You have tissue in your uterus that your body needs to get rid of. It's messy and painful, and it could start today or next week. Most patients opt for us to remove it by dilating the cervix and scraping the uterus. That shortens the—"

"No." Monica pointed her chin up. "I'm not evicting the baby."

"Mrs. Drazen, I'm sorry, but there is no baby."

"Don't you tell me there's no baby!" She was pure kinetic energy. A blur. Her limbs were still but poised to shake the earth free of its orbit.

I put myself between the two women.

"There is a motherfucking baby!" Monica called from behind me.

I felt the same as she did. I felt all her anger and denial, but I couldn't allow myself to get lost in it. "Is there anything else, Doctor?" She had to get out before we were escorted out.

Unfazed by Monica's denials, Blakely took a card out of her pocket. "Call me if the pain is really bad. I'll prescribe something."

"Pain?" Monica's voice shot from behind me. "I can take pain. Just try me."

I took the card. This was it. So much had changed in the past four hours, I felt numb. I hadn't even had a chance to process flying to New York, then not flying to New York, then the baby, now the lack of the baby. It had been a day of miserable false starts, ending with the promise of pain for my wife. "Thank you."

"Have her take it easy, if possible. It's going to hurt."

<h1 style="text-align:center">CHAPTER 83</h1>

MONICA

TAKE IT EASY. What kind of bullshit was that? How was I supposed to take it easy? Was I supposed to sip piña coladas by the pool and wait for a miscarriage? Like la-di-da, let's take a jog and have a good laugh and watch TV and forget that my whole life, everything I thought I wanted, changed in the past two days. I'm supposed to pretend that didn't happen?

Well, fuck you, Doctor. Fuck you with a big bag of fucking fucks.

Once that fucking fuck of a doctor and her little nurse were gone, I flipped them a double bird, because fuck them and fuck that machine and fuck that room and fuck that hospital and fuck the lie I fucking wrote on myself.

"And fuck you," I said to Jonathan when he twirled my underwear.

"You should get the D&C," he said, looping the cotton panties around my ankles. "Let the doctor end this. She suggested it for a reason."

"No."

"What if you're in the studio when you start cramping?"

"Fuck the studio. I hate this hospital. I hate everything about it. It's a rat shithole. Everything is beige and pale pink. The decorator should be shot. And they could run fucking potpourri through the vents, and it would still smell like bleach and death."

He slid my underpants back on, and I let him, because I was too mad, too confused by my tangle of emotions to get dressed and get off the table. Jonathan pulled me into a sitting position.

"Don't fight me," he said, opening the door.

His voice was as definitive as ever, telling me my behavior before I had a chance to question it. I didn't know what he meant until he put his arms under me and picked me up, carrying me out the door and down the hall. I put my arms around his neck and rested my head on his shoulder.

"You don't have to look," he said, and I knew what he meant.

I closed my eyes and focused on his leather scent, pretending that bleach and medicine didn't hover around the edges, ignoring the ding of the elevator and the whispering of nurses and doctors in their parallel language. It was so familiar and so foreign, because though the sounds and smells were the same, this time I wasn't worried about Jonathan, or even myself. I was just angry, and disappointed, and touching the edges of grieving the loss of something I hadn't even wanted twenty-four hours ago.

"I'm okay," I said into Jonathan's ear as he carried me out of the elevator and across the lobby.

"I know."

"I'm not upset anymore."

"I know.

"You can put me down." I opened my eyes. He filled the frame of my vision.

"Nope. You're my wife, and I'll carry you where I like."

Lil waited in the roundabout, parked in the red zone as if it were a marker for Bentleys. She opened the back door, and Jonathan poured me in.

I didn't say anything the whole way home. I sat on Jonathan's lap, wrapped in him, my head on his shoulder. Somewhere on the 10 freeway, I felt a twinge, and it started. The doctor had been very explicit about what to expect, and I didn't know if I'd thought I'd be immune, or I didn't care, or if I simply underestimated what she'd meant by pain and bleeding.

But by the time Jonathan carried me to the door, I felt as if I'd been stabbed in the stomach.

"Monica?" He swung the door open.

"I think I should go to the bathroom."

"Are you all right?"

"Yeah."

He looked concerned, but he let me down, and I ran to the bathroom off our bedroom. It had a shower, and a bathtub, and a door that locked. It was a super fancy little corner of the world, and it had a view of the ocean, because what else did a girl need when her body was ridding itself of a blight. Right? I peeled off my pants and sat on the toilet, hunched in pain so bad, I felt as if my guts were being pulled and tied into a knot at the end of a balloon.

There was a soft rap on the door.

I couldn't do this in front of anyone. Not even him. Not even the man whose chest had been open before me. Not even the one whose bleeding heart I carried every night in my dreams. I was doing this alone, whatever this was.

I grunted when the air went out of the balloon and the stretching and knotting started again.

"Monica," he said through the door, "I'm calling for pain killers."

"I'm fine!" Why did I say that? I wasn't fine.

"You were with me in the hospital," he said. "You have a distorted view of pain."

"Don't take this the wrong way," I said, barely able to breathe. "You are the love of my life, but get the fuck away from the door."

"No, I will not leave you." He used his dominant voice, and I didn't give a single shit. "Open it."

"*Go jogging*!" I screamed it not because I wanted to scare him, but because the pain intensified by an order of magnitude. I put my head in my hands, and the blood started.

CHAPTER 84

JONATHAN

THE DOOR WAS LOCKED. Not that I gave a shit on a practical level. A bobby pin could fix that. I could knock the door down or unscrew the knob. I was sure the staff kept a chainsaw somewhere in the garage. Or hedge clippers. I could have broken that lock with my spit, to be honest. That was how wound up I was. I put my fist on the door for one last threat, but before I pounded it, I heard her hiccup then sniff. As badly as that made me want to get into that bathroom, I imagined a sudden bang on the door would only startle her. What would be the point of that?

"I'll tell you what," I said.

No answer. Just breathing.

"I won't break this door down. But I'm staying right here." I sat with my back against the door, my forearms on my knees.

She groaned, and I heard her pregnancy ending in a rush. She made an N sound that stretched out like a rubber band.

"Monica?"

"Women have gone through this for centuries, okay? Generations. Just... if you're going to sit at the door like an eavesdropper..." She stopped, and I could only imagine why. "I'll let you know when I'm through."

The last word ended in a squeak. If I broke down the door, I could hold her hand. Or bring her a painkiller. I could be *doing something* instead of sitting against the door and imagining what she was going through. I felt trapped and incompetent. I wanted to grab my fitness as a husband back.

That was it. I wasn't leaving her alone.

Bobby pins. I needed just one to open that door. I went to her dresser. The surface was cluttered with a picture of her parents, a crochet runner, a calendar. I opened her nightstand drawer. Old pictures. Sunglasses. Pens. Little notebooks. What the fuck? Where were her bobby pins?

It hit me hard, deflating me. The bobby pins were where they belonged. In the goddamned bathroom.

I stood by the door, ready to break it down, and I heard her on the other side. She was humming the "Star-Spangled Banner" of all things. I put my hands on the door. She groaned the lyrics, and I heard a sickening splash.

I couldn't take the door down. I couldn't do that to her, but I couldn't leave her either.

She was the heart patient, and I was the lonely young woman trying to grasp onto anything I could to make something happen. Would I have gone into Paulie Patalano's room to pull the plug? Maybe. Maybe I would have. Because if this kept up for weeks and was a matter of life and death, yeah, I'd take that door down with a chainsaw even if it scared the shit out of her. I'd take the door down and shove it up someone's ass.

But it only *felt* like life and death. It wasn't.

I put my forehead to the door just as she sang "*...and the home of the brave.*"

"Brava," I said.

"Go away," she replied so softly I could barely hear her.

"Is 'America the Beautiful' next?"

"Not until the seventh inning."

"I'll wait out here all day."

"I wanted this baby, Jonathan. Once I found out, I did. But before that... do you think not wanting it... it's so stupid."

"You didn't miscarry because you didn't want it. You didn't scare it away."

"We'll try again. Right?"

She needed that hope. Hope was her power, her way of coping. She'd do reckless things to keep it alive. She'd murder and betray. She'd be brave and strong, all in the name of hope. If I could take her hope and let it feed me, I might have a nourished life, no matter its length.

"Yes, Monica. We can try again. Right away. Once you're better."

Another groan, and she started the "Star-Spangled Banner" again.

I put my hands on the door as if that was at all soothing to the woman on the other side. The song passed, and silence followed, interrupted by a few sniffs, a few breaths, a few hummed bars of something I couldn't identify. I sat at the door and listened. I didn't know how else to care for her but to make that door into my love, touching the wood as if it was skin, comforting her through it, making her safe with space and matter between us. I didn't know how much time passed before she spoke.

"Are you there?"

"Yes."

"I can't flush. I just... I can't."
"Do you want me to do it?"
A long pause followed.

CHAPTER 85

MONICA

This was ridiculous. Everything about it. Me on the toilet for over an hour, cramping as though it was my job. The crime-scene-worthy mess. My compassionate and gorgeous husband standing outside, asking me if I'd like him to flush the baby.

I should just do it. Then I could run into the shower, do a quick clean up of the floor and outside of the bowl, and exit looking fresh. I knew this would continue for a few days, but not like this. Not to the point of non-functionality. I felt finished. I felt as if the worst was over. I felt empty.

"Monica?"

I couldn't do it. It wasn't a baby. It was tissue that had formed because my body had fooled itself into thinking there was a baby, but it was a terminated mission. My uterus just hadn't gotten the memo. So I should just flush instead of being a cliché of a woman who'd just had a miscarriage.

"I'm unlocking the door," I said. "Just wait until I call you to come in okay?"

"All right."

"And I'm warning you, ahead of time, it's not pretty."

"Consider me warned."

The bathroom was huge, and it had a separate bath and shower. Blood dripped on the edges of the toilet from when I'd cramped so badly I'd moved away from the seat. Otherwise, the room was as pristine as Jonathan's staff could make it.

I unlocked the door and turned on the shower. It was hot in half a second. I didn't know how he did that, but money got rid of even the smallest

inconveniences of thermodynamics. I stripped, stepped in, and clicked the
door shut.

The water flowed over my face, scalding hot. I wanted it hotter. Second-degree
burn hot. I wanted to sterilize myself from the baby that wasn't a baby. I wanted to
forget the feeling of something real and human dropping from me to its death.

When the water flowed over me fully, a stream of red-stain went down the
drain. It was too much. I didn't think I could stand it. I was broken and useless.
What had felt real, wasn't. And now I was expected to—

The door clicked open, and Jonathan stood in the shower entrance, fully
dressed.

"I'm sorry," I said. "I forgot to call you."

He stepped into the shower, water slapping onto his shirt, sticking it to his
skin. Darkening and flattening his hair. He put his arms around me and pressed me
to him. His lips brushed my shoulder, and his hands pressed against me as if he
wanted as much of himself touching as much of me as possible.

"I love you," he said.

"I—" I choked up the rest of the sentence, because I felt lost and empty, and he
was still there. He was my sky. Through blood and breath, sin and sorrow, I was his
sea, and wherever the horizon was and the world ended, we were there, together.

What had I done to deserve this? Repeatedly and often, I'd failed to deserve
him. I'd resisted him, tried to deny him a family, then I'd failed to carry his child. I
wasn't worth him getting his clothes wet, but I needed him. I needed him so badly.
To fail for him and to try again, because having been pregnant for those hours, I
couldn't see any future past giving him children.

I clawed at his back and pressed my face to his shoulder. He rocked me under
the hot water, sodden and strong, even after my legs couldn't hold me.

"Come on," he said, shutting off the shower, "before I flood the floor."

He carried me for the third time, his feet squishing on the marble tiles. The
bath was running, and the lights were dimmed. He laid me in the tub.

"I'm sorry," I said.

"For what?" He leaned over the tub, his clothes still soaked, and submerged a
sponge. He didn't even roll up his sleeves; he just got them wetter.

"For letting the baby go."

"You know I'm not going to accept that apology."

"I feel like I failed you. And hours after getting you all excited. God, I'm such a
fuckup."

He put his fingertips to my lips. "Stop."

But it was too late. My eyes filled up, and the skin behind my face tingled. "I
can't. I can't stop thinking that—" I heaved a breath. "That it's my fault. That I
killed it."

He soaped the sponge. "If that were possible, there wouldn't be any unwanted
pregnancies."

I was Teflon, immune to logic, sense, and evidence-based reality. I couldn't shake the feeling that I was somehow at fault for this disaster. I couldn't answer him with the straight fact that despite the pure reason of his assertion, I was poisoned. Blighted. My body wasn't fit for a child.

He put the sponge between my thighs and cleaned off the last of the blood. His name was still there, and he rubbed until it was gone while I laid my head on the side of the tub and cried.

What shame. Lying in a tub with my legs spread, weeping while my husband scrubbed our baby from between my legs. But despite what the scene may have looked like, I wasn't ashamed. I was open, raw, and comforted.

"Thank you," I said. "You're good to me."

He put his hand flat on my abdomen. "You wrote something here too. It's darker." He ran his wet hand over my cheeks, wiping away old tears to make room for the new ones.

"There was a shower in between."

"I'm going to have to work to get it off."

"I don't want to look."

"Don't." He picked up a scrubby thing, tossed it, chose something softer, and put soap on it. He was all business. I looked at the ceiling as he scrubbed.

"Do you want to hear the last stupid thing that went through my head?" I said.

"If you're willing to hear my stupid thing after."

"I thought, 'This happened because I wrote it backward.'"

"That is stupid."

"What was your stupid thing?" I asked.

"That next time we should tattoo *Jonathan's baby,* and it'll stick."

I laughed through my tears. That was Jonathan, a poet in love and a realist in life, thinking superstitious nonsense, just like me.

"Are you cold?" I asked when he put the scrubber down. "Your clothes are soaked."

"I feel trapped in a bag."

"You do look a little vacuum-packed."

He laughed, and I laughed with him. He stood and peeled off his clothes, getting down to the pure magnificence of him. I didn't know if I could ever be away from him again. I needed him.

"They're going to restart the track in a week," I said, holding out my arms.

"I think you'll be okay by then."

"Come with me."

He stepped into the tub without answering.

"Jonathan," I said as he leaned his back on me, and I wrapped my legs around his waist.

"I heard you."

"Please. Don't leave me alone. Don't make me choose. I can't do it anymore."

He leaned his head back and kissed my cheek. "I own you, and I take care of my property. Every minute of the day."

"Say that means you'll travel with me."

"It means wherever you go, I'll be by your side. I'm going to take such good care of you, you're going to get sick of me. You're going to tell me to stay home, and I won't."

"Thank you," I whispered, laying my cheek on his shoulder. We stayed there until the water got cold.

<h1 style="text-align:center">CHAPTER 86</h1>

EIGHTEEN MONTHS LATER

MONICA

"Today?" Laurelin cried as she zipped my dress. "You agreed to do a show *today?*"

"Tonight, actually." I held up the strapless top with my forearm.

"You're supposed to get swept off your feet to a foreign land." Her face was red with irritation and her fists were tense. She was quite the romantic, our nurse.

"I am. After the show. Two songs in my wedding gown. Darren and I will blow the roof off the place, then I'll go on my honeymoon." I kissed her cheek, and when she tried to push me away, I kissed her harder.

"Come on," she said. "Let me get this on you."

Laurelin struggled to get the zipper up, cursing. Her pale blue gown hung on her like a sack, as if its lack of efficiency made her body repel it. She, Yvonne, and three of Jonathan's sisters were my bridesmaids, and they tittered around the waiting room, drinking tea and fussing with their makeup.

My hair was braided, of course, and twisted into a bun. Leanne had fashioned a veil of twisted tulle and beadwork, knotted it into the plait, and let it fall to the floor. I wasn't into finery, but the dress was gorgeous. Rock star gorgeous. Underneath it, I had a custom-made lace garter set with enough hardware and straps to suspend me from the Eiffel tower. I couldn't wait for Jonathan to see it.

I hadn't let him have me in two weeks, which hadn't been easy for either of us.

But I wanted to be wild with desire on our wedding night, and I wanted to torture him as much as he tortured me.

During the weeks after my miscarriage, I couldn't. I had been bleeding drop by drop, and I felt so raw and hurt, I couldn't let him near me. I hated my own skin. Then, one day, as we were getting on the Gulfstream to New York, the rawness left, and I wanted nothing more than his body inside me. He was gentle at first, but once he realized I was all right, he went back to the rough bastard I always knew.

He'd barely left my side since. Where I went, he went, and if he had to travel, I followed him. We brought Laurelin if we had to, and she brought the baby and her husband and kid sometimes.

Jonathan with a baby was magic. He opened up. His sense of humor turned to silly faces and funny noises. And yet, I couldn't give him one. There was nothing. Not even a threat or a tickle. Just us. We started talking about adoption, because he only had so long and I wanted joy for him before his heart gave out.

"Any word from Mr. Gevers?" Laurelin asked, as if reading my mind.

Andre Gevers was a Dutch man, and the first recipient of an artificial heart made by what we privately called the Swiss Project. Jonathan had funded the research, and though he still promised nothing as far as allowing an artificial heart to be used on him, if it worked, I knew he wouldn't say no to a life.

"Stable. The fake heart seems really happy in there." I held my hand up with my fingers crossed so tight, I nearly pulled a tendon.

"Two weeks doesn't mean it won't be rejected," Laurelin said. "I'm not trying to be negative, but medical research… there are a lot of failures before something sticks."

"It's going to work. He's going to be an old man."

"Gevers or Jonathan?"

"Yes."

"My brother was born an old man," Margie said, appearing next to me in the mirror, wearing a feminine-cut tuxedo. She was the best woman. We'd been at a loss for men, so she, Sheila, and Fiona were groomsfolk, along with Eddie and Darren. "Your dress isn't as puff pastry as I feared."

"You look perfectly marriageable yourself." I said.

"That's what I'm told." She handed me the loose bouquet of flowers. "You ready?"

"Thank you, Margie. For everything. I've always felt taken care of with you around."

"My pleasure. Now go."

All my sky-blue girls waited at the exit, and I followed them through the stone hallway and into the courtyard. The security detail followed us, as visually conspicuous as they were silent. I didn't know if I'd ever get used to being famous. It had been a year since my EP hit, and seven months since the full album. I was already having daily wrestling matches with my belief that I was a freak and a fraud, and Darren and Jonathan had to pull me away from them.

In the middle of the chaos and changing expectations, there was Jonathan, always at my side in public and always my master and king in private. We'd planned a wedding between plane rides, concerts, family functions, the management of a handful of hotels, and enough lovemaking to make my whole life a honeymoon.

Jonathan's divorce made him ineligible for a wedding in a Catholic church. Fortunately, Episcopalians were less strident, and St. Timothy's was more than happy to do the honors. The church was a huge stone edifice crusted with stained glass and surrounded by old trees in the center of Los Angeles. I got to the narthex, where my mother waited in a dress she tried to look modest in. It didn't work. She was too beautiful, and she carried it like a cross. She kissed me on the cheek and held me. I was overcome by the seriousness of it all. Yes, I'd been married for two years, and yes, this was all a big redo for the sake of his family and tradition, but those stones and brass fixtures had seen generations of brides. And the pews, from what I could see, were full of people.

"So much for an intimate event," I mumbled.

"Oh, please, Monya," my mother said, "you had no chance of that."

She took my hand, and we were hustled to the back of the line.

St. Timothy's had a huge organ, and at the first note, a hush fell over the congregation. I waited at the end of the line with my mother as the bridesmaids and groomsfolk walked down the aisle. David and Bonnie were right in front of me with the rings and a basket of rose petals.

"You ready, Mom?" I asked as Margie and Laurelin went.

"I hoped I wouldn't have to give you away. I hoped I'd meet someone to replace your father."

"No one could replace dad."

The music changed, and I took my mother down the aisle so she could give me away. I was so excited I wanted to run, but my mother took it slow. Too slow.

"Come on, Ma."

"You only do this once," she whispered.

I felt like a kid held back from the tree on Christmas morning. I knew what Jonathan looked like. I knew what his tux looked like, how it fit, how the white tie blended with the white shirt and how the line of the sharply cut black jacket made a perfect triangle from his throat to his waist, like an arrowhead to... well, I admit I was thinking of my wedding night.

Cameras had been confiscated. I couldn't look at all the people watching me. But I felt their eyes on me. Felt their good wishes.

Once I got halfway down the aisle, I could see Jonathan, because he'd stepped toward the center to see me. Margie tried to pull him back, but it was a wasted effort. Jonathan did what he wanted, when he wanted, and how he wanted, and he apparently wanted to watch me rush down the aisle.

Could my heart continue to melt every time I saw him? Would the day come when he had no effect on me? When I took his presence for granted? I couldn't imagine that. He was so straight, so perfect, carrying the formal suit as if it was the most natural thing he could put on his back. The man I'd met had returned, slowly but surely. His sudden visions of his heart rejecting him were gone, and my dreams and fear had collapsed under the weight of our intimacy. He was stronger, fitter, more dominant than ever, and he was my perfect life mate.

"Hey," I said when I reached the altar, and he took my hand. "How are you doing? You look nice."

"Nice? I'm surrounded by cross-dressers, and they all look better in a tux than I do."

I put my fingers over my mouth to stifle a laugh.

As the congregation sat behind us, Jonathan leaned over and whispered in my ear. "I own you. I'm going to take a belt to you just because I can."

"Jonathan, we're in church." I shut out the white noise of the church, the ministrations of the bellicose bishop in his sixties, and the rustlings of the choir.

"This is just a building," Jonathan said so low I could barely hear him. "Worship is later. I'm going to tie your legs over your head with that pretty veil, and I'm going to beat and fuck you so hard the words, 'Oh, God,' are going to summon the heavenly host."

His words went right between my legs. We stood at the altar as people talked about us, as a service was said in our honor.

I didn't know if there was a mic somewhere that could pick us up, so I turned and spoke directly in his ear, my breath to him, my vocal chords disengaged. A butterfly couldn't hear me. "I'm singing later. Be gentle with my throat."

His hand twitched. I was expected to know he was aware of all my needs, including my need to sit at a meeting, walk in front of people, or sing. He knew when to be gentle and when to score my skin because he was inside every part of my life, and any lack of trust warranted a delicious spanking.

"Good thing you don't sing with your ass," he whispered back.

I spit out a nervous laugh that every mic caught, and Jonathan's smile broke into a chuckle. The bishop looked at us, and the congregation stared. I waved and curtsied.

The bishop looked motioned us front and center.

David held out the red pillow with our rings. They'd been designed as tight coils, like key rings, to remind us of our first wedding rings and the circumstances they'd been given under. But they were gold, and they fit right, which would be a nice change. Jonathan and I positioned ourselves across from each other, and he took the smaller ring.

The bishop cleared his throat. "Mister Drazen, repeat after me. I, Jonathan Drazen—"

"I, Jonathan Drazen,"

"Take thee, Monica Faulkner—"

"Take thee, Monica Faulkner." Jonathan was smiling, the ring hovering over my finger, and I could practically hear the gears in his head turning.

"To be my wedded wife," the bishop said.

"To be my wedded wife," Jonathan said before he turned to the bishop. "You know we memorized this, right?"

"That would be the first time in my forty years of officiating weddings."

Laughter floated up from the congregation, and I put my head down to stifle a big giggle.

"We thought it was kind of important," Jonathan said.

"Get on with it then."

"Where were we?"

"Having and holding," the bishop said.

"Thank you," Jonathan squeezed my hand and continued. "... to have and to hold from this day forward, for better for worse, for richer for poorer, in sickness and in health, to love and to cherish, till death do us part." He dropped his voice, as if expressing seriousness, but also to create a web of intimacy around the words. "I own you. Like the sky owns the stars. You are mine." He slipped the gold key ring on my finger.

"You memorize yours too?" the bishop asked, looking at me over his half-moon glasses.

"Yes." I picked up the ring. "You ready, Drazen?"

"Yes."

"I, Monica Faulkner, take thee, Jonathan Drazen, to be my wedded husband, to have and to hold from this day forward, for better for worse, for richer for poorer, in sickness and in health, to love, cherish, and to obey till death. Your name is written on my heart."

I heard the murmurs. Jonathan and I had kept the word obey in my vows because we knew what we meant. He was my master in the bedroom, and I obeyed his commands. We knew the limitations between us, and these were our vows. We neither explained nor excused them.

And thus, both standing on our own two feet, before God and our families, with the news media waiting outside, we were wed.

CHAPTER 87

JONATHAN

SHE WAS MOST kinetic in stasis. With her energy contained by my will and her desire to please me, she was a sizzling box of energy, and the longer I kept her there, naked and still, the closer to her skin her arousal came.

She stayed still for me, the streets of Paris below, on the first night of our honeymoon, her nipples hard in the chilled air. I was behind her, which was all she knew. She didn't know when I'd move or what I was doing. I could hear her heartbeat, and her breath, which she tried to keep even but failed.

She was mine. I owned this body, this heart. I wanted to put my fingers and tongue inside her, my cock, everywhere all at once. Every act of ownership felt incomplete to the totality of my love. I'd married her for the second time only a day before, and I'd marry her a hundred times more, but our bond was in our consummation. I was hers, and she was mine, and we only came close to the expression of the depth of it when I broke her patience, her resolve, her expectations, soothed her heart, and broke her again.

I came around her, fully dressed, to watch her naked body as it shifted, to watch her eyes try to stay focused ahead. She was so good, objectifying herself for me, becoming an owned thing so we could play the games that were an expression of our deeper truth. She owned me. I was an object for her pleasure.

I sat in the chair in front of her and brushed my fingertips across her breasts. She shuddered. My plan was to get her on her knees and take her throat, then it could go one of three ways, with every step leading to a new game plan, depending on her level of obedience. Every plan led up to the both of us quivering together. But as I ran my fingers from her breasts to her belly, something changed.

Something about her.

I kissed her navel, pulling the diamond bar with my lips.

She'd gained weight since starving herself in Sequoia. On our honeymoon, she was a little heavier than when we'd met. I knew what her body looked like and what it felt like. My hands and mouth discerned her shapes in all their perfection. And as she stood by me, groaning as my tongue traced circles around her navel, I perceived a change as subtle as the sea.

"Monica," I said.

"Yes?"

"I don't want to alarm you."

She stiffened. "Are you okay?"

"*Shh*. I'm fine. As are you." I looked up at her. She looked straight ahead, as she was supposed to, and I stood so I could look her in the eye.

"What is it?" she asked, meeting my gaze.

"I don't want you to get excited for nothing." A senseless desire. No matter what I did, I was going to get her hopes up. I was going to risk causing her disappointment and pain. I couldn't protect her from that. The greatest gift I could give Monica, a wedding gift for our life together, was hope.

She broke the silence. "Tell me, or I swear I'll—"

"You'll do no such thing."

She set her mouth in a tight line and put her hands on her hips. Scene over.

I took her by her chin and risked her dashed hopes. "I think you're pregnant."

CHAPTER 88

monica

He was impossible. From the minute he'd run across Paris for a pregnancy test, to him cancelling everything on my behalf, to the doctor's appointment where I couldn't understand a word they were saying, he was the most impossible man I had ever met.

"I'm fine!" I said in the square across from the doctor's office. It had a church, and a statue, and pigeons everywhere. The sky was the color of the sidewalks, and the air was so wet it stuck to me. "I'm not even a little sick. I feel better than ever. I could run a marathon, so back off."

"The doctor said you should take it easy," he said. Mr. Easygoing in a blue polo, houndstooth scarf, and a wool coat was taking control of the situation. It calmed him to be in charge, which was fine, up to a point.

"That's totally not fair. You could tell me he said I have to wear a clown suit on Tuesdays, and I wouldn't even know."

"A clown suit? Even you couldn't make that sexy."

I crossed my arms and turned to face him. Pigeons flew up in the fog. The square was just starting to get crowded with the lunchtime rush, and we were ignored.

"You should have gotten me an English-speaking doctor," I said.

"I got you the best."

"Well, I felt left out. I felt like you all were talking about me like I wasn't there. And of all people, you should understand how shitty that is."

He stepped forward and cupped my cheeks. "Do you remember that heartbeat?"

The whooshing sound, like an angel walking on a heavenly treadmill, had come

879

through the sonogram loud and clear. I admitted that a tear fell from my eyes. Maybe two. Maybe I'd wept right there.

"So?" I said with a choke.

"What language was that?"

I shook my head. No language obviously. I wanted him to get to his point.

"It was our baby's," he said. "It was the language of life. Who cares what the doctor and I said? Who cares about how I want to take care of you? You want to fight about something? Let's fight about what you're having for lunch."

I smiled and turned my face into his hand, kissing the palm that was warm despite the December cold. "I want one of those ham croissants with the sour cheese."

"And a salad."

"Fine."

"And after, you take one of the prenatal vitamins."

I made a yuck face. The doctor had given me bullet-sized vitamins that smelled terrible. But I'd take them. Jonathan was my inspiration for keeping up a regimen. I'd take them every day on a clock, but I didn't have to pretend to like it.

"I could lose it again," I whispered.

"You won't. I have a feeling this one's going to stick."

He gathered me in his arms, and we held each other in a Parisian square, rocking back and forth for blissful minutes.

EPILOGUE

MONICA

I WOKE UP ALONE, and I panicked. I had that heavy feeling from sleeping longer and harder than I was used to. I felt drunk, hazy, and worried. The baby was supposed to be next to me or in the little cradle next to the bed, and Jonathan was supposed to be in the next room, but god damn if I couldn't smell him in the sheets.

"Jonathan?" I mumbled.

Was I still dreaming? Or was the air actually thicker? I knocked a glass of water from the night table. Cold water splashed on my leg. Not a dream. This was real.

How had I slept? I shouldn't have. The fact that I hadn't slept in three days notwithstanding, no decent person should sleep when their baby was as sick as mine was. Light flickered at the corner of the bedroom, under the bathroom door, and voices... no, a single voice. My husband, singing. God, he was terrible.

I opened the door.

The bathroom was washed in candlelight, and he was running the sauna with the door open, so I walked into a hot cloud. Jonathan was in the tub with little Gabrielle, all of three weeks old, face up on his thighs. I crossed my arms.

"You're not supposed to be around her while she's sick."

He ignored me and nuzzled the baby. "Can you say good morning to Mommy?" he cooed.

Gabby snorted then sneezed.

"Jonathan, I'm serious. At least wear a mask. You're immunosup—"

"I'm sterile enough for an operating room, and she's not contagious anymore."

He wielded an ear thermometer. I took it and crouched on the side of the tub. The little screen said 99.1.

"Oh," I said, "that's good. Do you think it's over?"

"I don't know." He dotted the baby's nose. "Are you going to let Mommy sleep, little girl?" She made an *ahhh* sound, and Jonathan turned to me. "She says yes, but she's reserving the right to change her mind."

"When did you learn to speak baby?" I ran my finger over his cheek, stripping away the water droplets.

"I live in Los Angeles."

We'd had a trying few days, with Gabby posting a 104.5 fever. Her pediatrician had come over late in the night, gotten it down to 101, and gone home. We could call him any time, but he said the ER wasn't necessary just yet. A few hours later, we were woken by the night nurse. The baby was spiking again.

It wasn't the nurse's fault, but we dismissed her anyway. The worry and responsibility were ours, and though we had the resources to hire out the exhaustion, we decided to own it. These were our moments of aggravation and pain; we wouldn't pay someone else to stand in for being together as a family. So we stayed up all night and cared for Gabby in shifts that didn't happen, because neither of us rested. I did the night nursing, or Jonathan gave her a bottle, grumbling about wearing gloves and a mask. We were still working out a routine that my body would accept, but those moments with her were so precious, I didn't care what time of day they were.

Gabby wiggled, still not knowing what her arms were for, grabbing at air with her tiny fingers. She had a full head of black hair, and though her eyes had the blue cast of a newborn's, they'd turn a shade of brown.

I submerged a big yellow sponge in the warm water and squeezed it over my daughter. Water fell over her chest and round belly, shining as if she'd been lacquered.

"I want redheaded babies," I said.

"We can try again, but unless both parents have red hair, it skips a generation."

"Why?"

"Dominance. It's in your genes."

"You're a jerk."

Gabby opened her mouth and turned her head, squeaking. She was just learning to cry. She could scream, squeak, sneeze, and smile, but we hadn't gotten to full-blown crying without a full-blown fever.

"Uh oh," Jonathan said. "She's calling Mommy."

I peeled off my shirt and underpants. My body was still misshapen from the pregnancy, but my husband eyeballed me as if I were the only woman in the world. Slowly, my figure was returning as if his kind attention was teasing it out.

I picked up the baby under her arms. She loved the water and jerked her tiny legs angrily when I took her out.

"Patience, little girl," I said.

Jonathan held his arms out for me. He was still magnificent, wearing nothing more than a scar and an erection that would go unattended until the baby was down. I got into the tub, sitting between my husband's legs. He wrapped his arms around me, and I positioned baby Gabrielle at my breast.

Jonathan rubbed my back, kissing my neck as I nursed. I was in some heavenly place where I was cared for physically and emotionally, turning this warm tub into a slice of well-being.

"Mister Gevers called," Jonathan said.

"Oh, did you thank him for the bunny and flowers?"

"Yes. He wants us to come out there. He wants to meet the little girl."

"I'm not travelling with a newborn."

"It's not that hard. I did it for ten minutes once."

"He and his wife can come here again. I'm not going anywhere yet." I leaned into him, and he wrapped his arms around us. "Not until I'm good and ready."

"Yes, mistress." He kissed my shoulder.

Little Gabby nursed her little heart out. I was so in love with her, more in love than I'd ever thought possible. I leaned my head against my husband's chest, letting the soft warmth of the water envelope me, and somewhere in my half-sleep, I became a part of it, growing into a universe where I was loved and where I loved. Where I was needed and where I was allowed to need. In our tight realm of three, I dreamed myself expanding into this tiny, infinite universe, perfect in its balance and stability.

I opened my eyes when Jonathan tucked my hair behind my ear and kissed my neck. So perfect was the silence, and our baby, sated and sleeping in my arms, mouth cocked open, the edges pointed in a smile.

Flesh of my flesh, love of my love, broken and tied back together with the strings of my heart, these are mine. And whatever life may bring, whatever tests and tortures, I am complete, and competent, and ready to go to battle in their defense.

But for now, there is only peace.

Your next stop on the Drazen drama is with Jonathan's sister Theresa and mafia capo Antonio in **COMPLETE CORRUPTION.** *It's FREE in Kindle Unlimited!*

Antonio is a beautiful killer.

He's a prodigy of a thief and as violent a mafia hitman as ever walked the earth.

He's about to complete the final act of vengeance against the men who hurt his sister and take his rightful place at the head of the Los Angeles mob...
when *she* appears.

Like a predator catching sight of his prey, his attention is consumed by Theresa Drazen.

A proper lady.

An heiress.
A refined, upstanding member of society.
He wants to tear away her manners.
Melt her cold gaze in hot screams.
Own her completely.
The things he wants to do to her are more criminal than anything he's ever been accused of.
And when Antonio wants something, he gets it.
Get **_COMPLETE CORRUPTION_** free in Kindle Unlimited now!